Musical Encounters

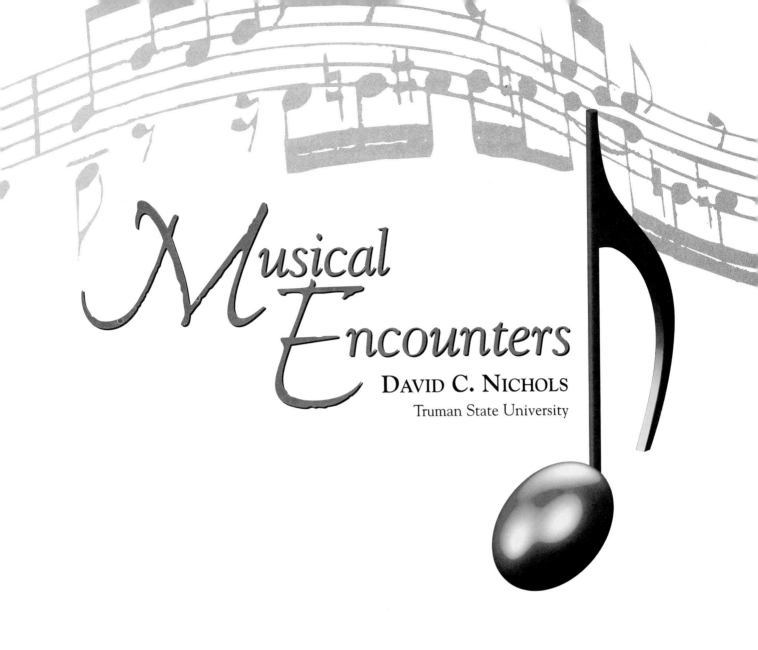

Musical Encounters

DAVID C. NICHOLS
Truman State University

Prentice
Hall

Upper Saddle River, New Jersey 07458

Library of Congress Cataloging-in-Publication Data

Nichols, David C. (David Clifford)
    Musical encounters / David C. Nichols.
        p. cm.
    Includes bibliographical references and index.
    ISBN 0-13-207457-5
    1. Music appreciation. I. Title
MT90 .N53 2001
780–dc21   00-042796

Editorial Director: Charlyce Jones Owen
Senior Acquisitions Editor: Christopher T. Johnson
Editorial Assistant: Evette Dickerson
Editor-in-Chief of Development: Susanna Lesan
Development Editor: Elaine Silverstein
Creative Director: Leslie Osher
Art Director: Kenny Beck/Maria Lange
Interior Designer: Kenny Beck
Color Inserts: Laura Gardner
Cover Designer: Kenny Beck/Maria Lange
Cover Image Specialist: Karen Sanatar
Cover Art: Kandinsky, Vassily (1866–1944), "Komposition 4,"
    1911, abstract, oil on canvas. Kunstsammlung
    Nordrhein-Westfalen, Duesseldorf, Germany/ Art
    Resource, NY. © 2000 Artists Rights Society (ARS),
    New York/ADAGP, Paris.

Marketing Manager: Sheryl Adams
AVP, Director of Production and Manufacturing:
    Barbara Kittle
Manufacturing Manager: Nick Sklitsis
Prepress and Manufacturing Buyer: Benjamin D. Smith
Production Editor: Jean Lapidus
Photo Researcher: Abby Reip
Image Permissions Coordinator: Carolyn Gauntt
Formatting and Art Manager: Guy Ruggiero
Artist: Lorena Cerisano
Copy Editor: Michele Lansing
Indexer: Murray Fisher
Proofreader/Photo Credits: Helena DeKeukelaere

This book was set in 10/12 Goudy by TSI Graphics, and was printed
and bound by Courier Companies, Inc. The cover, endpapers, and color inserts
were printed by Phoenix Color Corp.

©2001 by Prentice-Hall, Inc.
A Division of Pearson Education
Upper Saddle River, New Jersey 07458

Printed in the United States of America
10 9 8 7 6 5 4

ISBN 0-13-207457-5

Prentice-Hall International (UK) Limited, London
Prentice-Hall of Australia Pty. Limited, Sydney
Prentice-Hall Canada Inc., Toronto
Prentice-Hall Hispanoamericana, S.A., Mexico
Prentice-Hall of India Private Limited, New Delhi
Prentice-Hall of Japan, Inc., Tokyo
Pearson Education Asia Pte. Ltd., Singapore
Editora Prentice-Hall do Brasil, Ltda., Rio de Janeiro

This book is dedicated to those colleagues, students, and musicians of all ages who are finding that their distinctions between "legitimate" and "other" music are becoming more blurred as time passes.

CONTENTS

𝒫ART II
ART MUSIC: MUSIC AS INTRINSIC VALUE   93

*P*ART III
MUSIC AS A SOCIAL FORCE

239

PREFACE

When I first started teaching college some thirty years ago, the central purpose of music appreciation courses was to train uninitiated students to appreciate art music so they would come to like "legitimate" music. The implicit message was that music not belonging to the European-American tradition was secondary and therefore not worthy of serious study. As a lifelong student of our culture and as a career musician who finds constant personal fulfillment in an art form that I call my own, I have gradually come to realize that we all need to broaden our perspectives.

Diversity and change are two themes that seem to emerge whenever a discussion of our modern culture occurs. The social, political, and economic institutions of the world are weaving ever-changing webs of relationships and experiences as a new century begins. These interactions are not only reflected in the world of business and government, but they are at the very core of the cultural and aesthetic expressions coming from the people. *Musical Encounters* grew out of an awareness of these changes. It is founded on the principle that music is part of the fabric of life.

Diversity, Change, and the Listening Process

The structure and content of *Musical Encounters* focuses on three fundamental concepts: diversity, change, and developing listening techniques and attitudes necessary to accommodate a modern, eclectic musical taste.

Diversity

As the new millennium begins, the world of music reflects a broad diversity, not only from an ethnic/world music viewpoint, but also from the immense proliferation of many types of music that reflect contemporary culture. Never before has so much new music been available to the consumer; yet, at the core of concert music in the United States remains the traditional canon of musical literature.

A basic assumption of this book is that all musical expressions have a place in our society and, even though parameters of study eventually have to be drawn in any systematic study of music, it is helpful to approach listening to music from several avenues, especially those that reflect our current common use of music.

Chapter 3, *Focus on Listening: Vocal Music from Around the World*, for example, introduces the reader to a consciously diverse array of vocal music and focuses on the amazing versatility of the human voice in Western and other cultures. It allows students to hear sounds that may be outside of their personal comfort zones and shows them that even the voice—the most fundamental of music-producing "instruments"—can create sounds that are deemed appropriate in diverse social and cultural settings. Here students are invited to cross the line from merely using music to reinforce their own social status into an experience of listening to music that represents "other" perspectives and functions. The exclusive use of vocal music in this chapter is a deliberate choice. The voice is the common denominator among all music of the world.

Change

Musical styles are developing and merging at an ever-increasing speed, demanding more and more attention from the serious listener. A strong connection between change and music is the idea that functions of music, which are diverse in nature, are also changing as a society creates new roles for music in its ongoing development. How music functions and how music is marketed and supported in present and past cultures is also fundamental to perspectives in music.

Musical Encounters supports both a world of change and a tradition of music that has earned the name "Classical Music." As students study and experience the 71 recorded musical selections in this book, they will see that cultural change is always reflected in the music of any time period. Here is where music history becomes especially significant—as do art history, literary history, and other related studies.

The Listening Process

Fundamental to any study in the perspectives of music is the development of an educated musical ear. No matter what musical genre, style, or expression a person listens to, a standard set of listening techniques is used. Each person's brain processes music according to the skills, references, and abilities unique to him or her. The approach to listening in *Musical Encounters* enhances the student's abilities to hear musical gestures both in isolation and in larger contexts. The preparation of this, in Chapter 2, allows the students to hear examples of melodic contours, textures, chord progressions, rhythmic organization, and formal structure in a variety of settings. The intent is to help the student reach the conclusion that intelligent listening is relevant to all types of music—not just classical musical expressions. It is directed toward breaking down the barriers between high art and low art, and it also makes the learner aware of musical expressions from the non-Western world.

How do we accomplish this "global" approach to music? We first do so by acquiring the skills necessary to hear and perceive music. Music is a specialized art. As such, it requires that we learn some rudimentary concepts. The listening techniques developed in this book are founded on years of working with music at all levels. They are designed to make the student aware of both the vertical and horizontal aspects of music as it unfolds. We hear music in two dimensions: one involves the split-second event of the moment, the other relates to the unfolding of sounds in time. The student will develop an awareness of these dimensions of music and the necessary skills to perceive them as we examine a variety of musical expressions. The end result will be that, no matter what type of music the student listens to, he or she will be able to perceive "what is going on" in the music.

Design and Content

This text is organized into three parts. **Part I** targets building listening skills founded on a knowledge of a basic music vocabulary. It also exercises these skills by sampling musical expressions from around the world. Finally, it examines the artistic, social, and economic forces supporting music in our eclectic society. It identifies significant institutions, ensembles, and movements in modern musical cultures, and it illustrates these with listening examples.

Part II of *Musical Encounters* focuses on Western art music and discusses music of the Baroque, Classical, Romantic, and Modern eras. Here again, as in Part I, enhancing listening skills is integral to all discussions. Chapter 5, which centers on Baroque Music and the three principal composers, Bach, Handel, and Vivaldi, concentrates on principles of counterpoint and layering, and teaches the music student listening techniques that are structured on simultaneously occurring events. In Chapter 6, when music of the Classical Era is discussed, the concepts of repetition and contrast are emphasized. The following chapters reinforce these two principles of organization and apply them to the music of the nineteenth and twentieth centuries.

Maintaining a strong emphasis on the listening experience and music literature, Part II pays special attention to the aesthetic impulses and social and economic trends that gave rise to compositions and musical practices during the past 400 years. The emphasis here is away from "low-cal" music history. Instead of attempting to include every genre, major composer, and musical development throughout history, this book is designed to help the reader focus on selected issues and compositions, and to develop a skeletal framework of knowledge and musical experience for a lifetime of learning.

Part III, the final section of *Musical Encounters*, is topical in its organization. If offers the professor and students various choices for further study and the sociology of music. For the learner desiring to step outside of the world of classical Western art tradition, it also presents a fascinating look at music that crosses cultural lines. This new approach to content organization in a music appreciation textbook offers options for tailoring a specific course to the needs and interests of the faculty and students. It reinforces the concept that our musical culture is indeed diverse in nature.

Accompanying this text is a set of four compact disc recordings that is coordinated to serve as a basic listening experience for the student of music. Whenever possible, entire movements or compositions are used so the owner of the recordings will have a basic library of music for future use.

The appendices include a glossary of terms, an introduction to musical criticism, and a general outline of music history, which includes a list of the principal composers of Western art music.

This book is designed primarily for the college classroom, but it will also be useful to those interested in self-study. The suggestions for assignments can be adapted to all age groups and should provide intellectual stimulus regardless of age, education, or career orientation. The recordings accompanying the textbook offer a basic library of music that will provide hours of listening enjoyment.

Musical Encounters will involve the student in music in the following ways:

1. Listening skills will be developed. The student will be invited to increase his or her perception of music through a system of active learning experiences.

2. These listening techniques will be applied to a broad scope of music. The student's skills will become part of his or her everyday encounters with music.

3. An awareness of music's role in the social and economic fabric of modern life will develop. This awareness will be founded on a historical perspective and on an acquaintance with significant works of music, both past and present.

Musical Encounters considers all music legitimate. It assumes that as the student expands his or her life experiences to include more music, a greater variety of sounds, including classical or "art" music, will be appreciated. As the student's interest grows toward becoming an active consumer of art music, as well as pop music, he or she will also become aware of the various sociopolitical forces that drive and support the world of music.

The underlying principle of *Musical Encounters* is that the study of music in the university should reflect the eclectic society that is now such a part of modern American life. Although the main emphasis of this book is on the music of Western civilization and its "classical" and popular expressions, examples of music drawn from several world cultures are used to enrich the listening experience and to increase awareness of how various peoples organize sound into music according to their unique tastes, practices, and traditions. Music, that most versatile art, is thus both universal and specific in its scope.

ACKNOWLEDGMENTS

Because of the enthusiasm of my colleagues who teach perspectives of music and their interest in seeking new ways to approach the art of teaching music in the classroom, I was able to enlist help in testing the content and ideas of this project. The attitudes shown by the students and the encouragement of the administration at Truman State University played a central role in bringing this book to reality. I consider myself fortunate to be surrounded by such people.

Special thanks go to Professor Thomas Trimborn, who shared his creativity generously, and to Professor Michael Hooley, who taught from the manuscript but did not live to see the final realization of this project. Debra Fortenberry Priest was an invaluable aid in the initial editing process.

Wayne Spohr of Prentice Hall, who first suggested that I submit my ideas for publication, has offered continual support. He is a credit to his profession. Elaine Silverstein, the development editor, and Jean Lapidus, production editor, were remarkable both for their professional expertise and their infectious enthusiasm.

My personal source of strength in this project, however, is my wife, Vonnie. Perhaps those who know her will see some of her spirit reflected in these pages.

The author wishes to thank the following reviewers for their helpful suggestions: Professor Cindy Gould, Northern Arizona University; Professor Barbara Harbach, University of Wisconsin-Oshkosh; Professor F. M. Gilmore, Missouri Western State College; Professor David B. Welch, Ramapo College of New Jersey; Professor Donald A. Williams, Marshall University; and Professor David Chevan, Southern Connecticut State University.

David C. Nichols
Kirksville, Missouri

ABOUT THE AUTHOR

David Nichols, Professor of Musicology and Coordinator of Graduate Studies in Music at Truman State University, is active as a musicologist, a conductor, and a teacher of conducting. Trained as a historical musicologist with a Ph.D. from Indiana University, Professor Nichols has concentrated his research on the shaping forces of musical style in the eighteenth, nineteenth, and twentieth centuries. His eclectic abilities as a teacher, scholar, conductor, and a clarinetist/saxophonist have had a major influence upon both his interpretation of music and his interest in the sociology of music and its relationship to the world of concert music. His performance experience ranges from orchestral and choral conducting to directing musical theatre, church music, and performing as a jazz musician.

David Nichols' professional activities in guiding the music curriculum in liberal studies at his university and being part of Truman State University's Liberal Studies Program development have broadened his personal philosophy toward the study of music in the modern university. *Musical Encounters* is the result of a life-long interest in teaching students who represent a diverse array of interests, backgrounds, and academic disciplines. It projects the attitude that all music is "legitimate," and should be studied from perspectives that include both aesthetic and sociological considerations.

PART I

Foundations for Experiencing Music

THE many kinds of music available for our enjoyment address a broad spectrum of audiences and fulfill many different functions. Each small segment of society can claim a musical expression of its own. There are many varieties of rock music, subtle subcategories of jazz, and several types of country music. Each religious movement seems to have a musical expression that is congruent with its worship style. Music establishes mood and enhances drama in movies, television shows, and commercials. And, of course, the world of art music also presents a kaleidoscopic arrangement of musical styles for the appreciative listener's ears.

Since music is universal and is used by so many people perhaps you wonder why it is necessary to take a class in learning how to appreciate music. Part I of *Musical Encounters* will attempt to answer this question by providing a vocabulary of music and a foundation for listening techniques using a broad array of musical examples. The musical examples found in these chapters will provide background knowledge by illustrating compositional techniques and performance styles. In addition, they will expand musical experiences. Perhaps you have never heard Native American songs, contemporary African music, or Renaissance madrigals. The techniques for intelligent listening to music are universal—they are as relevant for the music of other cultures and time periods as they are for contemporary jazz, rock, and country.

Musical Encounters will open the door to lifelong enjoyment in the realm of sound and ideas. The intellectually active listener is one who enjoys hearing familiar musical styles and who also continually seeks out new listening experiences.

This text will help broaden your listening experiences. You will become more aware of the music you hear every day, and you will develop the skills you need to evaluate that music. As a result, you will find yourself enjoying music at a higher level than ever before. You will also understand the different purposes music can serve: to give pleasure, to heighten emotion, to influence behavior, to strengthen feelings of togetherness among peer groups, and even to stimulate the intellect. As an informed, experienced listener, you will discover that music will become an important avenue of personal enrichment for the rest of your life.

An Introduction to the
Study of Music

ACCORDING to most accounts, we are a nation of music lovers. The United States has ninety-five major orchestras with budgets of over $1,000,000 each, plus many other regional and metropolitan orchestras, ninety-nine opera companies with budgets of $500,000 or more, and numerous state and local arts councils that support classical concerts.[1] Recent industry reports indicate that over $12.5 billion is spent annually in the United States on musical recordings of various types. Virtually every college and university has at least one active chorus, a wind ensemble, an orchestra, and various chamber groups as part of its music program, and a course in music appreciation is taught at most institutions.

What is the reason for this widespread popularity? Why does virtually everyone seek out some sort of music?

Answers to these questions are as varied as the world of music itself. Perhaps music touches our feelings, our memories, and our intellect in a way that nothing else can. We can enjoy many kinds of music in many different ways. Music is at the same time very personal and universal in its language.

Perhaps the universality of music can be explained by examining its many functions. Music is a means of personal and emotional expression, both for the performer and the listener. It is also a vehicle for communicating ideas and ideologies. It can enhance and intensify written languages. Music reaches out across the world, into and out of all cultures, classes, and peoples.

Chapter 1 will take you into the world of music by looking at the ways in which we perceive music. Its goal is to demonstrate that how you listen to music affects your ultimate experience. You will also discover two general ways of organizing music, and you will begin to understand how to interpret this phenomenon of sounds organized in time. Musical perception will be addressed by defining and discussing the meaning of **musical style** and by illustrating its role in understanding the music of various historical periods, past and present.

And so we begin our journey toward enhanced listening. Whether you have studied music before or are completely inexperienced, you will find new and exciting ways to open your life to music and to experience new musical encounters.

WHAT IS MUSIC?

Music is often defined as sound that is organized by humans. This definition suggests that all music has some sort of structure. When a person hears music, it is the play of the elements of sound (pitch, rhythm, loudness or softness, tone colors, etc.) that influences the listening experience.

Viewed from a broader perspective, however, music is more than organized sound. It is a means of social communication that humans use to express various ideas, concepts, and emotions. Music often carries with it extra-musical values. These may be emotional (or affective), such as expressions of joy, triumph, anger, anxiety, or despair. They also may be descriptive, such as musical passages that imitate the wind, the rippling of a brook, or the firing of guns. Or, the intended values of a composition may be purely abstract. Such music is written with the primary goal of creating an interesting progression of sounds and a skilled manipulation of musical materials. It needs neither stories nor pictorial symbols to have relevance; it is an art form with intrinsic value. It speaks for itself. Music can be thought of as the translation of ideas into a medium that results in sound to be received and interpreted by living, thinking beings. In our study of music, we will examine structures and styles of music, and we will also look at the ways in which music functions as a means of communication. The questions we will try to answer about each work we listen to are: What makes this given piece or style of music special to us? How is this music used to reflect people's tastes, attitudes, and needs?

$\mathcal{W}$AYS OF LISTENING TO MUSIC

Much of the music in our everyday lives goes by unnoticed. Some people have developed the habit of having MTV on, or a radio playing whenever they are at home; they become so accustomed to the background sound that their consciousness blocks it out. Music is part of the sound/noise environment in supermarkets, hair salons, doctors' offices, and shopping malls. People jog to music, study to it, and even go to sleep to it.

Listening to music is often a very personal matter; just as there are many different kinds of music, there are also several ways in which people hear music. Different people also listen for different reasons. Composers, performers, and producers of music, being aware of this, create music to satisfy varying market needs. Whereas some people are satisfied to listen to only one style of music, many in today's society use music in a variety of ways and thus find that their tastes are ever expanding.

The famous American composer Aaron Copland (1900–1990) wrote *What to Listen for in Music*, in which he analyzed the listening process. His contention was that listening experiences could be divided into three general planes of activity.[2] The first level refers to the kind of listening where the hearer simply allows the music to flow through the ears and passively "bathes" in the music. This represents a kind of relaxation aided by music.

The second level of experiencing music, according to Copland, occurs when the music stimulates the listener to think of pictures or images, or to have some sort of emotional reaction. Whenever you hear Elton John's *Candle in the Wind*, you are experiencing Copland's second-level experience.

And, finally, Copland states that the third level of listening—the purely musical plane—is one in which the listener perceives the interplay of musical materials. The listener isolates various techniques of composition used by the composer and draws relationships between the various components of the composition. In short, the listener comes to digest and understand the end result of the composer's efforts by being able to recognize the details of the composition.

The point of identifying these levels of listening systems is to show that we can develop our musical perceptions so we can participate at various levels of involvement, and we can listen to music to move from a passive experience to an active one. At times we all enjoy music by simply letting it wash over us without probing its depth of style. Some styles of music, on the other hand, are produced in such a manner that we must listen with a more consciously attentive ear. People with well-developed listening skills feel that they experience music both emotionally and intellectually. Their involvement with music is accurately described as active, not passive.

Music can stir in the listener excitement and relaxation, joy and sorrow, tension and release, and feelings of calm or disruption. It can underscore and intensify poetry, vivify drama, complement movement and dance, and break through the boredom of everyday life.

For our introductory exercises in listening perception, we will examine two works that illustrate very different approaches to musical organization. They are chosen to reinforce the relationship between the various planes of listening discussed above.

The first listening experience is the well-known love song "Maria" from the Bernstein/Sondheim musical *West Side Story*. It is a soliloquy, a solo in which the main character Tony thinks aloud about his love for Maria, whom he just met at a dance. He is the founder of a New York teen gang, the Jets. Maria, who has recently immigrated from Puerto Rico, is the sister of Bernardo, who leads the rival Puerto Rican gang, the Sharks. These two gangs struggle to establish their domains in a crowded, inner-city setting; their hatred is intensified by their different ethnic backgrounds. The intense love between Tony and Maria flies in the face of this rivalry, and it is the focus of *West Side Story*.

Maria (Natalie Wood) and Tony (Richard Beymer) discover love in the Bernstein/Sondheim musical *West Side Story*, 1960. Photo by: Roger Viollet. Source: Liason Agency, Inc. ID # 359419*033.

Listening Guide 1

"Maria," from *West Side Story*
Leonard Bernstein and Stephen Sondheim

Broadway musical song
1957
Original cast recording sung by Jim Bryant
CD No. 1, Track 1 (2:34)

To Consider

As you hear this song for the first time, sketch down any ideas you might have, using the following questions as a guide. What aspects of the music catch your attention upon first hearing it? Consider the following when you listen to this number:

1. What is the general character of this song?
2. What is the specific mood or attitude suggested by the lyrics?
3. How does the music reinforce the mood of the poetry?

Ma - ri - a, I just met a girl named Ma- ri - a,
  and suddenly that name, will never be the same to me,
Ma - ri - a, I just kissed a girl named Ma- ri - a,
  and suddenly I found, how wonderful a sound can be.
Ma - ri - a, say it loud and there's music playing,
  say it soft and it's almost like praying,
Ma - ri - a, I'll never stop saying Ma - ri - a[3]

In our introductory listening to this song, we have surveyed the general mood of the music which, of course, reinforces the lyrics. Now listen to the music a second time with the intent of considering a more detailed approach.

1. Which syllables of the lyrics receive a stress (called an **accent**)?
2. What is the function of the slow and free section at the beginning of the song? Does this idea ever return? If it does, is the return of the opening idea the same length as the beginning?
3. Describe the combination of meter (regular beat groupings) and rhythm (length of notes) that Bernstein uses to establish the main section of the song. Does the steady beat play a role in the formal structure?

The following listening guide will help you identify these musical features.

0:00	The song opens with Tony singing a type of melody that uses a number of syllables of text to very few notes. The horn accompaniment is very sparse. Its character is one of an introduction, because its sustained style leads you to anticipate music that has more motion and a greater variety of notes. (In opera, this is called a **recitative.**)
0:30	The main melody of "Maria" begins. The first phrase identified with "Maria" is repeated before the melody leads into contrasting material. Notice that the main part of the song (where the singer breaks into "Maria! I've just met a girl named Maria") is supported by a beat that suggests a Latin dance. The regular beat pattern stops with the words, "say it soft and it's almost like praying."
1:16	After the singer finishes the first statement ("I'll never stop saying Maria"), the orchestra picks up the original melody. Tony sings new material that is superimposed on the orchestral music, while the singer continues to expound repeatedly on the word "Maria."
1:39	Voice and orchestra join in the same melody.
2:10	Material from the introductory recitative is used to stop the motion of the song and to create a graceful and an emotional ending. Tony ends with the same phrase that was stated the first time through the lyrics.

You have experienced several of Copland's levels of listening in this exercise. Your first impression was one of mood (did words like "tender," "melancholy," "awestruck," or "magic" come to your mind?). No doubt you bypassed the first level of listening and became emotionally involved with the song. The third level of listening, the "musical plane," began when you realized that the opening and closing parts of the song related to each other, and that the regular beat pattern accompanying the main section ("*Ma-ri-a, I just met a girl named Ma-ri-a*") sounded like a dance rhythm that might have been a subtle reminder of Maria's Puerto Rican origin. You also began to listen to the role the instruments played in relationship to the singer—when the orchestra played the same melody Tony was singing (called **doubling**) and when it went its separate way. With these realizations, you have actually begun to analyze the music.

MUSICAL STYLES AND THE LISTENING PROCESS

Our first musical example follows many conventions of composition that are common to centuries of Western musical composition, based on a general concept that music progresses according to principles of repetition and contrast. Commonly, the composer presents one or more central musical ideas (another word for a musical idea, in this sense, is **melody**). Then the composer manipulates these ideas to produce a work of continuing interest to the listener. These manipulations may take many forms, but in general, they represent a working out of ideas, which comes to a logical conclusion at the end of the work. In this traditional approach to composition, the central ideas (also called **themes**) are repeated, or **recapitulated,** at the end of the work.

Recapitulation in music refers to a restatement of a section of music, sometimes with modifications, which occurs after a contrasting section has been presented.

In our example from *West Side Story,* we heard the use of introductory material repeated at the end to round out the composition. We also heard the same melody move from the vocal line to the orchestra while the singer performed new material layered over the central melody. This work is based on principles of repetition and contrast.

This concept, however, is not universal to the entire world of musical expression. In another approach to musical structure, the music seems to gradually evolve in ways that give it a feeling of continual transformation without overt contrast. Many non-Western cultures enjoy these musical expressions (especially those in Asia and Africa) as we shall soon see.

Some composers of art music in the twentieth century purposely steered away from the traditional concepts of statement, contrast, and restatement and created expressions that emphasized this concept of gradual transformation in their music. In Chapter 10, we will see how contemporary American composer Philip Glass establishes a musical atmosphere in his *Façades* by creating ever-changing subtleties that draw the listener's ear to an awareness of gentle change. Never knowing what to expect, the listener must be constantly alert to the various directions that the music takes as it occurs (akin to the alertness one feels when driving down a mountain road filled with curves).

For an example of music based on a continual working out of melody and rhythm, without symmetrical regularity, let us listen to a work by African composer Hamza el Din (b. 1929) titled *The Gondola.* This work was introduced to the United States audience in the early 1960s at the Newport Folk Festival and subsequently recorded in 1965. Since then, Hamza el Din has become widely known as a troubadour for Sudanese music throughout the world. His songs and instrumental compositions, often inspired by memories of his native land, have grown in popularity as an awareness of his musical language grows.

Musical Encounter

Hamza el Din and the Oud

Hamza el Din has devoted much of the past four decades to promoting the music of his native land, Nubia, Sudan, an area near the southern Egyptian boundary that borders the Nile River. Hamza, one of the first African musicians to gain worldwide recognition for his artistry, is an accomplished oud player and singer. In the 1960s, his performances were heard by popular American folk singers Joan Baez and Bob Dylan, who recommended to the Vanguard record company that his songs be recorded. Hamza el Din now resides in the San Francisco Bay Area and is a regular performer in world festival

Hamza el Din playing the oud. Source: Jack Vartoogian.

concerts. His instrumental music also includes a percussion instrument, the tar, which he recalls was the only instrument found in Wadi Halfa, his native village, when he was a young boy.

The oud (also known as 'ud), a plucked lute, is one of the most significant stringed instruments in the Arab world. It is distinguished by its large, resonating body, its short neck, and a peg box that bends back from the neck of the instrument.

This instrument was named after the wooden plectra, or pick ('ud = wood), which was first used to pluck the strings; later, quills from eagle feathers were used because they gave a more pleasing sound. The **oud** is the ancestor of the European lute (al'ud, or in Spanish, laut), having come to Europe via the route from Northern Africa to Spain in the thirteenth century. In early times, it was thought that the oud produced sounds that could heal diseases.

Although the most elaborate instruments of this family have sound holes ornamented with elaborate carvings and fancy inlays on the body, fingerboard, and neck, as well as gracefully carved peg boxes, less elaborate folk ouds also are commonly found throughout the Middle East and North Africa. The oud is capable of producing melodies that move lightly over drones—or repeated low notes, musical gestures that are imitated in Hamza's composition for the string quartet.

Hamza el Din captivates his audiences not only with his songs and instrumental pieces for the oud, but by the descriptions that he gives concerning the genesis of his music. He is inspired by scenes, either imaginary or real, from his native village of Wadi Halfa, a village that became submerged by the waters of the Nile River when the Aswan High Dam project began in the early 1960s. He relates that when the Aswan Dam was finished, he was in New York. When he returned to the newly-created village that was built to replace his former town, he remembered the lost feeling that he shared with the other village natives. Turning to music for consolation and solace, he recalls that as he played his oud, impressions of his past came flooding back.

One well-known composition by Hamza el Din inspired by past memories is *Escalay* (*Water Wheel*), a work commissioned by the Kronos String Quartet, an ensemble that frequently ventures outside the traditional repertoire of the string quartet and seeks out innovative compositions for its programs. It appears in their popular recording *Pieces of Africa* (1991). The **string quartet** consists of two violins, a viola, and a cello, and it is a standard instrumentation which

Map of Africa showing the Sudan, Hamza el Din's homeland.

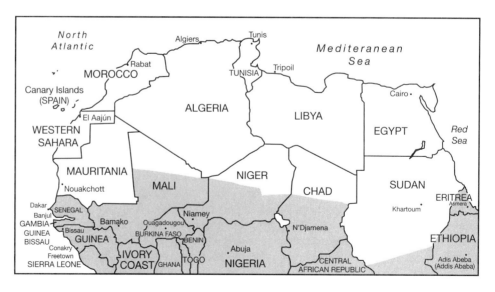

composers have used since the eighteenth century. The four musicians forming Kronos Quartet are interested in expanding into new musical territory the standard classical repertoire. They enjoy performing a variety of modern compositions, including music from around the world.

In writing *Escalay*, Hamza el Din remembered the monotonous hours of boyhood days when he and others labored to draw water from the community well by coaxing an ox, connected to a water wheel pump by a long pole, to walk in repetitive circular trips around the well. At the beginning, the music establishes a mood of tentative motion that eventually becomes faster and more repetitive. Its rhythmic pattern, however, is constantly changing ever so slightly. Hamza el Din soon introduces some short melodic gestures which represent a song that the boy sings—a collection of segments strung together in a seemingly endless melody. The composer is deft at translating the sounds of the oud to the modern string quartet, whose members combine **pizzicato** (or plucked) string performance techniques with the use of the bow.

Wherever Hamza el Din travels throughout the world, his perceptions of local landscapes and other personal experiences often remind this poet musician of his homeland. Such is the case with *The Gondola*, a work which came out of his travels to Italy. When he was riding in a gondola in Venice, the composer's mind shifted to days from his past when he would float on the Nile River. The feeling of being suspended between the water and the sky returned to him, and he composed an instrumental piece for the oud which represented this feeling to him and helped him recall his native culture.

The Gondola is truly an international piece of music, for Hamza el Din incorporates into it rhythmic figures inspired by the Italian saltarello dance without ever losing the character of Nubian musical style. The composer even imagines the intrusion of a motor boat in the middle of this work, which momentarily interrupts his feelings of nostalgia.

istening Guide 2

The Gondola
Hamza el Din (b. 1929)

Composition for the oud
Ca. 1964
Recorded by Hamza el Din
CD No. 1, Track 2 (4:32)

To Consider

Approach listening to this work for the oud with the awareness of music that seems to be continually evolving into something different. Consider the following questions as you listen, remembering the composer's comments about the origin of this piece.

1. Can you describe the character of the opening notes? Does the melodic material sound as though it is introductory in character, or does it sound like a definite melody, easy to remember? How can you tell?
2. Is there a point when you begin to sense motion and an increasing sense of momentum? How does the composer achieve this?
3. What do you think forms the gondola reference that the composer speaks of? Does it sound like something you would expect to hear in Italy, or is it an impression expressed in the composer's own native musical tongue?

0:00	Notice how the piece begins with a single melodic idea that rises and falls but is not repeated verbatim. The lowest pitch is played often enough to establish it as an important foundation and reference point for our listening.
0:35	Although motion picks up momentarily, frequent pauses and interruptions create a character of anticipation. There is no attempt at symmetrical phrases—the music sounds like improvisation.

0:54 The melodic fragments begin to take on the character of a theme, only to pause again. The bass note is played again and again as the foundation of the melody.

1:14 A feeling of motion continues, but it is still irregular as various melodic gestures come and go.

2:11 Each successive short melodic idea ends on the same fundamental bass pitch. Soon we begin to anticipate this note; it becomes a guidepost for our listening.

2:45 A new part of the work grows from the tentative beginnings and breaks into a regular rhythm. This section begins Hamza el Din's abstract reference to the Italian dance, the saltarello, and what he imagines to be sounds of a motorboat.

3:34 Although the listener anticipates a return to the tentative, peaceful, improvisatory character found at the beginning of the piece when the music slows to a stop, the work doesn't return to its opening material. The saltarello dance rhythm is not easily dismissed; the nostalgic memories of blue skies over the Nile is replaced by the realities of the Venetian gondola ride.

Listening to a work organized on repetition, such as *The Gondola*, requires a different approach from listening to a song with a melody that contains patterns of regularity. Here attention tends to focus on the moment; the mesmerizing effect takes the place of reference to a principal melodic or harmonic idea. The repetition creates only the anticipation of hearing more of the same. It seems that the work could go on forever; the ending could be placed at random, or the piece could continue for hours.

We have examined two different approaches to the manipulation of musical materials from two unrelated compositions by composers separated by different continents and cultures. They use repetition and contrast in their music in sharply contrasting ways. Needless to say, both of their compositions are effective and valid.

Reflect back on our two listening experiences, and you will realize that you have experienced music at both the emotional level and at the more analytical musical plane that Aaron Copland speaks about. Your pre-knowledge of *The Gondola*'s source of inspiration—Hamza el Din's memories of being suspended floating on the Nile that are interrupted by the sounds of a motor boat as he rode in a Venetian gondola—provided a reference for this piece. The perception of the manipulation of the musical elements (rhythms, melodies, the use of incessant bass notes) gave you deeper analytical insight into the composition.

*M*usical Encounter

The Mozart Effect: How Music Affects the Brain

*I*n the early 1990s, two scientists postulated that listening to music might have an effect on the functions of brain waves. To test their theory, they administered a spatial-temporal test to a group of college students after the students listened to a ten-minute segment of the Mozart *Sonata in D Major for Two Pianos*. Another group of students listened to relaxation music, while a third group took the exam without any musical prelude. The group of research subjects who listened to Mozart before their exam scored eight to ten points higher on the test than did the other participants in the experiment.

Spatial-temporal reasoning includes both the recognition of objects as being the same or different and the ability to form mental images of physical objects. Scientists recognize this as part of a higher brain functioning that is crucial to being successful in fields such as mathematics, physics, and engineering.

The pioneering research into the influence of music on the brain was carried out by Dr. Gordon Shaw, a physicist, who teamed with psychologist Dr. Frances Rauscher. These two scientists discovered that electronic brain activity, when fed into a synthesizer, created patterns of sound resembling different types of music. The next step in their inquiry was to determine whether or not brain neurons were stimulated when a subject listened to music. Drs. Shaw and Rauscher then began experimenting on preschool children to see if music influenced their brain development. The results were astounding.

One of the four control groups of children was given piano lessons, another computer lessons, a third singing lessons, and a fourth no lessons at all. At the end of six months, the piano students performed 34 percent better on the spatial-temporal ability tests than did any other group. Drs. Shaw and Rauscher called this phenomenon "The Mozart Effect."

According to brain scientists, the nerve cells that send messages throughout the brain are electrically charged and create paths, or circuits, in the process. The more a child is exposed to certain types of music—especially classical—the richer the brain network becomes.

Many other experiments correlating the shaping forces of music on developing higher-level thinking abilities are currently underway. Some involve the use of the electroencephalogram (EEG), which detects and records brain waves from the surface of the skull. Other researchers are using magnetic resonance imaging (MRI) and positron emission tomography (PET)—electronic devices commonly used to measure physical functions and activities of the brain. These studies focus on a variety of musical experiences, from children's participation in music-making to the effects of music listening on cognitive and spatial-temporal skills.

For several decades, music educators have believed that music instruction has positive effects on children's general brain development, but recent research may give scientific proof of these earlier postulations. Present and future studies will either reinforce or discourage conclusions concerning the effectiveness of music on building brain power in children, but as the twenty-first century dawns, it appears that there is indeed proof of a positive correlation between certain musical activities and intellectual development.

One of the strongest believers of music's magic is Zell Miller, who, as the governor of Georgia in 1998, proposed that his state set aside $105,000 so that each newborn child in Georgia could be given a CD of classical music upon leaving the hospital. Governor Miller made this public statement: "No one doubts that listening to music, especially at a very early age, affects the reasoning that underlies math and engineering and chess. I believe it can help Georgia children to excel." [6]

Did your enjoyment depend on knowing the background of the work? Not necessarily. The composition stands alone in the light of musical scrutiny. Hamza el Din was successful in beginning a work with a minimal amount of material and then building it slowly until its repetitive nature made you lose track of time and become immersed in the music itself. There can be no doubt, however, that being able to create your own mental picture of the composer's source of inspiration enhanced your appreciation of this effective composition.

The musical encounters that you will experience throughout this book will focus on the interesting relationships between content and structure—relationships that you have now experienced. (We have identified these initially as hearing music at the "emotional" and the "purely musical" levels of perception.) Music is indeed a phenomenal art, for it combines emotional, intellectual, and structural avenues of expression so effectively that, although they can be isolated by analysis, these components of music work together in a wonderfully interdependent way.

MUSICAL STYLE AND HISTORICAL PERIODS OF MUSIC

The two composers whose work we have listened to so far, Leonard Bernstein and Hamza el Din, represent radically different musical styles. Before we continue, we need to clarify the term **style,** which refers to traits of composition that are consistent with that composer. The way in which a composer organizes the musical elements in a composition, whether classical music or popular songs, results in a style that speaks for that individual composer. The musical style of a composition is the final result of the way in which various elements of music are presented and manipulated by the composer.

Although the musical style of a composition refers to its composite construction, the way in which a piece of music is performed, or the **performance style,** also is an important part of musical presentation. Every type of music carries with it certain expectations of performing style. For example, pop performers or performing groups work hard to establish a style of performance that will distinguish them from others. Pop star Mariah Carey has a unique way of adding short notes and expressive inflections to her melodies. The late Frank Sinatra's distinctive voice quality, the way he stressed certain syllables of the lyrics, and his low, soothing singing was easily recognized by millions of his fans—so much so that "crooner" became a household word because of his popularity.

In the world of pop music, of course, styles change at an ever-increasing rate, as the producers of popular music struggle constantly to present new material to the public. Each artist or group develops its own style (usually called "sound") in order to be distinguished from others, while at the same time maintaining enough common features with other performers to maintain an identity with a common style. The contrast between uniqueness and commonality gives rise to a vitality and an excitement that seems to be an important part of the pop world.

Although the term style can correctly describe music of all cultures and venues, its use in reference to a **composer's style** (as opposed to a **performer's style**) can be clearly illustrated by citing examples from the Western concert repertoire.

One composer, for example, may write music that features jagged rhythms intended to unsettle the listener's sense of rhythmic regularity (Stravinsky). Another may use very dissonant harmonies (Schoenberg). Someone else may simulate, or even quote, folk tunes (Copland). We recognize the music of J. S. Bach for its tightly interwoven melodic lines (counterpoint) and regularity of rhythm; we see in Mozart music that is based on subtle turnings of melodic and harmonic elements within the accepted conventions of materials.

These techniques of composition and the composers associated with them will be the major part of our following study. A discussion of musical style, whether at the level of the individual composer or a larger perspective of groups of composers having similar approaches, usually involves an examination of many elements of music (often called parameters of style). We will identify these elements in Chapter 3, as they are the basis of our study in subsequent chapters.

As we examine the music of different Western historical eras and different countries, some general features representing these times and places emerge. These observations have given rise to the concept of "schools" of compositional practice that often enable us to group together several composers. By doing so, music historians have been able to identify the most significant stylistic features of a given period of time.

Although this book is not a music history textbook, you will find frequent references to the broad epochs of the development of music through the ages: the Medieval (800–1450), Renaissance (1450–1600), Baroque (1600–1750), Classical (1750–1825), Romantic (1825–1900), and Modern (1900–present) eras. These dates are approximations, and the end of one historical style period may invariably overlap with the beginning of another.

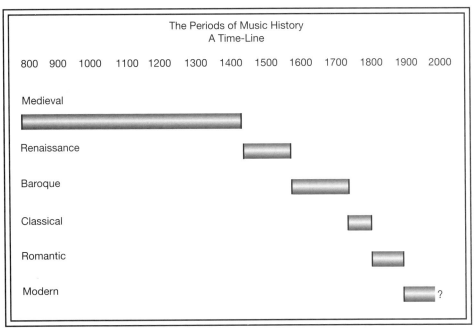

The Periods of Music History.

To illustrate the concept of a popular musical style from an earlier period of history, we will examine a composition from more than 450 years ago. It is a piece that has endured through history, for it is still frequently sung by small choral groups. It was the **French chanson,** popular among the nobility in France during the Renaissance. (*Chanson* is the French word for song.) Claudin de Sermisy (ca. 1490–1562), the composer of the chanson *Tant que vivray (So long as I am in my prime)*, was typical of court composers in the sixteenth century in that he wrote both music for the church and music for entertaining in the courts of the king. Sermisy worked in the French courts of Francis I and Henry II; he also was employed by the Sainte-Chapelle Cathedral in Paris. During his career, he wrote more than 175 chansons and approximately 110 choral works for the church. In addition to composing for the church, his duties included training and conducting choirs, organizing musical performances of various types, and singing at special festivals.

♪istening Guide 3

Tant que vivray (So long as I am in my prime)
Claudin de Sermisy (ca. 1490–1562)
Poem by Clément Marot

French chanson
Ca. 1530–1540
Recorded by the Ensemble Jannequin
CD No. 1, Track 3 (2:14)

Composers of sixteenth-century French chansons always wrote their music in such a way that the lyrics could be easily understood. They were typically written for four voice parts and were sung by small groups of perhaps two people on each part. Claudin de Sermisy was known for his ability to capture the spirit of the text, and this feature is what we will try to discover in this musical encounter. Read the words as you listen to *Tant que vivray* and see if you can detect features that relate the words to the music. (The lines of the poem are numbered for your reference when discussing the questions concerning the musical style of this chanson.)

Tant que vivrai en âge florissant,	So long as I am in my prime	1
Je serviray d'amours le roi puissant	I shall serve the great god of love	2
En fais, en dits, en chansons et accords.	In deeds and words, song and harmony:	3
Par plusiers fois m'a tenu languissant,	Oft he has left me to languish	4
Mais apres deuil m'a fait rejoissant,	But, after sorrow, has brought joy,	5
Car j'ai l'amour de la belle au gent corps.	For I have the love of a beautiful woman.	6
Son alliance, C'est ma fiance.	Her betrothal is pledged to me;	7
Son coeur est mien, Le mien est sien.	Her heart is mine, And mine is hers.	8
Fy de tristesse, Vive liesse,	Away with sorrow, Long live joy,	9
Puisque en amour, A tant de bien.	For in love there is so much pleasure.	10
Quand je la veulx servir et honorer;	When I wish to serve and honor her,	11
Quand par escript veulx son nom decorer;	When I wish to write her name's praises,	12
Quand je la veoy et visite souvent;	When I see her and visit her often,	13
Ses enviewx n'en font aque mormurer,	The envious only complain;	14
Mais notre amour n'en scauroit moins durer	Nevertheless, our love will endure	15
Autant oup plus en emporte le vent.	As long as the winds blow.	16
Malgré envie, Toute ma vie	In spite of envy, All my life	17
Je l'aimerai, Et chanterai.	Shall I love her; And I shall sing;	18
C'est la première, C'est la dernière	This is the first, This is the last	19
Que j'ai servie, que j'ai servie, Et servirai.	That I have served, and shall serve more.[7] 20

To Consider

1. Upon your first hearing, you probably noticed that the music repeated itself in certain places, although the lyrics continue to the next line. Can you detect this pattern of repetition?
2. How many lines of text are stated before the music repeats?
3. Is this pattern consistent throughout the two sections of the chanson?
4. Do the patterns of musical repetition help emphasize or clarify the lyrics in any way?
5. What is the poetic significance of the singers repeating the last lines of each section of the poem?

You have already discovered that this love song has a charm that still is apparent some 470 years after it was composed. As we examine points of musical style, this charm becomes even more evident.

0:00 The chanson begins with all of the four voices singing the words at the same time—like that of a hymn. Notice that there are slight pauses in the music to allow the singers to breathe with the flow of the lyrics.

0:21 Beginning with the fourth line of the poem, the music repeats and is identical to lines, 1, 2, and 3.

0:41 Notice that the line starting with "Son alliance" (line7) begins a slightly different musical setting. It seems to pick up in energy. The two lines (7 and 8) now form a musical unit which is repeated in lines 9 and 10.

0:51 "Puisque en amour" (line 10) is sung twice to reinforce the most meaningful line of the poem's first half—"For in love there is much pleasure."

The musical treatment in the second section of the poem is identical to the first. Did you notice that several words received some additional notes as the music progressed? These occurred in the final lines of each musical statement ("dits"—*words*, in line 3; "l'amour"—*love*, in line 6; "veoy"—*see*, in line 13, etc.). Do you think the composer added these notes simply for musical variety, or did he want to underline those words in the poem? If you were to become acquainted with more chansons of this style, you would discover that yes, indeed, composers of this music frequently emphasized key words in the lyrics.

Our musical encounter with a Renaissance French chanson has shown us several things about the style:

1. The words are set with care and clarity.

2. Certain patterns of musical repetition are present, even when the poem does not contain repeated lines.

3. Important words receive added musical attention by the composer.

4. The general mood of the poem is reflected in the music.

Your ability to discuss music will increase as you learn the vocabulary of music, which we will explore in Chapter 2. It is interesting to note, however, that elements of musical style can be identified even before you become acquainted with the technical terms of music. Now let us look at a painting to see what we can learn about style in art.

The painting, *Lady Musicians,* is particularly interesting to our study because it is a painting of three ladies performing Claudin de Sermisy's chanson, titled *Joyssance vous donneray* (*You bring joy [to me]*). The painter is identified only as "The Master of Female Half-Lengths." Art historians have placed this early sixteenth-century painting as having come from Antwerp; its anonymous artist took his name from this painting, named *Lady Musicians.*

The Master of Female Half-Lengths, *Lady Musicians,* also known as *The Concert* (the Harrach Collection, Schloss Rohrau, Vienna).

What can we tell about the style of this painting? *Lady Musicians* appears to be a rather realistic depiction of musical performance. We observe, for example, that the finger positions of the flute and the lute players are accurate. The notes of the manuscript are clearly documented as being from Sermisy's chanson. Notice the close attention to detail in virtually every part of the painting, from the delicate folds in the ladies' clothing to the intricate carving in the wood panel behind the musicians. There is no doubt about the social class of these women: their clothing, the dignity of their posture and facial expression, and even the tilt of their heads suggest propriety. They have similar hair and clothing styles, yet each woman appears to be an individual.

The general shape of the figures, the use of light to enhance the depth of the painting, and the balance of the subject matter suggest that this anonymous painter was influenced by some of the great Flemish painters, such as Hans Memling, Jan van Eyck, and Rogier van der Weyden. In painting, as in music, artists have a remarkable influence on each other. Their styles are certainly individual, but their works often share stylistic characteristics and thereby prove that they can be grouped with other artists.

What does our examination of *Lady Musicians* tell us about the performance practice of Sermisy's chansons? First, they were intended to be performed by people of class and good breeding. We also know that they were often played as well as sung. We can see that the performers were careful about their dress and about their performing demeanor. So by examining the music itself, we have determined the composer's style; the unusual existence of a painting depicting a work of Sermisy's being performed gives us insight into the style of performance practice. And, of course, the components of the painting lend information regarding the painter's style and technique.

By examining many compositions written during the Renaissance, and by studying various contemporary documents, including books, paintings, letters, and other manuscripts, we can determine that Renaissance music was performed by small ensembles. The Renaissance performance practices in music were vastly different from those of other times.

The concept of style, then, is not only an important feature of music, but it relates closely to activities in the other arts and in literature. Discovering these relationships is always one of the fascinating benefits of exposing oneself to the artistic world—and in observing how one functions as a complex, fulfilled human being.

SUMMARY

Music is universal and is enjoyed by all people. It can serve a variety of functions in a society, and listeners can respond on a variety of levels. Although music is commonly defined as organized sound, in reality, it is a form of communication capable of stimulating emotions. It also is used to rekindle in the listener personal experiences, to reflect tastes, attitudes, and needs, and even to describe actual events or fictional stories.

People often enjoy music at different levels of perception. Aaron Copland suggests that these levels are: the sensual level, where a person bathes in the sound without being aware of the manipulation of musical materials; the emotional level, where the listener is experiencing emotions and other stimuli as the result of hearing the music; and the purely musical level, which occurs when the listener is able to perceive the composer's techniques of composition with regard to structure and style.

The musical examples used in this chapter explored these levels of perception. In "Maria," from *West Side Story*, you heard how the composer intensified the word "Ma-ri-a" by using appropriate accents and rhythms. You also experienced the formal concepts of repetition and contrast. In Hamza el Din's *The Gondola*, you began to understand the continual unfolding of the music not governed by symmetrical concepts of repetition and contrast.

Finally, you were introduced to the concept of musical style and how styles in music parallel other art forms throughout history.

EY TERMS

accent
composer's style
doubling
drone
French chanson
musical style
oud
performance style
performer's style
pizzicato
recapitulation
recitative
string quartet
style

CHAPTER 2

The Language of Music

$\mathcal{I}$N Chapter 1, we learned that music is a means of communication—a unique way of organizing sounds into meaning. Even though music has the power to communicate directly to the listener without words, composers, performers, and consumers have found it necessary to develop a musical vocabulary that enables them to give performance directions, to discuss musical composition, and to define the elements of music. When asked to describe what happened in the musical examples found in Chapter 1, you no doubt were searching for words that could adequately represent what you heard.

People who strive to improve their listening skills and widen their musical experiences soon recognize that musical perception carries with it a specialized vocabulary. The components of music, often called elements of music, must be perceived and processed by the ear and the mind as the listener experiences music.

Whenever we listen to sounds, whether music, traffic, the ocean, the deep breathing of the person sleeping next to us, nature, or the city, we are either consciously or unconsciously aware of patterns that make up that listening experience. The continual development of this awareness is at the center of learning how to hear music.

This chapter contains a systematic approach to integrating the elements and structures of music with the listening experience. Throughout the chapter, recorded examples are used to illustrate specific components of musical composition. If you are relatively new to an in-depth approach to listening, the basic knowledge you will acquire here will greatly enhance your ability to enjoy and understand music of all kinds.

Our study begins by isolating four basic components of a musical sound (pitch, duration, intensity, and tone color) and uses these components as a gateway not only to understand how musical sounds are notated but also to see how a wide range of musical instruments offers the composer an almost limitless array of tone colors for use in a composition.

Next, the discussion and illustration of musical elements (melody, harmony, rhythm, meter, tempo, volume, texture, and form) will add meaningful enhancement toward musical perception.

$\mathcal{F}$OUR PROPERTIES OF A MUSICAL NOTE

Each note of music contains four basic components: **pitch** (the frequency of a sound,) **duration** (the length of the sound,) **intensity** (the volume of a sound,) and **timbre** (the characteristic tone quality or color.) The listening experience begins with your perception of how these fundamental components of sound are manipulated by the composer and the performer. The basic discussion of notation included here will help you not only understand some of the theoretical aspects of the art of music, but will assist you in following the written musical examples that occur throughout this book.

Pitch and Pitch Notation

Whenever a material vibrates at a specific frequency, it puts into force a movement of sound waves that our ears hear as pitch. These pitches can be measured in the number of vibrations, or cycles per second (cps) and can be identified by their frequency. The common designation for these units of measurement in cycles per second is **Hz,** named after Heinrich Hertz (1857–1894), the physicist whose theories led to the development of the wireless telegraph and radio.

The human ear is capable of detecting sounds ranging from 15 Hz to 20,000 Hz (cps), but it has a much narrower range of accurate pitch discrimination. The lowest note on the modern piano is 27.5 Hz; the highest is 4,186 Hz. Any sound that cannot be comprehended as a specific pitch is called **noise.** We will see later in this book that noise is also a legitimate component of music.

The piano keyboard.

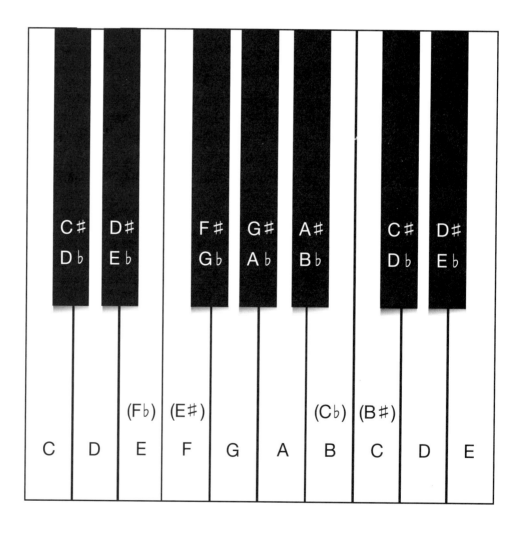

Long before pitches could be measured by their cycles per second, they were named by using the first seven letters of the alphabet (A-B-C-D-E-F-G). This practice, which developed gradually over several hundred years, is still used today. Therefore, instead of calling a specific pitch "440" (its frequency,) we call it "A."

If the frequency of a tone is doubled, another similar tone will be produced, but at the sound of one **octave** higher. (An octave is an interval between notes created when the top note sounds at exactly double the frequency of the bottom note.) Conversely, if a string vibrates at one-half the frequency of the original tone, it will sound one octave lower. Thus the frequencies of 110, 220, 440, and 880 Hz and so on are all called the same pitch name ("A"), with each separated by the interval of one octave.

The division of the octave into twelve parts, resulting in twelve separate pitches, also has ancient roots in the evolution of European music. The two procedures (the naming of notes by using seven letters of the alphabet and the development of twelve pitches belonging to the octave) obviously do not coincide. Therefore, a third notation practice gradually evolved so that all of the pitches of the twelve divisions of the octave could have names. Three symbols are used to alter the pitches of the seven notes (A through G) and to represent the remaining five notes of this octave division. The symbol (♭), the **flat,** was used to lower a pitch, while the **sharp** (♯) raised it. These are called **accidentals.** A third accidental was eventually used to cancel either a sharp or a flat—the **natural** (♮).

Notation is the term associated with written (and printed) music. As was the case with the naming of pitches, the notation of music developed over centuries. Its present form uses a system of five horizontal lines and includes the four spaces between those lines. This system is called a **staff.** Pitches are notated consecutively on those lines and spaces. **Clef signs**—symbols that appear at the beginning of musical notation—are used to indicate which notes are represented on the staff. The two most common clef signs are the **treble clef** (𝄞), or the "G" clef, and the **bass clef** (𝄢), also known as the "F" clef. Notice that the treble clef is an elaborate form of the letter "G"; the bass clef also evolved from the letter F. They are positioned on the musical staff to indicate the location of the pitches G or F, and thus are reference points for the rest of the lines and spaces.

Now that we have been introduced to pitch names and notation, let us read a well-known French folk tune to see how pitch notation works. (We also will refer to this example later when we discuss rhythm and meter.) This example is written in the treble clef and begins on the note C. Sing along (using the syllable "la") as you read the music and you will notice that, as the notes rise on the staff, the notes you sing will also be in a higher range. Notice also that short lines are added to extend the staff when the range of the notes exceeds the five lines and four spaces on the staff. These are called **ledger lines** and can be used either above or below the staff, as the music requires.

The Grand Staff.

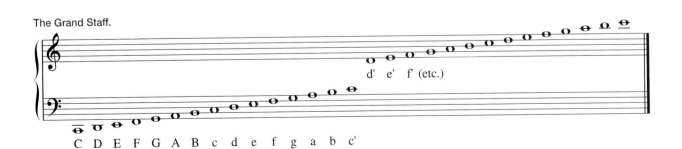

Are You Sleeping, Brother John?

Duration: An Introduction to Time Values

Just as music requires an accurate pitch system that can be notated and shared among people, so does it need a way to measure the lengths of the notes. The length of musical tones is measured by a system of notation that always relates to a basic **pulse,** or beat. The **beat** is a recurring pulsation that serves as a reference point for time values in music. Its name comes from the very pulse of the human body; in fact, in medieval times, it was thought that the human pulse (the *tactus*) should be used to set the general speed (or **tempo**) of sacred music. This concept of "appropriate tempo" has, of course, been extended to include a wide variety of speeds, from very slow to very fast, which is used to fit the demands of the music.

To experience the beat or the pulse of a melody, sing the following patriotic hymn, *America,* and clap on the beat. For our illustration only, the beats are marked with a vertical line above the notes. (This is not a common notational practice.) Try this exercise at different tempos.

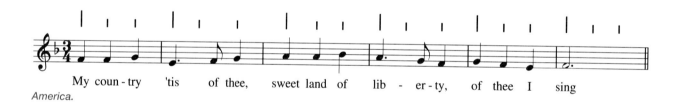

My coun-try 'tis of thee, sweet land of lib - er-ty, of thee I sing

America.

A sophisticated system of notation has evolved that permits a wide span of note lengths to be written down. The rhythm in music provides an unending variety to the feeling of motion in a piece of music. (**Rhythm** is the overall sense of movement in music.) The rhythmic notation system is based on a few fundamental principles. These involve the pulse, the individual **note values** in relation to the pulse, and the **meter,** or the grouping of these pulses into larger recurring sets. We will explore the concepts of duration in music first by becoming acquainted with the individual note values.

Common note values used in modern music are the whole note (∘), the half note (♩), the quarter note (♩), the eighth note (♪), the sixteenth note (♬), and the thirty-second note (♬). Faster or slower notes are, of course, possible and occur with less regularity than those mentioned here. An elaborate system of rhythmic notation is used to designate varying lengths of notes.

The following illustration is a chart of common note values and their relationship to each other.

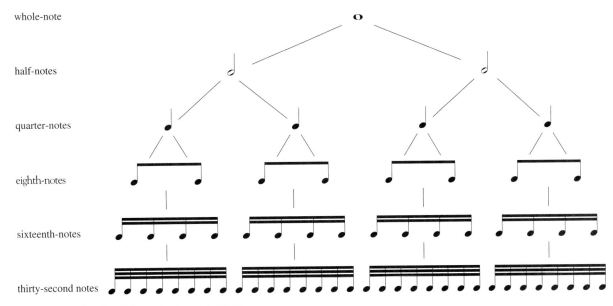

whole-note

half-notes

quarter-notes

eighth-notes

sixteenth-notes

thirty-second notes

Note values and their relationships to each other.

In the majority of musical scores, beats are grouped into larger sets for ease in reading and also for patterns of implied stress or accent. These sets of pulses are called **measures** and are notated in music by vertical lines connecting the top and bottom lines of the musical staff.

Almost any note value may be designated as the unit of pulse. Both the number of beats per measure and the rhythmic unit representing the beat are shown at the beginning of the musical score in a device called the **time signature** (also known as the **meter signature**.) In this set of two numbers (resembling a fraction without the line separating them), the top number indicates how many beats per measure occur in the music, and the bottom number indicates which note value gets the pulse. $\begin{pmatrix} 2 & 3 & 4 \\ 4 & 4 & 4 \end{pmatrix}$

Whereas the rhythmic value receiving the beat is irrelevant to the listener, the meter, or number of beats in a measure, often is a significant factor in hearing the music in a meaningful way. For example, the strong feeling of beat that you get when you listen to a rap performer is created by the regular grouping of two beats per measure and the strong accent placed on the second beat. Later in this chapter you will experience a technique commonly used in jazz that momentarily upsets the feeling of meter.

The example below demonstrates the common note values and their relationships in a simple metrical setting. The two sharps (♯) at the beginning constitute the **key signature,** an indication for the performer to raise all notes indicated (F and C) throughout the piece. A natural sign (♮) can be used if the composer wishes to cancel the sharps in any given note.

Note values in the context of a musical score.

The Vocabulary and Function of Volume in Music

The volume of a tone can range from the ear-splitting level of a rock concert to the softest lullaby. The terms composers use to indicate volume, called **dynamic markings,** originated in Italy and have become standard throughout the world.

Common Dynamic Markings

pianississimo	ppp	very, very soft
pianissimo	pp	very soft
piano	p	soft
mezzo-piano	mp	moderately soft
mezzo-forte	mf	moderately loud
forte	f	loud
fortissimo	ff	very loud
fortississimo	fff	very, very loud

In addition, two common words are used to indicate changes in dynamics: **crescendo** (a gradual increase in volume) and **decrescendo** (a gradual decrease in volume).

These expression indications are just some of many that are found in musical scores. In practice, the strength of volume often relates to the size and acoustics of the hall and the character of the music. The fluctuations of volume, used artistically with manipulations of other elements of sound, are key ingredients to stimulating musical enjoyment. The absence of dynamic contrast in music, like the absence of volume inflections in speech, leads to monotony and makes the music or speech sound impersonal and mechanical. Composers and performers, always aware of this, are careful to use dynamic contrasts to emphasize the artistry of a musical phrase, to delineate formal structure, and to build points of emotional climax and relaxation. As your listening becomes more specific in nature, you will become increasingly aware of the role that dynamic shadings play in musical expressions.

Timbre and the Colorful Sounds of Music

If musical sounds consisted only of pitches, rhythms, and various shades of volume, listening to music could be a very boring experience. The property of music that gives composers tremendous possibilities for manipulating sounds into colorful music is timbre, the characteristic quality of sound. Timbre is often compared to color in art, in fact, the term **tone color** is another way to describe timbre.

Timbre is determined by several basic principles. The way the tone is produced determines its basic sound characteristic. The second component of timbre is its **resonance,** or the manner in which the vibrations of sound are projected through the air. For example, notes that are produced by the human voice result from the controlled vibration of the vocal cords—two small membranes located in a person's neck. The small variance in the thickness and length of these cords, along with the unique way in which the sound is projected through the head and chest cavities and the mouth of the person singing, creates the resonance of that sound. Together, these two factors produce a sound characteristic of a specific person's voice. In Chapter 3 we will discover that the voice is capable of producing an amazing array of musical sounds. Timbre plays a major role in this variety.

The thousands of musical instruments in existence around the world provide an even greater array of timbral possibilities. We will explore these by identifying groups of instruments that share common ways of sound production, keeping in mind that our major focus in *Musical Encounters* is on listening.

If a comprehensive collection of musical instruments from around the world were to be assembled, the diversity of shapes and materials represented would be amazing. One interesting feature that instruments of all cultures have in common, however, is that sound is produced either by bowing and plucking, striking, or blowing on and through the instruments. Instruments are classified into three basic groups: wind instruments, stringed instruments, and percussion instruments. These three instrument types can be described more specifically by examining the exact way in which sound is produced by them. Let us consider the sources of these instrumental timbres by sampling some instruments from each category.

Musical Encounter

Overtones and the Overtone Series

*T*he Greek philosopher-mathematician Pythagoras (fl. ca. 500 B.C.) initiated a discovery that eventually lead to an awareness that, when a string vibrates, it not only vibrates over its entire length, but there are simultaneous vibrations of segments of the string that follow exact mathematical ratios. These vibrations, called **partials,** also produce pitches, although they are usually not audible to the human ear as such. These other tones are called **overtones,** or **harmonics.** Along with the principal or fundamental frequency of the vibrating string, these overtones make up the characteristic timbre, or tone quality, of that specific vibrating string. The relative strength of the overtones produced by a specific vibrating string depends on several factors, including the material used in the string, the thickness of the string, the diameter of the string, and its tension.

The acoustical phenomenon of the overtone series applies not only to strings but to any resonating body that gives off specific frequencies. Thus it also applies to woodwind, brass, and pitched percussion instruments.

The timbre of a sound is determined by the way in which that sound is produced—through a reed, lips buzzing into a brass mouthpiece, or mallets hammering on wood bars, as well as by the shape of the instrument. Each family of instruments and, to be more specific, each individual type of instrument, has its own configuration of overtones.

If a single vibration were to produce a sound, that would result in a **pure sound.** However, nearly all instruments produce a **composite sound** that consists of a fundamental pitch and several overtones. These overtones are created in a specific mathematical relationship to the fundamental pitch, and they produce what is known as the **overtone series.** The musical example below illustrates an overtone series based on the pitch C. In Chapter 3 we will encounter a culture whose women singers learn to produce not only a fundamental pitch but several of the overtones simultaneously.

The overtone series.

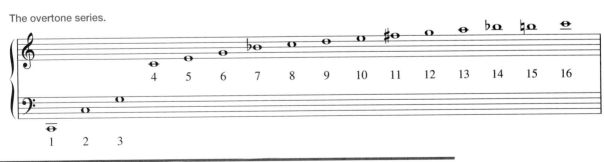

Wind Instruments

Wind instruments (**aerophones**) date back to prehistoric times. Archeologists have uncovered end-blown flutes dating from the Stone Age in places as disparate as Denmark, in South America, and in Asia. The timbres of these instruments, often associated with the supernatural, were used to influence the gods in matters such as weather, the fertility of crops, and even in death ceremonies. The functions of primitive trumpets—often fashioned out of bone, wood, or ivory—were also determined by their characteristic sound. Widely used in ceremonial and signaling functions, these instruments are found throughout the world.

Each characteristic tone color of various wind instruments is determined both by the shape of the instrument's tube and by the way in which the initial sound is produced. A cone-shaped instrument attached to a double reed (such as the oboe) produces a bright and nasal sound, whereas a cylindrical instrument played by blowing over an open hole (such as the modern orchestral flute) produces a more "airy" sound.

Music is created on wind instruments in one of the following ways:

1. By blowing across an open hole in a tube (as in the flute that you have heard in bands and orchestras), or in a whistle device called a "beak," a sharp edge in the blow hole that splits the air column before it goes into a tubular instrument. (If you were taught to play the recorder in grade school, you were playing a whistle flute.) These instruments, whether open-holed instruments or beaked instruments, go by the generic term "flute."

2. By a vibrating reed or reeds, which is either attached to a mouthpiece (such as in the clarinet or saxophone), or a double reed, which is usually inserted into the mouth and held by pressing the lips together on the reed (as in the oboe and the bassoon).

3. By buzzing the lips into a cup-shaped mouthpiece. Sound is produced in this manner by the entire family of brass instruments (trumpet, horn, trombone, and tuba).

The Woodwinds: oboe, saxophone, flute, clarinet, bassoon (in foreground).
Source: David C. Nichols.

The woodwind family of instruments is the most diverse category of wind instruments, and therefore, it represents a wide range of tone colors. For that reason, these instruments function well alone. When played as a choir, their sounds blend without sacrificing individual timbres.

Flutes, ethnic flutes, and whistles produce sound when a player blows an air stream into an edge, which splits the air stream and causes a vibration. In embouchured flutes (orchestral flutes, shakuhachi), this edge is an open hole in the instrument, and the lips of the player direct the air stream precisely into the edge of the hole to produce the sound. With beaked flutes (recorders, whistles, and some varieties of ethnic flutes), the air stream is automatically aimed. The lowest notes of the flute are soft; the higher one plays, the more brilliant the notes become.

Conversely, the sounds of the double reeds (the oboe, the English horn, and the bassoon) become thinner as they are played in the higher ranges. The lowest notes are the broadest and most protrusive. The slightly nasal sound of these instruments adds an edge to the woodwind choir.

The clarinet, the single-reed instrument, offers a tonal perspective to the orchestra that both blends well with the woodwinds and provides a mellow solo tone quality. It is a sound that may not soar above the entire orchestra, but it can project through the thick orchestral texture when called upon. It, like the flute, is a flexible instrument, capable of playing fast and difficult passages with ease. The unique tone of a saxophone, also a single-reed instrument, is created when the air column vibrates through its cone-shaped (conical) body.

Brass Instruments

The tonal role of brass instruments in the symphony orchestra is broad, but since all brass instruments are played with a cup-shaped mouthpiece, there is a stronger continuity of tone in the brasses than in the woodwinds. Sound is produced in brass instruments by the lips of the player "buzzing" into the mouthpiece, thereby creating vibrations to be amplified by the horn.

The horns (also called "French horns") are the most versatile brass instruments in terms of timbre. At times they are used as blending instruments, carrying the inner notes of chords. Horns also are capable of playing moving, haunting solos.

The trumpet is the soprano of the brass choir. Its power to project is legendary. Its structure is well suited to brilliantly tongued passages, and it often presents fanfare-like music. At times the trumpet gives off a feeling of aggressiveness, in contrast to the rather passive and round tones of the horn section.

Brass Instruments: Horn, tuba, trumpet, trombone (in foreground). Source: David C. Nichols.

Beethoven was the first to use trombones in the orchestra. He introduced them in his fifth symphony when he was trying to expand the expressive capabilities of the symphony. Like the horns, trombones frequently play a dual role of either playing supporting harmonies or solo passages.

The tuba functions as the foundation of the brass orchestral sound. While it traditionally was used in a rather restricted role of the strong bass note in full chords, modern composers are exploiting its melodic capabilities.

Stringed Instruments

The earliest and simplest example of a stringed instrument (or **chordophone**) is the musical bow, which is still used in some cultures in Africa and South America. Other early examples of chordophones are harps, which were used in Egypt and the Sumerian cultures some 5,000 years ago and have remained popular in one form or another until the present time. Since these early examples, many types of stringed instruments have developed and evolved. The lute, for example, which is thought to have originated in the Mesopotamian regions in central Asia, is the ancestor of the guitar and the modern orchestral instruments—the violin, viola, cello, and double bass.

Sound is produced on chordophones by strings that are stretched tightly (often attached to some sort of structure such as a box, which gives them resonance) and set in vibration by plucking, bowing, or striking. The tone quality of the modern piano, perhaps the most widely used string instrument in the music of Western cultures, is determined by the size of the instrument and the length and thickness of the strings. The modern grand piano has about 225 strings, averaging 180 pounds of pressure each (totaling about 40,000 pounds of pressure on the steel frame). Its tone color is much richer than that of a small spinet piano, with its shorter strings and smaller body.

The Japanese koto. A Japanese musician, wearing regional attire, plays a koto. Japan, ca. 1890s. © Michael Maslan Historic Photographs / CORBIS. ID # IH072205.

In our musical encounters, we will hear many examples of stringed music from Western cultures—both from the concert and the popular folk repertoires. These tone colors are familiar to almost everyone living in the Western Hemisphere. To expand our experience in instrumental timbres, we will now listen to a short example of a **koto,** a popular concert instrument from Japan's long musical tradition. This instrument is classified as a **long zither**—a type of chordophone that has numerous strings stretched over a basically flat, boxlike body. The koto also has bridges that can be adjusted along the body of the instrument to tune it; the player plucks the string on one side of the bridge while pressing on the string on the other side of bridge, thereby causing slight changes in string tension and therefore, subtle changes in intonation.

The string section of the traditional symphony orchestra forms its largest body of like instruments. Of the three instrumental families making up the orchestra (strings, wind, and percussion instruments), the strings are the most consistent in timbre. Each instrument type (violin, viola, cello, and string bass) has four strings of varying thickness that are stretched over a bridge attached to the body of the instrument. This bridge conveys the vibrations to the wooden "box"—which functions as the amplifier for the sound. The relative sizes of the four instrument types offer a continuous scale of pitches from the lowest (double bass) upward to the cello, the viola, and the violin, respectively. From the lowest rattle of the bass to the highest shrill note of the violin, there is a characteristic "string timbre." This sound forms the foundation of the symphony.

Listening Guide 4

A Message for a Solo 30-String Koto *(Sanjü-gen Dokuso No Tame No Messëji)*	Solo composition for koto About 1990 Recorded by Miyashita Shin CD No. 1, Track 4 (4:45)

To Consider

1. Notice the diversity of timbres in the opening few seconds of this work. Have you ever experimented with plucking or hitting the strings of a piano to produce percussive sounds?
2. What is your reaction to this piece? Do the tone colors of the koto seem strange to you? Is it difficult for you to place this large instrument in a musical role similar to that of the grand piano in Western cultures?
3. As you listen to this, notice how your ear becomes adjusted to the subtleties of tone colors available in this one instrument.

Once again you have been exposed to the concept of diversity in music—this time within the realm of music produced by vibrating strings. We, of course, have barely begun to hear the extreme ranges of timbres that can be produced by musical instruments. This range is made even greater by the hundreds of percussion instruments. So before we leave the concept of timbre in music, we will describe the categories of percussion instruments.

Percussion Instruments

The third grouping of instruments is even more varied than either stringed or wind instruments, for literally, anything used to create musical sounds that are not made by aerophones or chordophones can be called percussion instruments. This, of course, includes instruments that make noise (sounds without a definite pitch).

Timbre, a significant part of each musical note, is also a component of nonpitched sounds, and it deserves our attention here.

Two fundamental types of percussion instruments are **idiophones**—instruments made of naturally sonorous materials, and **membranophones**—instruments whose sound is made from hitting a skin or other membrane stretched over a resonating drum. From the first time people created simple rhythms by clapping their hands together to the subtle and intricate rhythms of African drummers, jazz drummers, and percussion ensembles in concert halls, humankind has felt the need to explore sound colors beyond the realm of voices, winds, and strings.

Stringed Instruments: Double bass, viola, violin, cello.
Source: David C. Nichols.

To describe the diversity of idiophones in music around the world, the following designations have been developed:

1. Stamping idiophones: instruments sounded by banging them on a surface, such as the ground or another hard surface (sticks, tubes, tap shoes). Stamped idiophones refer to the surface that produces the sound (boards over pits, for example).

2. Shaken idiophones: rattles, shakers, jingles.

3. Percussion idiophones: instruments that produce sound when struck by a stick or a beater (xylophones, gongs, marimbas).

4. Concussion idiophones: instruments that produce sound when two or more similar parts are struck together (cymbals, clappers, claves).

5. Friction idiophones: instruments sounded by rubbing (musical saw or musical glasses).

6. Scraped idiophones: instruments that have a notched or an irregular surface and are rubbed by a stick (washboard, guiro).

7. Plucked idiophones: instruments that have flexible tongues that are plucked (Jew's harps, sansas).

The percussion section in the Western symphony is enjoying an ever-increasing role in contemporary music. Some percussion instruments, such as the marimba, the

Percussion Instruments:
Timpani. Photo by: C Squared
Studios. Source: PhotoDisc, Inc.
Drum kit. Photo by: C Squared
Studios. Source: PhotoDisc, Inc.
Marimba. Photo by: C Squared
Studios. Source: PhotoDisc, Inc.

xylophone, the piano (a stringed instrument sometimes considered a percussion instrument because the hammers of a piano strike the strings), and the timpani, play specific pitches. Other instruments (snare drums, cymbals, claves, triangles, woodblocks, etc.) are not specifically pitched, although there is a range of "high" and "low" sounds within some of these nonpitched instruments.

MUSICAL STYLE AND CRITICAL LISTENING

What significance does a discussion of pitch, scales, harmony, rhythm, and timbre (as represented by the instruments of music) have for persons wishing to enhance their listening experience? As you listen to the wide spectrum of music represented in *Musical Encounters*, you will undoubtedly notice that these properties of sound are the basic tools the composer uses to shape musical composition. As you will soon see, pitch relates directly both to melody and harmony. Duration relates to rhythm and meter, while intensity is the basis for the shaping of dynamic levels found in the unfolding of music. Timbre is the foundation for the entire palette of tone colors the composer uses.

In this section we will examine these elements of music and relate them to musical style, using listening examples from a variety of sources as our illustrations. By the end of this chapter, you will have acquired a good working vocabulary of music.

Before we can discuss concepts of melody and harmony, two very important organizational concepts of music must be considered. First is the structure of **scales,** and second is the identification of the relation of one note to another on the staff, or **intervals.** We will consider intervals in more detail when we discuss harmony, but in order to understand scales, it is necessary to identify two basic intervals, the **half step** and the **whole step.** If you play any key on the piano and follow it with any adjacent note, you have played a half step. It is the smallest interval found on the piano (and in most of Western music). The whole step is formed by playing two notes separated by a half step. Scales are constructed by combining various patterns of half steps and whole steps.

Scales: The Building Blocks of Music

Virtually every culture throughout the world has developed patterns of pitch organization that serve as building blocks for its music—whether written down in notation or handed down aurally from generation to generation. These patterns of notes are called scales. A scale is a pattern of ascending or descending notes that consists of a prearranged order. Musicians shape their composition by combining pitches from these scales either horizontally (forming **melody**—the succession of pitches) or vertically (forming **harmony**—when two more notes sound at the same time).

The most common types of scales used in Western culture—and in all countries whose music is influenced by Western musical developments—are the following:

1. The **chromatic scale,** which consists entirely of half-step intervals. (Play every note, including the black and white keys on the piano, and you will create a chromatic scale.)

2. The **major scale,** which has the pattern of intervals: W-W-H-W-W-W-H. (H = half-steps; W = whole-steps)

3. The **minor scale,** which is distinguished by a lowered third step, resulting in this pattern: W-H-W-W-H-W-W. This particular pattern has become known as the **natural minor scale.** To create more variety in the use of minor scales with regard to harmony, several patterns of minor scales developed that alter the fifth and sixth scale step. For our listening, however, we will emphasize the lowered third interval as the identifying sound of the minor scale.

Three commonly used scale patterns: Chromatic, Major, Natural Minor.

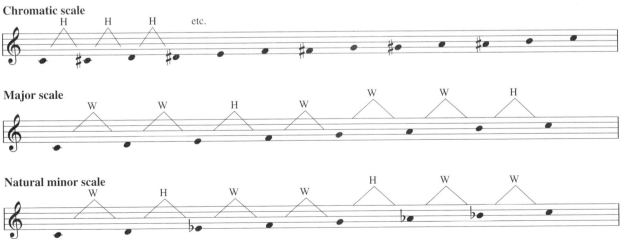

To demonstrate a melody that is based on a major scale, sing again the tune *Are You Sleeping, Brother John?* Notice that all of the notes are drawn from the C major scale. (Play the white notes on the keyboard, beginning with C, and you have played the C major scale.) Another famous melody that is based on the major scale is the Christmas tune by George Frideric Handel, "Joy to the World."

The traditional African-American spiritual, *Go Down Moses*, is a melody based on the minor scale. Sing it, and you will notice that it uses the minor scale to depict the severity of the words. Not all minor melodies are sad or somber, but many times the minor scale is used to underscore somber ideas. The following musical example shows the melody and also the scale from which it is taken.

Horizontal Line in Music: Melody

Melody can be defined simply as the linear succession of pitches. In the traditional music of Western cultures, the melody is most frequently the central focus of a composition. Forms ranging from the simple accompanied song to the symphony are frequently composed around melodies (in full-length musical forms, recurring melodies are called **themes**).

How does the ear perceive melody? It is often the most obvious element of music: it is "the tune," the theme. It is what carries the words in a song, the part that instrumentalists love to play, for listeners always perceive it as the most important part of a piece.

Any good melody must be written with a logical concept of linear continuity; it has some arrangement of notes that makes sense to the listener. Logic in melody frequently occurs by **contour.** For example, a melody may have a smooth shape (**conjunct** contour), in which the notes rise predictably to a peak and then return downward; or, it may have a jagged (**disjunct**) contour that gives it unpredictability.

As we examine several melodies in this chapter, we will define several features of melody that, if we are aware of them, will increase our ability to listen. We will see how **phrase structures** (a division of a musical line into cohesive musical segments) and scales (a scheme of musical notes assembled in ascending or descending order according to a prescribed order of intervals) are used to shape the character of a melody.

Go Down, Moses.

Go   down,   Mo - ses,   way   down   in   E - gypt's   land;

tell   old   Pha - raoh   to   let   my   peo - ple   go!

G minor scale

Amanda McBroom:
The Rose.

Amanda McBroom's title song for the movie *The Rose,* made popular by Bette Midler, illustrates two of these features. We will see the role that both phrase structure and scale patterns play in shaping this melody.

Perhaps the most obvious element of this melody is that it falls into even phrases, according to the poem. In fact, the concept of a musical phrase develops out of the idea of a complete sentence of speech. Notice that parts of the melody are repeated to form a pattern. Its form is *a, a, b, a'*. The three *a* parts have the same beginning notes; the first *a* section ends with an upward turn of the line, and the *a'* (called *a-prime*) phrase ends with a downward turn. The *b* phrase starts with a different pitch than do the *a* phrases; it gives contrast to the already established formal pattern. Notice that the musical phrase structure and the poetic rhyme scheme do not coincide in this song.

Musical Phrase Structure		Rhyme Scheme
a	Some say love, it is a river that drowns the tender reed,	*a*
a	Some say love, it is a razor that leaves your soul to bleed.	*a*
b	Some say love, it is a hunger, an endless aching need.	*a*
a'	I say love, it is a flower, and you its only seed.[1]	*a*

How about the relationship of the notes to each other? The *a* phrases of this beautifully simple melody are constructed from segments derived from a major scale. Whereas the *a* phrases of "The Rose" form a conjunct contour (meaning that the range of the notes is close together) using the first four notes of the scale, the *b* section ventures a bit further afield and uses pitches 3, 4, 5, and 6 of the scale. (This melody never uses the seventh note of the scale—a most unusual tune in this sense.)

Listening Guide 5

I Hate Music
Leonard Bernstein (1918–1990)
Lyrics by Leonard Bernstein

Song for soprano and piano
1943
Recorded by Christa Ludwig, soprano;
  Charles Spencer, piano
CD No. 1, Track 5 (1:10)

*C*ontrast the conjunct contour of "The Rose" to the disjunct contour of the humorous song, "I Hate Music (But I Like to Sing)" by Leonard Bernstein. Here the composer creates a melodic line that skips from low range to high and back again to make a hateful exclamation. Then, the next statement, "But I like to sing," is given a still disjunct but nevertheless **lyrical** treatment. (The term *lyrical* refers to music that is very smooth and connected, regardless of the contour.) Notice how effectively Bernstein uses the disjunct contour of pitches to illustrate the words.

To Consider

1. In addition to the contour (shape) of this melody, what other components of this song help relate the music to the lyrics?
2. What role does the piano accompaniment play in enhancing this song?
3. How would you describe the general character and mood of this work?

Leonard Bernstein: *I Hate Music.*

Vertical Structures: Harmony

Harmony in music is the simultaneous sounding of notes. The current usage of harmony makes no attempt to distinguish sounds that are "pleasing" from those that disturb the ear. Harmony occurs whenever two or more different musical tones are produced at the same time. To state it another way, if you were to take a vertical slice out of any moment in a composition, you would extract a harmonic unit.

Basic to any discussion of harmony is a measurement of the individual notes in a harmonic unit in relationship to each other. We measure the distance between notes by counting the lines and spaces separating the two notes—including the notes themselves. The distance between two pitches is called an interval. We have already become acquainted with half steps and whole steps. A common way of indicating intervals is to count the lines and spaces between two notes on the musical staff. The following diagram illustrates the use of this terminology in identifying intervals. Intervals of the third, sixth, and seventh are called **major intervals** or **minor intervals,** depending on whether or not they belong to the major or

The C major scale, with brackets indicating intervals.

minor scales generated by the lowest note of the interval. The intervals of the chromatic scale (comprised of half steps) are called **minor 2nds.** Whole steps are called **major 2nds.**

The **triad** is a chord made up of three notes spaced at the interval of a third from each other. (Frequently some of the notes of a triad are doubled at octaves—the resulting chord is still called a triad.) Traditional **chord progressions,** or the succession of chords, are formed from a pool of triads built on each note of the scale (the following example shows triads built on the notes of the major scale).

Triads constructed on notes of the major scale.

Three of these chords are identified as primary chords. They are triads built on the first, the fourth, and the fifth notes of the major scale. You will notice that any note of the scale can be found in at least one of these chords. These chords are called the **tonic** (I), the **subdominant** (IV), and the **dominant** (V). The I, IV, and V chords are the first ones a person learns when learning to play the guitar. Many folk songs—and early rock and roll, for that matter—are based almost exclusively on these three chords.

THE VOCABULARY OF HARMONY IN TRADITIONAL WESTERN MUSICAL CULTURE

Interval: The distance between two notes; one calculates this by counting the lines and spaces on the musical staff between each note, including each note.

Chord: Any simultaneous sounding of pitches. In its more conservative context, chords refer to harmonic units that are primarily third related, but that may have additional notes of varying consonance or dissonance.

Triad: Harmonies whose notes are arranged in intervals of thirds.

Arpeggio: Notes of a chord played one at a time.

Progression: The movement from one chord to another in logical succession.

Consonance: Harmonies that are characterized primarily by the intervals of thirds, fifths, and octaves. Consonant sounds are conceived of as pleasing to the ear, and they often create feelings of relaxation and a release of tension.

Dissonance: Harmonies that include intervals of seconds and sevenths. Dissonant sounds often create feelings of tension and excitement in music.

Tonic: The central pitch or harmonic focus of a composition or a segment of a composition.

Dominant: A triad built on the fifth scale step of a given tonal center.

Subdominant: A triad built on the fourth scale step of a given tonal structure.

Cadence: A series of chords or melodic pitches that points toward the ending of a phrase or a composition.

Key: The central harmonic focal point (tonal center) in a section or a composition.

Modulation: The shifting from one tonal center, or key, to another in a composition.

Chromaticism: Intervallic relationships of half steps, or semitones.

To illustrate the use of the I-IV-V chords in a simple but effective setting, we will refer to the melody by Ladysmith Black Mombazo, "The Lion Sleeps Tonight."

This song has a prominent bass part that outlines the first, fourth, and fifth notes of the scale, the roots of the principal harmonies. The repetitive nature of the song is reinforced and enhanced by these ever-present notes and the harmonies that they generate. You may notice that the melody contains notes from these chords also.

listening Guide 6

The Lion Sleeps Tonight
George David Weiss, Hugo Peretti, and Luigi Creatore

Recorded by Talisman A Cappella
CD No. 1, Track 6 (3:22)

To Consider

1. Can you sing the bass line of the piece as it unfolds?
2. As you sing these pitches, do you notice that you can begin to predict the chord changes as they occur? If you are able to do this, you are beginning to develop a sense for chord progression.

Time Words: Meter, Rhythm, and Tempo

Time is very important to music. Composers manipulate elements of time to produce particular effects: they may develop feelings of regularity by using repetitive note values in a logical order or may surprise the listener with unpredictable accents. Time is what separates the art of music from the visual arts, for music consists of sounds that unfold in time. We will briefly survey three aspects of temporal, or time, organization to see how they affect our musical perception. These are meter, rhythm, and tempo.

Earlier, when we spoke of the duration of a note, we introduced the idea that music moves by beats, or pulses, and that commonly these pulses are gathered into regular groupings called meter. At times, meter is implied or hidden; the listener cannot always detect how many pulses are included in a measure. Often, however, the meter is made

The Star-Spangled Banner.

clear by the use of accents—a slight dynamic stress on a given note. Commonly, the first note of each measure is accented slightly. For example, sing "The Star-Spangled Banner" and you will notice that the accents of the poetry and the music create metrical groupings of three pulses each.

Meter is notated in the musical score by a meter signature, a set of two numbers, one over the other. The top digit indicates the number of pulses per measure; the digit on the bottom designates which rhythmic value gets the pulse. A 3/4 meter, for example, means that there are three pulses or beats to the measure and that the quarter note receives the pulse. The most common meters are 2/4 (**duple meter**), 3/4 (**triple meter**), 4/4 (**quadruple meter**), 6/8 (**compound duple meter**), and 9/8 (**compound triple meter**).

TIME WORDS

Pulse:	The basic beat of music. The pulse is used as the basis for all movement in music.
Meter:	The regular grouping of pulses into measures.
Duple meter:	The grouping of pulses into units of two.
Triple meter:	The grouping of pulses into units of three.
Quadruple meter:	The grouping of pulses into units of four.
Compound meter:	Pulse groupings that involve a combination of duple and triple meters.
Mixed meter:	The use of several different meters in succession.
Rhythm:	The temporal value of a note.
Tempo:	The speed of the pulse.
Syncopation:	The interruption of the natural relationship between meter and rhythm by accenting fractional parts of the pulse.
Dotted rhythms:	Notes whose temporal values are lengthened by fractional amounts.

Duple Meters

Meter, however, is by no means always constant in music; many twentieth-century composers practiced a technique called **mixed meter** in which they changed the metrical patterns of their music in order to upset the regularity of accents. The effective use of mixed meter often has the effect of drawing the listener into the music.

A fascinating element of music is rhythm—the duration of each note. There are, of course, almost limitless possibilities of rhythms available to the composer. Rhythms always relate to the pulse and are measured either in multiples or fractions of that pulse. Some note values will be longer than a pulse, and some shorter. As we saw in the section on duration, we use a variety of note values to indicate rhythm. Basic note values may be changed by placing a dot after the note, thereby increasing the value to that original note by one-half.

Although feeling for meter is most often created by accenting the first note of a measure (as we saw with the "Star-Spangled Banner"), at times composers sometimes work against this natural feeling of meter without resorting to mixed meter. They do this simply by accenting notes other than the primary beats of the measure. In this way, they can agitate the emotional flow and intentionally create effects that disrupt the listener's expectations.

Jazz composers take advantage of this disruption perhaps more consistently than do many others. In fact, syncopation, or the use of misplaced accents (the interruption of the natural relationship between meter and rhythm), is one of the distinctive features of jazz. To illustrate the use of syncopation in music, we will listen to the Rob McConnell big band setting of the cabaret song "Just Friends." Notice how syncopation plays a significant part in the arranger's ideas.

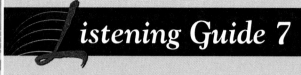

Listening Guide 7

Just Friends
John Klemmer and Sam Lewis

Jazz Ensemble ("Big Band") arrangement
Recorded by the Rob McConnell Band
CD No. 1, Track 7 (6:12)

*T*his example illustrates the energy that can be generated by a strong rhythmic placement of the pulse off the beat. The 32-measure tune is played ten times in various forms. Typical of jazz arrangements is the statement of the melody in a clearly recognizable form, both at the beginning and at the end. In this manner, the straightforward presentations of the melody frame this jazz arrangement with the inner statements acting as variations on the melody. The form is easy to follow because the phrase lengths of the tune never vary; the meter also serves as an anchor—the rhythmic freedom works both with and against the beat. As you listen, be aware of the strong role that syncopation plays here:

0:00   Introduction, followed by a unison statement of the melody in homorhythmic chords (the individual parts move with the same rhythm) by the saxophones; brasses join in accompaniment.

0:43   Rhythm section drops out, saxes and brass play the melody in block chords with heavily syncopated rhythms.

1:20   Tutti (all instruments playing together) statement serves as an introduction to an improvised (or spontaneously created) trombone solo.

1:54   Trombone solo continues, now with the saxes playing accompaniment.

2:28   Tutti statement serves as an introduction to the sax solo.

3:02   Sax solo continues, now with the rest of the saxophone section playing accompaniment.

3:38   Trombone sections plays melody in unison with bass; hi-hat cymbal and snare drum form the accompaniment.

4:12   Tutti statement serves as an introduction to the trumpet solo.

4:45   Trumpet solo continues; saxes play a rising scale passage as accompaniment.

5:19   Final statement consists of the melody and rhythmic accompaniment being traded back and forth between the sax and brass sections.

5:56   The arrangement ends with accented, syncopated chords.

Tempo

Tempo is simply the speed of the pulse. When you talk about a song that is just right for slow dancing, you are describing its tempo. Tempo is usually measured in beats per minute, thus giving composers and performers an accurate rate of the pulse. Since music is at times an inexact science, many tempo indications are general in character and are not exact measurements of the beat in relation to real time. The most common ones are listed next.

TEMPO TERMS

Adagio—very slow
Lento—slow
Andante—walking
Moderato—moderately
Allegro—fast

Vivace—very fast
Presto—extremely fast
Accelerando—increase tempo
Ritardando—decrease tempo

The Weave of Musical Lines: Texture

Texture, the relationship of musical lines to each other (or the "weave" of musical lines), takes into account the phenomenon that in addition to harmony—a vertical dimension involving the simultaneous sounding of pitches—music also has a horizontal dimension. That our minds and ears are capable of discerning both horizontal and vertical levels of music simultaneously is one of the great mysteries of human perception.

The three major groupings of musical textures are **monophony, homophony,** and **polyphony.** The first, **monophony,** or **monophonic texture,** occurs when only one performer is playing or singing. Think of a single, unaccompanied voice or a bugle playing taps. There is no accompaniment, no harmony; needless to say, its use is rather restrictive. The two other fundamental textures of music in our culture are used with great regularity and deserve careful examination.

Homophony, or more specifically, **homorhythmic texture** (homo means "the same"), occurs when all of the parts that are being played or sung move with the same rhythms. Perhaps the most commonly found homorhythmic texture is in traditional four-part hymns or patriotic songs, such as *Abide with Me* or *America*. Once your ear is aware of this texture, you will be surprised how frequently composers resort to homorhythmic texture, even for short sections within a long composition.

Let us examine a striking example of homorhythmic texture by turning to the choral repertoire of seventeenth-century England. Henry Purcell (1659–1695), the greatest English composer of the Baroque period, wrote the anthem *Thou Knowest, Lord, the Secrets of Our Hearts* for the funeral of Queen Mary in 1695. It moves through the text without any voice part straying from a rhythmic structure common to all parts. Purcell intensifies the worshipful purity of the text with his homorhythmic setting.

Listening Guide 8

*Thou Knowest, Lord, the Secrets of Our
    Hearts*
Henry Purcell (1659–1695)

English anthem
Recorded by the Cambridge Singers,
    John Rutter, conductor
CD No. 1, Track 8 (2:05)

This is an example of an **English anthem,** a short choral work originally intended to be sung in the services of the Church of England. It is written for an ensemble consisting of four types of voices categorized by their abilities to sing in different ranges. The highest voice part is called **soprano,** the second part is **alto,** the third part is **tenor,** and the lowest part is **bass.** *Thou Knowest, Lord, the Secrets of Our Hearts* is written in **four-part harmony,** indicating that the parts form chords or harmonies when they are all singing together.

Thou knowest, Lord, the secrets of our hearts:
Shut not thy merciful ears unto our prayer;
But spare us, Lord most holy,
O God most mighty,

O holy and most merciful Savior,
Thou most worthy Judge eternal,
Suffer us not, at our last hour,
For any pains of death
To fall from thee.
Amen.

To Consider

1. Did you notice how all parts move together in the same rhythm? How does this homorhythmic texture help enhance the mood of the text?
2. Do any of the parts deviate even slightly from this principle of texture? If so, when?
3. Does the composer emphasize any important words in the text by any special techniques? (Pay special attention to the settings of "Shut not . . ." and "Suffer us not . . .")

The most contrasting texture to homorhythmic settings is **polyphonic texture**—music characterized by independent musical lines. Here each of the parts maintains its individual character, although when all of the voices are sounded together they produce logical harmonic sonorities.

To illustrate polyphonic texture, we will remain in the genre of choral music and will stay with the same composer, Henry Purcell. His five-part setting (he adds a second soprano part here) of a text taken from Psalm 79 (*Lord, How Long Wilt Thou Be Angry?*) not only illustrates the effective use of independent voice parts but shows us how a quick change in texture to a homorhythmic setting can enhance the meaning of the words.

Listening Guide 9

Lord, How Long Wilt Thou Be Angry?
Henry Purcell

English anthem
Around 1680
Recorded by the Cambridge Singers,
   John Rutter, conductor
CD No. 1, Track 9 (4:08)

*T*he text for this supplicatory anthem is taken from the Old Testament, Book of Psalms, No. 79. As you follow the listening guide, you will be aware of the changes in texture that the composer uses to underline the text.

Lord, how long wilt thou be angry: shall thy jealousy burn like fire for ever?
O remember not our old sins, but have mercy upon us, and that soon: for we are
   come to great misery.
Help us, O God of our salvation, for the glory of thy Name: O deliver us, and
   be merciful unto our sins, for thy Name's sake.
So we, that are thy people, and the sheep of thy pasture, shall give thee thanks for
   ever: and will always be shewing forth thy praise from one generation to another.

(Psalm 79, vv. 5, 8, 9, 13)

0:00 The anthem begins with the basses singing alone. Soon the tenors and then the women's voices enter, each starting at the beginning of the Psalm verse.

0:50 The second phrase of the text is set with a new melodic entry.

1:49 The cry "Help Us, O God!" is set homorhythmically to emphasize the meaning of the words. "O deliver us" becomes more polyphonic, an effort to underline the struggle for deliverance.

3:16 "So We, that are thy people . . . " returns to a polyphonic texture with voices entering and leaving the texture with freedom. The voices weave around each other until they come together in a strong, final chord.

Form in Music

So far we have established a vocabulary of music by discussing the fundamental elements of musical composition. We now can perceive the roles of melody, harmony, meter, rhythm, and tempo as they unfold in the textures of music. There is a final consideration that represents the summation of all of these elements. It is the element of **form.**

In its most elemental description, form in music relates to patterns of repetition and contrast. Form takes into account all elements that lend structure to a piece of music. In our listening examples so far you have seen general patterns of organization that various composers and arrangers have created. "The Rose," for example, was organized around the structure of the poetry. The jazz arrangement of "Just Friends," although it contained ten statements of the song, contained three sections where the soloists each took two statements of the tune to complete a solo, thereby deemphasizing the simple concept of repetition of the 32-bar melody. Their solos were expanded from 32 measures to 64 (including the tutti introductions). You might say, therefore, that the form of "The Rose" was an A-A-B-A song, and that "Just Friends" was a theme with variations.

Composers tie together their melodic, harmonic, rhythmic, and textural ideas with an overall scheme of composition. Many composers establish a plan for their music before they begin to compose—akin to drawing a blueprint before one begins a building construction project. Furthermore, throughout the development of art music, certain general structures have become popular—general recipes as it were—for musical composition. Just as the jazz arranger uses syncopation to work both with and against a standard beat, many composers create ingenious variants within traditional formal structures.

And how about the listener? The ultimate goal for the listener is to be able to sense concepts of formal structure in music without having to make an intellectual exercise out of it. In other words, an understanding of form should help you enjoy a piece of music as it unfolds. It should not be the final goal of listening. The listening experiences in this study will support this goal. We will treat some examples very specifically from their formal standpoint; for others, we will emphasize different aspects of music. Whatever we do, however, we will always return to hearing how the composer manipulates the musical material. That, after all, is fundamental to the art of music.

Listening Guide 10

Symphony No. 35 in D Major, K. 385,
  Mvt. 3
Wolfgang Amadeus Mozart (1756–1791)

Minuet and Trio for orchestra
1782
Recorded by the Bavarian Radio Orchestra
Rafael Kubelik, conductor
CD No. 1, Track 10 (3:05)

The music of Wolfgang Amadeus Mozart (1756–1791) offers us a prime opportunity to observe a compositional technique influenced strongly by formal considerations. We will turn to the third movement of his *Symphony No. 35 in D Major*, also known as the *Haffner Symphony* (named after the family of Sigmund Haffner, burgomaster of Salzburg), to show how all of the principal elements of music come together in delineating formal structure. This movement is called a "minuet and trio"—a concert form that evolved from a popular seventeenth- and eighteenth-century dance. The minuet is a graceful dance in 3/4 meter, paired with a less assertive trio.

First listen to this movement while you follow the section-by-section description in the following listening guide.

To Consider

1. As you listen to this symphonic movement, do the patterns of repetition set up an anticipation of things to come as the piece unfolds?
2. Can you feel a sort of "question-and-response" concept in the phrases? (The first four measures state the question, the second four provide the response.)
3. Notice how contrasting volume levels (dynamic changes) have an effect on how you perceive the musical form.

A: Minuet

0:00 Violins present the principal melody without introduction. The first four measures of the theme are presented *forte*, and are answered by four more measures, played *piano*. These eight bars are repeated.

0:23 The second part of theme I occurs (eight measures; once again, four measures of *forte*, four of *piano*). This is followed by a return to the *a* section of theme I, also repeated.

B: Trio

1:08 Theme of the trio begins an 8-measure statement, this time all played *piano*—also repeated. (Notice that the trio is in a new key.)

1:30 The second part of the trio theme occurs: eight measures plus a 4-measure transition to the repeat of the opening of the trio.

A: Minuet

2:30 The minuet repeats in its original form, but this time no repeats are played. The minuet returns to the original key of D Major.

You may have noticed in the above example that there are several contributors to creating form in this movement. The melody was divided into symmetrical phrases of eight measures each; each 8-measure phrase was again divided into two parts of four measures. Changes in dynamics aided the comprehension of the phrase division. The trio theme is new and contrasts to the driving theme of the minuet and is more placid in nature. The trio was presented in a different key than the minuet sections.

As your listening experience grows, so will your ability to perceive (almost subliminally) how various works of music are put together. Remember, the listening process is one of continual development. As long as life lasts, not even the greatest musical ears are ever finished probing the depths of musical subtleties and structures.

UTTING IT ALL TOGETHER

Vertical and Horizontal Dimensions of Music and the Listening Process

Music unfolds in time. In this way, it is different from the visual arts, such as painting and sculpture, for one cannot simply take a mental snapshot of a piece of music the way one can a painting. Furthermore, there is no exact correlation between music and the visual arts concerning perceptions of height, width, and depth. However, music can be perceived easily by using the symbols of dimension, for the unfolding of music in time involves both horizontal and vertical considerations. As you hear a piece of music, you may think of it flowing from one moment to another. This represents the horizontal dimension of music; the vertical dimension consists of both the simultaneous sounds that occur at any given moment (the harmony) and the way in which the composer relates simultaneously moving parts to each other (texture).

So what does this mean to the listener? First, constantly improving the ability to sense form—patterns of repetition and contrast and the sensations of tension and release that occur—is an ongoing goal of the intelligent listener. Second, being able to grasp the various layers of sound in a piece of music adds to the understanding of the dimensions of music.

In Chapter 5 you will see how composers of the Baroque period (such as Bach and Handel) frequently built their compositions on principles of independent voice parts that worked both with and against each other. You will hear separate lines as they drive the music forward, lines that are independent but that form logical harmonies as they are sounded together. The music of the Baroque Era frequently involves techniques that emphasize polyphonic textures; sometimes this polyphony is intensified as it occurs in contrast to homorhythmic sections.

The music of the Classical Era (music represented by Haydn, Mozart, and Beethoven), on the other hand, emphasizes the structures where contrast and repetition are obvious to the listener. This music is dominated by sections in which principal melodies (or themes) stand out to the ear. The contrasts created by their statement, development, and return make the listener anticipate musical gestures before they occur.

Although Baroque Era music is used in this book to discuss concepts of counterpoint and layering, and classical music is illustrated to underline techniques of repetition and contrast, the two contrasting approaches to composition are certainly not mutually exclusive. As you consider both the horizontal and vertical dimensions of music presented in Chapters 5 and 6, you will find that your understanding of these two elements will grow and that you will come to enjoy all music at a higher and deeper level of appreciation.

SUMMARY

By considering the four properties of a musical note (pitch, duration, intensity, and timbre), we can comprehend the acoustical foundations of music. Pitch, although it can be measured scientifically by cycles per second, is conveniently identified by using the first seven letters of the alphabet. The lengths of notes and their organization have evolved over the centuries into a universal notation system that uses the beat, or pulse, as its basic unit of measure. Intensity is simply the volume of music. Timbre, or the tone quality of music-producing bodies (or instruments), is a term used to describe the characteristic sound of voices and various instruments.

The basic properties, in turn, help form the fundamental elements of musical composition, namely melody, harmony, meter/rhythm/tempo, and texture. The final element of musical composition is the way in which all elements are organized into larger structures. In music, we call this form.

Our musical perception is dependent on knowing these fundamental concepts of music. This knowledge translates into greater listening skills and hence into greater enjoyment.

KEY TERMS

accelerando
accidentals
adagio
aerophones
allegro
alto
andante
arpeggio
bass
bass clef
beat
cadence
chord progressions
chordophone
chromatic scale
chromaticism
clef signs
composite sound
compound duple meter
compound meter
compound triple meter
conjunct
consonance
contour
crescendo
decrescendo
disjunct
dissonance
dominant
dotted rhythms

duple meter
duration
dynamic markings
elements of music
English anthem
flat
form
four-part harmony
grand staff
half step
harmonics
harmony
Hz (Hertz)
homophonic texture
homophony
homorhythmic texture
idiophones
intensity
interval
key
key signature
koto
ledger lines
lento
long zither
lyrical
major interval
major scale
measures
melody

membranophones

meter

meter signature

minor interval

minor scale

mixed meter

moderato

modulation

monophonic texture

monophony

natural

natural minor scale

noise

notation

note value

octave

overtone

overtone series

partial

phrase structure

pitch

polyphonic texture

polyphony

presto

progression

pulse

pure sound

quadruple meter

resonance

rhythm

ritardando

scales

sharp

soprano

staff

subdominant

syncopation

tempo

tenor

texture

themes

timbre

time signature

tone color

tonic

treble clef

triad

triple meter

vivace

whole step

CHAPTER 3

Focus on Listening:
Vocal Music from
around the World

THE RUDIMENTARY NATURE OF VOCAL MUSIC

MUSIC'S first function in prehistoric times was communication. No doubt the earliest human ancestors discovered that a variety of vocal sounds—perhaps grunts, shouts, cooing inflections, and gentle sighs—could bring about a range of reactions in another person. A baby's first cry is, in fact, a most effective use of the voice.

Vocal communication is something that humans share with many forms of animal life. We have come to realize that some animal "songs" are highly sophisticated forms of discourse.

The human voice, however, is our focus. Throughout time, the voice has been the central vehicle for musical production; it is the "speech mechanism" of music. In that sense, it is rudimentary.

The voice is the primary instrument of musical expressions throughout the world. The use of the voice, as used in this panorama of world music, offers us a glimpse into different cultures. By examining songs both in their cultural contexts and from the standpoint of pure sound, we can come to a better understanding of the way in which various cultures use music to express themselves. The universal language of music has many dialects, and to comprehend music as a phenomenon that transcends national boundaries, you must become aware of these differences.

So far in this book, we have seen that all music is equal and has similar goals. We have separated the various elements that go into all music and have put them together again in a brief study of form. Now we will look at a variety of vocal music. Our purpose is twofold: the first is to show the very different means that people of different cultures use to adapt the voice to meet the tastes and demands of their particular genre or culture; the second is to help you sharpen your listening skills by calling attention to differences in sound manipulations that are all part of music. After completing this chapter, you should be ready to listen perceptively and study music free from preconceived notions that music that is new to you is either "weird" or "bad."

Several musical examples involve instruments. It is always interesting to be aware of the relationships of tone color between instruments and voices. We will explore these connections in this music.

Perhaps we also will discover that the "proper" way to sing depends on the demands of the particular type of music being sung. Here again our study will turn to an examination of musical styles. We cannot escape this important aspect of music.

AMERICAN FOLK MUSIC: PERFORMANCE PRACTICE

A folk song is music that comes from the common people—the *folk*. In many instances, it is not composed by formally trained muscians but grows anonymously from people who communicate their everyday emotions, rituals, and pleasures in song. Anonymity, however, is not always a condition for defining folk music. We will see that Stephen Foster, for example, became famous in America some 100 years ago because of the immense popularity of his songs. Some of his best-known songs are *Oh, Susanna; My Old Kentucky Home; I Dream of Jeannie with the Light Brown Hair;* and *Beautiful Dreamer.*

Most folk songs were passed down through the generations aurally—one person taught the song to another, and that person in turn passed it on, sometimes altering the music or words slightly to the singer's personal taste. In this way, traditional folk music is similar to gossip. One does not often know what the "original" version is, because each version holds our interest. For example, there are literally hundreds of versions of the song *On Top of Old Smokey.*

The folk music of some cultures, like that of the *shamisen* singers of Japan, for example, is unaffected by art music. In other parts of the world, however, the lines of distinction are not as clearly drawn. In Italy, for example, the music of opera—a cultivated art form—at times shows a very strong influence from Italian folk song, and vice versa. American folk music, like its sister expressions throughout the world, reflects a straightforward treatment of folk poetry, thus it is influenced strongly by the everyday speech patterns of the language. There is no attempt to imitate forms of cultivated music; the music and the performance are simple and plain by design.

A most important aspect of this musical expression is the singer. Each folk singer imparts a personalized signature to a song and seeks to develop a unique interpretation, much in the same way that a good storyteller does. The *lilt* of the melody (subtle accents and variations in dynamics), the tempos, the instrumental interludes between verses (if instruments are used), the way the words are accented, and even slight changes to the melody are all part of that individual style. Also, many folk singers develop a personal technique of ornamentation. Although personal in nature, these embellishments fall within an acceptable range of stylistic traditions of performance practice.

There are many types of singing voices in the realm of folk music. There is no widely accepted standard of tone quality for this type of music as there is in opera, for example. One could say that the common thread of the American folk song tradition is its insistence on simplicity and unaffected voice qualities. These qualities are strongly apparent in the following listening guide selection.

Angelina Baker is a song written by the most prominent creator of the nineteenth-century American folk song, Stephen Foster (1826–1864). Foster is a prime example of a tunesmith who never studied music in the formal sense, but who still emerged as a well-known figure in the

Laura Boosinger. By permission of Laura Boosinger. Photo by Jock Lauterer.

musical world. Several of his 189 songs became very popular. One of them, *Swanee River*, was sung throughout the United States by Christy's Minstrels—a four-member group that performed song-and-dance routines to the strumming of banjos and the percussive rattling of bones. As a result of this broad exposure, *Swanee River* sold 40,000 copies the first year of its publication.

When Laura Boosinger sings *Angelina Baker*, she conveys a melancholy mood in a context of purity and naïveté. The performer never allows her voice to rise above a moderate level of dynamics. You may also notice certain parts of the song where Boosinger gently slides into a note. When she does this, however, she always seems to do it with care; too much sliding around might destroy the meaning of the words and might also betray the general character of the song.

istening Guide 11

Angelina Baker
Stephen Foster (1826–1864)

American folk song
1850
Recorded by Laura Boosinger, folksinger
CD No. 1, Track 11 (4:30)

Now, way down on the old plantation,
   That's where I was born,
I used to spend the whole creation
   Hoe'n in the corn.
Well, first I'd work and then I'd sing.
   Happy all the day,
'Till Angelina Baker came
   And stole my heart away.

Chorus:

Angelina Baker, Angelina Baker is gone.
   She left me here to weep a tear
And beat on the ole' jawbone.
Well, first I'd work and then I'd sing.
   Happy all the day,
'Till Angelina Baker came
And stole my heart away

Chorus:

Now, Angelina was so tall
   She could not see the ground.
She had to use a telescope
   To look out on the town.

Chorus:

Now, early in the morning
In a lovely summer day
I asked for Angelina, but
They say she's gone away.
N' I don't know where to find her, so
I don't know where she's gone.
She left me here to weep a tear,
And beat on the old jawbone.[1]

Chorus:

To Consider

As you listen to this song, try to identify the vocal techniques the singer uses that add support both to the meaning and the feeling of the text. Some questions that you might ask yourself as you listen are:

1. How does the range of dynamics support the phrase structure of the text?
2. Do you detect any ornamentation in her singing?
3. Does the range of the melody support the feeling of the lyrics?
4. This song has instrumental interludes. Do you think that their use prepares your ear for the

The type of breath support that many folksingers use is relaxed and unforced. A sense of ease permeates the performance. Some people like to call this type of singing "natural." Its effortlessness is deceptive, however, for the singer must have good control of his or her voice to make it sound that easy.

Did you notice, for example, that the slight **glissando** Boosinger uses is echoed in the banjo when it plays the interlude, the instrumental music between verses? (A glissando occurs when a voice or an instrument "slides" up to or away from a specific pitch.) Such a practice achieves a continuity in the musical style. It is one of the significant aspects of mountain music, and it is totally appropriate for the style. To use a similar practice in the European art songs of Schubert or Brahms (which we will hear in Chapter 7) would, of course, be totally out of place.

THE SPIRITUAL: PERSONAL EXPRESSIONS AND POIGNANT TEXTS

The songs of Stephen Foster represent a significant style of American music, namely, the extensive tradition based on a European ancestry. Another strong heritage of folk music in North America stems from the African-American tradition. We will explore this avenue of music by listening to a well-known spiritual.

The **spiritual** is a religious folk song characterized by expressions of deep emotion. Cultivated extensively by African Americans in the South, its poetry served as a vehicle both for expressing religious faith and for sustaining hopes of relief from daily troubles, and ultimately release from slavery. This genre of music grew steadily in the nineteenth century with the proliferation of camp meetings and the development of black churches throughout the Southern United States. Although some scholars believe that many African-American spirituals were adaptations of existing religious songs of the white churches, their transformations were so complete that it is almost impossible for scholars to sort out those "original" black spirituals from those that developed out of the white folks' repertoire.

Whatever the original sources, the spiritual exuded simplicity of textual treatment. The poetry frequently deals with double entendre. For example, the songs that speak of crossing the River Jordan—meaning going to Heaven—are code terms for slaves who were escaping to the North. In similar fashion, texts dealing with the train going to Heaven were adaptations of the chariot that carried Elijah to Heaven but also referred to the underground railroad. Songs mourning the plight of the children of Israel and their trials provided easy reference points for the slaves.

This music carried with it certain stylistic features: it tended to have short, repetitive, melodic phrases. It was (and is) common for spirituals to be sung accompanied by body movement; scales are frequently gapped—some notes are omitted; and the element of rhythm always played a major part in the musical expression. Many times some notes are flatted with "blue notes"—especially on the third and seventh notes of the scale, and singers frequently slide from one pitch to another in order to create strong feelings of emotion (this practice is called **smearing**).

Scholars of African-American music history have identified several elements of music derived directly from African roots. For example, features of music that are commonly and accurately ascribed to the African tradition are complex rhythms, melodic scale patterns and nuances that frequently defy the European classical melodic shapes, use of short, repetitive, melodic segments, and a strong, aural tradition of musical performance.

European-American influences on black musical expressions have emerged in a basic harmonic language—the language of Western civilization, and the broad influence of Christianity, which was imposed on the slave population in eighteenth-century America. Interestingly, however, the religious music of the white populace was never adopted verbatim, but it was altered to the point of being reinvented by the black culture in America.

*L*istening Guide 12

Joshua Fit the Battle of Jericho
Traditional African-American spiritual

Recorded by Mahalia Jackson
1955
CD No. 1, Track 12 (2:05)

*W*e will focus on the performance tradition of the spiritual for this selection. This tradition is widespread in practice and rich in meaning. You will see how drastically dissimilar this performance tradition is from the European-based folk tradition, for its style requires a totally different kind of vocal production as well as a different approach to text pronunciation.

One of the great interpreters of the spiritual was Mahalia Jackson (1911–1972), whose music is readily available in record shops. In listening to her 1955 recording of the traditional spiritual, *Joshua Fit the Battle of Jericho*, we catch a glimpse of the tradition of elaborating on a given melody that is not only common to the "gospel style" and the spiritual but actually is a practice stemming from Africa.

The text is drawn from the Old Testament account of Joshua besieging Jericho (Joshua, Chapter 6). It is a free interpretation of the biblical account:

Refrain:　　Joshua fit the battle of Jericho, Jericho, Jericho,
　　　　　　Joshua fit the battle of Jericho, and the walls came tumblin' down.
　　　　　　Joshua fit the battle of Jericho, Jericho, Jericho,
　　　　　　Joshua fit the battle of Jericho, and the walls came tumblin' down. (Hallelujah!)

Verse 1:   You may talk about the men of Gideon,
                And you may talk about the men of Saul,
                But there(s) none like the good ol' Joshua
                And the battle of Jericho (Hallelujah).

Refrain: Joshua fit the battle of Jericho, etc.

Verse 2:   Up to the walls of Jericho,
                With sword drawn in his hand,
                Go blow them horns like Joshua
                The battle is in my hand.

Refrain: Joshua fit the battle of Jericho, etc.[2]

The tradition of spiritual performance in the African-American tradition is that each singer develops some sort of interpretation that personalizes the performance and indicates that the text has become a part of the inner spirit of the singer. These interpretations are especially noticed in slower songs.

To Consider

1. Can you describe the vocal style of Mahalia Jackson? Does she "slide" in and out of some pitches, or does she seem to sing all notes in the same manner?
2. How does the rhythm of the musical line fit the rhythm of the lyrics? Does the singer use any special effects to make the rhythm more obvious to you, the listener? Does she treat the pronunciation of the words in any special way?
3. What type of scale is used as the basis for this melody?

Mahalia Jackson makes this spiritual her own by treating it as follows:

a) She alters the melody on the opening phrase from a chromatic line to a simpler interval of a fifth.
b) A slight accent is sometimes added to the word "Jericho," which adds to the upbeat feeling. The word becomes "Jericho-uh."
c) "Hallelujah!" is inserted as a fill between text phrases.
d) Certain pitches are "dipped" into and "slid" away from the original note.
e) Rhythms are altered: "Gideon" is syncopated strongly, for example. This up-tempo performance combines the techniques of two-beat style jazz, wherein the first and third beats of the measure are reinforced by the bass and the after beats (2 and 4) are played by the hi-hat cymbal and snare drum. (As the piece progresses, you will note that the accompaniment goes into a 4-beat style, wherein the bass plays on each beat of the measure, which provides an intensified drive toward the end of the song.)

The spiritual (along with its secular counterpart, the blues) represents the soul of the African-American tradition. Its vitality is apparent in today's musical world, for it occupies a central place in the solo and choral repertoire of our country. This lively tradition is not only being preserved, it is experiencing an evolution of its own, for many gifted arrangers of spirituals are emerging and are adding to the libraries of choirs throughout the United States. Especially noteworthy are Albert McNeil (whose Albert McNeil Singers represent the best of African-American choral music) and three college choral conductors and arrangers: Andre Thomas of Florida State University, Robert Ray of the St. Louis Conservatory of Music, and Moses Hogan of Dillard College in New Orleans.

Musical Encounter

The Voices of Jazz

When "jazz" became a popular term in the late teens and early 1920s, it most often referred to instrumental solos that were improvised when dance bands would stray from the written music and allow individual players to add their personal creativity and expressions to the music. Before long, musicians such as trumpet player Louis Armstrong added their voices to the improvisation, and jazz singing united with the jazz band.

True jazz singers communicate musical inflections of jazz by bending pitches, by slurring rhythms that often work against the steady beat, and even by altering pronunciations of the lyrics to exaggerate meaning. Some jazz singers, such as Sarah Vaughan and Mel Tormé, developed a singing style called **scat**, in which various speech syllables are used to present the sounds of jazz. In a sense, these singers bridged the gap between the voice and solo instruments when they created sounds that imitated the articulation of horns.

Individual singing artists, like instrumentalists, took popular songs of the times and made them their own by changing the notes of the melodies, altering rhythms, and giving special inflections to the words. Take, for example, the George Gershwin song *Embraceable You*. Vaughan's rendering of the tune revealed a silky voice, with a small, quivering vibrato, sliding gracefully from one note to another. She often added her signature to tunes by beginning phrases slightly before the beat, sometimes starting on high notes that she reached for and always hit with extreme accuracy, altering the original tune. Vaughan's vocal stylings were undoubtedly influenced by her contemporaries, such as saxophonist Charlie 'Bird' Parker—although his improvisatory performances of Gershwin's famous hit strayed farther afield from the tune than did Vaughan's. Another great jazz/blues singer from the same era, Ella Fitzgerald, presented *Embraceable You* in a dreamier style, her voice modulating to deep, throaty tones to emphasize important words at the ends of phrases—the concluding words of the romantic poetry. Fitzgerald was truer to Gershwin's original notes than was Sarah Vaughan, but both singers' performances show an awareness of instrumental jazz styles. Likewise, jazz players such as Parker and trumpet player Miles Davis or tenor sax player Coleman Hawkins borrowed freely from vocal inflections when they played ballads. Instrumental soloists played like singers; singers sang like horn players.

Traditional singers of jazz were influenced by the classic jazz song tradition. In addition to Sarah Vaughan and Ella Fitzgerald, singers of this style were Billy Holiday, Betty Carter, and Carmen McRae, and more recently, Diane Schuur. Famous classic jazz male singers such as Billy Eckstein and Joe Williams are now joined by a younger generation such as Kevin Mahogony, a blues singer who is equally at home singing jazz. Other younger jazz singers such as Cassandra Wilson, Dianne Reeves, Diana Krall, and the amazing John Pizzarelli—who sings jazz licks while simultaneously playing the exact notes on the guitar—are influenced by a broad array of musical styles, both from the present and the past.

The voices of jazz, sometimes considered a heritage from the past, are being reborn to emerge as fresh entities in the diverse world of popular music. Influenced by such post–modern expressions as modern rock styles or rap, these singers demonstrate the versatility of the human voice as an instrument of jazz, and they are shaping new directions in a historical musical arena.

THE NATIVE AMERICAN VOICE

The vocal timbres typically found among singers of European-American folk music are frequently linked to the "natural" quality of the speaking voice, as illustrated in the Stephen Foster song *Angelina Baker*. We will now examine another musical expression from a very different American culture, one that illustrates the same relationship between singing and speaking. By contrasting the vocal music from the Northern Plains Indians with that of the European/American folk song, we can readily hear that the human voice is indeed capable of producing a variety of vocal timbres. The ethnic and cultural background that gives rise to the music is always significant in shaping a person's idea of ideal sound.

Music has always been an integral part of the lives of Native American cultures, as it has been of all cultures. Although diverse styles and practices of music among Native American people reflect the many different cultures, as well as the individual differences, music has always been a primary vehicle for the transmission of creation stories, oral history, and mythology, as well as an accompaniment to religious ritual, entertainment, and dancing.

A group of Native Americans beat a drum and sing at a powwow in Wisconsin.
© Arvind Garg / CORBIS.
ID # IH078189.

Native American cultural practices, which were long ignored or even actively suppressed by most European Americans, are now receiving more attention. Ethno-musicologists, like others who study the arts and culture, are attempting to explore and understand a wide range of cultural perspectives. Many fundamental principles held sacred by Western musicians—such as major and minor scale patterns commonly used in creating melodies, or even the way instruments are tuned—are not characteristic of many non-Western musical cultures.

For example, much of the music of Native American cultures reflects the use of **vocables** (non-lexical syllables, or "nonsense syllables"), melodies drawn from four-note or five-note scales, and performance practices that include shouting and gliding into and out of specific pitches. Drums, rattles, and other percussion instruments frequently are central to the music. Western concepts of **intonation**, where all members of a vocal ensemble strive to produce the same pitch, are not significant in most Native American cultures. Although melody instruments are sometimes used, they are not commonly utilized in organized ensembles.

This means that the norms for listening to music from other cultures must be different if one is to approach world music with understanding. Music, however, can speak for itself. The *Rabbit Dance*, our selection for the Native American voice, speaks to us strongly about the sound predilections of Native American culture.

This encounter with a Native American musical expression illustrates that music, the so-called "universal language," speaks in many different dialects. Being able to analyze the sound of various musical expressions constitutes the first step in understanding what is "beautiful" to others, and perhaps, in making it sound beautiful to ourselves. It is a prime goal of our study.

Listening Guide 13

Rabbit Dance
Northern Plains Indian Song

Native American love song
Recorded in 1975
Recorded by Carlotte Heth on location
CD No. 1, Track 13 (3:16)

The *Rabbit Dance* is a social dance of merriment in which women are allowed to choose their partners. The couples cross their hands in front of them and dance around a drum. This song has the following English text:

> Hey, Sweetheart, I always think of you.
> I wonder if you are alone tonight.
> I wonder if you are thinking of me.

To Consider

1. Can you describe the timbre (or tone quality) of this Native American singer?
2. How do you account for the fact that the men who are singing the song do not exactly sing all of the same notes together? Do you think this is intentional or accidental?
3. What role do the drums play in this piece?
4. Are there any vocal devices or inflections that relate to the beat of the drums?
5. What is your initial reaction to this song in terms of mood? Do you think it is sad? Melancholy? Contemplative? What standards can you use to come to these conclusions?

Drums begin the "Rabbit Dance," and soon a leader establishes the general range of the song, which uses the higher range of the voice (a common practice in the music of Northern Plains Native Americans). The men who are singing know the melody; although they are not in perfect unison, it is clear that even the vocalized introduction is a well-known tune.

The English words are sung four times and are framed by an introduction. The vocal timbre of the singers is nasal, and the desired dynamic level is rather loud. Notice that the voices create pulsations throughout the song, even in the middle of syllables in the English text. This provides a unique consistency with the rhythmic accompaniment of the drums, but the vocal pulsations (created by the kind of diaphragmatic pressure one uses during a shout) and the beats coming from the drums are not intended to fall on a basic underlying pulse but are irregular. The meter of the percussion suggests a triple meter (1-2-3, 1-2-3).

VOCAL TECHNIQUES IN ROCK

A very different approach to singing is used by Roger Daltrey of The Who, a rock group that rose to popularity in the 1960s, enjoyed immense success throughout the 1970s, and whose recordings still command a respectable part of today's rock nostalgia market.

The song *Won't Get Fooled Again*, for example, illustrates a vocal timbre that is strident in character. In order to achieve this, the singer constricts his vocal chords and sings in a high vocal range and a loud dynamic range. This sound is as calculated as was

Pete Townshend jumps as he plays the guitar with The Who in concert, 1976. Roger Daltry appears at the left.© Neal Preston / CORBIS. ID # PN002930.

the folk expression you heard in the recording of the Stephen Foster song *Angelina Baker*. The general tone color of the singer's voice matches the mood of the song. A second feature of this kind of music is that the nasal quality of the voice is entirely congruent with the strident sounds of the electric guitar and the keyboard. It becomes part of the general timbral quality of the song. Obviously a crooner with a soft voice does not belong in a rock group.

In this song the voice is used both as a pitched and as a non-pitched instrument. The Who were at the cutting edge of this practice, where the singers move in and out of a specific pitch level and many times intensify their music by shouting or screaming. The end result is one of excitement, overt emotional expression, and energy.

JAPANESE SHAMISEN HAIYA SONG

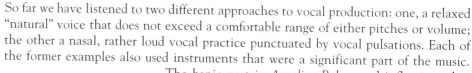

A geisha plays the shamisen while kneeling on a straw tatami mat. © Michael Maslan Historic Photographs / CORBIS. ID # IH063980.

So far we have listened to two different approaches to vocal production: one, a relaxed "natural" voice that does not exceed a comfortable range of either pitches or volume; the other a nasal, rather loud vocal practice punctuated by vocal pulsations. Each of the former examples also used instruments that were a significant part of the music.

The banjo part in *Angelina Baker* used inflections that the singer also employed. (The drums in *Rabbit Dance* provided a model for the dynamic pulses of the voice.)

We now will turn to an example as different from the others as is possible to find, but one that shares some of the features of the previous examples. In Japan, the traditional folk timbre of both voice and instruments is often described as "nasal" by listeners whose ears are accustomed to Euro-American folk and classical music.

The song we will listen to, *Kagoshima Otsu-e Bushi*, is a traditional song sung throughout the Japanese province of Kagoshima. This particular version is a victory song of a sumo wrestler. It is distinctive because at times the singer moves away from pitched singing into a normal speaking voice.

The banjo-like sounds come from a **shamisen** (also called a **gottan**)—a stringed instrument consisting of a wooden box to which a neck is attached, with strings strung similar to those of the American banjo. The shamisen differs from the banjo, however, because it is made of a wooden box rather than a skin (or in the modern banjo, a plastic sheet) stretched over a frame. The shamisen is of all-wood construction. You will notice, however, that the sound produced by the shamisen is similar to the dry sound of the banjo.

Listening Guide 14

Kagoshima Otsu-e Bushi
Traditional Japanese song describing a victorious sumo wrestler.

Recorded by Toridamari Tadao, vocalist and shamisen player.
1991
CD No. 1, Track 14 (4:55)

This song is sung throughout Kagoshima, and it exists in many different versions. The recording that you will hear consists of a song called *A Victory Banner of a Sumo Wrestler*, and it includes half-spoken, half-sung monologues that indicate the satisfaction of the wrestler having won his match.

To Consider

1. How would you describe the vocal timbre of this singer?
2. Does the singer always use "regular" pitches, or does he use notes that are unusual to the Western ear?
3. Relate the melodies played on the shamisen to those that are sung by Toridamari.
4. Are some of the same embellishments or ornaments used by each? Does this practice relate to that used by Laura Boosinger in *Angelina Baker*?
5. Judging from the way the song is presented, can you detect a concept of form in this music?

0:00	The song begins with a preliminary strumming of the shamisen.
0:10	The singer begins his tale; if you listen carefully, you can hear that the top string of the shamisen is being played to follow the general contour of the vocal melody. This most likely indicates that the melody being sung is not improvised. Also notice that the shamisen melody and the tune that the singer is singing is not exactly the same melody. This practice of presenting two variants of the same melody simultaneously is called **heterophony**.
1:29	A new section of the song begins. The singer is now telling the story of the wrestling match using spoken dialogue. (This resembles a recitative in Western opera.) The emotions of the story compel him to speak faster, his voice rising to climactic points.
3:30	Shamisen strumming signifies a return to the song. The final part of this performance is sung once again in heterophonic style with the shamisen.

The general formal organization of this song is A-B-A, with the B section containing the spoken dialogue.

THE XHOSA CULTURE: OVERTONE SINGING FROM SOUTH AFRICA

Some traditional African cultures practice a vocal tradition that is unknown in the West. This technique involves producing several notes at the same time by singing the fundamental note (the lowest pitch) in a gruff voice in such a manner that higher notes (called overtones) become audible. It is practiced by the women of the Xhosa culture, who live in the very southeastern part of South Africa, adjacent to the Sotho and Zulu societies. This

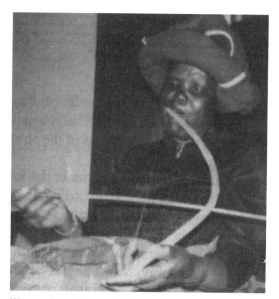

Woman from Xhosa singing with mouth bow. Source: Journal of the International Library of African Music, Vol. 7, No. 1, 1991.

highly specialized technique is learned by Xhosa women through the aural tradition; there are no written descriptions of how to produce this sound.

Xhosa overtone singing was "discovered" by ethno-musicologist David Dargie in 1980, but it is not known how long the practice has been in existence. According to Dargie, a woman learns the technique by singing in a very gruff voice until she is able to focus on producing overtone pitches. When this happens, she then is able to smooth out the gruffness and, by manipulating her mouth, she can bring out the higher pitches, which form a melody over the lower, more guttural sounds. At times one can hear three pitches being produced at the same time! Xhosa people call this technique *UMNGQOKOLO*.

Yet another sound you will hear are the "click words" in the Xhosa language. When sung, they generate percussive rhythms.

Although our musical example of overtone singing comes from South Africa, there are several other areas of the world in which a similar practice occurs. For centuries the monks of Tibet have intoned prayers using this method of sound production. The overtone singing tradition is also cultivated by women of some ethnic groups of Bulgaria.

*L*istening Guide 15

Nondel'ekhaya
Folk song from Xhosa, South Africa

Recorded in 1985
Recorded by Dr. David Dargie
CD No. 1, Track 15 (4:00)

The term *Nondel'ekhaya* in Xhosa refers to someone who is "married at home"—a woman who is raising a family at home without a husband. This song consists of short phrases of text that are sung alternately by a leader and a follower. Translations are as follows:

Hey! Nondel'ekhaya! She says the beer is finished.
Oh! I am sorry for the unmarried young ladies.
Oh! They took my place, they were as strong as me.[3]

You will hear a recording made by Dargie in 1985 of thirteen women singing this traditional song. Some of the women in the ensemble sing in a natural voice, some use the *UMNGQOKOLO* technique of producing a very low-pitched sound with another melody above. Before the ensemble begins, one young lady is recorded demonstrating *UMNGQOKOLO* alone, because when all thirteen women sing together, the texture is so thick that it is hard to hear this special technique. Listen for the very low tone that becomes audible at times in the song. That is the bass (drone) note for the overtone singing. The recorded example that you will hear is only a segment of this song, which continues for over fifteen minutes.

Another fascinating vocal technique used by Xhosa people is that of producing sounds by placing a mouth bow near the singer's mouth and creating sounds that set up sympathetic vibrations on the string of the bow. Again, multiple pitches can be generated. After the women's song is over, you will hear a demonstration of the gourd-resonated bow technique. These musical examples show the extreme diversity of sounds that this South African culture has developed by use of the human voice. The CD recording demonstrates these in the following order:

A: A solo demonstration of the UMNGQOKOLO technique.
B: A group of thirteen women singing, some using UMNGQOKOLO.
C: A demonstration of a gourd-resonated bow.

To Consider

1. Describe the various types of vocal production that you hear in the women's song.
2. Is there a general rhythmic plan to this song? If so, what is it?
3. Can you hear an overall plan to this piece of music, or does it continually evolve through short patterns of repetition?

THE VIRTUOSO VOICE IN ITALIAN OPERA: THE COLORATURA ARIA

We now shift to an example of Western art music, which represents an entirely different function and way of cultivating the human voice. Its intent is to display virtuosity (great technical skill).

The most intensely trained voice in Western musical culture is that of the opera singer, particularly that of the **coloratura** soprano. The word coloratura in the eighteenth- and nineteenth-century operatic tradition signifies the rapid scales, trills, arpeggios, and other ornaments that are freely used in solo arias (the Italian word is equivalent to the English "air," or song). These vocal gymnastics are highly difficult to execute, and when properly sung, they add virtuosity and flair to the music.

One major goal of coloratura singing is a total consistency of tone quality throughout the vocal range, from the lowest note to the highest. In other words, the singer must be able to leap from the lowest notes to the highest notes with the greatest of ease. In addition to a highly flexible voice capable of singing fast passages with accuracy and a consistent tone, a skilled operatic singer must be able to project the sound over the orchestra to the far corners of the concert hall. And, of course, it is always important to sing the notes on pitch as written and with accurate rhythms, as well as to act out the appropriate character and emotions.

Listening Guide 16

"Sempre libera," from La Traviata
Giuseppe Verdi (1813–1901)

Coloratura aria from an Italian opera
1853
Recorded by Tiziana Fabriccini, soprano
La Scala Chorus and Orchestra
Ricardo Muti, Conductor
CD No. 1, Track 16 (4:18)

"Sempre libera" from Giuseppe Verdi's opera *La Traviata* is one of the most famous coloratura arias from the nineteenth-century repertoire. In this opera, the heroine, Violetta, discovers that Alfredo, the hero, has secretly been in love with her for some time when he finally declares his devotion to her at a party in Paris. After musing about what married life would be like, Violetta sings that she must remain free (*sempre libera*) so that she may pass from pleasure to pleasure.

American Coloratura Soprano Beverly Sills. © Wally McNamee / CORBIS. ID # WL007861.

This aria places many demands on the singer: the text calls for a performance style that is carefree and flamboyant; the music is difficult—one must execute the light trills and rapid scales with ease and accuracy, and one must conform to the rhythmic structures laid out by the orchestra. (A **trill** is the rapid alternation of a principal note of the melody with an adjacent pitch.) As you listen, follow the text and note how the composer created trills and scale passages to help illustrate the carefree nature of the passage. The text is as follows:

Sempre libera degg'io	Forever free, I must flit
Folleggiare di gioia in gioia.	Wildly from joy to joy.
Vo' che scorra il viver mio	I want to spend my life
Pei sentieri del piacer.	On the pathway of pleasure.
Nasca il giorno, o il giorno muoia,	Whether it be day or night
Sempre lieta ne' ritrovi. Ah!	I will ever be found. Ah!
A diletti sempre nuovi	In places of delight,
Dee volar il mio pensier!	Always seeking newer joys![4]

To Consider

1. Which words are *embellished*, or ornamented? Do the high pitches of the melody correspond to significant words, or do you feel that the text settings are rather randomly placed?
2. How does the soprano keep these difficult passages contained within the context of the aria?
3. Can you describe the relationship of the vocal melody to the music played by the flute, or by any other instruments?

SUMMARY

In summary, the seven styles we have considered represent a small sampling of the enormous variety of musical sounds that the human voice is capable of producing. Over the centuries and across the world, musical expressions have emerged that are so different from one another that it seems that there are no common features to draw them together. However, each expression is a highly cultivated one—each musician, regardless of geographical or historical location, performs along specifically delineated guidelines, and each seeks a certain kind of sound.

To say that each musical expression is equal to the other does not, however, indicate that rock, folk music—whether European based or Native American based—and coloratura opera arias require the same level of musical training or performance skills. There is no question that the amount of training required to sing the difficult passages in a Verdi opera aria requires more years of training and practice than does singing lead in a rock band, for example. On the other hand, the operatic voice attempting to sing rock would clearly be inadequate in most cases. The musical encounter we had with the Xhosa culture of South Africa illustrated that virtuosity is not limited to being able to sing scales with lightning-speed accuracy. The technique of producing several pitches at the same time by one voice is indeed another specialized singing technique requiring much development.

Thus we come to appreciate and enjoy both virtuosity and appropriateness of musical style—no matter what type of music we experience. As we grow in musical experiences and listening skills, we come to learn what is expected of certain musical venues and also what goes into producing performances and compositions that are truly outstanding.

As students of music and musical cultures, it is always worthwhile to expand our understanding by learning what these musical conventions are. In that way, our musical tastes develop not by isolating one very specific type of music and dogmatically identifying with it, but by encountering many ways of music making.

KEY TERMS

coloratura
glissando
gottan
heterophony
intonation
shamisen
smearing
spiritual
trill
vocables

CHAPTER 4

Musical Performance and the Music Industry

MUSIC, that "universal language," that basic means of expression found throughout the world, is market driven in one way or another. The three major components of music production—the composer, the performer, and the audience—form a musical environment invariably linked to and supported by a variety of economic and social conditions.

Several fundamental questions may come to mind when you study the forces behind music. What factors create the need for a specific type of music? How do composers decide what kind of music to write? Who supports them in their endeavors? How does music reflect the aesthetic, cultural, and economic structures in any given society? And, finally, what is it about some music that allows it to bridge periods of time and place and makes it of universal interest to so many people, regardless of race, gender, nationality, geographical location, or social class?

The answers to these questions are as varied as history itself. For example, in our own modern culture, there are several different ways to make a living as a composer. To be successful in the areas of pop music, musical theater, and film music, modern composers must find a direct, immediate outlet for their music in order to make a living. Their careers may be precarious until they are established, for there are no guarantees connected to their work. It is not uncommon for these composers to find odd jobs to support themselves while they are getting established.

Although composers of art music frequently share the same pressures for success as pop composers, many have combined their professions as composers with a college teaching career, thus they are more financially secure. Of course, there are trade-offs: college professors/composers must spend many hours teaching and only have limited time to write. And, even though the composers of pop, theater, and film music have no guarantees of financial success, if their music becomes popular, the financial rewards far outstrip those of the professor/composer.

Two distinctly different but related forces drive the music market in all cultures, past and present. The first is a cultural factor, for music speaks for humankind. Music reflects the thoughts, concerns, expressions, and tastes of people, ranging from the most profound ideas and artistic languages to the most banal utterances of a society. The second force significant to music is the economic factor.

To illustrate this, let us consider two very contrasting composers/performers from two very different times in history. Wolfgang Amadeus Mozart, whom we have already met, lived in a culture where he was expected to dress in a specific way, conduct himself in courts according to prescribed behavioral patterns, and produce music that would satisfy the nobility for which it was written. His music reflected the philosophical concepts of the Enlightenment, which stated that music is "the art of pleasing by the succession and combination of agreeable sounds." This definition of music, given by an English writer, Charles Burney, in his *General History of Music* (1776), reflects

Elton John in "concert dress." New York, 8/16/1976: Elton John opening the seven-day concert singing "Grow Some Funk of Your Own." © Bettmann / CORBIS. ID # BE022326.

the nature and even the style of music that was acceptable at that time. Mozart had to conform to the social environment of the time in order to be successful. On the other hand, his genius allowed him to push the boundaries of cultural expectations, and he became a shaper of the very expectations and stylistic conventions under which he composed.

Also, consider Elton John, one of the most successful composers and performers of pop music in the last part of the twentieth century. Elton John's performance dress, his signature look, which included outlandish eye glasses, and his style of music, ranging from raucous rock to tuneful ballads, all fit the many faces of mainstream pop and rock. He, like Mozart, knew "what sold," but his genius was instrumental in forming the direction of pop music in the late twentieth century. Both Mozart and Elton John represent prime examples of both the social and economic sides of music marketing.

How music is supported in our modern American society is not only a practical issue for composers, publishers, and performers, it has become an object of political discussion that reaches the highest levels of government. Whether or not tax monies should be spent to support art music or government agencies should censor pop music lyrics are both issues that we will examine in Chapter 11.

Regardless of its origin and function, all music must meet the needs of its public in order to survive. Some musical genres are market driven in the narrowest commercial sense (such as the current pop music market), while others are supported by less direct principles than, "If it doesn't pay for itself, it shouldn't exist." All composers share a wish to have their music performed.

The professional performing artist and the audience are, of course, inseparably linked. Whether the source of income comes from the nobility or the church, as it did three centuries ago, or whether the performing artist is dependent on live concerts, CD sales, and MTV contracts, as is the current situation with pop artists, performing musicians always must keep their source of income in mind when they are choosing their programs.

In addition to music written for professional performers, there is another market source for music that provides a healthy portion of revenue for the music industry—the amateur music market. Throughout the Western world, the centuries-old tradition of amateur music making is still thriving. Music is practiced in the home, played and sung in private gatherings, clubs, schools, churches, temples, and synagogues throughout the modern culture.

In this chapter we will examine some of the forces that sustain music in our culture, past and present. Although the focus of this chapter will be on Western performance practice, the same economic forces affect music all over the world—all musicians have to eat. The first part of this chapter looks at the economic and social factors supporting art music and includes a discussion of the well-established institutions (including ensembles) that are vehicles for musical expression. The second part examines the world of pop music and identifies forces that drive and sustain that immense industry. Since the primary focus of *Musical Encounters* is on listening, we will sample some of these musical expressions as we proceed.

MAJOR PERFORMING INSTITUTIONS

Even though music in our culture is amazingly diverse and the performers and performance practices point to a wide array of musical expressions—composers, performers, and concertgoers still depend on some well-established types of ensembles that provide continuity and give shape to music in our time. In the concert world of art music, these "institutions" of music are often resident companies of a certain number and type of musicians—such as symphony orchestras, opera companies, wind symphonies, choruses or, in a larger venue, ballet troupes.

In this chapter we will examine these institutions as part of the music industry environment. We will look for answers to questions such as: What are the basic characteristics of sound that make up these groups, and why are so many people attracted to them? What are the cultural factors supporting a musical institution? What economic influences are significant in sustaining the market for a particular type of ensemble or segment of the musical environment?

Choral Ensembles

Of all musical groups in existence today, the choral ensemble is the most accessible to the average person interested in becoming involved in making music. We have already discussed singing as being rudimentary to music, but let us consider further the current state of vocal music in our culture. Our pop music culture has become more and more a spectator phenomenon. The extensive use of electronic technology, while it has been important in spreading the music of entertainment everywhere, has taken away much opportunity for the average person to participate as a performer. To "do" pop music, one should have thousands of dollars of equipment.

In spite of major shifts in music production techniques among the pop cultures, the choral ensemble remains at the center of vocal performance. Choral music is found today in public schools, higher education, churches, and in combination with symphony orchestras. With such widespread use, one cannot identify a specific "style" or "form" of choral music. Throughout our culture, groups of people with similar musical interests band together to form choral ensembles. Whether the stimulus to sing comes from gospel music, traditional and modern madrigals, "barbershop" groups, church and synagogue choirs, or large ensembles that are affiliated with symphony orchestras, a compelling urge to sing permeates parts of our society.

The majority of choral groups in the United States are filled with amateur singers who have a strong desire to make music. Many of these people learned to sing in public and private school systems, while others grew up in homes where music was a strong part of the family culture.

Perhaps it is the very simplicity of its nature that fosters the continuing interest in choral music. Or, it may be that singing and listening to choral music provides personal aesthetic fulfillment, and also can be used as a vehicle for religious worship, expressions of patriotism, and support for the rituals of life. Common to all choral music is the use of the human voice in its natural ranges: soprano (the highest type of voice), alto (a lower-ranged female voice), tenor (the high male voice), and bass (the low male voice). Of course, some voices defy gender characterization. There are male sopranos and altos, some using a **falsetto** voice, a special vocal technique of producing unusually high notes by using only the inner edges of the vocal chords.

The SATB (soprano/alto/tenor/bass) choir forms the center of choral composition. To obtain a more varied timbral range, composers often divide each voice category into two parts, thereby designating first and second sopranos, altos, tenors, and basses. Choral

A family participating in the singing of a madrigal.
© Bettmann / CORBIS.
ID # SF7873.

conductors determine who sings these parts, not by singing ability, but by testing each voice to see how it becomes stronger or weaker as the voice moves upward or downward on the musical scale. "Deep" and low male voices, then, sing the lowest bass part. Voices that seem to become stronger as the range goes upward, in turn, sing the highest parts in the music.

Most prominent composers have written works for chorus. During the Renaissance (ca. 1450–1600), choral music rose to unprecedented heights in the church. Secular (nonreligious) music also abounded during this time. Each country in Europe developed its own type of ensemble music. Our generic term for these vocal ensembles is **madrigal groups**. Modern chamber ensembles usually have twelve to twenty singers who perform a wide variety of music, from the English and Italian madrigals of the sixteenth century, to carols, and even to arrangements of popular ballads, show tunes, and traditional folk songs.

To illustrate the versatility of choral music as it is practiced in our modern culture, we will sample music from two different traditions: the madrigal repertoire of the sixteenth century and a modern arrangement of a slave lament sung by a prominent gospel choir.

A classic English madrigal is *Now Is the Month of Maying* by Thomas Morley (ca. 1557–1602), who lived and wrote in London and cultivated the popular music genres of his time, including both sacred and secular music, although he earned much of his living by serving in the Chapel Royal as organist and choir director. Morley's composition achieved great popularity during his lifetime, for he published extensively. The style of his music and of his contemporaries is closely related to the traditional Christmas carols that are so widespread in European–American culture. Today, English madrigals are a popular year-round form of music sung by high school, college, and amateur choirs throughout the country.

istening Guide 17

Now Is the Month of Maying
Thomas Morley (ca. 1557–1602)

English madrigal
1595
Recorded by the Cambridge Singers,
  John Rutter, conductor
CD No. 1, Track 17 (1:55)

Now is the month of maying,
When merry lads are playing,
  Fa la la la la
Each with his bonny lass
Upon the greeny grass
  Fa la la la la

The Spring, clad all in gladness,
Doth laugh at Winter's sadness,
   Fa la la la la
And to the bagpipe's sound
The nymphs tread out their ground.
   Fa la la la la

Fie then! Why sit we musing,
Youth's sweet delight refusing?
   Fa la la la la
Say, dainty nymphs, and speak,
Shall we play barley-break?
   Fa la la la la

To Consider

1. What interesting rhythmic patterns did the composer use to help underline the carefree attitude of the text?
2. You will notice that the first two lines of each "verse" are repeated. Why is this an effective compositional device?
3. The "fa-la-la" refrains are typical of many English madrigals. Do you know a Christmas carol that uses these syllables? What is the significance of the fa-la-la refrains to the music?

A striking feature of this compositional style is the clarity of the individual voice parts. Whether the texture is woven with independent voice parts or is presented in homorhythmic chords, one can easily hear each part. This music is well suited to amateur singers' voices: the ranges of the voices are comfortable; the rhythms, although they are interesting and frequently lively, are not difficult, and the chord structure is easy to grasp by the performers and the listeners. Subject matter for madrigals varies, but love is often the stimulus for the lyrics.

A more recent offshoot of the madrigal group is the **show choir**—a group of singers that combines music with choreography and sings arrangements of popular jazz and romantic ballads, or cabaret music.

The **gospel choir** is certainly one of the most overtly expressive types of choral ensembles in our modern culture. Stemming from the African-American spiritual tradition, this music has a unique performance practice. Its function is to give voice to a common expression of emotion and faith shared by those participating.

Albert McNeil is the founder and conductor of the Albert McNeil Jubilee Singers, a gospel choir that specializes in music of African-American origin and influence. McNeil believes that Negro spirituals have strong links to African musical traditions, and he cites the strong rhythms and call-and-response practices as having come from Africa.

Although the Jubilee Singers is a professional choir of thirty-six singers (they tour with fourteen singers), most gospel choirs consist of amateurs. You can hear gospel choirs wherever there is a strong community of African Americans throughout

Singer Darren Day and cast of *Summer Holiday* at the Apollo Theater in London, July 1997. © Robbie Jack / CORBIS. ID # RJ002412.

Gospel choir. Source: Stone.
ID # eb3269-001.

the United States. Their fervent, vibrant performances are hallmarks of the performance style.

Let us sample a gospel choir by listening to a recording made by the Jubilee Singers. *I Cannot Stay Here By Myself* is an arrangement of a slave lament. The lyrics are simple, but the emotional content of the song is intense and meaningful.

The most traditional choral music is the **concert choir**, a large group of singers whose repertoire was originally written for the chorus. Hundreds of works exist, both for unaccompanied choir and for chorus and orchestra. This tradition became very popular in the nineteenth century when, during

*L*istening Guide 18

I Cannot Stay Here By Myself
Hall Johnson, arranger

African-American spiritual
Recorded by the Albert McNeil Jubilee Singers
CD No. 1, Track 18 (4:16)

I cannot stay here by myself,
Oh, I cannot stay here by myself, by myself
I'm going away, the Lord knows where
I cannot stay here by myself.
Sometimes I weep like a willow
Sometime I moan like a dove, like a dove
I'm going away, the Lord knows where
I just can't stay here by myself.
I cannot stay here by myself, (Oh Lordy, what shall I do?)
I cannot stay here by myself (Oh Lordy, where shall I go?)
I'm going away, the Lord knows where,
I just can't stay here by myself.[1]

To Consider

1. What is the function of the choir as it hums the opening chords?
2. Can you identify the expressive devices that intensify the lyrics of the song? What is the role of the chorus after the soloist enters?
3. Notice the subtle reference to the song *Swing Low, Sweet Chariot*, which the arranger added between the second and third verses of the song.

4. In the final verse, the chorus sings the lyrics of the song, while the soprano soloist sings a personal response (this is an example of the "call-and-response" tradition stemming from African folk music). Did you notice that the melody was sung by both men and women in different vocal ranges? This musical practice adds more expression to the words, which by now have been repeated enough so that you anticipate them.

5. Do you think the repetitive nature of the lament adds to or detracts from its effectiveness?

the Industrial Revolution, common people often formed choral organizations for recreation and fulfillment, thereby establishing the practice that choral music was the music of the people and not confined to esoteric cultural groups. Later in this book, we will sample this great repertoire.

Musical Theater from Opera to Broadway Musicals

The ancient Greeks discovered the effectiveness of combining music and drama. Ever since, people have been creating various types of musical theater to entertain, to stimulate thought, and—in general—to allow people to reflect on the human condition.

Musical theater is, after all, about people. Popular topics and emotions such as love, hate, jealousy, the use and abuse of power, the human capacity to care, and the human need for laughter constitute the germinal foundations for the dramatic arts. And, of course, the use of music intensifies the drama.

Opera, the most universal form of musical theater, combines soloists, choruses, and orchestral music in a setting of elaborate staging, costuming, lighting, and scenery. The demands of opera are immense: great singers also need to be fine actors; composers must not only be capable of writing dramatic music, but they must always be aware of the demands that the stage puts on the musical form itself.

Two general categories of text settings in opera are the **recitative** and the **aria**. The recitative is characterized by melodies that have a narrow range of notes so that the words of the text are presented in the style of a recitation. The accompaniment is very sparse. Composers commonly set dialogue in recitative style. The aria is a type of operatic song in which the singer is allowed the opportunity to display maximum emotion and vocal technique in an attempt to intensify the meaning of a poem or another type of poignant text. Since its inception in the early 1600s, opera has undergone continual development and change in the hands of hundreds of composers.

In Chapter 3, you heard an aria from the late-nineteenth-century Italian composer Giuseppe Verdi. You will recall that "Sempre libera" from *La Traviata* was filled with difficult scale passages and ornamentation that called upon the utmost performing skills from the soprano. With this knowledge and experience as a background, we shall return to the very earliest years of opera in Italy to discover the origins of this dramatic

The English National Opera performance of *Orfeo*, March 1992. Source: © Robbie Jack / CORBIS. ID # RJ001208.

form. We will listen to an excerpt from the first complete opera that has been preserved. Written by Claudio Monteverdi (1567–1643), one of the most significant composers representing the transition from the Renaissance to Baroque styles in music, the opera *Orfeo* is still performed by modern opera companies.

Monteverdi stands in history as one of the great musical innovators. His early compositions were steeped in the traditions of the high Renaissance, musical practices that included the organization of musical textures into a sort of seamless unfolding of melodic lines. He then helped establish new musical expressions that are now recognized as having major historical significance. His forward-looking attitudes toward his art resulted in his composing the greatest of early operatic masterpieces.

Orfeo, la favola in music (*Orpheus, a Musical Fable*), his opera of 1607, served as the germ for several later operatic practices:

1. It utilized a new style of musical texture in which a solo singer was accompanied by a single harmonic instrument (such as a lute, a harpsichord, or an organ) and a bass instrument, which played the lowest melodic line of the chordal accompaniment. This style, called **monody**, is the musical ancestor of operatic solos.

2. His opera included a full orchestra comprised of some forty players. The music written for the orchestra often enhances the drama of the text.

3. The opera incorporates a chorus, inspired by the traditional chorus of Greek drama but also resembling the madrigal, or four-part song, a musical form popular in Monteverdi's time.

4. *Orfeo* exhibits a strong concept of chord progression (a logical sequence of harmonies) that helps set the stage for several centuries of harmonic evolution.

*L*istening Guide 19

**"Tu se morta," from *Orfeo*
Claudio Monteverdi (1567–1643)**

Opera excerpt
1607
Recorded by Chiaroscuro Ensemble
Nigel Rogers, conductor
CD No. 1, Track 19 (2:42)

*T*his, the most famous excerpt from Monteverdi's *Orfeo*, is the lament that Orpheus sings when he discovers that his love Euridice has died. (He subsequently goes into the underworld in an attempt to gain her back.) Particularly interesting are the chord progressions and the use of chromaticism to express the anguish of Orpheus. The embellishments, such as the trill at the end of the piece, also provide the singer/actor an opportunity to portray the emotions of the text. As you listen to this music, put aside feelings that this music is "different" and allow yourself to concentrate on the text. You will discover that the monodic style of Monteverdi remains a valid vehicle for music drama—even though it was composed nearly four centuries ago.

Tu se' morta, se' morta, mia vita,	You are dead, dead, my life blood,
ed io respiro; tu se; da me partita,	And yet I live; you have left me,
se' da me partita per mai più,	And are gone from me forever,
mai più non tonare, ed io rimango—	Never to return, yet I remain————
no, no, che se I versi alcuna cosa ponno	No, no, if verses have any power,
n'andrò sicuro al piú profondi abissi,	I shall go bravely to the deepest abysses,

e intenerito il cor del re dell'ombre,	And having mellowed the heart of the king of shadows,
meco trarotti a riveder le stelle,	I will take you back with me to see the stars again,
o se ciò negherammi empio destino,	Or if cruel fate will deny me this,
rimarrò tecco in compagnia di morte!	I will remain with you in the company of death!
Addio terra, addio cielo, e sole, addio.	Farewell earth, farewell sky, and sun, farewell.[2]

To be sure, opera has changed considerably since its inception in the early 1600s. Its versatility as a musical form is attested to when one considers that opera always reflects the musical environment, the dramatic interests, and even the available technological developments representative of each time period in history.

One significant development is the use of voice, both for spoken dialogue and for singing. Forms such as **opera buffa** (comic opera) in Italy, **singspiel** in Germany, **opera comique** in France, and **comic opera** in England were the first to use these mixed techniques. These forms are all characterized by a mixture of spoken and sung dialogue.

The **American musical**, building upon less formal treatments of text, grew to immense popularity in the early decades of the twentieth century. Broadway, a street in New York City lined with theaters, became the center for this art form. Since the subject matter of musicals usually has uncomplicated plots, and the music unfolds in the form of songs that often do not require the level of virtuosity demanded by opera, the musical became the musical theater of the middle classes in America. Although opera still flourishes in opera houses and in universities, the musicals written by Rodgers and Hart, Rodgers and Hammerstein, Lerner and Loewe, and Bernstein and Sondheim are performed on stages throughout America, from high school gymnasiums to Broadway itself. The two most successful composers of musicals in recent years are Stephen Sondheim (b. 1930), composer of *A Little Night Music, Sweeney Todd*, and *Into the Woods*, and Andrew Lloyd Webber (b. 1948), best known for *Jesus Christ Superstar, Cats, Phantom of the Opera*, and *Evita*.

The musical hit *Les Miserables*, by Alain Boubil and Claude Michel Schoenberg, was first produced in London and soon became an international sensation among musical theatergoers. Its story, based on the nineteenth-century novel by Victor Hugo, tells of the life-and-death struggles during the great social and political upheaval of the French Revolution. *Les Miserables* opened in London in the fall of 1985 and has been playing in the-

Movie still from *Les Miserables,* with Frederic March, released in 1935. © Bettmann / CORBIS. ID # BE076826.

aters around the world ever since. It has been translated into fourteen different languages. The cast calls for a wide range of characters; the original cast included actors/singers who had rock opera experience, such as Colm Wilkinson, Patti Lupone, and Shakespearean actors Roger Allam and Alun Armstrong. Its breadth of musical expressions complements the telling of the profound and emotional story.

The immense popularity of *Les Miserables* resulted in an unprecedented number of performances in its first ten years of existence. By 1995, it had been presented over 22,000 times by twenty-nine companies to audiences of over 42 million people! Performances were held in twenty-three countries throughout the world.

Chamber Music Groups

If you want to experience great music in a more intimate setting than the opera house, the musical theater, or the symphony hall, you will find the chamber music performance rewarding. In virtually any large city or university town in the United States, there exists an active chamber music environment. Chamber music often is played in private homes and in recital settings. In this way it differs from the large forms of music such as the symphony, for most chamber music is written to be played one player per part. Each player is thus an independent member of the musical texture. For that reason, musicians find great personal enjoyment in playing chamber music. The feeling is more intimate than playing in an orchestra, and the musicians often feel as though they are having a musical conversation with each other, for this music often passes musical ideas—melodies and rhythmic figures—back and forth in shared commentary.

What is chamber music? It is concert music written for a small group of musicians—usually one player or singer to a part. Its name comes from the concept that people perform it in a "chamber," or a small performing hall.

Chamber music is written for different combinations of instruments, but several have become standard. The **string quartet** is undoubtedly the most common genre of chamber music. It evolved concurrently with the string section of the orchestra and consists of two violins, a viola, and a cello. (The double bass is a bit cumbersome, and the sound is too deep to balance the other instruments.) It first attained great popularity in the eighteenth-century European courts, but now the string quartet has become a regular component of the artistic life of the people. Franz Joseph Haydn (1732–1809) wrote many quartets for the Esterhazy family in Austria; his quartets, along with those of Mozart and Beethoven, established this genre. Today, several important professional string quartets, including the Julliard String Quartet, the Emerson Quartet, and the Kronos Quartet (a group dedicated to performing modern music), perform and record regularly.

We will turn to the sound of a string quartet in our discussion of chamber music. It is a single-movement composition, *Alla Marcia* (or, "Like a March"), by English composer Benjamin Britten (1913–1976). The instruments play melodies that respond to each other almost in a conversational mode, sometimes interrupting each other in their haste to be part of the music.

One interesting sound feature of the string quartet is that the timbres of the four stringed instruments in the ensemble are produced in the same way: the violins, the viola,

The Emerson string quartet.
Source: Jack Vartoogian.

and the cello all are elaborately designed wooden boxes with curved surfaces designed so the sound waves bounce around and are therefore amplified. Each instrument has strings that are either bowed or plucked. Therefore, the string quartet sounds like one large instrument capable of playing from very low to very high.

Listening Guide 20

Alla Marcia (Like a March)
Benjamin Britten (1913–1976)

Single-movement composition for string quartet
1933
Recorded by the Endellion String Quartet
CD No. 1, Track 20 (3:23)

Britten's *Alla Marcia* is a playful march that sounds like a processional. It starts very quietly, emerges into a busy texture where melodies and rhythms scurry around, and ends as though it were trailing off into the distance.

To Consider

1. Describe the beginning of this march-like piece in terms of texture. How does the composer set up his musical conversation? How many instruments are involved at the beginning?
2. Can you hear when other instruments join in? What type of commentary is made? Does it accompany a melody, or is it an additional melody?
3. What gives the work its march-like character? What instruments sustain this feeling?
4. Finally, can you feel when the piece is about to end? How do you know when this is about to happen?

The following listening guide will help you hear how composers write melodies and rhythms in chamber music in such a way that the instruments seem to carry on conversations with each other.

0:00	The very opening measures start with a single repeated note accompanied by a pizzicato (plucked) rhythm in the cello. The march-like feeling is set up in this way from the very start.
0:08	Soon a violin presents a playful melody. The viola then begins to add another layer to the beat established by the cello and plays on the "after beats." When you hear this, you will feel the energy level of the march increase.
0:46	By now all four instruments are playing. The first violin soars above the others, clamoring for attention.
1:00	Now, two melodies compete with each other. The cello continues to supply the steady beat of the march, but now it plays with the bow.
1:33	The texture soon becomes one of various instruments commenting on the violin melody.
1:55	The texture relaxes somewhat, creating an anticipation of new material. The viola takes up the plucked rhythm, and the second violin plays a simple melody. Soon the cello furnishes the pulse, and the middle instruments play on the "after beats." The momentum picks up again for a short time.
2:30	The weave of voices becomes simple again and returns to the feeling of the opening measures, with a sustained note in the viola, the violin stating parts of the melody, and the cello providing the beat.
3:00	It is now apparent that the march is ending with the same single note repeated against the plucked cello rhythm.

Other established instrumental combinations are the **piano trio** (piano, violin, and cello), the **piano quintet** (string quartet and piano), the **string quintet** (usually a string quartet with an added cello), and the **woodwind quintet** (flute, oboe, clarinet, bassoon, and horn—the horn, although a brass instrument, lends a blending quality to the timbres of the woodwind instruments). Although eighteenth- and nineteenth-century composers did not write for this group, the **brass quintet** has risen to popularity among the audiences of recent decades. Performing a repertoire ranging from sixteenth-century music originally written for brass instruments to arrangements (called **transcriptions**) of music written originally for other instrumental combinations, this instrumentation of two trumpets, horn, trombone, and tuba, has proven to be a highly versatile and attractive ensemble.

The Symphony Orchestra

The symphony orchestra is the most widespread professional institution for art music in the United States. Perhaps you will recall from Chapter 1 that ninety-five orchestras report budgets of over $1,000,000. The American Symphony Orchestra League, the national professional organization for symphonies, reports the existence of 1800 orchestras in the United States (including adult, youth, collegiate, and chamber orchestras). Since its development in eighteenth-century Europe, the symphony orchestra has gained and retained a universal popularity in the concert world—which now has spread to non-Western countries such as Japan, Korea, and China. In later chapters of *Musical Encounters*, you will examine orchestral works from various composers and historical eras.

Let us explore the characteristics of sound belonging to the symphony orchestra, for after all, it is the sound itself that is the reason for the ongoing life of this institution of music. The symphony orchestra is made up of four general groupings (or families) of instruments: the woodwinds (flutes, oboes, clarinets, and bassoons), brass (horns, trumpets, trombones, and tuba), percussion (a wide variety of both pitched and non-pitched instruments whose tone is produced by striking or scraping), and strings (violins, violas, cellos, and double basses.) Typically, a major professional symphony orchestra consists of about 120 musicians, but this number varies according to the requirements of individual compositions written for it.

The art of setting music for this ensemble, called **orchestration**, is a major consideration for the composer. Whenever we hear orchestral music, we become increasingly aware of the subtleties of timbre, pitch, range, and volume that are possible in orchestral composition.

What is the attraction of the symphony orchestra then? It is that the orchestra's vast tonal and timbral resources represent the widest practical palette of sounds available to the composer. Although electronic technology now makes an even more varied sound spectrum possible, and the world of popular music has become dominated by electronic instruments, it seems, at least for the present, that **acoustical instruments** (or instruments that do not rely on electronic amplification to produce sound) have earned a permanent place in the ears of the concertgoing public.

The various instrumental families in the orchestra are arranged on stage to make the most of their tonal capabilities. A basic seating chart, indicating the sections of the orchestra is given on the following page. This arrangement may vary somewhat, according to the demands of the works being played or the wishes of the conductor, but most orchestras are arranged in this manner.

The economic and social conditions in the United States during the middle and late twentieth century provided an excellent environment for symphonic music in many ways. European orchestral traditions in some ways were more restrictive than those on the American continents. Great music from past European masters (Mozart, Beethoven, Brahms, etc.) dominated the repertoire—especially in the major cultural centers such as Vienna. It also was traditional that orchestras were made up of males only.

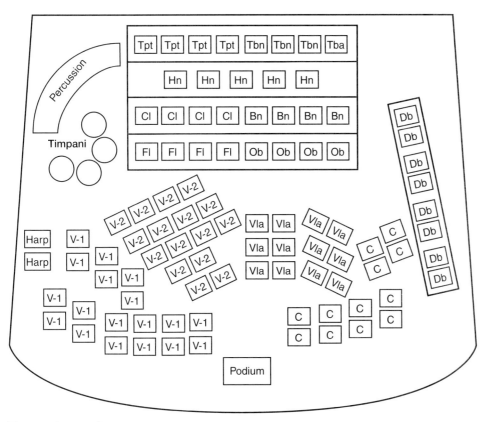

The symphony orchestra.

In the second half of the century, however, these male-exclusive practices in orchestral music began to change—especially in the United States. Currently, when a position for an orchestral player becomes available in a symphony, auditions are held in such a way that the players are judged only on their playing ability and the type of sound that they produce, and not on any other factors, such as gender, race, or national origin. In the United States, starting salaries for players in major symphonies range from about $60,000 to $90,000. Such symphonies have annual budgets of over $10 million. Of course, many musicians play in regional symphonies and orchestras in smaller communities at a fraction of the salaries offered by the New York Philharmonic, or the Chicago, St. Louis, Boston, Los Angeles, Philadelphia, and Cincinnati orchestras.

$\mathcal{P}$OP MUSIC PERFORMANCE

Pop music is all about keeping up with the times. It is generated by performing artists who are skilled at presenting their ideas in formats immediately accessible to a specifically targeted audience. In past years, it was common for observers of the pop music scene to speak of "disposable music," meaning that what is popular today certainly will be replaced by something different tomorrow. In reality, modern pop music represents much more than that. It originated as an expression of the common people, for it speaks in a language understood by many. In spite of the commercial nature of its production and distribution, it remains a significant part of today's musical culture.

During the past two decades, a growing number of musicologists and sociologists have taken pop music seriously and consider these musical expressions a significant cultural benchmark. We will examine the rock and pop culture of the second half of the twentieth century in an attempt to understand the forces behind its creation, the musical directions it took, and the influences it had on shaping our diverse culture.

Rock: Then and Now

Rock 'n' roll began as a youth movement in the 1950s—the most pervasive movement of its kind in popular music history. It offered a means of expression through which teenagers could declare independence from the older generation, a way to find group identity through a form of cultural expression that adults found difficult to digest. When Elvis Presley developed his undulating choreographic performance style, this gesture was met with such disdain that the cameramen on the *Ed Sullivan Show* were instructed to show Elvis only from the waist up in his 1956 appearance on national television. That evening, the *Ed Sullivan Show* received one of its highest audience share ratings ever.

Historians of rock 'n' roll trace its roots to a combination of influences: rhythm and blues, blues "shouters," gospel, boogie-woogie piano music, hill-billy country music, and honky-tonk music. The term *rock and roll* was a concept coined by Cleveland disc jockey Alan Freed in 1954. Freed was an ingenious shaper of popular taste. He promoted music that was clearly directed toward teenagers and their concerns in life. Songs about love, sexual identity, and personal expressions of freedom—some intense, some lighthearted—formed the spirit of rock. A general attitude of energy permeated the entire rock 'n' roll industry.

The popular music industry grew to immense proportions in the third quarter of the twentieth century. Fueled by a spirit in which members of subcultures sought new identity, several styles of music emerged and flourished. At first these styles seemed to speak for a specific group, but soon the energy of this music spread, was intermingled, and became an ever-growing force of expression and entertainment. Millions of recordings cut by hundreds of artists singing and playing in many different styles brought life to this industry.

Portrait of Elvis Presley, seated, singing and playing a Gibson guitar, 1957. Photo by: Frank Driggs. Source: Archive Photos. ID # G1863/093/F11K82E.

Those artists representing different significant strains of pop music in the late 1950s and the following two decades included Elvis Presley, Chuck Berry, James Brown, the Beatles, Bob Dylan, and Jimi Hendrix. Presley brought a combination of country and western, rhythm and blues, and Southern gospel singing to the new arena of pop music. His strong personality eclipsed many other musicians. Today he is widely referred to as the "King of Rock 'n' Roll." Berry was successful in combining an African-American blues tradition with lyrics that appealed to teenage American values and interests. Brown was the "Godfather of Soul"; the Beatles represented the British invasion into the American rock scene, while Dylan represented the poet/songwriter coming from the white folk tradition. Finally, Hendrix was the prototype of the hard-rock culture that eventually became a hallmark of the 1970s.

Let us sample two songs from this group of influential shapers of pop music in the quest for understanding this energy that created a musical culture of its own. We will examine songs performed by Berry and Brown. (The music of the Beatles is discussed in Chapter 13, *Music and Romance*.)

The story of Berry's influence and rise to prominence in this new music market serves as a prime example of the early rock 'n' roll environment. When Charles Edward Anderson "Chuck" Berry (born 1926) began playing the guitar at the Cosmo Club in East St. Louis (1952), he had no idea that his music was to become a central part in a

PLATE 1:

*G*ian Lorenzo Bernini
(Italian, Naples 1598-1680),
"Ecstasy of St. Theresa," 1652.
Santa Maria della Vittoria, Rome /
Canali PhotoBank, Milan /
SuperStock. ID # 1039/15074/N/P36D.

PLATE 2:

*P*eter Paul Rubens (Flemish, 1577-1640),
"The Assumption of the Virgin," c. 1626.
Oil on panel, 1.254 x .942 (49 3/8 x 37 1/8 in.);
framed: 1.575 x 1.257 x .082 (62 x 49 1/2 x 3 1/4).
National Gallery of Art, Washington.
Samuel H. Kress Collection. ID # 1961.9.32.(PA)1393.
Photograph © Board of Trustees,
National Gallery of Art, Washington.

PLATE 3:

*B*althaser Neumann, Ceiling of the "Kaisersaal," scenes from the life of German Emperor Friedrich Barbarossa (1122-1190). Photo by: Erich Lessing. Source: Art Resource, NY. ID # S0096762.

PLATE 4:

*J*acques Louis David (French, 1748-1825), "Oath of the Horatii (Le Serment des Horaces)." Musée de Louvre, Paris / SuperStock. ID # 1158/922/I/P20J.

PLATE 5:
Eugene Delacroix (French, 1798-1863), "Liberty Leading the People." Musée de Louvre, Paris / ET Archive, London / SuperStock. ID # 862/1189/I/P30G.

PLATE 6:
Caspar David Friedrich (German, 1774-1840), "Two Men Viewing the Moon," 1819/1820. Gemaldegalerie Meue Meister, Dresden, Germany / A.K.G., Berlin / SuperStock.
ID # 463/7096/N/P7B.

PLATE 7:

*J*ohn Singleton Copley (American, 1738-1815), "Watson and the Shark," 1778, oil on canvas, 1.821 x 2.297 (71 3/4 x 90 1/2 in.); framed: 2.413 x 2.642 x .101 (95 x 104 x 4 in.). National Gallery of Art, Washington. Ferdinand Lammot Belin Fund. ID # 1963.6.1.(PA)1904. Photograph © Board of Trustees, National Gallery of Art, Washington.

PLATE 8:

*F*ranz Liszt plays before the royal family of Austria. Archivo Inconographico, S.A. / CORBIS.

new musical expression destined to become a multibillion-dollar industry. By 1955, he had written the song *Maybelline*, a rhythm-and-blues style tune that became number 1 on the R & B charts.

Within the next six years Berry succeeded in writing ten more Top 10 hits: *Thirty Days, Roll Over Beethoven, Too Much Monkey Business, Brown Eyed Handsome Man, School Days, Rock and Roll Music, Sweet Little Sixteen, Johnny B. Goode, Carol,* and *Almost Grown*.

What is the significance of Berry's music on America? First, he was the most dominant African American in the early days of rock. He was a key figure in bringing the tradition of rhythm and blues, mixed with a bit of country and western, into early rock 'n' roll. His guitar riffs were drawn from the music of the blues; his lyrics were pop poetry at its best—unpretentious, direct, and without hidden meaning.

Berry used the guitar as both an accompaniment and a tool in musical dialogue, for his guitar "licks" often responded to a particular phrase of the words. Whereas many of his rhythm and blues contemporaries used horns as a backup for the guitar and vocals, Berry more directly relied on the guitar. His piercing electric guitar style influenced many rock artists to come.

If Elvis is the "King of Rock 'n' Roll," then Berry is the "Father of Rock 'n' Roll," in recognition of his personal influence on early rock. Some believe that the roots of rock stem more from rhythm and blues than from country. Many students of pop culture suggest that influential New York disc jockey Alan Freed renamed R & B "rock 'n' roll" to capture the audience of white teenagers. However, Berry, guitarist and singer, was also Berry the lyricist. Through his lyrics Berry reached out to a broader audience than the traditional rhythm and blues crowd. His poetry reflects the romantic ideals of teenage America in the 1950s. Songs such as *School Days, Almost Grown, and Sweet Little Sixteen* were entertaining dance tunes that crossed lines of ethnicity and musical styles. As a result, this "rockabilly" music became popular with R & B, country, and pop audiences, and Berry was in the middle of it all. *Oh, Baby Doll* is typical of this expression.

*L*istening Guide 21

"Oh, Baby Doll"
Chuck Berry (b. 1926)

Rock 'n' roll song hit
1957
Recorded by Chuck Berry with Lafayette Leake, piano
Willie Ditson, bass; Fred Below, drums
CD No. 1, Track 21 (2:33)

Baby doll, when the bells ring out the summer free,
Oh, Baby Doll, will it end for you and me?
We'll sing old *Alma Mater* and think of things that used to be.

I remember so well back when the weather was cool,
We used to have so much fun when we were walkin' to school,
If we'd stop off to hear the latest songs they sing,
And we'd just make it in before the bell would ring.

Baby Doll, . . .

When the teacher was gone that's when we had a ball,
We used to dance and play all up and down the hall.

We had a portable radio, we was ballin' the jack,
But we'd be all back in order when the teacher got back.

Baby Doll, . . .[3]

To Consider

1. If you were to write a cultural/musical analysis of this song that would attempt to explain its appeal to the teenage American market in the 1950s, what would you write?
2. What gives this song a feeling of energy?
3. Discuss the level of complexity/simplicity in the chords that Berry plays on the guitar.
4. What elements make it sound "quaint" to the modern ear?

The music of Berry and his contemporaries probably sounds quaint to your ears. Frequently the songs used only a few basic chords, and the amplification systems for the instruments were inexpensive and uncomplicated.

When R & B music was absorbed into the pop field and became part of the rock 'n' roll scene, an intense expression of "soul" music began to be heard by the entire rock 'n' roll audience, both black and white. For much of the African-American culture of the 1960s, "soul music" meant "black music." Bobbi Jean Lewis, a writer for *Soul*, a newspaper dedicated to reporting news related to this segment of society, wrote:

> Soul is the music that tells it like it is . . . this isn't really a long way around of explaining rhythm and blues, because that's what R & B is. It communicated the soulfulness of the Negro people. The Beatles don't own it, and neither do the Stones or the Animals or any of the other British groups, which have invaded American shores. But these English long-hairs cut their musical teeth on American rhythm and blues.[4]

Before long, however, the term took on a more general meaning for a lot of musicians. It referred to a general feeling of intensity, an aesthetic that admittedly had its roots in the music of the black culture but that could be emulated by non-black musicians as well.

What is this elusive factor of "soul" in pop music? We will try to discover the answer to that question as we listen to James Brown as he shares a performance of *Try Me* with Robert Palmer. The R & B style of Brown is much more direct, more hard-core expressively African American than was the music of Berry.

Brown was born in Macon, Georgia, in 1933 and moved to Augusta with his father when he was four. He lived in a brothel with his aunt and was raised in poverty. His musical talent became apparent when, as a young boy, he sang and danced for soldiers returning home from World War II and worked as a shoe-shine boy. His life was full of music and trouble. He spent some time in a reform school and emerged in the early 1950s resolving to make a living as a musician. His first song, *Please, Please, Please*, released in 1956 when Brown was twenty-three years old, reached number 6 on the rhythm and blues charts and sold more than 1 million copies. In the following years, Brown made many recordings and went on to influence the future of R & B. Like Presley and Berry, Brown also carries a title—"The Father of Soul." Brown also was recently accredited as being the "Godfather" of the rap and hip-hop generation.

The soul movement in the early 1960s blossomed into a large market for pop music, because it reflected a growing awareness among young African Americans that a new cultural identity was being formed. Performing artists and groups became associated with the movement. Joe Tex sang the blues, the Supremes sang in a well-polished pop style, and jazz musicians such as Ramsey Lewis played music with a distinctive "black" sound. By the end of the decade, groups such as Diana Ross and the Supremes, the Temptations, and Smokey Robison and the Miracles crossed racial lines of popularity, and the music industry once again experienced an expansion into new musical—and commercial—success.

Listening Guide 22

<table>
<tr><td>

Try Me
James Brown (b. 1933)

</td><td>

Rhythm and blues
1959
Recorded by James Brown and Joe Palmer
CD No. 1, Track 22 (4:00)

</td></tr>
</table>

Try me, try me,
   Darlin', tell me
I need you,
   Oh yeah
Try me, try me
   And your love will always be true
Oh . . . I need you.

Hold me, hold me,
   I want you right here by my side
Hold me, hold me
   And you, love, we won't have
Ah . . . I need.

(Interlude)

Hold me
Walk with me,
   Talk with me
I want you
   To stop my heart from cryin'

Walk with me
   Talk with me
And your love
   Will stop my heart from cryin'.
Oo, I need you.

(Reprise)

Walk with me.[5]

To Consider

1. What is unique about the way Brown delivers the lyrics of the song?
2. How does the rhythm and accent of the band reinforce this style?
3. Can you describe the underlying principle of meter? What beats of the measure receive the strongest beat?

0:00   "Try Me" begins with a strong emphasis (accent) on the 2nd and 4th beats of the measure. This is the most important element of the "funky" sound of the song. This is called a **backbeat**. If you listen carefully to the rhythm in the band you will hear that each beat of the measure has three subdivisions. This is an example of **compound meter**: *one*-ta-ta, *two*-ta-ta, *three*-ta-ta, *four*-ta-ta. Furthermore, notice how the band emphasizes the fourth beat of the measure by playing each subdivision louder than those of earlier beats.

1:07 The second verse, "Hold Me," begins. By now you have settled into the song and are feeling the backbeat. The pauses Brown takes after each short phrase of the words add to the character of "soul," as do the short comments he gives between the lines of the lyrics.

1:50 An instrumental interlude is played by a saxophone duet. The singer reinforces the end by interjecting, "Hold me."

2:35 The third verse, "Walk with me," begins. Its repetition now feels very comfortable to your ears as you anticipate each phrase of the words. A big ending is given to the song.

4:21 Just as you think the song has ended, Brown and the band play a reprise of the third verse in a very effective and dramatic ending to this soulful, funky, love song.

Meanwhile, yet another trend was emerging that added diversity to the pop scene. When the Beatles arrived in America, something began to change in the rock industry. The audience for the new version of rock 'n' roll seemed to expand almost overnight. The songs of the Beatles seemed to contain more poetic imagery than the repertoire of the then-current rock and roll, and the musical techniques evolved into a more sophisticated style (we will discuss this further in Chapter 13). It was as though songs were being written with an "art-music attitude" instead of a totally "low-brow" concept. The market for rock was beginning to widen.

From 1965 to the 1970s, pop music proliferated in different directions. Folksingers wrote songs about the social ills of the time. War protest songs were sung by Bob Dylan, Joan Baez, and the Kingston Trio. Lighter songs in the folk vein also were popular, as were more wistful tunes, all of which originated either out of a songwriter's personal experience or fantasy. Simon and Garfunkel sang *Feelin' Groovy*, Jim Croce sang of saving *Time in a Bottle*, and Harry Chapin recorded the tragi-comedic song, *30,000 Pounds of Bananas*. You will encounter more music from this era in the later chapters of this book.

A mainstream of rock, coming out of the 1970s decade, can be generically labeled **hard rock**. Its driving backbeat is reinforced by high-tech electronic amplification—often reaching the levels of intentional distortion. The spirit of hard rock is one of extreme energy, a search for freedom of expression, and a feeling of teenage independence. The downside to the hard rock culture is that performers are often linked to the drug culture that surrounds the music. Several of hard rock's greatest stars have succumbed to drug overdoses.

The pop music industry in the final two decades of the twentieth century became the most eclectic market ever to exist in modern history. New submarkets developed both for those listeners who always desired to be on the leading edge of musical development and for those who wanted to retain their favorite recordings and artists. The term "classic rock" was coined for an aging generation of rock 'n' rollers. Many categories of current rock music expressions currently exist alongside this classic rock. New forms of pop music, such as rap and hip-hop, developed from a variety of influences. Their forms of expression speak for a significantly large segment of modern teenage America. Techno music reflects capabilities for electronically generated music. To some modern ears, it sounds impersonal; to others, it is refreshingly modern and forward sounding.

An Elective Musical Selection

Your final musical selection in this chapter is an open one for you to explore. You are invited to choose a recording or a music video from any current rock group, listen to it, and discuss the following considerations with your friends:

*T*O CONSIDER

1. Based on your encounters with music so far, can you describe the basic premises of this music? Describe the types of singers/instruments that make up this piece. Does it have a form? Is it repetitive? Is there a melody connected to this song?

2. What features of this music reinforce its success as a commercial venture in the music industry? Why is this music attractive to you?

3. Do you feel the musical style of this particular piece is derived from any sources you may have encountered in this study?

4. How are the emotions, feelings, and attitudes (if any) of the singer or songwriter translated into music in this song? Can you describe the song as "personal," "emotional," or "commercial"? (Find your own descriptive words).

The Recording Industry

So far in *Musical Encounters* we have noticed that the socioeconomic foundations of music are dominated by two important themes—diversity and change. No segment of the music industry reflects this more accurately than the recording industry.

One aspect of this change is the technology of sound reproduction, which is in constant evolution. Thomas Edison built his first phonograph in 1877 using a mechanical system whereby vibrations were cut into a wax cylinder and read by a needle attached to a horn-shaped mechanism that amplified the sound. In the 1920s, Joseph Maxwell perfected a new electromagnetic system of recording sounds onto a carbon disk, and by the middle of the decade, over 1 million recordings were produced each year. In the arena of popular music, the improvement of gramophone discs fostered a market for sales that rivaled the sale of sheet music. The 1920s experienced the development of specialized segments of a commercial market directed toward individual tastes in music. "Race records," "hill-billy" music, the music of "crooners" such as Bing Crosby and, later, jazz recordings catered to the individual tastes of millions of Americans. In the 1930s and 1940s, big band jazz added to this burgeoning market. By the end of the 1940s, the recording industry, and its close relative, the radio, had surpassed the sale of sheet music as principal delivery systems of modern popular music.

Classical music was recorded by major symphonies, opera houses, and various other performing groups and artists in spite of the technological restrictions of the limited length of recording possibilities and the tone quality of recordings. With the advent of the long playing record (the "LP"), however, even these restrictions were overcome, and in the 1950s, virtually all major professional performing ensembles cut recordings, often led by famous conductors and played or sung by artists of world renown. Arturo Toscanini (1867–1957), the fiery interpreter of the music of Beethoven, Wagner, and Verdi, recorded in the studios of the National Broadcasting Company (NBC). His famous interpretation of the Verdi opera *Falstaff* and his recordings of the nine Beethoven symphonies remain classics of musical interpretation to the present time.

During the 1970s, compact discs (CDs) were made possible by the introduction of digital recording technology, and in the following decades, the music industry expanded at a greater pace than ever before. Although six labels dominate the large-sales market, hundreds of independent companies (called "labels" in the industry) create music for specialized markets and widen the possibilities for all possible tastes and all people.

In the late 1970s, sales of recordings dipped somewhat, but the industry was revitalized when music videos and music TV channels became common. The 1980s and 1990s were decades of international expansion, giving rise to a "world music" perspective. In Japan, for example, individual labels catering to the Japanese teenage market produced recordings under the categories of electronica, pop, cutesy pop, tsunami pop (a culturally mixed style, including music sung in French), rock, avant-rock, and hip-hop.

A survey of compact disc sales in 1998 revealed an interesting trend in music listening, when it was discovered that movie soundtracks were selling at an astonishing rate. Movie soundtracks are often made up of several different styles of music recorded by various artists. The success of this format has led industry analysts to believe that the tastes of many people are moving away from buying CD recordings by a single artist and toward a variety of music on one recording. The tasteful selection of music for movies such as *When Harry Met Sally* (1989), *Sleepless in Seattle* (1993), *Titanic* (1997), and *Midnight in the Garden of Good and Evil* (1998) resulted in the sale of millions of compact discs. For example, by mid-1998, the CD soundtrack sales for *Titanic* exceeded 10 million units. The soundtrack market for the six-month period January–August 1998 contributed heavily to the gross CD sales of over 502 million units amounting to a total sales of $5.8 billion.

Listening to music by using computers linked to the Internet is the most recent development in the music industry. Music has become so accessible that one can sample music ranging from sound bites and snippets of a recording to entire recordings themselves. Computer technology enables people to download music at an affordable cost. The Internet has become a vehicle for advertising, for purchasing music, and for listening to music. Digital distribution is the technology of the present and the wave of the future. The Internet has the potential to offer music with less production and distribution costs than conventional music markets.

Musicians can profit from this technology, for their music can be transmitted directly to the market. Some artists may choose to give away songs over the Internet in order to promote recordings and albums. And the digital transmission of music offers the ultimate delivery system for markets anywhere in the world. A person wishing to hear the music of Northern India can listen to it in McCook, Nebraska, instantly and anytime, through the Internet.

Driving Forces in MTV Programming

Music Television (MTV) came about in 1981 as a music industry collaboration between Warner Communications and American Express, who subsequently sold it to Viacom, Inc. The originators of this form of music communication wanted to create a TV network that would predominately feature music videos to a huge teenage audience already defined by the rock music industry. Linked to the cable network system, it rapidly became a success across the United States.

What gave rise to this new music industry? Foremost were the technological developments in the film and sound recording industry, which presented a vehicle for the production of music videos. Second, network television was not prepared to air some of the rock that contained lyrics or video gestures that might be considered offensive to the general television audience. MTV was less subject to executive censorship than was mainstream TV. Also, the development of a network directed toward a specific critical mass of public—the teenage market—once again solidified the success of such a venture. Like early rock and roll, MTV presented a format for the ever-rebellious youthful perspective.

The MTV of the early 1980s was dominated by music videos and music clips. These videos were imaginative, were at times sexually suggestive without being pornographic, and were defiant toward the older generation. To further enhance the appeal, host personalities provided zany commentaries on the music; they represented the video counterpart to the radio disc jockey. The recording industry was interested in MTV because it offered a way to advertise CD recordings of the artists whose songs appeared in video form. The pervasive presence of television sets throughout the country offered the most effective way to address a gigantic audience of viewers and listeners—with no additional purchase. Television advertisers also saw a here-to-fore unimaginable opportunity for direct advertising. The power of MTV became so strong that many artists were signed to exclusivity pacts so that their releases would appear only on MTV for limited lengths of time before they were released as CD recordings, thereby further guaranteeing their success and power. In 1992, both Bill Clinton and Al Gore appeared on separate MTV shows in an effective campaign strategy.

MTV programming underwent an obvious metamorphosis as the 1990s progressed. In an effort to capture an even broader share of teenage and young adult viewers, programmers expanded the music video format to feature more commentary, interviews with college-age students at sunny vacations spots, call-in programs directed toward discussions of dating, and regular news programs. In an effort to further challenge the limits of taste in the early 1980s, an increasing number of heavy metal and rap videos were aired. Soon there was a demand for a separate music video channel, and VH1 was formed in 1985 in an effort to return to a more mainstream popular music format. In the 1990s, CMT, another video music channel, became popular, this one aimed at the new country music audience.

MUSIC AND ECONOMICS: HISTORICAL PERSPECTIVE

A glance back in history indicates that elements providing social and economic support for music vary from era to era. In fact, it is some of these support systems that indicate the passing from one historical era to another. For example, we know from surviving historical evidence (music manuscripts, written descriptions of music, and written records) that music which was developed for use in the church (**sacred music**) dominated **secular music** (or nonreligious music) during the Middle Ages.

As the centuries progressed, however, new types of music were developed, and a broader segment of the population became exposed to music. This in turn increased the demand for even more and varied musical expressions. Stated in commercial terms, the market for music expanded. In that sense, it is no different from the history of any other form of communication, whether literature, art, or drama. The arts are all driven by other types of global development: commerce, technology, governmental and political influence, and social conditions. When we view music from its cultural and economic perspectives, in addition to examining and experiencing its aesthetic qualities, we begin to comprehend its value to our lives as well as to the lives of others, past and present.

In medieval times, the establishment of Christianity as the central religion in the Roman Empire provided the medium for the development of a musical tradition and practice that dominated the cultivated musical scene for centuries. By the time of Pope Gregory (r. 509–604), the Roman Church emerged as the central representative of Christianity in the Western world. Along with that came the formulation of a **liturgy**— an order of worship—which included music as a central component. For centuries the Church was satisfied with music consisting of a single melodic line (called Gregorian chant because of the strong role that Pope Gregory had in its development), but by the late ninth century, attempts at polyphony (music that had two or more musical lines) were underway. These early attempts at part music were called **organum**, a type of musical composition in which the composer (usually anonymous) used an established Gregorian chant for one part, and then added a freely-composed part to that chant line.

The Church during the Middle Ages was the center of learning. It was here that monks could learn to read, write, and record history. Musical development also flourished in this environment, for the founder of the Catholic liturgy learned early on that music was a beneficial adjunct to ritual and worship.

The development of musical notation in Western culture—also a product of those working within the Church—allowed the passage of music to occur outside of the oral tradition. Rhythmic notation developed from the natural stresses of poetry; as notation became more precise, so

Troubadour plays six musical instruments. © Historical Picture Archive / CORBIS. ID # HT003281.

did the rhythmic structure of the music. The development of notation therefore not only expanded composers' musical resources, it expanded the market for music, for it gave composers the opportunity to share their music with others in written form.

Music was not limited to the Church, however, for nonreligious poetry also was set to music and performed by minstrels of various classifications. Often these were itinerant musical entrepreneurs who traveled from village to village peddling their music. Some of these musician/poets were part of a lower social class, called **jongleurs**, but during the twelfth and thirteenth centuries, there was a movement of poet/musicians that developed sophisticated expressions of secular music and poetry. Its poetry was often strophic in nature and showed careful attention to patterns of repetition and rhyme scheme. These **troubadours**—who were active in the region of Champagne in Southern France—and **trouvères**—minstrels from the area around Paris—often wrote poetry about love. Their poems reflect the dignity and intellect of "refined love"—an attitude born not out of physical desires and passion but out of the concept that love is the source of all goodness. They were supported by the aristocracy; their poetry and songs comprised a major part of the entertainment and enlightenment of court life in the Middle Ages.

We know that this music of secular poetry and songs was considered significant, for not only the names of these poet/musicians were recorded and preserved—names such as Bernart de Ventadorn (ca. 1130–ca. 1190), Marcabru (ca. 1110–after 1150), and Guillaume XI, Prince of Acquitaine (1071–1177)—but a large repertoire of their poems and melodies survived to modern times. Over 6,500 troubadour and trouvère poems and approximately 1,600 melodies have been found. Many songs and poems were undoubtedly not written down.

A recent discovery of manuscripts in libraries in Paris, Rome, and Modena indicates the existence of women troubadours, called **troubairitz**, who were active in Southern France from about 1145 to 1225. The troubairitz were aristocratic ladies—some of whom were even patrons of troubadours—who engaged in the art of poetry and music. At least eighteen have been identified by name.

By the early Renaissance, the French poetic forms of the **rondeau, ballade**, and **virelai** were firmly established. These fixed forms, with standardized patterns of repetition and contrast, became sources of lyrics both for composers and singers.

During the Renaissance (1450–1600), the demand for church music expanded to include even more music in the service—special music that involved trained singers. **Polyphonic Masses**, music in several voice parts based on words from the liturgical service called the Mass, were composed and sung in churches throughout Europe. As Christianity was exported to the New World, so was the very music that gave it meaning. As early as 1532, a musician/priest, Pedro de Gante, established a school for native children in Mexico for learning church music.

Although the Church remained a major supporter of music in the fifteenth and sixteenth centuries, the wealthy nobility, the cultural and economic elites, began to figure even more prominently as a co-sponsor of composition and practice. Many new types of music were added—dances, instrumental works, love songs in various structures, popular poetry set to music—music that reflected a culture burgeoning with discovery and adventure. Each country in Central Europe developed its own popular forms of music for entertainment and personal participation: in France, it was the **chanson**; in Italy, the **madrigal**, in England, the **English madrigal** and the **ayre**.

Having musical skills became one of the hallmarks of a sophisticated person during this time. Baldassare Castiglione of Mantua addressed this issue in a 1528 monograph called *Il Cortegiano* ("*The Courtier*"). Castiglione was a member of a noble family and was well known in his time as a poet and cultural chronicler. He wrote:

> I am not pleased with the Courtier if he be not also a musician, and besides his understanding and cunning upon the book, have skill in like manner on sundry instruments. For if we weigh it well, there is no ease of the labors and medicines of feeble minds to be found more honest and more praiseworthy in time of leisure than it. And principally in courts, where ... many things are taken in hand to please women withal, whose tender and soft breasts are soon pierced with melody and filled with sweetness. Therefore no marvel that in the old days and nowadays they have always been inclined to musicians, and counted this a most acceptable food of the mind.[6]

The English translation of Baldassare Castiglione's comments was made in 1561 by the English nobleman Sir Thomas Hoby. Although its language is dated and difficult to grasp, this document shows that certain things were expected of a sophisticated person of this time, namely, that every "courtier" should be able to sing and play various instruments. Castiglione testifies to the ability of music to be emotionally uplifting, and he also suggests that women are attracted to musicians. (Elvis Presley's magical charms obviously have historical precedent!)

Music by now had become popular and socially acceptable, if not desired. Church services were filled with music sung and played by well-trained musicians. Centers for training boy singers were developed by metropolitan cathedrals, and budgets were created by the church hierarchy to maintain composers and performers.

The significant developments in the European musical world were given an immeasurable boost by an advancement in technology—the invention of the printing press. Some six decades after Gutenberg's revolutionary invention of printing from movable type, Ottaviano Pettruci developed a system of printing music. His *Harmonice Musices Odhecaton A* (Venice, 1501) changed the world of music forever, for now multiple copies of compositions could be marketed to an ever-expanding audience. It is interesting to note that the *Odhecaton* contained ninety-six settings of secular music intended for sale to all of those who could afford it. Within a short period of time, other printing houses began producing music. Music now had become an industry as well as an art.

The following centuries witnessed a rapid growth of the music market; new forms of music evolved to serve an ever-increasing functional base, new and improved instruments were built, instructional books on learning how to play and sing emerged, and a larger percentage of Europe's population became involved in music when public concerts began to be held. Opera was born in Florence, Italy, early in the seventeenth century—a new form of music that was destined to grow in popularity until it spread from Italy to France, Germany, England, and eventually to all corners of the Western world.

Other new forms of music attracted large numbers of people. In eighteenth-century England, the **oratorio**—a multimovement form for chorus, soloists, and orchestra—was becoming the rage, primarily due to the efforts of German-born composer George Frideric Handel. His masterpiece, the *Messiah*, of 1741, enjoyed

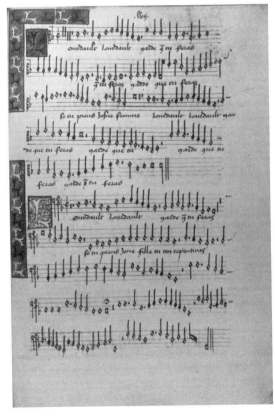

Page from the *Odhecaton* of Petrucci. Source: The University of Chicago Press.

Jan Vermeer, "A Young Woman Standing at a Virginal," ca. 1670. Oil on canvas, 20 3/8 x 17 13/16 in. (51.7 x 45.2 cm). © National Gallery Collection; by kind permission of the Trustees of the National Gallery, London / CORBIS. ID # NG001985.

many performances during his lifetime and is still the most popular work for large chorus in the history of music. Dance forms such as the **allemande**, the **sarabande**, the **courante**, and the **gigue** (to name only a few) were gathered together and performed as suites.

Baroque wind instruments that gave more variety to the music—and therefore made music more attractive to the audiences—were the **recorder**, **flute**, **oboe**, **bassoon**, and **trumpet** (which, incidentally, did not have valves until the nineteenth century). In addition to the stringed instruments that we associate with the modern Western orchestra—the violin, viola, cello, and double bass—the **lute** was a popular instrument of that time. Today, lute playing is almost a lost art, but in the seventeenth and eighteenth centuries, many solo performers played recitals for wealthy patrons, the public, and for their personal enjoyment.

The market for lute playing, however, was soon eclipsed by the harpsichord and the pipe organ, two keyboard instruments that were more versatile in function than the lute (and easier to learn to play at an acceptable level of proficiency). Composers targeted their compositions toward these instruments. One popular publication for the **virginal**—an English version of the harpsichord— was the *Fitzwilliam Virginal Book*, circa 1612. This book contained 297 compositions by many English composers and was a "best-seller" in the industry. Many of the compositions were based on well-known tunes, and the music was relatively easy enough to be played by well-trained amateur musicians.

Pipe organs were to be found in every church, and the harpsichord was used extensively in every imaginable musical setting, including homes, public performances, and official ceremonies. Virtuoso performers on the high (clarino) trumpet and the organ became famous for their abilities. One of the most skilled organists was Johann Sebastian Bach, who was known for his unusual dexterity in playing the pedal keys with his feet. (We will encounter Bach and his music in Chapter 5.) Composers wrote music to meet the performance abilities of these specialists. Opera continued to grow in popularity and complexity.

What about the role of women in the Renaissance and Baroque musical cultures? Evidence suggested by paintings from this era suggests that it was considered proper for a lady to learn how to sing, play the lute, flute, or other instruments such as the harpsichord and organ. We also know from church records that girls and women were not allowed to sing in church choirs—either the Roman Catholic Church or the churches spawned by the Reformation, such as the Lutheran and Anglican churches. This tradition continued well into the eighteenth century. In 1706, for example, J. S. Bach was brought before the church council in Arnstadt, where he worked as the church organist and choir director, for inviting a "stranger maiden" to "make music in the church," even though he had presumably asked permission and had limited his music making to rehearsal only.

Perhaps a low point in history for women church musicians occurred when Pope Innocent the XI issued the following edict in 1686:

> Music is completely injurious to the modesty that is proper to the (female) sex, because they become distracted from the matters and occupations most proper for them. Therefore, no unmarried woman, married (woman), or widow of any rank, status, condition, even those who for reasons of education or anything else are living in convents, or conservatories, under any pretext, even to learn music in order to practice it in those convents, may learn to sing from men, either laymen or clerics, or regular clergy, no matter if they are in any way related to them, or to play any sort of musical instrument.[7]

In spite of the stern papal edict, some isolated women composers, such as Bianca Martia Meda, an Ursaline nun who lived outside of Milan, Italy, exercised their creative impulses to produce music. Recent research has discovered that compositional activity by women composers throughout the seventeenth and eighteenth centuries was more widespread than was originally thought.

For much of the Baroque Era, the church was the only place where the common people could hear music by skilled composers—and church music represented the highest quality of music. Gradually, entrepreneurs began to realize that people would pay money to attend public concerts. One of the earliest continuing series of public concerts was organized by a London coal merchant, T. Britton, in 1678. For thirty-six years, Britton held public concerts in a room above his place of business. Composers of both vocal music and instrumental ensemble music found a commercial outlet for their compositions, for they would routinely receive a percentage of the ticket sales for their music.

Another series of concerts of historical importance were the *Concerts Spirituel,* first conceived by A. Philidor in France. These concerts, which ran from 1725–1789, consisted of religious music and were organized around Easter observances. The *Concert Spirituel* society became a model for other series in various countries of Europe.

By the dawning of the Classical Era, public concerts were part of the musical scene in Europe. Composers could earn a living in several ways (usually through a combination of activities). They could prepare compositions to be played at a concert, with part of the gate receipts going to them; they could write on commission, either from a publisher or from a wealthy individual; they could be paid a stipend by a wealthy person (a patron); they could receive royalties from a publisher for their works; or they could work in a church as an organist or a choir director. Many composers also gave music lessons and performed in public for added income. Mozart, for example, actively pursued all of these means. Today we call a musician who does not receive a salary from a single institution a freelancer. Many composers throughout history lived in this manner, and many still do today.

A discussion of how composers survived in relation to their artistic environments will be continued later in this book. We will see how Beethoven struggled to develop independence from a patronage culture and how Verdi's popularity in Italian opera elevated him to a national figure and a symbol for unification of Italy.

During the nineteenth century, the established European concert music culture became the model for the expanding world of art music in both the Northern and Southern Hemispheres of America. Fueled by immigrants from countries where musical cultures were widespread, such as Germany, Italy, and France, the market for cultivated music began to grow. New York was the first North American city to develop a philharmonic society (the origin of the New York Philharmonic Orchestra) in 1842. In 1881, St. Louis became the first city west of the Mississippi to have a resident symphony orchestra. A Chicago businessman, Norman Fay, was responsible for initiating the Chicago Symphony Orchestra when he invited the famous conductor Theodore Thomas to come to Chicago to start an orchestra in 1891. San Francisco had to wait until 1911 (five years after its devastating earthquake) for its own symphony.

The concept of a **pops orchestra**—a symphonic orchestra that specializes in performing music that is "lighter" than the usual symphonic repertoire (including orchestral arrangements of show tunes, popular songs, ballads, and dance music)—was brought to Boston by Henry Lee Higginson, the founder of the Boston Symphony Orchestra. In the summer of 1885, Higginson initiated a summer concert series in Boston, fashioned on similar concert experiences he had had while a student in Vienna. The idea became so popular that a permanent orchestra was formed, the Boston Pops. You have no doubt seen the Boston Pops on television in special programs such as the 4th of July concerts.

But what about music in our times other than symphony orchestras? We know that never before has the music industry experienced such diversity. Our culture is inundated with music of many types and expressions. Nonetheless, one condition seems to remain constant in the world of music. Musical production (composition, performing, and now, recording) is driven by its audiences. The venues of music are stimulated by diverse concepts such as technology, intellectual curiosity, and individuality, and the "commercial" market of pop music is directed toward gross sales in millions of dollars.

Fortunately for the composers of art music, their success is not always determined solely by the commercial markets of published music, record sales, and performance royalties but is supplemented by other sources. Major symphony orchestras, for example, often offer competitive "composer in residence" programs, whereby composers are given a salary to write music for a symphony and to be present as a consultant to symphony conductors. An elaborate system of grants to fund individual composition projects has been developed over the years. Many of these grants are funded by contributions from businesses, single individuals, or associations, while others are government sponsored. In Chapter 13, we will read about the National Endowment for the Arts (NEA), its history and its current status. During recent decades, the NEA has been instrumental in supporting the arts throughout the country. Arts councils in the various states also have programs that support both the creation and performance of music. These programs ensure that the arts reach a wide segment of the population.

Examples of associations not connected to tax monies are the American Society of Composers and Publishers (ASCAP), the Broadcast Music Industry (BMI), and the SESAC (originally named the Society of European Stage Authors and Composers, the SESAC has changed its function to a performing rights organization, but it has retained its initials). **Performing rights organizations** are businesses designed to represent composers and publishers and their right to be compensated when their music is performed in public. By obtaining a license from groups such as the BMI or SESAC, music users such as television stations, radio stations, restaurants, hotels, and malls can legally play any song in the organization's list of music. This concept is unique to our times; when music making was only done "live," there was no need for such organizations. Now, however, with so much music being played through recordings, the producers of music can receive royalties not only on the sales of their recordings but on the actual playing of them over public, profit-making media.

The American Composers Forum is one of several organizations funded by private foundations, often sponsored by business corporations. One of the ways organizations such as these support music is by offering grants to help composers underwrite the cost of their work. Many of them average in the $2,500 range.

Whereas many basic functions of music remain constant, new expressions emerge that reflect an exciting, ever-changing society in a global world.

We will examine some of the forums for music that are popular in our time. Much concert music is written for types of musical ensembles that have been in place for over 100 years, such as the symphony orchestras that pervade the country. We will later become better acquainted with them and with the practices surrounding the music that they perform. In Chapter 11 we also will consider the evolution of pop music—because it provides us with a window through which to observe our behaviors, attitudes, and overt expressions.

Musical Encounter

Music Technology via the Internet

Music lovers and buyers of recorded music can now be a part of a new industry that is revolutionizing the way music is marketed and delivered. Anyone who has access to a computer can call up a musical company specializing in Internet sales and demos to hear a sample or even a complete cut of a recording. Companies such as MP3.com (www.MP3.com) offer thousands of recordings in hundreds of categories of music—from children's to metal, pop, punk, rock, rap, and classical. The complete on-line listing for this company, for example, offers over 280 subcategories of musical styles! One can locate recordings through a browsing system which is sophisticated but easy to use and which includes genres and subgenres, main regions, and artist/labels, and alphabetically by artist. Other features include: bios on performing groups and stars, as well as the opportunity to e-mail a cut from a CD to a friend, or link into other Websites in the music industry. One can even buy concert tickets through this Website.

Recording artists who formerly signed contractual agreements with recording studios are seeing this new venue as a chance to connect directly to listeners without having to go through a recording company, thereby not only speeding up the process for disseminating their music but also allowing them to take a greater share of the royalties from their work. (A typical recording contract with a major record producer normally nets the recording artist around 10 percent of the retail cost of the CD—from $1 to $2 per CD.) Cductive Digital, a company linked to MP3, advertises that it has cutting-edge music by such artists as Sleater-Kinney, Built to Spill, Danielle Howle, the Donnas, Dujeous, Skeme Team, Mr. Life, DJ Spooky, Goldie, and Bad Meets Evil.

The artist, who signs an agreement with the Internet music company, can record a song, upload it immediately, and have it ready instantly for the public to hear. The customer, after hearing the song, may choose to buy it—also through the Internet connection. It is even possible to custom order a CD containing cuts from various recordings.

Rapper Chuck D, leader of the group Public Enemy and a strong proponent of the new Internet technology, said there could be "a million artists out there and 500,000 labels or more." Although some critics are worried about the possibility of lower technological standards creeping into this system, proponents of Internet music marketing point out that the demands of the public will regulate this technology through their demands for high recording quality.

The potential for musicians reaching a vast audience is almost unlimited. One artist, Alanis Morissette, made a recording available through the AT&T Internet music site (www.a2bmusic.com)—a company that does not allow copying—and was surprised to discover that her song was downloaded by computer users/listeners 285,000 times. Computer links to ticket sales netted her 22,000 concert ticket sales to her public concerts.[8]

SUMMARY

Two forces drive the music market in all cultures, past and present. The first is a cultural factor, for music speaks for humankind and is a vibrant voice that communicates thoughts, concerns, expressions, and tastes of people at all levels of society. Economic factors represent the second aspect upon which musical practice is dependent for survival.

Throughout history, the composition of music and the marketing of music have been inseparable factors. These forces may vary from era to era and may differ from each other depending on the social and economic stimuli of a culture. During the Middle Ages, for example, the Church was a driving force for music. The use of music in the liturgy of the Catholic Church aided the processes of consolidation, when a standard repertoire of chants gradually emerged in the Roman rites. Led by the support of the nobility and assisted by the technological advances offered by the printing press, Renaissance musical styles and forms expanded.

In subsequent periods of history, one can point to specific support systems to understand more fully the close relationship between cultural and economic factors in music. Opera emerged as a significant form of expression in the Baroque Era; the symphony became a principal form of music as the orchestra was standardized in the Classical Era. As the centuries progressed, musical environments expanded in the realm of art music to include an ever-growing number of amateur musicians who discovered the joys of making music in one form or another.

Standardized forms (genres) of music exist today as vehicles for audiences to appreciate great music. Among these institutions are choral music, musical theater, the symphony, and chamber music. These groups have enjoyed a strong lasting power because they provide the means for composers to express their ideas in forms that are meaningful to a variety of people. They are easily adaptive to the many musical expressions of ever-changing societies.

By observing both the cultural impetus for composition and the way music is created, sponsored, distributed, and received by the audiences, we can get a better sense of the role of music in the lives of all people, past and present.

Diversity and change also are an important part of the pop music scene. The world of pop music reflects directly the concerns, interests, and tastes of common people in everyday life. As such, it is very directly market driven, for its composers, producers, and artists exist from the profits it produces.

The twentieth century brought about a sophisticated, deliberate commercial music culture. This is especially true in the pop world. Rock 'n' roll developed in the 1950s from several different influences, including country and western and rhythm and blues. The teenage market quickly responded to the energy and strong beat of this new music. Soon, other elements of pop music were added to the cultural/social mix. Soul music was identified with the African-American expressions of power and excitement, and folk ballads were composed and sung by musicians such as Bob Dylan and Joan Baez, whose songs often were directed toward the social problems of the time. The 1960s witnessed the British invasion—rock 'n' rollers from England who added a certain sophistication to the lyrics of rock, in spite of their free-spirited philosophies of life. Rock became a vehicle for rebellion and experimentation in the 1970s in the hands of Jimi Hendrix, Mama Cass, and the Rolling Stones.

A primary factor in the socioeconomic nature of music is technology. Whether it is the development of notation in the Middle Ages, the advent of music printing during the early sixteenth century, the invention of the radio, music recordings, or the computer industry in the twentieth century, music has always been linked to the technical processes that produce and disseminate it.

The electronic age, with its advanced systems of amplification, recording technology, and computer technology, presents new potential to the music industry on a continuing basis. Two of the most recent developments, MTV and the use of the Internet to deliver music around the world at any time, have exerted a strong impact on the music industry. The electronic age also has influenced musical styles of modern pop music with the addition of yet another style of rock—that of techno music.

KEY TERMS

acoustical instruments
allemande
American musical
aria
ayre
backbeat
ballade
bassoon
brass quintet
chanson
comic opera
concert choir
courante
English madrigal
falsetto
flute
gigue
gospel choir
hard rock
jongleurs
liturgy
lute
madrigal
madrigal groups
monody
oboe
opera buffa
opera comique
orchestration
organum
performing rights organizations
piano quintet
piano trio
polyphonic Masses
pops orchestra
recorder
rondeau
sacred music
sarabande

secular music
show choir
singspiel
string quartet
string quintet
transcription
troubadours
troubairitz
trouvères
trumpet
virelai
virginal
woodwind quintet

PART II

Art Music: Music As Intrinsic Value

So far in *Musical Encounters* you have learned basic listening techniques that have opened a door to a new world of musical experiences. You have heard a variety of musical expressions and have seen that music is a many-faceted art whose audience includes a broad spectrum of people representing diverse perspectives. Also, you are now aware that music may be either purely commercial or artistic, or it may succeed in appealing to both the marketplace and to the artistic sense. All music, whether pop or high art, shares a common bond, for in order to survive, it needs a receptive audience, and therefore it has a commercial component.

Part II of *Musical Encounters* focuses on the Western art, or concert tradition, and discusses the music of the Baroque (1600–1750), Classical (1725–1825), Romantic (1825–1900), and Modern (1900–present) eras. Here again, as in Part I, you will be encouraged to enhance your listening skills as you increase your knowledge of major composers, their music, and the styles of their compositions. As you read *Musical Encounters* and listen to the accompanying CDs, keep in mind that this book is designed to help you develop a skeletal framework of knowledge and musical experience for a lifetime of learning. Chapter 5, which centers on Baroque music and three major composers, Bach, Handel and Vivaldi, concentrates on principles of counterpoint and layering and teaches the music student listening techniques for music structured on simultaneously occurring events. In Chapter 6 we will concentrate on musical styles based on the principles of repetition and contrast as they relate to the aesthetic orientations prominent in the Classical Era. The four chapters that follow reinforce these two fundamental approaches to organization and apply them to the music of the nineteenth and twentieth centuries.

Maintaining a strong emphasis on the listening experience and music literature, Part II also treats the music of the past 400 years with special attention to the aesthetic impulses and social/economic trends that gave rise to compositions and musical practices. You will see that master composers such as Bach, Handel, Haydn, Mozart, and Beethoven not only left us with great music for our enjoyment but also established compositional techniques that served as the foundation for music in the nineteenth and even the twentieth centuries.

The more you understand how composers write and the context within which they work, the more enjoyment you will find in hearing music (which is, of course, our ultimate reason for studying music). At the same time, you will understand how music functions as an integral part of every society in any given historical period, past and present. So let us begin our encounter with great music and the people who gave us this music to hear and enjoy.

CHAPTER 5

Music of the Baroque: The Age of Bach, Handel, and Vivaldi

*T*HE three composers represented in Baroque Era music—Johann Sebastian Bach (1685–1750), George Frideric Handel (1685–1759), and Antonio Vivaldi (1678–1741)—typify Baroque music in its full-blown, mature state. Although each had an individual style of composition, the structural and aesthetic features found in their music

illustrate a broad approach to artistic thought that is commonly accepted to have begun at the beginning of the seventeenth century. Musical styles, however, do not develop in isolation; they are influenced by social factors, political structures, and economic conditions—trends and practices that often extend beyond the borders of a particular country or region and emerge as defining characteristics of a large geographical area, in this case, Western Europe.

Making connections between various art forms is sometimes an easy task, while at other times one has to mentally stand back from the art to see broad relationships. In the Baroque Era (ca. 1600–1750), for example, we will come to understand that ornamentation in Baroque music, such as the common use of **trills** (the rapid alternating of one note and a note immediately above or below it on the scale), is broadly related to the exuberant detail in a sculpture—such as Gianlorenzo Bernini's (1598–1680) *The Ecstasy of St. Theresa*, or the decorations on buildings or ceiling frescoes created by architects such as Balthasar Neumann (1687–1753) or Giovanni Battista Tiepolo (1696–1770). The complex musical textures of the **fugue**—a style of Baroque music in which a subject or a melodic idea is presented in various voice parts one at a time in the manner of a round, in a texture that weaves the various parts in and out of each other—can be compared to the busyness and motion found in the lines and subject matter of a painting by early Baroque master Peter Paul Rubens (1577–1640).

*T*HE BAROQUE PERIOD IN THE OTHER ARTS

The term *baroque*, in its original sense, refers to something that is irregular (as in the shape of a baroque pearl—which is not perfectly round), or to artistic creations that are overly ornamented or "grotesque." Whereas the term once carried with it negative connotations of poor taste, it is now commonly used to refer to works of art that are highly ornamented, flamboyant, and dramatic. These general aesthetic principles describe creative activity that occurred between ca. 1600 and 1750 in many different media—architecture, painting, sculpture, decorative arts, and music. Of course, there was a broad range of both individual and national expressions within this large time span.

A good example of ornamentation in baroque architecture may be seen in St. Peter's Cathedral in Rome. The canopy over the altar of St Peter's tomb was designed by Gianlorenzo Bernini. Its four columns are decorated with intricately shaped vines that wind around twisted columns and support a canopy of bronze that in turn supports

Tourists stand beneath Baldachinno sculpted by Bernini, with a view of the Throne of Saint Peter in Glory, also by Bernini, in Saint Peter's Basilica in Vatican City, October 1989.
© Owen Franken / CORBIS.
ID # OF007123.

several angels in various poses. The base of the canopy resembles a cloth valance with tassels. Every surface is covered with detail in a dramatic statement of ornamentation and motion—a sort of visual counterpoint.

Another famous work of Bernini's that illustrates further the concept of baroque design is the sculpture *The Ecstasy of St. Theresa* (See Color Plate No. 1). This masterpiece depicts an angel piercing the heart of Theresa of Avila, a sixteenth-century saint, who wrote this about her spiritual experience:

> The pain was so great that I screamed aloud; but at the same time I felt such infinite sweetness that I wished the pain to last forever. It was not physical but psychic pain, although it affected the body as well to some degree. It was the sweetest caressing of the soul by God.[1]

Notice that the sculpture contains a high amount of dramatic action and is given a theatrical background by the rays of gold, depicting light from heaven. The robes worn by the angel and St. Theresa contain a large number of deep folds; the busy textures of this marble sculpture underline the feeling that this is an action frozen in time.

Motion is also the word that comes to mind when one views the paintings of Peter Paul Rubens (1577–1640), a Flemish painter of extraordinary dramatic flair. His works, ranging from depictions of sacred events to secular subjects, most often show characters whose actions are caught in mid-motion, such as an action photograph. Skies are turbulent, the subjects' clothing is often flowing, horses are rearing on their hind legs, and the canvas is filled with contrasting colors, shapes, and figures in a combination of violence and ecstasy.

Again, one can relate the busyness of line and motion in a Rubens painting to the counterpoint of music found in the fugue or the grandiose and flamboyant sounds of the toccata. Much as the ear is drawn to the intricacies of melodic shapes when listening to contrapuntal music, the eye is drawn from one event to another when viewing a Rubens painting.

The frescoes that adorn the ceilings of the Residenz, the elaborate home of the Prince-Bishops of Würzberg, which was begun in the 1720s, serve as further examples of the exuberance of baroque design. The court architect, Balthasar Neumann (1687–1753), commissioned a prominent artist, Giovanni Batista Tiepolo (1685–1766), to decorate several ceilings, including a grand staircase during 1749–1754. Tiepolo's ceiling paintings are filled with images of heavenly figures flying through beautiful skies, as though the ceiling represented windows through which one could view the heavens.

In our discussion of the music of the Baroque Era, we will come to hear that concepts of continual motion, elaboration by ornamentation, and busy textures created by counterpoint all form a major part of the baroque style. In that sense, they relate directly to the art and architecture of the period, for the general effect of both visual and musical arts of this time was highly dramatic and full of detail.

COUNTERPOINT AND LAYERING IN MUSIC OF THE BAROQUE

One of the most important ways of putting music together is to present two or more melodic ideas at the same time. This compositional device is called **counterpoint**—a technique of composition where musical lines are structured so they can be heard independently from other parts in the musical fabric. It may be compared to listening to two people speak different sentences simultaneously—but, in music, it is easier to comprehend because of rhythmic, intervallic, and harmonic relationships between the independent parts. We have already encountered concepts of counterpoint in our discussion of polyphonic texture (Chapter 2).

The extensive use of counterpoint is one of the most significant features of Baroque music. Its significance is further increased for the music listener when one considers that Baroque-style counterpoint is used as the basis for hundreds of musical expressions since the eighteenth century. Before we listen to counterpoint in a major work of

Folk songs, *Three Blind Mice* and *Are You Sleeping, Brother John?* in score form with chord symbols written underneath the music.

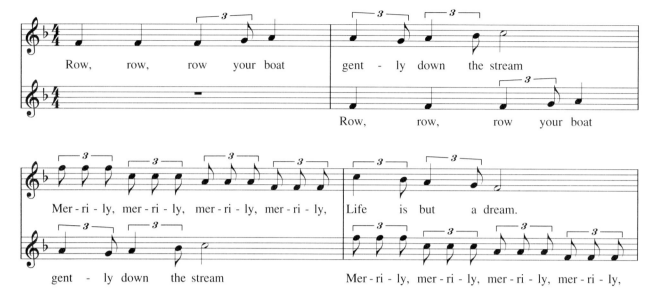

Imitation, "Row, Row, Row Your Boat"

J. S. Bach, we will examine some underlying premises of counterpoint by using children's folk songs as a point of reference.

Try singing *Three Blind Mice* while someone else is singing *Are You Sleeping, Brother John?* You will notice several things. First you hear each melody as being very separate, but somehow the two tunes work together.

Why is this? The reason is simple: both tunes share a harmonic structure, for identical chords support each melody, and the chords change at the same time for each tune. On the preceding page, the musical example demonstrates this concept. Notice how: (1) the tonic (C Major) and dominant (G Major) chords in these simple tunes fit both melodies at the same time; and (2) how the rhythm created by the chord changes is reflected in the final "ding, dong" of *Are You Sleeping, Brother John?* and in the last measures of *Three Blind Mice*.

Playing or singing two different melodies at the same time is one kind of counterpoint. A common type of musical arrangement in which counterpoint is used is a **round**. In a round, one person starts the tune, and a second person waits to begin until the leader finishes the first line. The third and fourth singers follow in like fashion, until several people are singing different phrases at the same time. When a melody is presented in this way, with each part entering with the same tune at consecutive intervals of time, this is called **imitation**. The round (such as *Row, Row, Row Your Boat*) is the simplest form of imitation in music.

Layering is a more complicated way of presenting several musical concepts at once. This technique often involves more than the simple statement of melodies in counterpoint. Often larger units of sound are presented in counterpoint to create a complex but comprehensible musical structure. For example, one group of people could sing *Three Blind Mice* while another group sang *Are You Sleeping, Brother John?* thereby performing layers of two different but congruent musical gestures. If a composer were to arrange the songs each with four-part harmony (soprano, alto, tenor, bass) and set each song with an instrumental accompaniment, the entire composition would fit together. Later in this chapter, we will see how Bach took basic contrapuntal ideas and enlarged them by using the technique of layering.

Composers have used contrapuntal techniques for hundreds of years. It was during the seventeenth and eighteenth centuries, however, that the techniques of contrapuntal composition were perfected—so much so, in fact, that modern composers study the works of Bach and his contemporaries in order to understand this significant concept of musical organization. This period of time is known as the Baroque Era; its music, art, and architecture have aesthetic elements that invite comparison. Before pursuing these interesting connections, we will examine a piece of music that illustrates clearly the concepts of counterpoint and layering.

Listening Guide 23

Toccata and Fugue in D Minor, BWV 565
Johann Sebastian Bach (1685–1750)

Composition for organ
Before 1708
Recorded by Otto Winter
CD No. 2, Track 1 (5:00)

The *Toccata and Fugue in D Minor*, BWV 565, for organ by Johann Sebastian Bach, is one of the most flamboyant, loud, and exciting pieces of music written during the time; it is also one of the best written. (The BWV number in Bach's music refers to the catalog of his works, abbreviated in German as the *Bach Werke Verzeichnis*.) Bach was living in Weimar during this time and had a job as the church organist there. He was a virtuoso organist and no doubt dazzled and even shocked some of the faithful worshipers with his organ settings of Lutheran hymns. This music served two functions: (1) Organists usually began the church service with some sort of special work; and (2) The powerful pipe organ created the biggest sound available to listeners at that time and served as a concert experience during the church service, for at that time in Germany, church and concert music was virtually inseparable—especially for the common people.

As the title implies, the *Toccata and Fugue* consists of two parts, written in two different styles. The **toccata** is a Baroque form of keyboard music that often features rapid scales and other patterns of notes to create a flamboyant work of virtuosity. Furthermore, a feeling of freedom is established by the use of pauses, which break up the patterns of notes that fly by in a blur. Its texture is not always easily defined, but its style is clearly recognizable because of its ostentatious nature.

The fugue, on the other hand, is a disciplined style of music in which a tune (called a "subject") is presented in imitation, and it is often spun out with other contrapuntal melodic lines (called "counter subjects") in a web of polyphonic texture. The term fugue is derived from the Latin word *fuga*, meaning "flight"—a reference to one line chasing another. The secret of listening to a fugue is to follow the theme, or the subject, as it winds in and out of the musical texture. You will find yourself anticipating an entrance of the subject and, toward the end of the fugue, you will even hear when the entrances overlap. A common technique in fugal writing is the use of **episodes**—sections where the counterpoint originally generated by the subject continues with melodic material not drawn directly from the main subject. A third feature of many fugues occurs toward the end, where composers frequently closely overlap entrances of the subject and create an effect of tumbling toward the end of the piece.

To Consider

When you listen to *Toccata and Fugue*, turn the volume up on your stereo and imagine that you are in a cathedral with very high vaulted ceilings—a sound chamber that allows the sound to bounce around before it decays. The organ pipes cover one entire end of the church, and when the organist chooses to raise the level of volume on the instrument (by pulling "stops" of the organ causing many pipes of different timbres to play at once), the sound is almost deafening.

1. Notice how the composer offsets the very dramatic opening statement with pauses that allow the sound to reverberate throughout the church. From the very start of this work, it is obvious that this is a dramatic piece of music.
2. Bach combines scales, chords, arpeggios, and melodies made up of repeated figures, and occasional trills in a setting that exploits the entire sound range of the pipe organ. As you listen to this work, notice how his music complements the capabilities of the instrument.
3. Finally, be aware of the contrasting nature of the toccata and the fugue. (You will hear the beginning of the fugue in this excerpt.) Notice that the toccata frequently contains dramatic pauses and more changes of tempo, whereas the fugue seems to be a continual working out of counterpoint.

0:00   The very flamboyant opening measures establish the key of d minor with rapid scale fragments and strong chords.

0:37   A short melodic phrase made up of sixteenth-note triplets (three notes per unit of pulse) undulates its way upward and forms the principal melodic idea for the toccata. Notice how the composer achieves a feeling of growing momentum as the music stops and restarts in this section.

2:18   Here the tempo becomes very fast as motion builds toward the end of the toccata; huge chords signal the ending.

3:02   The fugue begins with a single part played by the left hand, and soon, the second entrance of the fugue subject (the theme) enters in above it. A steady rhythmic pulse, created by the sixteenth notes of the subject and accompanied by the eighth notes of the supporting line, establishes the motoric pulse that is often associated with the instrumental music of the Baroque Era. The third entrance of the fugue subject is barely audible because of the continuous nature of the motion here. The entrance of the fourth statement of the subject, however, is very obvious, because it is played on the pedals. Throughout the rest of the fugue, the heavy bass gives dimension to the work as it enters and leaves the texture. (The recorded example ends after the fugue begins.)

Now that we have experienced what is perhaps Bach's most famous work and have seen how counterpoint was used by this master composer, we will consider some of the other compositional practices that were in style during the Baroque Era.

OTHER ASPECTS OF BAROQUE MUSIC

As you listen to the music of the Baroque Era, you will become increasingly aware that counterpoint is not the only distinctive quality of music from this period of time. Other elements of composition that deserve attention are harmony, texture, and rhythm. In attempting to discover the primary features of a baroque style, we must always keep in mind that each individual composer approaches composition with a slightly different approach from another. There are commonalities of techniques that emerge, however. We will pursue these before we listen to more music of Bach, Handel, and Vivaldi.

Harmony and harmonic practice during the Baroque Era are characterized by a strong emphasis on the tonic, the subdominant, and the dominant (I, IV, and V) chords with the secondary chords (triads built on other steps of the scale than the first, fourth, and fifth notes) also used to add variety and interest. However, the harmonic practice that distinguishes Baroque musical practice from those before and after it is the regularity of chord progression that occurs. If you analyze the scores of many works from this period, you will soon see that chord changes occur at very regular times. For example, almost every first beat of a measure may have a new chord change; or maybe the frequency of the chord change happens twice in each measure, such as on the first and third beats of a 4/4 measure.

This technique of regularity of chord progression (called **harmonic rhythm**) helps produce that steady lilt (in the case of a slower piece of music) or the rhythmic drive (in a faster work) that typifies much Baroque music. Some composers, such as Bach, are known for a faster harmonic rhythm where chords change once or twice each measure. Others, such as Vivaldi, used a slower rate of chord change. These are the subtle differences between composers.

In complementing the feeling of regularity, composers also created a feeling of **motoric rhythm** by writing music that included a regular beat. Furthermore, while some instruments played the fundamental beat of the music, others were playing faster notes—subdivisions of the basic pulse.

We will see that much of twentieth-century jazz is founded on the same principle. The bass may play "walking notes" on the beat, and the drummer will play the bass drum on the first and third beats of a 4/4 measure and on the hi-hat (pedal) cymbals on the offbeats (two and four). Meanwhile, a melodic instrument or keyboard will play elements of regular harmonic change and melodic lines that further reinforce the concept of steady pulsating music.

While much Baroque music pushes along in a regular rhythm, there are some forms of music that contrast this regularity. The selection we just heard, Bach's *Toccata and Fugue in D Minor*, for example, started with a piece (the toccata) in which the rhythm stopped and started in order to build suspense and drama. The recitative, speech-like declamation found in operas, cantatas, and oratorios—forms of vocal music in the Baroque era—also uses a freer principle of rhythmic organization. The rhythms in these forms are primarily drawn from the natural, rhythmic flow of the text.

Textures in Baroque music also often complement the feeling of regularity. The independent voice parts of counterpoint help propel the music along. Some composers, such as Handel, enjoyed contrasting the use of polyphonic texture with homophonic, or homorhythmic sections. (For a review of textures, please see Chapter 2.)

Another feature of the music of the Baroque Era that was common and is easily heard is the **polarity of outer voices**—a technical way of saying that the top part and the bass part in the music seem to be more prominent than the middle part. Early in the seventeenth century, when opera styles were being developed, a practice arose that supported this concept of polarity. Composers used a device known as **figured bass**—a kind of musical shorthand to notate the outside parts of the music. The melody was notated on one musical staff, while the bass line was written on the lower staff along with symbols that indicated the chords. Harpsichord players reading this music partially improvised by adding notes belonging to the chords, as suggested by this figured bass system. The flute sonata on the following page illustrates the figured bass.

Word painting is perhaps one of the most fascinating aspects of composition used by some composers from this time. It refers to creating musical gestures that help underline, or illustrate, key words or concepts in a piece of vocal music. If, for example, a composer was setting a phrase of text that spoke of a soul descending into Hell, he or she might write a melody that moved downward. Conversely, if the words spoke of a soul rising to Heaven, an upward-moving melodic line would be appropriate. Instrumental accompaniments also were used to help depict the words. Such is the case in a soprano aria, "I know that my Redeemer liveth," from Handel's *Messiah*, where the text

An editor's realization of the figured bass. Jean Baptiste Loeillet, *Sonata in C Major for Flute and Cembalo.*

Excerpt of "I Know That My Redeemer Liveth," from the *Messiah* by George Frideric Handel.

says, "and tho' worms destroy my body, in my flesh shall I see God," and the composer uses dotted rhythms in the violins to signify the gnawing away of the flesh by the worms. Notice in the musical example above, that the violins play a repeated melodic gesture that moves back and forth between two notes. This is Handel's way of underlining the meaning of the words—a good example of word painting.

Our introduction to features of Baroque music would not be complete without a discussion of the types, or genres, of music popular during the time. We have already discussed the significance of opera up until this time period. Opera was drama set to music, and it included parts for the orchestra, such as the overture—a piece that introduced the opera; arias—extended solos and duets that allowed the singer to exhibit advanced vocal techniques and to elaborate on a textual idea; recitatives—numbers usually preceding an aria in the style of a recitation with a very sparse accompaniment; and **choruses**—numbers where a larger group of singers performed on texts that embellished the opera plot. Other forms of music developed that were based on the principles of opera, which served different venues of the music market in the Baroque Era.

One such related genre is the **oratorio**, an extended concert work consisting of several musical numbers including recitatives, arias, and choruses, often begun with an instrumental overture and having some instrumental interludes. Another type of music closely related to the oratorio is the cantata—a shorter work, also consisting of solos (recitatives and arias) and frequently several movements for chorus.

In sacred music, the polyphonic settings of the texts of the Mass and other liturgical sources (taken from the words of religious rituals) were set to the accompaniment of organ and orchestra. They often were more choral in nature than the oratorios, but they also included passages for solo voice.

Instrumental music was written to be played independently from vocal or choral music. **Trio sonatas** consisted of music for two melodic instruments with the accompaniment of a keyboard instrument and a bass instrument. **Solo sonatas** were composed for popular melodic instruments, such as the violin, flute, or oboe. The **solo concerto**, a work for a solo instrument and an instrumental ensemble, was the forerunner of the classical concerto—a form that will be considered in Chapter 6.

Keyboard music in the Baroque Era was written for the pipe organ, the harpsichord, and occasionally for the clavichord (a keyboard instrument in which bars of metal strike the strings and produce a very soft sound). Popular forms for the pipe organ—the common instrument used in churches (especially in the Protestant churches of Germany)—were the **prelude**, the fugue, the toccata, and various forms of **hymn** settings, also called **chorale pre- ludes**. In the late Baroque period, these forms proliferated into several variations of genres, and the world of music became increasingly diverse as the eighteenth century wore on.

In France, the harpsichord, called the *claveçin*, was the instrument of choice for composers wishing to create delicate, sophisticated music that reflected the refinement of courtly music. This music frequently avoided the tight counterpoint of the fugue—a form popular in Germany—and was characterized by a wide variety of trills and other ornaments.

Counterpoint in the Music of Bach and Handel

When one compares and contrasts the musical styles, lives, and creative output of composers Bach, Handel, and their contemporaries, it is possible to formulate an accurate overview of the unity and variety of Baroque music. These composers serve as examples of the musical practices prevalent in the first half of the eighteenth century.

Musical Encounter

François Couperin and the Claveçin

*T*he claveçin (or harpsichord) was a keyboard instrument that attained great popularity in France during the seventeenth and eighteenth centuries. A forerunner of the piano, the harpsichord produces a tone by a method in which a plectrum—originally made from a goose quill or a piece of leather—plucks a string when a key on the keyboard is pressed. The resulting sound has a distinct attack, much like that of a guitar string when it is plucked with a fingernail or pick. French harpsichords were often painted, and their cases were ornamented with gold leaf; artists would be commissioned to paint scenes or even portraits on the inside of the lids of these elaborate instruments.

François Couperin was an important composer for this popular instrument. His claveçin music typically has an ornamented melody (which is played by the right hand) and a left-hand bass line, which outlines the harmonic structure of the piece. Occasionally other notes are added to fill in these harmonies. The counterpoint between the melody and bass is heard as the interplay of two horizontal lines—both dependent on each other but still maintaining their own individuality of direction.

Much of Couperin's claveçin music is based on dance forms and rhythms; the practice of grouping dances such as the allemande, courante, sarabande, minuet, passpied, and gigue into **suites** was a common one during the seventeenth and eighteenth centuries in keyboard and instrumental music. Each dance had its own characteristic meter and rhythmic style that was easily recognized by the audience. The allemande, for example, is always written in duple meter, usually starts with a short upbeat, and contains short running figures that are passed through various parts of the texture. The courante is in 3/2 meter; the sarabande is also in 3/2 meter, but it has a characteristic rhythm that emphasizes the second beat of the measure.

Harpsichord. Source: Hubbard Harpsichords.

Couperin composed twenty-seven suites of dances for the clavecin, which he called **ordres**. Some of his works—especially those that do not adhere strictly to dance forms—bear programmatic titles that give hints about the composer's intent. Their light, transparent textures are well suited both to the harpsichord and to the French culture of the time.

This short piece, titled *The Queen of Hearts*, is typical of Couperin's compositions for the clavecin. They are easily performed by musicians with intermediate keyboard skills, but they have rather demanding ornaments that must be executed accurately in order to interpret correctly the composer's intentions. During the late Baroque Era, the art of ornamentation—especially in France—became a highly developed performance practice; each ornamental sign carried with it a specific meaning. So, although we see in Couperin's *Queen of Hearts* what is essentially a three-part texture, the embellishments add another dimension to this elegant music.

François Couperin: *La Reine des Coeurs* (*Queen of Hearts*). Source: Bibliothek Nationale, Paris.

Nowhere is both the splendor and the attention to detail commonly associated with the Baroque aesthetic so amply illustrated in music as it is in the works of Bach. Bach's music was directed by a well-schooled sense of musical craftsmanship; in fact, according to his students, Bach felt that anyone, given the proper training and discipline, could compose music that was of an acceptable quality. Bach's music, however, shows more than mere craftsmanship. His ability to infuse his counterpoint with melodic and harmonic inventiveness places his works above mere craftsmanship.

The Sources of Bach's Style: Background

Bach was born into a family of musicians; in fact, his musical lineage can be traced back to 1561. When a male was born into the Bach family, it was expected that he would become a musician. Bach's uncles, his cousins, and even his sons were musicians, most of them practicing in Northern Germany.

So, like his relatives, when Bach was a boy, he was instructed in several instruments. Although he sang in St. Michael's Church at Lüneburg when he was fifteen years old and played violin in the Saxe-Weimar court, the organ became his favorite, and by age nineteen, he secured a position as an organist in the Lutheran Church at Arnstadt.

His interest in church music and organ performance inspired him to travel 200 miles to the northern town of Lübeck to hear and study with a famous organist, Diedrich Buxtehude. Later, he had the opportunity to replace the aging Buxtehude, but he found out that if he accepted the position at Lübeck, he was expected to marry Buxtehude's daughter as part of the arrangement. Instead, Bach married one of his cousins, Maria Barbara, in 1707. They had seven children before Maria Barbara died. His second wife, Anna Magdalena, bore him thirteen more. Only six of Bach's children survived him. Life was not easy in the eighteenth century; death always seemed to be lurking nearby. Bach's religious music reflects this aspect of life, for it is filled with references to death and the hope of eternal life that his religious faith provided.

With the exception of a five-year stint as a court composer and musician to Prince Leopold of Anhalt at Cöthen, Bach spent his entire professional life working for churches. His final appointment was as the *Kapellmeister* (director of church music) for the St. Thomas Church and subsidiary churches in the city of Leipzig, a post that he held for twenty-seven years.

Over 1,000 compositions by Bach have been preserved. He is the major composer of organ music and of sacred cantatas in all of history; his other sacred vocal works (motets, Masses, passions and oratorios—various types of compositions all containing sacred texts) exhibit his consistency of genius. He also composed instrumental works that are standard repertory for violin, flute, oboe, cello, and keyboard players. His music is so popular that it has been arranged for almost any combination of instruments. It is not uncommon to hear saxophone quartets, synthesizers, clarinet choirs, or even jazz and rock groups playing his music.

There is no doubt that Bach's way of life contributed to the shaping and consistency of his musical style. His employment at Leipzig, for example, was not dependent on whether or not people would pay to hear his music. He was hired to play the organ, to compose for church services and for special occasions, to teach in the parochial school, and to organize church music for several city churches. Thus he was free to practice his craft of composition according to his own intellectual, spiritual, and emotional inclinations.

His music is therefore filled with counterpoint, where melodic lines are tightly woven around each other. One can imagine that his audiences—churchgoers steeped in the Northern German traditions of Lutheran chorales and organ music—became educated to the level of his music until it became the expected norm. Their ears became accustomed to listening for the main subjects in Bach's fugues, or the way in which he wove well-known hymn melodies into his musical framework. We also can speculate that the people who heard Bach's compositions on a weekly basis were unaware of the greatness of his genius; he was, after all, a humble church musician fulfilling his duties as an employee of the church. Had Bach been alive in modern times, he would have had an agent, a publisher who would advertise his compositions, and probably a TV audience. But his craft speaks for itself—and has for over two and one-half centuries. His compositional style that has served as a model for many composers in the past 250 years is worth investigating further. An examination of his music reveals some very basic approaches to composition and also serves as an excellent training ground for developing listening skills.

Listening to Bach's Music: Basic Approaches

The craft of Bach's musical compositions relied on several basic principles: melodic material is organized around a strong, harmonic framework; rhythms support the concept of independent lines in a contrapuntal texture; and several layers of musical activity are often presented simultaneously.

Bach manuscript, *Branden-burg Concerto No. 2.* By per-mission of Barenreiter Music Corporation.

We have already experienced this approach to composition in *Toccata and Fugue in D Minor*, the introductory example of contrapuntal music at the beginning of this chapter. A further look at another masterwork by Bach will reinforce knowledge of this approach to musical organization.

Bach wrote a collection of six compositions in the style of the **concerto grosso**, a form of Baroque music in which a small group of instruments (the **concertino**) is featured against a backdrop of the entire ensemble (the **ripieno**). Bach sent these works to Christian Louis, the Margrave (Marquis) of Brandenburg in 1721, in the hope of securing a job offer. Although the position in the Brandenburg court never materialized, Bach's attempt to incur the favor of the Margrave resulted in some of the most often played and recorded instrumental music from the Baroque Era.

Listening Guide 24

Brandenburg Concerto No. 2, Mvt. 2
Johann Sebastian Bach (1685–1750)

Baroque concerto grosso
1721
Recorded by Tafelmusic,
Jean Lamon, Conductor
CD No. 2, Track 2 (3:45)

The second movement of the *Brandenburg Concerto No. 2* uses only the concertino section of the ensemble, minus the trumpet, which is featured in the other two movements. This popular slow movement is built on a very regular change of chords, one per measure, a bass line played by the harpsichord and cello that outlines these chords, and an upper structure of three solo instruments playing in imitative counterpoint.

As you listen to this, think of hearing the movement in two layers: (1) the imitative melodic lines that are passed back and forth by the flute (recorder), the oboe, and the violin; and (2) the harmonic background that is provided by the bass melody and the harpsichord playing harmonies outlined by the cello.

To Consider

Some further features of this music that typify it as belonging both to the Baroque style of music and to the music of Bach are:

1. The melody is spun out from a simple subject having a distinctive character. Notice how this tune rises one-half step, pauses for a beat and one-half, and then falls—through a trill—down by a minor third.
2. A steady beat is maintained by the bass line playing even eighth notes.
3. A feeling of regularity (a motoric pulse) is enhanced by chords changing once per measure. This is called a **regular harmonic rhythm**.
4. After a solo instrument plays the opening subject, it then plays melodic lines that support another instrument's entry. This secondary material, the countersubject, occurs in virtually all contrapuntal music.

Sources of Handel's Style: The Biography of an Impresario

Unlike Bach, who worked in a rather limited, well-defined setting for most of his life, Handel was a cosmopolitan figure whose musical fortunes depended on both public support and aristocratic favor.

Handel was deeply involved in musical theater during much of his career. To be sure, he wrote organ works and compositions for solo instruments, but his primary efforts for years focused on composing, producing, and directing opera. When his operatic style fell out of fashion, he turned his attention to the oratorio and achieved further fame and fortune with public concerts.

Born and raised in Germany, George Frideric Handel (1685–1759) traveled extensively during his early years as a musician. Although his father wanted him to be a lawyer, Handel's desire to be a musician won out. In 1706, for example, he went to Italy to learn the most popular techniques of Italian opera, and he stayed there for nearly four years. His travels not only put him in touch with an eclectic sampling of musical tastes during the early eighteenth century, they also allowed him to meet influential people. His career in Italy was fostered both by aristocrats and powerful church authorities; among them were the Prince Ferdinand de' Medici, Francesco Ruspoli (a wealthy nobleman), and Cardinal Grimani. While in Italy, Handel met many prominent composers and learned by listening to performances of their works. Many believe that Handel met Prince Ernst August of Hanover, brother of the Elector (who later became King George I of England), in Venice.

His success in Italy led to an appointment in Hanover (Germany) as the chief musician at the court of George Louis, the Elector. During this time, Handel traveled to England, where he was received graciously at Queen Anne's court and produced several operas.

Handel's life was altered considerably in 1714, when George Louis, Elector of Hanover, a German, became King George I of Great Britain. Handel moved to England, where he received generous support from the king and queen. The composer found the environment pleasing to his artistic practices, and he became a central figure in the musical life of England—so prominent, in fact, that he spent twenty-six years there and became an English citizen in 1727.

He experienced both the exuberance and challenge of a prominent musician. His operas were highly successful in spite of occasional financial problems, which arose from the closings of various opera companies and from the competition from a new, less formal musical production. The Beggar's Opera, composed and produced by Johann Pepusch and John Gay, ushered in a new style of musical theatre that soon became so popular that it cut into Handel's profits. Appointments to significant musical positions kept coming,

George Frideric Handel. Source: © Archivo Iconografico, S.A./ CORBIS. ID # CS002882.

however. During his lifetime, Handel was a composer to the Duke of Chandos, the Royal Academy, and the Chapel Royal.

When he died in 1759 at age seventy-four, his body was interred at the Westminster Abbey. Thousands of people attended his funeral.

The music of Handel that has remained the most popular with today's listeners and performers includes the oratorios *Messiah* and *Judas Maccabeus*; the choral works *Ode for St. Cecilia's Day* and the *Chandos Anthems*; and the operas *Guilio Cesare*, *Rodelinda*, and *Tamerlano*. His instrumental music is world famous and ranges from the delightful sonatas for flute, recorder, oboe, and violin to his ensemble compositions using the forms of the concerto grosso and the trio sonata. Most popular are his suites for orchestra, titled *Water Music* and *Music for Royal Fireworks*.

Listening to Handel's Music: The *Messiah*

It took Handel only twenty-four days to write his masterpiece oratorio, the *Messiah*. This work resulted from Handel's interest in supporting charities and from a proposal that he aid in fund-raising efforts by producing a series of concerts in Dublin. He wrote the *Messiah* between August 22, 1741, and September 14, 1741. Using a combination of techniques borrowed from the opera, he structured this gargantuan work, which is several hours long, around the story of the prophesy, life, and ministry of Christ—a popular subject both in his time and for centuries since. The oratorio consists of movements for orchestra, for soloists, and for chorus that flow in a logical fashion and are often based on a historical event or person. The *Messiah* contains a text drawn largely from the King James version of the Bible and from the common book of worship used in England at the time, the *Anglican Psalter*, and it was assembled by the librettist Charles Jennens.

The *Messiah*, from its first performance in the spring of 1742, was a hit with audiences; today it is undoubtedly the most popular large choral work in the repertoire. Its popularity lies not only in the subject matter but in the way in which Handel composed it. To borrow a phrase from the computer world, it is "user friendly." It appeals directly to the listener, because the music and the text are easily understood. This multimovement work flows gracefully from one type of composition to another—from recitative to aria to chorus. Nowhere does the counterpoint become overburdening. Handel's intended audience was certainly more diverse than Bach's, and an overly learned contrapuntal style might have stood in the way of the public's appreciation and acceptance of the music. Furthermore, the orchestra parts frequently enhance the vocal lines by playing exactly the same notes as the singers are singing (a technique called doubling), thereby adding both to the dynamic power and the comprehensibility of the music.

We will discover the accessibility of Handel's *Messiah* by examining a recitative, an aria, and a chorus that occur in succession early in this work. Finally, we will hear the chorus that ends Part II of the *Messiah*, the "Hallelujah" chorus, one of the greatest showstopping numbers of all time. According to legend, King George was in the audience during a performance of the *Messiah*, and he stood when he heard the "Hallelujah" chorus—whether out of respect or out of the need to stretch is not entirely clear. Upon realizing that the king was standing, however, the entire audience immediately rose to its feet. Audiences have been following this tradition ever since, whenever this famous chorus is sung during a performance of Handel's *Messiah*.

Listening Guides 25–27

Messiah (excerpts) **George Frideric Handel (1685–1759)**	Oratorio 1741 Recorded by Le Grande Ecurie et la Chambre du Roy, Jean-Claude Malgoire, conductor
	"Comfort Ye, My People" (recitative) "Ev'ry Valley Shall be Exhalted" (solo aria) CD No. 2, Track 3 (6:42)
	"And the Glory of the Lord" (chorus) CD No. 2, Track 4 (3:10)
	"Hallelujah" (chorus) CD No. 2, Track 5

*H*andel set the text from Isaiah 40, "Comfort Ye, My People," using a declamatory or speech-like style of music called the recitative—where the words are set with only one or two notes a syllable, and where the accompaniment uses only a few instruments as accompaniment. In opera, the recitative was frequently used for conversation between two characters or for providing a narration of events. A recitative is typically followed by an aria, where the music is more elaborate, the singer is called upon to sing more extended passages on some of the syllables, and the accompaniment is a more important part of the musical texture.

The chorus, "And the Glory of the Lord," is one of the most popular numbers in the *Messiah*, and it is often performed alone by choirs, as is the universally known "Hallelujah Chorus."

To Consider

1. As you listen to "Comfort Ye, My People," and the following aria, "Ev'ry Valley, . . ." notice the musical contrast between the recitative and the aria. Describe the musical structures that create this difference in style.
2. Notice specifically the word painting that occurs within the text, "The crooked straight and the rough places plain." Handel chooses two words, "crooked" and "plain," to underline by composing melodic contours to match these words.
3. Can you describe the changes in texture that occur in both the choruses "And the Glory of the Lord," and "Hallelujah"? How does the composer achieve a sense of drama and magnitude with these textural changes?

G. F. Handel: The Messiah (excerpts)

Recitative:	Comfort, comfort ye, my people saith your God, Speak ye comfortably to Jerusalem, and cry unto her that her warfare is accomplished, that her iniquity is pardoned. The voice of one crying in the wilderness: Prepare ye the way of the Lord, make straight in the desert a high place for our God.
	(Isaiah 40: 1–3)
Air:	Ev'ry valley shall be exalted, and ev'ry mountain and hill made low, the crooked straight, and the rough places plain.
	(Isaiah 40: 4)
Chorus:	And the glory of the Lord shall be revealed. And all flesh shall see it together, for the mouth of the Lord hath spoken it.
	(Isaiah 40: 5)
Chorus:	Hallelujah, for the Lord God Omnipotent reigneth, Hallelujah! The kingdom of this world is become the Kingdom of our Lord and of His Christ, and He shall reign for ever and ever, Hallelujah! King of Kings, and Lord of Lords, and He shall reign for ever and ever, Hallelujah!
	(Revelation 19:6; 11:15; 19:16)

---

25 "Comfort Ye . . . " (CD No. 2, Track 3)

0:00 Orchestra plays an introductory melody independent from the solo voice melody.

0:16 Recitative begins with solo voice and is answered by the strings with the same melodic fragment. The orchestra then continues with its own melody.

1:20 "Speak ye comfortably to Jerusalem" is set to a melodic sequence. "And cry unto her" is set to a very dramatic leap of an octave.

"Ev'ry valley . . . "

3:02 This time, the orchestra's melody is the same as the solo tenor's musical line.

3:38 "Exalted" is set to a sequence of melodic figures that gradually rises in pitch, thereby underlying the text.

4:04 The melodic setting of "ev'ry mountain and hill made low" ends in a low pitch, again illustrating the meaning of the words.

4:09 "The crooked straight" is set to a disjunct melodic figure, whereas "the rough places plain" is illustrated by smoother, conjunct melodic figures.

26 "And the Glory of the Lord . . . " (CD No. 2, Track 4)

0:00 The orchestra presents the opening melody that provides the melodic material for the entry of the alto section.

0:11 The alto section is answered in a powerful homorhythmic setting sung by the rest of the chorus, thereby establishing a pattern where one phrase of the text is presented by a single section of the chorus (such as the altos or tenors) and is answered by the entire chorus reaffirming the most important parts of the texts with loud, homorhythmic statements. The orchestra parts double various choral parts to reinforce the choral texture without competing with it.

27 "Hallelujah" (CD No. 2, Track 5)

0:00 This chorus, which occurs at the climax of Part II of the *Messiah*, begins with a full orchestral introduction. The orchestral introduction foreshadows the choral opening with identical musical material.

0:10 The chorus enters with a loud shout of "Hallelujah" in homorhythmic texture. After individual voice parts sing "For the Lord, God Omnipotent reigneth," the whole chorus answers "Hallelujah" in strong, chordal statements.

1:16 "The kingdom of this world . . . " is sung softly to contrast to the loud, shouting interjections.

1:35 The most polyphonic part of this number occurs with the text, "And He shall reign for ever and ever . . . " However, the texture seldom exceeds two parts singing contrary to each other at the same time.

1:57 "King of Kings . . . " is treated as a trumpet fanfare. The trumpet in the orchestra plays a brilliant scale flourish in the center of this section, which underlines the trumpet-like nature of the chorus here. "Forever and ever" is elaborated on in a gesture of emphasizing the concept of eternity. The drums (timpani) provide added grandeur by emphasizing the strong rhythms of this section.

3:26 The work ends with a final, slow, and profound statement of "Hallelujah." The IV-I cadence sounds like a grand Amen.

What are the musical characteristics of Handel's style that make it so accessible to such a wide audience? First, one can easily hear how he contrasts short sections of polyphonic texture (where he introduces melodies in imitation throughout the four sections of the choir) to large statements where all voices "shout" out an important part of the text in homorhythmic texture. He takes great care to give musical meaning to the most important words of the text. To underline this technique with further drama, Handel has the instruments of the orchestra double the vocal parts.

As we have come to expect from the music of this time, Handel's melodies are frequently "spun out" with sixteenth-note extended passages where a solo singer sings many notes to one syllable (called **melismas**), but here again he tempers this technique with pauses in the melodic line. His bass lines are strong, and the listener is always aware of the harmonies as they progress from one chord to another. His harmonies are the simplest when he sets powerful passages of text; he often relies on rhythms to provide the real interest. (Predictable chord progressions underlining strong rhythmic ideas are found in many popular musical expressions, especially in the blues and in early rock 'n' roll.)

*M*usical Encounter

Women Stars of Baroque Music

*O*pera, the form of musical drama that began in the early Baroque Era, played a major role in the rise of women composers and performers. The marketplace for secular musical forms grew, due in part to the support of the courts and major aristocratic families such as the Medici family of Florence, Italy, and also due in part to public opera performances, such as the ones Handel was involved with in England. In Chapter 4 you learned that the Church was reluctant to allow women to become involved in choirs and instrumental ensembles, believing that they would interfere with the concentration on sacred worship. The very nature of opera, with its emphasis on the dramatic depiction of both male and female characters, however, required the presence of women, thus several women musicians rose to prominence during this most significant phase in history.

Francesca Caccini (1587–1640), a member of the Medici Court in Mantua, was a singer, a lute, guitar, and harpsichord player, and a composer. Her father, Guilio Caccini (1545–1618), is known as one of the shapers of opera, for he was a member of a group of intellectuals in Florence that met and discussed the possibility of developing a new form of music that would effectively combine elements of drama and music. This new form, opera, was the result.

Francesca sang in the premiere performance of *Euridice*, written by her father, Guilio, and Jacopo Peri, one of the very works to qualify as opera. Guilio Caccini's major impact, however, was in solo song, for he demonstrated a new style of music by publishing *Le nuove musiche* (*The New Music*), a collection of works for solo singer with the accompaniment of a harpsichord and cello, which became common performance practice in Baroque Era music.

Francesca Caccini's most famous appearance was at the wedding of Maria de' Medici and Henry IV, King of France, in 1600. The king was so impressed that he declared this Italian guest "the best singer in France." Her successful career continued as a well-paid singer in the Medici Court, and in 1617, she went on a concert tour to several major cities in Italy.

Although her role as a singer was important during her lifetime, it was her opera/ballet, *The Liberation of Ruggiero* (*La Liberazione Di Ruggiero*) that gave her prominence in the history of music. Caccini called her work a balleto—a popular stage genre during the time that featured dance rhythms, the prominent importance of its libretto, and the use of word painting—which pointed more directly to the opera than to the balleto. It called for five sopranos, two altos, seven tenors, and one bass in singing/acting roles, and it also contained parts for several choruses. The first performance of *La Liberazione* was reported in a diary of the Medici Court in 1625.

Francesca Caccini's opera is significant to music history for several reasons. It is the first opera written and published by a woman; furthermore, it was the first Italian opera to have been performed outside of the country, for in 1682 it was produced in Warsaw, Poland.

In 1607, Francesca married Giovanni Baptiste Signorini Malaspina, also a musician and touring partner. During the following years, she regularly appeared as a featured singer both in the Medici Court and in the Church of Santa Nicolo in Pisa. "La Cacchina," as she was called by her admiring public, was a popular teacher of music as well. It is assumed that she remarried after her husband died in 1626, for the court records contain a notice that one Francesca Caccini, wife of a senator, died in 1640.

Two other singers whose lives serve as examples for the coming out of women as professional performers toward the end of the Baroque period are Francesca Cuzzoni (ca. 1698–1770) and her rival diva Faustina Bordoni (1700–1781). Cuzzoni made her singing debut in Parma, Italy, in 1716, and then she appeared in Venice opposite Bordoni in 1718. During her early career, her title was "Chamber Virtuoso to the Grand Duchess Violante of Tuscany." Her singing career took her to nearly all of the leading opera centers in Europe: London, Bath, Genoa, Paris, Modena, Bologna, Venice, Rome, Hamburg, Vienna, Stuttgart, and Amsterdam. Her fame as an accomplished singer is well documented and attested to by the many leading operatic roles she played. Her notoriety for living a flamboyant lifestyle—including the accumulation of large debts—is equally known in history.

The records of Cuzzoni's fame contain several accounts of her performing personality. Like many rock stars of the twentieth century, Cuzzoni was not immune to controversy. One famous incident occurred when she arrived in London for her King's Theatre debut, where she was to sing the female lead role in Handel's opera, *Ottone*. When she discovered that a particular aria was not composed specifically for her, she refused to sing it. Legend has it that Handel, himself in a rage, picked her up, went to a window in the theatre, and threatened to drop the unruly prima donna to the ground below. She recanted and sang to an enthusiastic audience, many of whom paid up to seven times the original ticket price just to hear her.

Cuzzoni's strong personality clashed with Bordoni's, the other great soprano of the time, when, at a performance of *Astianatte,* an opera by Giovanni Bononcini (1670–1747), Cuzzoni and Bordoni became involved in a scuffle on stage during the performance—all of this in the presence of the Princess of Wales. The audience participated eagerly in the rivalry and encouraged the fighting divas with ovations, catcalls, and whistles.

Bordoni, an Italian, also debuted in France at the home of an ambassador to Rome. Her career was first centered in Venice, where she appeared regularly for some nine years as a leading soprano. Her reputation for singing, acquired not only in Venice but also in Reggio, Modena, Bologna, Rome, Naples, Munich, and Vienna, earned her a position at King's Theatre in London, where she debuted in 1726.

Charles Burney, a musical journalist and historian who documented the musical life of England from his firsthand experience, admired Bordoni's voice and her character. He said that she had "perfect intonation and breath control," and he also spoke of her as a genuine, sensible person with excellent acting ability. Other reviewers remarked about her articulate, brilliant execution, her ability to pronounce words very rapidly, the power of her voice, and her ability to express emotions, whether fury, love, or tenderness.

Bordoni was married to Johann Adolf Hasse (1699–1783), a German-born composer who spent many years in Italy and was for several decades the most admired composer of Italian serious operas. Before moving to Italy, Johann and Faustina lived for a while in Vienna, where Faustina became one of the favorite musicians of the famous patron of the arts—and a musician herself—the Empress Maria Theresa (1717–1780).

Caccini, Cuzzoni, and Bordoni are just a few of the women from the Baroque Era who emerged as public figures and began to broaden the musical culture of Europe. Elizabeth-Claude Jacquet de la Guerre (1666–1729) captured attention as a child prodigy on the harpsichord and went on to become a composer who wrote in many popular genres of the day, including operas, cantatas, chamber music, and keyboard works. Upon her death, Louis XV of France had a commemorative medal struck in her honor. Barbara Strozzi (1619–ca. 1664) was a well-known musician who was at the very center of early opera activities in Venice. Her fame in Italy was based not only on singing and compositions (she was active both as a leading lady and as a composer of vocal music) but also on her flamboyant social life.

Even though women composers remained a rarity for years and were outnumbered by men many times over, a modern awareness of women's role in music has grown to new heights in the past quarter of a century.

ℬAROQUE TEXTURES IN JAZZ

The concept of counterpoint and layering, established in the Baroque Era, is such an attractive technique of composition that composers throughout history have been drawn to it. Furthermore, counterpoint has been a useful tool for many modern musicians, both within and outside the world of concert music. We will digress from a historical consideration of Baroque music to discover that the same listening skills that one uses to hear a fugue by Bach are applicable to listening to many jazz expressions.

Perhaps one of the strongest parallels that can be drawn between a historical style and a seemingly unrelated genre of music are between Baroque counterpoint and jazz. The melodic lines of **Dixieland jazz**, often played by the clarinet, the trumpet, the trombone, or the tenor saxophone, are conceived according to principles of independent counterpoint. They are played over the accompaniment of a bass instrument (a tuba or string bass) and over chords thumped out by a banjo or a piano. As the name indicates, Dixieland is a jazz form that grew out of the South during the first two decades of the twentieth century. Although its instrumentation varies from group to group, the concept of contrapuntal improvisation is a common feature of the Dixieland style.

The Modern Jazz Quartet (often called MJQ by jazz aficionados) frequently uses concepts of counterpoint in its arrangements and performances. *Delaunay's Dilemma* illustrates the relationship between Baroque counterpoint and jazz. This jazz group consists of vibes (vibraphone), piano, acoustic string bass, and drums.

In summary, let us see what much of jazz has in common with Baroque music:

1. The concept of motoric rhythm is shared by each. Motoric rhythm refers to the regular simultaneous presentation of both the basic pulse and its subdivisions.

2. Melodies are frequently "spun out" in a continuous fashion, often developing into a counter subject that supports a head motive.

3. Regular harmonic rhythm—chord changes that occur with predictable frequency—is another common feature. The regular occurrence of chord progressions creates a steady foundation and an accompaniment to the melodic lines.

The Modern Jazz Quartet performs at Birdland, NYC, November 11, 1954. John Lewis, Percy Heath, and Milt Jackson. Photo by: Bob Parent. Source: Archive Photos. ID # G1829/014/F11H2Z2.

Listening Guide 28

Delaunay's Dilemma
John Lewis, arranger

Jazz arrangement
Performed by the Modern Jazz Quartet
CD No. 2, Track 6 (3:00)

To Consider

Listen for the interplay of counterpoint in this composition based on the English carol, "God Rest Ye, Merry Gentlemen." Describe the progress of the arrangement in terms of texture and use of melody. Before you read the description in the listening insert, consider the following:

1. How does the composer "set up" this piece at the beginning? What is the musical function of the bass at the very start of this piece?
2. Can you tell when the introduction is over and the main part of the arrangement begins? What determines this?
3. How and when is counterpoint used?
4. What devices does the composer use to signal that the end of the work is coming?

0:00	A four-measure introduction lets the listener know that the vibes (vibraphone) and bass will be the central instruments in this jazz tune.
0:06	The "head" of the tune (first part of the melody) is presented by the vibes for eight measures. It's repetition signals the first two sections of the A-A-B-A form—typical of many jazz tunes (also known as "song form").
0:29	The B section of the tune is stated, followed by the return of A.
0:50	Now, the working out of the tune begins; the vibes and the bass engage in counterpoint reminiscent of Baroque music.
1:01	The counterpoint begins in earnest. Notice the steady, motoric pulse, which gives a solid foundation for the improvisation.
1:55	As the music continues, notice that the function of the piano is to provide the harmonic backdrop for the counterpoint. You are probably aware of the steady harmonic rhythm as you begin to feel comfortable with this traditional jazz style.

4. Several melodic concepts are often presented simultaneously. Different parts seem to go their separate ways, but they still relate to each other through the harmonic framework underlining the music.
5. A strong bass line gives depth to the music. In jazz, the piano, bass, and drums furnish this foundation; in Baroque instrumental music, it is the harpsichord (or organ) and the cello (or string bass).

Antonio Vivaldi and *The Four Seasons*

In the 1970s, the movie *The Four Seasons* was produced, in which Antonio Vivaldi's composition by the same name was used as background music; and so began the Vivaldi revival in America. *The Four Seasons* (the composition) is actually a set of four concertos for violin and small orchestra, each containing three movements. They are an example of **program music** in that they contain descriptive elements depicting spring, summer, fall, and winter.

Vivaldi, one of the most prolific composers of the Baroque Era, was trained and or-
dained as a priest, but his interest leaned away from saying Mass and more toward musical
composition. Although he was troubled by illness throughout his life (some more cynical
historians feel that he often became ill whenever he was asked by the Church to work as a
priest and not as a musician), his many compositions attest to his energy. Over 450 of his
concertos survive, plus forty-nine operas, twenty-five sonatas of various types, and many
sacred choral works, including cantatas, motets, and oratorios—music that is enjoyed by
modern audiences everywhere.

He was assigned to direct the musical program at the Conservatory of the Pietà in
Venice. The conservatory was essentially an orphanage for girls—a well-organized school
where Vivaldi developed some excellent performing ensembles. Venice during this time
was a center for musical performance and entertainment, and tourists from all over Europe routinely came to this city to experience the exciting life that characterized its environment. The first conservatories were developed in orphanages—charitable residences
for abandoned, indigent, or illegitimate children. Musical shows were presented for the
tourists by residents of these orphanages, and Vivaldi was assigned to the major girls' orphanage in the city. We know that his music was popular during his lifetime, for he was
asked to compose music for various occasions, not only in Venice but also in Rome,
Verona, and Florence.

Vivaldi's thirty-seven years as the director of the music program at the Pietà orphanage provided him with a source of income, a means to develop his own musicians, total
control of his own performing ensembles, and a public to hear his music. The level of ex-
cellence that the performers attained is obvious when one examines the vast repertoire of
music that was written for performance during these years. One such work is the famous
set of four violin concertos, *The Four Seasons*, the subject of our next selection.

Listening Guide 29

"La Primavera," ("Spring"), **from *The Four Seasons*** **Antonio Vivaldi (1678–1741)**	Baroque violin concerto Published in 1725 Recorded by Tafelmusic Jean Lamon, violinist and conductor CD No. 2, Track 7 (3:35)

*W*e will examine the first of Vivaldi's *Four Seasons* concertos to discover the charm of this very
active composer. A basic premise of his music is that Vivaldi gives the listener a strong feeling of chord progression; he does this by changing his harmonies at a rather deliberate pace, thereby
allowing the listener to "keep up" with his harmonic progressions. Over this the solo violin plays
strong thematic material, often in counterpoint with the first violins of the orchestra. Vivaldi is also
well known for his melodic sequences and his use of scales and arpeggios in his melodies.

To Consider

1. How does Vivaldi use repetition at the beginning of this piece to set up the listener for further
   musical events? Listen carefully to the very opening measures, and see if they return from time
   to time.
2. Describe the texture of this work at the beginning. Does it seem to be contrapuntal in nature
   or homophonic?

3. Can you hear the strong bass line of the orchestra throughout this movement? What type of dimension does it add to the music? Does it add to the predictability of chords and phrase endings?

0:00	The opening melodic motive in the string section is the central theme of this movement. Notice the echo effect that is created by musical material being passed between the full ensemble (tutti) and a smaller group of players, the concertino.
0:36	The solo violin enters with music suggesting the twittering of birds. The solo violin and first violins of the tutti trade these ideas.
1:10	The tutti orchestra returns: again, notice the alternation between the tutti and the concertino.
1:53	The solo violin depicts a quick storm by rapidly ascending scales and frantic arpeggios. The string section reinforces this with tremolos (short, fast, back-and-forth bowing created by moving only the wrist of the bow hand).
2:19	Once again, an exchange of the tutti and the concertino. Counterpoint is created between the solo violin and the first violins of the orchestra.
3:16	Final tutti is followed by the closing statement in the concertino.

SUMMARY

For hundreds of years, contrapuntal techniques have been used by many composers. It was during the seventeenth and eighteenth centuries, however, that the fundamental techniques of contrapuntal composition were perfected—so much so, in fact, that modern composers study the works of Bach and his contemporaries to understand this significant concept of musical organization. This period of time is known as the Baroque Era; its music, art, and architecture have aesthetic elements that invite comparison.

Counterpoint is used in a variety of ways by composers according to the genre of music in which they write and depending on their personal, stylistic tastes. The weave of voices in the fugues of Bach is very closely knit. Handel used imitative counterpoint much more sparingly in the choral movements of his oratorios. The French composer Couperin embellished his counterpoint with trills and other ornaments to present a light texture of two or three parts in his works for harpsichord (claveçin).

The approach to composition involving independent lines working both with and contrary to each other is an attractive technique not limited to the music of the Baroque Era. Modern jazz performers frequently use techniques of counterpoint in their music. Playing independent lines over regularly changing chord progressions is a basic technique used in jazz composition and performance.

KEY TERMS

chorale preludes
chorus
concerto grosso
concertino
counterpoint
Dixieland jazz
episodes
figured bass
fugue
harmonic rhythm
hymn
imitation
layering
melismas
motoric rhythm
oratorio

ordres
overture
polarity of outer voices
prelude
program music
regular harmonic rhythm
ripieno
round
solo concerto
solo sonatas
suite
toccata
trills
trio sonata
word painting

Repetition and Contrast: The Classical Style

*I*N Chapter 5, we saw how counterpoint, the most important characteristic of Baroque music, fit in with larger patterns in art, architecture, and society in general. In this chapter, we will take a similar view of the music of the Classical period. We will see that the defining trait of this musical period, repetition and contrast, was an important

pattern that guided the development of special forms of music that served both the composers and the public with comprehensible, artistically balanced music. Concepts of balance and propriety, so significant to the Classical Era, provide the links to the Western Classical tradition of this time. In this chapter you will also see how this music continues to touch us today, although we live in an entirely different cultural milieu.

Although patterns of repetition and contrast are found in almost every musical expression of music in Western cultures, the music of Haydn, Mozart, and Beethoven illustrates these principles with the most clarity; therefore, we will turn to this rich source to further our awareness of these fundamental compositional techniques. We will examine the cultural milieu from which this music originated. Music of the Classical Era, with its emphasis on structural clarity, is just a reflection of a larger philosophical approach to thinking.

In Chapter 2, you heard an example of classical music, the third movement of Mozart's *Symphony No. 35 in D Major*. Recall that the melodies of this work are shaped in symmetrical phrases in units of 4, 8, and 16 measures, and that their structure forms a sort of question-and-answer effect. Furthermore, the larger formal organization (an A-B-A structure) is clear to the listener, even upon the first hearing. Everything about this symphony suggests that the beauty of the music is conceived within the framework of order and logic. We will pursue these approaches to musical style in depth after we consider the social and aesthetic forces that shaped the music of this period in history. Our investigation will lead us into examining the life experiences of Haydn, Mozart, and Beethoven, for it seems that the better we come to know the composers, the more our interest grows in their music.

Many people throughout the years have been drawn into the world of concert music by first hearing the music of the Classical Era. Its appeal is universal and timeless.

One of the most appealing aspects of the art of music is its extreme versatility. The many functions of music have already been documented in previous pages. In this chapter, we will focus on music that does not depend on outside literary references for its existence. It is called **abstract music** or **absolute music,** for it is not written to tell a story or to evoke specific pictorial images in listeners' minds. The ideas that flow from the composer's pen through the performers' voices or instruments are conveyed through the artful arrangement of sounds—melodies, harmonies, and textures that play directly upon the ears of the listeners. Composers working in the late eighteenth and early nineteenth centuries produced works that illustrate this type of composition in its best context. It is called the music of the Classical Era.

The compositions chosen for examination in this chapter are works structured around principal themes or melodies. The accompaniments (the harmonies and textures) are written in such a way that they enhance rather than compete with these main themes. Musical materials are often presented in patterns of repetition and contrast that maintain the interest of the listener.

We will begin our study by examining the spirit of the times that gave rise to this musical expression.

THE MEANING OF CLASSICISM IN MUSIC

Many people today use the term "classical music" to refer to a broad category of concert music separate from folk, pop, country, jazz, or any other stereotypical style of music. More accurately, however, "classical music" represents a style that was developed primarily in the time of Mozart, Haydn, and Beethoven, or during the mid-eighteenth to early nineteenth centuries. This music followed certain principles of style that link it to the aesthetic qualities of classical Greece and Rome: an emphasis on formal structure, balance, objectivity, and logic. These aesthetic qualities, first associated with the Greek and Roman cultures, became the model for later expressions that we now call "classical."

The mid-eighteenth century in Europe was strongly influenced by a philosophical movement called the Enlightenment. During this era, people began looking at life from a perspective of Nature and Reason. They saw human progress as being brought about by human reason and the application of natural laws on human behavior. Their models often were drawn from ideas expressed by great thinkers of ancient times. Aristocrats, philosophers, artists of various types, and politicians tried to strive for an ideal world shaped by the elegance of intelligent thought.

Jean Jacques Rousseau (1712–1778), one of the most influential and controversial philosophers of this era, advocated freedom from the absolute authority imposed by church and state. His writings show an insistence on free will and individual rights, and he passionately defended reason—a philosophical stance that grew out of the age of the Enlightenment and included figures such as philosophers René Descartes, John Locke, Voltaire, and Emanuel Kant, scientist Isaac Newton, and political philosopher and jurist Charles de Montesquieu. The *Encyclopédie* (1751–1772), published in Paris by Denis Diderot, aimed at synthesizing all currently significant contributions to human thought and was an influential source for the educated population of the time.

The *philosophes,* as this group of thinkers was called, developed an approach to reason that was based on the principles of reexamining and questioning all known values and ideas. Kant's motto, "Dare to Know," typified their approach to life. They sought to discover truth through unlocking the laws of the universe. In nature, they found a balance, a logic, and a means for understanding their contemporary culture.

An examination of paintings from this era serves to underline these aesthetic principles. One artist whose works typify an approach to painting guided by the concepts of balance, structure, and objectivity—a noble simplicity—is Jacques Louis David (1748–1825). In his famous work *The Oath of the Horatii,* David draws on classical history to show how logic and reason prevailed at a crucial moment in history when Rome and Alba Longa staged a combat between three individuals to prevent a war. (See Color Plate #4) The classical structure of the painting is shown in the three arches that frame the scene and the balance resulting from the placement of the three sons on the left and the weeping women (the sisters of the Horatii) on the right. The symmetry of the work originates out of a classical concern for the balance of subject material. The painting has political overtones and is inspired by the revolutionary spirit of the times; Louis XVI commissioned this work in his campaign to foster the moral improvement of France.

Music of this era shows a balance not unlike that found in David's works; its manifestations are shown in the formal structures that composers used as standard architectural schemes for their works. Smaller, more detailed stylistic features also point to the composer's concern for objective thought: melodies often are constructed in symmetrical phrases, and the placement of strong harmonic progressions based on the tonic key and its dominant helps delineate the form. This concern for structure is further enhanced by the composer's use of dynamic changes. Frequently crescendos are used toward the end of sections. This, along with strong I-V-I chord progressions, brings a definite sense of closure to individual sections of music.

Today we listen to this music for its intrinsic value. It speaks to us with its creatively shaped melodies, its interesting use of harmonies that always relate to tonal centers, and its beautiful sense of balance. Western classical music has become, for many people throughout the world, the ultimate combination of musical thought and emotion. Its organization and structure appeal to what seems to be a natural sense of balance; its melodies, harmonies, and rhythms play on our ears and emotions. This music of another era has become the music for our time—and for all times.

GENRES AND FORMS OF MUSIC

Types of music for voice—operas, sacred and secular choral works, and solo songs—are genres of music that were established in the previous centuries and readily adapted to the stylistic features of classical music. Opera houses flourished, and choral music, which was written primarily for the church, was also finding its way into secular settings. Music for the solo voice gained in popularity as well, as the piano became more and more prevalent, for solo vocal music was most conveniently supported by the piano, an instrument undergoing constant technological improvements during this time.

The most exciting developments in the musical world, however, were taking place in the area of instrumental music, for it was during the Classical Era when the symphony orchestra became a popular ensemble, and works comprised of three or four contrasting movements, called "symphonies," were written. These compositions show a general approach to formal organization that also occurs in other types of instrumental music.

The many genres of instrumental music were written with similar structural plans. Typically, larger forms of instrumental music were organized into either three or four movements. This so-called "sonata form" usually started and ended with fast movements; the middle movements were composed to provide contrast. Often a slow tempo was written for the second movement. If there were two inner movements to the work, the third movement would usually be in triple meter—also to add contrast. Furthermore, standard internal structures were developed that many composers used to organize their works. Far from being mere molds into which composers poured their melodies, harmonies, and rhythms, these formal schemes functioned both as general structural guidelines for the composer and as listening guideposts for the consumer of music.

Chamber works such as the string quartet (for two violins, viola, and cello), the piano trio (for piano, violin, and cello), and the piano quintet (for string quartet and piano) are genres that share the multimovement concept and certain formulas of repetition and contrast with the symphony. Thus the symphony, the string quartet, the piano trio, and the piano quintet are terms associated both with the ensemble and with the music that is written for them.

Music for the solo piano became widely accepted as composers and performers cultivated the ever-widening sonorities of that developing keyboard instrument. **Sonatas** for various instruments with piano accompaniment were written to meet an ever-increasing demand for compositions as more and more people learned how to play instruments. A typical sonata has three or four movements; the first movement might be in **sonata-allegro**

form and would have a fast tempo, the second movement would normally be composed in a slower tempo and might have an A-B-A structure, and the final movement would again return to a fast tempo and be in a repetitive form such as a rondo.

The classical form of music known as the **symphony** resembles the sonata—except, of course, it is written for a symphony orchestra. Most often, symphonies had four movements, for they included a dance-derived movement, the **minuet and trio,** as one of the inner movements. We have already encountered this when we listened to the third movement of Mozart's *Symphony No. 35* in Chapter 2.

Mozart made famous the **piano concerto,** also typically a three-movement structure. The piano concerto, like the solo concerto, also uses internal forms similar to sonatas, symphonies, and chamber music but adapts their structures to accommodate the solo instrument. Many composers followed in Mozart's footsteps and produced not only keyboard concertos but concertos for both stringed and wind instruments.

FORMAL SCHEMES OF MUSIC IN THE CLASSICAL ERA

Let us examine briefly some of these formal schemes. We have already encountered the minuet and trio form in our introduction to the role of form in music. Another significant blueprint for music is commonly called the sonata-allegro form, or the "first movement form." It fundamentally involves three major sections: in the first section, major themes are presented (called the "exposition"); in the middle section these materials are broken up into smaller ideas and passed through the ensemble with a series of key changes (called the "development"); then, they are repeated in their simpler form (the recapitulation). Later we will examine the sonata-allegro form in more detail in Mozart's *Symphony No. 40 in G Minor.*

Other structures that were frequently used by classical composers are the **ternary form** (ABA), the **rondo form** (ABACADA—or a similar variant), and **theme and variations** (where a central melody is first presented in a simple statement and then used as a source for a series of embellishments). The **minuet and trio form** is another type of ABA structure, where the theme of the minuet represents the A sections, and the trio is the B section. It was common for the trio to be presented in a different key than the minuet.

These patterns of repetition and contrast provided logic and predictability to the music of the time. The artful manipulations of the musical material in classical music still capture our attention and interest and provide a great source of musical enjoyment.

ECONOMICS OF MUSIC DURING THE CLASSICAL ERA

In the mid-eighteenth century, artistic taste was fostered by rich people, such as kings and nobles, and developed by talented composers, painters, sculptors, and writers. The aristocracy supported both creators of the arts as well as performers. Franz Joseph Haydn, for example, lived for over thirty years at the grand Hungarian estate of the Duke of Esterháza, east of Vienna. His patron and employer, Paul Anton Esterházy, maintained an orchestra, an opera theater, and a marionette theater. Concerts were frequently given, and chamber music was performed almost daily. Esterházy often took part in these events, for he himself was an accomplished musician.

A musician during this time would do well to earn an appointment at such a court, and many did just that. Another option for employment was the church. For centuries, churches throughout Europe maintained boys' choirs as well as some instrumental musicians for use in various worship services and ceremonies. By tradition, young boys with strong musical talent would be sent by their eager parents to live in the dormitories of parochial schools. There they could live and serve as musicians while being educated by the church. Often, when their voices changed, the boys were no longer needed and were sent out to seek their fortunes elsewhere.

As the century progressed, composers found themselves less dependent on a single patron and began earning their living by piecing together several types of ventures: they sometimes scheduled concerts of their music, would charge an admission fee, and would hope to come away with a profit after paying all of the expenses. (This, of course, is what popular rock bands do today.) They also earned money by publishing their compositions. Sometimes a publisher would buy a manuscript outright from the composer; at other times, the composer would establish a royalty contract with a publisher. The ideal for composers, however, was to find a wealthy patron who would commission compositions. At times, aristocrats would invite artists to live in one of their properties free of charge.

Since the musicians' livelihoods depended on the church, the patronage system, and the public audience, the types and styles of music that were written and performed were strongly influenced by those sources of income. (While this is also true to a certain extent in modern times, today's composers of concert music, on the other hand, are often supported by teaching positions at universities. They feel free to write music in any style that they wish. Many current art music composers also recognize that they are writing for a much more specialized, therefore smaller, audience.)

A close parallel to the eighteenth-century life of the composer is our current-day freelance composer. These people must find an audience willing to listen to and pay for their compositions. This was true for two classical composers, Mozart and Beethoven. Today's composers also are commissioned by wealthy individuals, organizations, or corporate sponsors to produce a specific type of musical composition for a designated purpose.

FRANZ JOSEPH HAYDN: THE FATHER OF THE SYMPHONY

Many people confuse the sound of Haydn's music with Mozart's. Haydn, like Mozart, wrote in all of the known genres of his time. He wrote music that had well-defined forms, phrases, and harmonies. Although a close examination of his music reveals some very interesting idiosyncrasies, his music speaks for the Classical Era and the Age of Reason. In many ways, Haydn was a pioneer in establishing a classical musical style. The two instrumental forms that he cultivated and shaped over his lifetime—over eighty string quartets and 104 symphonies—served as models for other composers, including his most famous successors, Mozart and Beethoven. During his first years at the Esterházy court, his orchestral musicians began to call him "Papa Haydn" because of his genial personality and gentle leadership—although he was barely twenty-nine years old at the time. In retrospect, Papa Haydn fit him quite well, for his influence on the symphony as a genre of music has since earned him the title "Father of the Symphony."

Haydn's early experiences with music were in his home, where his parents sang folk songs for their own enjoyment. When he was still a young boy, one of his relatives persuaded his parents to send him to Vienna to a school where he could find good musical training. Haydn eventually became a choir boy at St. Stephen's Church in Vienna. He was forced to leave at age sixteen when his voice changed and he was no longer of use to the choir.

After an intense period of musical study, a time when his musical reputation was growing but his financial status was most tenuous, Haydn finally procured employment directing a small orchestra at the court of Count Ferdinand Maximilian Morzin.

His major career break came shortly after his twenty-ninth birthday, when he became part of the Esterházy court. Prince Paul Anton Esterházy, the reigning prince, soon became not only a patron but a good musical friend of Haydn's. It was at the Esterházy court, in eastern Austria (now near the Hungarian border), that Haydn spent his life composing and performing music for guests and residents at Esterháza—until 1790, when Paul Esterházy died.

By that time, the composer was famous throughout Europe. His music was especially well received in England, so much so, in fact, that an influential impresario, Johann Salomon, hired Haydn to write some symphonies for public performance there. Haydn's last twelve symphonies (called the "London Symphonies") are the result of this commission. They are his best-known works and reflect the mature writing of a composer whose musical resources had been expanded from a small court orchestra to a larger public orchestra.

Symphony No. 103 illustrates well Haydn's symphonic writing, for it incorporates features found in several of his late symphonic works. This composition, written in 1795, makes dramatic use of the wind instruments—an instrumental section of the orchestra for which Haydn wrote superb music. Other works by Haydn that show his well-honed sense of folklike charm and use of subtle orchestration include the *"Lark" String Quartet, Opus 64, No. 5* and the popular *Concerto for Trumpet in E Flat.*

Among his most famous choral works are the large works with orchestra, *The Creation, The Seasons,* and *The Seven Last Words of Christ,* as well as a series of Masses and other sacred works. Like many of his contemporaries, Haydn wrote for many different occasions in many genres. Although his dramatic music is not performed much today, his choral, instrumental, and keyboard works are part of the major performing repertoire all over the world.

In 1798, Haydn composed the folk song that was to become Austria's national anthem, *Gott erhalte Franz den Kaiser* (God, Preserve the Emperor Francis), in a strong statement of patriotism (the tune was adapted by Hitler to become *Deutschland über alles*). The text, in a translation done by Haydn's English friend, Dr. Charles Burney, is as follows:

> God preserve the Emp'ror Francis
> Sov'reign ever good and great;
> Save, o save him from mischances
> In Prosperity and State!
> May his Laurels ever blooming
> Be by Patriot Virtue fed;
> May his worth the world illumine
> And bring back the Sheep misled!
> God preserve our Emp'ror Francis!
> Sov'reign ever good and great![1]

Haydn, "Gott Erhalte Franz dem Kaiser," the Austrian National Anthem.

Musical Encounter

The Court of Esterházy and Franz Joseph Haydn

In the late 1760s, Miklós Joseph Esterházy, who had succeeded as head of the family upon the death of his brother Paul, moved his summer residence to a recently built castle in the country. Schloss Esterházy, a beautiful mansion overlooking the Neusiedler See (a large lake) in northwestern Hungary, was the center of artistic activities for the noble family from early spring to late autumn. Franz Joseph Haydn and his musicians were also in residence there during this extended season to provide the nobility with suitable artistic entertainment, in the form of chamber music, small opera productions, symphonies, and even sacred music.

Here Haydn showed both his sense of humor and his political savvy when he wrote his *Farewell Symphony*, first performed late in the 1772 season. Evidently that season was so enjoyable for the prince that he delayed ending the summer activities well beyond the normal time. Only after the prince released the musicians for the summer could they return to Vienna to their wives and children (families of musicians were not given summer housing at the estate). Haydn, poignantly aware of this, decided to persuade the prince to end the season, not by directly approaching him and discussing the issue, for that would be a serious breach of protocol, but by writing a piece of music that would remind his noble boss of the situation. Thus, in the last movement of the symphony the musicians gradually leave the stage, a few at a time, with their instruments in hand, until only two violinists are left to finish the movement. Haydn's ploy worked, and the prince decided that it was time for all to return to Vienna for the winter.

The rural setting of the Esterházy summer residence was ideal for the magnificent architecture of the Schloss Esterházy. Built in an Italian Renaissance style, this castle has 126 guest rooms, two great halls for receptions or balls, a nearby library with 7,500 volumes, and a theater large enough to seat an audience of 400. The original swamp that surrounded the building site was drained, and a series of gardens decorated with sculptures, well-manicured flowers, and game preserves was created to envelope the senses of both residents and guests. The elegance often was compared to the splendor of Versailles, the lavish home of French kings, about twelve miles southwest of Paris.

The Esterházy family frequently invited the most prominent actors, performers, singers, poets, and artists here to help create an ideal environment both at Schloss Esterházy and at Eisenstadt, their winter residence. Haydn was at the very center of this life for almost thirty years. Even with this ideal setting, he often longed for a broader world, and he found it when he went to London toward the end of his life.

WOLFGANG AMADEUS MOZART: A TWENTIETH-CENTURY PERSPECTIVE

If Mozart had been born in 1956 instead of 1756, would he have been another Andrew Lloyd Webber? Perhaps. Both musicians showed precocious talent at an early age; they also had fathers who guided their early musical development and their exposure to the public. Mozart worked in opera—the type of music most popular in his time, and also the most lucrative; Lloyd Webber's genre is musical theatre. (Had he been living today, would Mozart have made as much money for *Don Giovanni* as Lloyd Webber did for *Phantom of the Opera?*) But parallels such as this can be frivolous, and of course they can be taken too far.

The musical environment of the eighteenth century would not have allowed Mozart to take up pop music as a viable profession. The social institutions supporting music in Europe were based on either the court or the church. Public concerts, which were only in their infancy, could provide only part of the composer's income. The genre closest to pop music during Mozart's time was musical theater, and there were some operas that provided very light entertainment. Opera plots often involved sexual intrigue, broken and mended relationships, the interplay of wit between people in disguise, and many other topics addressed in our times, not only by soap operas but by popular song texts. (In the eighteenth century, however, nothing was explicit.) Innuendo and suggestion were *en vogue*. Mozart was quite interested in this culture of entertainment, and he wrote well for it.

Now, more than two centuries after his death, Mozart is a household name throughout the world, East and West. Millions of people have seen the movie *Amadeus*, which was based on his life and music. Further millions have heard his music in concerts and listen to recordings of his compositions. Why is he so popular? It is simply because his music has endured for centuries. The spirit of his music is one of energy, of incredible logic, and of clarity that appeals to all people throughout history.

Profile of a Genius

Wolfgang Amadeus Mozart was born in Salzburg, Austria, on January 27, 1756. His father, Leopold, was a violinist in the private orchestra of the Archbishop of Salzburg. During the year of Wolfgang's birth, Leopold published the first major book written on violin playing. A year later, he was appointed the assistant director of the Archbishop's orchestra and was also named court composer. So it is readily apparent that Wolfgang was born into an ambitious and a musical household. It comes as no surprise that the son of Leopold Mozart would be exposed not only to a vast amount of music but to a strong work ethic. It was this combination of elements that paid off for the young Mozart.

Wolfgang not only experienced music from his father, but he learned from his older sister Maria Anna (called "Nannerl" by Mozart in later years). Maria Anna, who was less than five years older than Wolfgang, was also a talented musician.

Although we know little about Nannerl, we know with certainty that Wolfgang was a child prodigy. His father first noticed Wolfgang's intense attentiveness during Nannerl's music lessons when Wolfgang was only three years old. A court trumpet player, Schachtner, a friend of the Mozart family, wrote about Wolfgang's eagerness in learning arithmetic, his phenomenal ear, with which he could remember pitches with total accuracy even a day after he heard them, and his high concentration level during music lessons.

In the month of Wolfgang's sixth birthday, his father took him and his sister to Munich (ninety miles away) to play before the Elector (the Prince), who received the two young children warmly. Shortly afterward, Leopold took the children to Vienna, where the Emperor was so taken with the *kleiner Hexenmeister* (little magician) that he had him play the keyboard first with only one finger and then with the keyboard covered. Wolfgang not only charmed the Emperor but also sat in the Empress's lap and hugged and kissed her.

Although we are fascinated by his genius as a child performer, it is Wolfgang's compositional gift that has given him immortality in the world of music. His earliest work is the *Minuet and Trio in G Major* for piano, dating from 1762 (Mozart was only six). During the next twenty-nine years of his life, he produced some 626 compositions. This means that he composed a new work on an average of one every eighteen days—and this includes full-length operas, large choral works, and symphonies!

Wolfgang Amadeus Mozart's life has always been surrounded with mystique, much of it taking on mythological proportions. It is most commonly known that he wrote several times to a fellow Mason, Michael Puchberg, for personal loans, and it is therefore assumed that Mozart was essentially penniless during his last years. (The Masonic Order, also known as Freemasonry, was an organization of men founded on the humanitarian teachings of the time. It was a highly structured organization that included rituals and symbols, but it was founded on the principle of love for all mankind, a positive attitude toward man and life, and a broad concept of God's role in the universe. Many eighteenth- and nineteenth-century intellectuals were members of the Freemason movement, including Haydn, Mozart, and Beethoven.)

Another popular myth about Mozart is that he was poisoned by his jealous enemies. Some pointed to Antonio Salieri, a leading court composer, as the perpetrator of the crime. For years it was thought that his funeral was poorly attended because the weather was bad on the day of his burial. Further myths surround the story of his wife Constance, whom early historians painted as being a simple sex object for her famous husband and whose main concern was money.

All of these long-held opinions have either been proven to be overstated or spurious by recent scholarship, and although such fantastic stories have over the years contributed to the Mozart mystique, their debunking does not change the attractiveness of his music.

Mozart's life was centered around two cities. He lived in Salzburg, the place of his birth, until he was twenty-five. Although his life in Salzburg was filled with composing, performing, traveling, and meeting both nobility and the public, he realized that he needed to move to Vienna if he was to become truly successful. And so, in 1781, against his father's wishes, he moved to the cultural center of the empire.

It was in Vienna that Mozart married. His wife, Constance Weber, was devoted to him and to his career. In the nine years of their marriage they had six children, only two of whom lived beyond childhood. After Mozart's untimely death at age thirty-five, Constance worked hard to promote her husband's music.

The Mozarts loved to entertain. Wolfgang felt that he must dress well, because so much of his living depended upon the wealthy class of people. He earned a living from giving private music lessons, from composing on commission, from gate receipts of his music at concerts, and partially from the publication of his music. We know that his family moved from apartment to apartment in Vienna. Mozart's letters also tell us that, in times of financial difficulty, he depended on a fellow Masonic lodge brother for loans and support.

Mozart wrote for every performing combination popular in Vienna. His music ranges from music for the church to compositions for the musical theater, symphony orchestras, chamber groups, and solo performance, both vocal and instrumental. His music is so popular today that it is hard to single out his most successful genre. We know from his letters that composing operas and symphonies occupied much of his attention. He also established the piano concerto as a major genre of music. He enjoyed performing his own works with various orchestras as a pianist and conductor.

Mozart's Melodic Tools

There exists in Mozart's music certain features that are consistent. First, he was always interested in writing beautiful melodies. As one becomes more familiar with his works, a concept of clarity and logic becomes apparent. Mozart's talent for alternating feelings of excitement and tension with moments of relaxation is unmatched in all of classical music.

We will examine some of these features in two of his compositions. Foremost in our minds will be the question, "How does Mozart achieve feelings of tension and release in his music?" To answer this question, we will examine Mozart's melodic materials, his use of harmony, and his concept of formal design.

Listening Guide 30

Concerto for Clarinet in A Major,
  K. 622, Adagio
Wolfgang Amadeus Mozart (1756–1791)

Clarinet concerto
1791
Recorded by Robert Marsellus, clarinet, with the
  Cleveland Orchestra, George Szell, conductor
CD No. 2, Track 8 (7:40)

*A*lthough we would do Mozart an injustice to reduce his melodies to simple formulas, it is appropriate to identify several of the devices he used repeatedly as the cornerstone of his writing technique. For example, most of Mozart's tunes contain material derived directly from scales and arpeggios. He often arranged his phrases in **melodic sequences** (a melodic fragment repeated at a different pitch level) and embellished his phrase endings with **ornamentation.** These features, which we already alluded to in our earlier discussion of melody, represent the tools of his craft; when we understand how they were used, we can begin to glimpse inside the composer's creative mind.

We can see these features clearly in the slow movement of Mozart's *Concerto for Clarinet and Orchestra.* We will see how these major building blocks of melody are used and combined to form Mozart's melodic style.

To Consider

Listen to the presentation of the melody in "Adagio" from the beginning of the work to the end of the first section, where the clarinet ends the section with a chromatic scale and a trill. Listed below are five features of melody that are important in understanding Mozart's style. See if you can distinguish between them as you listen.

1. Melodic notes are taken from triads (chords). Can you identify one chord (triad) that is the most prominent in the first eight measures? How does the composer's choice of notes help create the basic restful mood of the melody?
2. Passing tones are a principle part of the melodic structure. (A passing tone is a note that comes between two chord tones presented in stepwise progression.) How does the placement of these tones lend interest to the tune?
3. Scale passages form a significant part of the melody. Did you notice that the opening section of this movement has a lot of notes drawn from either a major scale or a chromatic scale?
4. Ornaments provide added character to the music. Ornaments, also called embellishments, are printed in smaller notes in the melodic line. What purpose do you think they have in this music?
5. Melodic sequences provide structure to phrases. Sequences are formed when a short melodic fragment is repeated at a different pitch level. How does the use of sequences in this melody establish a feeling of familiarity with the music?

0:00	The first eleven notes all belong to the tonic chord, with the exception of two notes, which are called "passing tones." Notice that a single chord (the tonic) underlines the first four measures of the piece, thereby strongly establishing the key center. The primary chords (I-IV-V-I) constitute the harmonic vocabulary.
1:14	The clarinet begins a line constructed of scales that is presented in melodic sequence.
1:50	The orchestra repeats the music first played by the clarinet.

Wolfgang Amadeus Mozart: "Adagio" from the *Clarinet Concerto in A Major, K. 622* (Solo clarinet in A, measures 1-54).

2:25 Now the clarinet plays a line based on a more extended use of the arpeggio. Scales and turns are part of the melodic construction. A chromatic scale, topped off by a trill, ends the first section of the movement.

4:10 Arpeggios and scales lead into the short cadenza.

4:29 The cadenza—a solo passage without orchestral accompaniment—breaks the motion of the music and adds a feeling of anticipation to the return of the principal melodic theme.

4:40 The opening musical material returns.

6:24 The movement begins to draw to a close—again on melodies created from scales and arpeggios. The music ends on the gentle strokes of the tonic triad.

A second listening to "Adagio" in its entirety will put all of these elements into an artistic context. Notice the crucial placement of ornaments—trills, turns, and grace notes—with which Mozart dresses up his melodic lines. These figures add to the elegance of the tunes and also boost the musical ideas to their completion. As you listen to the entire movement, concentrate especially on identifying triadic figures (including arpeggios), scale fragments, melodic sequences, and ornaments.

Formal Organization in Mozart's Music

Having experienced Mozart's melodic structures, we will deepen our listening ability by considering other ways in which this composer presents his ideas. One of his most famous works is *Symphony No. 40 in G Minor, K 550*. This work was written in the summer of 1788, a particularly productive year for Mozart. In the short span of June, July, and August of that year, he not only composed the 39th, 40th, and 41st symphonies, but he also wrote two piano sonatas, a violin sonata, a trio for piano, violin, and cello, the *Adagio and Fugue in C Minor* for string quartet, and two vocal works.

We are in awe of Mozart's ability to produce compositions so quickly. One factor that will provide insight into Mozart's tremendous writing facility is that he used well-established conventions of formal organization in his works. Perhaps this partially explains his ease of composition. Formal schemes such as the sonata-allegro form, the rondo form, the sonata-rondo form, the minuet and trio form, theme and variations, and the **da capo** (A-B-A) structure so prevalent in operatic melodies were resources upon which composers drew during this period. Mozart was no exception.

How ingeniously the composer treated these standard forms—forms that the listeners of the time could recognize—is, of course, what separates the best composers from the more commonplace ones. In the movie *Amadeus*, this point is made clearly when Mozart plays a keyboard excerpt by Salieri after having heard it once, but then he shows Salieri and the attending courtiers how it could be improved (a very effective moment in the film, although fictional).

Listening Guide 31

Symphony No. 40 in G Minor,
   K. 550, Mvt. 1
Wolfgang Amadeus Mozart (1756–1791)

Symphony
1788
Recorded by the Cleveland Orchestra,
   George Szell, conductor
CD No. 2, Track 9 (8:09)

*U*ndoubtedly the most familiar classical form for larger movements is the sonata-allegro. This form is commonly used as a first movement in symphonies, sonatas, and string quartets, and it is even found in modified structure in the concerto.

The three main structural components—the exposition, development, and recapitulation—are clearly delineated in this movement of *Symphony No. 40*. Keep in mind that our goal is to develop an awareness of the structure of Mozart's music through the listening experience. Before one becomes bogged down with the technical details of form in classical music, it is beneficial to realize that the central function of form is to provide logic to patterns of repetition and contrast. This is most easily heard in the melodies, but other elements of music, such as rhythm, dynamic contrast, and instrumentation, are also components of this approach to musical logic.

First remember that melody is the prime element here. When you listen to this work, try to recognize the two main melodic building blocks for this movement. They are as follows:

Theme A

Theme B

W. A. Mozart, *Symphony No. 40 in G Minor, K. 550*, Mvt. 1 (A and B themes).

Mozart uses these two melodies (called themes) in such a way that he is able to alternate feelings of movement or excitement with moments of release or relaxation. This is perhaps the most ingenious part of his work.

You have probably noticed that this symphony is in G minor, which means that the principal key area of the symphony is based on chords constructed from a minor scale. If one plays a major triad G-B-D, for example, and then lowers the middle note (to G-B♭-D), a G minor triad results.

As you listen to the first movement of this symphony, experience the feelings of movement and repose that are incorporated into the main themes and reinforced by other material which, for lack of a better term, we can call linking material. Listen to see what kind of musical devices are used to support these melodies.

Exposition

0:00   The first theme begins without an introduction. Notice the symmetrical phrasing of the theme and its repetitions. The full orchestra brings in the closing material, played forte and supported by scale passages.

0:53   Theme B enters (B-flat major); again, the phrasing is symmetrical and the theme is repeated—as was the first theme. A closing idea crescendos, underlined by scales and a repetition of I-V-I chord progressions.

2:02   The exposition is repeated verbatim.

Development

4:08   Two chords announce the development. At first, it sounds like another repetition of the opening material, but soon sharply stated scale passages permeate the texture. The two-note motive from theme A is passed around in different orchestral parts.

Recapitulation

5:24   The music reverts to the sounds of the beginning of the movement. However, the closing material of this section seems to be more complex than before.

6:37   The B theme is once again presented, but in a minor key. Again, tension mounts as scale passages crescendo. The I-V-I progressions signal an approaching finality.

Coda

7:52   The music slips into a brief coda, but soon the final chords end the work.

After working through this movement and becoming aware of the use of form, listen to the work again and see if you can feel the contrasts between tension and release that are such an important part of Mozart's music. The more you hear his music, the more you will be aware of the skill Mozart had in expressing subtle shades of tension and release.

Studying this aspect of Mozart in detail will pay off in understanding and enjoying his music. Whatever the formal plan of his music, this element always shines through. Remember, when listening to Mozart, an awareness of formal structure is made much easier if you listen most carefully to the melodies first and how they are supported by the accompaniment second.

BEETHOVEN AND HIS TIMES

Ludwig van Beethoven (1770–1827) occupies a pivotal position in music. He was born into a musical system where professional musicians were looked upon as servants of the nobility or church. Their functions were well defined, and their compositions were not expected to go beyond the realms of aristocratic taste. By the end of his career, Beethoven had established himself as an independent artist who not only exercised the freedom of personal expression but was also rewarded financially for it, thereby paving the way for future generations of composers.

In the year Beethoven was born, Mozart was fourteen and had already written five operas, twelve sacred vocal works, thirteen symphonies, and many songs and keyboard pieces. Haydn was thirty-eight and firmly established at Esterháza. Napoleon Bonaparte, whom Beethoven first admired because of his goals of freeing people from oppressive government, and then repudiated when he declared himself Emperor, had been born in Corsica one year earlier.

Beethoven's birth predated the Boston Tea Party by three years to the day. This event, a protest against England's practice of taxing the colonies without giving the people a voice in the government, illustrates the spirit of independence in the air. When Beethoven was born, Thomas Jefferson had just become a member of the Virginia legislature and at age twenty-four, he introduced (unsuccessfully) a bill that would allow slaveholders to emancipate slaves—another example of the prevailing mood of the times.

Of all the musicians who have risen to fame over the years, Beethoven is the most often cited example of a composer who broke the restraints of patronage and servitude and elevated the position of composer to a higher plane. In that way, he was a child of his times, for his life exudes a strength of character and independence so often connected with major figures from his era. Although he worked with and for the aristocracy, he established a spirit of independence from them, at one time even referring to them as the "princely rabble." The self-reliance he was forced to develop as a youth was translated to his art at a later stage in his life. Similarly, Beethoven was not afraid to push the bounds of formal organization in his music, to dare his audiences to follow a more complex manipulation of melodic ideas, and to explore an expanded dynamic and harmonic language of music.

Beethoven disputed both the social and musical conventions of his time. In that way, he is a revolutionary, a product of a time of overt change. His life and works reflect attitudes in which classical ideals, forms, and emotions are gradually replaced by stronger emotional statements. New compositional practices reflecting these attitudes became the shaping forces of a new aesthetic period known as romanticism. While we consider Beethoven a classicist—primarily because the genres of music that he cultivated were already established, and because of his interest in formal structure, melodic and motivic manipulation, and general balance that his works achieve—he is a transitional figure into a new era.

The revolutionary attitudes we detect in Beethoven's life and works were not an isolated phenomenon. Concepts of personal and political freedom, liberty, and equality permeated the European (and American) culture in the late eighteenth and early nineteenth centuries. The impact of the French Revolution was felt throughout the Western world, and the resultant spirit of change was reflected in the arts of the time. The subject matter in the art of this period often depicted realistic action inspired by current social and political idealism—a romantic glimpse of a moment caught in time.

This spirit is well illustrated in *Liberty Leading the People*, a painting by French romanticist Eugène Delacroix (1798–1863). (See Color Plate #5) Written to commemorate the July 28, 1830 revolution that had just brought Louis-Philippe to the French throne, this painting is strongly political in nature. Delacroix, who had been a member of the National Guard, portrayed himself as the figure in the top hat. The person with outstretched hands holding the tri-color flag is Liberty, a heroic figure symbolizing the bold, daring spirit of revolution that was so prevalent in the early nineteenth century. Delacroix's depiction of Liberty as a partially dressed woman was highly controversial during the time— yet another manifestation of the painter's bold, romantic approach to his art.

The Universality of Beethoven's Music

Beethoven's music addresses all humanity. It stands alone as an intrinsic entity of sound that expresses both logic and feeling. His tempestuous spirit of individuality inspired music that retains its excitement almost 200 years after it was written. His tempos vary from lightning fast to deliberately slow; his melodies build to intense emotional climaxes. His formal concepts, however, were born out of the Classical Era, and his art shows an intensive interest in structure. For that reason, he is still a product of the Classical period in music. Many, however, see him as a transitional figure to the next broad movement in aesthetic history—the Romantic Era.

Why is Beethoven's music considered universal, and why does it continue to move us so deeply today? These questions could be answered in many ways, but we will first approach them from the standpoint of the emotional nature of his music. His music is often flamboyant and daring, and its sharp, dynamic contrasts hold the attention of even the modern listener, whose ears are accustomed to cacophonous background noises and loud amplification. Perhaps it is not the volume of his loud sections nor the absolute silence of his soft passages but their relationship to each other that makes this music so riveting.

The genres of music Beethoven cultivated also became the popular vehicles for concert music for centuries. Most of his orchestral works (nine symphonies, various overtures and dances) call for a larger orchestra than Haydn's and Mozart's, not only in numbers but also in the way the instruments are used. Beethoven frequently featured wind instruments in his orchestral textures; his use of trombones in three of his symphonies (Nos. 5, 6, and 9) and his fondness for the piccolo (Nos. 5, 6, and 9) and the contrabassoon (Nos. 5 and 9) show his taste for the expansion of sounds both at the high and low ranges of wind timbres.

When Beethoven wrote choral works intended to impress his audience with grandiose concepts of sound, or when he wished to create huge, dramatic statements of grandiose texts, he used the full symphony orchestra. In the *Missa Solemnis*, for example, he not only drew upon a classical orchestra augmented by four horn and three trombone parts, but he also included the pipe organ. His use of chorus and solo singers in the *Symphony No. 9* set a precedent for many composers of later times.

Beethoven gave us more than large symphonic and choral works, however. His solo and chamber works provide us with both intimate and powerful glimpses of musical expression; they make us aware of our own ability to respond to his sounds. His chamber works, like his orchestral and choral works, have become standard repertoire for concert performance. He wrote some seventy-four chamber works for instruments, including string quartets; trios for piano, violin, and cello; quintets for two violins, two violas, and cello; and various other combinations of instruments. His solo compositions not only include many works for piano (Beethoven was himself a pianist) but sonatas for the violin, viola, and cello. His many songs for piano and voice (numbering around eighty-six) present both pleasure and challenge to the modern singer.

Like Mozart before him, Beethoven cultivated the concerto form. His five piano concertos and his single violin concerto combine the individual expression of the solo instrument with the power of the orchestra—a fitting genre for this composer.

The Shaping of a Musical Giant: A Biographical Sketch of Beethoven

Beethoven's attitudes of independence and freedom fit him well, for they were born of a life of challenge. No one would have predicted that the newborn Ludwig van Beethoven, the man destined to expand the horizons of music in Europe, would amount to anything special. His father, Johann Beethoven, was a musician, a singer in the court at Bonn, but he also was addicted to alcohol.

Ludwig's childhood was filled with the tirades of his father, who recognized his son's musical talent and wanted to exploit it for profit, as had Mozart's father. According to contemporary reports, Ludwig was frequently the target of his father's insults and angry outbursts. Because of Johann's eagerness to profit from his son's musical skills, Ludwig's formal education was cut short. The young Beethoven had no formal schooling after his eleventh year. As a result, his math skills were elementary, and his knowledge of foreign languages (namely French and Italian) was acquired by practical experience and never developed to a level of sophistication. Thus the prospects for Ludwig van Beethoven to become a man of stature in his field of endeavor were indeed slim.

The people who helped shape Beethoven's success as a composer come from a variety of backgrounds. Like many other budding composers, Ludwig sought out successful composers for criticism and suggestions.

Christian Gottlob Neefe, court organist for the Elector Max Friedrich in Bonn, earned a place in history because he was Beethoven's first, and perhaps most significant private teacher. Sometime in 1781, in Beethoven's eleventh year, the distinguished Neefe began teaching Ludwig on the keyboard; one of his principal vehicles for instruction was the collection of preludes and fugues by J. S. Bach, the *Welltempered Clavier*, thereby providing Beethoven with a basic knowledge of counterpoint. It also was most likely Neefe who urged Beethoven to go to Vienna, the city where Mozart had realized his success, in order to further his career.

During the first twenty-two years of his life, while he was living in Bonn, Beethoven acquired remarkable keyboard performance skills and a solid working knowledge of orchestral and vocal music. And, although his Opus 1 is dated from 1793–1795, it is widely accepted that he was very busy composing prior to his moving to Vienna.

Once in Vienna, the aspiring composer sought out Franz Joseph Haydn for lessons. It was not their first meeting; two years prior, Haydn had traveled through Bonn, and Beethoven had had an opportunity to show the revered master a cantata that he had composed. Only scant historical detail exists about the two musicians' relationship, but we know that Beethoven had taken coffee with Haydn at a Vienna restaurant, for he made note of it in a diary. Ludwig paid tribute to Haydn by dedicating his Opus 1 trios to him in 1795; the first three piano sonatas, Opus 2, also bear a dedication to Joseph Haydn. We know too that Beethoven sought out additional training in composition from a well-known teacher and composer, Johann Albrechtsberger. His other private teachers during the early Vienna years were Johann Schenk and Antonio Salieri, the opera composer and now-famous rival of Mozart.

The list of aristocrats and nobility who supported music in and around Vienna is long, and only a few need be mentioned to illustrate their importance to Beethoven's life. In Vienna, Beethoven supported himself by giving piano performances in the salons of the wealthy, teaching, dedicating works to patrons from which he received remuneration, selling his compositions either to publishers or offering "subscriptions" to acquaintances, and organizing public concerts. Beethoven succeeded in all of these activities, thanks to an aristocracy that not only supported the arts but felt a strong need for their presence. Among these were Count Ferdinand Waldstein, Austrian Prince Josef Franz Maximilian Lobkowitz, Archduke Rudolf, and Prince Ferdinand Kinsky.

Beethoven, who was conditioned to adversity at an early age, underwent a sobering experience in his early thirties; he realized that he was losing his hearing. In 1802, he wrote a letter to his brothers Caspar and Johann in which he outlines his mental anguish upon discovering this problem. The letter, known as the *Heiligenstadt Testament*, states,

> But only consider, that, for the last six years, I have been attacked by an incurable complaint, aggravated by the unskillful treatment of medical men, disappointed from year to year in the hope of relief, and at last obliged to submit to the endurance of an evil, the cure of which may last perhaps for years, if it is practicable at all. . . . If I strove at any time to set myself above all this, oh how cruelly was I driven back by the doubly painful experience of my defective hearing! Yet it was not possible for me to say to people, "Speak louder—bawl—for I am deaf!"

The lengthy letter goes on to describe the circumstances of his torment, and it speaks of death:

> I hasten to meet death with joy. If he comes before I have had occasion to develop all my professional abilities, he will come too soon for me in spite of my hard fate, and I should wish that he had delayed his arrival. But even then I am content, for he will release me from a state of endless suffering.[2]

Beethoven did not die in his twenty-eighth year but lived until age fifty-six. His deafness, which became total by his thirty-sixth year, was only one of the several afflictions that besieged him. His illnesses ranged from continuing gastric problems to typhus, rheumatic fever, eye infections, and fevers. He looked upon these as something to overcome with a strong will.

He was intensely devoted to composition, so much so that he was often gruff with his acquaintances. His intellectual interests were evident in the books that he owned and read, including the Greek classics and the latest literature from his times.

Beethoven found great personal fulfillment in being in the country and communing with nature. His personal philosophy was no doubt shaped by his feelings for the beauty of nature, and although there seems to be no evidence that he worshiped regularly at church, he nonetheless seemed to recognize God as an omnipotent presence. His most famous sacred work, the *Missa Solemnis*, is a passionate and an elegant statement of the fundamental tenets of Christian faith, composed by someone fully acquainted with the aesthetic meaning of the text.

Form and Content: Listening to Beethoven's Music

The following selection is perhaps the most famous symphony in the history of music. In this work, Beethoven achieved an ideal balance between the intellectual concepts of structure and an emotional expression that is remembered for a lifetime by those who come to know it.

Listening Guide 32

Symphony No. 5 in C Minor, Op. 67
Mvt. 1, Allegro con brio
Ludwig van Beethoven (1770–1827)

1808
Performed by the Cleveland Orchestra
George Szell, conductor
CD No. 2, Track 10 (6:05)

*B*eethoven's Fifth Symphony grows out of one rhythmic motive. The first four notes that begin this popular work are undoubtedly the most famous in music history.

Beethoven: Opening motive
to *Symphony No. 5,* Mvt. 1.

Its basic idea is very simple—three short notes followed by a long note; some people call it a knocking motive. The danger to the composer is that such an idea can become overrepetitive. It may bore instead of inspire; it may be received by the listener as trite. We will see how Beethoven avoids the pitfalls by using this simple concept artfully.

The composer not only used this rhythm thirteen times in the first twenty measures of the first movement, but he unified the entire symphony with it. Each movement contains reference to this motive. This usage is called **cyclical.** A melody or musical idea is said to be cyclical when it appears in several different movements of a multimovement work.

In the "Allegro con brio" (fast, with brilliance), we can observe Beethoven's ability to create a feeling of power, his means of building and sustaining tension, and his highly developed skills in manipulating feelings of motion. Beethoven uses the orchestra with greater versatility than is found in the works of earlier composers. At times he features a solo instrument; at other times, the entire orchestra is pounding out a rhythm. As you listen to this movement, be especially aware of the instruments that furnish the accompaniment for the principal themes. For example, discover how Beethoven cleverly provides linear continuity by having the woodwind instruments play sustained pitches arranged in chords.

To Consider

1. One of the most fascinating aspects of this movement is the way in which Beethoven passes around different melodic material from instrument to instrument. What does this technique accomplish with regard to your musical interest?
2. What musical devices are contained in this work that help you predict when principal sections of the piece are coming to an end?
3. How does Beethoven create tension in this work? How does the development section compare to the exposition, for example, with regard to tension and the feeling of motion?

Exposition

0:00 The two statements of the opening motive provide a tonal framework for the movement, although one cannot tell whether it is C minor or E-flat major until the accompanying instruments present a C minor chord.

0:46 The horn interjects a brief introduction to theme B, now given to the woodwinds. Its character is typically a second subject quality—more lyrical than the opening four-note motive. The tonality has now changed to B-flat major. Notice that the accompaniment uses the germ motive in the bass line.

1:09 The volume and rhythmic excitement builds into a tempestuous closing statement for the exposition.

1:28 The exposition is not repeated verbatim in this performance; the conductor chooses to go right to the development section.

Development

1:29   The development section is dominated again by the four-note germ motive. Listen to the sustained woodwinds, which offer some contrast to the pounding insistence of the central idea. Notice the role that arpeggios play in the development.

Recapitulation

2:53   The central idea returns in full orchestra. Beethoven soon adds a variant to the recapitulation by assigning the oboe a line that momentarily stops all motion. It is almost like a brief cadenza.

3:49   The second subject is now presented in a minor key (in keeping with the standard expectations of the sonata-allegro form).

Coda

4:35   The extended coda is one of Beethoven's trademarks, and this coda begins in a false recapitulation—where the listener is led to believe that the music is once again returning to the opening. Just as it seems this movement is going to last for a long time, Beethoven ends it with strong tonic and dominant chords.

In this selection, we have seen how Beethoven uses the principles of repetition and contrast in manipulating various elements of composition. His contrasts occur through changes in dynamics, tempo, accompanimental rhythms, range of instruments and register, and—in his orchestral works—instrumentation. Beethoven's range of expression is much more broadly drawn than is Mozart's, so much so that his music is now recognized as being seminal to the Romantic Era of music history. In spite of their differences, both Mozart and Beethoven show a finely developed sense of expressive nuance.

CLASSICAL MUSIC OF SOUTH INDIA

To the average American citizen, the term "classical music" conjures up images of musicians performing on a concert stage, playing or singing music originating from Western European influences. Although this world of classical music offers a lifetime of musical exploration to the curious mind and ear, it is important to realize that so-called classical traditions are not unique to the European culture but also are cultivated in various regions throughout the world.

In this chapter so far we have encountered the music of Western Europe, which is organized around patterns of repetition and contrast and is representative of the era of Western music history known as the Classical Era. Earlier we discussed the rather confusing term *classical* and pursued its various meanings connected to music. We know that the music of Haydn, Mozart, and Beethoven emphasizes structural principles that were universally adhered to in that particular musical culture. Their music, however, is not only classical from the standpoint of structures and aesthetic content, but because it is a living statement of abstract thought in music.

Significant to our increasingly broad perspectives of music is the knowledge and awareness that classical concepts are not unique to the Western culture. Like people of Western European tradition, many other cultures have strongly cultivated art music that has survived over the centuries.

To sample such an expression from a world perspective we will consider classical music from South India—music of the Karnatak culture. India's rich musical culture is represented both by folk styles and classical music; its music follows strong traditions, both in its compositional practices and in the way in which it is performed. The Karnatak

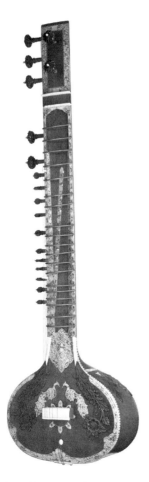

Sitar (North India). Photo by: C Squared Studios. Source: PhotoDisc, Inc. ID # OS34094.

culture centers primarily in South India and is contrasted by the Hindustānī tradition in the north. These two musical cultures have much in common, but they are separated by the strong Muslim influence that is prevalent in the northern regions.

Just as certain underlying principles of composition exist in the classical music of Mozart and Beethoven—concepts such as repetition and contrast, homophonic and polyphonic textures, clarity of formal structure, and so on—similar principles are common to classical music in India. Both Hindustānī and Karnatak music stem from the same ancient tradition, and both are founded on the concept of **rāgas**—the melodic system comprised of several hundred entities, or gestures. A rāga actually includes a variety of concepts in a unique relationship: a selection of pitches often in a distinctive melodic shape, a system of ornamentation, a basic scale of pitches, varying from five to nine notes, and concepts of emotion that relate to the ordering of pitches in the melody (commonly referred to as **modes**). The rhythm of the music is called the **tāla,** a term that means "the palm of the hand" and refers to the musical beat.

Musicians must study diligently to learn the many basic rāgas, the complex practices of ornamentation, which, along with the repertoire of rhythmic patterns of the metric system (called tāl, or tāla), form the basic musical elements of this music and also reflect the aesthetic theories of the Indian culture. The famous Ravi Shankar, for example, studied with the guru Baba Ustad Allaudin Khan for several years before he emerged in 1955 as an accomplished artist and creator of Indian music. He is internationally known as a **sitar** artist.

The basic texture in both Hindustānī and Karnatak music is a single line of melody, a drone, and rhythms played by a drum. This characteristic ensemble is basic both to instrumental and vocal music and is often augmented by a second melodic stringed instrument which accompany either a vocal or an instrumental solo. The sitar and the sarod are two popular plucked lute-type instruments common to the Hindustānī culture, as is the sārangī, a bowed lute. The drone is produced by the tāmbūr, and the most frequently found drum is the tabla—a set of two drums handbeaten by one player.

Instrumental traditions in South India include the ghatam, a clay pot, a tambourine-type instrument called the kanjīra, and a double-headed cylindrical wooden drum, the mridangam. In the south, the **vīna** replaces the sitar as the most popular soloistic string instrument; the Western-style violin also is used to support vocal music, but the tuning and the playing technique are adapted to Karnatak musical styles.[3]

The golden age of Karnatak (South India) music occurred in the eighteenth century, when several principal composers/performers emerged. In South India, composers Muthusnamy Dikshitar (1775–1835), Shyama Shastry (1762–1827), and Tyagaraja (1767–1847) have often been compared to the "Three Great B's" of European music: Bach, Beethoven,

The Vina (Southern India). A Hill School painting from Bilaspur depicts Madhava with Vina in a forest, ca. 1725. National Museum of New Delhi. © Angelo Hornak / CORBIS. ID # AH001293.

and Brahms. Their compositions originally were patronized by the higher classes, and only the privileged strata learned the intricacies of structure and expression of this music and also learned to perform it. Now, however, a much broader audience enjoys the classical music of India—an audience that includes even the Western world.

The following selection, a performance of a rāga and tāla composed by classical composer Tyagaraja (1767–1847), illustrates an approach to musical composition from a culture totally different from the Western tradition. It is performed by two virtuoso musicians, Shri Emani Shankara Sastry, a vīna artist, and Shri Madras A. Kannan, a percussionist, playing the mridangam. Both are held in highest respect in South India and represent many years of private study and public performances.

Listening Guide 33

Vara Narada Narayana: Rāga
Vijarasri Adi: Tāla
Tyagaraja (1767–1847)

Instrumental composition from South India
Recorded by Shri Emani Shankara Sastry, vīna,
and Shri Madras A. Kannan, mridangam
CD No. 2, Track 11 (5:16)

This rāga is performed on the vīna, a seven-stringed lute. The vīna's sound case is made of hardwood from the bread tree; its neck is a fingerboard having two bands of wax that support twenty-four bars, or frets. Four strings are for the melody; the remaining three are used to produce rhythm.

The drum, which plays the tāla—or the structural rhythmic formula—is the mridangam, a tunable double-headed drum. One head is often tuned to the fundamental note of the piece, called the **Sa,** and the other to the tone a fifth above the Sa, named the **Pa.** We are reminded here that in Western music, the same pitches are treated as primary (the tonic and the dominant).

To Consider

1. As you listen to this composition, be aware that this classical music of India is not structured on the principles of stating a theme, manipulating that theme, and repeating, or summarizing, it.
2. Can you describe some general features of this music as they relate to the unfolding of time? How does the composer sustain your interest—even if you are totally unfamiliar with this music?
3. Can you identify certain pitches that seem to be the cornerstone of the vīna melodic material? After hearing two or three minutes of this music, did you feel the persistence of these pitches?

0:00	The opening three repeated notes appear to function as an introduction and are soon given accompanimental support from the drone strings of the vīna.
0:10	The mridangam enters, adding another layer to the work and playing rhythms that are independent from the rhythmic elements of the vīna but seem to complement the general flow of the music as it unfolds.
0:45	If you listen carefully, you will come to realize that the pitches of the drum (the mridangam) are the same pitches around which the melodies of the vīna are structured.
0:53	A short section begins in which the vīna works out ornamented material without the support of the drum.
1:05	Gradually, the mridangam punctuates the musical texture, careful not to compete with the vīna at this point. A rhythmic element in the drone strings becomes apparent in this section.
1:58	Mridangam rhythms now become increasingly complex as the composition acquires a new level of excitement.
2:31	Now the drum begins to capture moments of prominence under the persistence of the two principal pitches of the vīna (pitches E and B).

A second listening will reinforce the existence of a conscious structure in this rāga and tāla. To the musical audience from South India, the inherent formal practices are no doubt as obvious as are the concepts of exposition-development-recapitulation to those well grounded in the classical music of the Western culture. Our musical encounter with South Indian music has a common ground for its first point of entry—a structural scheme. To the Western ear, the repetitive effect of the drone, the inflections of pitch that are part of the system of ornamentation, and the complex relationship between the melodic gestures and rhythmic content are fascinating points of exploration.

SUMMARY

The music of the Classical Era in Western civilization is characterized by close attention to the principles of balance, clarity, and logic, which are manifested in music as patterns of repetition and contrast. This general approach to musical composition and aesthetics mirrored the general feeling of the times, for philosophers, artists, and composers sought to discover and develop basic rules for life based on Nature and Reason. Toward the end of the eighteenth century, however, these attitudes that were so much a part of intellectual and political thought found strong direction through an emphasis on the individual and hence on freedom. The resulting revolutionary spirit further supported concepts of individuality and gave new life to the culture.

In music, a significant byproduct of the movement that began as the Enlightenment and moved into revolutionary concepts is the large body of artfully constructed music that was created by composers of this era. This "classical" music has served a public with endless musical pleasure for centuries, and it will no doubt continue to do so for the foreseeable future.

The classical traditions of Western culture, however, are by no means the only traditions from the past that survive in the world of music. An example of a living classical culture is the musical practices of India—a land in which the music of both Hindustānī and Karnatic traditions continues to flourish, as new performers become skilled in the musical practices and literature of the past and combine them with contemporary approaches to their art.

KEY TERMS

abstract (or absolute) music
cyclical
da capo
melodic sequences
minuet and trio
minuet and trio form
modes
ornamentation
Pa
piano concerto
rãgas

rondo form
Sa
sitar
sonata
sonata-allegro form
symphony
tāla
ternary form
theme and variations
vīna

CHAPTER 7

The Spirit of Romanticism

So far in *Musical Encounters* we have concentrated on listening techniques, on the broad diversity of sounds that comes under the rubric of music, and on two fundamental approaches to composition—counterpoint and repetition and contrast. We also have discovered that musical styles and practices do not exist in isolation but rather result from broader aesthetic and cultural trends. For example, we observed how the concept of ornamentation and complex textures was expressed in the music of Johann Sebastian Bach and also in the art of Gianlorenzo Bernini during the Baroque Era. We also saw the concern for balance in a painting by Jacques Louis David and in the musical structures of Wolfgang Amadeus Mozart.

In Chapters 7 and 8, our focus is on Romantic art music, an aesthetic movement that flourished in the nineteenth century, and on the relationship of music to emotions. Using techniques of composition derived from both Baroque counterpoint and Classical repetition and contrast, composers in the Romantic Era found ways to extend musical expressions to new emotional heights and to explore new techniques. In order to be successful musicians, they were aware—either consciously or intuitively—of the opportunities presented to them by their specific cultural environments. In that sense, they were both products of their own time and shapers of their own destiny, for their compositions helped express their private thoughts as they in turn spoke for the aesthetic tastes of their times.

As in earlier chapters, the internal structures that composers develop in the creation of music will be examined. We also will consider the dimensions of music that have to do with the references the listener might bring to enhance the enjoyment of music. These may be in the form of emotional reactions that are stimulated by certain musical gestures, by memories and reminiscences of personal events that the listener recalls when hearing the music, or in some cases, by a story that served as a starting place for the composer to create. In other words, it is possible to enjoy Hector Berlioz's *Symphonie Fantastique* on a purely musical level, by noting and appreciating the themes, harmonies, orchestration, and nuances of dynamics and tempo. However, the listening experience is greatly enhanced by a knowledge of the specific background information—in this case, the ability to imagine feelings and images stimulated by the story that inspired the music, which Berlioz expected his listeners to bring to the work.

During the Romantic Era (ca. 1815–1900), composers exploited a fascinating duality of music—both its attractiveness, as a purely abstract expression of sound manipulation, and its ability to evoke basic emotions, images, and memories in an almost pictorial way. The interplay between abstract (or absolute) music and pictorial (or program) music is a strong feature that links a broad array of forms, styles, and performance practices in nineteenth-century music. Although music of all periods reflects emotions and may be inspired by ideas coming from outside of the realm of pitches, rhythms, and other musical elements, it is the intensity with which nineteenth-century composers linked music to emotion that gives Romanticism its characteristic spirit.

ROMANTICISM IN THE ARTS

The libertarian and egalitarian ideals of the French Revolution often are cited as forces in the late eighteenth and early nineteenth centuries that gave rise to the aesthetic movement known as Romanticism. In the previous chapter, we saw an example of this revolutionary spirit as envisioned by Romantic artist Eugène Delacroix when he depicted Liberty as a woman leading a revolutionary battle.

Expressions of romanticism, however, go beyond the ideals of the French Revolution, for they also are influenced by a growing interest in a return to nature and an emphasis on the goodness of humanity. Even when artists, novelists, poets, and musicians looked back in history for sources of inspiration for their paintings, stories, poems, and compositions, they gave their creative works a personal interpretation that allowed their public a glimpse of their emotions and inner thoughts.

Such emotions are apparent in Franz Schubert's song based on Goethe's poem *Die Erlkönig*—the subject of our first musical selection in Chapter 7. This poem creates a vivid image of a father holding his dying son tightly in his arms as he rides his horse through a dark and windy night in a futile attempt to find security. Frequent references to the wind, the misty clouds, and the darkness set an emotional stage for the story.

In his painting *Two Men Contemplating the Moon,* Caspar David Friedrich (1774–1840), Germany's leading Romantic painter, captures a night scene reminiscent of the pictorial image created by Goethe's poem (see color plate No. 6). The two men—the subjects of the painting—are overshadowed by the size of the rocks in the foreground and by the haunting effect of the sprawling tree limbs framing them. The moon is far away, a distant glimmer casting an eerie light on the scene. By enveloping his subjects in an exaggerated view of the night setting around them, Friedrich is successful in establishing a strong emotional content, even though no action is depicted in this painting.

The American pioneer of Romantic art, John Singleton Copley (1738–1815), created a different type of emotional experience in his *Watson and the Shark* (1778), an action painting based on a real-life experience of a young British sailor who was attacked by a shark while swimming in the Havana harbor. (The date of this painting predates the time commonly associated with the Romantic movement in music, but it is consistent with the beginnings of the era in literature and art.) Copley, a native of Boston, moved to London two years prior to the American Revolution, and he was recognized widely for his portrait painting. His style, however, was more down to earth than that of his contemporary, Gainsborough, and he ventured into the realm of Romantic expression with his *Watson and the Shark*. This painting, now his most famous work, was commissioned by Brook Watson, the young man who was attacked by a shark but was rescued after having lost his foot in the incident. Watson went on to become a prominent businessman, a member of Parliament, a Commissary General to the British armies in America, and eventually, Lord Mayor of London. (See Color Plate #7)

Art historian Horst Waldemar Janson describes *Watson and the Shark* in the following manner (notice the references to past literary and biblical references in Janson's interpretation of the painting):

> [Copley] made every detail as authentic as possible (here the black man has the purpose of the Indian in *The Death of General Wolfe*) and utilized all the resources of Baroque painting to invite the beholder's participation. The shark becomes a monstrous embodiment of evil, the man with the boat hook resembles an Archangel Michael fighting Satan, and the nude youth flounders helplessly between the forces of doom and salvation. Copley may also have recalled representations of Jonah and the Whale: these include the elements of his scene, although the action is reversed (the prophet is thrown overboard into the jaws of the sea monster). The charging of a private adventure with the emotional and symbolic qualities of myth is highly characteristic of Romanticism.[1]

Although one can find many examples of the Romantic aesthetic in paintings dating from the late eighteenth and early nineteenth centuries, the Romantic movement's strength lies in the great outpouring of literature from this time. In England, the publication of the *Lyrical Ballads* (1798) by Wordsworth and Coleridge fostered an attitude that poetry results from "the spontaneous overflow of powerful feelings." In Germany, a movement known as *Sturm und Drang* (*Storm and Stress*), a perspective that popularized a nostalgic reexamination of history (particularly medieval times), paved the way for the Romantic Era. Writers such as G. E. Lessing, J. G. Herder, Schiller, and Goethe contributed many Romantic writings to a growing market of readers that was eager to explore imaginary fantasies. Romantic literature in France is represented by the works of Victor Hugo, Chateaubriand, Alexandre Dumas, and George Sand (the female author and Chopin's friend, who wrote under a male pseudonym). In America, the works of Emerson, Thoreau, Poe, Whittier, Longfellow, Whitman, James Fenimore Cooper, Hawthorne, and Melville pursued various avenues of Romantic expression. These writers succeeded in capturing the personal involvement of the readers—not only their intellect, but their emotions—in such effective ways that the market for prose and poetry expanded to new dimensions.

Let us define the concept of Romanticism by looking at a poem. Why discuss poetry in a book about music? Simply because music and literature often are inseparable to the Romantic aesthetic. We will read *When I Have Fears that I May Cease to Be*, written by the English poet John Keats in 1817, and we will attempt to gain insights from it that can be used to define a broad concept of Romanticism.

Consider these questions as you read this poem. Was the poet old or young when he wrote this? What two basic concerns emerge from the writer as he contemplates death? What images—word pictures—does Keats use to describe his thoughts?

When I have fears that I may cease to be
   Before my pen has gleaned my teeming brain,
Before high pilèd books, in charactery,
   Hold like rich garners the full ripened grain;
When I behold, upon the night's starred face,
   Huge cloudy symbols of a high romance,
And think that I may never live to trace
   Their shadows, with the magic hand of chance;
And when I feel, fair creature of an hour,
   That I may never look upon thee more,
Never have relish in the faery power
   Of unreflecting love;—then on the shore
Of the wide world I stand alone, and think
Till love and fame to nothingness do sink.

The perspective a young person brings to the realities of life is a theme that seems to recur in nineteenth-century art, as it does in this Keats poem (incidentally, Keats died at age twenty-six). His two concerns—his dreams—are stated in the last line: they are love and fame. The fame Keats desires is one built on his individual achievements, the expression of his own voice. The idea that each artist had something unique to contribute, as seen in this poem, was a strong feature of the Romantic movement. Each composer, poet, or artist worked hard to develop an individual creative expression that would offer a unique contribution to posterity. As a result, it is sometimes difficult to identify a few specific characteristics that describe all poetry, art, or music stemming from these times, for each creative artist contributed a unique perspective to his or her art.

The concept of a suffering artist often is linked to this Romantic spirit of individuality. The artist—that person of genius who must cope with a sensitive psyche, a special problem, or, at least, the burden of having a gift of creativity that cries out for fulfillment—is a phenomenon that occurs with regularity throughout the nineteenth century. For example,

Scenes from Weber's opera *Die Freischultz,* based on the German folkballad, *The Wild Huntsman;* Act III, Scene 6. © Bettmann / CORBIS. ID # S5742D.

Beethoven had to deal with the problem of deafness and continuing ill health, Schubert struggled against the ravages of syphilis, Frenchman Berlioz was tortured by his love for an English Shakespearean actress, whom he eventually married but with whom he never found long-term happiness, and Schumann fought bouts of depression that led him to attempt suicide. Chopin's respiratory problems, which first manifested when he was twenty-eight, not only affected his romance with novelist Mme. Dudevant (who wrote under the male pseudonym George Sand) but furthered the image of the suffering artist.

The idea that artists must suffer, that art is born of struggle, that good—whether truth, liberty, or fraternity—comes from human effort and travail is a concept that seems to emerge time and time again in the early nineteenth century. Whether or not a romantic composer labored under the burden of some affliction, it was popular at this time to illuminate the most difficult hardships of everyday life and to use the resulting emotions as a stimulus for creative work.

Fantasy was a popular word during the Romantic movement. It carried with it connotations of one's ability to extend the imagination freely into unknown and exotic places. Some people were taken with fantasies of the supernatural world; creative minds often engaged in imaginative portrayals of unreal situations (opera is a perfect genre for this). The pioneer of German opera, Carl Maria von Weber (1786–1826), for example, composed an opera based on a blending of folk elements and the magic of the supernatural. In *Der Freischütz* (*The Free Shooter*), the main character, Max, uses magic bullets in a shooting competition so that he might win the post of head ranger and capture the hand of a maiden, Agathe, in marriage. At midnight, seven magic bullets of silver are cast amidst magic cantations and mysterious ritual; they are supposed to always hit their mark. One of them, however, goes astray and hits Agathe—but she is protected by a bridal wreath that had been blessed by a hermit with supernatural powers.

Exotic combinations of fantasy set in the context of everyday human experiences were popular during the early Romantic era; they represented a freedom of thought that only creative imagination could express. An interesting development in early nineteenth-century culture was the flowering of popular writers and poets such as in Sir Walter Scott, Lord Byron, and Goethe, whose works inspired the public's greater awareness of literature. This increased interest in literature in turn stimulated the senses with sharp imagery and imagination. Some of the most sensational works of literature of all time, such as Mary Shelley's (1797–1851) *Frankenstein,* were written during this period.

Frankenstein, perhaps the greatest Gothic Romantic novel and the first science fiction novel, is about the creation of a monster by scientist Victor Frankenstein, who hopes to create a new species but instead gives life to a Satan figure who swears revenge on his creator and on the human race. His only salvation is through the creation of a partner and a mate, an Eve figure. Shelley's classic novel is a story that can either be read for its superficial excitement and drama—and it is indeed an effective story—or can be seen as a symbol of deeper meaning, such as Victor's anxiety and his ultimate parental abandonment to an unknown creature, or as a play between good intentions and the evil results of tempting fate. The depth of insight that the nineteen-year-old Shelley infused into this work also suggests that the young author was fully aware of life's calamities and uncertainties.

(Her perspective as a woman on such aspects as the anxiety of creating life has been a widespread topic of discussion for modern scholars.) Whatever the level of appreciation one experiences with this work, it has never failed to attract a large readership; it also has been the subject of at least forty-two movies.

A fantastic theme also is embodied in the Romantic work *Ivanhoe*, a romance by Sir Walter Scott (1771–1832), first published in 1791. It is about a knight who, upon returning from the Crusades, finds himself thwarted and disinherited in the pursuit of Lady Rowena. The images created by Scott involve scenes of peril and rescue, of chivalry and pageantry, which stimulated the minds of his readers as their imaginations carried them off to other lands and ancient times.

OMANTIC MUSIC: ITS FORMS AND STYLES

Romantic music reflects the society out of which it arose, just as musical expressions from all times reflect their social contexts. The widespread taste for vivid description found in Romantic literature also appears in the musical forms that evolved to meet the same prevailing aesthetic appetites. Composers, the agents for shaping the public's musical tastes and practices, provide their personal creative genius based on their times, and they develop musical forms and styles relevant both to their work and audience. Sometimes they find existing forms useful; other times they invent new structures in their ongoing efforts to serve their artistic and practical senses. In the nineteenth century, both approaches were used with success.

Although the well-established classical forms of music survived in the nineteenth century, the spirit of the times required some new expressions. The **art song,** popularly referred to by the German word **lied** (and its plural form **lieder**), underlined the relationship between poetry and music. Lieder are songs in which poems are set to music for solo voice and piano accompaniment. This is illustrated in Schubert's *Erlkönig* later in the chapter, and we might observe that no genre of music could be more suited to a setting of a Romantic poem than the accompanied song. The feeling of intimacy created by a solo singer and a solo instrumentalist effectively captures the personal spirit of Romantic poetry. Other genres of music came into being during this time, a result of the strong popularity of literature and Romantic imagery.

One such interesting type of music is called the **character piece,** which refers to a composition for piano that has descriptive titles but no real story connected to it. Felix Mendelssohn (1809–1847) was well known for this kind of "musical poetry" in which he could create a specific mood by writing appropriate melodies and harmonies. He called these **songs without words.** Character pieces were written with many different titles, and were very popular in private gatherings and in small recitals (called salon music).

At the other end of the spectrum is the genre called the **program symphony.** The program symphony is created to stimulate in the listener a pictorial response. At times the music is quite descriptive; at times it may be designed to establish a mood. Later in this chapter we will examine a program symphony by Frenchman Hector Berlioz (1803–1869).

A third, related type of Romantic music that again exhibits a strong taste for Romantic images and literature is the **symphonic poem**—an extended, single-movement work for symphony orchestra that often carried with it a "program." This music, initiated by Franz Liszt (1811–1886) in the second half of the century, was clearly inspired by literature. Composers found that audiences were especially drawn to this type of music, as they were drawn to epic romances. The parallel between the two genres—one literary and one musical—is certainly no coincidence.

Romantic Era composers found opera an ideal form for the dramatic blending of literature and music, and they built their stories around both contemporary subjects and

Romantic interpretations of past historical events and personalities. The music—as well as the length of the operas—grew to increasingly large proportions until, at the end of the century, German composer Richard Wagner (1813–1883) brought together four gargantuan music dramas in a cycle intended to be performed as one super musical festival. Other vocal musical genres of the past that were effective tools of Romantic music were the oratorio, large choral works with soloists and orchestra, including the traditional Mass texts, and other choral works, either with or without orchestral accompaniment.

Are all forms of music in the nineteenth century connected to a story or a specific mood? Certainly not, for the concert world was acquainted with music of the past; the abstract music of Haydn, Mozart, and Beethoven established strong precedents that composers continued to follow. Preexisting musical forms such as the symphony, the concerto, the solo sonata, and chamber music were readily adapted to nineteenth-century musical aesthetics and were used extensively by a wide variety of composers. Thus the forms of the past survived alongside the newly developed Romantic forms, for the audiences of the time were highly receptive both to abstract music and to programmatic expressions.

How did the old forms of music survive alongside newly developed genres in the nineteenth century? Together these musical structures met the aesthetic needs of the times by offering two perspectives: one was the miniature—represented by the lieder, the character piece for piano and other related short works for solo instruments and piano—and the other was the grandiose, represented by opera, oratorio, symphonies, concertos, and extended solo sonatas. Some composers were equally comfortable writing in both concepts, while others specialized in one genre. Chopin, for example, cultivated the character piece for piano, but he also wrote concertos and sonatas. Schubert is famous not only for his hundreds of songs with piano accompaniment (lieder) but also for his symphonies, his extended piano sonatas, and his chamber music. Opera composers Richard Wagner and Giuseppi Verdi are best known for their extended dramatic works (although they too composed within other genres).

Beethoven set the stage for the expanded symphony with his *Symphony No. 9*. Romantic composers, ranging from Schubert to Berlioz to Mendelssohn, Schumann, Brahms, Bruckner, Tchaikovsky, Dvorak, Sibelius, and Mahler, followed his lead and wrote symphonies that often lasted from forty minutes to over an hour in performing time. The attention span of the concertgoer was sustained by the emotional ebb and flow of the music that was built on logical, but extended, concepts of musical form. Symphonies were not only born of beautiful melodies and exciting harmonies, they also included difficult passages of virtuosity, both for individual instruments and for entire sections of the orchestra. The dynamic range of the symphony orchestra, now expanded to 100 players (and even more on some occasions) and the use of new instruments (such as the E-flat soprano clarinet, the English horn, the contra-bassoon, and the tuba), provided the composer with the tools to keep the listener awake and aware during the symphonic concert.

$\mathcal{M}$USICAL STYLE

Most music of the nineteenth century shares a strong interest in beautiful melody set in a context of expanded harmony. The most memorable melodies from this era were often vocal in nature—even when written for instruments—in that their notes seem to flow from one to another as though they could be sung. Instead of concentrating on melodies that contained short rhythmic motives to be used in later development, composers of Romantic melodies emphasized a contour with climactic peaks and smooth phrases. At times, melodies are irregular in their phrases—extending on for many measures (as we will see in Berlioz's *Symphonie Fantastique*). At other times, they are short, compact, and innocent in design, as in some of Schubert's lieder.

The three primary chords of tonality, the tonic (I), the subdominant (IV), and the dominant (V), still serve as the basis for tonality in the majority of nineteenth-century music, but now other chords—based not only on other steps of the scale but on chromatic alterations of these triads—became more widely interspersed with primary harmonies. The result was chord progressions that were more colorful and varied and less rigid and predictable.

For a look at the melodic and harmonic functions typical of Romantic music, let us examine the first eight measures of Chopin's *Prelude in B Minor, Op. 28, No. 6.* Notice that the composer has the left hand play the tune, while the right hand plays chords and sets up the rhythmic accompaniment. The climax of the melody, which occurs in measure five, is supported by colorful, chromatic chords as it works toward the end of the phrase.

Chopin, *Prelude in B Minor, Op. 28, No. 6* (meas. 1-8, with fingering indications).

Techniques of Baroque music, such as the fugue and melodies spun out from a single rhythmic idea, were not as popular in Romantic music. If you listen carefully to concert music from the nineteenth century, however, you will be able to hear moments of counterpoint from time to time.

One outstanding feature of music in the nineteenth century is the expansion of instrumental music and the experimentation with orchestral colors. It became the focus of many composers. This expansion of sounds can be compared to the enormous changes in our times brought about by the synthesizer and by computer-generated music. Prior to the 1900s, before electronic technology was developed, composers relied on acoustic instruments, and they found that the combination of various timbres produced by the instruments yielded a wide array of interesting sounds and gave them an extended palette of tonal colors with which to paint their musical pictures.

Finally, significant to nineteenth-century music is the element of contrast between simplicity and difficulty as related to performance. At times, the musical expressions were almost naively simple—gentle tunes played or sung in comfortable ranges of the instruments and voices, set to common rhythms and phrase structures. In other instances, the music became extremely difficult and demanded great skill from the performers. This contrast, which is not unlike the contrast between the miniature and the grandiose forms of music, gave the music a diverse and an exciting quality.

A NEW AUDIENCE FOR MUSIC

An interesting phenomenon happened in the musical world in the nineteenth century—the public concert came into its own. In fact, the ramifications of this primarily European development spread across the Atlantic to the United States. Whereas at first most great performances in America came from imported musicians and instruments, soon choral societies began springing up, and toward the end of the century, Americans began to see the founding of symphony orchestras, opera companies, and philharmonic societies—organizations that firmly established concert life in our country.

But the public concert was not all that was popular during this time. The availability of music written for the individual player or singer, the publication of instruction books in music, the growing number of people teaching private music lessons, and the proliferation of musical instruments were all factors that supported a healthy musical environment. And, of course, live music was the only performance option, one of the few types of entertainment available before television, radio, movies, or recordings.

Musical Encounter

Piano Manufacturing and Marketing in the 1800s

As the electric guitar would revolutionize popular music and serve as the springboard for rock and roll in the 1950s, the piano influenced the world of music in the nineteenth century. As the century progressed, the piano underwent technological developments—such as the use of heavier steel framing, stronger tension on the strings, and a more sophisticated action—that improved its tonal quality, dynamic range, and responsiveness to the pianist's subtle touch. In its improved condition, the post–Beethoven piano became so popular that manufacturing companies sprang up in many major cities and turned out pianos by the thousands for an eager public. For example, by 1824, there were fifty piano makers in London; by 1834, Parisian piano maker Pleyel & Co. had 250 employees and produced an amazing 1,000 pianos a year; the competing firm Sébastian Erard made 400 instruments with 150 workers. Using manufacturing techniques developed as part of the Industrial Revolution, mass quantities of instruments were created. Improvements in the action, tone, and general expressive possibilities of the piano were a constant process.[2]

The mass manufacturing and sale of pianos was not limited to Europe either. Boston, Philadelphia, and New York became the leading musical centers in the United States. In 1829, almost 2,500 pianos were sold in these three cities alone, most imported from Europe. Using techniques developed in Europe, American builders soon began manufacturing instruments on a large scale. In Boston, the Chickering Company competed with the best European pianos. By 1860 (the year of the first national statistics on manufacturing), 21,000 pianos were built in the United States.[3]

Beethoven's piano (1803) at the Beethoven house in Bonn, Germany. © Bettmann / CORBIS. ID # BE035980.

Composers met the demand for music by writing feverishly for an expanding market: art songs (lieder) and character pieces for piano, as well as sonatas, and concertos were bought, practiced, and performed privately and publicly at an increasing frequency. The rising middle class, because of the Industrial Revolution, found music accessible to them. Composers began to depend more and more upon the public and less upon the generosity of the nobility for their source of income.

Music had now become much more of a "universal language" than ever before. When one considers the various forces that came together to foster musical growth, it is easy to understand why music was a suitable vehicle for the emotional, artistic, intellectual, and entertainment needs of a populace coming into a greater awareness of life's offerings.

FRANZ SCHUBERT: POPULAR SONGWRITER

The genre of music that most directly illustrates the Romantic concept of linking literature and music is the lied, and lieder are best illustrated by the works of the early nineteenth-century composer Franz Schubert (1797–1828.) During his short life, Schubert composed over 600 lieder, using the poetry of contemporaries such as Wolfgang Goethe, Heinrich Schiller, and Henrich Heine, as well as poets from the past, such as Shakespeare. In his lieder, Schubert takes great care to relate the poetry to the music, often by using the piano to create imagery to support the story of the words, or to underline the emotion of the text. Thus the piano is not a mere accompaniment but an integral part of the composition.

Schubert's position in history is a curious one, for although he lived in Vienna, the musical center of Europe at the time, he also lived in the same city where Beethoven was the supreme composer. Our modern perspective—some 200 years after Schubert's birth—allows us to comprehend his significance, but the Viennese public of the early 1800s never came to understand fully the genius of this composer. For Schubert, establishing a place in Beethoven's city was not easy, and he never came to enjoy financial success.

His father was a schoolteacher and an amateur cellist; early in his life, his parents discovered his talent for music and arranged for him to take violin, piano, organ, and singing lessons. At age eleven, he auditioned for and was accepted in the Vienna court choir, a position that included the best professional training available for youths at the Imperial and Royal City College—a highly select boarding school. (The internationally known Vienna Boys' Choir had its origins with this tradition.) There Schubert distinguished himself as a singer and as a budding composer; his earliest song was written in 1811, his first symphony in 1813, and his first Mass in 1814. By the time the young composer reached his late teens, his composition skills were well honed and mature. (In 1815, for example, he composed 145 songs. His *Erlkönig*—the subject of our next musical selection, was written during this year; it earned him widespread recognition six years later, when it was finally published.)

Schubert's creative successes, however, did not find a financial correlative, for he was forced to leave the college in the fall of 1813. Bowing to familial pressure, he enrolled in a training institute for elementary teachers, and, by 1814 he was teaching at his father's school. He soon experienced the conflict between carrying out the drudgery of his duties in the schoolroom and trying to find time to develop a career as a composer. During this period of his life, Schubert's songs were beginning to attract the attention of many, but Beethoven, the master composer in Vienna, failed to give him his enthusiastic support—which would have furthered his career remarkably. Neither his meager income from publishing nor his teacher's salary provided him with a comfortable living; in 1816, he applied unsuccessfully for a position as a music master in a training school for elementary teachers in another city. Instead, he moved in with a friend, Josef Witteczek, who later became a major resource for Schubert followers, for he collected a large repertoire of Schubert's first editions, memoirs, and manuscripts. The house where Schubert and Witteczek lived soon became the center of small gatherings and private concerts, which became known as *Schubertiade* (or The Schubert concerts).

In 1819, after his father obtained a post as master of a school at Rossau, a district adjacent to Vienna, Schubert left his friendly atmosphere and took a teaching job in his father's new school, but he never found teaching fulfilling. There he suffered from bouts of depression, and worried about becoming a "thwarted musician."[3] Wherever he lived, however, he continued to compose new works. This was also true when he moved for a while to Hungary, where he taught the children of Count Johann Esterházy. He complained, "At Zseliz I am obliged to rely wholly on myself. I have to be composer, author, audience and goodness knows what else. Not a soul here has any feeling for true art, or at the most the countess now and again."[4]

With the end of the summer season of 1819, and with the end of the Esterházy's vacation season, Schubert returned to Vienna, where he moved in with another friend, Mayrhofer. Here the composer enjoyed a very fruitful, active musical life, and compositions kept flowing from his pen. His works included many songs, works for chorus, piano pieces, and symphonic works, but he still was unable to profit substantially from composing. In 1821, when he had already written over 600 works, a public performance of *The Erlking* attracted the attention of the publishers Cappi & Diabelli, and they agreed to publish twenty of his songs.

Throughout the remainder of his life in Vienna, Schubert, in spite of his momentary financial successes, lived the life of a struggling artist. His problems were further exacerbated by bouts of syphilis—a common, incurable sexually transmitted disease—that he contacted in 1821, and he often experienced depression and extreme discomfort as a result. His final illness came in the form of typhus, to which he succumbed on November 19, 1828. At his request, he was buried close to Beethoven's grave—ironically, the two composers had only met once; in 1888, both composers' graves were moved to a central location in the Vienna Zentralfriedhof. The remains of Schubert, Beethoven, and Brahms (who died in 1897) now reside in neighboring proximity.

Schubert's works comprise forty volumes in their modern edition. Today, his songs, piano sonatas, symphonies, chamber works, and Masses are performed throughout the world wherever Western culture has reached. His *Unfinished Symphony*, so named because it has only two movements, rivals the symphonies of Beethoven in fame. His lieder became the model for many composers who followed him.

Engraving of *The Erlking.* Erlkoenig works mischief by frightening children, theme of Schubert's famous song. German woodcut, 1840.
© Bettmann / CORBIS.
ID # PG16258.

*L*istening Guide 34

Erlkönig (The Erlking)
Franz Schubert (1797–1828)

German lied
1815
Recorded by Dietrich Fischer-Dieskau, with Gerald
   Moore, piano
CD No. 2, Track 12 (4:17)

---

*T*he *Erlkönig (Erlking)* is in the form of a **ballad**—a long narrative musical setting of a poem
that tells a story. This song includes four characters: a narrator who introduces and concludes
the story; the Erlking, a messenger of death who is luring a child away; the child, who is slowing
dying; and the child's father. In the poem, the father is on horseback riding frantically through the
night with his dying child in his arms. As he tries to find help for his son, the Erlking, the angel of
death, is hovering and speaking to the child.

One can hear the galloping of the horse from the very first measure of this song, for Schubert
represents it with repeated triplet figures (three notes to one beat) in the right hand of the piano.
The sound is mysterious and foreboding—the short, G-minor melodic fragment interjected in the
bass line helps establish the general mood of the piece.

Franz Schubert, *The Erlking* (piano, meas. 1-4).

This Romantic poem contains several elements that held fascination for the public at that
time: death related to youth and a mysterious element of the supernatural, in the setting of a "dark
and stormy night." The poem contains both action and dialogue. Notice how skillfully Goethe is
able to bring his story to life through this device.

Wer reitet so späte durch Nacht und Wind?	Who rides so late through night and wind?
Es is der Vater mit seinem Kind;	It is a father with his child;
Er hat den Knaben wohl in dem Arm	He holds his boy fast in his arms
Er fasst ihm sicher, er hält ihn warm.	He clasps him tightly, he keeps him warm.
"Mein Sohn, was birgst du so band dein Gesicht?"	"My son, why are you hiding your face so in fear?"
"Siehst, Vater, du den Erlkönig niche?	"Father, don't you see the Erlking is near?
Den Erlenkönig mit Kron' und Schweif?"	The Erlking with his crown and wand?"
"Mein Sohn, es ist ein Nebelstreif."	"My son, it's only a misty cloud."
"Du liebes Kind, komm, geh' mit mir!	"You dear sweet boy, come go with me!
Gar schöne Spiele spiel' ich mit dir;	Such pleasant games I'll play with thee;
Manch' bunte Blumen sind an dem Strand,	Many bright flowers are growing there,
Meine Mutter hat manch' gülden Gewand."	My mother has many golden clothes to wear."

"Meine Vater, mein Vater, und hörest
du nicht,
Was Erlenkönig mir leise verspricht?"
"Sei ruhig, bleibe ruhig, mein Kind:
In düren Blätterb säuselt der Wind."
"Willst, feiner Knabe, du mit mir gehn?
Meine Töchter sollen dich warten schön;
Meine Töchter führen den nächtlichen
Reihn'
Und wiegen und tanzen und singen
dich ein."
"Mein Vater, mein Vater, und siehst
du nich dort
Erlkönigs Töchter am düstern Ort?"
"Mein Sohn, mein Sohn, ich seh' es genau:
Es scheinen die alten Weiden so grau."
"Ich liebe dich, mich reizt deine schöne
Gestalt;
Und bist du nich willig, so brauch' ich
Gewalt."
"Mein Vater, mein Vater, jetzt fasst er
mich an!
Erlkönig hat mir ein Leids getan!"
Dem Vater grauset's er reitet geschwind
Er hält in dem Armen das ächzende Kind,
Erreicht den Hof mit Müh' und Not;
In seinen Armen das Kind—war tot.

"Oh, Father, my father, can you not hear,

The Erlking's voice in my ear?"
"Be still, stay calm, my child:
It's the wind in the leaves that you hear."
"Sweet child, won't you come with me?
My pretty daughters will wait upon thee;
Each night they will show you new places
to go
And rock you, and dance with you, and sing
you to sleep."
"Father, my father, don't you see over there

The Erlking's daughters in the foggy air?"
"My Son, My Son, I only can see
The glistening of the old willow tree."
"I love you, your beauty excites me so

That if you are not willing, I'll force you
to go."
"Oh Father, my father, he's after me now!

The Erlking has done me terrible harm!"
The horrified father rode quickly on
Holding close his moaning son,
He reached his home in panic and dread;
And in his arms the child—was dead.[5]

The challenge for Schubert was to depict four characters with one singer. Listen to the song and consider the following questions concerning the relationship of music to poetry:

To Consider

1. What musical function does the rhythm of the piano part play in the story (in addition to representing the galloping of the horse through the night)?
2. Does his changing of modes from major to minor have any relationship to the poetry?
3. How does Schubert depict the son's growing fear of the Erlking?
4. How does the composer make use of the broad voice range of the singer to help delineate the characters?
5. What vocal or dramatic techniques does the singer use to enhance the drama of this song?

Schubert's use of repeated triplets to represent the galloping horse, his use of G minor to create a sinister atmosphere, his switch to B-flat major for the enticingly sweet song of the Erlking, and the plaintive repetition of the child's cry "My father, my father!" are all devices that link the music to the poetry. This descriptive use of music became extremely popular in the nineteenth century and enhanced the concept of Romanticism.

HECTOR BERLIOZ: PROGRAM MUSIC

Now that we have seen how Schubert makes a more elaborate story come alive in a song by using musical devices to intensify the drama, we will move to a larger genre of music, the symphony, to see how another composer tells a story with his music.

French composer Hector Berlioz (1803–1869) is well known for his program symphonies—symphonies that describe a story or an event. Berlioz, a Romantic prototype, was a colorful person who represented the leading edge of musical experimentation during his era.

Berlioz's memoirs paint an image of a man of drama, exaggeration, and flamboyance. His thoughts and points of reference are distinctly different from what we are accustomed to today. Here, for example, is an excerpt from the first paragraph:

> During the months which preceded my birth my mother never dreamt, as Virgil's did, that she was about to bring forth a laurel branch. Nor, I must add—however painful the admission to my vanity—did she imagine she bore within her a brand of fire, like Olympias, the mother of Alexander. This is extraordinary, I agree, but it is true. I came into the world quite normally, unheralded by any of the portents in use in poetic times to announce the arrival of those destined for glory. Can it be that our age is lacking in poetry?[6]

Of course Berlioz expects the reader to answer this question, "No!" The two references to the literary past contained in this paragraph are a mere sample of what is to come, for Berlioz, the composer known for his brilliant use of the orchestra and for his contributions to program music, was impassioned by literary images, fantasies, and traditions. His love for both literature and pictorial imagery is shown in his music and in his writing; he enjoyed a life as a music journalist and critic in addition to his life as a composer and conductor. A close look at his literary and musical creative works reveals a larger-than-life personality with a penchant for a flamboyant emotional life. In this Berlioz represents the aesthetic code of his time.

Berlioz's romantic character can be seen in almost every facet of his life and activities. His personal life was filled with drama; his life's story is one of extreme passion, longing, frustration, and rage at broken relationships, primarily due to his unusually active imagination and indomitable spirit.

To please his father, Berlioz started medical school, but he soon deserted his medical studies for a career in music. After trying medical school for a short time, he wrote:

> Become a doctor! Study anatomy! Dissect! Take part in horrible operations—instead of giving myself body and soul to music, sublime art whose grandeur I was beginning to perceive! Forsake the highest heavens for the wretchedest regions of earth, the immortal spirits of poetry and love and their divinely inspired strains for the dirty hospital orderlies, dreadful dissection-room attendants, hideous corpses, the screams of patients, the groans and rattling breath of the dying! No, no![7]

Although he stayed in medical school for two years, until he achieved his bachelor's degree in physical science in 1824, his decision to quit medicine resulted in his father abruptly cutting off his allowance. This disrupted his relationship with his parents for years to come. Now, in his twenties, Berlioz was often forced to borrow money from friends, but he pursued music with a passion, and he was especially impressed with the operas of Gluck. He also fell madly in love with pianist Camille Moke, and when he found out that she had married, he vowed to get his revenge by shooting both wife and husband! Fortunately this sentiment was only a dark fantasy.

Soon he became infatuated with Harriet Smithson, a Shakespearean actress from Ireland, when he saw her perform the role of Ophelia in *Hamlet* in 1827. His pursuit of

Smithson reached a level of intensity that approached mental derangement, for he often referred to Harriet as Ophelia, Juliet, or Desdemona—leading characters in Shakespeare's plays *Hamlet, Romeo and Juliet,* and *Othello* (all of whom, incidently, met early and untimely deaths). Berlioz began a frenzied courtship that was at first totally unsuccessful, and at one time, caused him to attempt suicide. During this time of despair, he composed his *Symphonie Fantastique,* based on the story of a musician who, trying to poison himself, accidentally falls into an opium dream and dreams that he has killed his beloved Estelle. For Berlioz, the distinction betweeen Estelle and Harriet was often blurred, and he continued to seek the attention of his real-life obsession. Finally, with the fame of his *Symphonie Fantastique* in 1830, he won an introduction to the famous actress. In spite of their language barrier, they were married in 1833. The marriage, however, was tumultuous, and after Harriet died in 1854, Berlioz married Marie Recio, a soprano for whom he had written several works. His new marriage was cut short when his wife died of a heart attack at age fifty-four. Later, in a moment of despair, Berlioz wrote:

> I am in my sixty-first year; past hopes, past illusions, past high thoughts and lofty conceptions. My son is almost always far away from me. I am alone. My contempt for the folly and baseness of mankind, my hatred of its atrocious cruelty, have never been so intense. And I say hourly to death: "When you will." Why does he delay?[8]

Berlioz began writing music at age fifteen, and he continued writing until 1864; his most active years of production were in the 1830s and 1840s, a time when Romanticism in music was beginning to flourish. He wrote five operas, four symphonies, five concert overtures, and several other compositions and arrangements for orchestra, many choral works, songs with various combinations of accompanying instruments, works for solo voice and orchestra, and arrangements of other composers' works.

His best-known compositions are the cantata *L'enfance du Christ (The Childhood of Christ)*; the *Grand Messe de Morts (Requiem Mass,* a setting of the Catholic liturgy for the dead); the large choral/orchestral work *La damnation de Faust (The Damnation of Faust)*; the three operas *Benvenuto Cellini, Les Troyans (the Trojans),* and *Béatrice et Bénédict;* and his orchestral music. A program symphony that followed *Symphony Fantastique* is *Harold in Italy*—a work that features a viola soloist. *Romeo and Juliete,* Berlioz's third symphony, was among his favorite compositions. This work and his fourth symphony, the *Grande symphony funebre et triomphale,* include chorus in the tradition set by Beethoven in his Ninth Symphony. The concert overtures of Berlioz also are part of the standard symphonic repertoire of modern orchestras. Favorites are *Le carnaval romain (The Roman Carnival Overture)* and *Le roi Lear (King Lear).*

Berlioz was interested in creating music that spoke for itself, but its sources were frequently related to a literary stimulus. His program music was always inspired by a story and depicted the events of that story musically. It is interesting, however, that if one chooses to ignore the story, his music can stand alone; furthermore, Berlioz himself intended it to be self-sufficient, for he was well acquainted with Beethoven's great abstract symphonies, and he modeled himself after Beethoven. When he heard Beethoven's Third and Fifth symphonies for the first time, he said: "Beethoven opened up before me a new world of music."[9]

Berlioz's *Symphonie Fantastique* approaches Beethovian proportions. It carries the subtitle, "Episode in the Life of an Artist." Berlioz wrote the following program as a listener's guide to this work:

> A young musician of unhealthily sensitive nature and endowed with a vivid imagination has poisoned himself with opium in a paradoxysm of love-sick despair. The narcotic dose he had taken was too weak to cause death but it has thrown him into a long sleep accompanied by the most extraordinary visions. In this condition his sensations, his feelings and memories find utterance in his sick brain in the form of musical imagery. Even the beloved one takes the form of melody in his mind, like a fixed idea which is ever returning and which he hears everywhere.

I. Dreams, Passions: Largo; Allegro agitato e appassionato assai.

At first he thinks of the uneasy and nervous condition of his mind, of somber longings, of depression and joyous elation without any recognizable cause, which he experienced before the beloved one appeared to him. Then he remembers the ardent love with which she suddenly inspired him; he thinks of his almost insane anxiety of mind, and his raging jealousy, of his re-awakening love, of his religious consolation.

II. A Ball: Allegro non troppo.

In a ballroom, amidst the confusion of a brilliant festival, he finds the beloved one again.

III. Scene in the Meadows: Adagio.

It is a summer evening. He is in the country musing when he hears two shepherd-lads who play, the ranz des vaches (the tune used by the Swiss to call their sheep together) in alternation. This shepherd duet, the locality, the soft whisperings of the trees stirred by the zephyr-wind, some prospects of hope recently made known to him, all these sensations unite to impart a long unknown repose to his heart and to lend a smiling color to his imagination. And then she appears once more. His heart stops beating, painful forebodings fill his soul. "Should She prove false to him!" One of the shepherds resumes the melody, but the other answers him no more . . . Sunset . . . Distant rolling of thunder . . . loneliness . . . silence.

IV. March to the Scaffold: Allegretto non troppo.

He dreams that he murdered his beloved, that he has been condemned to death and is being led to the stake. A march that is alternately somber and wild, brilliant and solemn, accompanies the procession. The tumultuous outbursts are followed without modulation by measured steps. At last the fixed idea returns, for a moment a last thought of love is revived—which is cut short by the death-blow.

V. Dream of a Witches' Sabbath: Larghetto; Allegro.

He dreams that he is present at a witches' dance, surrounded by horrible spirits, amidst sorcerers and monsters in many fearful forms, who have come to attend his funeral. Strange sounds, groans, shrill laughter, distant yells, which other cries seem to answer. The beloved melody is heard again, but it has its shy and noble character no longer; it has become a vulgar, trivial, grotesque kind of dance. She it is who comes to attend the witches' meeting. Friendly howls and shouts greet her arrival . . . She joins the infernal orgy . . . bells toll for the dead . . . a burlesque parody of the "Dies Irae" . . . the witches' round-dance . . . the dance and the "Dies irae" are heard at the same time.[10]

How does Berlioz tell this elaborate story musically? He does not tell it through an event-by-event musical description of the words. Instead the composer plays on one's ability to correlate the key emotional words in the program to the sounds he produces. Notice, for example, the emotional buzz words in the first movement: "uneasy," "nervous," "somber," "depression," "joyous elation," "love," "religious consolation" (and there are more). Throughout this work, Berlioz suggests these by a constantly changing array of melodies, rhythms, tempos, and orchestral combinations that allow the listener to create the relationships to the general story.

This referential technique of listening is fostered more specifically in Berlioz's program music by the use of a melody or motive identified with a specific person or an idea. This melody, called the **fixed idea** (or, in French, the *idée fixe*), recurs in each movement, woven into the musical texture with great imagination. A single melody used throughout various movements of an extended work is known as a cyclical melody. You will remember that Beethoven used this concept in his Fifth Symphony (although not in connection with a programmatic idea). The concept of linking a cyclical melody to a programmatic idea was Berlioz's contribution.

In *Symphonie Fantastique*, Berlioz uses a fixed idea to represent a girl who is the object of the young musician's love. Most scholars believe that Berlioz's fantasy was partially autobiographical and that the fixed idea in his *Symphonie Fantastique* refers to Estelle, a young lady with whom Berlioz fell madly in love when he was twelve. (We have already seen that the Estelle image is also connected to Harriet Smithson; this confusion is not unusual for Berlioz.) Berlioz saw her one summer when he was at his grandfather's place in the mountains outside of Grenoble. Estelle, who was older than Berlioz by six years, became for him a symbol of love that remained with him throughout his life. An excerpt from his memoirs, expressed in a colorful excess of wording and ideas typical of the Romantic literary style, illustrates his feelings:

> The moment I beheld her, I was conscious of an electric shock: I loved her. From then on I lived in a daze. I hoped for nothing, I lay awake whole nights disconsolate. By day I hid myself in the maize fields or in the secret corners of my grandfather's orchard, like a wounded bird, mute, suffering.[11]

The "Estelle melody" in *Symphonie Fantastique* is a traditionally shaped tune with phrases based on a recognizable melodic and rhythmic idea. Berlioz used familiar conventions of melodic construction: (1) melodic segments that outline a triad; (2) use of scale fragments; (3) melodic sequences; and (4) "question-and-answer" phrase structures.

Hector Berlioz, *Idée fixe* from
Symphonie Fantastique, Mvt. 1.

Listening Guide 35

"March to the Scaffold" from
***Symphonie Fantastique*, Mvt. 4**
Hector Berlioz (1803–1869)

Program symphony
1830
Recorded by the Berlin Philharmonic
Daniel Barenboim, conductor
CD No. 2, Track 13 (4:46)

In the fourth movement, the "March to the Scaffold," Berlioz suggests in his program that the young musician thinks briefly of his beloved just as the guillotine falls. To illustrate this in the music, the "Estelle melody" is cut short by a fortissimo chord played by the full orchestra, which is followed immediately by pizzicato (plucked) strings playing three notes suggesting the severed head falling into a basket. (Remember, when Berlioz wrote this, memories of the guillotine and of the French Revolution were vivid in the public's mind.)

As you listen to this movement, keep in mind that, although Berlioz's program is a powerful part of the music, the composition is structured to stand alone. Its presentation and development of contrasting themes, its interesting orchestral colors, and its concepts of tension and release earn it a place in the standard classic orchestral repertoire. You can listen to this music on two planes: the referential or programmatic, and the purely musical. That, of course, underlines once more the artistry of Berlioz's program symphonies.

To Consider

1. What kinds of rhythmic stress patterns in the music suggest a march in the beginning of this piece? Is it a continuous march, or does it stop and start up again. How can you tell?
2. As you follow the listening guide below, can you identify each program feature as it happens? How does knowing the story and listening for musical elements that describe the program change the way you listen to, and make it different from, the way you usually listen to abstract symphonic music?
3. Berlioz manipulates three primary elements of music to achieve his musical drama: melody, rhythm, and dynamics. How does he use each of these elements to lead you through the story?

0:00	Basses and timpani establish a somber march rhythm. The procession can be heard approaching from far away.
0:27	Cellos and basses present the principal melody representing the hero being led along the march; the bassoon offers counterpoint, suggesting the gossiping of the bystanders.
0:54	The low strings represent a mob that jostles to get a closer view of the condemned man as the violins play the halting melody. The chattering of the crowd continues, represented by the bassoon.
1:39	The second theme—a fanfare-like melody—appears in the brass and woodwinds. The march to the gallows takes on the air of morbid pomp and festivity.
2:11	A third short theme, like a trio of a march, enters: woodwinds and brass exchange figures. The staggering hero is briefly referred to. This section contains elements of various themes, leading toward the climax of the procession.
3:16	A fortissimo statement of the hero's theme tells us that he has arrived at the gallows.
3:41	Dotted rhythms in the strings played under short figures in the winds suggest an angry crowd anxious to get on with the execution.
4:14	The fury is interrupted when the clarinet plays the beginning of the "Estelle melody," signifying the tender memory of the hero's beloved. The melody ends abruptly with the falling of the guillotine and the resulting bouncing of the severed head into a basket.
4:25	The movement concludes with drum rolls and strong chords that provide finality to the completed execution.

Musical Encounter

Berlioz: A Show Business Pioneer

One of Berlioz's dreams was to assemble a huge orchestra consisting of several hundred players, for he wanted to have at his fingertips the broadest, loudest array of sounds available. Because Berlioz was a popular conductor, he had several opportunities to assemble such a large orchestra. His most memorable experiment in mass concerts was at the Exhibition of Industrial Products building in Paris in 1844. Berlioz collaborated with Viennese waltz king Johann Strauss in producing a gala festival consisting of 1,022 performers. (The orchestra numbered

"Caricature of Hector Berlioz Leading an Orchestra in 1846." Color engraving. The Pierpont Morgan Library / Art Resource, NY. ID # SO083402.

some 500; the chorus made up the rest.) Berlioz organized two assistant conductors and five chorus masters, plus seven additional time beaters, all of whom conducted together. The program consisted of music by eleven composers, including three pieces by Berlioz. Berlioz recorded in his memoirs that the musical exhibition was brought off not only without mishap but also with success.

Always a serious student of the orchestra, Berlioz's creative mind pushed the limits of this science of sound. Like many innovators throughout history, Berlioz often was criticized for his ideas—". . . the hideous noise of trombones . . . of ten able-bodied men thwacking at kettledrums, of tubas and cornets, of double drums, cymbals and tam-tams."[12] In truth, however, his explorations into orchestration techniques launched a special consciousness toward developing new sounds in musical timbres. Berlioz the Romanticist is also Berlioz the visionary.

To provide added color and tonal resources to his music, Berlioz introduced new instruments to the orchestra (most of which are now considered standard). The small E-flat soprano clarinet added a shrill top range, the harp supported a blending effect and also provided opportunities for intimate solos, the contrabassoon—which Beethoven had so successfully used—added depth to the woodwind sound, and the tuba afforded a strong bass. But the mere adding of instruments to the orchestra was only as effective as the imagination of the composer, and Berlioz proved a most inventive acoustician in the way he used the instruments of the orchestra (so much so, in fact, that he wrote a treatise on orchestration). His underlying flair for show business, for spectacle, and for interesting sounds have earned him a place in history.

CHOPIN AND THE GOLDEN AGE OF THE PIANO

If Berlioz took a classical form, the symphony, and modified it to suit the Romantic ideal, Frédéric Chopin (1810–1849) took a "classical" instrument—the piano—and brought it into the very center of Romantic music. He did this by creating works that were perfectly suited to the special capabilities of the piano and were also suitable to the tastes of a public ever more eager to hear passionate, but flamboyant, music.

Chopin's advantage was that he was a skilled performer. Much of his music requires advanced abilities, but at the same time it is written so that it lies well under the fingers of the pianist. Chopin, his Hungarian contemporary Franz Liszt (1811–1886), and German virtuoso Sigismond Thalberg (1812–1871) shared the musical spotlight for piano performance in mid-nineteenth-century Europe. Unlike Lizst and Thalberg, who were both known for their extroverted lifestyles and musical bravura, Chopin was more introverted and his music more intimate.

Chopin was born in Poland into a family that had immigrated from France. His father, a French tutor in the homes of Polish nobility, provided his precocious son with a rigorous education, including piano lessons. At age six, Chopin was writing verses and studying piano, so successfully that those around him thought he would be "Mozart's successor." Later in life, his father wrote to him, "The mechanics of playing took you little time . . . it was your mind, not your fingers, that kept busy."[13]

Chopin's first public appearance was shortly before his eighth birthday, when he played a concerto by Polish composer Gyrowetz. His formative years, spent training with the director of the Warsaw Conservatory, were highlighted by a feature performance of a concerto by Moscheles (a popular composer of the time), the publication of his Opus 1, the *C Minor Rondo,* and the gift of a ring from Russian Tsar Alexander I, who heard him play while on a diplomatic visit to Warsaw. Although his musical training concentrated on art music forms composed in the Viennese classical tradition, while he was still in his teens, Chopin also developed an interest in Polish folk music.

After he passed with distinction his final examinations at the Warsaw Conservatory, Chopin was ready to enter the larger arena of concert life and composition and to make his living as a musician. He was invited to Berlin in 1828, where he met Mendelssohn and heard Italian operas of Rossini for the first time. A year later, he traveled to Vienna, where he played some of his own works, including an improvisation on a Polish folk song, and he was enthusiastically received by the snobbish Viennese audience. A lengthy concert tour of Germany and Italy soon followed. He returned to Poland, a nineteen-year-old pianist/composer who had already made his mark in countries that were unusually critical of new performers—especially those from a foreign land. Back in Poland, he fell in love with a young singer, Konstancia Gladkowsky, but his unrequited love for her, although a source of inspiration for compositions, often left him in deep despair.

In 1830, when Warsaw was on the brink of revolution, Chopin left for Paris. His first successful public appearance as a pianist in Paris took place in 1832, where the leading music critic of the time declared his *F Minor Concerto* to have "an abundance of original ideas of a kind to be found nowhere else."[14] Chopin soon became part of the inner circles of Parisian music, but he soon discovered that he was not fit to be a concert virtuoso. A nagging respiratory illness and his underlying gentle nature worked against such a career; his Hungarian counterpart Franz Liszt and German sensation Sigismond Thalberg were, after all, much more flamboyant, and they excited the audiences with their virtuosity. In all, Chopin, the pianist, performed for the Parisian public a mere thirty times.

But Chopin did not sink into oblivion, for his compositions and his reputation as a piano teacher earned him admission to the highest aristocratic society. His public personality was reserved and dignified. Privately, however, Chopin was infuriated by the uneducated taste of the concert going public in Paris. He understood that only the most sophisticated music lovers would understand the nuances of his music—such as the meticulous pedal technique that allowed the performer to sustain notes with subtle accuracy. In a letter to a friend, he wrote, "All the same it is being said that I played too softly, or rather, too delicately for people used to the piano-pounding of the artists here."[15] Another letter of his contains the comment, "I don't know where there can be so many pianists as in Paris, so many asses and so many virtuosi."[16]

The sensitive nature of Chopin's playing was matched by his fragile health; early in his life he contracted tuberculosis, a disease that plagued him until it claimed his life at the young age of thirty-nine. Some biographers feel that his image as a gentle artist was enhanced by his physical condition, and one can only speculate that his mental attitude bore the scars of his ill health. Chopin wrote, "I laugh, and in my heart, as I write this, some horrible presentiment torments me. To live or to die seems all one to me today."[17]

Chopin's life was enhanced by several love affairs, the most lasting of which was his relationship with novelist Aurore Dudevant, better known by her *nom de plume* George

Eugene Delacroix (French, 1798-1863), "Portrait of Frederic Chopin," detail. Musee du Louvre, Paris/A.K.G., Berlin/ SuperStock. ID # 463/4061/N/P18F.

Sand. Sand was a controversial figure in Parisian artistic life, for she lived out some of the ideals that her novels contained, namely, a philosophy of free love unincumbered by marriage. She had several romantic liaisons after she left her country squire husband Casimir Dudevant, in 1822, including French poet Alfred de Musset and Chopin. After their first meeting, Chopin remarked that her appearance was not to his liking, and he declined an invitation to a house party that she held in 1837. He soon changed his mind, however, and by 1838, the young composer and the famous novelist were lovers. Chopin spent ten years living with Sand and her two children. Some of the time was spent in Majorca, some in luxurious surroundings in Paris, where Sand often entertained artists, writers, and musicians. During this period, the famous Delacroix painted Chopin's portrait.

In spite of his ailing condition, the years Chopin spent with Sand resulted in some of his best works. By 1846, however, the relationship between the two lovers cooled; Sand's two children had grown up and began to cause problems, and Maurice, one of the sons, tried to make his mother break off her liaison with Chopin. Family rivalries were complicated when Solange, the daughter, entered a quarrelsome marriage with sculptor Auguste Clésinger. By 1847, Chopin's break with Sand was complete, and he was devastated; his health deteriorated rapidly, and he lost all interest in composition. He gave one final concert in Paris in February 1848, one week before the revolution broke out. Chopin then traveled to England at the invitation of Jane Stirling, a wealthy student, and he was welcomed into the English society. During his last year of life, Chopin struggled to face the rigors of travel and of social obligations required of a celebrity of his stature. He eventually returned to Paris and died in the fall of 1849, surrounded by friends and his sister Ludwika.

Chopin represents a curious combination of elements of Romanticism based on a firm foundation of earlier music. He never lost his interest in the music of Mozart—which he had learned as a child, and the concepts of balance—so central in Mozart's music—had a lasting effect on him. His compositions using the classical forms of the sonata and the concerto were successful, but he found his musical voice in the character piece, a large variety of relatively short compositions mostly written for the piano, which may appear under various titles. The character piece was the chief vehicle for Romantic pianistic expressions of a wide variety of emotions and moods. Chopin's character pieces carry titles such as prelude, etude, mazurka, polonaise, waltz, impromptu, nocturne, ballade, fantasy, albumleaf, and scherzo.

Chopin's works, which run the gamut from highly virtuosic—fast and loud—to deeply lyrical, quiet, and contemplative, transmit a romantic sentiment tempered by a well-developed sense of musical structure.

To illustrate this range and variety, we will examine the *Ballade in G Minor, Op. 23.* The use of the term **ballade** for a piano piece is a curious one, for it is most often associated with a narrative poem—one that tells a story, such as the poem Schubert used in *The Erlking.* Chopin's ballades for piano have a vague connection to narrative poetry, but they are not programmatic. They exist as abstract music, neither inspired by nor descriptive of an existing piece of poetry. Such is the nature of the Romantic mind.

Listening Guide 36

Ballade in G Minor
Frédéric Chopin (1810–1849)

Character piece for piano
1836
Recorded by Murray Perahia
CD No. 2, Track 14 (5:25)

The *Ballade in G Minor* has several sections whose relationship to one other is most apparent upon first hearing. Let us approach this composition by listening on the "sheerly musical plane" (to borrow Aaron Copland's term) to find out how Chopin shapes this popular piano piece. As you listen to this excerpt (the complete work is approximately nine minutes long), chart the principal sections and describe the musical material that characterizes them. The listening guide will help you do this.

The two principal melodies in this work are structured traditionally. Notice how their phrases rise and fall symmetrically. The presence of recognizable rhythmic concepts and tuneful ideas in this ballade gives us a feeling of structure.

Frédéric Chopin: *Ballade in G Minor, Op. 23.* (Themes A and B).

But then, after these melodies are implanted in the ear, something spontaneous happens. The music seems to forsake its clean shape and goes off into expressive, free, and often virtuosic passages. The listener never knows exactly what is happening but is carried away with the excitement, oblivious of symmetry and balance. And then, unexpectedly, the simple melodies return.

Once more remembering Copland's concept of "levels of listening," listen to this ballade a second time for its emotional and expressive content. How does the composer create effects in your ear and mind as this piece unfolds? What musical reference points trigger in you the responses of repose, motion, anticipation, surprise, or resolution? When considering these questions, you can glimpse the "Romantic spirit" that is the driving force behind the music.

To Consider

1. What melodic concepts and rhythmic devices go toward building patterns of repetition and contrast? (Listen to this work first before you refer to the listening guide below.)
2. This piece opens with a serious introduction. What musical devices create this feeling?
3. From time to time in this work, the right-hand melodies seem to "break away" from the restrictions of the two principal melodies. What effect does this have on your listening experience?
4. How do these principal melodies serve as the foundation for this ballade? What is the relationship between these melodies and the occasional flamboyant bursts of virtuosic piano technique?
5. Describe the range of reactions you feel during this piece. What specific musical devices prompt these reactions?

0:00 Introduction: the character is intentionally indefinite. A forte beginning outlining a B-flat chord resolves into a quiet statement suggesting a dominant (V) harmony.

0:37 The A theme: a traditionally shaped melody is presented with simple afterbeat accompaniment. Soon this tune, with its symmetrical phrasing, is extended harmonically and melodically. The "classical" nature of the melody is lost, as the energetic impulses dominate and point toward a conclusion.

2:01 Closing material: strong, virtuoso ideas lead to the end of the first section. Again, cadences are extended, and melodic concepts are repeated with various accompanying figures.

3:57 B theme: this lyrical second theme, like the A theme, is first presented simply. Soon, however, the quiet, expressive material gives way to more bombastic treatment.

4:02 The A theme returns briefly.

4:33 Now the B theme enters in octaves, accompanied by full forte chords.

5:20 The music breaks into a fast, waltz-like passage with brilliantly figured scale passages in the right hand. This material begins to signal the end of the work. The final four minutes of this ballade (not included in this recording) contain material from both principle themes. The final section begins: fast and loud passages alternate with contrasting pianissimo chords. After a few deceptive endings, the final chords are reached by chromatic scales beginning at either end of the keyboard and converging in the middle range.

Obviously, Chopin's *Ballade in G Minor* contains strong elements of contrast. Dynamics and tempo vary throughout the work; the composer draws upon a wide variety of rhythmic concepts; and the range of pitches is also wide. However, one more fundamental type of contrast provides the key to the composer's mind: the interplay between control (or structure) and freedom (or "fantasy," to use a popular term of the early nineteenth century).

By moving back and forth between the realm of logical structure and fantasy, Chopin exercises our emotional responses. Never does the music become monotonous, yet we always feel we have "something to hang onto." This feature, illustrated so well in the *Ballade in G Minor*, is frequently present in his music. His musical intuition, gained in part from the study of Mozart's music, expressed itself in a style that combined elements of classical thought and romantic abandon. That, coupled with Chopin's unmatchable knowledge of the capabilities of the piano, has no doubt been the chief contributing factor to his immense popularity over the years.

So far in *Musical Encounters* we have become acquainted with composers who have written in a broad spectrum of musical genres. Chopin represents a contrast to these musicians, for he wrote almost exclusively for the piano. His vast contributions of character pieces, along with his two concertos and three sonatas for piano, are joined by nineteen songs on Polish texts, three chamber works with cello (written for a friend), and a piano trio (violin, cello, and piano). In a relatively short span of thirty-two years, he wrote some 248 works.

CLARA WIECK SCHUMANN

It is not uncommon for composers to be accomplished performers. Bach, Handel, Mozart, Beethoven, Schubert, and Chopin were all excellent keyboard performers, according to contemporary reports. Clara Wieck (1819–1896), however, began her career as a virtuoso pianist. Her innate musical talent, nurtured by rigorous training, resulted in her becoming a recognized concert artist at a very early age. She gave her first solo piano recital in Leipzig, Germany, at age eleven. A year later, her father arranged a concert tour for her that took her to Paris; by age sixteen, she was acclaimed throughout Europe as a teenage phenomenon.

Although Wieck's fame was based on her performing abilities, another talent that developed early in her life was a gift for composition. Her Opus 1, *Four Polonaises*, dates from 1830. In her seventeenth year, she completed her *Piano Concerto*.

Her marriage to composer Robert Schumann (1810–1856) took place only after a three-year battle with her father. The social laws of the time necessitated that the couple could not marry without the approval of the prospective bride's father, and Friederich Wieck saw absolutely no promise in Schumann's future. Schumann, nine years older than Clara, came to live with the Wiecks as a roomer in 1830, and by 1837, he asked Friederich Wieck for the hand of his eighteen-year-old daughter. Friederich's wrath toward Schumann became strongly overt, and eventually the two men met in court where it was decided that Robert and Clara could marry.

Clara Schumann's activities as a touring musician were soon changed into that of a wife and mother who found herself providing support for a moody, flamboyant husband, whose genius was plagued by fits of depression, and by raising eight children. Nevertheless, she managed to continue her musical life. She gave public recitals and also taught at the Leipzig Conservatory, maintaining a private studio for select students.

Portrait of the German pianist and composer Clara Schumann, wife of Robert Schumann. © Archivo Iconografico, S.A./CORBIS. ID # CS005849.

With such an active private and public life, it is no surprise that Clara Wieck Schumann was not a prolific composer as were the other pianist/composers, Franz Liszt, Fréderic Chopin, and her husband Robert. Her twenty-seven opus numbers are dominated by works for the piano and songs (lieder) for voice and piano, but also include two works for orchestra and piano and a few chamber compositions. At times her music reflects the brilliant pianistic virtuosity for which she achieved fame as a child. Other moments in her compositions show her capacity for lyricism, influenced perhaps by her deep understanding of the expressive potential of the human voice and the strong tradition of lieder, which was prevalent around her.

Clara Schumann's *Trio for Piano, Violin, and Cello in G Minor, Op. 17*, Mvt. 3 provides an excellent example of this musical expression, for it is born out of a well-honed knowledge of the expressive capabilities of the instruments for which it is written, and displays the basic lyrical nature of its composer. The tempo marking for the third movement of the *Trio* is marked Andante, which means that the music moves at a rather slow pace; one can expect such a movement to contain beautiful melodies that explore the expressive range of the three instruments. As you listen to this lyrical piece, you will soon realize that the main concept of this music is the interchange among the voices, as the instruments pass melodic ideas back and forth and alternately assume supporting roles.

istening Guide 37

Trio for Piano, Violin, and Cello in
  G Minor, Op. 17, Mvt. 3
Clara Schumann (1819–1896)

Piano trio (1846)
Recorded by the Macalester Trio (Donald Betts, piano;
Joseph Roche, violin; Camilla Heller, cello)
CD No. 2, Track 15 (5:35)

To Consider

1. Describe the musical activity at the very beginning of the work. What instrument presents the melody? Can you tell what meter the piece is in? How is the meter established?

2. As the various instruments enter, what is their relationship to the interplay of melody versus accompaniment? Does one instrument dominate the texture?

3. Can you feel a change of emotional content when the middle section of the piece begins? (The movement is in a simple A–B–A structure.) What subtle rhythmic devices does the composer use to indicate this change?

The following guide will assist in your understanding and appreciation of this movement.

0:00	The central melody is presented by the piano solo. Notice how Clara Schumann keeps the accompaniment from obscuring the tune. The left hand of the piano plays a bass note on the first beat of each measure and chords on the second and third pulses.
0:38	The violin enters, repeating the melody already introduced by the piano. The accompaniment now changes to arpeggios.
1:10	Now it is the cello's turn to play. Its melody sounds like a continuation of the principal melody. This subsidiary melodic idea is soon supported by the violin, which creates a duet with the cello. The piano resumes its simple accompaniment style established during the first measures of the piece.
1:42	A stronger, more agitated second theme heralds the beginning of the middle section. Notice how the mood change is a subtle one; it fits into the overall spirit of the entire movement. Dotted rhythms, more frequent melodic exchanges among instruments, and slightly louder dynamics help establish this gently contrasting center to the movement.
3:28	The cello "sings" the first theme to signal the return of the A section, playing to the accompaniment of arpeggios in the piano.
4:04	Supporting material is played by the violin, as the three instruments extend the lyrical nature of the movement with their thematic interchanges.
4:34	A closing melodic idea suggests that the movement is about to end. Once more, each instrument alternates between presenting melodies and providing accompaniment. The movement eventually slows and cadences on several repeated chords.

 GENDER AND NINETEENTH-CENTURY COMPOSERS: FELIX AND FANNY MENDELSSOHN

Robert and Clara Schumann earn the distinction of being the most dynamic professional musicians who formed a two-career marriage. Although it was not unusual in the nineteenth century for a woman to rise to the status of a virtuoso performer, it was uncommon for one to attain prominence as a composer. Clara Schumann was a pioneer in what was often considered a "man's" world. Her persistence as a composer was undoubtedly due to her natural instinct to record her creative abilities on paper, and as a result she left behind a strong legacy of music.

Another pair of composers/performers contemporary to Robert and Clara Schumann were a brother and sister, both of whom were active composers in Germany during the first half of the century, Fanny Mendelssohn Hensel (1805–1847), and her brother Felix Mendelssohn (1809–1847). Their story provides insight into the culture of the gender of the time, for although Fanny composed over several hundred works in her lifetime, she remained relatively unknown until recent decades.

Like Clara Wieck Schumann, Fanny (Cäcilie) Mendelssohn was an accomplished pianist and composer. Although her father discouraged her career as a composer because of the social conventions of the time, her husband, painter Wilhelm Hensel, encouraged her creative activities. Six of her songs were published under her brother's name, but many of her works were left unpublished and still await public exposure.

A composer who initially was best known for her songs, Fanny Mendelssohn Hensel has recently emerged as an interesting figure in Romantic studies, not only for her musical activities as a pianist and a composer, but also as an example of the role of women in nineteenth-century musical society. Younger brother Felix Mendelssohn was the object of their father's encouragement in the world of music, for Abraham Mendelssohn felt strongly that becoming a composer was not an appropriate career for a woman. Although her creative muse could not be contained, she did not submit any of her works for publication as long as her father was alive, even after her husband urged her to do so. Hensel, whom she married in 1829, was an artist and supported her work as a musician.

During her lifetime, Fanny Hensel's published works were limited to two genres: several of her lieder appeared in print (she wrote over 250), as did a few compositions for piano. Her famous brother Felix published six of her songs under his name; three each appear in his songs, Opus 8 and 9. Fanny Hensel was active from 1838 as a pianist, composer, and participant in weekly musical events that were held in the Mendelssohn household. She also directed a choral ensemble.

"Sehnsucht," published as Felix Mendelssohn's Op. 9, No. 7, is a musical miniature consisting of seventeen measures that are repeated for the second verse of the poem. It is written in a comfortable range for the amateur singer; the piano part also is very easy to play.

A reading of this song will show that the piano doubles the voice at times but still maintains an independence that allows the solo voice to draw the attention of the listener. As you listen to someone play and sing this, notice that even in this short song exists a mid-section with a temporary key change. This song, as simple as it is, still exhibits a rather sophisticated concern for the text and harmonic progression. Its simplicity is its charm. Its subtle harmonic structures and its treatment of the voice and piano relationship are its art.

Fanny Mendelssohn Hensel, *Sehnsucht (Longing)* Op. 9, No. 7. Source: Edwin F. Kalmus.

Fern und ferner schallt der Reigen	The dance sounds fade farther and farther away
Wohl mir! Um mich her is Schweigen	It's true! Silence is all around me
Auf der Flur.	In the meadow.
Zu dem vollen Herzen nur	Rest will not appear to those
will nich Ruh' sich neigen.	With heavy hearts.
Horch! Die Nacht schwenbt durch die Räume.	Listen! Night is suspended in space.
Ihr Gewand durchrauscht die Bäume.	Its robes rustle the trees.
Lispelnd leis.'	Soft whispers.
Ach, so schweifen liebeheiß	Alas, thus ends my love's passion
Meine Wünsch' und Träme.	My hopes and dreams.[18]

The music of Fanny Mendelssohn Hensel is slowly emerging as the musical world is becoming aware of her talents. Besides her songs and piano works, a *Trio in D for Violin, Cello, and Piano, Op. 11* is currently enjoying popularity, as is her *Oratorio on Biblical Themes* for SATB chorus, soloists, and orchestra.

Fanny Mendelssohn Hensel was a strong supporter and biographer of her famous brother Felix. She was a central figure in the musical life of Berlin, both as a pianist and as an organizer of public concerts.

The life of Felix Mendelssohn (1809–1847) is in stark contrast to the romantic image of the emotionally unstable and sometimes suffering artist, which is often expected of nineteenth-century artists, poets, and musicians. Mendelssohn was the son of a prosperous banker, Abraham, and he was able to pursue the life of a professional musician and composer without financial worries. He was heir to a tradition of family pride, and from his letters to his father, we can ascertain that Felix intended to make his mark on the world through diligent work. His father had strong opinions, not only concerning family life (we have referenced his attitudes toward Fanny Mendelssohn Hensel earlier) but concerning the importance of a thorough education for his son. So Felix became well-grounded in philosophy, the classics, gymnastics, and music.

It was music that spoke most directly to Mendelssohn's spirit. At an early age, he not only began to study piano but studied composition as well. By age thirteen, he had written a quartet for strings and piano; by age seventeen, he wrote his first masterpiece, the *Overture to Shakespeare's "Midsummer Night's Dream," Opus 21*.

During his formative years, Mendelssohn met many influential people, including distinguished composer, conductor, and teacher of composition Carl Friedrich Zelter (1758–1832). One of Zelter's interests, which he shared with Felix Mendelssohn, was the music of J. S. Bach, and soon Mendelssohn's interest grew to the point where he decided to embark on a project to revive the music of the great Baroque composer, who, until that time, was known only to relatively few people. In 1829, Felix Mendelssohn mounted a performance of Bach's masterpiece, the *St. Matthew Passion*, and the Bach revival began.

Mendelssohn's foray into the choral music of the Baroque Era had a profound effect on his own compositions, and he later adapted the oratorio form to his own musical creativity. In 1836, he composed an oratorio entitled *St Paul*. His other famous oratorio, *Elijah*, followed. Mendelssohn's contributions in furthering the tradition of combining orchestra and chorus in large compositions played a major role in the concert life of mid-nineteenth-century Germany. Since Felix Mendelssohn also was a highly sought after conductor as well as a composer, he was able to program many choral/orchestral works by composers such as Bach, Handel, and Haydn.

One factor that gave rise to the sustenance of choral music performance in the nineteenth century was the popularity of the amateur choral organizations that seemed to spring up everywhere. During the Industrial Revolution, when so many people worked long hours in the factories, it was not uncommon for people to seek fulfillment by singing in large choirs—some of which were organized by industrial leaders themselves. Singing associations became so popular that, according to contemporary reports, every small town seemed to have two or three. Music festivals—events where concerts were given by several societies—became popular.

Felix Mendelssohn's contributions to instrumental music include a substantial list of works for orchestra, including five symphonies, many works for piano, chamber ensembles of various types, and organ pieces. His vocal works run the gamut from lieder to oratorios, cantatas, and other choral settings.

SUMMARY

The musical culture of the nineteenth century reflected the public's taste for expressions that could arouse emotions, invoke mental images, and stimulate memories. Music was composed to appeal directly to the emotions of the listener. This romantic music was dominated by clearly established melodies and colorful harmonies written in the context of both large forms such as operas to musical miniatures such as art songs (lieder).

Instrumental music often bore descriptive titles that functioned to guide the listener into a general attitude or fantasy. Although standard genres of music that had been established prior to the nineteenth century were still cultivated by composers (symphonies, concertos, and chamber music, for example), new forms evolved that would more directly support the spirit of Romanticism. The character piece was a type of composition for piano with descriptive titles. In the symphonic poem, the orchestra created images and suggested stories according to the composer's stated intentions.

First and foremost, however, was the dominance of melody over all other aspects of music. It was melody—often a singable tune—that drove the various forms and genres of music and nourished the romantic tastes of the public and the expressive urges of the composer. Expressive melody is the link that provides aesthetic continuity among the songs of Franz Schubert, the program symphonies of Hector Berlioz, the character pieces of Fréderic Chopin, and the chamber music of Clara Schumann.

The varied genres of music, ranging from intimate works for voice and piano to flamboyant symphonies and lengthy, elaborate opera productions, were illustrative of the broad market for music that existed in the nineteenth century. To accommodate the growing demands for music in this Romantic Era, composers used forms from the past as molds for their creative ideas and developed new genres of music. The intermingling of the old with the new is also reflected in the subject matter that stimulated the arts in the Romantic Era. Poets, novelists, artists, and musicians frequently breathed an air of contemporary interpretation into well-known classical stories.

KEY TERMS

art song
ballade
character piece
fixed idea
lied (lieder)
program symphony
songs without words
symphonic poem

The Expansion of
the Romantic Ideal

$\mathcal{M}$usic rouses a series of intimate feelings, true but not clear, not even perceptual, only most obscure. You, young man, were in its dark auditorium; it lamented, sighed, stormed, exalted; you felt all that, you vibrated with every string. But about what did it—and you with it—lament, sigh, exalt, storm? Not a shadow of anything perceptible. Everything stirred only in the darkest abyss of your soul, like a living wind that agitates the depths of the ocean. (Johann Herder)[1]

The spirit of Romanticism, born from the political and social philosophy of the French Revolution and expressed in the poetry, novels, visual arts, and music during the following decades, was well established by the middle of the nineteenth century. German Romantic poet and philosopher Johann Herder's description of the power of music to inspire intimate feelings recognizes that this quality, as real as it is, is nonetheless nebulous and often defies specific description. This idea was firmly entrenched in the aesthetic consciousness of the mid-nineteenth-century artistic world, and it formed a basis of understanding for all of those who enjoyed music. Composers were no longer reacting against a classic aesthetic of reason and nature but were involved in the established practice of stimulating emotions through their music in the most imaginative ways. Romantic music stood on its own and could communicate directly to the soul without the outside stimulus of imitating Nature and Reason.

We have seen that the freedom of music to express nearly all emotions gave rise to a wide variety of styles and forms of music. At times, composers breathed new life into classically balanced forms of music from the past, while at other times, they invented new concepts of structure. Sonatas and symphonies existed alongside character pieces and symphonic poems. In practical terms, it was this diversity of structure that allowed the composer to be an individual, for composers were no longer restricted to writing within a framework of music intended to please an esoteric audience of noble patrons but were writing to connect directly to the emotions of the mass audience.

Thus, the Romantic ideal became more than a philosophical movement, for its expansion called for an impressive array of performing venues. In Europe, which served as the model for all of Western culture, performing organizations of various types were supported by a public that had become accustomed to including music as part of its routine and that had discovered the romance of musical expression. Public concerts were available that featured symphony orchestras, vocal and instrumental soloists with great virtuosic skill, chamber music, and various forms of choral music, from large oratorios to compositions based on folk songs. The piano became a popular instrument in many homes, and many people sought out good teachers and music conservatories where they could improve their musical skills.

The most popular vocal genres in music in the last half of the century were lieder, small choral ensemble works, operas, and large choral works based on religious texts, as well as instrumental compositions including solo sonatas and short pieces for solo instrument and piano, chamber music—ranging from three to eight players—small orchestral ensembles, symphonies, overtures, symphonic poems, and music derived from ballets. Works for piano dominated the keyboard repertoire, although some composers carried on the tradition of organ music.

In this chapter we will examine some of the Romantic masterworks coming from European cultural centers as well as the music originating in several other countries. Some of these are compositions inspired by literary sources—a practice that began early in the 1800s and continued throughout the century. Rimsky-Korsakov's opera *Le coq d'or (The Golden Cockerel)*, for example, is a musical setting of a fantastic story about the consequences of misguided behavior. Other works represent the logical progression of genres in the hands of composers whose melodic and harmonic vocabularies are enriched by the prevailing musical styles. We will see how Brahms's music combines the balance of a classically oriented perspective with the lush Romantic concepts of harmony and melodic nuance. Guiseppe Verdi's music illustrates the art of beautiful song as well as an inventive approach to orchestral accompaniment designed to intensify the sentiments of the melody and lyrics.

Pursuing the concept of orchestration further, we will listen to the overture to the *Nutcracker Ballet* and sample the genius of orchestration of Peter Ilyich Tchaikovsky. The *Nutcracker* also illustrates the importance of melody to late Romantic Era music—a feature common to all of the musical selections in this chapter.

A remarkable expansion of musical activities also was happening in countries outside of the traditional European cultural centers such as Germany, Austria, France, and Italy. Some, such as the United States, looked strongly to Europe for its inspiration. Others, such as Russia, struggled to develop musical expressions that spoke their own national language but still conformed to the structures and genres of established concert music.

Although the forms of music that had been established in the early part of the nineteenth century continued to be popular, composers became more individualistic as time progressed. For example, the way in which Verdi approached opera, ranging from the subjects he chose to his musical structures, and even his orchestration, differed immensely from Richard Wagner's. Each symphony composer put his own stylistic stamp on his music.

The three examples of instrumental chamber music in this chapter stem from three different approaches to musical composition: first, a work for small chamber orchestra is inspired by the national dance rhythms of Czechoslovakia, which unmistakably and purposely identifies its composer Antonin Dvořák with his homeland; second, a transcription for violin solo of an opera aria by Russian nationalist Rimsky-Korsakov confirms that melodies were often so carefully constructed according to the lyrics that even when they were played by an instrument, the relationship of the melody to the words was apparent; and last, we will hear a work of "absolute" chamber music written by Amy Beach, the most significant woman composer from the United States during the turn of the century.

These musical selections, along with the musical encounter discussing Richard Wagner's role in opera history, are presented to show both the diversity and the Romantic intensity of music expression in the second half of the nineteenth century. Literary concepts, beautiful melodies, expanded harmonies, and artful orchestration combine to present music that has intensive expressive qualities and broad audience appeal.

JOHANNES BRAHMS: ROMANTIC EXPRESSIONS IN CLASSICAL MOLDS

During his lifetime, Johannes Brahms (1833–1897) was known as a musical conservative, for he frequently shaped his musical forms according to established classical models. He loved to develop rhythmic motives in his works, furthering the traditions of Beethoven's compositional style. (For a review of the function of rhythmic motives in Beethoven's *Symphony No. 5*, see Chapter 6.) Brahms's treatment of dynamics, or the manipulation of volume levels, was not as influenced by Beethoven's music as was his use of motivic development, for his musical personality was not as bombastic as was Beethoven's. For example, in Beethoven's Fifth Symphony, excitement often is created by loud chords crashing in on the ears; Brahms prefers to build up to his dynamic high points.

Another contrast between Brahms and Beethoven is in the element of harmony. Brahms's harmonies are often classified as "warm"—meaning that he spaced the notes of his chords in such a way that a general blending effect resulted. This was accomplished by placing the third of a triad (such as an E in the C major chord) in the same octave as the bass note (C). Brahms was a master of sustaining a mood in his larger works; in his shorter compositions, such as his songs, he established the general emotion of the work in the very first measures and shaped it artfully throughout.

Brahms's life, like his music, is an interesting blend of a conservative perspective and romance. He was born in 1833 in Hamburg, Germany, where his father earned a modest living by playing horn in local dance orchestras and eventually playing double bass (string bass) in the Hamburg City Orchestra. His father introduced him to music, and Johannes learned so quickly that, by the time he was ten years old, an American agent tried to arrange a concert tour in the United States for him as a child prodigy, but his piano teacher spoke against it and Brahms remained in Hamburg. Soon, Brahms also began studying composition, and while he was still in his early teens, he began to earn money by playing at various music functions around the city. He gained practical experience as an arranger and a composer for symphonic instruments by writing for the Alster Pavilion Chamber Orchestra, a professional contact that his father arranged. Another facet of his training came when he was hired to play in taverns, where he performed the waltzes, polkas, and German folk songs, the popular music of his time. This influence becomes apparent when one experiences Brahms's lighthearted waltzes, such as the *Liebeslieder Waltzes* (*Lovesong Waltzes*) for piano, or even the way he treated the waltz, as in the third movement of his *Symphony No. 3 in F*.

Johannes Brahms, *Symphony No. 3*, Mvt. 3 (measures 12-24, 1st violin).

Another influence appearing in his later compositions was his fascination with Hungarian music—a musical craze that invaded Hamburg, born out of political events. In 1848, political revolutionaries seeking a change in the Hungarian government were defeated and fled through Germany and directly through Hamburg to immigrate to the United States. The spirit of revolution—which swept Europe during this year and was fired by flames of discontent coming from bad harvests, famines, epidemics, and complacent governmental leaders—also reached into Hungary. Ferenc Kossuth, a Hungarian statesman, writer, and master of public opinion, led a movement demanding a separation of Hungarian government from the other Hapsburg provinces. The defeat of this effort drove many to leave the country; as a result, Hungarian culture, including its exotic music, spread into Germany.

Brahms met Hungarian violinist Eduard Hoffmann (known by the Hungarian equivalent, Reményi) in 1850 after he heard a phenomenal performance by this virtuoso. Reményi, after having heard the seventeen-year-old Brahms play the piano, invited him to be his pianist on a concert tour. In this manner, Brahms learned the performance practices of Hungarian music, such as the drastic changes in tempo found in the Hungarian dance, the *czardas*.

Armed with a broad musical background, an exceptional talent for performance and composition, and solid training, Brahms was established as a professional musician by the time he reached his twenty-first birthday. By that time, his list of compositions included seven works for piano, including three sonatas and a set of thirteen variations on a Hungarian melody; nineteen songs for solo voice and piano, and a piano trio (for violin, cello, and piano). He was well known as a pianist, and he had met some of the most powerful influences in music at that time, including the famous violinist Joseph Joachim, Franz Liszt, and—most important to his future—Robert and Clara Schumann.

His relationship with the Schumanns had many facets and turns over the years, for Brahms was enamored with Robert's musical gifts and influence, and he also fell in love with Clara. Although she was fourteen years his senior and remained married and devoted to her husband (even through Robert's nervous breakdown and attempted suicide in 1854), Clara became a close friend of the young composer. After Robert's death in 1856 (Brahms was twenty-three, Clara thirty-seven), his passion bordered on an obsession, and his love for Clara never abated, even though it was temporarily repressed when Brahms became infatuated with Agathe von Siebold in 1858, a relationship that nearly resulted in marriage. His long-standing devotion to Clara, however, convinced Brahms to end his courtship with Agathe; instead, he immortalized her by writing a composition using a theme made of pitches drawn from letters in her name, A-G-A-(T)-H-(the German term for B♮)-E in his G *Major Sextet, Opus 36,* for two violins, two violas, and two cellos.

Creating melodies based on words or phrases did not end with Brahms's tribute to Agathe von Siebold, for after having decided that he would never marry—in spite of his love for Clara Schumann—he adopted the philosophy "frei aber froh" ("free but happy"), and later he represented this theme in several compositions with the pitches F-A-F. The most famous composition using Brahms favorite motto is his *Symphony No. 3.*

Johannes Brahms: *Symphony No. 3* begins with his motto, F-A-F. These notes represent "frei aber froh" ("free, but happy") and an autobiographical comment on the composer's personal philosophy of life as a bachelor.

In 1862, Brahms moved to Vienna, the city of Haydn, Mozart, Beethoven, and Schubert. He was accepted warmly into the close-knit musical culture, where his career continued to blossom with new performances of his compositions. Brahms soon became interested in adding conducting to his professional skills, and when the head of the Vienna Singakademie died, he was appointed as its musical director and conductor. At thirty years of age, Brahms became the conductor of Europe's most prestigious choral society, where he conducted music composed by famous masters such as Heinrich Schütz, Giovanni Gabrieli, Johann Sebastian Bach, Ludwig van Beethoven, Felix Mendelssohn, and—of course—his own compositions.

Brahms's years in Vienna were the best ones of his life, and he was extremely busy composing, conducting, and performing as a pianist for the best audiences in Europe. He wrote in nearly every popular genre of music, except opera. In 1876, he was offered an honorary doctorate from Cambridge University, but since he was expected to accept it in person, which required his crossing the English Channel, he refused it, for Brahms had an aversion to traveling by boat. Joachim, who also was offered the prestigious award, attended the ceremony and arranged for the performance of Brahms's *Symphony No. 1* at the ceremony, which Joachim conducted. In 1879, the University of Breslau conferred upon him the honorary doctorate in music; this time Brahms accepted and honored the occasion with his *Academic Festival Overture*.

In the spring of 1896, Brahms heard of the death of his beloved Clara Schumann, who had been suffering from increasing deafness and had finally succumbed to a series of strokes, and he rushed to Bonn to attend her funeral. During that summer, Brahms's friends began to notice a change in his complexion, and it was discovered that he had cancer of the liver. He died on April 3, 1897, less than one year after Clara's death.

Brahms's lieder provide a succinct example of the composer's expressive warmth, and illustrate his ability to capture the central mood of a poem in a short musical gesture. For example, by the time you have heard the brief piano introduction to *Wie bist du, Meine Königen*, you will already begin to feel the romantic expressiveness of this love song. His songs have long been part of the standard performing repertoire, and they represent a continuation of the romantic traditions established by Schubert and Schumann. Brahms's music, like that of Robert Schumann's, reflects careful consideration of the relationship between voice and piano.

*L*istening Guide 38

Wie bist du, meine Königen **Johannes Brahms (1833–1897)**	German lied (art song) 1864 Recorded by Dietrich Fischer-Dieskau, with Gerald Moore, piano CD No. 2, Track 16 (4:31)

*W*ie bist du, meine Königen (My Queen, you are so wondrous) is a love song based on a Persian poem translated into German by Georg Friedrich Daumer. Composed when Brahms was in his early thirties (1864), it shows the gentle expressiveness of his romantic capabilities. The form of the music carefully follows the words. Brahms treats the four quatrains (four-line stanzas) of the poem in an A-A-B-A structure. Notice how the third quatrain states the conflict of the poem and how that conflict is represented in the musical setting. Especially memorable is the repeated word "wonnevoll" (wonderful), which ends each stanza of the text.

Wie bist du, meine Königen, Durch sanfte Güte wonnevoll! Du lächle nur—Lenzdüfte wehn Durch mein Gemüte wonnevoll!	How wonderful you are, my queen in your tender goodness! If you but smile, spring fragrances waft through my soul rapturously.
Frisch augeblühter Rosen Glanz vergleich 'ich ihn dem deinigen? Ach, über alles was da blüht ist deine Blüte wonnevoll!	The radiance of newly-blossomed roses, shall I compare it to yours? Ah, more than anything else that blooms is your bloom wonderful!
Durch tote Wüsten wandle hin— und grüne Schatten breiten sich, ob fürchterliche Schwüle dort ohn' Eńde brüte, wonnevoll.	If you walk through barren deserts greenery will spread its shade— even though terrible sweltering heat there endlessly broods—delightful, wonderfully delightful!

Laß mich vergehn in deinem Arm!	Let me perish in your arms!
Es ist in ihm ja selbst der Tod,	In them, indeed, is death itself—
ob auch die herbste Todesqual	even though the bitterest pangs of death
die Brust durchwüte, wonnevoll!	Rage through my breast—wonderful, wonderfully wonderful![2]

To Consider

1. When does Brahms double the voice with the top piano line, and when do the two parts harmonize?
2. How does the piano interlude after each quatrain of the piano relate to the vocal melody?
3. Can you describe the phrase structure of the vocal melody?

Having listened to this small masterpiece, one might wonder where Brahms's link to classical concepts occurs in his works, for *Wie bist du* certainly seems to be part of the romantic lieder tradition that we have already experienced, and it is. If we examine, however, the broader scope of Brahms's music and his approach to composition, we see that he belonged to two different aesthetic camps. Perhaps the significance of this factor to our study is to underline the concept, once again, that artistic expression rarely fits neatly into categories of stylistic and aesthetic description. Music seems to reflect the human trait that individuals, although they belong to a certain school of thought, most often retain subtle uniqueness.

What is Brahms's uniqueness? Many people see in Brahms's music a desire to express his melodic and harmonic warmth into forms that are drawn from classical models. Aside from his lieder, Brahms worked within the classical forms: symphonies, sonatas, string quartets, concertos, and variations. His music shows a strong concern for balance and proportion, not only in its larger, formal structures but also in the way its phrases are shaped. For example, Brahms frequently used the sonata-allegro form (the "first-movement form," which we studied in Mozart's *Symphony No. 40 in G Minor* and in Beethoven's *Symphony No. 5*) in the first movements of his large instrumental works. His careful attention to the symmetry of that form can be illustrated by a simple chart showing the number of measures he devotes to each section in his *Symphony No. 1 in C Minor*. The three central sections of the movement are nearly identical in performance time; the development section, true to the classical concept of its structure, is the most texturally, melodically, and harmonically complex section.

Introduction	Exposition	Development	Recapitulation	Coda
40	150	151	152	17

No. of measures:

A formal diagram of Brahms's *Symphony No. 1 in C Minor*, Mvt. 1.

In Brahms's lieder, one can detect this sense of balance—often generated by the manner in which the composer sets the regular phrases of the poetry. The influence of classical symmetry in Brahms's music is even more apparent in his larger works, such as in his four symphonies. Here Brahms breathes new life into traditional formal schemes by his lush harmonies and by underlining his melodies with subtle swells and diminuendos of dynamic nuance. It is easy to hear the ebb and flow of the dynamic markings in each phrase of the music: it always seems to start softly, crescendo to a subtle peak, and then subside. Brahms's attention to balance and his Romantic expressiveness and nuance give the impression that he intuitively combined two approaches to musical aesthetics—Classicism and Romanticism—and proved that they need not be separate entities.

Brahms's compositions include over 380 songs; a large collection of both sacred and secular choral works, including the well-known *German Requiem* and some beautiful compositions for women's voices; four symphonies; several other orchestral works, two concertos for piano, one for violin, and one for violin and cello together; numerous chamber works; and compositions for piano. His sonatas for violin (three), cello (two), and clarinet (two) are among the best expressions in their respective genres.

GIUSEPPE VERDI AND THE ITALIAN OPERA TRADITION

Dramatic lyricism—the result of setting emotionally charged lyrics to melodies involving a wide range of pitches and dynamics for mature, well-trained voices—is at the core of Verdi's operas, and his operas are the central repertoire of nineteenth-century Italian music. Furthermore, the name of Giuseppe Verdi (1813–1901) was so honored in his country that the nation turned his name into a political slogan: "Vive Verdi" came to mean **V**ive **E**mmanuel **Re D'**Italia ("Long live Emmanuel, King of Italy"). This slogan was used to stir sentiment toward Italy's unification and to honor its future king, Victor Emmanuel II. During the reign of Victor, and under the capable leadership of the king's premiere, Camillio Cavour, the eight different states constituting the political and geographical divisions in the Italian peninsula were successfully brought together in 1861 in its first meeting of parliament. Cavour worked hard and effectively to stir the Italian people toward developing pride in their country and urged them to centralize finance, commerce, travel, and military power.

Verdi's gift of melody, his choice of librettos, his talent for reaching into the souls of the Italian public, and his instinct for fostering Italian traditions and national pride, made him one of the most powerful forces in the music of his time. Verdi spoke for Italy.

For a composer to be such a political and social force through music, one would expect the subjects of his operas to be consistently drawn from the folk traditions of Italy, but that is not the case. He drew upon many sources from various historical periods for his libretti—from Shakespeare (*Macbeth, Otello, Falstaff* from Shakespeare's *Merry Wives of Windsor*) from operas influenced by French grand opera (*Simon Boccanegra, Un ballo in maschera, La forza del destino, Don Carlos,* and *Aïda*) from common stories relating to Italian culture, sometimes his own life (*Rigoletto, Il trovatore,* and *La traviata*), and from others containing acts of heroism.

Verdi's references to political and personal events were not always direct, but their sentiment was understood by the Italian audiences. For example, in *Nabucco* (*Nebuchadnezar*), he wrote a chorus depicting the dreams of the captive Hebrew people: "Fly, thought, on golden wings," which became an instant hit, for the Italian audience immediately identified the plight of the Old Testament Hebrews with their own, for at that time Northern Italy was under the control of the Austrians. The music became an Italian cry for political freedom.

He studied music from an early age, and at age eighteen, when he decided to apply for admission to the Milan Conservatory—a center for opera training—he was refused entrance because he was considered too old. Undaunted, Verdi moved to Milan, home of the La Scala Opera company, and he succeeded in having his first opera *Oberto* accepted at age twenty-six. By now the composer had been married for four years and was the father of two children.

However, Verdi's life was not always one of joy. Early in his career, after he had secured a commission to write two operas for the La Scala Opera in Milan, he experienced a series of personal tragedies that almost destroyed him. He had just begun working on his new commission when he began experiencing chest pains, symptoms of small heart attacks. Furthermore, he ran short of money, the producer of La Scala shunned his request for an advance payment on the opera, and his wife had to pawn her jewelry to pay the rent on the family's apartment.

These problems were soon overshadowed by the events that occurred within several months. In April 1840, Verdi's little boy became ill and died in his mother's arms. A few days later, his daughter also died of undetermined causes. And, on June 3, Verdi's wife, to whom he had been married for only five years, developed a "violent inflammation of the brain" and died. Later in his life, he described the misery of the most horrible three months of his life:

> In the midst of these terrible griefs I had to write a comic opera! *Un Giorno di Regno* (*A Reign of a Day*) did not please; part of the fault lay no doubt with the music, but part also with the performance. With my soul tortured by my domestic misfortunes, chagrined by the non-success of my work, I felt certain that it was hopeless to look to art for consolation, and I decided I would compose no more.[3]

Fortunately for Italian opera and for millions of operagoers, Verdi's resolve to forsake composition was short lived, for he soon accepted a commission to set the story of Nebuchadnezzar. *Nabucco* was the beginning of Verdi's new life. It not only launched him to fame as an opera composer but also was the source of personal enrichment, for during the rehearsals of *Nabucco*, he became acquainted with leading soprano Signorina Giuseppina Strepponi. Their extended friendship over the following sixteen years resulted in their marriage, which took place on August 29, 1859.

American opera singer Leontyne Price of the Metropolitan Opera in dress rehersal for *Aida* at the Paris Opera. Source: Hulton Getty / Liaison Agency, Inc.

Verdi's compositional technique can be summarized by the following general approaches: His melodies achieve their dramatic character through his attention to supporting strategically the highest points of melodies with the loudest dynamic levels, an ingenious aptitude for instrumental doubling, and a strong sense for the expressive capabilities of the operatic voice. He strove to depict human drama through simple, beautiful vocal melodies. His orchestral accompaniments do not compete with the voice. Rather, they support the vocal line by artfully combining various instruments with the voice. Whatever his choice of instrumentation, it always supports the drama—the moments of intense dynamics, the emotionally quiet passages, and the flamboyant gestures of unrestrained feeling all enhance the story line and add to the drama of the piece. He refrained from assigning dramatic innuendos and hidden meanings to his orchestral themes, in contrast to his German contemporary Richard Wagner. His music is straightforward.

A typical Verdi opera has four sections: either four acts, or three acts with a prologue. Sometimes each act is divided into several scenes, which allows the drama to take place in separate settings and in different moments in time. The second and third main sections usually contain finales where a chorus, functioning as a crowd of people in the drama, brings the act to a close. It was also common for Verdi to have a quiet, introspective aria in the third act. And, of course, the opera began with an overture that always established the emotional character of the opera. This structure gave a dimension of predictability of form and provided a solid foundation for the drama.

The example from Chapter 3, "Sempre libera" from *La traviata*, shows Verdi's lighthearted, colorful side. His expressive nature can also be seen in the opening aria from *Aïda*, "Celeste Aïda," a love song sung by Radames, captain of the Egyptian guard, to the beautiful Aïda, who is living as a slave in the Pharaoh's court, but who in reality is the daughter of the Ethiopian king.

Listening Guide 39

"Celeste Aïda," from *Aïda*
Giuseppe Verdi (1813–1901)

Opera aria
1871
Recorded by Richard Tucker, tenor,
CD No. 3, Track 1 (3:22)

Verdi sets this short aria to a very simple yet well-planned accompaniment. The aria unfolds in a basic A-B-A form. The vocal melody begins in a comfortable range for the singer, rises to a high point that requires strong breath support and projection, and then descends by the interval of a third back to its point of origin. Then, in typical operatic fashion, the final phrase of the text is repeated twice as Radames's love song ends on a climactic high note.

If you listen carefully to the instrumental doubling, you can hear how Verdi supports the drama of this aria. At the beginning, he uses a flute to play a duet line with the singer only for the opening notes of the melody. Verdi is able to create a feeling of intimacy by giving the impression that Radames is singing alone—almost without accompaniment. The strings accompany with short pizzicato chords that avoid competing with the singer for attention (much like a piano accompaniment here). As the aria moves to the middle section, the strings begin to support the lines with added parts, providing an emotional backdrop for the words, "You are the radiance of my life."

Finally, the opening phrase of the melody enters, this time doubled by the cello in exactly the same range as the singer (once more a typical device of Verdi's). Notice how this doubling gives added emotion to the line without requiring the singer to exert any added—and unnatural—stress. Verdi's talent as an orchestrator lies in his keen sense of economy. He used the full orchestra only when it was called for by the action and excitement of the drama, and he used small combinations of instruments at other times. In a genre where it often seems that "more is better," his economy of instrumentation many times proves the opposite to be true.

As you listen and are aware of the orchestra's role in this aria, also pay attention to which words receive the strongest emotional stress (either involving range or rhythmic duration).

To Consider

1. By now you have learned to listen to the correlation between the musical line and the text. In this instance, how is Verdi considerate of the words in creating his melodic contours?
2. What is the relationship between the high notes of the melody and their placement within the meter?
3. What orchestral devices does Verdi use to underline this aria?

Celeste Aïda, forma divina,	Celestial Aïda, heavenly creature,
Mistico serto di luce e fior,	Mystical halo of light and flowers,
Del mio pensiero tu sei regina,	You are the queen reigning over my thoughts,
Tu di mia vita sei lo splendor.	You give my life radiant splendor.
Il tuo bel cielo vorrei ridarti,	I want to return you to your lovely sky,
Le dolci brezze del patrio suol;	To the gentle breezes of your father land;
Un regal serto sul crin posarti,	To set a royal crown on your head,
Ergenti un trono vicino al sol.	And place you on a throne next to the sun.[4]

Musical Encounter

The Music Dramas of Richard Wagner

To Richard Wagner (1813–1883), the ultimate aesthetic expression was one that fused dramatic poetry with music (singing and orchestral) into a highly integrated artistic genre. The **music dramas**—his term for these tightly constructed operas—brought German opera to its absolute heights of Romanticism. While some nineteenth-century composers developed smaller forms such as the art song or the brief character piece for piano, Wagner moved in the other direction—toward gargantuan artistic structures that lasted several hours.

Not content with writing individual stage works, each with its independent subject, Wagner combined four into a cycle. These music dramas, *Das Rheingold* (*The Rhinegold*), *Die Walkure* (*The Valkyrie*), *Siegfried*, and *Götterdammerung* (*Twilight of the Gods*), revolved around a complex plot and combined to create his famous *Der Ring des Nibelungen* (*The Ring of the Nibelungs*). Wagner intended this series of operas to be performed on consecutive nights. He worked on this gigantic project intermittently for twenty-six years before his opera cycle was complete (1848–1874). So that the Ring Cycle (as it is commonly called) had an appropriate place for performance, Wagner conceived of building an opera house specifically for the production of his music dramas, and such a theater was built. The Bayreuth Theater was completed in 1876. Its modern version stands today, and is the world center for Wagner performances.

Just as Wagner pushed the physical limits of opera into a new and larger genre of art by expanding its length, linking four music dramas together, and increasing the size of the opera orchestra, he also led the musical world into new harmonic practices. His music frequently strays into harmonic ambiguities through the use of extended chromaticism, which suspends the feeling of tonic and dominant—traditionally the two defining chords of tonal centers. The emotional range of the music takes us into new areas, because the listener's anticipation of resolution is increased as the chromatic chords play out. (This compositional technique is well illustrated in the *Prelude* to his opera *Tristan and Isolde*.) In this sense, Wagner was a revolutionary.

Wagner's personal lifestyle matched his flamboyant spirit of creativity. He grew up with the theater as part of his life; his early years were influenced by actor/singer/dramatist Ludwig Geyer, who was part of the court theater in Dresden. (Geyer, incidentally, became Wagner's stepfather shortly after Karl Friedrich Wagner, Richard's legal father, died. Richard was fifteen months old at the time. Some people, including the philosopher and friend of Richard Wagner, Friedrich Nietzsche, believed that Geyer was Wagner's biological father.) At the age of twenty-three, Richard married actress Minna Planer; his twenty-five years with her proved turbulent, for on several occasions, Minna left Richard to live with other men. The two were separated from each other permanently in 1861.

Three other women most prominent in Wagner's life were Jennie Laussot, an English woman married to a French businessman; Mathilde Wesendonk, the wife of a wealthy merchant and the source of his inspiration for *Tristan und Isolde*; and Cosima von Bülow. Wagner married Cosima, the daughter of Wagner's friend and contemporary Franz Liszt, in 1870. Before their marriage and while Cosima was still the wife of Hans von Bülow, they had three children together: Isolde in 1865, Eva in 1867, and Siegfried in 1869.

Richard Wagner (1813–1882) German composer. Wagner composing in his Bayreuth house Villa Wahnfríend. Print by Rudolf Eichstaedt, about 1890. Source: Photo Researchers, Inc. ID #: GU 3385.

Wagner spent most of his life in Germany but also lived for short periods in London, Paris, and Zurich. He was educated at Leipzig, worked as a chorus master for operas in Würzburg, directed operas at Königsberg and Riga, and wrote and produced music dramas in Dresden, Munich, and Bayreuth. His life reads like a modern-day soap opera, for it was full of political, financial, and marital intrigue. In 1840, he was thrown into debtor's prison in Paris; in 1849, he had to flee Dresden to escape prison because of his political activities. Both Wagner's life and his music speak for a time in which romantic fantasy and individuality superseded restraints of common practice.

Wagner's music is German in every sense. The majority of his plots are drawn from Nordic or Germanic mythology and glorify the rich heritage of Wagner's homeland. The plot of *Tännhauser*, for example, is set in Wartburg and involves a singing contest in which the hero, a minstrel, wins the love of the maiden Elisabeth. *Die Meistersinger von Nürnberg* is an opera that recreates the story of Hans Sachs, the sixteenth-century cobbler who achieved fame as a singer and composer of German folk songs. Wagner shaped the libretto for *Lohengrin* from Wolfram von Eschenbach's epic *Parzifal* and from Grimm's fairy tale *Swan Night*. Its plot is typical of the romantic German penchant for mixing elements of mysticism, in which magic spells, divine and earthly love, and symbolism combine to create a fantasy filled with romantic imagination.

Wagner's operas and music dramas also build on the strong German/Austrian tradition of symphonic music, for the role of the orchestra is elevated from being a mere accompaniment and commentary to actually becoming involved in the drama. To accomplish this, Wagner invented the concept of **leitmotif,** whereby characters, ideas, and even emotions are represented by identifiable melodies. These musical fragments (akin to the *idée fixe* of Berlioz's—but much more involved) are not immediately perceptible to the casual listener but give added dimension to those who know Wagner's works thoroughly.

$\mathcal{P}$ETER ILYICH TCHAIKOVSKY: RUSSIAN ROMANTICISM

Russian composer Peter Ilyich Tchaikovsky (1840–1893) is a central figure in the late Romantic Era, and his works are among some of the most popular with audiences around the world. Although he was born and educated in Russia, he maintained aesthetic ties to Western Europe throughout his life and considered Mozart his musical inspiration. In spite of that, his musical expressions are ultraromantic. His compositions are known for their beautiful melodies that soar to immense emotional heights. Although he identified with European musical practices such as formal clarity, his ballet music often comes out of the spirit and folk traditions of his country. Another aspect of his talent that makes his music so attractive is his inventive use of orchestral color.

Tchaikovsky's European orientation was not unique or unusual among artists in Russia, for historically, Russian culture contains both Eastern and Western elements. When Peter the Great (r. 1682–1725) was the czar of Russia, he established diplomatic and commercial ties with Western Europe, thereby opening the door for cultural influences. It was Catherine II the Great (r. 1762–1796), however, whose interests firmly established a foothold for European culture in Russia. She imported literature, philosophy, science, art, architecture, and music from the West. Russian nobles attended Italian opera, some dressed in Russian furs, others in the latest Parisian fashions. Moscow under Catherine's influence became an international city.

Tchaikovsky's musical training began tentatively, for his parents wanted him to become a lawyer, not a musician. It was not until he was in his early twenties that Tchaikovsky entered serious musical study at the Conservatory in St. Petersburg. His first professional appointment came in 1866, when the famous pianist Nicholas Rubinstein organized a conservatory in Moscow and offered him a faculty position there as professor of harmony.

Throughout his life, Tchaikovsky considered himself an international composer, although many feel his music reveals his Russian personality. His most famous works are orchestral and are written in forms common to the European concert stage, such as symphonies and concertos; he also wrote opera, choral works, vocal solos, and chamber music. His last three symphonies (nos. 4, 5, and 6); his three ballets, *Swan Lake*, *Sleeping Beauty*, and *Nutcracker* and his overtures *Romeo and Juliet*, *The Year 1812* (known as *The 1812 Overture*), and his short piece *Italian Capriccio* are frequently played throughout the world. His three concertos for piano and his violin concerto also are common literature. *Eugene Onegin* and *The Queen of Spades* are his best-known operas.

Tchaikovsky's approach to Romantic expression is poles apart from Brahms's warm sentiments; his music seems to exude more overtly passionate feelings. His melodies run the gamut from lighthearted Mozartian playfulness to dark emotion. His melodic gift and his ability to exploit the timbral capabilities of the orchestra are his two best-known stylistic features.

Composers who write music for ballet often arrange their dance compositions for concert performance as well, thereby increasing the market for their music. Tchaikovsky's ballet music is particularly well suited to this practice, for it is organized into a series of short dance numbers, many of which can stand alone as musical compositions. He abstracted two suites from his most famous ballet, the *Nutcracker*, and they are played either in whole or in part by symphonies throughout the world. The *Nutcracker Suite No. 1*, a work about twenty-two minutes long, comprised of eight numbers drawn from the ballet, is perhaps the most famous ballet music of all time, for both its story and Tchaikovsky's music appeal to people of all ages. The overture to this suite is the focus of the following musical selection.

The *Nutcracker* ballet is based on a fairy tale about a young girl, Clara, whose magical godfather, Drosselmeier, gives her a beautiful nutcracker doll as a Christmas present. Although she wants to stay up late on Christmas Eve, she falls asleep clutching her prized gift, and with a little help from Drosselmeier, she dreams fantastic dreams involving a mouse king, who tries to kidnap her, and a group of soldiers who, along with the Nutcracker, come to rescue her. The Nutcracker becomes her Prince Charming, and he takes her away to his enchanted land of the Snow Queen, of Snowflakes and Candyland, where they see the Sugar Plum Fairy and the waltzing flowers. The magic story ends when Clara wakes up under the tree on Christmas morning, still holding her nutcracker doll. Her dreamland friends are gone, and she is surrounded by her family.

The story of the ballet is a much happier tale than the story upon which it is based, a rather morbid tale by E.T.A. Hoffman called *The Nutcracker and the Mouse King*. Hoffman's tale, intended for adult readership, was rewritten by Alexander Dumas and turned into a children's story. This version was brought to the attention of Tchaikovsky by Marius Petipa, the senior ballet master of the Russian Imperial Ballet, and the famous *Nutcracker* ballet was then created.

The Dance Prism Company performs a scene from Tchaikovsky's *Nutcracker* at Mechanic's Hall in Worchester, Mass. © Kevin Fleming/CORBIS. ID # KF006233.

*L*istening Guide 40

"Nutcracker" Suite, Op. 71a, Overture
Peter Ilyich Tchaikovsky (1840–1893)

Overture to ballet
1889
Recorded by the Philadelphia Symphony Orchestra
Eugene Ormandy, conductor
CD No. 3, Track 2 (3:31)

*I*t is customary for ballets to begin with a piece played by the orchestra, which functions as an introduction to the dance. The overture often presents musical material that foreshadows the general attitude and musical style of the ballet, thus it offers an excellent opportunity to preview the composer's approach to melodic construction, harmonic treatment, orchestration techniques, and other musical devices.

Your first impression will no doubt be that the music is indeed dance-like in character. It has definite accents on the first beats of each measure, and one can easily envision dancers moving with decisive steps on these pulses.

To Consider

1. Describe the phrase structure of the opening to this overture. How does melodic repetition help establish the feeling of regularity in this work?
2. How does Tchaikovsky use the various families of instruments in the orchestra to delineate the form of the phrases?
3. What role does syncopation play in the musical energy of this overture?
4. This overture is based on two melodic concepts (seen below). How does the way in which these two themes are presented create a strong sense of balance? Can you identify the basic pattern of repetition and contrast upon first hearing this piece?

Theme A

Theme B

Principal themes from Tchaikovsky, *"Nutcracker" Suite, Op. 71a,* Overture.

0:00 The overture begins with the strings playing theme A, an 8-measure melody made up of two 4-measure parts. Its repetition is enhanced by a running note (sixteenth note) accompaniment in the violas.

0:19 The flute picks up the excitement of the rapid counter melody and then passes it on to the clarinet. This running figure is soon broken up into smaller fragments and tossed back and forth between the first violins and the flutes.

0:37 Now the woodwinds take up the theme, playing the A theme in a homorhythmic statement (all of the parts that support the theme are playing with the same rhythms). The strings provide the running-note background.

0:52 The second theme B begins—a legato melody that climbs up the scale to the top of an arch-shaped line. It ends with a sixteenth-note component, which links it musically to the material accompanying the A theme.

1:30 The climax of the middle section is reached when the violins, violas, and piccolo create a frenzy of sixteenth notes and drive to a cadence, or logical ending.

1:44 The A theme returns in what sounds like an exact repetition of the beginning of the work. (By now you are able to anticipate coming musical events, such as the passing back and forth between the woodwinds and strings of melodic fragments, syncopated chords that enliven the energy, etc.)

2:35 The B section begins again with the melody played by the strings, in a repetition of its original presentation.

3:14 Now one can sense the upcoming ending of the overture: sixteenth-note passages tumble toward the end, supported by repeated chords played with regular rhythm.

MUSIC AS A TOOL OF NATIONALISTIC STATEMENT: NICOLAI RIMSKY-KORSAKOV AND THE RUSSIAN ERA

In the second half of the nineteenth century, composers intentionally linked their compositions to the native musical resources of their own countries. This movement, called **nationalism,** promoted a feeling of national and ethnic pride and was especially popular in countries outside of the traditional Western cultural centers, such as Germany, France, and Italy. Hence nationalistic music found popularity in countries such as Russia, Czechoslovakia, Bohemia, Norway, Finland, and Spain. Eventually, in the early twentieth century, nationalism became part of the musical expression of American composers, as we will see when we discuss the music of Aaron Copland in Chapter 10.

Composers writing nationalistic music often drew upon their country's rich folk music heritage as sources for their compositions. They imported folk melodies and folk dance rhythms that infused their music with nationalistic character. In our examination of Russian music, we will see how Russian folklore and musical nuances are used to create music that reflects national expressions.

Another way of directing musical expression toward one's country is to describe scenes or historical events through music. This, of course, is relatively simple with operas. With symphonic poems, however, the composer must create musical gestures that remind the audience of a thought or scene. Nationalistic music is, in that sense, program music directed specifically toward expressing patriotism.

The nationalistic movement in Russia emerged around 1875, when five composers announced their intention to create a national musical language in concert music. The impetus for this concept was the strong spirit of national consciousness current in their country following the enactment of the *Act on the Emancipation of the Peasants from Serfdom* in 1861. This law liberated some 22.4 million serfs from lifetime servitude.

The resulting political and social upheaval, with its promise and its problems, created a strong sense of national consciousness reflected in politics, society, and the arts.

The "Russian Five" composers, as they soon came to be known, were mostly learned amateurs. Mily Balakirev (1837–1910) was the only professional in the group who owned a partnership in the St. Petersburg Free School of Music. Alexander Borodin (1833–1887) was a chemist; César Cui (1833–1918) was a teacher of French and later a professor of engineering; Modest Mussorgsky (1839–1881) worked as a clerk in the Ministry of Communications before becoming a professional composer; and Nicolai Rimsky-Korsakov (1844–1908), eventually the most famous of the group, was a naval officer before becoming professor of composition at the St. Petersburg Conservatory. Unlike Tchaikovsky, whose music was more abstract and intentionally cosmopolitan, the Russian Five championed nationalistic expressions.

Nicolai Rimsky-Korsakov combined a variety of Russian folk music practices, including oriental influences, with a remarkable talent for orchestration. His music is therefore colorful, flamboyant, and descriptive of national sentiment. Many consider his fifteen operas, most of which are based on Russian legends, his best works. Besides his fifteen operas, his works include fourteen works for chorus, thirty-three orchestral compositions (the most famous are *Capriccio Espagnol, Scheherezade,* and the *Russian Easter Festival Overture*), fifteen chamber works, twenty-five compositions for piano, and eighty-eight songs. He also collected and harmonized 140 Russian folk songs.

Rimsky-Korsakov's last major opera, *Le coq d'or* (*The Golden Cockerel*), is based on a folk legend by the great Russian novelist, poet, and playwright Alexander Pushkin (1799–1837). The following musical selection is an excerpt from this popular opera and exhibits the composer's skill at writing melodies that not only accentuate the characters in the story but express sentiments of national origin.

Russian poet, novelist, and playwright Alexander Pushkin, is shown listening to tales told to him by his nurse. Pushkin's stories inspired compositions by several Russian nationalist composers. Source: CORBIS.

Le coq d'or is about the aging King Dodon (a czar) who, in spite of his past as a fierce warrior and conqueror, wishes to live in peace, but whose territory is constantly threatened by enemies. He encounters an astrologer who gives him a golden rooster. The astrologer tells the king that if he places the golden rooster at the highest point of his palace, the rooster will magically warn of danger and will direct the king's armies to where to engage the enemy before the domain is attacked. In gratitude, the king offers the sorcerer gifts, which he refuses, saying that wealth has no satisfaction for him. He bewilders the king by asking him merely to honor their friendship in the future.

One day the rooster warns that trouble is near, and the king dispatches the eldest of his two sons to lead an army and to seek out the source of trouble. Shortly after, the rooster again warns of trouble, and the king sends his second son to take another battalion into battle. Finally, after hearing no news about either of the two military forays, the king prepares to go into battle himself.

Dodon comes upon a devastating battle scene and discovers that his two sons have killed each other in conflict. As he is mourning the loss of his sons and the defeat of his armies, a tantalizing queen emerges from a tent and seduces the king. The king asks for her hand in marriage and takes her back to his castle.

The king's triumphant return to his village with his chosen queen is marred by a sense of foreboding. As the crowd cheers the king and celebrates his assumed victory on the battlefield, the astrologer reappears. He reminds the king of his promise to grant him any wish, and he informs him that he wants to marry the woman he sees before him—King

Dodon's new love, the Queen of Shemakâ. Horrified, the king tells the sorcerer that he will give him half of his kingdom instead of the hand of his bride to be. The king commands his guards to take the irritating sorcerer away. Before the king's men can carry out his orders, the astrologer reminds the king of his promise. The king, in his anger, strikes the wizard with his scepter and kills him.

At that moment, a distant peal of thunder is heard, and the golden rooster cries out, "Cock-a-doodle-doo! Danger lies in wait for you!" Descending upon the king, the rooster pecks him on the head, and the king falls dead.

Amid the chaos that follows, the queen can be heard laughing. When order is restored, both the Queen of Shemakâ and the golden cockerel have mysteriously vanished.

Listening Guide 41

"Hymn to the Sun," from _Le coq d'or_
(_The Golden Cockerel_)
Nicolai Rimsky-Korsakov (1844–1908)

1907
Opera aria arranged for solo violin and piano
Recorded by Jasha Heifitz, violin,
    with Emanuel Bay, piano
CD No. 3, Track 3 (3:03)

Abstracting famous melodies from well-known operas as a basis for solo instrumental arrangements was a common practice in the nineteenth century. This selection is an arrangement for violin and piano of a beautiful song sung by the magical Queen of Shemakâ as she emerges from the tent on the battlefield and is discovered by King Dodon. Her song is filled with melodic inflections influenced by Russian musical sources: the first part of the melody consists of short phrases that present a simple melodic and rhythmic idea. The exotic Eastern character is created by the fast, ornamented passages that supplement the long notes at the ends of phrases. These flourishes often contain chromatically altered notes (a practice of raising or lowering a pitch that normally belongs to a consonant chord within the tonality), which suggest the hypnotic character of the mysterious queen and also provide musical hints that she is from Eastern lands. The words she sings reinforce this musical observation:

> All hail to thee, oh sunlight gleaming!
> With joy I greet thy glad return,
> Of Eastern lands long dreaming,
> Thy loving message fain would learn!
> Recall again each fragrant flower,
> The valleys fair, and rich with dew,
> Where throated birds, in rapture shower
> Their wonted songs forever new!
> Say, when at night, those Eastern daughters
> Intone a low lament of love,
> The viol floats o'er distant waters,
> While myriad stars peep out above.
> Beneath the veil enchantment lending,
> With am'rous gaze and smile serene,
> They wait for one, his footsteps wending,
> To greet again some magic queen?

The couch is set, in patience biding
The holy sacrifice of old;
To sacred arbor, softly gliding,
He shall enjoy your charms untold!
The couch is set, in patience biding
To sacred arbor, softly gliding,
He shall enjoy your charms untold!
Ah, enjoy, enjoy your charms untold![5]

The opening descending line depicts the queen as she appears. She then begins singing a song that repeats the same melodic phrase at the beginning of each stanza of the poem. The violin and piano version of this song uses the first and third stanzas and adds an appropriate ending. As you listen to this transcribed song, notice how the melody captures the spirit of the poem. The close connection of musical line to poetic meaning is one of the outstanding features of much nineteenth-century music, and it is one of the outstanding features of this lyrical, seductive tune.

In the opera, the Queen of Shemakâ's song initiates the temptation of King Dodon and the beginning of his downfall.

To Consider

1. Read the lyrics of the song as you listen to the violin. How does the composer express the general sense of the words?
2. As you listen to this melody, can you hear elements of the tune that trigger any suggestions of exoticism in your mind? (Notice that there is a main melody to the song, and at some phrase endings, the composer adds quick melodic gestures built around scales that are uncommon to the majority of concert music that we have heard so far.)
3. One of the adjustments to the song that the violin arrangement shows is the way in which the melody is first presented in the lower range of the violin and is then played one octave higher when it returns the second time. (The original song, sung by the Queen of Shemakâ, is the same octave at each repetition.) What musical or dramatic effect can you detect as you listen to this compositional practice?

The Golden Cockerel is Russian in character, not only because Pushkin's story depicts the simple daily lives of historical Russia but because Rimsky-Korsakov's music contains melodic and harmonic materials suggestive of Russian folk songs. In that sense, it is nationalistic music, for it says to the listener, "I am from Russia!" This type of nationalism obviously is not intended to make a strong political statement; rather, it expresses a national musical language. It gives artistic integrity to the country of its origin and thereby fulfills the composer's wishes to be considered a "Russian" composer.

Rimsky-Korsakov's concentration on expressing Russian musical culture in his works was not always conscious, for his wide repertoire includes works of abstract music not inspired by patriotic allegiance. However, the forces that shaped him and his musical psyche were dominated by folk melodies and rhythms that surrounded him as a youth. They can be compared to a local accent that one acquires unconsciously that often dominates one's life, no matter how far removed from a home environment. Rimsky-Korsakov was not only aware of his native musical accent, but he cultivated it in his compositions.

It is this conscious exploiting of one's musical heritage that identifies composers as "nationalistic." The practice of using melodies, phrase structures, and rhythms drawn from folk melodies is common to nationalistic composers in different countries. In the following selection, we will become acquainted with a composition by Dvořák that has universal appeal, but, like Rimsky-Korsakov's *Golden Cockerel*, also bears the composer's native musical accent.

CZECH MUSIC AND THE MAINSTREAM

Nicolai Rimsky-Korsakov and the other members of the Russian Five were not the only composers to use elements of folk music in their works and write compositions that reflected their national origins. Two such composers emerged in Czechoslovakia (an area in Central Europe, now divided into the Czech Republic and Slovakia) in the late nineteenth century whose music gained international reputation. Their position in the musical world is interesting, for both are well known for their compositions which consciously reflect their homeland. Their nationalism is expressed in well-established musical styles of mainstream composers. It is precisely these established techniques that offered them entrance into the highly selective concert society of Europe. They are Bedřich Smetana (1824–1884) and Antonín Dvořák (1841–1904).

Smetana was responsible for elevating world awareness of Czech music, particularly with his cycle of symphonic poems titled *Má Vlast* (*My Country*), written to honor his homeland. His compositions include operas, orchestral works, chamber works, songs, and works for piano solo. Although his patriotic zeal is most obvious in his later compositions (those written after his fortieth year), his personal style of composition has become identified with Czech music, regardless of his own patriotic intentions. His melodies do not often quote folk music, but his melodic style stems from the music of his country.

Smetana's musical accomplishments no doubt paved the way for his successor and fellow countryman, for by the time Antonín Dvořák was ready to enter the arena as a composer, the European musical world was already accustomed to embracing music originating from Bohemia (part of Czechoslovakia). Dvořák's first successful work was for chorus and orchestra, *Hymnus* (1873); two years later, he was awarded the Austrian state prize for his *Symphony in E-Flat*. Smetana himself had introduced the work in Prague a year earlier. From the relatively early age of twenty-four, Dvořák enjoyed success and was championed by such prominent contemporaries as Liszt, von Bülow, and Brahms.

Dvořák's musical talent was not limited to composition. Initially in his career he played both violin and organ, and as his fame as a composer spread, he frequently conducted his own works. While he was still in his mid-twenties, he was appointed to a professorship at the Prague Conservatory. In 1874, he was invited to go to London to conduct his *Stabat Mater* (a work for chorus and orchestra based on a liturgical text), and the success of this performance led to several other invitations to England. When he was fifty years old, he was awarded honorary doctorates by Cambridge University and by the Czech University in Prague.

His career led him to the United States in 1892, when he became the artistic director of the National Conservatory in New York. During his three-year stay in the United States, he visited several Czechoslovakian communities, including Spillville, Iowa, the present-day site of a museum in his honor. While in the United States, he developed an interest in African-American music that influenced his compositions, especially the *New World Symphony*.

Dvořák's achievements and fame did not rest on his uniqueness as a Czech nationalist composer, although he wrote several Slavonic dances and rhapsodies and used folk songs and dance forms in some of his music. His music was influenced heavily by Brahms, and it expressed a tasteful balance between vivid emotionality and skillful manipulation of melodic motives and harmonic subtleties.

Listening Guide 42

Serenade for 10 Wind Instruments,
   Violoncello, and Double-Bass in D Minor,
   Op. 44, Mvt. 4
Antonín Dvořák (1841–1904)

1878
Chamber music
Recorded by the Marlboro Festival Chamber Orchestra
CD No. 3, Track 4 (5:25)

Dvořák's *Serenade for 10 Wind Instruments, Violoncello, and Double-Bass in D Minor* (for two oboes, two clarinets, two bassoons, contrabassoon, three horns, cello, and doublebass) is often thought to have been inspired by the composer's deepest, darkest thoughts, for much of the music is somber in character. Whether or not one can attribute this to Dvořák's "Czech character" is, of course, a matter of conjecture. What can be heard as nationalistic influences, however, are the regularly repeated phrases of the themes, which resemble Czechoslovakian folk songs. The instrumentation suggests a work designed to be performed in open air, perhaps in a garden. *Opus 44* is the first work in a series of compositions inspired by the composer's Slavonic impulses—impulses inspired by such Czech dances as the *soudedská* (the "neighbors' dance" in 3/4 meter), which is found in the second movement, as is a faster, romping dance called the *rejdovák*.

The fourth movement is a fast piece based on a melody that falls into short, rhythmic, even phrases, typical of Czechoslovakian folk music. But it is music that is treated with symphonic techniques from the arena of concert music. This movement offers the opportunity to hear how music inspired by a folk-like melody can be melded into the forms of a symphonic tradition in a way that preserves the qualities of both cultivated and folk music.

To Consider

1. As you listen to the opening melody, can you identify the rhythmic motive that becomes a building block that ties this piece together? Notice how the closing short rhythmic motive is used as the music progresses. Its folk-like character is created by the short phrases and the simple, accented rhythms.
2. One of the most important features of this fourth movement is the technique of passing melodic gestures back and forth between instruments. Can you describe which instruments are most prominent in this technique?
3. What roles do the cello and bass play? Are they melodic or accompanimental?
4. How does the composer present the melodies in such a way that you, the listener, begin to anticipate their return?

0:00   The first four notes of the Finale are distinctive in that they serve as a germ for the entire movement. As the movement opens, notice that all of the instruments are playing in homorhythmic texture. The initial theme is eight measures long and is divided into two half phrases of four measures each.

0:12   A five-note melodic gesture, which grows out of the first theme, is presented by the oboe; it is then tossed to the clarinet and the bassoon. Soon, other short melodic fragments develop and are played by various instruments. This type of interchange between instruments stems from classical symphonic compositional technique. Repeated eighth notes in the horns provide a backdrop for this activity.

1:02   A new folk-like theme enters in the clarinet, accompanied by dance rhythms in the bassoons, horn, and cello. Gradually the texture thickens until all instruments are playing. The activity swells to a fortissimo and then diminishes in preparation for another new section. Various melodic and rhythmic motives based on previously stated melodies keep the motion alive.

2:19   A slower section suggests a change in the form. The solo clarinet presents another melody, this one based on an arpeggio followed by a quick rhythmic dance motive.

3:31   An elegant, stately march begins; all instruments play in homophonic texture once again. Again, as in earlier music, the phrases of the melody are shaped in short units.

4:27   The final section of the movement begins with an "Allegro molto" melody in the character of a dance. Gradually the texture builds until all instruments play together to bring this sprightly movement to a close.

Dvořák, *Serenade.*

Dvořák's music often combines simply constructed melodies that sound like folk songs and dances with skilled manipulations in orchestration. His compositional techniques reflect both an awareness of his country's musical heritage and the well-established conventions of Western concert music.

AMY BEACH: AMERICAN PRODIGY

In order to be considered "modern"—in other words, alive—must we of today rule out the great inspiring force of emotion, and cling exclusively to the intellectual? Surely we may be allowed to reach out in both directions—the intellectual and the emotional. (Amy Beach)[6]

The concert traditions established by the European masters made as strong an impact on music in the United States as they did throughout the European continent. As audiences for concert music continued to grow in the United States, so did the number of composers writing for them. But the works of these American composers often had to compete with those of famous Europeans for performing time, and progress toward an independent American musical expression was slow. However, as the works of European composers continued to dominate much of the concert venue on this side of the ocean, there were some American pioneers whose music was performed alongside these famous composers. One of these pioneers was Amy Beach.

Mrs. H. H. A. Beach, nee Amy Marcy Cheney (1867–1944), was born in New Hampshire into a well-established family and raised in Boston. Boston, the cultural center of the United States in the nineteenth century, was an ideal place to nurture and educate a child prodigy. According to family reports, Amy's ear for musical memory was phenomenal; before

she was two years old, she could improvise a second part to a melody. As a child, she was able to
play back a hymn on the piano after one hearing,
and she could accurately identify any pitch she
heard. Her early studies in music were with her
mother, a pianist and singer, and soon her parents
secured music instruction for her with some of the
best-known teachers in Boston. By age sixteen, she
made her concert debut in Boston, playing a piano
concerto by Mocheles and a rondo by Chopin. She
quickly became recognized as one of the most
gifted pianists in Boston and gave frequent, full-
length concerts during the next few years, often
performing new music.

One well-known aspect of Amy Cheney's life
was her marriage to Boston physician Dr. Henry
Harris Aubrey Beach. Amy was eighteen and already an established concert artist; Beach was forty-
three and equally well known in the field of
medicine. Their life was one of opulent comforts
and was filled with music and a strong emphasis on
the arts, for Beach also enjoyed playing the piano
and singing. Amy proudly took the name Mrs. H.
H. A. Beach as her professional name.

Throughout her marriage, Amy continued to
perform and compose. Her husband encouraged
her musical activities, but since he viewed it as
his duty as a husband to be her sole source of fi-
nancial support, he encouraged her to donate her performing fees to charity. (According
to Jeanell Wise Brown, Amy Beach's biographer, this was misinterpreted by many to mean
that Beach discouraged his wife's career as a professional performer and composer.) His
wealth allowed Amy to concentrate on performance and composition, free from the need
to teach private lessons.

Portrait of composer and
pianist Amy Marcy Beach
(1867-1944). © CORBIS.
ID # IH000719.

In this setting of professional and personal success, Amy Beach was a musical pioneer,
for in 1892, when her *Mass in E-Flat* was performed by the Handel and Haydn Society of
Boston, she enjoyed the distinction of being the first American woman composer of a
major-length work. During the same year, the Symphony Society of New York, now the
New York Philharmonic, performed a cantata of hers—another first. Amy Beach also was
the first American woman to compose a symphony; her *Gaelic Symphony* was premiered
by the Boston Symphony Orchestra in 1896.

In all, her published compositions number over 300 and include songs (the largest part of
her output), piano works, chamber works, including a popular violin sonata, choral works, a
one-act opera, and a piano concerto. Amy Beach's musical style stems from a Romantic aesthetic, for she was not part of the movement embracing modernism, nor was she part of the
nationalistic movement. Because of her nineteenth-century stylistic orientation, after her
death in 1944, her music was not given widespread consideration by performers and writers of
music. The "new" musical conventions of the mid-twentieth century were well established.
That traditional music, dearly loved by listeners and musicians alike, was represented by the
works created by famous nineteenth-century composers. There was no place in this modern
musical scene for the work of a Romantic twentieth-century composer, and a woman at that!

In recent decades, in light of changing attitudes toward music and music history, the
music of Amy Beach has found a new audience. Inquisitive listeners who have ventured
outside of the standard repertoire have discovered what Amy Beach's contemporaries
found—a treasury of musical expression conveyed within a Romantic framework.

Listening Guide 43

Romance, Op. 23, for Violin and Piano
Amy Beach

Solo composition for violin and piano
1893
Recorded by Joseph Silverstein, violin,
  with Virginia Erskin, piano
CD No. 3, Track 5 (5:38)

*A*my Beach wrote this work for well-known violinist Maud Powell for performance at the 1893 Columbian Exposition in Chicago. Its premiere was so successful that the audience demanded to hear the work a second time. *Romance* is Amy Beach at her best during the early years: her sense of lyricism is apparent in both the violin and the piano. Interesting in this work is the interchange between the two instruments, similar to the close melodic relationship between voice and piano in Romantic lieder.

To Consider

1. What role does the opening melodic motive play in the work?
2. How does the right-hand (treble) melody of the piano relate to the violin theme?
3. What is the overall formal scheme of this composition?

0:00	Piano introduction foreshadows main motive of melody. Violin enters with symmetrically phrased tune. When the violin reaches a high range, it holds a note, and melodic interest is transferred to the piano.
1:20	Piano plays interlude, signaling a second section.
1:27	Violin begins with section B, faster, more difficult, but still lyrical in nature.
2:00	The closing ideas of the B melody are extended through the melodic sequence.
2:50	The climax is reached, punctuated by forte chords on the piano.
3:14	In a quasi-cadenza, the violin turns the B section toward its conclusion.
3:42	The A section returns; the piano plays simple chords in accompaniment.
4:30	Again, the ending is prolonged by repetition and sequence.
5:05	The coda (or ending) begins. The violin and piano draw the piece to a close with descending melodies and a gradual decrescendo.

What is Beach's place in the world of concert music? She holds the distinction of being the first American woman to be recognized by the public as a serious composer. Her works were performed by those eager to seek out new music in a culture that, although it readily accepted female performers, looked upon women composers with skepticism. Second, her contribution to the repertoire of late Romantic music in America is now being recognized for its intrinsic value.

Beach received many laudatory reviews during her lifetime, both in America and Europe. Some nineteenth-century music critics, however, refused to take her compositions seriously because she was a woman. George Upton, in his 1880 book *Women in Music*, states: "Not only are women too emotional and lacking in stamina to write music, but a woman's mind simply cannot grasp the scientific logic of music making."[7] Another similar comment was made fifty-three years later by Carl Seashore, the psychologist who pioneered the musical aptitude test: "A woman is equal to man in terms of talent and ability, but her fundamental urge is to be loved and adored as a person, nothing more."[8]

Beach did not find it part of her personality to challenge such attitudes publicly. The international fame she garnered through both her brilliant piano performances and compositions certainly transcended issues of gender. Her music is now occupying an ever-more prominent role in the repertoire of concert music.

Summary

The late Romantic Era in music history is characterized by composers who developed individualistic styles that were often focused on beautiful melodies supported by extended harmonic practices. Following the example of earlier composers such as Beethoven and Berlioz, composers continued expanding the palette of orchestral colors by using inventive instrumental combinations in their orchestral music.

Whether their music contained musical features stemming from their national heritage, such as writing melodies in the style of folk songs or using rhythms from native dances, or whether their compositions were driven by a cosmopolitan approach to composition, these composers succeeded in creating musical expressions that were both highly emotional and skillfully constructed. The public, which now included people from a broad spectrum of society, found emotional satisfaction and aesthetic fulfillment in the musical venues ranging from intimate solo song or chamber music performances to large orchestral works and lengthy operas.

The Romantic ideal thus represents a wide spectrum of forms, styles, and approaches to composition, serving a diverse audience—all linked together by the basic aesthetic philosophy that music exists primarily to inspire feelings in the hearts of individual listeners.

Key Terms

leitmotif
music dramas
nationalism

The Twentieth Century: Winds of Change

WHAT IS NEW ABOUT TWENTIETH-CENTURY MUSIC?

OUR encounters with music so far have demonstrated that variety and change are two of the most exciting features of our art. As composers react to each other's work and to their social and political environment, their works reflect influences that come from many different sources. This is especially true of the music of the twentieth century, for the urge to experiment with new expressions and experiences is the central feature of the post–Romantic aesthetic.

What influenced composers of the early twentieth century in their desire to be new and different? This question has been answered in many ways from many different perspectives, but it remains clear that the drive to be new was a phenomenon specific to music. In the early twentieth century, various forces came together—political, social, and scientific events that superficially seemed totally unrelated—in such a manner that they changed the culture. By exploring several of these cultural developments, we can comprehend the changes in music that underline the recurring theme of change and diversity in our culture.

FORCES IN TWENTIETH-CENTURY LIFE: TECHNOLOGY, WAR, AND SOCIAL REFORM

The history of Western civilization is not a slow, even metamorphosis, for occasionally specific circumstances emerge and converge with others to form seminal events in the history of change. One such historical milestone in the Renaissance, for example, was the invention of the printing press. Gutenburg's printing press, upon which he published the Bible on movable type in 1455, revolutionized the world of learning, for it eventually enabled the mass production of books, the major vehicle for the advancement of information until the development of electronic media in the twentieth century. Printing, like any other major technological development, also had its effect on music and the arts. We have already seen how the Industrial Revolution of the nineteenth century resulted in the mass production of pianos, making the instrument available to thousands of people. As a result, composers cultivated lieder for voice and piano, many types of chamber music, and thousands of solo piano compositions.

The Industrial Revolution was in full swing by the beginning of the twentieth century and was constantly expanding as techniques of manufacturing became more sophisticated. Perhaps the most significant development at the turn of the century was transportation. The decades following the completion of the transcontinental railroad line in 1869 experienced a remarkable growth in railroad travel, as lines were developed to all parts of the United States. After World War II, domestic and international commercial air travel expanded, as propeller-driven airplanes became larger and more efficient. The advent of the jet airliner in 1958 made international travel even faster. Increased expediency in travel resulted in the faster blending of people from all parts of the world; as people began to travel more extensively, they came into contact with diverse cultural backgrounds, perspectives, and experiences. This diversity led to an open attitude toward change as more and more people expanded their cultural horizons.

The two World Wars had a lasting effect on the arts and culture. Both wars brought Europeans and Americans closer together, for millions of Americans served in various locales throughout the world; as a result, they experienced not only the horror of war but found their association with foreign cultures an expanding force in their lives. Intense expressions of nationalism in politics, often cited as a cause for the World Wars, became unpopular as an aesthetic basis for music and the other arts as a new internationalism emerged.

Another important change in the beginning of the century was the women's movement. The women's suffrage movement, aimed toward giving women equal political rights and privileges with men, was given strong impetus in 1890 with the merging of two active woman's organizations, the Stanton-Anthony group and the Stone-Beecher organization, into the National American Woman Suffrage Association. In the first decades of the twentieth century, several states gradually gave women the right to vote in public elections, and in 1919, Congress approved the Nineteenth Amendment to the U.S. Constitution, which states that, "The right of citizens of the United States to vote shall not be denied or abridged by the United States or by any State on account of sex."[1]

The traditional role of women in society, as well as public and private attitudes concerning women, changed again during World War II, when hundreds of thousands of women were called upon to serve the war effort in various capacities; their activities ranged from active (non-combative) duty in foreign war zones to working in manufacturing plants within the United States. Throughout the twentieth century, the women's movement continued to be the harbinger of progressive social reform. Such attitudes also carried over into the arts, and gradually more women entered the arena of composition in music. (In Chapter 10, we will discuss the leadership role that the composer Pauline Oliveros played in the women's liberation movement during the 1960s.)

What significance does the advancement of travel and technology, the World Wars, and the women's movement have on our discussion of twentieth-century

Mrs. Hervert Carpenter, bearing an American flag in a parade for women's suffrage in Manhattan. © Bettmann/ CORBIS. ID # BE001015.

music? They are all part of the cultural environment of diversity and change. The forces that gave rise to these elements and the residual effect of their activities essentially made the world smaller. New ideas and experiences became a greater part of the life experience for millions of people. Tolerance and acceptance of change gradually gave way to a thirst for change. This spirit in turn influenced composers, artists, and the public to move into new artistic territory.

Musical Encounter

Early Developments in Electronic Music

New developments in music technology during the early twentieth century began with the rather isolated development of electronic inventions that began to offer the composer a larger palette of sounds than was formerly possible with acoustical musical instruments. Two pioneering instruments capable of producing musical tones electronically were the **Theremin** (exhibited in the Moscow Exhibition in 1920), a tone generator in which pitch and volume are controlled by the proximity of a player's hands to two antennae, and the **Ondes Martenot** (1928), a keyboard instrument with two loops of wire, called ribbons, which emits slurred, sweeping sounds. Like many inventions, when these instruments were first developed, they captured the attention of relatively few people, because many thought that they were interesting but basically insignificant gadgets. Some eight decades later, however, we now understand that these pioneering instruments were at the forefront of a gargantuan movement toward electronically generated sound—a movement that is taken for granted in the early twenty-first century.

Today's composers, always eager to create new sound combinations, can draw upon sound that is electronically generated by computers and synthesizers, either to supplement or replace totally conventional methods. By the end of the twentieth century, computers had become the standard tool of composition for composers in all genres of music. In the world of commercial music, in fact, the music for many television advertisements is now totally generated by electronics.

The recording industry has evolved from imprinting sound wave vibrations on a wax cylinder, through recording music on wire recorders, tape recorders, and flat disks made from various materials read by a stylus, to digital and laser technology. In the last decades of the 1900s, developments in computer technology have allowed the transmission of music through the Internet, thus adding another means of accessibility to the dissemination of both recorded and live music production.

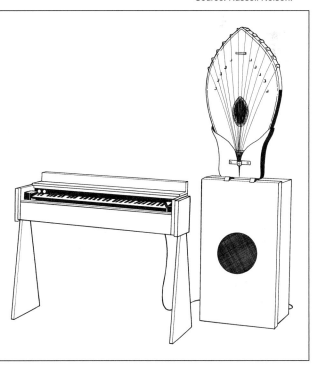

The Ondes Martenot.
Source: Russell Nelson.

The Arts and Modernism in The Early Twentieth Century

The music, art, and literature of the early twentieth century reflect a spirit of **modernism,** a broad movement in the arts whose adherents made a conscious effort to break with the past. Like many "isms" that became so popular in the twentieth century, modernism began as a shared attitude among artists and soon gave rise to a variety of expressions. Composers, writers, and artists each sought ways to contribute to this new spirit, and several developed new and different approaches, or various "movements." In the world of painting, for example, terms such as *symbolism, fauvism, expressionism, cubism, primitivism, futurism, dada,* and *surrealism* emerged, each identifying schools of thought and practice. In music, the major modernist movements were **impressionism**, most closely associated with Debussy; **primitivism** and **neoclassicism**, both found in works by Stravinsky (and other composers); **expressionism**; and the compositional technique that grew out of it, **serialism**. We associate the latter two with Arnold Schoenberg.

Artistic activity blossomed and flourished in France toward the end of the nineteenth century. In the visual arts, impressionist artists discarded the photographic reality of earlier art work and created personal interpretations of their subjects. One painter, Claude Monet (1840–1926), completed the 1874 work *Impression: Sunrise,* and the term impressionism was coined when Louis Leroy, an art critic for the French paper *Charivari,* wrote a hostile review of Monet's painting. Monet and his contemporaries Edouard Manet (1832–1883), Auguste Renoir (1841–1895), and Edgard Degas (1834–1917) soon were linked to the term by the common approaches of their art.

Impressionist art is known for its reinterpretation of reality; the artist becomes a lens through which the viewer sees the subject. At times outlines blur into the background, details recede, and figures blend into each other; the play of light appears at times unreal. A shimmering effect achieved by blending colors in unusual ways is frequently felt in these works. Upon viewing an impressionist painting, one is drawn to the painting itself and becomes aware of colors, brush strokes, and unique perspectives.

Notice, for example, the role that light plays in Monet's *On the Bank of the Seine, Bennecourt* (1868). The bright sunlight on the village across the river causes strong but blurred reflections on the water. The skirt of the girl, sitting on the bank, is not strongly defined by specific outlines but blends into the surrounding grass and flowers. Even the trees have a certain indefinite nature: the leaves and the bark consist of color patches. The reality of the subject is altered by the artist's delivery. (See Color Plate No. 9.)

Stravinsky's works are frequently linked to **cubism**, particularly to the works of Stravinsky's contemporary, the Spanish painter Pablo Picasso (1881–1973.) During his cubist period, Picasso distorted reality by presenting figures and objects in geometrical shapes and by presenting several views of his subject matter simultaneously. Thus elements such as the eyes, ears, and nose seemed to find new places on the subject's face. Picasso's *Three Women,* an early cubist work (1907–1908), shows these tendencies. In this work, the artist presents his subjects in the context of geometrical shapes that clearly replace naturalism. However, in spite of this distorted, nonrepresentational approach, the viewer is aware that the painting is of three humans. (See Color Plate No. 10.)

The early works of Stravinsky, such as *Le Sacre du Printemps,* are linked to the short-lived movement in art, primitivism. This connection is represented in music through the subject matter that inspires the work, and at times, through the use of driving, repetitive rhythms that recall primal images. It illustrates the excitement of the times toward new and diverse inspirational points for the arts.

The translation of the concept of the Noble Savage—a romantic image that inhabitants of "primitive" cultures were somehow purer than people affected by the diversity of modern life—was evident in the life and works of Paul Gaugin (1848–1943) and began an approach to art that further demonstrated diversity and change in the early twentieth century.

Gaugin left the sophisticated environs of Paris first for rural areas in France and later for Tahiti, where he found his Utopia. According to Gaugin, Tahiti represented a place unaffected by the colonialism of European culture, and therefore it offered a fresh perspective on life. His paintings reflect the simplicity of a "carved look" and the influence of the native art of the South Seas.

Paul Gaugin, *Te Po*, 1890.
Burstein Collection/CORBIS.

Expressionism, an art style that explores the psychological and emotional content of the work, is most often associated with German artists in the early twentieth century. Influenced by the popularity of Sigmund Freud's theories, these artists exaggerated colors, subjects, and shapes and distorted facial expressions to communicate extreme emotions. In music, the works of Arnold Schoenberg often are linked to this school of thought. Later in this chapter we will see how Schoenberg's serial compositions revolutionized much of modern music. He also was a gifted painter, and his works show the influence of the expressionist movement in art.

The works of Norwegian artist Edvard Munch (1863–1944) generated so much controversy at the 1892 Berlin exhibition that a group of young artists formed an association called "The Berlin Secession." Munch's works were influenced by earlier artists who often depicted strong emotions in their art, such as Goya, Toulous Lautrec, Van Gogh, and Gaugin, but Munch's works seemed to carry the concept of strong expression one step further. Munch, who suffered from a mental disorder and received electric shock treatment for depression in 1892, depicted one of his favorite themes in *Anxiety*.

So many movements in the arts emerged during the early twentieth century that this could be called the "Era of Isms." Instead, this period is characterized by an enormous energy toward change by the generic term *modernism*. The literature of the times also reflected the spirit of modernism. One of its central figures is the poet and playwright T. S. Eliot (1888–1965), whose poem *The Waste Land* is a classical example of the modernist aesthetic in literature. This poem, which was edited by Eliot's contemporary, the equally famous Ezra Pound (1885–1972), was published in 1922 in the literary magazine *The New Criterion*. It represents the desolation of modern industrial life by using fragmented narrative and vague allusions that add dramatic power to the poem. (Eliot's line, "Ich bin keine Russin" translates to "I am no Russian, I come from Lithuania—real German.")

Edvard Munch (1863–1944), "Anxiety," 1894. Munch Museum, Oslo, Norway. Erich Lessing/Art Resource, NY. ID # S0077526.

THE WASTE LAND

I. The Burial of the Dead (excerpt)

April is the cruellest month, breeding
Lilacs out of the dead land, mixing
Memory and desire, stirring

Dull roots with spring rain,
Winter kept us warm, covering
Earth in forgetful snow, feeding
A little life with dried tubers.

Summer surprised us coming over the Starnbergersee
With a shower of rain; we stopped in the colonnade,
and went on in sunlight, into the Hofgarten,
And drank coffee, and talked for an hour.
Bin gar keine Russin, stamm' aus Litauen, echt deutsch.
And when we were children, staying at the archduke's,
My cousin, he took me out on a sled,
And I was frightened. He said, Marie,
Marie, hold on tight. And down we went.
In the mountains, there you feel free.
I read, much of the night, and go south in the winter.[2]

The fragmented collage of ideas presented in Eliot's lengthy poem is accompanied by fifty-two footnotes, written by the poet, which explain the symbolism of the work. His truncated poem is full of symbolism, including the Grail legend, the *Canterbury Tales*, the Old Testament, Wagner's opera *Tristan and Isolde*, Dante's *Inferno*, and many more. *The Waste Land* was not only new because of its style and idea, but because it was the first work in the history of published poetry with extensive footnotes. Its publication caused a major stir in the literary circles of the time. Some years later, poet William Carlos Williams described its influence on poetry as that of "an atom bomb."

The following musical selections explore the attitude of newness that was pervasive throughout Western culture in the dawning of the new century 100 years ago. Additionally, these examples illustrate the expansion of approaches to composition that gave new variety to the world of art music. Twentieth-century composers experienced a new freedom born out of a new world order, and their compositions revealed this freedom. As you listen to works by Debussy, Stravinsky, Schoenberg, Copland, Bernstein, and Larsen, you become more deeply aware of the array of styles, perspectives, and compositions that awaits the individual wishing to explore the music of the recent past.

*T*WENTIETH-CENTURY MUSIC

The music discussed in this chapter of *Musical Encounters* was selected to illustrate how six twentieth-century composers contributed to the large repertoire of art music performed in our concert halls and transmitted through recordings. This sampling of music illustrates that music is a flexible expression capable of challenging, exciting, and pleasing the modern ear.

New forms, new rules of composition, and new ways of producing sound became the hallmark of modern times. If we seek continuity in the music of the twentieth century, we will soon become frustrated, for the element of change is the only constant found. Musical evolution—to the point, at times, of revolution—is a fundamental feature of modernism.

Because all modernist compositions must compete with works of the past for audience attention or approval, it has been important for each modern composer to establish a unique style to establish a place on concert programs. The result is a tremendous proliferation of styles and sounds. In the twentieth century, composers became explorers of brave new worlds of sound, sometimes to the extent that they left their listeners behind! On the other hand, a new audience emerged, one that was always looking for innovative ideas and sounds.

Although artists and composers rebelled against their Romantic roots, the works of early modernists often contained enough traditional references to provide the viewer or listener with points of comparison with expressions of the past. Compositions inspired by aesthetic perspectives such as impressionism, primitivism, expressionism, and neoclassicism were all built upon past musical practices and depended on the listener to recognize such musical gestures. For example, Debussy the impressionist used traditional chords in a new way to de-emphasize strong tonic-to-dominant relationships, and Stravinsky alternated sections containing singable melodies with dissonant, nonmelodic sections to emphasize the contrast between gentleness and raw, primitive emotions.

This chapter explores these trends of modernism by examining six compositions that span a total of seventy-five years, beginning in 1910 and ending in 1985, and share a common approach to composition, in that their new and unusual components are set within the framework of traditional musical practices. Three of the six musical selections are by composers from the United States and reflect America's prominent role in twentieth-century concert music. The most recent composition from this group is Libby Larsen's *Overture—Parachute Dancing* (1985), a work for orchestra structured around short, melodic gestures representing leaping dancers.

CLAUDE DEBUSSY AND MUSICAL IMPRESSIONISM

The music of Claude Achille Debussy (1862–1918) reflects some of the qualities of impressionist painters. In his classic work, *Prelude a l'aprés-midi d'une faune* (*Afternoon of a faun*), he creates effects of blurred reality in the way he handles the orchestra. His techniques of writing became sources of inspiration for others who were looking for an escape from nineteenth-century concepts of endlessly soaring melodies and lush harmonies. Debussy's music, far from being totally revolutionary, represents a link from romanticism to modernism, just as the impressionist painters are a link between traditional representational art and modern, abstract forms.

Debussy was born into a family with an unstable income and undisciplined child-rearing attitudes. He was soon sent to live with an aunt, who encouraged him to take piano lessons, and thus unknowingly launched his future career. His teacher, a former student of Chopin, recognized his talent. By his tenth birthday, the young Debussy was enrolled in the Paris Conservatory. The following seven years were filled with piano lessons and training in music theory, and Debussy participated in many piano competitions.

While a teenager, Debussy expanded his horizons when he was employed by a wealthy Russian woman, Nadezdha von Meck (well known in history as a major patron of Tchaikovsky's), who hired him as a household pianist and teacher for her children. His job took him to various summer residences in Italy, Vienna, and Moscow. This cosmopolitan experience had a strong influence on Debussy, for later in his life, he became interested in musical expressions from cultures outside the realm of European-based compositional styles.

In 1884, Debussy was awarded the Prix de Rome for his cantata *L'Enfant Prodigue* (*The Prodigal Son*); this prize provided him with living expenses in Rome for two years. It was here that he had opportunities to meet other laureates in the various arts—painting, sculpture, and music, which furthered his world attitudes. However, his basic nature, which tended toward introversion and cynicism, made him feel uncomfortable and disappointed in the Italian experience, and he returned to Paris.

In his twenties, Debussy became fascinated with Russian orchestral music and symbolist poetry, particularly the works of Mallarmé. He made a trip to Bayreuth (Germany) and heard Richard Wagner's *Parsifal* and became exposed to Asian music at the Paris Exposition in 1889. The following years were spent writing works that reflected these influences, and he began developing a distinct style of music, which soon became associated with the impressionist artists. In 1893, he wrote his only string quartet, a composition that has become a standard for modern string quartets; one year later, his *Prelude a l'aprés-midi d'une faune* for orchestra was finished. This also is a seminal work in its genre and is the most performed and recorded impressionistic orchestral composition. His most prolific production of music slowed in 1915, when his rectal cancer (diagnosed in 1909) became severe. His last trip abroad in 1914 was to London, and he continued to make plans to travel to the United States, England, and Switzerland, but he returned to Paris in acute pain. In spite of his physical condition, between the years 1915 and 1917, he produced a set of etudes for piano, three pieces for two pianos, titled *En blanc et noir,* a cello sonata, a sonata for flute, viola, and harp, and a violin sonata.

Debussy's best-known compositions, however, come from his earlier period. In addition to his string quartet and *Prélude a l'après-midi d'une faune,* a list of these masterworks include *Nocturnes* for orchestra (1899); *Pelléas et Mélisande,* his only opera; *La Mer* and *Images I, II,* and *III* for orchestra (1905–1908); two books of preludes for piano (1910–1913); and the ballet *Jeux* (1912).

Let us examine some of Debussy's impressionistic techniques, keeping in mind that he, like Claude Monet, disliked the term *impressionism.* They were both far too individualistic and independent to be linked to an "artistic movement" defined by the critics.

Several musical features of Debussy's music show his ingenuity for being a gateway to the twentieth century. He was fascinated by the scale systems used in Eastern music. He often used fragments of unconventional scales in addition to the major and minor systems in his music.

His approach to harmony and chord progression also was different from well-established conventions. Debussy often avoided strong chord progressions that were created by dominant-to-tonic chord movement. Instead, he frequently used a technique called **planing,** which used a stream of chords in parallel motion. The resulting effect was a nebulous de-emphasis of the harmonic flow. It enabled him to become more of a "color composer," for in the passages where he used planing, the listener is drawn away from strong chord progressions and is allowed to focus on the subtle gestures that suspend time and sustain a serene mood. If we carry the analogy between Debussy's chord streams and colors, we might describe his music as representing pastels rather than fire engine red, hunter green, or black. His colors are different from the bright, bold sounds that we will experience later in this chapter when we hear Leonard Bernstein's *Candide Overture.*

Claude Debussy, *The Sunken Cathedral* (measures 1–4) and the pentatonic scale from which it is derived.

Pentatonic scale

Listening Guide 44

The Sunken Cathedral (La Cathédral engloutie) from *Preludes for Piano*, Book 1
Claude Debussy (1862–1918)

Composition for solo piano
1910
Recorded by Paul Crossley
CD No. 3, Track 6 (6:00)

*T*he Sunken Cathedral is part of a collection of twelve short works for piano that Debussy published as *Preludes, Book 1*. Each piece has a picturesque title, but most often the titles are only indirectly programmatic, for Debussy makes few attempts to tell a story with these works.

The most popular prelude from this collection is *The Sunken Cathedral*, a composition set in A-B-A form that comes closer to being programmatic than many of his other preludes. Debussy's point of departure for this prelude is an ancient legend from Brittany, a peninsula that juts out into the Atlantic in Northwest France, where, according to the tale, a city lies under the sea just off the coast. It is said that once each year the ruins of this city, called Ys, are visible when the sea goes out during the spring tide, only to be covered again for another year as the water returns.

Debussy draws only vaguely upon this legend in his *Sunken Cathedral*, for he suggests that a cathedral emerges from the sea in a foggy mist, the bells toll, and then it slowly recedes back into the water. This prelude parallels the concept of impressionistic art perfectly, for it calls forth images of shimmering water and the reflection of the cathedral on the sea.

To Consider

1. As you listen to this work, try to hear it on two levels: one, the programmatic concept of a cathedral rising and receding in the mist; the other, on a more musical plane. Describe Debussy's unique treatment of chord movement and the effect created by his use of the sustaining pedal on the piano.
2. The composer's directions to the performer indicate that the music should be played with "profound calm," as though one were creating an atmosphere of a "sweet, sonorous mist." What musical devices are used by Debussy to allow the pianist to create this atmosphere? What role do the sustained notes of the left hand play in this process? Can you feel a strong meter here, or does the rhythmic organization grow gradually from the right-hand chords?
3. As the work progresses and you begin to hear the faster rhythms of the left hand, a short, three-note motive appears at the top of the left-hand musical phrase. How does Debussy use this as a building block in this section? (This is the climax point in the music resulting from the composer's directions, where he tells the pianist to "emerge from the mist little-by-little." It is at this point where one can imagine the ancient cathedral becoming visible.)

0:00 The prelude begins very softly with a sustained chord spanning five octaves and a melodic segment created by other chords rising in quarter-note rhythms. The motion is calm; the pianist connects all notes with as little spacing as possible between them.

1:48 The rhythm of the left hand, which up until now had been very sustained, starts to pick up momentum as triplet figures emerge. The cathedral is now emerging from the mist. Soon the left-hand rhythms become even more prominent as a quick three-note rhythm tops out the rising left-hand line, grows into a gesture of four sixteenth notes, and leads to a forte statement reminiscent of the opening measures.

2:21 The strongest, loudest part of the prelude suggests that the cathedral is now in plain view. The melody heard at the beginning is realized in its entirety and is played in both hands "fortissimo, but without harshness."

3:16 A four-measure segment suggests the tolling of the cathedral bells as the music becomes very soft once again.

3:25   Now the middle section begins, there is a key change, and the musical texture becomes thinner. At first, a single melodic line is played over the constantly sustained bass notes. Slowly, more parts are added, so once again complete chords are heard in parallel motion.

4:48   The final section begins with the shimmering effect of flowing eighth notes of the left hand. The chords of the right hand play a soft passage marked, "like an echo of the phrase heard previously." It signals that the cathedral is once again being swallowed up by the rising tide.

5:27   Gentle, wide-spaced chords appear in a direct reminiscence of the opening measures, thereby giving a logical ending to this gentle, impressionistic composition.

What is modern about this composition? We can imagine that the person listening to this prelude in 1910, the year of its publication, would notice that the way in which the chords were presented was certainly different from standard practices. Instead of driving toward a cadence with a dominant (V) to tonic (I) relationship, they move in parallel motion with apparently no urgency to cadence. This chord planing was one of Debussy's attempts to create something new out of well-established material—namely, the triad.

A second novel feature about his work is that it contains no strong melodies accompanied by supporting material. The opening phrase is a series of chords, the top note of which forms the melody. Its phrasing is not complete until the climax of the work is heard (when the cathedral has emerged totally). The general form also is blurred by linking sustained notes in the bass, and the listener is not often aware of the A-B-A structure that emerges until well acquainted with the work.

To our modern ears, these musical features may be very subtle, for we are accustomed to hearing much more flamboyant, radical changes in musical practices. At the beginning of the century, however, this music sounded innovative and fresh to the ear steeped in nineteenth-century Romantic music.

IGOR STRAVINSKY DISCOVERS PARIS

The spirit of innovation that underlines the music of Debussy is carried out in a bolder fashion by Igor Stravinsky. More than Debussy, contemporary critics labeled him a modernist and even accused him of "practicing a cult of wrong notes," for many did not understand his harmonies and rhythms, which by now are considered principal developments in the evolution of modernism.

Although Stravinsky (1882–1971) was born and educated in Russia, he first achieved fame in Paris, a major cultural center during the early twentieth century. It was Sergey Diaghilev, the Russian impresario and director of the Russian Ballet (*Ballet Russe*), who catapulted Stravinsky to worldwide attention when he commissioned several ballets from the young composer. These three ballets, *L'Oiseau de feu* (The *Firebird*, 1910), *Petroushka* (1911), and *Le Sacre du Printemps* (*Rite of Spring*, 1913), showed that Stravinsky would have much to say about the development of the music of the future. Diaghilev's idea of presenting exotic Russian ballet in Paris linked strong artistic traditions in both countries, for France and Russia were two of the world's prominent ballet centers. The *Ballet Russe* was billed in Paris as an exotic import, and audiences flocked to see its performance.

Stravinsky's roots were founded in traditional music. His father Feodor was a famous bass singer in the Imperial Opera of St. Petersburg, so Igor grew up around professional musicians and became acquainted with great music at an early age. Nicolai Rimsky-Korsakov invited the young Stravinsky to study with him, and for the five years prior to Rimsky-Korsakov's death, Stravinsky composed under his guidance.

By 1908, the year of Rimsky-Korsakov's death, Stravinsky's musical apprenticeship was over, and he was ready to become a professional composer. His *Symphony in E-Flat, Opus 1* shows Stravinsky's technical skill but does not reflect the experimental features of his music, which soon became evident. Like his older Russian contemporaries, Alexander Glazunov and Rimsky-Korsakov, Stravinsky used the orchestra skillfully, and, following the lead of his older compatriots, his early works were constructed in traditional symmetrical phrases of four, eight, and sixteen measures.

Like Picasso, Stravinsky's search for new expressions was founded upon recognizable elements that he manipulated in new ways. However, instead of manipulating figures and objects, as visual artists did, Stravinsky altered rhythmic and metrical structures, melodic ideas, and textural elements to offer modern approaches to music. Even his approach to using instruments was novel. For example, he expanded generally accepted concepts of instrumentation. He began exploiting nasal qualities of woodwind combinations and muted brass, he used strings in unconventional roles by assigning them parts that were non-lyrical, and he increased the importance of percussion instruments. (When he was composing *The Rite of Spring,* he surrounded himself with percussion instruments in his small apartment.)

A significant part of Stravinsky's musical personality is related to his ideas of rhythmic organization. The rhythmic elements of his music are often irregular, made up of mixed meters, syncopations, and ostinatos (short, repeated melodic and rhythmic figures) that suggest a regularity which at times is suddenly interrupted by the addition of a single eighth note or an unexpected accent.

Stravinsky's harmonic language often involved two simultaneous centers. At times, he composed aggregate chords made up of two unrelated triads (called polychords); at other times, his music seemed to suggest two different key centers. This is similar to the way Picasso presented his subject simultaneously from multiple viewpoints.

Stravinsky's melodic style also can be compared to the cubist style in art. Many times, Stravinsky's melodies are mere fragments of tunes. Stravinsky enjoyed presenting fragmented melodic ideas alongside clear, easily understood melodies—the type one can hum after having heard the music. We will see this technique used in our examination of *Petroushka*.

Listening Guide 45

Petroushka (Scene 1)
Igor Stravinsky (1882–1971)

Music from the ballet
1911
Recorded by the New York Philharmonic,
Zubin Mehta, conductor
CD No. 3, Track 7 (5:35)

*O*ne very appealing feature of Stravinsky's contribution to modernist expression is his unique manner of mixing traditional elements of music with innovative musical gestures. Stravinsky's music, which was clearly written for a musically literate audience, often lures the listener into a comfortable reference to conventions of music—such as regular, rhythmic pulses—only to interrupt them abruptly with an unpredictable element. The result is a heightened sense of awareness; the listener cannot become complacent. We can see this approach to writing in his ballet of 1911.

THE STORY OF PETROUSHKA

Petroushka is derived from a Russian folk tale set in St. Petersburg during the 1830s at a pre-lenten (Shrovetide) celebration. The ballet opens with a crowd scene filled with entertainment events of the fair: a musician plays the hurdy-gurdy, two rival ballerinas dance for the public (accompanied by organ grinders) drunken sailors appear and dance with their arms linked, a weight lifter shows his skills, sophisticated folks and peasants alike watch the spectacle as the actors and performers try to earn a few coins for their efforts. Finally, the crowd parts as a magician enters and gestures mysteriously toward a stage area. The curtains part, and three life-size puppets begin to dance. Suddenly they come to life and dance among the crowd, and gradually, they become human and take on human emotions and personalities. Petroushka, the clown, is flamboyant and nervous; the Ballerina is aloof, impersonal, but beautiful; and the Moor is colorful, crude, and dull.

The two middle scenes of the four-tableau ballet center on the interaction of the three main figures. The second scene shows Petroushka in his little room; as he experiences emotions for the first time, he realizes that he is ugly. When the Ballerina is pushed into his room by the magician, Petroushka falls in love with her, but she leaves without responding to him.

A parallel scene happens in the third tableau, where the Moor is shown lying on his back, playing with a coconut, when the magician opens the door to his room and the Ballerina enters, playing a trumpet. The Moor, too, falls in love with her, and dances an awkward dance first around her and then with her.

Petroushka soon enters and is jealous of the Moor and his dancing partner. The Moor throws Petroushka out of the room and continues his fascination with his beautiful acquaintance. However, she soon becomes frightened and exits.

The final scene is once again at the Shrove-tide fair where the fairgoers experience more spectacular entertainment. As the celebration continues, Petroushka rushes out on stage followed closely by the Moor, who is brandishing a scimitar. The Moor strikes Petroushka, who falls dead, but not before he gestures his love to the Ballerina. The crowd gathers around the fallen body as the Moor slinks away and quietly flees.

As the reality of Petroushka's tragic death settles on the crowd, they demand that the magician be brought to explain the recent events. As he parts the crowd and approaches Petroushka, his gestures indicate that he thinks the people are crazy. He picks up Petroushka, who is once again a limp puppet. As he drags the puppet off the stage, the orchestra plays the opening measures of the music identified with Petroushka, and the magician looks over the rooftops of the fair booths to see the ghost of Petroushka jeering at him.

Let us examine the first scene (called a tableau) of Stravinsky's innovative musical structures. The composer uses a flurry of dissonant instrumental sounds under a syncopated flute figure to depict the crowd at the fair. (Shrove-tide is traditionally the boisterous three-day period before the beginning of Lent, a penitential season in the Christian church calendar. Mardi Gras is a Shrove-tide celebration.) New musical material sets the stage for various groups of characters as they come into the focus of attention.

In his *Autobiography*, Stravinsky reported that he wanted to write an orchestral piece that featured the piano. He said,

> In composing the music, I had in my mind a distinct picture of a puppet, suddenly endowed with life, exasperating the patience of the orchestra with diabolical cascades of *arpeggi*. The orchestra in turn retaliates with menacing trumpet-blasts. The outcome is a terrific noise which reaches its climax and ends in the sorrowful and querulous collapse of the poor puppet.[3]

This "noise," as Stravinsky calls it, is made up of several instruments playing unrelated, repeated figures. This layering of sound effects, on one level of listening, illustrates the activity of the crowd at the fair; on the sheerly musical level, it presents a counterpoint of ideas and propels the motion of the passage.

To Consider

1. What musical activities make up the different layers of composition that occur simultaneously in this work? (The listening guide below will assist you.) How does this technique of composition affect your listening—your attention span?
2. Can you detect changing meters as they occur? Notice how some of the music is written in duple meter, while other melodies that enter are in triple meter. As Stravinsky interchanges these ideas and the orchestra quickly adjusts to the complex rhythmic and metrical demands of the piece, you will no doubt begin to hear how everything fits together so logically, in spite of the diverse musical content.
3. As prominent melodies emerge, tap your finger to the rhythm and meter. What happens to the flow of the beat, and how does this feature of the music influence your anticipation of musical gestures as the piece unfolds?

0:00	A flute opens with a motive built on an ascending fourth over a flurry of alternating pitches in the woodwinds. Additional melodic fragments enter that also become part of the basic melodic material of the first scene.
0:08	The violins play melodic fragments characterized by descending thirds. The piano interjects a staccato motive.
0:21	The strings play a percussive, syncopated melody; the oboes, then the trumpets, join the commentary with other rhythmic figures.
0:54	The brass section plays a Russian sailor's dance. Notice the irregular phrasing of this segment.
1:46	Finally, a lyrical waltz melody appears, only to be interrupted by syncopated jabs.
2:06	A second appearance of the waltz is more successful. This time the interruptions do not stop the waltz. It evolves into a trumpet tune representing the dancers at the fair.
3:33	Syncopated material based on the opening motives returns, illustrating the busy crowd scene.
3:58	The sailor's dance reappears. Various melodic fragments overlap and succeed one another.
5:28	A snare drum solo ends the tableau and leads into the next section, where the Showman appears.

The success of *Petroushka*, with its interrupted melodic fragments, led to the even more adventuresome composition, *Le Sacre du Printemps* (*The Rite of Spring*). This work, which premiered in Paris in May 1913, literally caused a riot when members of the audience found the music and the ballet obscene and unmusical. With this work, it appeared that Stravinsky had overstepped his bounds as a modern composer. The reviews were scathing! One said:

Vaslav Nijinsky shown in *Le Pavillion d'Armide*, 1909. © Bettmann/ CORBIS. ID # PG8389.

> The music of *Le Sacre du Printemps* baffles verbal description. To say that much of it is hideous as sound is a mild description. There is certainly an impelling rhythm traceable. Practically it has no relation to music at all as most of us understand the word.[4]

In reality, *Sacre* was and is one of the most ingenious orchestral works of the twentieth century. Its melodies are inspired by Russian folk music and often consist of a small range of pitches; Stravinsky sets them by continually shifting notes, strong rhythms, and mixed meters that defy a steady pulse, and he uses novel orchestration techniques to create a work that always seems fresh, even to those who are well acquainted with his compositions.

As for the uprising at the premiere, it was probably due not only to the unusual music—which had precious few singable tunes—but to the unconventional choreography of Vaslav Nijinsky. The ballet depicts a pagan rite in ancient Russia in which a virgin is chosen to be sacrificed to ensure the fertility of the earth. Nijinsky, a gifted dancer and choreographer, set the story to movements that were totally new to the classical world of ballet. Thus the modernism of the musical score was matched by the dance patterns.

By the end of World War I, Stravinsky began to seek ways to incorporate into his music influences from past eras of style, especially the Baroque and Classical eras. He had returned to France after having spent the war years in Switzerland, and he was interested in expanding his musical reference points from a Russian perspective to a more universal outlook.

In 1919–1920, again at the suggestion of Diaghilev, he composed the ballet *Pulcinella*, which was based on the music of Italian Baroque composer Giovanni Baptiste Pergolesi (1710–1736) and on several of Pergolesi's contemporaries. His research into Pergolesi's music inspired him to adopt some of the techniques of Baroque music, such as elements of counterpoint and phrasing. Of course, Stravinsky's melodic structures, his approach to rhythm and meter, and his orchestration retained their unique character. This approach to musical composition—the inclusion of earlier stylistic elements into a contemporary idiom—came to be called neoclassicism, another important twentieth-century style.

Stravinsky lived a long life filled with musical and financial success. He moved to the United States in 1940, settled in Hollywood, California, and eventually became a U.S. citizen. Continually looking forward and always interested in developing fresh ideas, he was the model for many composers in the modern era. In 1953, two years after he wrote his great neoclassical opera *The Rake's Progress*, Stravinsky once again changed his approach to composition and began using the serial technique that had been developed by Arnold Schoenberg. His last works are characterized by extreme austerity and are highly structured around abstract mathematical principles. His music, which in his early career had caused a great deal of controversy because of its daring flamboyance, became introspective and cerebral at the end of his life.

What follows is a selected list of works (with English titles) that not only represents Stravinsky's musical genius but shows the wide versatility of his musical expressions over the years:

Ballets: Stravinsky composed suites from these works for concert performance: *The Firebird* (1910); *Petroushka* (1911); *The Rite of Spring* (1913); *Pulcinella* (1920).
Symphonic works: *Symphony in C* (1940); *Symphony in Three Movements* (1945).
Instrumental compositions: *Octet for Wind Instruments* (1923); *Concerto in E Flat* ("*Dumbarton Oaks*") (1938); *Ebony Concerto* (1945).
Stage works: *The Soldier's Tale* (1918); *The Rake's Progress* (1951).
Choral works: *Symphony of Psalms* (1930); *Mass* (1948).
Vocal solo and instruments: *In Memoriam Dylan Thomas* (1954).

RNOLD SCHOENBERG: THE NEW VIENNESE SCHOOL

If France laid claim to being one of the prominent cultural centers of Europe during the early twentieth century, Austria certainly was in contention for similar recognition. After all, Vienna had been the center of music for decades: Haydn, Mozart, Beethoven, and Schubert had laid the cultural foundations there (in retrospect, some call it the "First Viennese School"). In 1874, a child was born in Vienna who was destined to start a "Second Viennese School."

After a rather nondescript childhood during which time he took violin lessons and experimented with writing short pieces of music, Arnold Schoenberg (1874–1951) became acquainted with three prominent Viennese friends who profoundly influenced his future: Oscar Adler introduced him to music theory; David Bach expanded his experience through a combination of philosophy, mathematics, literature, and music; and Alexander von Zemlimsky taught him composition and counterpoint. In this way, Schoenberg entered the cultural life of his city and soon became part of its core.

Schoenberg's career as a musician grew out of his talent as a music theorist. After having achieved some success at writing music typical of his time, he soon became interested in pushing the limits of his art by discovering new ways to organize harmony. In

1908, after having written the first three movements of his *String Quartet No. 2 in F# Minor,* he decided to abandon the use of key signatures for the last movement. He added text to this movement, a poem to be sung by a soprano, stating, "I feel the air of other planets." This new air came to be known as "atonalism," and it began yet another approach to musical composition that had a strong impact on the music world. (Atonalism refers to music in which one cannot hear a specific tonal center or key.)

Schoenberg eventually called his concept of harmony "the emancipation of dissonance," for he wanted all tones to have equal harmonic weight in his music. This means that the age-old practice of music that was centered around a key center (with tonic and dominant chords and chromatic substitutions) was replaced by a system completely free of such references.

Of course, the public criticized him. To add to the notoriety of his dissonant harmonies, Schoenberg also came up with the idea of *Sprechgesang* (*speech-song,* also called *Sprechstimme*), in which a singer "speaks" approximate pitches within a wide range without actually landing on any given pitch. His famous work of 1912, *Pierrot Lunaire* (*Moonstruck Pierrot*), uses this technique. It is a collection of twenty-one poems by expressionist poet Albert Giraud, set in German translation to an instrumental ensemble of piano, flute/piccolo, clarinet/bass clarinet, violin, and cello. Like Stravinsky's *Le Sacre du Printemps,* this work caused a major upset in the concert world. A music critic from the *New York Courier* wrote this scathing diatribe against the composer and his experimental composition:

> Arnold Schoenberg may be either crazy as a loon, or he may be a very clever trickster who is apparently determined to cause a sensation at any cost. His *Pierrot Lunaire* is the last word in cacophony and musical anarchy. Some day it may be regarded as of historical interest, because it represents the turning point, for the outraged muse surely can endure no more of this. Schoenberg has thrown overboard all the sheet anchors of the art of music. Melody he eschews in every form; tonality he knows not, and such a word as harmony is not in his vocabulary.[5]

A third novel contribution to sound exploration that Schoenberg created was Klangfarbenmelodie, or the technique of creating linear continuity by continually shifting the tone colors, or timbres, of an instrumental ensemble. This technique is a substitute for melody as it is normally perceived, and it compels the listener to focus on a different kind of sound orientation.

Although Schoenberg thoroughly explored the concept of emancipation of dissonance in the first decades of the century, he still felt a need to develop a more specifically defined set of compositional tools to achieve his goals. During a period of time when he wrote very little music, from 1917 to 1923, he met with a group of musician friends on a regular basis where new music of various composers of the time was played, analyzed, discussed, and debated. This intense involvement with other musicians stimulated Schoenberg to devise a system of writing that became the hallmark of his middle and late works. This approach, called serialism, allowed Schoenberg to express his aesthetic goals in a practical method of composition.

Serialism is a technique of composition in which the entire work is based on a series of notes composed from the chromatic scale. This series (also called a **tone row,** or **set**) is often treated in the following ways:

1. The general guideline is to use all notes of the series before any are repeated.

2. The notes of the series may be used melodically (horizontally), harmonically (vertically), or a combination of the two.

3. The series may be altered by use of **permutations** (generating a new series by inverting it, i.e., if the original series contains an interval of an ascending fifth, the inversion would be a descending fifth).

4. The series and its permutations may be transposed to any pitch level.

Schoenberg's serial system included the concept of using the tone row (or set) in **retrograde** (backward), in **inversion** (where the direction of each interval is in the opposite direction of the original tone row), in **retrograde inversion**, and in **transposition** (transferring the row to a different pitch level). These are indicated in the following example by: (O) = original set; (IT) = inversion transposed; and (I) = inversion.

a) Chromatic scale

b) Tone row of the _Trio_

Arnold Schoenberg, _Trio,_ from _Suite für Klavier,_ Op. 25 (1925): a. chromatic scale; b. tone row of the _Trio._

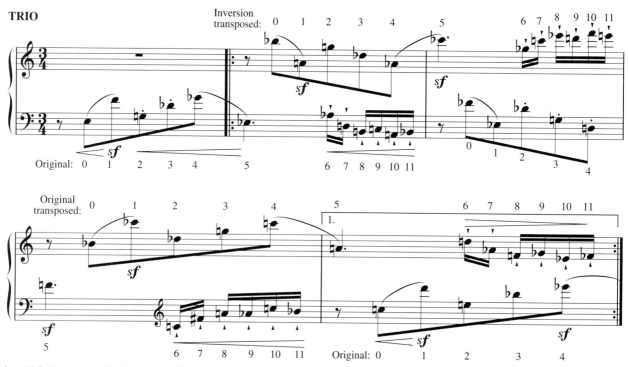

Arnold Schoenberg, _Trio,_ from _Suite für Klavier,_ Op. 25 (1925). This excerpt illustrates Schoenberg's use of the tone row. Notice that the left hand plays the original version of the row, while the right hand presents a transposition of the inversion.

Listening Guide 46

"Minuet and Trio", from *Suite für Klavier*, Opus 25
Arnold Schoenberg (1874–1951)

1925
Section from a five-movement suite for piano
Recorded by Glen Gould, piano
CD No. 3, Track 8 (3:52)

To Consider

1. Although there are no singable melodies and no references to familiar triads in this, Schoenberg achieves cohesiveness in this short piano piece. Can you identify some aspects that, even upon first hearing, tie it together and give it a feeling of completeness?
2. How do you interpret the change of character that happens when the Trio begins? Is this strongly perceptible, or do the Minuet and the Trio feel like one section, in spite of the repetitions?
3. How does the lack of familiar compositional elements (other than their form) draw your attention to elements such as melodic contours and short, rhythmic motives?

0:00	Although the Minuet is in a 3/4 meter, Schoenberg obscures the meter by avoiding strong beats at the beginning of the measures.
0:52	After a brief ritardando (a slowing down of tempo), the Minuet continues toward a strong climax, which is signaled by a loud ascending sixteenth-note bass figure and answered by a descending treble gesture.
1:35	The Minuet ends peacefully; the Trio follows after a short pause.
1:46	The Trio begins with a disjunct left-hand melodic gesture; it is immediately countered by a right-hand melody descending from the opposite direction.
1:57	The repeated sections of this short Trio happen so quickly that the ear almost fails to identify them as they fly by. Perhaps Schoenberg is not as concerned with the listener's perception of form here as he is with the awareness of the contrary motion of the right and left hand melodic lines in this two-part texture.
2:18	In keeping with the classical Minuet and Trio form, the Minuet returns, providing an element of symmetry to this miniature serial composition. (Our introduction to the Minuet and Trio form was the third movement of Mozart's *Symphony No. 35*.)

Serial composition, while seeming very mathematical and mechanical to critics, actually offered the composer a new way of organizing the pitches of a composition, while at the same time allowing a vast array of possibilities. Schoenberg and his two leading pupils, Alban Berg (1883–1935) and Anton Webern (1885–1945), created many viable works and thereby solidified a school of thought and practice that served as a compositional foundation for many composers to follow.

Schoenberg's influence is felt in several ways. His popular compositions include the orchestral works *Verklärte Nacht* (*Transfigured Night*) (1899), a work written in a more traditional style, which shows his connections to earlier musical practices of chromaticism within a tonal framework, *5 Pieces* (1908), and *Variations* (1928). His pioneering work for band, *Theme and Variations* (1944), is often performed by university wind ensembles. The early choral works, *Gurrelieder* (1901) and *Friede auf Erden* (1907), are part of the advanced choral repertoire of today. In his later years, Schoenberg wrote three works for narrator and orchestra that were quite effective (he abandoned the concept of *Sprechstimme* in these works): *Kol Nidrei* (1939), *Ode to Napoleon* (1943), and *A Survivor from Warsaw* (1947). Of his four stage works, his opera *Moses and Aaron* (1951) is the best known.

In addition to the above-mentioned large works, Schoenberg composed several songs with piano, and he also wrote two sets of songs with orchestra. His chamber works for various combinations of instruments (including the famous chamber piece with solo voice, *Pierrot Lunaire*, of 1912) and his piano works are a significant part of his creative output.

Schoenberg's contributions to modern music did not end with his theories of composition and his music, for he also was a conductor, an author of several books on music, and a master teacher of music theory and composition. His teaching career began in 1903 in Vienna and ended with his retirement in 1944 from the University of Southern California. By immigrating to America, Schoenberg became part of the growing significance of the United States being recognized as a cultural center of the Western world.

THE EMERGENCE OF THE UNITED STATES AS A WORLD LEADER IN CONCERT MUSIC

We have already noted that two major composers we have singled out for study spent the last years of their careers in the United States. Schoenberg came to the United States in 1935 and Stravinsky came in 1940. Each came for his own reason, but each was aware of the potential of moving to a thriving, growing, and healthy artistic environment. Other prominent European composers who raised the consciousness for modern music by coming to America were Richard Strauss (1864–1949), Gustav Mahler (1860–1911), Sergey Rachmaninoff (1873–1943), Sergey Prokofiev (1891–1953), and Paul Hindemith (1895–1963). Some, like Strauss, spent a short time in the United States, usually a result of attending or conducting performances of their works, while others accepted professional positions as conductors (such as Mahler) or university professors (Hindemith) before returning to their homelands.

What was it about the American musical environment that attracted European composers to America? One obvious reason was that many European intellectuals immigrated to the United States to improve their living conditions (especially those, like Schoenberg, who came to the United States in the 1930s and 1940s to escape the Nazis and World War II). A second factor that enticed European musicians to cross the Atlantic was the symphony orchestras, opera houses, and public concerts that began to flourish in greater numbers than ever before. Toward the end of the nineteenth century, permanent orchestras were established in Boston (1881), St. Louis (1881), and Chicago (1891); they were preceded by the New York Philharmonic, whose precursor, the Symphony Society, was founded in 1842. Soon, most major cities in the United States could boast their own orchestra: Philadelphia formed its orchestra in 1901, Minneapolis in 1903, and Cleveland in 1918. Supported by William H. Vanderbilt, the New York Metropolitan Opera opened in 1883 with sixty-one performances in its own opera house and fifty-eight more on tour.

Supported by private foundations and by the public, art music performances soon were a common part of life in U.S. cities. Many champions of art music were either European immigrants or their descendants; for example, many German musicians came to America after the 1848 revolution in their homeland and formed cultural communities in the new land.

As a result of the rising interest in music, schools of music also became popular in the late nineteenth and early twentieth centuries. In 1891, Antonín Dvořák was brought to America by a wealthy patron, Mrs. Jeannette Thurber, to assume the directorship of the National Conservatory of Music in New York. The Eastman School, opened in Rochester, New York, in 1921 and, named after its leading benefactor, George Eastman, of the Eastman Kodak Company, soon led the way in training musicians of the highest professional caliber. Following was the Julliard School in New York City; conservatories, both public and private, were established in virtually every metropolitan center. In the early decades of the century, states started to include music appreciation courses, chorus, band, orchestra, and music contests in the public school systems. In 1940, an *Outline of a Program for Music Education* was adopted by the newly formed Music Educator's National Conference, the nationwide organization for music education. Currently music is being taught for credit throughout the United States.

A major element in the rise of musical activity beginning in the 1940s resulted from the devastation of the European culture during World War II. Many concert halls, opera houses, and other places where music flourished had been flattened by the bombs of modern warfare, and the basic focus on survival and restoration after the war hindered a healthy artistic environment. Fortunately, however, the artistic nature of humankind eventually prevailed, and the arts in Europe soon resurfaced to resume its prominent role in the lives of the European people.

Alfred Einstein, a German musicologist (and cousin of the famous scientist Albert Einstein), published his reaction to the war and its effect on music in 1939. He wrote the following about America's role in music:

> America's position is at once fortunate and difficult. It is the only country really on the sidelines. The hospitality which it has offered so many musicians from old Europe, has its complications, the invasion must be "digested." But America has already digested many invasions, and it will soon find out which of the new arrivals it can utilize and which not. Be that as it may, as long as the war continues, America will be a refuge, the only refuge, for this freedom. . . . America has an opportunity, a splendid duty, not only to produce good music, but to foster good music no matter where it may originate. It has the opportunity and duty of tolerance. And tolerance in matters of art has always borne lasting fruit. [6]

By the middle of the twentieth century, the United States had all of the ingredients necessary to rival any European cultural center. Many leading European composers migrated to America in search of better personal and professional opportunities. Numerous professional symphony orchestras and opera companies provided artistic outlets both for composers and audiences. Schools of music existed in universities throughout the country offering training for musicians, a large concert venue for performance, and educational opportunities. And public schools in all states of the union offered children exposure to music.

The following musical selections are just a sampling of prominent American composers and their music and serve to illustrate how concert music in the United States took on a life of its own in the twentieth century.

ARON COPLAND POINTS TO AMERICAN FOLKLORE

Like virtually every composer of note in the early twentieth century, Aaron Copland (1900–1990) explored several avenues of musical style, including serialism, in search of a personal expression. Instead of following the paths of European composers, however, he developed an approach to music that is seen today as being both cosmopolitan and decidedly American. His music is now heard not only in the concert hall but in television commercials—a sure sign of acceptance in the modern world.

Copland was born in Brooklyn, New York, and received his early musical training by taking piano lessons. By age seventeen, he became interested in writing music and began to study in Manhattan with Rubin Goldmark, then a prominent teacher and composer with musical roots from Vienna. Under the tutelage of Goldmark, Copland learned traditional harmony and counterpoint. However, his adventuresome spirit soon led him to seek broader horizons, and in 1921 he went to Paris. His most significant training as a composer was acquired there with Nadia Boulanger—the most famous teacher of composition in the century, with whom Copland felt he could explore new ideas. Looking back on the years with Boulanger, he said:

> She was really a remarkable personality and an extraordinary musician. She knew everything about music you'd want to know: the oldest music, the newest music . . . a studio was not just a place where we studied with her, it was a kind of musical center of Paris. She had her Wednesday afternoon classes for her students, and after the class was over, all the musical greats of Paris came for tea! I met Stravinsky there and I met Milhaud and Poulenc and the younger composers . . . I even shook hands with Saint-Saëns in that place. She really launched me on my way![7]

Through Boulanger's influence, Copland received his first big professional break. His teacher introduced him to Sergey Koussevitsky, who had just been appointed music director of the Boston Symphony. Koussevitsky suggested that Copland write a symphony for organ and orchestra with the idea that Boulanger should perform the organ part. (Copland later rewrote this work without organ, and it became his *Symphony No. 1.*) After the 1925 New York performance of this work, conservative conductor Walter Damrosch turned to the audience and said, "If he can write like that at twenty-three, in five years he'll be ready to commit murder!"[8]

Today, a decade after his death, the musical public does not remember Copland as being a revolutionary composer, however. He now seems to speak for America more than any other composer. His best-known, most accessible works deal with American subjects: the ballets *Billy the Kid* (1938), *Rodeo* (1942), *Appalachian Spring* (1944); *Lincoln Portrait* (1942), scored for orchestra and narration to Carl Sandburg's text; and *Fanfare for the Common Man* (1942).

What is it about Copland's music that makes it American? The most tangible element is melody. In his early ballets, he introduced well-known cowboy tunes. Copland was from New York City and had little, if any, firsthand experience with Western folk tunes. His knowledge of American folk music was gained through published folk song collections. Aside from the quotation of tunes in his works, he developed a melodic style in which "open" intervals—frequently fourths and fifths—became symbolic of the big skies and vast spaces of America.

His use of syncopation and his strong accents—both on and off the primary beats of the measure—gives tremendous energy to his music. Much of his rhythmic vitality also stems from jazz. Copland, like Stravinsky before him and Bernstein after him, was strongly attracted to the inspirational and stylistic resources that American jazz could lend to concert music.

Listening Guide 47

"Buckaroo Holiday," from *Rodeo*
Aaron Copland (1900–1990)

Music from the ballet
1942
Recorded by the London Symphony Orchestra,
Aaron Copland, conductor
CD No. 3, Track 9 (7:41)

The 1942 ballet *Rodeo*, with scenario and choreography by Agnes de Mille, was a commission from the Ballet Russe de Monte Carlo and was first performed in New York City. The ballet tells a story of the problem that confronted the typical American girl of the frontier—how to get a suitable man. The work was successful from its opening night (it received twenty-two curtain calls). Recognizing the success of *Rodeo*, Copland immediately adapted four dance episodes from the ballet for an orchestral suite and thereby contributed a new and exciting work to the standard orchestral repertoire. The first of these four episodes, *Buckaroo Holiday*, uses two melodies that Copland found in the John and Alan Lomax collection of folk songs, *Our Singing Country*.

Sis Joe (as used in "Buckaroo Holiday")

If He'd Be A Buckaroo

Aaron Copland: Two themes from *Rodeo*.

Copland used part of the song *Sis Joe* as the basis for the powerful bursts of sound that occur a few minutes into the dance. The principal melody of "Buckaroo Holiday," however, is *If He'd Be a Buckaroo*. The listening guide will identify these sections.

On the purely expressive plane of listening, this music is brash, bold, and optimistic. Its energy, derived both from the syncopated presentation of the melodies and judiciously chosen combinations of instruments, is hard to ignore. The story of *Rodeo* and the images Copland paints with his music give it an American expression.

To Consider

When you listen, be aware of these three fundamental considerations:

1. What effect does Copland's use of syncopation and strong accents have on your natural tendency to antipicate upcoming musical gestures?
2. The open instrumentation often groups instruments from various families in novel ways. Copland's distinctive sound is frequently described as having a wide-open sound. What specific musical devices do you hear that create this effect?
3. Describe the general ebb and flow of the motion in this piece. How does this contribute to the energy of this dance?

0:00	The dance opens with an introductory theme comprised of converging scale patterns set in an energetically syncopated rhythmic context.
0:43	An abrupt change of character and tempo provides a brief lyrical section in which flutes and muted horns are answered by muted trumpets and bassoons. Although these short phrases are lyrical, they are nonetheless syncopated.
1:45	The tempo increases with a 23-measure vamp (a repeated phrase) that heightens anticipation.
2:08	A powerfully accented theme (derived from the second half of a cowboy melody, *Sis Joe*) is punctuated by the bass drum and slapstick. (A slapstick is a percussion instrument made of two flat boards hinged together. When the player moves it in a quick, whipping motion, it creates a sound like the cracking of a whip.)
2:20	The opening scale theme returns, perhaps hinting that this will function as a link between various themes of the piece.
3:23	The two-beat rhythm introduces the central melody of *Buckaroo Holiday*; the cowboy tune, *If He'd Be a Buckaroo*, is played by the trombone. The even phrases are broken up by moments of silence, thereby upsetting the feel of even rhythm and meter.
3:53	The trumpet plays the *Buckaroo* melody. Notice the humorous stop-and-go presentation and the artful exchange of instrumentation here.

4:06 The *Buckaroo* melody continues, this time in a harmonic setting, suggesting two different tonal centers a fifth apart.

4:43 The central theme is now treated in imitation, and one begins to feel that the dance is coming to an end.

4:59 Another lyrical section extends the music. New material is mixed with accompanying rhythms and motives derived from the now-familiar tunes.

5:30 Large chords serve as an interlude to a section based on the previous *Sis Joe* section.

6:42 The final section once again features the *Buckaroo* melody set to an accompaniment of motives taken from various sections of the dance.

To classify Copland simply as a composer who writes music inspired by American subject matter is, of course, a gross injustice. His life work includes two operas, six ballets, twenty-nine works for orchestra, two concertos, twelve chamber works, one composition for concert band, fifteen piano works, two for organ, eight choral works, ten sets of songs for solo voice and piano, four incidental compositions for stage, seven film scores, and two television scores.

His personality was one of openness and accessibility. Whether he appeared as a conductor at his music concerts or gave formal lectures on music, he exuded the same attitude that his music contains—uncompromising standards that nonetheless held wide public appeal. He proved to the world of concertgoers that it is possible to be both modern and popular. In the last decades of his life, his fame took him all over the world as a representative of American music.

Copland enjoyed a close professional friendship with conductor/composer Leonard Bernstein—the next subject of our study. Bernstein, eighteen years younger than Copland, forms an interesting parallel to his senior colleague, for the two musicians shared similar attitudes toward their art.

*L*EONARD BERNSTEIN: AMERICAN ECLECTIC

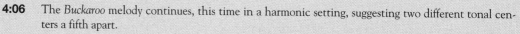

One can accurately assume that talent is a fundamental part of a composer's profile, and there can be no doubt that the composers we have studied thus far in *Musical Encounters* exhibit aptitude far beyond that of mere musical dilettantes. Few modern composers have been so broadly talented, however, as Leonard Bernstein (1918–1990). As a conductor, Bernstein brought tremendous vitality and interpretive insight to musical performance. As an ambassador for music, he is unmatched in his articulate, pithy insights into the music of all historical periods and styles; his televised concert/lecture series with the New York Philharmonic in the 1950s pioneered music appreciation programs for television. His compositions range from ballets and operas to Broadway musicals, from sonatas to symphonies, and from art songs to choral works.

Bernstein received his musical training at Harvard and at the Curtis Institute, where he studied piano, conducting, and composition. He also studied conducting with Sergey Koussevitzky at the Berkshire Music Center in Tanglewood, Massachusetts, where Koussevitzky was so impressed with his work that he appointed Bernstein as his assistant in 1942. His most famous career opportunity came in 1944, when he was called upon, on short notice, to substitute for the great conductor Bruno Walter, who suddenly became ill and was unable to conduct a major concert of the New York Philharmonic. Bernstein's brilliant performance, coupled with the recognition that he had prepared the scores in an extremely short amount of time, catapulted him to fame. During the next forty-six years, he conducted virtually every major symphony orchestra in the world. His appointment as the New York Philharmonic's musical director and chief conductor in 1958 (a position he held until 1969, when he was made conductor laureate for life) was his longest tenure with one orchestra. He was active until the very last months of his life; he died only weeks after announcing his retirement, due to poor health.

As a conductor, Bernstein was flamboyant, energetic, and often controversial. His gestures at times were larger than life. His flair for "show business" made him a target for occasional criticism, but his superior musicianship and conducting technique made him one of the most sought-after conductors in the world and earned him the respect of professional players everywhere. During his time with the New York Philharmonic, he filmed a series of Young People's concerts and became known to television audiences throughout the United States. Bernstein, like Copland, was a key figure in expanding the audience for classical music, both in the United States and in foreign countries. The famous series of lectures he gave at Harvard during the 1973 season is a monument to his musical insight. The lectures are available both in book form and in videotape under the title *The Unanswered Question.*

Bernstein's compositions reflect his broad abilities and interests. His use of jazz rhythms, brilliant orchestral effects, and daring dynamics is all part of his style. His music, although sometimes profound, never seems pretentious or dreary, a trait he shares with Copland.

New York, March 1, 1977: Leonard Bernstein conducting the Philharmonic Orchestra with Russian pianist Lazar Berman. © Bettman / CORBIS. ID # U1894361.

Listening Guide 48

Overture to *Candide*
Leonard Bernstein (1918–1990)

Overture to a Broadway musical play
1956
Recorded by the New York Philharmonic Orchestra,
Leonard Bernstein, conductor
CD No. 3, Track 10 (4:21)

One of Bernstein's most popular short works for orchestra is the overture to his musical play *Candide.* This work, based on Voltaire's famous satire, ran for only seventy-three performances on Broadway; nonetheless, its short overture has attained a permanent place in orchestral music. The full-length work, with a revised libretto, is now frequently performed by opera companies, and the overture is frequently played in transcription form by college and university concert bands.

This lively overture is founded on some familiar structural principles: it is based on very distinct, recognizable melodies (three, in this case), and the structure contains elements of repetition and contrast. Its modern character is created by the lively syncopations, the changing meter, and the energetic, and sometimes irregular, rhythms.

To Consider

1. As you listen to this work, describe the nature of the themes. For example, what is the character of the first melody? What musical devices give it an energetic quality? How do the second and third tunes contrast with the first?

2. What effect does the character of the second theme have on your listening experience? Were you led by the composer to anticipate a change in character? (Notice how the second melody is more lyrical than the first, although its tempo is brisk.) Count the beats of the tune as they occur, and you will discover that the meter is mixed (one-two, one-two, one-two-three, etc.).

3. What correlation do you see between the rhythmic and metrical energies of Stravinsky's *Petroushka*, Copland's *Rodeo*, and Bernstein's *Candide Overture*? If you listen to them in sequence, you will notice that each one has moments when the meter changes unexpectedly and "distorts" the "natural" feeling of the music. This feature is one of the most exciting characteristics that links these three composers.

0:00	After an attention-getting beginning, the first melody group begins in the strings. The busy theme contains asymmetrical phrases punctuated by strong, syncopated rhythms. Its diatonic (step-wise) melodic contour tempers these elements, however. The central melodic idea is followed by three sub-themes: one characterized by syncopated rhythms, the second by three accented notes at its beginning, and the third, an answer that ends in quick scalar flourishes.
1:15	The contrasting B theme enters. This tune has more regular phrases, although they are still not totally symmetrical. Notice that Bernstein uses a centuries-old technique of presentation: the melody first appears in one instrument group and then is repeated several times, each time being played by more instruments until the full orchestra is participating.
2:10	The A theme group returns, first in the flute/piccolo and then in the full string section. The restatement of the A group is less dynamic than it was in its original version.
2:40	A reappearance of the B theme, first in the woodwinds and then in all instruments, anticipates new melodic material.
3:09	The third melody (the C theme) enters over an after-beat accompaniment. Its contour is drawn from a triad. Again, the style of repetition and treatment of orchestration are consistent with earlier practices in this piece, but the imitative treatment of the theme adds new interest.
3:26	Closing material begins with a dance-like passage underlined by the snare drum. The final moments incorporate elements of the A and B themes.

Much of the charm of Bernstein's music lies in the quickness with which he presents one idea after another. This is music for the alert listener, but it is also music written for a broad audience. Esoteric statement and pioneering compositional theory are not important to this composer. Inventiveness and craft of composition, however, are clearly present at all times.

A mere examination of the titles of Bernstein's works reveals his eclectic attitude toward music. His symphonic works include three symphonies and many additional orchestral works with descriptive titles, and symphonic suites drawn from his stage and film music.

Bernstein's chamber works also reflect a wide range of musical approaches, some using classical forms and titles, while others have unique titles suggesting freedom from traditional chamber genres. His vocal and choral music includes works based on religious subjects, such as the *Chichester Psalms* for chorus, or the unconventional theater work *Mass*, which was commissioned for the opening of the John F. Kennedy Center of the Performing Arts (1971) and includes many styles of music from the times, including rock.

LIBBY LARSEN AND THE MODERN MAINSTREAM

> The hardest work for a composer is to find your own voice. When people have a calling and it's a life-time work, you never really know if you have found it—you are always searching. My framework always shifts. I want to communicate music to large groups of thinking people.[9]

Elizabeth ("Libby") Larsen (b. 1950) likes to talk about the small world of the professional musician. That world often consists of playing the classics of the Romantic repertoire many times over to an audience that is perceived as being adverse to new and challenging sounds. Early in her career she put forth the theory that the classical audience enjoys concerts for five fundamental reasons: the performance (where people can compare it to recordings or other interpretations); predictability (which helps the audience achieve a comfort level in its listening); entertainment; duration; and spirit. Her intention as a composer is to write music that is not necessarily governed by these traditional concepts but that still communicates to an audience. She puts it this way:

> Whatever I do I am acknowledging, and to some extent being influenced by, my audience. . . . And while the audience will not always get to decide the outcome, it will never cease to be a reality: since I've chosen *performance* for my piece, it must face the seats. I would like it to say something to, or at least smile or wave at, its audience.[10]

Perhaps Larsen's desire to create music that communicates well to her audiences stems from her musical background as a child growing up in a middle-class family in Minneapolis, Minnesota. She recalls that her parents were avid music fans, especially of Broadway tunes and "stride" piano (an early jazz style in which the left hand played a bass note on the beat and then would "stride" quickly to answer with a middle-range chord on the offbeat). Her experience in Catholic church choirs (before Vatican II) exposed her to singing Gregorian chant. In high school, she played in a rock band. Her eight years of piano study gave her insight into the classics. As an adult, her personal musical tastes reflect this healthy mixture.

Her gregarious personality and her philosophy of music have made Larsen a strong advocate for a spirit of mutual respect between the composer and the audience. She seeks to converse with others about music, whether they are students of music or interested music lovers. Her taste is eclectic, but her compositional technique is well defined. She recalls her childhood interest in taking watches apart, and she feels that music is like a watch, in that you can take it apart and put it back together again.

When she was contemplating a major in college, she decided that she either wanted to become a stockbroker or an opera singer. After learning that she did not have the performing gifts of a professional singer, and having been introduced to making music, she concluded that composition related in some way both to analyzing stocks and watch making: all three require a similar energy.

Larsen is a strong spokesperson for American music. In 1994, she and some of her colleagues in the Minnesota Composers Forum did a study of programming of American composers' music in symphony orchestras. They determined that a mere 4 percent of all orchestral programming in the United States was music by American composers, and that 50 percent of that consisted of music by Copland and Bernstein. There is little room for the remaining 2,500 serious American composers in the symphonic repertoire.

Listening Guide 49

Parachute Dancing
Libby Larsen (b. 1950)

Single-movement work for orchestra
1984
Recorded by the Bournemouth Sinfonietta,
 Carolann Martin, conductor
CD No. 3, Track 11 (6:22)

Thus far in Chapter 9 we have studied five modern works that contain memorable melodies treated in innovative ways. *Parachute Dancing* represents a continuation of this trend, with one major exception. Instead of writing complete melodies in this work, Larsen uses melodic and rhythmic fragments to represent her linear ideas. This is clearly more "modern" than Stravinsky's use of interrupted melodies in *Petroushka* or Bernstein's use of meter and rhythm to upset the flow of his melodies in his *Overture to Candide*. And yet, this fragmented concept of melodic and rhythmic jabs represents clearly the idea of dancers jumping on the wall, perhaps summoning their courage to make the big leap into the waiting crowd below.

Parachute Dancing, an overture for orchestra, illustrates Larsen's innovative approach to composition using the restrictions of a traditional orchestra. It was commissioned by the American Composers' Orchestra of New York, a group that champions new music by American composers.

The starting place for this work came to Larsen as she was reading about the history of flying. She came across a description of a practice in the sixteenth century, where a group of dancers would stand on a high wall, each holding a huge, silk umbrella. Accompanied by an outdoor band of instruments, they would begin dancing on the courtyard wall until, after having summoned their courage through music and dance, they would jump off the wall and float to the ground, their umbrellas which function as parachutes supporting their safe descent.

Parachute Dancing is based on short motives that represent random dance steps—some tentative, some bold—which are mixed in a general A-B-A form. Larsen chose this form so the listener could follow the progression of music as the piece became increasingly complex. The motives are more gestures than melodies, for they are dominated by their rhythm. Each gesture emerges and disappears into the musical texture at various points. According to the composer, these musical events represent the unsettled feeling the dancers experience before they work up their courage to leap from the wall.

In this work, Larsen designates points in the score at which various members of the orchestra stand up to present their motivic entrances. In this way, she introduces an element of movement into this piece, which after all is about motion.

As you listen to this work, you will hear a series of short motives, some that will be identified in the listening guide below. A few motives will reappear throughout the piece, while new ones enter as the work unfolds. You will hear a musical tapestry of sounds that seems to be constantly changing and moving onward toward points of climax. Short, rhythmic motives represent the quick dance gestures of the wall dancers as they work up their courage to leap into the air and float down with their parachutes. Another point of pictorial reference to the wall dancers occurs at the very end of the piece, when the the orchestra's descending glissandos depict the dancing parachuters jumping from the wall and floating to the earth below. (Glissandos are created by sliding between two notes; on the violin, this is accomplished by maintaining pressure on the string with the left hand while bowing with the right, and then moving it gradually to a new place on the fingerboard.)

To Consider

1. What techniques of orchestration does the composer use to help you sort out the short, rhythmic musical gestures? Discuss this in terms of instrumentation, articulation, and phrasing.
2. Can you detect any programmatic plan linked to the concept of dancers as they do their movements on the wall? Does the music intensify as it unfolds?

3. Why do you suppose the composer chose to end very quietly instead of with a strong fortissimo climax? What is the significance of the timpani at the very end?

0:00 The timpani starts the A section and establishes a feeling of motion. The short, disjunct motive played in thirds by the trumpets is the first "dance gesture." Other melodic fragments (trombones, strings, flutes) suggest additional dance gestures whose roles are temporarily secondary.

0:58 A crescendo, underlined by cymbals, introduces a motive of a repeated, single pitch (again played by the trumpet), which captures the listener's attention.

1:40 The B section begins with a pianissimo violin entrance; this material is now more lyrical than the beginning of the piece. Notice that the lyrical motives, which are passed from one instrument to another, are ascending. Larsen is conveying a suggestion of upward motion here.

2:45 Faster staccato gestures begin to appear, alternating and competing with lyrical gestures in an exchange of motion.

3:15 The timpani entrance signals a new section, reminiscent of the opening A section.

3:45 Gradually the texture becomes filled with various "dance gesture" fragments, overlaid in increasing complexity.

5:50 Suddenly, in a quiet moment, the violins play a descending glissando. The image of dancers floating down, landing softly on the ground, is created. The understated ending of the work is surprisingly dramatic.

Larsen's musical philosophy and practice balance forward-looking ideas with a solid foundation in compositional skills. She does not subscribe to one specific compositional school but is eclectic in her approach. Her success as a composer is proof that she is aware of her audience's taste, but it is not a success born out of compromise. The newness of her music is in keeping with her attitude about the future of art music in the United States. When she is asked, "What's ahead for the American composer?" she says, "Music will not die—it just gets reinvested with other value systems."[11] Perhaps this concept is at the core of modernism.

SUMMARY

Music in early twentieth-century music reflected modernist attitudes demonstrated by composers who sought new ways to express themselves. Modernist composers alluded to traditional musical practices but introduced shocking changes by creating new types of melody, harmony, and rhythm. New methods of composition allowed a new musical freedom.

As the century reached its mid-point, composers such as Aaron Copland and Leonard Bernstein began to create music that reached out to a broader audience. They wrote works that were unique, expressive, and palatable for an audience of eclectic, but nonetheless sophisticated, tastes.

KEY TERMS

cubism	neoclassicism	retrograde inversion
expressionism	Ondes Martenot	serialism
impressionism	permutations	set
inversion	planing	Theremin
Klangfarbenmelodie	primitivism	tone row
modernism	retrograde	transposition

CHAPTER 10

Post-Modernism:
A New Way
of Thinking

*T*HIS chapter focuses on radically innovative approaches to music within the cultivated, or concert, traditions. Composers known as "post-modernists" are those who have consciously moved outside of the mainstream of modernist music by offering music and musical ideas that both challenge the establishment and generate new possibilities of thought within the artistic musical world.

The term **post-modernism** is used to describe artists and their works whose attitude is, above all, diverse in its orientation. The characteristic of plurality—the side-by-side existence of a range of differing approaches and reactions to modern life and thought—is its major feature. During the 1960s, a tendency to be experimental and innovative—to be different from the past—swept the intellectual world of art music. A new breed of composers began to conceive of sounds that, instead of containing references to past styles, forged not only newer sounds but new, total experiences. Composers such as John Cage and Pauline Oliveros made us rethink the very definition of music—which only recently had been redefined as "any" organized sound. Oliveros, incidentally, represents post-modern thought, not only by her musical style but by her voice in the feminist movement—a very significant part of the post-modern world.

*T*HE 1960S AND THE EXPANSION OF THE POP CULTURE

The post-modern era in the United States was born out of a turbulent environment of war, political unrest, and drastic social change. The principal players in this movement included the youth and young adults in a way never before experienced in Western history. Social and political leaders emerged who were conversant with the pop culture of the day and, they not only used the popular media, music, and rhetoric of the people as a vehicle for their messages of protest and reform, they also shaped the very means through which the culture interpreted the events of the time.

During the 1960s, for example, the civil rights movement, under the leadership of Dr. Martin Luther King Jr. (1929–1968), pressed for an end to segregation in the schools and for protection of minority voting rights. King rose to national prominence when he organized the famous bus boycott in Montgomery, Alabama; he was a young man of twenty-six at that time. He led a peaceful protest march during the summer of 1963 in Washington, D.C., where he delivered his most famous speech, "I have a dream."

In the 1970s, however, the civil rights movement took on new dimensions, when members of the Black Panther Party, a black political activist group under the leadership of Huey Newton, decided that it was time to intensify social protest by carrying guns and

A Vietnam veteran attends an anti-Vietnam War rally at Valley Forge, PA, 1970. © Leif Skoogfors / CORBIS. ID # EF001343.

defying oppressive police. Civil rights activism and protests against the Vietnam War, were social movements that achieved widespread influence, not only because of their local impact but because they used television, art, and music in the delivery of their messages. (In Chapter 14, we will discuss the impact of music on the protests of the 1960s and 1970s.)

Another issue in the changing culture of the 1960s and 1970s was an intensification of the feminist movement and the sexual revolution. With the advent of the birth control pill came the attitude that sexual freedom was less risky, and with a more relaxed attitude toward sex, traditional sexual mores were challenged. In addition, feminists such as Gloria Steinem argued that the societal standards commonly accepted for the male population should be equal for women.

Feminists also created an awareness of the inequities women faced in the workplace, the home, and in society in general. The American public was made aware of a "glass ceiling"—a cultural aversion to allowing women to obtain the highest level of management in business—and the long process of changing that culture began. Although by the 1970s women were commonly hired as symphony musicians (a practice that was almost unheard of fifty years earlier), the focus on gender equality intensified.

The artistic expressions that became the voice of social change during this period were reflected less in the "high art" of the time than in the popular arts. The term *arts and entertainment* was coined in acknowledgment of this diversity. The rock 'n' roll of the 1950s evolved into the rock culture of the 1960s. Rock and its gentler sister expression the folk song became the most important forces in communicating the messages of war protest, gender equality, and civil rights. Large-scale rock concerts, protest marches, and peace rallies were the popular forums of the time, replacing the sophisticated concerts and formal public meetings of earlier eras.

The post-modern movement in the arts was not immune to the influence of the pop culture, for along with the reinvention of artistic and compositional techniques, it also restructured the very premise of "high art." Visual artists used pop materials and images in their art, perhaps less in defiance of former conventions than in an interest to express contemporary values. Robert Rauschenberg and Andy Warhol represent leading proponents of this approach to post-modern art.

In 1970, composer Donald Erb wrote a work for orchestra, electronic tape, and rock band, titled *Klangfarbenfunk I* (*Sound Colors I*), in which the hard beat of the rock band gradually emerges out of the symphonic texture and then recedes into the general mass of sound. Even Leonard Bernstein, whose music is not considered part of the avant-garde movement, was heavily influenced by the pop culture of the late 1960s and early 1970s when he wrote his *Mass*. This work uses both a symphony orchestra and a rock band; traditional liturgical texts are intermingled with rock lyrics when the celebrant of the Mass questions the religious traditions of the Catholic Church.

Some composer/performers, such as Frank Zappa, made their names in the pop world, but they also bridged the gap between the old labels that separated "classical" from "popular." (For a look at another side of Zappa's musical personality, listen to the recording made by French composer/conductor Pierre Boulez, titled *The Perfect Stranger*, on the Rykodisc label: RCD 106542.) Others, such as Phillip Glass, initially gained recognition as a composer and promoter of new music in the esoteric circle of modern music aficionados. In the middle and late 1990s, Glass's music became known to a much broader audience when the mass culture began adopting some compositional techniques that he pioneered.

Of course not all composers joined the post-modern bandwagon. Many found success and artistic fulfillment in cultivating a musical language more connected to the common musical heritage. Since one of the realities of music is that earlier music can live side by side with contemporary creations through musical performance, the avant-garde composers often appear to the public to be even more radical than even they consider themselves. The composers of the avant-garde, much like other creators of music throughout history, are many times simply exploring their individual capabilities of contributing unique expressions to an art that has room for diversity.

Whatever their musical language, these composers prove once again that music is not merely light entertainment (although it may be just that), but it is many times a reflection of thought that often forms a bond with the worlds of philosophy, literature, politics, and psychological perception. On the other hand, it often includes satire, irony, and according to some people, blasphemy, for it challenges both the ear and the mind, and it promulgates acceptance of the broadest possible array of musical expressions.

JOHN CAGE AND THE REVOLUTION OF THE MID-CENTURY

Occasionally in music history a figure comes along who not only breaks the conventions of the past but also forces other people to rethink their most cherished philosophies of the art. John Cage (1912–1992) is such a person. To many, his name is associated with the radical fringe of musical composition, for in 1952 he "wrote" a composition, *4'33"*, in which the performer was to sit in silence at the piano for the designated time suggested by the title. To others, this—perhaps his most famous composition—signaled the presence of a new philosophy of music in which the listener was equally (if not more) responsible than the composer for organizing and interpreting sounds. Cage's intent in *4'33"* was for each listener to concentrate strongly on whatever sounds occurred during the "work" and to organize the sounds into his or her own conceptual experience. Music is therefore redefined, for it becomes any listening experience that is perceived at a given time. Cage's music emphasized this philosophical position. Whereas his early compositions were directed at expanding the repertoire of sounds included in music, they were nonetheless products of the composer's control, since all musical gestures were included in his score—the customary and traditional practice of composition. As Cage's music and philosophy evolved, however, he devised methods whereby the composer could be more removed from controlling every element of sound.

How did Cage arrive at such an approach? We will see his progression from a young composer looking for new ways to produce sounds to a philosopher seeking new meaning in an ever-expanding concept of sound and visual perception.

Cage was born and raised in California, where as a young adult he studied composition with Arnold Schoenberg and Henry Cowell. He was attracted to the experiments of Cowell for prepared piano, and he caught the attention of musical audiences as a performer of that style, both in America and in Europe. Cowell and Cage "prepared" pianos by adding objects to the strings, such as rubber bands, paper clips, and glass tumblers, in order to alter the sound of the piano and expand its capability to produce novel effects. (Of course, this occurred before the invention of

Composer John Cage, 1970s.
Photo by: Camera Press Ltd.
Source: Archive Photos.
ID # 01-CAG-002/F11PEPA.

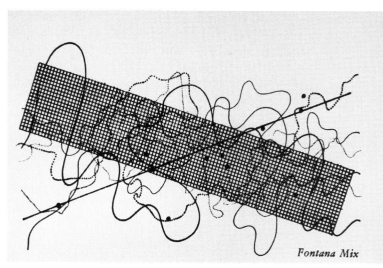

Fontana Mix

John Cage, the musical score, *"Fontana Mix"* © 1960. By permission of Henmar Press Inc.

the synthesizer—the most common modern way to create new sounds.) Cage's *Amores* (1943), two solos for prepared piano and two trios for three percussionists, is a standard work in that genre.

In 1942, Cage moved to New York and began a long association with the Merce Cunningham Dance Company as its music director. Already interested in art that went beyond mere musical composition, his instincts for expansive thought led him to study Zen Buddhism and the Chinese Book of Changes, the *I Ching*. His studies in oriental thought reshaped his ideas concerning the internal organization of musical elements within a composition. The Western concept of repetition and contrast, with its emphasis on chord progression, tension and relaxation, and harmonic drive toward the cadence (as in the music of Mozart, for example), was replaced with a philosophy of composition that strove toward the absence of forward motion. He was no longer interested in music that was governed by the idea that all composition should have a clearly delineated "beginning, middle, and end." For Cage, the underlying approach to virtually all Western music heretofore was now replaced with a sound that seemed to be suspended in time— music that did not have to go anywhere but could simply exist in a state of "being."

His compositional techniques involved **chance music**, whereby he developed schemes to produce sounds that were not predetermined. One of his works, *Music of Changes* (1952), for example, involved the tossing of coins. His *Atlas Eclipticalis* (1962) was written by superimposing a transparency on a map, making pinholes in the transparency where selected cities were found, and then superimposing the transparency over music manuscript paper where the pinholes became places where notes were located. In his chance (or **indeterminate**) music, he often left many avenues of performance open to the performer, such as the choice of instruments or voices, melodic ranges, and rhythmic interpretations. In this way the performer became an integral part of the creation of the music.

What is the purpose of such happenstance music? First it was to replace all formal structures in music with a free technique of composition; second, it illustrated the idea that music can consist of any sound (or any noise).

Admittedly, Cage's music is more talked about than performed in the concert world. Both professional performers and audiences find the degree of freedom in his music too radical for "practical" performance. His ideas, however, are taken seriously, and they have influenced many who have followed him. The idea of a static expression, where sounds are allowed to occur without the obligation of development or a linear concept of form, was adopted by many other postmodern composers. It was even popularized in the "New Wave" movement of the 1990s. Perhaps Cage's greatest impact on the musical world lies in the rethinking of how music is perceived.

Cage's works include compositions for piano, prepared piano, vocal music, music using electronic techniques, and audio visual works. He also was active as a painter; his art works exhibit the same attention to static expression as does much of his music. He formed long-term artistic associations with Merce Cunningham (dance), David Tudor (a pianist specializing in avant-garde music), and composers Morton Feldman and Christian Wolff. As an artist, he was influenced by Robert Rauschenberg. Cage referred to Rauschenberg's collage techniques that brought together common objects that were simply placed next to each other as "a situation involving multiplicity."[1]

Cage was the recipient of many prestigious awards in his life, including the Guggenheim fellowship and the American Academy of Arts and Letters award. In the last three decades of his life, he was in popular demand as a writer, speaker, and performer. He served as artist/composer in residence at Wesleyan University (Middletown, Connecticut); the University of Cincinnati; the University of Illinois; the University of California, Davis; and Harvard University (as the Charles Elliot Norton Lecturer, 1988–89). His books *Silence* (1961), *Notations* (1969), *Writings through Finnigans Wake* (1978), *For the Birds* (1989), and *I-VI* (the Harvard Lectures) provide vivid insight not only into his personal philosophies but into his valuable contributions to the literature of post-modern thought.

THE MUSICAL PERSPECTIVE OF PAULINE OLIVEROS

Listen to everything you can possibly hear both externally from the environment and internally from the memory, imagination, or internal environment (i.e., body sounds). Allow your attention to expand to include the most distant and faintest sounds without premeditating a pitch. (Pauline Oliveros)[2]

The philosophies of Cage and his redefinition of music and its functions have influenced musical thought among many forward-looking musicians. One of the most prominent of these composers is Pauline Oliveros (b. 1932), whose creative mind and enigmatic personality made a decided impact on the avant-garde in America.

Oliveros's early exposure to music included listening to her grandparents' radio and playing the piano. She started studying accordion when she was twelve years old, and four years later, she played it in a polka band. As a music major at San Francisco State College, she gained a high level of proficiency on the French horn. Her studies in composition, however, were unrewarding, for she, like so many modern composers from Debussy to Cage, found the rigors of traditional composition instruction too confining. She finally found a good teacher, Robert Erickson, at the San Francisco Conservatory of Music. Erickson encouraged her interests in new sound explorations, and Oliveros soon found herself developing an individual approach to music.

That approach followed several paths during her lifetime, but she was strongly motivated by her own listening experiences, sense perception, and consciousness studies. Her composing media involved, at various periods in her life, works for unique combinations of performers and instruments (piano, accordion, songs for soprano and horn, various chamber works, works for mixed chorus), electronic music, theater pieces (often involving combinations of acoustic and electronic instruments, light projections, and dancers), and works titled *Meditations*.

Throughout her life, Oliveros has been on the leading edge of musical experimentation. In one of her early works, *Sound Patterns*, she extended the sound possibilities of the human voice by using noises not commonly associated with music, such as lip pops, tongue clicks, lip flutters, and finger snaps. In this way she was imitating sounds available through electronic composition—an area that she soon explored.

When Oliveros first became interested in improvisation, the concert world was not accustomed to allowing the performer to be part of the creative process, except of course in jazz. Some of Oliveros's compositions in this arena were written for specific virtuoso performers on various instruments, sometimes with electronic tape background. Later she began writing and staging theater pieces, sometimes involving outdoor locations and including everyone in the area as performers. One such work, *Link* (1971), was intended to be performed on a college campus. It involved performers making a sound map where certain locations of environmental sounds are normally located. The performers stand near these sound sources and point to them; they often add to the "natural" sound sources by making sounds of their own that match the pitch of the environmental sound.

Of course, many people consider this musical fraud. The point of experimentalists such as Oliveros in carrying out such sound experiments is to heighten awareness of the sounds that occur naturally in the environment. Music thus becomes redefined and takes into account any sound experienced by the listener.

Pauline Oliveros with her accordion. Source: Jack Vartoogian.

Later in her career, Oliveros's work became introspective, and she drew on various types of meditation as inspiration. Her works in the 1990s represent some of the most creative postmodern sound experiments, and they have extended music into completely new arenas. Oliveros is indeed one of the key players on the post-modern musical stage.

Oliveros was an early champion of the women's movement. On September 13, 1970, she published an article in the *New York Times*, "And Don't Call Them 'Lady' Composers," in which she strongly attacked traditional attitudes toward women and women composers. Soon she became a principal spokesperson for the feminist movement in the arts. In her discussion, Oliveros points to the history of the European repertoire, which consists primarily of music of the past written by male composers. She says, "Certainly, no 'great' composer, especially a woman, has a chance to emerge in a society which believes that all 'great' music has been written by those long departed."[3]

Oliveros represents a voice both for the women's movement and for modern music and its acceptance by the public. Her electronic composition *Bye Bye Butterfly*—the subject of our next musical selection, presents a feminist perspective on *Madame Butterfly*, the famous early-twentieth-century opera by Giacomo Puccini. In Oliveros's composition, faint strains of the opera can be heard sounding through a texture of electronic sounds. Eventually the operatic music is drowned out by electronic sounds, thereby suggesting that the unfortunate circumstances such as those experienced by Cho-Cho San (translated in English as Madame Butterfly) should never happen again to any woman.

This famous opera, set in Japan at the turn of the nineteenth century, is about a Japanese girl who falls in love with an American naval officer, Lieutenant Pinkerton. According to custom, Pinkerton marries Butterfly and lives with her until he tires of her; he then returns to the United States to marry an American, free from all marital obligations to his Japanese wife.

After Pinkerton leaves for home, Butterfly suffers disgrace in her community when she gives birth to a son, whom she names Trouble. Butterfly waits patiently for her lover to return for her, and after more than two years, she learns of the arrival of Pinkerton's boat.

Butterfly's humiliation is complete when she finds out that Pinkerton has returned with his American wife with the intention of taking the child back to America. Butterfly sends a message saying that Pinkerton and his wife Kate can have her child if they return in a half hour. In the company of her faithful servant and companion Suzuki, Butterfly takes down from a shelf the ceremonial sword that bears the inscription, "Die with honor if you can no longer live with honor." She plunges the sword into her body as Pinkerton rushes back into her home.

The musical quotation in *Bye Bye Butterfly* comes from Act I of *Madame Butterfly*, where Cho-Cho-San sings to her friends about the joys of love:

Above the ocean, in the treetops,
   Once again we feel the breeze of spring-time.
No girl in all Japan can be happier than I am,
   Nor in the whole world.
Remember why I came here:
   It was love that had called,
And love is here to greet me.
Life now is forever,
   For death can never come
To those who are in love.[4]

Listening Guide 50

Bye Bye Butterfly (excerpt)
Pauline Oliveros (b. 1932)

Electronic tape composition
1965
Recorded by the composer at the
    San Francisco Tape Music Center
CD No. 3, Track 12 (4:00)

This work uses the technique of tape delay, in which two tape recorders are used to create a reverberation resulting in the overlapping of sound elements. Oliveros created this work using two Hewlett-Packard oscillators (tone generators), two line amplifiers, one turntable with record, and two tape recorders in a delay setup. She arranged the equipment, tuned the oscillators, and played through the composition in real time—which means that this recording is both a creation and a performance. The music has two basic components: one is a high, narrow band of white noise that sounds like radio static, and the other is excerpts from the Italian opera *Madame Butterfly* by Giacomo Puccini. The interchange between the static noise and the familiar strains of the opera creates a new sort of surrealism. The general organization of this work of about eight minutes is A-B-A, with the outer sections being dominated by electronic sounds, and the center section focusing on the opera.

To Consider

1. Although the means of sound production is unconventional to most music listeners' ears, some elements of composition are still easy to relate to. For example, Oliveros uses repetition of a single sound to generate anticipation. What other devices do you hear that call forth your responses to this composition?
2. How does the composer create a sense of depth in the opening section of this work?
3. When you hear the excerpt from Puccini's *Madame Butterfly*, do you hear it as a layer of sound that comes in under the electronic music, or does it appear to you a part of the contrapuntal texture of the work?

0:00	The composition begins with a long period of silence. After some 40 seconds in which no sound can be heard, a high-pitched sound wave emerges and rewards the listener's anticipation that was created by the silence.
1:01	Suddenly a low, pulsing sound enters, and one begins to perceive a feeling of depth. Pitches change, creating a free, sustained melodic line.
1:46	A strong, rhythmic wave enters. Now one feels that the work is beginning to gain momentum.
2:25	Low sounds enter, again adding a wider dimension to the complexity of sound.
3:02	A sustained high pitch, devoid of rhythm, suggests a change in the musical form.
3:24	The abrupt entrance of the voices comes in under the high, sustained pitch, and the B section begins. An ethereal, dreamlike sequence is created by the blending of electronic and vocal sounds.
3:57	The musical quotation from Act I of Puccini's opera breaks through the haze of sound. It is Butterfly's aria, in which she expresses her newfound feelings of love and joy.
5:00	The excerpt ends as electronic sounds rise to prominence.

GEORGE CRUMB: NEW NOTATIONS, NEW SOUNDS

The music of George Crumb (b. 1929) is firmly established in the repertoire of post-modern music emerging from the last three decades of the twentieth century. Although his approaches to composition are decidedly different from John Cage's or Pauline Oliveros's, Crumb's music demonstrates a strong dedication to music inspired by a variety of contemporary stimuli, from political, social, and cultural events to ideas generated by modern poetry. His musical language is widely recognized for its originality and innovative genius.

Born in Charleston, West Virginia, in 1929, Crumb received his advanced musical training at the University of Illinois, at the Berlin Hochschule für Musik, and at the University of Michigan. His dual career as a composer and professor of music has kept him in the forefront of the musical world. He has been the recipient of numerous awards, including two Guggenheim fellowships and the 1968 Pulitzer Prize for Composition for his *Echoes of Time and the River*. Six universities have conferred on him honorary degrees.

Crumb's highly personal musical style shows a tendency to explore instrumental sounds that are outside of the traditional composer's reference; he has expanded his use of traditional orchestra instruments to include mandolin, harmonica, musical saw, Tibetan prayer stones, Japanese temple bells, a harp threaded with paper, a toy piano, and amplified string instruments. His expansive sound resources also include nontraditional techniques of the voice, wherein the singer uses clicking sounds, singing into the piano to create sympathetic reverberations, and exploitation of isolated consonants and vowels. His knowledge of the sound resources of percussion instruments is exhaustive, and he relies heavily on a wide variety of percussion instruments in his works.

Many listeners agree that Crumb's music has both a haunting and a powerful impact on the emotions. In that sense, his music parallels the aesthetic effect of works by Spanish poet and playwright Federico García Lorca. In reading the works of García Lorca (who was killed by Nationalist soldiers in 1936 during the Spanish Civil War), Crumb came to realize this close, ethereal bond. His *Songs and Refrains of Death* and his *Ancient Voices of Children* both capture the dark character of García Lorca's expression.

Crumb's scores are easily recognized because of their visual originality. No unnecessary printed material is found on the page; instead, Crumb designs his scores both for musical practicality and visual meaning. Crumb, unlike John Cage, is conscious of time durations in his music, and he specifically indicates intervals of time—including moments of silence in his compositions. He sometimes uses numbers in his scores to indicate durations in seconds (called "real time" by composers), which either indicate points of silence or the time to be given to a specific musical gesture. Silence is for him a significant element of his style; it draws the listener toward the music by increasing the anticipation.

Crumb has succeeded in bringing experimental techniques into a musical expression that are comprehensible and attractive to listeners. Most of his music has been recorded and is readily available to the public. Although performers initially need to expend extra effort learning to read Crumb's music, they often report that the notation eventually adds to their understanding. Crumb has written several articles for musical journals and has lectured widely at universities across the United States, but his music speaks for itself.

Crumb wrote several well-known series of compositions. His *Makrokosmos* for piano appears in two volumes (1972 and 1973), each containing twelve works inspired by the zodiac. The innovative notation of these works makes their pages works of art in themselves. He also wrote four books of *Madrigals* (1965–1969) for soprano and several different combinations of instruments on the texts of García Lorca.

The Pulitzer Prize-winning *Echoes of Time and the River* is a work for orchestra supplemented by a mandolin and antique cymbals—the same instruments Crumb featured in his

Ancient Voices of Children. Its four movements, "Frozen Time," "Remembrance of Time," "Collapse of Time," and "Last Echoes of Time," provide clues about the programmatic atmosphere of the work.

Crumb's *Black Angels* (1970) for amplified string quartet is his commentary on the Vietnam War. The three movements are "Departure," "Absence," and "Return," and they include twelve episodes, each with a subtitle. The composer wrote it as a parable on our troubled world, and he indicates that the work "traces the voyage of the soul." His choice of the string quartet as a medium for this expression is curious, for traditionally this genre is considered a vehicle for abstract musical ideas. In addition to traditional performance techniques, Crumb calls for the string quartet members to shout, chant, whistle, and whisper at various points in the performance, as well as to play gongs, maracas, and crystal glasses. *Black Angels* is a very effective, vivid musical expression, full of symbolism. (The Kronos String Quartet has recorded this on the Elektra Nonesuch label.)

Ancient Voices of Children, a song cycle for soprano, boy soprano, oboe, mandolin, harp, electric piano, and percussion, uses selected poems of García Lorca in an approach freer than that of any other composer we have discussed thus far. At times the singer whispers the text in a barely audible voice; at other times lines from the poetry follow protracted vocalizations of syllables. In the first song, for example, preceding the first line of poetry is a lengthy vocalization anticipating the line "El niño busca su voz" ("The little boy was looking for his voice"). It is as though the composer literally translates the meaning of the poem into nonverbal sounds before the words themselves are sung.

Ancient Voices of Children: II, IV

II

Me he perdido muchas beces por el mar	I have lost myself in the sea many times
con el oído llena de flores recién cortadas,	with my ear full of freshly cut flowers,
con la lengua llena de amor y de agonía.	with my tongue full of love and agony.
Muchas veces me he perdid por el mar,	I have lost myself in the sea many times
como me pierdo en el corazón de algunos niño.	as I lose myself in the heart of certain children.

IV

Todas las tardes en Granada,	Each afternoon in Granada,
todas las tardes se muere un niño.	a child dies each afternoon.[5]

George Crumb, "*Ancient Voices of Children,*" © 1971. Used by permission of C.F. Peters Corporation.

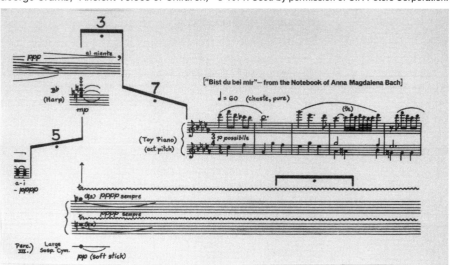

In his elaborate performance instructions, Crumb indicates that both the Spanish text and its English translation are to be printed in program notes. Since the words of the text are usually presented as part of the total sound collage and are not always understandable, it is essential that the listener read García Lorca's texts as the music is being performed. In this way, the listener becomes a participant in the work. The artistry of García Lorca's words is that they stretch the imagination with images both abstract and real.

$\mathcal{M}$INIMALISM AND BEYOND: STEVE REICH AND PHILIP GLASS

Minimalism first emerged as a movement in painting and sculpture during the late 1950s and early 1960s with the works of Jasper Johns and Robert Rauchenberg. In a reaction against the abstract expressionism movement, with its emphasis on subjective feeling and inner emotion, sculptors such as Donald Judd, David Smith, and Ad Reinhardt began creating "objectless" structures of solid geometric forms.

The premise of minimalism in art was to present neutral images—ones that were not inherently expressive. Minimalist artists often repeated identical units, used only one or two colors, and employed a minimum of materials. Minimalist art directs attention not toward the artist and his or her expression of emotions but toward the object itself; references to nature and narrative subject matter are eliminated. The object itself is the focus of the art. Inspired by the pioneering work of John Cage, minimalism in music surfaced full blown in the works of Philip Glass, Terry Riley, La Monte Young, and Steve Reich. These composers in turn influenced John Adams, Daniel Lentz, and David Borden. For

Donald Judd, "Untitled," 1968. Stainless steel and amber plexiglass, 14 ft. 3 in. total height; 9 in. high x 3 ft. 4 in. wide x 2 ft. 7 in. deep (each box). Empire State Plaza Art Collection, Albany, New York. Photo: Lee Boltin. © State of New York / CORBIS. ID # IH051798.

our brief look at this interesting form of artistic expression, we turn to Steve Reich and Philip Glass, for they have emerged as composers who have bridged the gap from the esoteric world of music/philosophy and have created music of interest to a broader public.

Steve Reich (b. 1936) was born into an American Jewish family in New York City. His mother was a pop singer and songwriter, his father a lawyer. Reich's memories of his childhood were dominated by the many train trips he took across the country when he was shuttled between his father's residence in New York and his mother's in Los Angeles. His parents divorced when Reich was only a year old, and Reich spent six months of the year at each home. His experiences living in two separate residences a continent apart offered him the opportunity to hear a variety of music, from Bach to bebop, and he developed an eclectic attitude toward music early in his life. As a teenager he was infatuated with the jazz music of Miles Davis and John Coltrane.

Armed with solid musical training, earned at Cornell University, with private study in composition at Julliard under the guidance of William Bergsma and Vincent Persichetti, and a master's degree from Mills College in California, where he worked with Darius Milhaud and Luciano Berio, Reich was ready to make his mark in music. In 1966, he formed a group known as Steve Reich and Musicians, a group of percussionists and keyboard musicians. (Incidentally, this composer with a golden pedigree in musical training was earning a living driving a cab in New York City at the time.)

Reich's interest in percussive sounds eventually led him to travel to Africa, where he studied African drumming with a master drummer of the Ewe tribe in Ghana. There, Reich became sensitive to the intricacies and complexities of the rhythmic structures of African music—rhythms that often exceeded the comprehension of audiences in Western culture.

Reich's focus on these rhythmic patterns, which are repeated over and over with slight variations, led to a minimalist approach to music, for by concentrating on rhythm alone, Reich stripped away all extra-musical references. His prolonged work *Drumming* (1970–1971) does just that. This composition, which uses four tuned bongo drums, three marimbas, female voices, three glockenspiels, a whistler, and a piccolo, employs the concept of repetition and metamorphosis to produce a mesmerizing effect. Instruments and voices fade in and out of the texture in this continuous sound.

Another technique pioneered by Reich is **phase shifting,** where repeated short musical gestures are played in unison by several players, and gradually, one or more of the parts begins to change, until there are several closely related rhythmic patterns that sound "out of sync" with each other. As the work progresses, these sounds eventually emerge again in unison. His *Clapping Music* of 1971, a work for two people who clap rhythms, illustrates this technique.

Although percussion ensembles play Reich's music with some regularity (*Pieces of Eight* is one of his most popular), the world of concert music has been very slow to adopt Reich into the standard repertoire. His influence on the pop world, with its more adventuresome attitude toward sound, has been greater. David Bowie, for example, feels that Reich influenced him to use acoustic instruments in his 1983 album *Let's Dance*. The repetitive tape looping techniques used by Peter Gabriel and Brian Eno and the Talking Heads also stem directly from Reich's work. (One loops a tape by cutting the desired sound segment from a reel-to-reel recording tape and fastening the two ends together. When it is played, the same segment is repeated over and over.)

Philip Glass (b. 1937) is far too much of an individual to fit neatly into one category of musical style. The roots of his musical expression lie in the minimalist movement. One of the most successful composers of the 1990s, Glass has forged a place for himself in the contemporary world, ranging from rock to chamber music to symphonic works to stage music to opera. The Philip Glass Ensemble, formed in 1986, has enjoyed immense popularity throughout the United States and Europe. He has been the subject of feature articles, both in professional journals and in popular magazines such as *Time*; Columbia Records signed him to an exclusive recording contract in 1982; and in 1985, he was named the *Musical America* Musician of the Year.

Philip Glass was born into a musically aware family: his father owned a record store in Baltimore. His musical awareness began in his home listening to his older brother and sister practice piano; he started taking flute lessons at the Peabody Conservatory when he was eight years old. His remarkable academic career and formative learning experiences included studies in mathematics and philosophy at the University of Chicago (when he was fifteen), studies in composition, first at the Julliard School with William Bergsma and Vincent Persichetti, and later with Darius Milhaud in Aspen and Nadia Boulanger in Paris. His interest in non-Western music led him to work and study with Ravi Shankar (the famous sitar player who introduced the music of India to Americans in the 1970s) and Allah Rakha, India's most prominent tabla (tuned drum) performing artist.

How do these influences show themselves in Glass's music? First, his firm knowledge of fundamental compositional techniques is seen in his well-developed abilities to manipulate the basic materials of music: his music reflects a conscious awareness of time elements, textures, and timbres. Second, his broad experience has allowed him to span the often separate worlds of popular and classical music (but not without raising the suspicions of more cautious classical musicians). And finally, Glass has consciously tried to write music that people like to hear, but at the same time to maintain a highly innovative personal style.

Much of Glass's music is static in nature. It is based on highly repetitive patterns and modules of sound that undergo subtle changes as the music proceeds in time—a structure whose roots are non-Western in origin and are also a benchmark of minimalism. The expected patterns of repetition and contrast governed by musical themes and punctuated by sudden changes in dynamics, textures, and contrapuntal elaboration are absent in his music, for Glass's compositions are directed more toward establishing a musical atmosphere than toward creating a narrative in sound.

However, far from being quiet background music akin to a musical wallpaper, his compositions often reflect the strong influence of rock. Glass lives and works in a world accustomed to a high sound level.

Listening Guide 51

Façades (excerpt)
Philip Glass (b. 1937)

Chamber music composition for two soprano saxophones, two violins, viola, cello, and double bass
1981
Recorded by the Philip Glass Ensemble
CD No. 3, Track 13 (7:20)

To Consider

1. As you listen to *Façades*, keep in mind that this music requires a very different approach to listening from other, more traditional works in the classical repertoire. Does its absence of development become obvious to you? What does Glass do to replace the techniques of counter point, motivic development, and contrast to which you are now so accustomed?
2. What happens to your sense of "real time" (your feeling for actual seconds and minutes) here? What do you think the composer's intentions are with this composition?
3. As the work unfolds, do you get a sense of when it will end, or could this go on indefinitely?

0:00	The repetitive underpinning of this work is established at the opening of this piece by triplet figures in the strings. The general pitch level of string patterns periodically shifts up and down by conjunct intervals of either a half step or a whole step.
1:11	The soprano saxophone enters with sustained notes that also shift by closely spaced intervals. The pulsation continues in the strings; occasionally a dissonance occurs, created when one part shifts tonally before the other moves to a new pitch level.
2:20	The saxophone adds a five-note scale passage leading to the sustained notes it plays. By now the listener's ear is so accustomed to repetition that this added gesture stands out from the rest of the texture.
3:19	The second soprano saxophone enters in a duet with the first, but it quickly recedes into the pulsating triplet figures.
4:27	Once again the saxophone plays sustained notes preceded by five-note scale passages.
5:33	A new pitch level, accompanied by a short variation on the saxophone line (this time emphasizing a lower note resolving upward), suggests a change in the music. A few moments of melodic interest occur as the saxophone expands its melody to include a few more notes.
6:32	The saxophone motion shrinks gradually to two notes and then to one sustained pitch; the pulsation continues under the long tones of the saxophone until the very end.

PLATE 9:
*C*laude Monet (French, 1840-1926), "On the Bank of the Seine, Bennecourt (Au bord de l'eau, Bennecourt)," 1868. Oil on canvas, 81.5 x 100.7 cm. The Art Institute of Chicago, Mr. and Mrs. Potter Palmer Collection. ID # E10368/1922.427. Photograph © 1998, The Art Institute of Chicago. All rights reserved.

PLATE 10:
*P*ablo Picasso (1881-1973), "Three Women," 1908. Hermitage, St. Petersburg, Russia. Scala / Art Resource, NY. ID # S0133566.

PLATE 11:
*R*obert Rauschenberg (American, 1925-   ), "Monogram," side view. Source: SuperStock. ID # 260/700/D/P1M.

PLATE 12:
*L*utenist and singers in a walled garden (1490-1500). From: Roman de la Rose, written and illuminated in Flanders, by an artist known as the master of the prayer books. By permission of The British Library. ID # 13787/1007577021.

PLATE 15:
"Charlemagne Hears Rolland's Horn."
Source: The University of Bonn.

PLATE 16:
Sheet music: "Over There" by George M. Cohan.

Another work of Glass's that uses a continual rhythmic pulsation is the second movement of his *Low Symphony*. Written in 1992, this three-movement work is based on the melodies of David Bowie and Brian Eno; its character, however, is strictly Glass. The symphony is based on the 1977 album by Bowie and Eno, titled *Low*. Its three movements are named after cuts on the album: "Subterraneans," "Some Are," and "Warszawa."

Glass's major successes include the album *Glassworks* (1982), which has sold over 100,000 copies, and his opera *Einstein on the Beach* (1975). His list of compositions include seven works for symphony orchestra, twenty-five compositions for various chamber and instrumental ensembles, nine choral/vocal works, eleven operas, and twenty-five miscellaneous compositions for plays, films, incidental music, and even opening and closing music for the 1984 Summer Olympics in Los Angeles.

One of his most recent works was a commission for the 1998 movie *The Truman Show*. "Truman Sleeps," an instrumental piece from the sound track, shows how Glass combines minimalistic components of repeated eighth-note figures in a slowing, changing harmonic scheme with short melodic ideas to create a feeling of static atmosphere. The principles of minimalism, once thought to be an esoteric experiment in sound, in the hands of Glass have now become part of the pop culture.

NEW AGE SPACE MUSIC AS A POST-MODERN EXPRESSION

Musical trends emerge first among the experimental composers of concert music and then become infused into more popular formats. For example, in the 1950s, **Muzak**—background music that was played in stores, offices, elevators, and so on—became a hallmark of the American musical environment. Muzak first consisted of symphonic arrangements of standard songs from Broadway musicals or Tin Pan Alley, tunes such as "Always," "Tenderly," "September Song," and "Autumn Leaves." Arrangers borrowed orchestration techniques from the music of Brahms, Dvorak, and even Debussy to create what became known as "wallpaper music."

Minimalism has also found a popular expression in the 1990s. This music, called *new age space music*, is the focus of regular FM programming and also has received its specially designated place on the shelves of music stores. Common to new age space music is the idea of constant repetition of short, rhythmic, melodic, and harmonic gestures that together create a feeling of timelessness—of suspended motion and sound in space (hence the name "space music"). Its function is to establish an atmosphere of sound, a backdrop of musical evenness, devoid of emotional extremes. It is relaxing and soothing, a respite from the active world.

One of the most successful creators of new age music for piano is George Winston (b. 1949). Winston's interests in music were influenced by the Top 40 rock and roll music of the 1960s (he played piano and organ in a rock band in Miami during the mid-1960s), by the stride-piano styles of traditional jazz players, such as Fats Waller, and by jazz pianist Vince Guaraldi's music for the *Peanuts* television specials.

Winston began composing when he was in his early twenties. His early compositions ranged from rock to blues to lyrical expressions drawn from his arrangements of standard tunes. Eventually he teamed with William Ackerman, a guitar player who formed the Wyndham Hill record company, and began writing music founded on minimalist concepts. He has produced several albums, including the popular recordings *Autumn* (1980), *December* (1982), and *Winter into Spring* (1982).

The rising popularity of music designed to soothe the listener into a sense of timelessness, with titles such as "Nature's Answer to Stress," represents an attitude to experiencing music that was first explored by composers such as John Cage and Pauline Oliveros.

This novel expression is now part of the popular culture. Even hardware stores now have displays of recordings of nature's sounds: whale songs, bird songs, sounds of waves crashing on the shore, rippling brooks, and falling rain.

Music based on minimalist techniques has been received with the greatest reluctancy by musicians and listeners whose tastes have been shaped by the traditional Western approach to music as a forward-moving progression of sound. Such people do not easily thrust aside their listening skills, which center around making continual references to past musical events in a piece and anticipating future gestures based on what they have already heard. Nonetheless, new age music and the recorded sounds of a static nature found a place in the late twentieth century.

The connections between Western music based on minimalistic devices and various musical expressions from around the world—especially those whose stylistic origins do not stem primarily from European roots—create a fascinating listening scenario. Throughout *Musical Encounters* we have experienced several works whose organization and general aesthetic approaches were of metamorphosis and gradual change as opposed to repetition and contrast. Listening to these works requires a similar approach to musical perception, an aesthetic that creates remarkable links between cultures that differ greatly from one another.

$\mathcal{S}$UMMARY

In their desire to create new musical expressions, post-modernist composers frequently seek to express sounds and ideas heretofore not considered as part of the world of concert music. Devices such as the use of silence, electronically generated noise, environmental sounds, unusual instrumental combinations, and minimalistic techniques of continual repetition, and the gradual metamorphosis of musical gestures are all part of the post-modernist approach.

Perhaps the end result of this music making is that the very definition of music is being expanded. Composers whose music falls into the somewhat nebulous category of post-modernist have received mixed reactions from members of the musical establishment. Their impact on the general contemporary musical culture, however, has been strong, for by offering us a chance to expand our points of reference in music, they have opened up to the world a new awareness of music's function in our diverse culture.

$\mathcal{K}$EY TERMS

chance music
indeterminate music
minimalism
Muzak
phase shifting
post-modernism

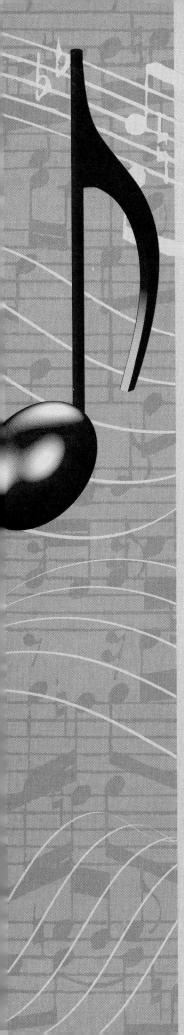

PART III

Music As a Social Force

$\mathcal{T}$HE final section of this book treats music as a force for social communication in our contemporary culture. The range of music you will hear is intentionally broad; various forms of popular music are found alongside compositions written for the concert stage. By breaking down the barriers between "high-brow" and "low-brow" music, we are free to consider how music functions as a tool for self expression, group expression, and social commentary. We will observe that music functions as social communication in virtually all genres, styles, and types of music.

By this time in your musical encounters you have probably become impressed with the immense versatility of music. This aural art that we defined simply as "the organization of sounds" has the capability of stimulating our perceptive intellect with intricate manipulations of notes, rhythms, and textures; it can entertain us with delightful sounds, arouse our emotions, play on our sentiments, or lull us to sleep.

This versatility of music in our modern cultures is underscored when we compare an eighteenth-century definition of music to our current usage. In 1776, English musician and scholar Dr. Charles Burney wrote a history of music in which he defined its function as "An innocent luxury, unnecessary indeed to our existence but a great improvement and gratification of the sense of hearing."[1] Today, Burney's definition is certainly inadequate, for it totally ignores the multifaceted nature of music's role, purpose, and practice in our contemporary culture. In recent years, music has stimulated strong discussion—dialogue that has even reached the federal government level—concerning elements of music that influence individual citizens. We call these discussions "culture wars," since they sometimes engender heated debate and involve specific subcultures of our society.

Our considerations regarding the sociology of the contemporary music scene in Chapter 11 will show how music serves as a cultural catalyst for peoples of a shared heritage.

We also will consider several ways in which music has become a topic for discussion by examining the culture wars that continue to add to the excitement of our times. The very fact that people line up so strongly on various sides of issues such as censorship and federal funding for the arts heightens our awareness of music's power as a communication medium.

In the final chapters of *Musical Encounters*, musical expressions directed toward feelings about love, religious attitudes, and emotions concerning war and peace form the basis of our discussion. Chapter 12 concentrates on the various ways in which music can express concepts of love and romance and shows how music enhances the universal emotion of love in culturally specific musical languages. Chapter 13 explores music and religious thought by considering the principal historical philosophies of a few selected contemporary religious practices, and it describes the music that reinforces these worship styles. The final chapter introduces music as a tool for dialogues concerning war and peace.

CHAPTER 11

The Sociology of
Music in Our Time

A MUSE WITH MANY FACES

Consider for a moment the many categories of music with which you are familiar. How many kinds of music can you name? If, by some strange stroke of your background, you had never heard any music, you could learn much by turning on the radio and listening to the many styles of music as you changed stations. Different stations not only feature segments directed toward one style, but many specialize in one kind of music. Radio stations feature alternative, heavy metal, classic rock, soft rock, rap, contemporary Christian, easy listening, country, "new" country, new wave, and classical music. And there is more! Think of the major role that MTV plays in the listening habits of many. MTV has replaced Top 40 radio as the most popular vehicle for music in the teenage and young adult markets. The advent of the compact disc also has fostered the expansion of music into everyone's life. Many American households receive over thirty channels of music through a television cable service or a satellite dish.

We may observe that never before in history has there been so much music available. Billions of dollars are spent each year in the United States in the music industry. What does this all mean to us? One consideration may be that our diverse society also has some specific needs for music. We may want to examine what role music plays in our culture—more than simply recognizing its large volume of acceptance.

MUSIC AND GROUP IDENTITY

Observers of the current decade describe life in the United States as multicultured. In fact, the term **multiculturalism** became a buzz word of higher education, industry, politics, and the media in the late twentieth century. Its common meaning refers to the many ethnic groups within a larger culture such as the United States. However, ethnicity is not the only force that brings people together; other groups also are present within our society, each with their own separate identities. After all, humans are social beings and, as such, they look for others to share their attitudes and tastes. They may be drawn together by religious beliefs, economic factors, political perspectives, or social and class structures. When these groups capture the attention of a larger public, they are often identified as subcultures.

Have you ever found yourself categorizing people you know by the type of music they listen to? Have you ever said, "She listens to country music all the time," or, "He's a Deadhead," or, "She's a jazzer"? You may remember the term "Headbangers," popular in the 1980s, which defined a hard-driving rock beat and associated violent head gestures. Such people are very focused in their musical taste and identity.

It is not surprising when we discover that the perspectives of one subculture may conflict with the viewpoints of another, resulting in tension between the groups. Some see these tensions as a natural phenomenon—something to be expected in the rapid process of social integration, which is occurring in our many-faced modern culture. Others may become so involved in voicing their perspectives that they find it hard to recognize the validity of cultural background other than their own. Music, the universal language, not only plays a large role in identifying these subcultures and interest groups, but it is often a forceful vehicle either for positive or negative statements about life experiences.

One positive function of music in our culture is that it often serves as an agent for coherence among people within a specific group. Young people in their teen years, for example, often turn to music to express their particular life concerns and emotions. In Chapter 4 we observed the immense musical industry directed toward the youth culture. Literally every subgroup of teenage culture can claim its own musical expression.

Besides the music of teenage America, many other groups are brought together by a specific musical style. People belonging to a similar ethnic background are frequently drawn to music that represents their heritage and lifestyle. There are so many different ethnic groups within the United States that to attempt to define them all and to discuss the music associated with each would take several books. Rather, we will sample one type of ethnic music that originated in another country, but that serves as a worldwide aesthetic catalyst for an entire people. The musical encounter of our choice—Celtic music—has attained a popularity which, although it comes from an ethnic source, has recently found popularity among a broad audience.

Music written for specific groups and subcultures may either originate as a natural expression of a group (as in the case of early blues songs, which came out of the African-American culture early in the twentieth century), or it may be a manufactured style created by the music industry (such as "contemporary Christian" music, which fuses religious words with existing rock expressions). Of course, not all music is directed toward a specific segment of our culture, and many people do not wish to associate with one subculture. We will now examine several facets of our culture where group identity is a strong factor and where music functions as a social force of communication.

Music and Ethnicity

Perhaps the most logical place to begin, when one considers how music enhances group identity, is to examine the music of a specific ethnic society. The United States, although it is a young country compared to European countries, is a composite of many cultures from around the world. Many Americans who are active citizens of the country at large still maintain pride in their ethnic origins and often convey this pride through music.

Let us examine one musical culture as an illustration of how music can express a specific ethnic personality. **Celtic music** not only represents an important ethnic heritage with deep and wide roots, but it is one that has recently found a broad listening audience throughout the world. Celtic music—the folk music that we commonly associate with Ireland and Scotland—has some very distinct characteristics that come from centuries of musical practice.

In reality, the Celts are a race that no longer exists. Furthermore, modern usage of "Celtic" includes references to a mystic influence that is loosely applied to a general aesthetic of some new age music. The nomenclature of "Celtic" is such a popular image that the music industry has discovered that the mere association with the word sells

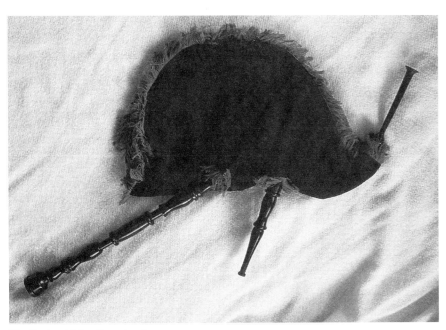

The Breton biniou (bagpipes).

recordings. In spite of the commercialization of Celtic music, it still retains strong musical accents that speak for people of a common, albeit widespread, ethnic background.

What is the reason for this popularity? Many people of Irish, Welsh, and Scottish ancestry find personal meaning in learning about their cultural heritage and discovering the rich heritage of legend, art, and musical practices of the Celtic culture. These traditions date back to the fifth and sixth centuries B.C., when Indo-European-speaking tribes spread across Europe and reached the British Isles, France, Spain, Macedonia, and Asia Minor. In medieval and modern times, this culture has survived in western France, Wales, the Scottish Highlands, and Ireland.

Celtic music often is identified by its instruments. If you venture to the Celtic section of a CD rack, you will find music that includes fiddles (violins), flutes, tin whistles (a simple whistle flute also known as the pennywhistle), bagpipes, harps, several types of accordions, bombards (folk oboes), guitars, drums (the bodhrán, a flat frame drum played with a double-ended stick), and bones (percussion instruments that produce a clicking sound when hit together; a similar sound can be made by striking two large animal jawbones together).

The fiddle is the most prominent instrument of Irish and Scottish music. Celtic music often involves rather fast, continuous fiddle melodies that allow performers to exhibit their skill at playing rapid passages. At times, fiddlers rest their instruments on their arms instead of placing it under their chins—the standard position for playing the violin. Simple flutes provide a light, airy timbre, while tin whistles are more shrill.

Bagpipes, instruments commonly associated with the music of the Scottish Highlands, originated in ancient times in the Far East, were recorded to have been used in Nero's time, and were prominent instruments in the Middle Ages. Various forms of bagpipes (often referred to simply as "pipes") are used in Celtic music. In Ireland, the **Uilleann pipes** are bellows powered and have a quieter sound than the Scottish bagpipes. In England, the **Northumbrian small pipes** are popular. Like the **biniou** of Brittany and the **gaita** of Spain, they are capable of producing softer sounds. The drone of the bagpipe family is an identifying feature of Celtic music.

The Celtic harp is very prominent in this music. It has retained a basic structure that stems from Old Testament times. These instruments, when played together, or in various combinations, create an aura of sound associated with Celtic ancestry. Moods of Celtic music range from mournful, sentimental ballades to the fast dance music of Irish jigs.

Our musical encounter with Celtic music involves a currently popular group from Ireland, The Chieftains. This group of instrumentalists and singers was formed in 1963 and, during the course of the last four decades, has performed all over the world. Their numerous recordings feature virtuosic performances on traditional instruments such as the uilleann pipes, fiddle, tin whistle, concertina, harp, bodhran, and timpan (a form of the hammer dulcimer). Although their music emanates from the common people, The Chieftains have expanded their realm of music to include guest appearances with chamber, concert, and symphony orchestras throughout Europe and the United States.

Sea Image is an original composition by Paddy Moloney, a member of The Chieftains, and one of its principal arrangers. This tune combines many of the traditional elements of Celtic music, from the mournfully slow melodies played over the drone pipes to the lively 6/8 dance rhythms typical of Irish and Scottish music.

istening Guide 52

Sea Image
Paddy Moloney

Instrumental composition in the Celtic style
Recorded by the Chieftains
1978
CD No. 3, Track 14 (6:11)

To Consider

1. Notice the constant changing of instrumental timbres. How does this compositional technique enhance your interest in the music?
2. As you listen to this work are you aware of a formal structure to this composition? Does the title, *Sea Images*, stimulate your mind to create mental images of what the music is depicting as the formal structure unfolds?
3. Can you describe this music, using musical terms? What meters do you encounter here? Are the phrases of the melody short or long, regular or irregular? Are the chords used essentially primary triads, or do you hear more complex chord progressions?

0:00	The music begins tentatively with melodic fragments entering over the drone of pipes and violin.
0:28	The bodhran (drum) introduces an element of rhythm which leads to a short, repeated melodic phrase presented by the whistle flute and uilleann pipes. The harp provides counterpoint.
1:07	The anticipation of growing rhythmic activity is temporarily halted as the fiddle plays a mournful phrase. It is the end of the introduction.
1:26	Now, the fiddle breaks into a dance tune and one begins to feel the regularity of the meter. Gradually other instruments enter as the texture becomes layered with busy musical material.
2:48	The bodhran signals a change in motion. The uilleann pipes slow the motion down temporarily and play a recitative-like passage punctuated by the drum and accompanied by the harp.

3:20   The whistle flute enters with melodic support and the recitative-like section ends with a sustained drone.

4:13   The dance rhythms return. Various instruments join together in playing the short, repeated phrases of the dance tune. Once more the texture becomes thicker as the participants provide slightly varied versions of the melodic phrase.

Music of Teenage America: Rock

The music of rock is such a prominent aspect of our youth society that it is a primary identifying factor of the teenage segment in the United States. When Bill Haley and the Comets created "Rock Around the Clock" in 1954 by setting lyrics to a well-known boogie-woogie bass line, little did they know that the energy from that recording would ignite a musical practice that would become known as "rock 'n' roll." Now that rock is entering its sixth decade, musical features have changed dramatically from the acoustically produced sounds of the 1950s. This adaptability is the key to survival, for current rock not only speaks for a large segment of today's youth, just as it did in the past decades, but it is also listened to by many adults.

Common to the rock movement is the expression of energy produced by its singers and musicians. Music for the rock generation is never a placid experience. Sound comes alive: guitars shriek, drums pound, singers shout out the lyrics to a steady stream of regularly pulsating rhythms, and musicians move on stage to choreographed movements. The resulting energy is one that has become synonymous with our youth culture.

Today's rock is vastly different from its early form. The musical style has changed and has become more diverse, and rock has become a major business, churning out billions of dollars each year. Rock also reflects the attitudes and perspectives of teenage America, which are much different than those of the 1950s. Some feel that the behavior of today's teenagers is strongly influenced by the type of music embraced by their particular peer group; critics of rock frequently have problems coping with high decibel levels, the general attitude and content of the lyrics, and the physical gyrations of the performers. They believe that the rock movement, having started as an energetic offshoot of dance music, has come to signify what is perhaps the central symbol of sexual freedom and teenage independence in recent times.

London, 2/6/57: Bill Haley and the Comets (Ruddy Pompilli, Al Rex, and Johnnie Grande) rehearse. © Bettmann/ CORBIS. ID # BE039990.

Listening Guide 53

Rock Around the Clock
Jimmy DeKnight and Max Freedman

Early rock song
Recorded by Bill Haley and the Comets
1954
CD No. 3, Track 15 (3:12)

Let us listen to one of the earliest rock 'n' roll tunes to discover some of the roots of this style. You may be struck by the extreme simplicity of this music if you compare it to today's pop expressions. As you listen, keep in mind that this music was a movement of amateur musicians who formed small groups to create music. Early rock 'n' roll was something that almost anyone could sing; it was typically backed up by guitar(s), drums, piano, bass, and whatever other instruments could provide melodic support.

To Consider

1. What specific musical elements of this song provide the "energy" commonly associated with rock 'n' roll?
2. Can you identify the chord progression underlying *Rock Around the Clock?* Have you heard it before? What does this suggest about the origin of early rock?
3. How do you think the lyrics reflected the teenage culture of the 1950s? What would be the significance of staying out all night in the 1950s compared to today?

Others, however, do not wish to group together all of the various rock expressions, nor do they agree that a large part of our youth can be identified with a particular style of rock. The reality of rock in current years is that it has found many different performance practices and has evolved into a variety of subcategories. Because of this variety, today's young people can choose from several musical and social agendas from within the contemporary pop and rock culture.

A question pertinent to our study of music as a vehicle for group identity is: do various types of rock speak for specific groups of teenagers in today's society? And, can we identify certain musical features of the different kinds of music that serve as a guidepost for the stylistic analysis of pop music?

It is commonly held that, in order to succeed in the current commercial market, rock artists must develop a unique style—an expression that distinguishes them from some other group. At the same time, however, certain parameters of expression remain constant. One cannot fall outside of the general "window" of style in any category of rock and expect to sell recordings. Connected with the musical style of a given group is an image. This is a composite of dress, facial attitude during performance, choreography, lighting, and personality mystique. Several general movements in the world of rock and roll can be identified as broad examples of this image.

A prime example of music that carries with it a specific image of sound and behavior is heavy metal. This is a type of rock characterized by electronic instruments amplified to an extremely loud range; the term "heavy metal" in reference to rock is purportedly borrowed from the writings of William Burroughs, a social iconoclast and Beat writer, who, with his literary associates Allen Ginsberg and Jack Kerouac, occupied a major place in shaping the counter-culture during the 1960s and 1970s. The Steppenwolf song, *Born to Be Wild*, written in 1968, used the term "heavy metal thunder" in referencing both the machinery of the motorcycle, and more subtly, the musical style of the song.

Born to Be Wild is all about motorcycles and the carefree spirit associated with the lifestyle of bikers in the 1970s. It is the title song of a Steppenwolf album that also includes *Monster*, a song of political commentary, and *Snowblind Friend*, an anti-drug song. Steppenwolf's leader, John Kay, was born in West Germany and immigrated to Canada in 1963, moved to New York in 1966, and finally settled in Los Angeles in 1968. Kay retired temporarily from the rock scene in 1972, after having been very active for seven years, but his success continues. His recordings have exceeded 20 million in sales; his songs were licensed for use in thirty-seven motion pictures and in thirty-six television shows. His song *Born to Be Wild* illustrates an infectious youthful energy and carefree attitude:

Get your motor running
Head out on the highway,
Lookin' for adventure
In whatever comes our way.

Here and God are gonna make it happen
Take the world in a love embrace
Fire all of your guns at once, and
Explode into space.

I like smoke and lightning
Heavy metal thunder
Racin' with the wind
And the feelin' that I'm under.

Like a true nature's child
We were born, born to be wild.
We can climb so high
I never wanna die.

Born to be wild
Born to be wild.[1]

Earlier expressions associated with behavior and attitude patterns are punk rock and acid rock. The movement known as **punk rock,** or simply punk, came about in the 1960s, and pushed teenage independence to new limits. The word "punk" was first attached to youthful groups who came to the United States in the wake of the Beatles and the Rolling Stones. Originally identified by greased hair and clothes with padded shoulders, this movement in the 1970s came to represent social offensiveness, where members blatantly set out to capture the attention of society through their behavior, appearance, noise, and language. The movement is not characterized by specific musical features but rather by a general attitude. Popular punk groups include the Sex Pistols, the Clash, and the Damned.

Acid rock is a loose designation for the heavily amplified rock that was part of the drug culture of the 1960s. Practitioners of this type of rock purportedly connected music to the concept of mind expansion. Its musical style frequently included electronic fuzz and feedback and gave the general impression of freedom and improvisation. Groups representative of this genre include Jefferson Airplane and the Grateful Dead.

A more recent type of music that grew out of the inner-city culture as a means of personal and group expression is **hip-hop.** Hip-hop is a movement that broadly describes the New York City, mostly black, pop scene (especially rap), and it includes break dancing, body popping, electronic sounds, and modern graffiti. The common mode of dress is designer training shoes and slick athletic warm-up clothes in bright colors. This expression has been exploited successfully by the advertising world. **Rap** is a related term that actually refers to a dance craze that originated in the 1970s and was cultivated first by New York City teenagers from the African-American and Latin communities. Its base is disco music that is altered by increasing the accent on the second and fourth beats of the measure (called a backbeat). Originally used as a background to break dancing, this music evolved into rap when the practice of reciting rhymed street poetry was added to the music. At times this pop expression takes on the air of improvisation, where the words flow rapidly in creative rhythmic patter and rhyme schemes. Rap, once the sole property of city African Americans, is now enjoyed by millions of teenagers of varying backgrounds across the country.

These poems are often written in strong language. It addresses the emotions, attitudes, and concerns of the writers/musicians in a direct manner, uninhibited by the conventions of formal speech and propriety. Street language vocabulary is at times specialized—many people from outside of this culture may not understand some of the words used; words are also used that are not considered socially acceptable to the American public.

The poetry of rap is often based on the true life experiences of the street. No subject is taboo. They often reflect the violence of the culture in the late twentieth century. Songs of hatred growing out of clashes with police, songs depicting gun fire, songs of beatings, and songs of uninhibited sexual expression are typical of this popular musical genre.

Just as music can express tender feelings of romance, of religious sentiments, and of patriotic feelings, it can also depict aggressive behaviors and attitudes. Rap songs frequently function in this manner. Such music provides a meaningful voice to the society from which it arises. It also allows a larger public to feel some of the emotions and experiences it describes.

The 1994 recording of the rap group Warren G and Nate Dogg *Regulate,* speaks of a violent street life in which the singer talks about pulling his "gat" (an assault weapon which, as he relates, holds sixteen bullets in the clip and one in the chamber) to "regulate" (i.e., shoot) some "brothas" who had robbed him. The poetry creates a vivid sense of the tough street life depicted here, as told in strong language and rhythm within the context of a specialized vocabulary. It is real-life drama.

Another popularly used term, **classic rock,** has come to be identified with mainstream rock 'n' roll from the 1960s, 1970s, and 1980s. Its adherents frequently consider this a slightly more sophisticated level of music than the extremes of rock, which seem to rise and fall with regularity.

For those who do not want to associate with any of the cliched expressions of rock, the designation, **alternative music,** has appeal. Once more, it is difficult to assign a specific compositional/performance practice to this type of music. Basically, recordings that fall into this category are typified by songs with lyrics that can be understood upon first hearing, by a general evenness of dynamic level, and by a relatively conservative mode of social expression.

The constant, driving energy of the rock era is the bond that links together many styles of this youthful music. At times, rock also expresses an inherent rejection of the boredom created by the "straight world." The following analysis, given by critic and writer on communication theory, Lawrence Grossberg, underlines a fundamental function of rock and roll. Grossberg states:

> The politics of youth celebrate change, risk, and instability; the very structures of boredom become the sites of new forms of empowerment. The powerlessness of youth is rearticulated into an apparatus in which it becomes the site of "pleasure" and power. The "pleasure" of empowerment/empowerment of "pleasure" is, furthermore, articulated around the material pleasures of the body. It is its emphasis on rhythm and dance, and its affirmation of sexual desire which may, occasionally, challenge the dominant gender categories. Rock and roll seeks pleasure in the different ways the body can be inserted into its social environment." [2]

Some people feel that rock is not only a delineator of groups and subcultures within our teenage population but is more generally an indicator of the generation gap between youth and adults. It is a tool of expression used by teenagers who are growing up—and away—from their parents. It is a way to say to their parents, "I'm different from you. I like different things, and I do not always express myself the way you do." (And some would argue that a certain amount of independence is healthy at this stage of maturation.)

However, since rock is now over two generations old, many parents of today's youth were participants in the earlier musical movements of rock 'n' roll. Their attitudes toward components of rock such as volume, abrasive lyrics, and general performance practices are not as critical as were those of parents in earlier generations.

We will examine some of the extreme attitudes that illustrate culture wars involving music in our contemporary society. The musical selections in this section are certainly different than those found in other parts of this book, for they are philosophical and ideological in nature. They are, however, very significant components of our musical world and are worth examining. The first area of interest concerns certain expressions of rock and how segments of the public view it as a social force. Our second excursion into the sociology of music will take us into the areas of censorship concerning music and lyrics. Finally, our sociological encounters with music will lead us to the ongoing discussion that stems from attitudes toward music and its aesthetic companion, art. This argument focuses on federal funding for the arts, and is often controversial.

Your encounters with attitudes about music in our culture will no doubt reinforce the central theme of this book. Diversity is perhaps the most prominent element of our entire society, and the world of music certainly reflects that diversity—both in the music itself and in attitudes concerning music.

$\mathcal{I}$ SSUES AND ATTITUDES TOWARD MUSIC AND ART IN CONTEMPORARY CULTURE

Rock and Rap: An Argument over Influences

Does rock and its more recent relative rap—especially "gangsta rap"—exert a negative influence on today's youth? If it does, how can that influence be measured? Should offensive lyrics be censored by governments? Should recording companies be required to post warning labels on offensive material? What are the roles and responsibilities of government, industry, parents, and schools in identifying the influences of music on young people?

These are all questions that have been bandied about for decades ever since Elvis Presley patented his famous gyrations, but they became more hotly argued in the 1980s and 1990s. It is interesting to observers of musical culture that especially in the last two decades of the twentieth century, controversies over private and public morality have focused strongly on music and its potential to influence others. To those acquainted with music history, this comes as no surprise, for in one way or another, music has always reflected the tastes and attitudes of a society; furthermore, music is no stranger to controversy.

Perhaps one of the most notorious diatribes against the teen rock movement is contained in a best-seller social critique by University of Chicago professor Allan Bloom, in *The Closing of the American Mind*.

> I do not suggest that it [rock] has any high intellectual sources. But it has risen to its current heights in the education of the young on the ashes of classical music, and in an attempt to tap the rawest passions . . . Rock has one appeal only a barbaric appeal, to sexual desire—not love, not eros, but sexual desire undeveloped and untutored. It acknowledges the first emanations of children's emerging sensuality and addresses them seriously, eliciting them and legitimating them, not as little sprouts that must be carefully tended in order to grow into gorgeous flowers, but as the real thing. [3]

Bloom's contention is that he is not primarily concerned with the moral effects of this music—whether it leads to sex, violence, or drugs. His stance is that the all-pervasive music of rock ruins the imaginations of young people and therefore has a negative impact on aesthetic education. The expressions of youthful longings and passions through the medium of rock, according to Bloom, conflict with those the adult world recognizes as wholesome. It is therefore essential that today's young people have a passionate relationship with art and thought that will provide a link between the "animal" and the spiritual.

Recent controversies have arisen over the degree to which rock groups can and should openly defy cultural and moral conventions in our society. The issues of moral rebellion, exploitation of women, and lack of respect for others have been at the center of these controversies. Do certain rock musicians cross the line of communal decency and morality by openly defying the values of our society, or are the extremes of such freedom of expression healthy for our culture? The lines of argument are drawn, not always between youth and adult, but also between people of all ages who feel strongly about public expression in the twenty-first century.

We will now examine several issues that have arisen in recent years concerning not only rock but other related facets of the arts during our times—issues that ultimately result in a discussion of whether or not free expression as guaranteed by the U. S. Constitution should be controlled, or at least labeled, when it crosses the bounds of what society considers acceptable subject matter.

During the 1980s, two prominent issues arose. One was whether or not certain types of music were detrimental to our youth culture; the other was whether or not artistic expressions should be supported by government funds. These issues, while seemingly unrelated, eventually focused on the public will versus private expression.

Although debates about the debilitating effects of rock and lyrics on our youth have been going on for decades, the activities of heavy metal groups Guns N' Roses and Judas Priest and those of the rap group 2 Live Crew typified much of the controversy raised in the 1980s and early 1990s concerning the social function of some rock. These three bands gained notoriety by issuing recordings containing lyrics that offended many on several broad social fronts. According to one news magazine editorial, recordings such as 2 Live Crew's *As Nasty As They Wanna Be* (1989) frequently

Congress shall make no law respecting an establishment of religion, or prohibiting the free exercise thereof, or abridging the freedom of speech, or of the press; or the right of the people peaceably to assemble, and to petition the Government for redress of grievances.

Article I (the First Amendment) to the Constitution of the United States.

conveyed messages that "1. Women are sexual objects to be used and abused by men. 2. Violence is an effective means of resolving conflicts. 3. It is O.K. to hate another class of people."[4] The Florida statewide prosecutor, in response to the critics of this album, made the strong case that *As Nasty As They Wanna Be* violated the state's obscenity and racketeering laws.[5]

In 1985, two youths wounded themselves (one of them fatally) after listening to the album *Stained Glass* by Judas Priest. Attorneys for the two families sought $6.2 million in damages from the rock group, claiming that the songs "warped and distorted and destroyed the minds"[6] of young people. The song, *Better By You Better By Me*, it was claimed, contained the subliminal message "Do It!"—a message that encouraged their sons to attempt suicide.

Nevada Judge Jerry Carr Whitehead eventually ruled that there was no scientific evidence to suggest that subliminal messages in music could prompt attempted suicide. His ruling stated that, "The scientific research presented does not establish that subliminal stimuli, even if perceived, may precipitate conduct of this magnitude. . . . The strongest evidence presented at the trial showed no behavioral effects other than anxiety, distress or tension."[7] The controversy, however, underlined an argument centering on the freedom of expression claimed under the First Amendment of the U.S. Constitution and the outcry of some to control material that is considered outside of the range of social acceptability.

In the mid-1980s, a group called the Parents' Music Resource Center (PMRC), in a reaction to objectionable rock lyrics, proposed that the government establish a rating system

"Judas Priest" Dave Holland, Glenn Tipton, Rob Halford, Ian Hill, and Scott Downing. © Lynn Goldsmith/CORBIS. ID # BE083473.

in the recording industry whereby recordings would be labeled where excesses of explicit sex and graphic violence occurred, or where references to drug and alcohol consumption or the occult were present. Hearings were held in Congress to determine whether or not this rating system should be established. Several parents as well as recording artists were called upon to testify.

Testimonies from John Denver and Frank Zappa typify the recording artists' feelings toward record labeling. The late John Denver, in a polite testimony, stated the following in reference to the proposal:

> Mr. Chairman, this would approach censorship. May I be very clear that I am strongly opposed to censorship of any kind in our society or anywhere else in the world. I have had in my experience two encounters with this sort of censorship. My song "Rocky Mountain High" was banned from many radio stations as a drug-related song. This was obviously done by people who had never seen or been to the Rocky Mountains. . . . To my knowledge, my movie *Oh God* was not banned in any theaters. However, some newspapers refused to print our advertisements, and some theaters refused to put the name of the film on the marquee.[8]

The late Frank Zappa, leader of the 1960s rock band The Mothers of Invention and an active composer and a verbal proponent of rock 'n' roll, was less polite. In speaking about the women who formed the PMRC, he said that no one forced them to bring certain kinds of music into their homes:

> Thanks to the Constitution, they are free to buy other forms of music for the children. Apparently, they insist on purchasing the works of contemporary recording artists in order to support a personal illusion of aerobic sophistication. Ladies, please be advised: The $8.98 purchase price does not entitle you to a kiss on the foot from the composer or performer in exchange for a spin on the family Victrola. Taken as a whole, the complete list of PMRC demands reads like an instruction manual for some sinister kind of toilet training program to house-break all composers and performers because of the lyrics of a few. Ladies, how dare you?[9]

Strong feelings on both sides of issues arising over the questionable lyrics in popular music have continued. More recently has been the "gangsta rap" recordings, which express strong feelings of racism and draw attention to social issues such as the high level of conflict between some components of the African-American community and the police forces in large cities.

During the 1990s, lawmakers in several states introduced legislation that allowed communities to rate music "harmful to minors." Some bills, such as the Concert Ratings Bill, introduced in Michigan on May 21, 1998, clearly spell out the subject matter of music that would qualify it as being unacceptable, and would allow authorities to refuse entrance to youths under age eighteen to concerts where such music is being performed. A different approach to regulation was introduced in February 1998 in California. This bill was designed to prevent certain retirement funds from investing in any industry that supported music that advocated sexual assault, bestiality, the illegal use of drugs, criminal gang activity, the denigration of females, or violence against a particular sex.

Whether or not bills such as these eventually become laws, it is certain that music is used by many as a way to communicate about a variety of subjects. Those who want to restrict it feel that it is inappropriate to express social injustices through music; the people who produce this music feel that they have a constitutional right to sing and play any kind of music that they wish, free from governmental intervention.

One thing is certain. Whatever the subject of controversy in our current society, music is a central medium of expression for individuals who wish to deliver a strong message.

A natural outgrowth of a pluralistic society such as ours is a diverse expression of attitudes toward the role of the arts in our lives. The discussion concerning what is appropriate as subject matter in the arts is not limited to music. The controversy also exists in painting, photography, and the other graphic arts. A major topic of discussion and debate that arose in the late 1980s was whether the federal government should support art that contained socially controversial material, and if it did provide financial support for such art, did the government have the right to censor the content of the artistic product by withholding funding from projects deemed inappropriate?

Controversies Concerning Federal Funding for the Arts

Public subsidy for the arts has never had the total support of all political persuasions. Opposition to government spending has been part of a conservative element in the nation's capital since it was first instituted. Several themes of arguments have persisted throughout the years. One such argument states that, as long as the nation has a deficit and as long as there are hungry and poor people in this country, money should not be spent on the arts. Other pockets of opposition to federal grants arise when a specific work that has received funding is targeted for criticism.

The following gives a synopsis of the development of the National Endowment for the Arts (NEA), the U.S. government program designed to support the arts nationwide.[10] The numbers of employees and program directors represent the status of the NEA during the mid-1980s.[11]

Musical Encounter

The National Endowment for the Arts

The concept of public funding for the arts in America was President Truman's idea. He called on the Fine Arts Commission to make recommendations for a federal program in support of the arts. President Eisenhower furthered the concept by calling upon Congress to create a Federal Advisory Commission on the Arts. The issue remained unacted upon until President Kennedy created the Federal Advisory Council for the Arts by executive order. The Council for the Arts was finally established under the Johnson administration in August 1964, but it was not until September 29, 1965, when the National Foundation on the Arts and Humanities Act was passed, that the foundation was laid for the actual monetary funding of projects. In November of that year, the first grants were awarded, some to dance companies and theatres and others to individuals such as composers, teaching artists, and choreographers.

The Arts Endowment staff includes a chairperson, who is appointed by the president of the United States; the National Council on the Arts, comprised of twenty-six members who hold office for six years, also appointed by the president; and panels of professional practitioners in the arts, numbering about 500 people, who are engaged temporarily as jurors and advisors. The Arts Endowment staff has some 300 civil service employees with program directors. In addition, a strong linkage exists between the federal and state arts organizations.

In 1992, the NEA received in funding $176 million (68 cents per U.S. citizen). A comparison of artistic activity between 1965, the year in which federal funding was first allocated, and 1992, when funding had been in place for almost three decades, indicates that a cultural explosion occurred in the United States after the founding of the NEA. In 1965, there were twenty theatres, fifty-eight symphonies, thirty-seven dance companies, and twenty-seven opera companies. In 1992, the NEA reported the existence of 420 theatres, 230 symphonies, 250 dance companies, and 120 opera companies.

The 1997 budget was reduced to $99 million. Furthermore, legislation was introduced, unsuccessfully, in the summer of 1997 to phase out the NEA entirely over a three-year period. The 2000 budget was $97.6 million.

It is the contention of the artistic world that the arts speak for humankind. Ryan O'Dougherty, the NEA's media arts director, states this position clearly: "The arts are not meant to be loved, they are meant to stimulate. They are meant to tell the truth . . . they are meant to keep us alert and alive to the problems in our culture at large."[12] Lobbyists from the political right and from some religious groups, however, feel that the taxpayer's dollar should not be spent on cultural statements in the guise of art. Their definition of art is that of "high" art—art that always uplifts, art that is above the commonplace. In the modern artistic community, however, high art and low art are being fused as never before, and many times the result is socially disturbing. Once more our culture is experiencing a dichotomy of definition. The question "What is art?" is now being answered with the

Musical Encounter

The Visual Arts and the NEA

*C*ontroversies erupted in June 1989, with the cancellation of the partial federally-funded *Awards in the Visual Arts 7* exhibition, sponsored by the Southeastern Center for Contemporary Art in Winston-Salem, North Carolina, which included *Piss Christ*, a work by Andres Serrano. This work is a photograph of a plastic crucifix immersed in urine, and it was the rallying point around which many critics of federal funding for artistic works gathered.

Whereas the artist argued that the use of bodily fluids such as blood, milk, semen, and urine in his works represented the fluids of life and were symbolic to him of violence, purity, life, and human waste, others viewed Serrano's choice of subject matter as offensive and inappropriate for federal subsidy.

In July 1989, the U.S. Senate voted to bar the NEA from using federal funds to "promote, disseminate or produce obscene or indecent materials, including but not limited to depictions of sadomasochism, homoeroticism, the exploitation of children, or individuals engaged in sex acts, or material which denigrates the objects or beliefs of the adherents of a particular religion or nonreligion."[13] It also barred grants for artwork that "denigrates, debases or reviles a person, group or class of citizens on the basis of race, creed, sex, handicap, age or national origin."[14]

Another heated discussion was generated when the Corcoran Gallery of Art in Washington, D.C., canceled a photographic exhibition by Robert Maplethorpe, whose exhibition, also with the support of the NEA, produced an art show containing several pictures that several U. S. senators considered pornographic.

More fuel was added to the Maplethorpe controversy when, on April 7, 1990, a grand jury in Hamilton County, Ohio, returned an indictment against the Cincinnati Contemporary Arts Center for displaying the Maplethorpe exhibition. The grand jury identified seven out of 175 photos in the show as being obscene, thus in violation of Ohio's state code on obscenity.

Incidents such as the Serrano and Maplethorpe controversies prompted much discussion on the role of federal funding in the late 1980s and early 1990s. The discussion spread from a concentration on content in federally funded art to the general question of whether or not the arts need federal support at all.

broadest possible definitions by some, while others feel that the concept of art is a limited, well-defined one.

The arguments surrounding federal funding for music typically do not stem from discussions concerning propriety in subject matter, such as they do in painting and photography. The major controversy over questionable subject matter in music occurs in the arena of pop music, and pop music is not funded by federal grants. Its venue is a commercial market. Composers of art music in our times have not been interested in pushing the limits of public taste with regard to sexual content, violence, and other topics that are offensive to many. Their areas of experimentation are primarily concerned with novel ways of manipulating the musical materials of their work.

Whether or not art music—operas, ballets, symphonies, chamber groups, vocal ensembles—should receive federal tax dollars to supplement its existence is an argument based on its primary functions. Some people feel that music is, after all, entertainment, and that it should exist on its own commercial success. "Let the people who want this music pay for it themselves" is a common argument. Others feel that the arts provide an ongoing cultural education and benefit and enhance the cultures they reach. Supporters of federal funding feel that the small part of the federal budget directed toward cultural enrichment is justified.

On May 11, 1992, the ABC news show *Nightline* featured a discussion of two opposing views about federal support for public television, a major producer of artistic and cultural programs in America. The conservative viewpoint offered was that, in a period of recession and during a time in which the cable television industry provides so many viewing opportunities that are supported by commercial enterprise, a network that receives partial federal funding is unnecessary. The statement was made that the Public Broadcasting Service (PBS) is an elitist concept, catering to the wealthy. The opposing argument was that the total amount of federal funds spent on public television is so minimal in relationship to the federal budget that it is worth continuing when its intrinsic value is assessed. A further argument in favor of federal funding was that the types of programming possible on PBS are frequently not feasible when one considers the nature of commercial television in which frequent interruptions for advertising must occur. The concept of PBS as an elitist network was refuted strongly by the argument that the majority of PBS viewers were indeed not the wealthy but were members of middle- and lower-income groups.

The ongoing controversy over federal funding for the NEA resulted in specific and drastic cuts in federal funding in the late 1990s. When the 104th Congress cut federal spending in the fiscal years 1996 and 1997, it also reduced funding for the NEA. Although the GOP's goal for 1996 was the elimination of funding for the NEA, the 1997 funding outcomes retained a $99 million allotment. The Clinton administration proposed a budget of $136 million each for the NEA and the National Endowment for the Humanities in the 1998 budget. In June 1997, however, the Economic and Educational Opportunities Committee met and passed legislation that would reauthorize a three-year phaseout of both organizations. The attempt to phase out these federal programs proved futile, but the debate still continues concerning this issue.

Although opinions vary on the nature and funding of musical and artistic events, it seems apparent that our culture enjoys access to a broader variety of music than has ever before existed in history. The concept of "low art" and "high art" (exemplified by the terms "pop music" and "classical music") is a result of this diversity. However, an interesting phenomenon has occurred in recent decades—the coming together of these two concepts, expressions that were formerly held to be in diametric opposition to each other. The vocabulary of "art" and "artists" now enjoys (and sometimes tolerates) the broadest possible interpretation, also perhaps due to the diversity of musical expressions currently fashionable in our culture.

SUMMARY

Music functions on many levels of human experience. Perhaps one of the most interesting ways to look at music is to examine its power to bring people of like interests, ethnic backgrounds, or religious beliefs together. Music brings coherence to a variety of people; its language can be subtle, tender, and reflective of cultural nuances, as found in the specialized instrumental music of Celtic music, or it can be bold, brash, and blunt, as in rap music.

When we consider these many functions of music and the various languages with which it speaks, we come to realize that all music is legitimate. While it is unrealistic to assume that many people would find all musical expressions attractive and useful in their lives, the appreciation of various perspectives of music within our vast cultural mix is a possible and an admirable goal for people in our multilayered society.

Active discussions continue to be waged on the appropriateness of depicting socially objectionable facets of our modern culture in music. The world of pop music and the various genres of visual arts have raised poignant issues with regard to our current social environment. Both "high" and "low" artistic expressions continue to raise public awareness of how we think about ourselves. The dialogue will no doubt continue throughout the twenty-first century.

KEY TERMS

acid rock
alternative music
biniou
Celtic music
classic rock
gaita
hip-hop
multiculturalism
Northumbrian small pipes
punk rock
rap
Uilleann pipes

CHAPTER 12

Music in Religious Thought and Practice

$\mathcal{I}$N Chapter 11, we saw how music functions to bring together people of similar perspectives. It serves as a social, political, and religious catalyst for virtually all segments of society, past and present. Indeed, in our study of musical selections throughout this book, we have seen that music functions in many ways. Now, as we turn to the topic of religious music, we will focus our attention on yet another way in which various types of music enhance religious emotions, beliefs, and traditions. Similarly, in Chapters 13 and 14, we will pursue two more areas in which music functions as a tool for conveying concepts that transcend mere entertainment. We will again see how music can function as a vehicle for social commentary.

Music functions as a significant component of religious ritual throughout the world. Its unique capabilities of stimulating intellectual and emotional responses allow it to function as a vehicle for enhancing the emotional meaning of worship and for instructing church members in religious doctrines. Most religions, whether branches of Christianity or encompassing other forms of religious thought, have developed a musical repertoire that reflects a particular system of religious practice.

This chapter illustrates yet another powerful function of music. It also reinforces a central theme of *Musical Encounters*, which is the concept that our culture, and the music that reflects it, is made up of many different perspectives. In religious music, the differences between two denominations of Christianity may be rather subtle at first glance, only to become much more pronounced when viewed in depth. In this chapter you may also be impressed with some of the vast differences both in philosophies and musical practice found in the religious music of today. For example, the contrast between the traditional music of the Lutheran Church and contemporary Christian musical expression is as large as one could possibly imagine.

How do we approach the study of music as a conveyor of religious attitudes and a companion to worship? Even though we are primarily interested in viewing musical practices as we encounter them in our everyday life, we will examine some of the origins of the ideas that gave direction to this music. Through a process of sampling contrasting forms of religious music and studying the cultural background of these various expressions, you will see how music can be used to reinforce religious beliefs as well as serve as an outlet for expressive worship and ritual.

For music to function as a meaningful component of religion, it must have two basic qualities. First, it must be an effective tool of communication. Second, it must have the power to influence human emotions. These two concepts are rooted strongly in ancient civilizations, and they are accepted today as basic components shared by many types of music.

The ancient Greeks believed that music had divine origins; in fact, the very word for "music" originated with the Greek *muse*, a term for any of the nine gods who ruled all song, dance, poetry, and drama. In his masterpiece of philosophy, *The Republic*, Plato described the Greek ideal of society as he conceived it. According to Plato, in this Utopian life, "Education in music is most sovereign," for "rhythm and harmony would find their way to the innermost soul and take strongest hold upon it, imparting grace."[1]

CHANTING AS A MEANS OF WORSHIP

Many religious cultures throughout the world use chanting to add meaningful dimensions to their worship. **Chanting** refers to singing a single-line melody, without harmony, without counterpoint, and originally without the accompaniment of instruments. With few exceptions, a chant also contains a free rhythmic structure with the absence of a regular meter. In some religious traditions, chanting is a convenient way to focus on the text; in others, chanting is a way of purifying the heart and achieving a higher state of consciousness. Chanting reaches from the Native American cultures of the plains to the Russian Orthodox Church. It is found in disparate places such as India, Africa, and Korea, as well as in liturgical churches in the United States and in traditional Jewish practice.

Our musical selections with chanting will take us to two traditions. We will listen to a chant as practiced in the Buddhist traditions stemming from Tibet in the Himalayan Mountains, and then we will experience the Roman Catholic Church practice of Gregorian chant, named after Pope Gregory (r. 590–604), who was responsible for fostering the practice of standardized chant throughout Christendom. As you listen to this music, you will come to realize the contrasting functions of these two chanting cultures.

Chanting and the Buddhist Liturgy of Tibet

Tibetan ritual music is totally egoless. Every other form of music touches the ego, with people slaving over their instruments for years to become very fast and acrobatic. A lot of the time, however, the music is forgotten when people are lost in their virtuosity.[2]

The form of Buddhism in the mountainous region of Tibet depends heavily upon music. This unique form of worship is characterized by monks singing in the lowest range of the human voice. Although monotone chanting is the norm in Tibet, the ancient art of multiphonic singing—the production of two or three notes by manipulating the over-

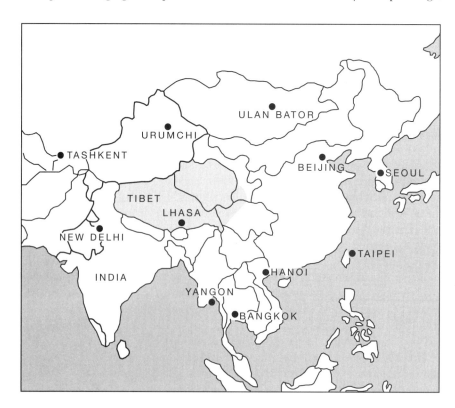

tones of a fundamental pitch—is also cultivated widely by Buddhist monks from this tradition. They believe that only those who have attained a level of selfless wisdom can develop this technique. (In Chapter 3, we heard overtone singing from a very different culture.)

Buddhist ritual often includes alternating singing and playing loud sounds on instruments in order to entertain and invoke the gods. This philosophy of sacred music dictates that some sounds are heard by the ear, whereas others are felt by the body or the mind. It categorizes sounds as pure (*Dra*), resonating (*Yang*), and those with word-like meanings (*kāā*). There are many different variations of religious practice among the various orders of monks in Tibetan monasteries, which number over 3,000, but they share a dedication to Buddhist philosophy, logic, and dialectic, balanced by the use of the Tibetan language. A common goal is the unification of the external and internal worlds, and music is the vehicle used in this process.[3]

Listening Guide 54

Sutra Reading from the Namgyal Monastery of Dharamsala
Buddhist Chant

Recorded by Buddhist monks of the Namgyal Monastery
CD No. 4, Track 1 (4:18)

The Namgyal Monastery at Dharamsala in North India originally existed in Tibet and was founded by His Holiness, the Dalai Lama III, during the sixteenth century. It was disbanded in 1959 by the Lhasa Uprising and reestablished in its present location in Himachal Pradesh in North India. Dharamsala is where the Dalai Lama currently lives in exile among his followers at the Dip Tse Chok Ling Monastery.

We will listen to a segment of a **sutra** reading for our musical selection of a Buddhist chant. The sutra is a collection of the discourse of the Buddha. In this ritual, the priests receive the teaching of the Buddha from a high priest and meditate with him on the **mandala** (a graphic symbol of the universe). In the sutra meditation, the sins and pollution of each individual are purified.

The monotone chant is led by the high priest, who is then joined by the group of monks in a response pattern. Inflections of the language create subtle changes of pitch that sound like ornamentation to the Western ear. These sections of chant are then interrupted by loud bursts of an instrumental group consisting of cymbals, hand bells, rattle drums, double reed instruments of the oboe family, long brass trumpets (played in pairs), and several types of drums. Hand clapping and finger snapping also are part of the Tibetan sutra reading ritual.

You will hear only a segment of the entire ritual, but this selection includes the two basic elements of this musical practice. The alternation of chanting and loud instrumental music goes on for a prolonged period in actual practice. At times the chanting speeds up, but it is always broken up by instrumental music. When one experiences the religious ritual in its entirety, all sense of time is suspended.

To Consider

1. When you listen to the monks chant, be aware of the rhythmic pulse of the readings as they create an "other-world" monotony. What patterns of regularity can you decipher from this music?
2. What principles guide the "pitch" inflections of this music? Do you think there are specific notes connected to this chant, or is the chant organized according to the general range of the monks' voices?
3. The loud interruption of instruments is designed to entertain the gods. Musically there are two layers of material: the first is the soft, rhythmic chanting; the second is the loud instrumental interjections. Do you think that these strong contrasts may have both theological and emotional bases as part of this worship ceremony?

Our encounter with this chanting not only illustrates yet another use of the human voice but gives us a brief glimpse into its use as a vehicle for worship. In this case, the vocal techniques employed do not approximate the sounds of speech but are intentionally different, in an effort to transcend the mundane world.

The European Tradition: Gregorian Chant

The word "tradition" is well suited to the chant of the Roman Catholic Church. It was founded in ancient Jewish practices, introduced as the early Christian faith was being organized into a structured religion, and has been practiced in varying degrees of intensity since the fourth century. Although the chant tradition is named after Pope Gregory, who was a strong supporter of the practice of chanting liturgical texts, its existence before his time has been well documented. Furthermore, the five most common parts of the **Mass**—the divine service of the Church—were not developed until several centuries after Pope Gregory's death. These are the *Kyrie* (*Lord, have mercy upon us*), the *Gloria* (*Glory be to the Father*), the *Credo* (the creed, *I believe in one God*), the *Sanctus* (*Holy, Holy, Holy,*), and the *Agnus Dei* (*Lamb of God*).

A specific source of information regarding the way psalms and prayers were chanted in early Christian worship in Jerusalem was recorded by the nun Etheria (also known as Egeria) in 385 A.D. Her document *Peregrinatio Etheria* (*Etheria's pilgrimage*) indicates that she took a pilgrimage from her convent, probably in northwest Spain, to find out what religious practices were like in the Holy Land. Her account of the early worship practices in the cradle of Christianity indicates the existence of organized daily rituals, called Offices, and the celebration of the last supper, called the Mass. Etheria mentions singing practices during the various services she attended. Her descriptions are quite specific and provide concrete information about the way in which the hymns, psalms, and other religious texts were presented. Often one person began a section of the text and was then joined by others who would "respond" to the leader with the rest of the text.

Damasus I (r. 366–384), an early church leader in Rome, began an organized process of liturgical development in the Roman Catholic Church. His work was influenced by St. Jerome, a priest who visited Jerusalem and returned with suggestions concerning liturgical practices based on the chanting of scriptures.[4]

What is unique about the music of chant? There can be no doubt that the practice of chanting was at first a utilitarian one. The singing voice could carry over a large congregation with much more clarity than someone simply reading the texts. It is assumed that over a period of time, certain portions of the worship were chosen as being appropriate for chanting, and common practices developed into traditions. In spite of its practicality, however, one cannot deny the existence of an emotional or an aesthetic dimension to chant. Musical sound often has the power to lift a person out of the everyday world of speech into another mode of thought. The flow of the Latin texts, coupled with the gentle melodies, presents an effective way to enhance the meaning of the words. In this way, chant serves both theology and emotion—the two elements we have consistently mentioned as being part of the music of worship throughout the world.

Introit for the First Sunday in Advent, from "Liber Usualis." Source: St. Bonaventure Publications.

istening Guide 55

Introit for the First Sunday in Advent
Gregorian chant

Recorded by the Choir of the Vienna Hofburgkapelle
Joseph Schabasser, conductor
CD No. 4, Track 2 (3:48)

*W*e will listen to a chant designed to be sung as the priest approaches the altar during the Mass. It is called an **Introit,** which literally means "entrance." Different parts of the Mass were named according to their functions in the service.

This Introit is for the first Sunday in Advent—a four-week season ending in the celebration of *Nativitas,* or Christmas. The text documents the faith of humankind, which looks toward the coming of Christ with trust and joy in spite of the perils of a troubled world.

Ad te levávi ánimam méam:	Unto Thee do I lift up my soul:
Déus méus in te confído, non erubéscam:	O God I trust in Thee, let me never be ashamed:
neque irrídeant me inimíci méi:	let not mine enemies triumph over me.
étenim univérsi qui te exspéctant, nonconfundéntur.	Yea, let none that wait on thee be ashamed.
Vías túas, Domine, demónstra míihi:	Show me thy way, O Lord:
et sémitas túas édoce me.	and teach me thy paths.
Glória Pátri et Fílio,	Glory be to the Father and to the Son,
et Spíritui Sáncto.	and to the Holy Ghost.
Secut érat in princípio	As it was in the beginning,
et nunc, et sémper,	is now and forever,
et in saécula saeculórum.	World without end.
Amen	Amen

To Consider

1. As you listen to this chant, notice that the choir repeats the first section of the text. What musical form does this repetition create?
2. Can you describe the shape of the melody of this Introit? Notice that there are frequent places in the melody where several notes are used on one syllable of the text. What emotional reaction does this practice bring forth?
3. The *Gloria Patri* is a standard part of all Introit chants. What religious function does it have? Why do you think it is part of all Introits?

*T*HE ROLE OF MUSIC IN WORSHIP: THE PROTESTANT TRADITION

Two qualities of music, usefulness as a tool for indoctrination and effectiveness as an aid to emotional expression, are at the core of music and religious thought in the Western tradition. When we study the interplay of these two dominant themes as found in various systems of religious worship, we can gain meaningful insight into the way people use music as part of their belief systems. The musical selections that follow will take us into several mainstream religious movements, some of which were founded in Europe or in the Middle East, but which are an integral part of our modern culture. You will see that the music of these various practices accurately reflects both the belief systems and emotional quality of each specific religion. Once again you will be reminded that music is particularly versatile in its ability to express a variety of emotions and to serve diverse functions.

Should church music be directed primarily toward emotional worship, or should its main focus be on expressing the teachings and doctrines of the church? Or, should church music be written and performed for its artistic (or in some cases, entertainment) value, or should it be directed toward church doctrines? These questions have concerned church authorities for ages.

In the sixteenth century, reformers throughout Europe became concerned about some of the practices in the Catholic Church, which until that time had been the only form of Christianity practiced in Europe. Among the reformers were Martin Luther in Germany and John Calvin in Switzerland, who founded religious movements that eventually led, either directly or indirectly, to the many denominations of Protestant churches which are in existence today. Although all Christian belief harkens back to biblical accounts of Christ's life and ministry, each denomination developed certain practices of worship and philosophical positions concerning Christianity that gave them a unique stance in the religious world.

Some theologians and musicians in the early Protestant churches were very strong proponents of high art compositions and thereby followed the lead of Roman Catholic Church practices. Catholic polyphonic settings of the Mass forms were written predominately for church choirs comprised of trained singers. One of these was Georg Motz, a school music director and head of church music in Tilse, Germany, in the late seventeenth century. He called congregational singing a "vile chorale clamor," and he was in favor of professionally trained choirs performing the musical functions in the church. Others were interested in totally reforming the age-old attitudes toward sacred music by suggesting that congregational singing become the norm. Their argument was that music should be simple so the words would be clearly understood. Christian Gerber, a theologian who published an article about church music in 1704, even went so far to say that God himself preferred music in which the words were easily heard. Gerber's position was that congregational singing is "more pleasing to the Highest than an artistic piece where the listener can understand nothing because of the noise of the instruments or else hear a word only now and then." He also wrote that singing hymns is the best way to praise God's deeds, because the whole congregation "is praising the greatness of God with one mouth."[5]

Such discussions may seem irrelevant to our modern world with its diverse attitudes and religious musical cultures, but they form an important part of the relationship of religion to music. Our modern culture offers such a variety of musical expressions in worship that almost anyone who is inclined toward religious experience can find both a faith and a musical practice appropriate to individual tastes and needs.

Many religious practices in today's world have deep historical roots. The following musical selections will take us back to several of the sources of Protestant church music—the Lutheran and Methodist traditions—to see how music helps express religious thought. Both religious denominations use the hymn as their central musical expression; one tradition comes out of Germany in the sixteenth century, while the other has its roots in England but actually flourished and grew in North America two centuries later. Even though these two religious denominations are from different centuries, their modern practice brings them together.

Martin Luther and the Chorale

When Martin Luther contemplated a new form of worship for his German congregations, he came upon an idea that religious hymns, called **chorales,** could be developed, which reflected the backgrounds and tastes of the German people. His hymns, and those of his contemporaries, were written in the style of songs that everyone knew. In fact, some of the tunes were borrowed directly from the nonreligious songs of the day. The chorale is the main musical expression of the Lutheran Church. Chorale texts were written not only as worship tools but as statements of the Christian doctrine. Originally these chorales were sung in unison without supporting harmonies. Soon, however, the practice of writing for four voice parts—soprano, alto, tenor, and bass—became standard. In recent times, Lutheran chorales have been commonly published for four voice parts in a homorhythmic texture (all parts have the same rhythm). This style became standard for the hymns of most Protestant churches throughout the centuries.

Furthermore, if one looks at the modern hymnals of several Protestant denominations, one will see that each church borrows freely from the other. For example, *Oh, For a Thousand Tongues to Sing*, the Methodist hymn that we will examine later in this chapter, is frequently sung in Lutheran churches (as well as in churches of other denominations) throughout America today.

However, if we compare the underlying attitudes of Martin Luther toward church music with John Wesley's (the founder of Methodism), and when we observe some of the different traditions of hymn usage in these two music traditions, we can conclude that there were fundamental differences between their philosophy of music and worship.

Martin Luther (1483–1546), the central figure of the Protestant Reformation and the founder of the Lutheran Church, had very strong opinions about music.

> I am not pleased with those who, like all the fanatics, despise music. Music is a gift of God, not of men. Music drives away the devil and makes people happy; in the presence of music one forgets all hate, unchastity, pride, and other vices. After theology I accord to music the highest place and the greatest honor.[6]

Luther's writings about music make it clear that he recognized the power of music as emotionally uplifting and useful for theological value. At age fifty-two, when he was already a famous reformer and professor of biblical theology at Wittenburg (Germany) University, he wrote:

> Experience testifies that, after the Word of God, only music deserves to be praised as the mistress and governess of the emotions of the human heart (regarding animals we say nothing here), by which emotions human beings are ruled and often torn asunder as if by their masters. A greater praise of music than this we cannot imagine. . . . It is out of consideration for this power of music that the Fathers and Prophets willed, and not in vain, that nothing be more closely bound up with the Word of God than music.[7]

Thirty-eight hymns by Luther are still in existence and used by Lutherans throughout the world. His knowledge of music was extensive; he was familiar with the principal composers of his day and spoke highly of the arts and their use in worship. Luther's attitude was quite different from Wesley's concerning highly cultivated musical arts, for he believed that the best of human efforts should be used in the glory of God. Even though Luther and Wesley lived in different periods of time, and people's attitudes are often influenced by their own particular cultural environment, there is a distinct difference in their attitudes toward music and worship.

It is interesting to trace the use of the Lutheran chorale both as a vehicle for worship and as a source for art music composition. In the Protestant churches, the Lutheran chorale has inspired more sacred compositions than any other form of Protestant music. Judging from Luther's comments on music, we can conclude that he would have approved.

The original form of the Lutheran chorale was a single melodic line. Many of the tunes came from the secular (popular) songs of the day. For example, the German popular song *Innsbruck, I must leave you*, a sad tune about a man having to leave the beautiful town at the foot of the Austrian Alps, and also having to leave his love there, became a hymn titled, *Oh World, I Must Now Leave Thee*, a song about approaching death. By the end of the sixteenth century, four-part hymn settings (soprano, alto, tenor, and bass) were common. Today, as in the late 1500s, hymns still appear in four-part texture.

Several general features of the Lutheran hymn made it accessible to worshipers during the Reformation years. First, the words were in German, the language of the people. The language of the Roman Catholic Church, in contrast, was Latin—the language of learning and diplomacy. Also, the words of the text were more personal than those found in the Roman church music of the day. Without compromising theological purity, Luther and his contemporaries wrote music that would appeal both emotionally and doctrinally to the faithful.

The four-part setting of the Lutheran chorale is appropriate for the type of service in which it is used. It is emotionally reserved and often performed within a limited range of dynamics. The melodic line is composed so the congregation can sing it without difficulty—notes are set in conjunct motion; musical phrases are regular; and repetition of melodic material is the norm. This music does not attempt to relate to an idiom of popular music.

Wake Awake, for Night Is Flying (*Wachet Auf, ruft uns die Stimme*) is a chorale from the Reformation era written by German Lutheran Minister Philipp Nicolai. It is based on the New Testament (Matthew 25: 1–13) parable of the ten virgins who were invited to a wedding feast. Five of the virgins prepared for the feast by bringing oil for their lamps. The other five were not prepared. When the bridegroom appeared at the door to let them into the feast, only those who had oil in their lamps were allowed into the wedding hall. The virgins in the parable represent humankind, and the bridegroom is Christ. The story of the ten virgins teaches that only those who have prepared themselves for Heaven will be accepted on the final day. In the Christian faith, oil frequently represents the Holy Spirit.

Lutheran chorale melodies have been used throughout the centuries as principal themes for several different forms of art music. During the Baroque period, hundreds of pipe organs were built in churches throughout Europe, and organ music flourished, especially in the Lutheran areas of northern Germany. Consequently, works for organ based on chorale tunes became popular. Modern organ compositions using chorales are still being written and are enjoyed in churches throughout the Christian world. It is common for organists to play chorale preludes—single-movement compositions for organ often based on hymns—before the church service each Sunday.

Lutheran hymn: Wake, Awake (Wachet Auf)

istening Guide 56

Wake, Awake, for Night Is Flying
Philipp Nicolai

Lutheran chorale
1599
Harmonization by J. S. Bach, around 1731
Recorded by the Vienna State Opera Orchestra and
      Chorus, Felix Prohaska, conductor
CD No. 4, Track 3 (1:50)

*S*ome of the best settings of Lutheran chorales were done by J. S. Bach who, you will remember, was a Lutheran Church organist and choir director in various cities in northern Germany. We will listen to one of the harmonizations that he set for his choir and a small group of instrumentalists. Then we will see how he used the same chorale as part of a choral movement in one of his cantatas. The chorale text is full of religious imagery and personal experience.

Gloria sei dir gesungen	Gloria be sung to you
mit Menchen-und englischen Zungen	with men's and angels' tongues
mit harfen und mit Cymbeln schon.	With harps and beautiful cymbals.
Von zwölf Perlen sind die Pforten	Of twelve pearls are the gates
an der Stadt; wir sind Konsorten	at your city; we are consorts
der Engel hoch um deinen Thron.	Or the angels high about your throne.
Kein Aug' hat je gespürt	No eye has ever sensed,
Kein Ohr hat je gehört	No ear has ever heard
solche Freude	Such a delight.
Des sind wir froh,	Of this we rejoice,
Io, io!	Io, io,
ewig in dulci jubilo.	forever in dulci jubilo.[8]

When you listen to this chorale setting, you may notice that the traditional Lutheran chorale is often somewhat different than other American Protestant hymns, because the musical phrases are frequently not as symmetrical as the American hymns and the harmony is not as predictable. This will become apparent to you after you study (and sing) the Methodist hymn *Oh, For a Thousand Tongues to Sing*.

To Consider

1. The setting of *Wake, Awake* that you are listening to is by Bach, and it forms the last movement of the cantata based on this melody, so you will hear an instrumental accompaniment to the hymn. As you listen, concentrate on the voices. Notice that the melody is always in the soprano part, the bass line always presents a strong contrast to the soprano, and the harmonies never become commonplace nor boring.
2. Can you deduce the form of the chorale? It comes from a German folk form developed originally by the **meistersingers** and **minnesingers**—the German counterparts of the troubadours and trouvères. You will hear the first musical phrase of the song repeated; then, new musical material follows. The form is A-A-B.
3. How does the contour of the melody support the opening words? Are there any other points of the text that may have influenced the composer writing the melody?

The cantata is another popular form of Baroque religious music that contains chorale melodies as melodic sources. The cantata is a multimovement form (varying from five to eight movements), usually written for a small chorus, soloists, an organ, and an instrumental ensemble. The most prominent cantata composer was Johann Sebastian Bach. Many of his cantatas are based on well-known Lutheran chorales and were sung by his church choir during the Lutheran worship service with him conducting from the organ bench. The church choir of Bach's time usually had about sixteen to twenty singers, not unlike modern church choirs. Usually an instrumental ensemble consisting of the same number of players as singers would also be part of the cantata performance.

Chapter 5 described the techniques of counterpoint used by Bach—techniques that both John Wesley and John Calvin found uncomfortable. The very fact that Lutheran chorales were so intertwined with art compositions—and that these pieces were intended to be used in the church service for the common churchgoer—underlines a basic philosophical difference between the founders of Lutheranism and other Protestant denominations with regard to the music of worship.

The following musical selection will provide a glimpse of Bach's skill in combining several layers of musical activity into a comprehensible piece of music designed for church use. The work is the sacred cantata based on the Lutheran hymn *Wake, Awake, for Night Is Flying*.

During his tenure as the head of musical activities of the St. Thomas Church in Leipzig, Bach was expected to provide cantatas for use in the Sunday church services. His works for this genre provide us with some of the best music written for small chorus and instrumental ensemble. Bach wrote for an orchestra of strings and some woodwinds, such as flutes, oboes, and bassoons, and, of course, organ. For festival days he often added trumpets and timpani.

Cantata 140 has a very interesting formal structure. Its seven movements are built around three verses of the Lutheran chorale. These verses form the first, the center, and the last movements and act as the pillars of the work. The inner movements consist of solo arias and recitatives; the text is a personal commentary on the parable of the ten virgins from the Bible, as previously discussed. We can compare them to windows of the structure through which we see the meaning of the established chorale text.

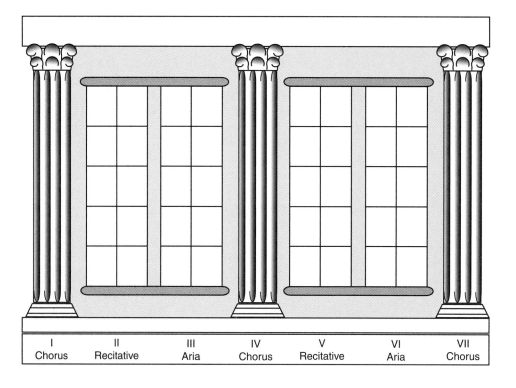

Cantata 140 diagram.

I	II	III	IV	V	VI	VII
Chorus	Recitative	Aria	Chorus	Recitative	Aria	Chorus

We will listen to the first movement to experience Bach's concept of counterpoint applied to a chorale-based composition. Bach built this movement in three layers: as you listen, keep these three basic layers in mind. It will help clarify the understanding of this work and serve as a reference point for this ingenious composition.

Listening Guide 57

Cantata 140, Wake, Awake
  (Wachet Auf,) Mvt. 1
J. S. Bach (1685–1750)

Church cantata using Lutheran
  chorale as cantus firmus
Recorded by the Vienna State Opera Orchestra and
  Chorus, Felix Prohaska, conductor
CD No. 4, Track 4 (7:10)

Wachet auf, ruft uns die Stimme	Wake, awake, for night is flying
der Wächter sehr hoch auf der Zinne,	The watchmen on the heights are crying
wach auf, du Stadt Jerusalem!	Awake, Jerusalem, arise!
Mitternach heisst diese Stunde;	Midnight hears the welcome voices;
sie rufen uns mit hellem Munde:	And at the thrilling cry rejoices:
wo seid ihr klugne Jungfrauen?	"Oh, where are ye, ye virgins wise?
Wohl auf, der Bräut'gam kömmt,	The bridegroom comes, Awake!
steht auf, die Lampen nehmt!	Your lamps with gladness take!
Alleluia!	Alleluia!
Mach euch bereit zu der Hochzeit	With bridal care, yourselves prepare
Ihr müsset ihm entgegen gehn.	To meet the Bridegroom, who is near."[9]

To Consider

1. The orchestra opens the movement by playing a melody supported by chords presented in dotted rhythms. Describe the aesthetic character of this music. Do you feel a sense of solid regularity created by the chord progressions and the rhythms?
2. The chorale melody is presented by the tenor section of the choir. How does its rhythm contrast with the instrumental ensemble's musical material?
3. What is the musical function of the soprano, alto, and bass sections of the chorus as they enter the musical texture?

The Calvinist Perspective of Religious Music

The most famous proponent of putting restraints on elaborate sacred music in history was the Protestant reformer John Calvin (1509–1564), who felt that austere devotion was not possible when instrumental music or polyphonic choral music was used in church. Calvin established the practice of monophonic (one line) singing of psalms among his followers. His attitude toward music was that "properly practiced it affords a recreation but it also leads to voluptuousness . . . and we should take good care that it does not furnish the occasion for dropping the reins to dissoluteness or for causing . . . disorderly delights."[10] In Zurich, Switzerland, Calvin's reforms were taken to such an extreme that the cathedral organist watched with tears streaming down his face as the cathedral organ was destroyed. In Bern, the organist/composer Hans Kotter was forced to become a schoolteacher because his organist position was dissolved.

Calvin's attitude about the role of music in worship was in direct opposition to Martin Luther's ideas about the use of music in the church and community. We have already seen how the Lutheran churches, stemming from Luther's ideas, used the chorale for worship purposes, both in congregational singing and as the basis for elaborate musical composition for organ, chorus, and various instrumental/vocal ensemble combinations. To Calvin, music should not detract from the message of the scriptures; to Luther, music—including elaborate contrapuntal compositions—had a definite role in enhancing religious thought and practice. The contrasting principles of these two sixteenth-century church leaders reinforce the concept that music is often at the center of discussion, for it is a most effective tool for expressing ideas of various kinds.

Charles and John Wesley and the American Hymn Movement

For our next musical selection with Protestant music, we will move forward to the eighteenth century to a time only a few decades later than the period during which Bach created so many musical masterpieces based on Lutheran music. Now we will examine another religious movement, Methodism, a Protestant denomination founded by two brothers in the United States during the colonial period.

The musical practices of hymnody in the Methodist movement provide a powerful example of how music can be used in religion. The timely emergence of the simple congregational song played a major role in developing a new style of worship that came out of England in the eighteenth century and soon spread to the colonies of America.

Methodism was a religious movement that began within the Church of England, and it soon became an independent Protestant denomination. It considered itself in the central stream of Christian spirituality and doctrine. The founders of this new style of worship, John Wesley (1703–1791) and his brother Charles Wesley (1707–1788), were Church of England missionaries to the Georgia colony, arriving in 1736. Although their efforts to establish centers of worship in America were not successful, prompting them to return to England, the Wesley brothers were instrumental in leading a revival movement in England. This movement eventually spread to the colonies and soon became an established religious body.

Charles is often referred to as the poet of Methodism; John is known as the philosopher and theologian. Together they collaborated on a musical tradition that was rich in doctrine and experiential content, or practical applications of Christianity. Charles wrote 8,989 religious poems, 6,000 of them appropriate for hymn settings. These formed the center of Methodist musical practices in the following centuries. The 1908 version of the Methodist hymnal, for example, contained 440 hymns by him.

John, the leader of Methodism, helped bring the hymns to their final form and worked strongly to establish the practice of hymn singing in the worship service. He also shaped the philosophy behind the hymns and was an outspoken voice for the proper practice of hymn singing. The preface of his 1761 collection of hymns, *Sacred Melody*, contains his instructions for congregational singing:

1. Learn these tunes before you learn any others; afterwards learn as many as you please.

2. Sing all. See that you join with the congregation as frequently as you can.

3. Sing lustily and with good courage. Beware of singing as if you were half dead, or half asleep; but lift up your voice with strength. Be no more afraid of your voice now, nor more ashamed of its being heard than when you sung the songs of Satan.

4. Sing in time.

5. Above all, sing spiritually. Have an eye to God in every word you sing. Aim at pleasing Him more than yourself, or any other creature.[11]

The tremendous flowering of poetry and song that came in the Methodist Church movement was met with strong opposition by the bishops of the Church of England. Prior to the Methodist revival, there was little congregational singing in Britain's churches. Anthems (such as the Purcell's *Lord, How Long Wilt Thou Be Angry*, which you heard in Chapter 2) were sung by choirs; Psalm singing—a simple, monophonic presentation of Old Testament poetry, also was popular. When the practice of hymn singing was instigated by Isaac Watts (another composer/author of hymns) and the Wesleys, it was met with strong opposition by existing church authorities.

The Church of England, with its formal traditions and liturgy, clearly did not meet the need of the Wesleys and their followers, for their newfound zeal in Christianity demanded a more direct style of sermon delivery, an intense emphasis on showing God's love in Christ amid the continuing crises of human existence. This was a religion for the common folk, and the Wesleys were able to build this movement on principles of scripture and reform. Their mission statement was quite practical in nature. It sought "to serve the purpose of living Christianity, the life of ministering love."[12]

The direct simplicity of this message was reflected in both the music and the words of the hymn. The Wesley hymns were founded on Scripture; the music was designed to be simple. It was written in four-part harmony, without chromaticism or counterpoint. The structure of the musical phrases was generated by the poetry.

The Wesley hymns were directed toward two basic concepts. First, hymns and hymn singing must be based on biblical sources; second, the music must be simple and direct. The music of the Methodist Church laid the foundation for a new style of American church music that was more closely related to popular styles than to art music. The Wesley writings emphasize the importance of the hymn texts. John Wesley described his hymnal of 1780 as "a little body of practical and experimental divinity."[13]

To understand this philosophy, let us examine one of Charles Wesley's hymn texts. (The music is provided as it appears in the most current Methodist Hymnal. Notice that the modern version contains some verses that are different from the early version (see page 272). This is typical throughout Protestant hymnody, regardless of denomination.) The hymn *Oh, For a Thousand Tongues to Sing* is by tradition the first hymn in the Methodist Hymnal.

As you read this hymn on the next page, glance at the references printed parallel to the lyrics, which indicate the scriptural source of the various lines of the hymn. It will show you how carefully the texts were shaped so that they would be true to the Scripture. These various references offer excellent sermon material for the minister; they also are designed to be used as instructional material for those interested in learning more about the Methodist approaches to Christianity and Christian living.

Hymn from Methodist Hymnal.
Source: Abingdon Press.

A Performance Experience:

To experience the following congregational song, try singing it with other members of your class. Have someone play the piano as part of your musical performance. On the first verse, everyone should sing the melody; for the other verses, sing the harmony if you are able. Your class probably represents a cross section of people, some of whom have singing expertise and some who do not. As you sing, listen to those around you, and you will feel what it is like to sing in a church service.

John and Charles Wesley shaped their hymn lyrics according to various biblical Scripture texts to ensure that their hymns reflected the true gospel of the church. The text of the hymn you just sang is printed below with the scriptural references from which the ideas of the song lyrics were derived. This will show the detailed care with which the Wesleys approached their hymn writing.[14]

1 O for a thousand tongues to sing
   My dear Redeemer's praise!
   The glories of my God and King,
   The triumphs of his grace!

Psalms 119: 172, "My tongue shall speak of thy word . . ."
Psalms 145:1, "I will extol thee, my God, O King."

2 My gracious Master, and my God,
   Assist me to proclaim,
   To spread through all the earth abroad
   The honors of thy name.

Matthew 9:31, "But they, when they were departed, spread abroad his fame in all that country."
Psalms 66:2, "Sing forth the honor of thy name: make his praise glorious."

3 Jesus, the name that charms our fears,
   That bids our sorrows cease—
   'Tis music in the sinner's ears,
   'Tis life, and health, and peace.

4 He breaks the power of canceled sin,
   He sets the prisoner free;
   His blood can make the foulest clean—
   His blood availed for me.

Isaiah 61:1, "He hath sent me . . . to proclaim liberty to the captives and the opening of the prison to them . . ."
Isaiah 1:18, "though your sins be as scarlet, they shall be white as snow."

5 Hear him, ye deaf; his praise, ye dumb,
   Your loosened tongues employ;
   Ye blind, behold your Savior come,
   And leap, ye lame, for joy!

Mark 7:31, ". . . he maketh both the deaf to hear and the dumb to speak."
Acts 3:8, "And he . . . entered with them into the temple, walking, and leaping, and praising God."

6 Look unto him, ye nations, own
   Your God, ye fallen race;
   Look, and be saved through faith alone,
   Be justified by grace!

Isaiah 45:22, "Look unto me, and be ye saved, all the ends of the earth; for I am God, and there is none else."
Ephesians 2:8, "For by grace are ye saved through faith"

7 See all your sins on Jesus laid:
   the Lamb of God was slain,
   His soul was once an offering made
   For every soul of man.

John 1:29, "Behold the Lamb of God who takest away the sins of the world."

Oh For a Thousand Tongues to Sing is an example of the musical simplicity of the Methodist hymn tradition. When you hear this played on the piano, notice how smoothly each voice part moves from one note to another. All voice parts are in very comfortable ranges. If you listen carefully to the bass line, you will probably be able to pick out the three primary chords of G Major; G, C, and D, as they are used to anchor the tonality of this song. Notice also that the phrases of the text fall into four-measure groupings in the music. All of these musical elements are in keeping with the goals that John and Charles Wesley established for the worship in their new evangelical church movement. Their intention was that no worshiper should ever be overwhelmed or confused by music that was too complex to understand. On the other hand, they did not want music to be trite and meaningless. Although it was to be simple and straightforward, it was also meant to show good musical taste and to have intrinsic beauty.

One of the Wesleys' contemporaries commented on the beauty of the Methodist hymns: "The song of the Methodist is the most beautiful I ever heard. Their fine Psalms have exceedingly beautiful melodies composed by great masters. They sing in a proper way; with devotion, serene mind, and charm."[15]

The success of the Wesleys and their contemporaries is evident in the longevity of these hymns, for they are still used throughout the world, wherever Methodism is practiced.

JEWISH TRADITIONS AND MUSICAL PRACTICE

Judaism is an ancient faith that originally came from the very cradle of history—ancient Mesopotamia. In the millennia since then, Jews have wandered the globe and adapted the musical traditions of the people who they lived among, setting their own ancient texts to melodies in many different styles.

Abraham Zvi Idelsohn, a scholar who spent his life studying Jewish music, wrote about the diversity of Judaism's practices. Idelsohn visited Jerusalem in 1906 in search of a central musical practice. He visited over 300 synagogues in Jerusalem and found more diversity than uniformity. He wrote: "The various synagogues were conducted according to the customs of the respective countries, and their traditional song varied greatly from one another."[16]

Like so many musical traditions and practices, sacred and secular music connected to Judaism and Jewish cultures is a blend of many influences. The music of the Jewish community reflects the broadly diverse history of this ancient culture. The singing of wordless melodies— a practice often used in offering prayers before meals, at weddings, or at celebrations during holy days—is drawn from the Hasidic tradition. For Hasidic Jews, music has a special quality of being able to draw oneself closer to divine knowledge. The Sephardic Jews, whose origins are in Syria, sing melodies that came out of Arabic melodies set to Hebrew texts.[17]

In the Ashkenazic tradition, cantors sing emotional, highly ornamented melodies, using rich tenor voices. Many American Jews are Ashkenazi, and they claim origins from areas other than the regions of the Middle East and the Mediterranean rim.

Perhaps the ability to absorb various musical cultures is a unique characteristic of Jewish worship, for in spite of the diversity of expressions, there remain some very strong traditions within Judaism. Jewish music has many sources and functions: it may exist in the form of a liturgical chant used in synagogues, or it may come from the folk music repertoire originating in Israel. Another source of Jewish music is modern composition written by composers who are inspired by Jewish faith and traditions.

Thus it is hard to define the "religious" music of Judaism as having a single function, for this music is performed for many different occasions. Jewish music around the world is linked by the melodies, rhythms, and themes that inspire it. Many of these traditions focus on ancient texts, which form the core of Judaism's music. One of these cornerstone texts is the *Shmà Israèl*, an ancient creed of the Jewish faith. It is a statement of commitment to a single God (in ancient times, most people worshiped gods who ruled over various aspects of Heaven and Earth), and it also is the strong admonition to transmit the knowledge and traditions of belief to future generations. The *Shmà Israèl* is a prayer that most devout practicing Jews commit to memory at a very early age.

Shmà Israèl Adonoy eleheynu Adonoy e<u>h</u>od	Hear, O Israel: The Lord is our God, The Lord is one.
Veohavto et Adonoy eloheyc<u>h</u>o bec<u>h</u>ol levovc<u>h</u>o u'vchol nafshecho u'vechol me'odecho	And thou shalt love the Lord thy God with all thine heart, and with all thy soul, and with all thy might.
Vehoyu hadevorim hoele asher onoc<u>h</u>i metsavecho hayom 'al levovecho	And these words which I command thee this day, shall be in thine heart:
Veshinontom levoneyc<u>h</u>o vedibarto bom besivtecho beveytec<u>h</u>o uvelechtec<u>h</u>o baderec<u>h</u> uvshochbec<u>h</u>o uvekumecho.	And thou shalt teach them diligently unto thy children, and shalt think of them when thou sittest in thine house, and when thou walkest by the way, and when thou liest down, and when thou risest up.

The strong traditions of the Jewish faith, a religion rooted firmly in the history of the Jewish people, are transmitted through its music. These traditions are taught to each child in the faith, and the music helps recall times past. Its style is unique and unites Jewish people around the world. Its scope not only includes music intended for the synagogue but for the home as well.

> Just as to the Jew religion meant life and life religion, so to him sacred song has been folk-song and folk-song, sacred song. In the folk-songs current among Jewish people there are included tunes for Bible texts or tunes based upon Biblical themes, for prayers, for religious poetry, melodies for meditation, for the elevation of the soul to its Creator, for rousing the spirit to ecstasy, . . . and, finally melodies which express the innumerable struggles and pains the Jew has suffered . . . Jewish folk-song, like Jewish life in the past two thousand years, nestles in the shadow of religion and ethics.[18]

The following musical selection is a setting of the *Shmà Israèl,* which uses only the first two lines of this ancient scripture as its text. It is sung by a children's choir and a soprano soloist, accompanied by an ensemble of accordion, piano, tambourine, violin, and bass. Upon your first listening, you will be impressed with the sentimental simplicity of the repeated eight-measure phrases. The melody follows a minor scale, the meter falls into three beats per measure, and the harmonies are comprised of primary chords. Repeated listenings, however, show an artful arrangement of structure with ingenious instrumental accompaniments and countermelodies.

listening Guide 58

Shmà Israèl
Arrangement of an ancient Jewish prayer

Recorded by Mina Blum, soprano, with the "G. Verdi" Childrens' Choir, Silvia Rossi, director, and the I Solisti di Parma ensemble
CD No. 4, Track 5 (3:01)

*A*lthough musical arrangements such as this are not intended for use in the synagogue, this music is nevertheless sacred to all those who ascribe to the Jewish faith. (Music in traditional synagogues is typically a monophonic chant.) The texts are enhanced by the simple melody, the rhythm, and the manner in which the instruments play the melodies and accompany the singers.

To Consider

1. The first time you hear this song, allow yourself to grasp its general mood in relationship to the words that are repeated several times: "Adonoy eleheynu Adonoy e<u>h</u>od, Shmà Israèl" ("The Lord is our God, The Lord is one. Listen, Israel"). How would you describe the character of this song?
2. After you feel that you know this song, listen for the musical devices the arranger uses to give continuity to this work. For example, how does the song begin? What is the texture for the first eight measures? Is there a rhythmic background to it, or is it simple and free?
3. What happens in the first repetition of the melody? Can you hear another tune (a counter-melody) being played? Which instrument seems to carry the main melody; which one plays the countermelody?
4. Did you notice that there are two basic phrases to this melody? With which notes of the scale does each phrase begin? (These melodic ideas are so similar that it is easy to hear them pass without realizing their differences.)
5. As you listen, can you chart out a formal structure for this song?

0:00	The accordion begins playing the simple melody, accompanied only by an occasional note of harmony, and a spoken statement from the soloist, "Shmà Israèl." It is in the character of an introduction.	[A]
0:22	The melody is taken over by the piano, accompanied by short chords on the accordion and sustained bass notes on the piano. Notice that this is where the rhythmic pulse of the song begins.	[A]
0:48	As the piano repeats the melody, the accordion now presents a countermelody. The tambourine adds a subtle pulse.	[A]
1:12	The second phrase of the tune is sung by the children's choir. Notice that it begins on a higher note than the first phrase (on the third scale step instead of the first).	[B]
	The eight measures of the B phrase are repeated.	[B]
1:53	The soprano soloist enters, singing with a wide vibrato, a performance style frequently found in Jewish solo singing.	[B]
2:15	The A phrase returns, played by the violin, accompanied by the subtle bass lines of the piano and short after-beat chords.	[A]
2:37	Finally the accordion returns to finish the song, playing to the accompaniment of a violin countermelody.	[A]

NEW TRADITIONS IN RELIGIOUS EXPRESSION

So far we have encountered religious music built on strong traditions and associated with a specific religious denomination or religious culture. Now we will examine a recent development in music that neither reflects one approach to faith nor one approach to musical practices. Instead, it is linked to the world of pop music, primarily to various styles of rock. **Contemporary Christian music** is a musical expression that uses lyrics and titles drawn from religious topics and expresses them in the modern music of rock and pop styles. Its appeal is to the young; its audience is found primarily within the United States.

For example, the compact disc cover of *Supertones Strike Back*, a contemporary Christian recording, features a picture of the seven band members in suits and sunglasses, striking the pose associated with the famous *Blues Brothers* film. The music has a very strong bass and percussive backbeat that accompanies lyrics presented in ska style. Funky horn lines backed by heavy metal guitars provide interludes between the words. Some of the tracks on the CD contain songs with melodies; the volume level is loud; energy is provided not only by the strident vocal technique but by the prominent beat.

CD cover: *Supertones Strike Back*. Courtesy BEC Recordings and Dayton Artist Agency, Inc.

Songs such as *Never Gonna Be As Big As Jesus, I'm Not the King,* and *Walk on Water,* recorded by Audio Adrenaline, are supported by a strong backbeat, electric guitars playing at nearly feedback levels, and heavy bass lines. The vocal style comes from the rock movement, with roots in the Rolling Stones' music. Proponents of this style are quick to point out the absence of a drug culture among contemporary Christian groups. The wholesome attitude that this music conveys and lyrics that express Christian concepts in modern youthful imagery are two factors that make this music attractive to a culture born into the world of rock.

The ballad *Take Me Back,* recorded by four female musicians who form the group Point of Grace, presents a more mellow approach to this musical expression. Point of Grace uses close harmony at times and is backed by electronic keyboards and synthesizers, a heavy backbeat, and a strong, strident bass line. This versatile group also uses acoustical guitars in some of its recordings. When acoustical instruments are employed, they are frequently used as lead-ins to a heavier electronic sound.

Listening Guide 59

Take Me Back
Pete Strayer and Robert Sterling

Contemporary Christian music
1995
Recorded by Point of Grace (Heather Floyd,
    Shelley Phillips, Terry Lang, Denise Jones)
CD No. 4, Track 6 (3:52)

The lyrics of contemporary Christian music are invariably directed toward the emotional experiences of the youthful culture to which they are addressed. *Take Me Back,* recorded by Point of Grace, carries with it a message that would make John Wesley proud, with biblical reference to the parable of the Prodigal Son; its language and musical style, however, communicate with the youthful audience of today.

> Been too long chasing selfish dreams
> Seeking only what my heart desires
> I've drifted so far away it seems
> From the truth that set my soul on fire
> How many times will it take for me to see
> That You're the only love my heart will ever need!

Chorus:
Take me back, take me back, Jesus
Take me back
To where I can know Your love.

Like the Prodigal far from home
Lost inside a world of my own choosing
Tried to make it on my own
Never realized all I'd be losing
I still remember just how it used to be
Lord, forgive my weakness
Come and rescue me.

(Repeat Chorus)

There's no one else I would turn to
You're the only one who can pull me through
You can pull me through.[19]

Point of Grace met at Quachita Baptist University in Arkadelphia, Arkansas, and formed a singing group. Their careers as recording artists began after they won the Overall Grand Prize, Groups competition at the Christian Artists Seminar in Estes Park, Colorado, in 1992. Since then they have released fifteen consecutive No. 1 singles on Billboard's Contemporary Christian chart. In 1998, Point of Grace began a tour of churches throughout the United States.

Our musical selection with contemporary Christian music illustrates the prominent use of electronic instruments typical of this genre. Keyboards, synthesized bass, and percussion combine with drums, piano, and guitars to create this modern sound.

To Consider

1. As you listen to this song, notice that the words are presented with clarity. What is the relationship of the accompaniment to the words?
2. Which pitch references in the synthesized keyboards relate to the vocal notes?
3. Does the underlying rhythm of the instruments fit well with the "Take me back" interjections of the chorus?
4. Can you describe the layers of this work? How many levels of musical activity can you identify?

For people who want to be active participants in performing contemporary Christian music in any corner of the world, hundreds of background recordings have been made and are marketed with sheet music. This innovative approach to music marketing has found great success, and the results can be heard in many churches throughout America where an alternative worship style is promoted.

When you consider the styles, background, motivation, and use of contemporary Christian music in our current culture, you will no doubt begin to understand that the onset of the new millennium is characterized by a convergence of many musical traditions. Sometimes the mixture of rock music styles is baffling to those associated with long-standing hymn traditions in Christian music. To others, contemporary Christian music offers a link between the secular and sacred world, between the traditional ideologies and innovative musical practices.

Contemporary Christian music reflects a pop culture that has penetrated the last bastion of traditional musical practices—religious music. Its message is emotional, it offers excitement to a whole generation of music consumers, and it guides them toward a religious experience that is practical and realistic.

*M*usical Encounter

Percussion Possessed: The Drums of Haitian Vodun

By Elsa Youngsteadt[20]

The ceremony takes place in a **Vodun** temple, somewhere in Haiti. Celebrants gather around the perimeter of the room; the drummers take their positions; priests and initiates begin scattering sacred liquid mixtures in various places throughout the temple; lengthy prayers follow. The drums are silent as the priest prays first to the Christian God, then to the Catholic saints, and finally to the pantheon of African gods, the *Iwa*. Under the influence of the Catholic Church, Vodun adopted the Christian God as the highest deity, the distant creator and most powerful god. To the followers of Vodun, this God rules the universe and is responsible for judging and if necessary, punishing the soul at the end of its life on earth.[21]

But Vodun also retained its more approachable pantheon of African gods. These beings are the essence of the Ancestors, whose wisdom and assistance may be sought regarding matters too trivial for the highest God. Although there are many gods representing many African geographical places of origin, two main types have emerged in Vodun religion: the *Rada* spirits are characterized by a beneficent nature that represents the emotional stability of the homeland; the *Petro* family of gods is predominantly a New World creation, an angry, fiery group of spirits that is an expression of the soul in slavery.[22]

When the prayers end, the drums play the first dance rhythm, and the singing and dancing to invoke the first of the series of *Iwa* gods begin. The dancers move around a pole, erected in the center of the temple, which represents the connection between the human and spirit worlds and is the point around which all dances revolve.

There are separate songs for each *Iwa*, which prepare the congregation for the spirit's presence—songs of invocation, of possession, and of farewell. Different rhythms are specific to each nation of *Iwa*, and the drumming is an essential element in inducing possession and maintaining ceremonial continuity.

Usually three experienced drummers, including a master percussionist, are joined by a gong player and a priest who plays a sacred rattle. One anthropologist described their function: "It is the drumming which fuses the fifty or more individuals into a single body, making them move as one, as if all of these singular bodies had become linked on the thread of a single pulse."[23]

Through the intensity of the master drummer's playing and the timing of his breaks from playing—the moments in the ceremony where the possession takes place—he controls to a great extent the occurrence of possession. Although the drummers are professionally trained and are not usually initiated into the religious society, they often become emotionally involved, to the point of being possessed. Through it all, however, they must maintain their skillful, intricate drumming patterns. If they lose concentration, they risk destroying the entire possession ceremony. One such episode was described by anthropologist Harold Courlander:

> (The drummer) sometimes drums himself into a genuine neurological hysteria; in such a state, he is likely to be something akin to a musical genius. Mouth open, eyes turned up and nearly closed, his drumming at such times may bring on unwanted possessions among the dancers. I have seen a drummer collapse, his body jerking, his head bobbing loose, bring on wholesale possessions and break up a dance.[24]

To the followers of Vodun, the drum is not strictly a physical object but a sacred spiritual being as well. Ritual activity for the drums begins even before the tree is felled: when the drum maker and his assistant go to select the tree, they carry a candle, draw a sacred image at the base of the tree, and offer food, liquor, and prayers. Only then may they fell the tree. Like all sacred objects, the drums are baptized after their construction, but they are the only objects to be dressed with special vestments for the ceremony.

It is believed that the initial ceremony and baptism are not enough to preserve the sacred powers of the drums, hence, they are resanctified from time to time in a ritual through which they are symbolically sent to Ifa, West Africa, the Haitian's image of the homeland. A lighted candle is placed on each drum, and food and drink offerings are scattered about them. Animals are sacrificed, and then the instruments are draped with a white sheet representing the purifying environment of Ifa. The servants enter a state of mourning for the temporary departure of the drums.

It is the music of the drums that brings about possession, which often occurs when the percussionist enters a *kase*, or a break in the drumming. If a servant or a drummer feels he is on the verge of a possession that is for some reason inappropriate, the phenomenon can be fended off by saluting the drums, or in the case of the drummer, by tapping his drum on the ground. This process emphasizes the nature of the drum as a spiritual entity not entirely under the drummer's control. Sacred drums are never used during secular musical activities.

Vodun, although it has been officially opposed by the Haitian government and the Roman Catholic Church, still remains the most prominent undercover folk religion of Haiti. In the 1950s through the 1970s, when "Papa Doc" and "Baby Doc" Duvalier ruled Haiti, many people immigrated to the United States, particularly to New York, where their religion continues to be practiced.

THE GOSPEL CHOIR

Another practice in religious music is the gospel choir, an adaptation of the spiritual tradition in America. Predominantly identified with African-American worship practices, this music, like so many musical expressions at the turn of the new century, has found broad audiences and participants.

Gospel choirs exist in churches and in institutions of higher education throughout the country. Their emphasis is on an emotional and a "personal" worship practice, not on traditional church denominations. Like contemporary Christian music, gospel choir music speaks for people who find fulfillment in singing, playing, and listening to music that is full of energy and related to pop expressions.

The traditions of the African-American spiritual have been addressed earlier in this book. Our musical selection with gospel choir music is based on a traditional spiritual. Its text, "Wade in the Water," is a traditional song referring to the story of Moses leading the children of Israel out of Egypt and away from the Pharaoh's captivity. The Old Testament account of this event, taken from the Book of Exodus (Chapter 14), relates that God separated the waters of the Red Sea to create a passage for the Israelites and then caused the sea to return to its normal state when the chariots of Pharaoh gave chase. Thus God "troubled the waters" to allow Moses' followers to escape. The significance of this story to the descendants of slavery in the United States is clear—it represents the strength of Jehovah in liberating humans from captivity.

The gospel choir Sweet Honey in the Rock recorded a modern version of this traditional spiritual at a Carnegie Hall recital on November 7, 1978. The arrangement of *Wade in the Water* uses performance practices long associated with "Negro" spirituals—call and response, vocal solos embellished with emotional exclamations, and forte statements of the entire chorus singing refrains.

Listening Guide 60

Wade in the Water	1987
Gospel choir arrangement of	Recorded by Sweet Honey in the Rock
a traditional spiritual	CD No. 4, Track 7 (7:18)

*T*his arrangement is for chorus without accompaniment. As you listen to this spiritual, you will notice that the basic premise of the arrangement involves soloists, who sing the verses, and the chorus, which provides a musical backdrop for them. Different soloists take their turns, adding personal embellishments of words, notes, and melodic inflections. The chorus functions not only in the role of providing the textual refrain "wade in the water," but it also sets up an underlying rhythm and sense of motion that propels the piece along.

This recording is a live performance at Carnegie Hall in New York City. It is introduced by the leader of the group, Bernice Johnson Reagon.

Chorus:

Wade in the water, Wade in the water, children
Wade in the water, God's gonna trouble the water.

Verses:

See those people dressed in white,
They look like the children of the Israelites.
See those children dressed in black,
They come a long way and they ain' turning back.

See those children dressed in blue,
Look like my people comin' thru.
See them children dressed in red,
Must be the children that Moses led.

Some say Peter and some say Paul,
There ain' but the one God made us all.[25]

To Consider

1. Describe the layers of musical activity in this song as the piece unfolds. What gives this arrangement its artistic shape?
2. Notice the steady, rhythmic organization. Can you describe how this is brought about?
3. What special inflections does each soloist give to create individuality of expression? How do these solo interpretations add to the spontaneity and general character of the work?

SUMMARY

Throughout history, music has been a component of religious thought and practice. It combines elements of theology (for it is heavily dependent upon its texts to express beliefs) and emotion (for music is emotional by its very nature).

Various church doctrines express their music in different ways. Traditional Protestant Christianity uses the hymn as the cornerstone of music. Other religious groups use chants, while still others utilize simple folk-like melodies in their worship practices. Frequently one can find elements of various cultural roots in the varied musical practices of a given religion. Such is the case in the music of Judaism, whose practices vary widely from place to place, but whose music reflects the strong heritage of the Jewish experience.

A recent development in religious music is the contemporary Christian movement, which is not aligned with any religious denomination but still is designed to convey the fundamental concepts of Christian faith. It comes from the pop traditions in our modern culture, and it has gained enormous popularity among the contemporary youth culture.

The gospel choir movement is another musical expression that combines elements of various musical backgrounds. Much of its music is founded on traditional spiritual musical practices, such as the alternation of soloists and chorus, the embellishment of music by improvised words, and added melodic inflections. It is a living, ever-changing, and spontaneous musical expression that, even though it stems from the African-American traditions, is enjoyed by many, regardless of ethnic origin.

The music of religion in the contemporary world reinforces the phenomenon of diversity and change that characterizes the modern world. It reflects the underlying principle that, whereas virtually all cultures use music to express themselves, the music itself is widely different from one expression to another. Music, the most elastic of art expression, is a most effective tool in human communication.

KEY TERMS

chanting
chorales
contemporary Christian music
Introit
mandala
Mass
meistersingers
minnesingers
Methodism
Shmà Israèl (Shema Israel)
sutra
Vodun

CHAPTER 13

Music and Romance

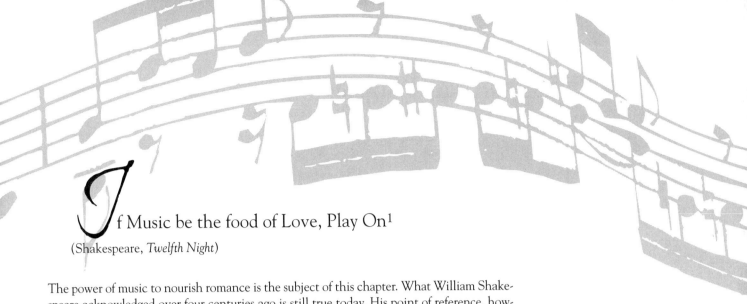

$\mathcal{O}$f Music be the food of Love, Play On[1]

(Shakespeare, *Twelfth Night*)

The power of music to nourish romance is the subject of this chapter. What William Shakespeare acknowledged over four centuries ago is still true today. His point of reference, however, was limited to the musical practices of his own English culture, therefore, he spoke for his particular society. Today music is still the food of love, but the musical menu is much more diverse than it was during Shakespeare's time. As a modern student of music, you will find that musical expressions of love may vary according to their unique cultural backgrounds. Our musical selections will take us through several styles of music, each with its own set of practices. We will experience some of the different cultural accents of our universal language, and we will look for common features in this music. By focusing on the music of romance, we can find a common subject for our inquiry, for songs of love are ubiquitous.

Because the music of love gives us such a deep insight into the minds of poets and musicians—people who speak for a society through their art—this topic is most appropriate for inclusion in our study of the sociology of music. Emotions, attitudes, and cultural practices are often communicated on a person-to-person level in the music of love.

And yet, expressions of love and romance are as universal as music itself. The way in which people express their feelings of love may differ greatly from one level of society or from one subculture to another, but there also are some similarities between these expressions. Music also has nuances that are unique to a given cultural environment, and features that appeal to a larger audience. The music of love must be both universal and personal—universal enough to address a segment of a culture and personal enough to allow one individual to relate to its message.

Both in vernacular (or popular) and in cultivated expressions (or art music), the formal characteristics of love music are frequently elementary enough to be understood by a broad audience. Thus each listener can project into the song past experiences, present longings, and future dreams according to the musical stimulus laid out by the music itself. The challenge for the composer/producer of love music then is to find musical formulae that are sufficiently common to reach a general audience and sophisticated enough to encourage individual ownership and identity. When a couple in love can truly say, "They are playing our song," the composer of that love song has indeed been successful.

$\mathcal{L}$OVE AND THE ART SONG

We will begin our study by considering love as it is expressed through an art song. Great works of art are often universal in scope and message; they have the capability of transcending both time and place. Many composers of art music write in such a manner that their music can be loved and understood by audiences everywhere. It is their wish that something of their efforts will become timeless, and that their music will become part of the standard repertoire of concert music. It is appropriate then that our first musical selection is of this venue.

The music of Ralph Vaughan Williams (1872–1958) has wide audience appeal. It is composed with a creative impulse and skill sufficient to keep it from becoming commonplace in the wide arena of art music. This gentleman's music was not considered on the leading edge of experimentalism in the first half of the twentieth century, but it has continued to gain in popularity in recent decades. It is easy to hear, performable, and emotionally charged and intellectually conceived. Vaughan Williams also had a finely developed sense of poetry and selected poems that were a good match for his sense of musical aesthetics and charm.

You will discover this special character when you hear his love song *Silent Noon*. This art song is from a **song cycle**, *The House of Life*, based on poems by Dante Gabriel Rossetti (1828–1882). A song cycle is a group of songs by a single composer, usually based on a common theme. The other songs included in *The House of Life* are *Love-Sight*, *Love's Minstrels*, *Heart's Haven*, *Death in Love*, and *Love's Last Gift*.

Rossetti was an Italian-born poet whose father immigrated to England and became a professor of Italian at King's College, London. Rossetti grew up in a bilingual environment, and his poem *Silent Moon* was originally written in English.

As you listen to Vaughan Williams's setting of this love poem, keep in mind that its composer wrote the song using well-established compositional techniques common to the heritage of Western art music. The concepts of repetition and contrast should be apparent to you as you hear this effective setting of Rossetti's love poem. Following a tradition established in the Classical Era, this song is for a solo singer with piano accompaniment.

Listening Guide 61

Silent Noon
Ralph Vaughan Williams (1872-1958)

Poem by Dante Gabriel Rossetti
Art song
1903
Recorded by Robert Tear, tenor,
    Philip Ledger, piano
CD No. 4, Track 8 (4:24)

Your hands lie open in the long fresh grass,
The finger points look through like rosy blooms:
Your eyes smile peace.
The pasture gleams and glooms
'Neath billowing skies that scatter and amass.

All round our nest, far as the eye can pass,
Are golden kingcup fields with silver edge,
Where the cowparsley skirts the hawthorn hedge.
'Tis visible silence,
Still as the hourglass.

Deep in the sun-searched growths the dragonfly
Hangs like blue thread loosened from the sky:
So this winged hour is dropt to us from above.
Oh, clasp we to our hearts, for deathless dower,
This close-companioned inarticulate hour,
When twofold silence was the song,
The song of love.[2]

To Consider

1. Before you listen to this song, read the words aloud to feel the rhythm and the freedom of the poetry.
2. As you listen to this love song for the first time, read the poem silently as you hear it, and see if you can detect in the music points that specifically reinforce places in the text.
3. What devices does Vaughan Williams use to provide a feeling of continuity? Are there any patterns of repetition in the music?
4. Can you hear the key changes that occur in this song? Do they provide points of interest? How do they relate to the poem?

0:00   The piano begins by stating an opening melodic idea. When the singer begins, you will notice that it is the main melodic idea of the song. (Try to remember this melodic idea—it will return later.) As you listen to the beginning section, notice how the piano supports the singer by doubling some—but not many—notes of the tune.

1:07   A new section begins with a change of key and a different pattern of accompaniment. The left hand of the piano part plays simple arpeggios over the steady quarter-note chords of the right hand. The text, "All round our nest . . ." is set to new musical material in the voice part.

1:46   Notice the dramatic rhythm and the stable, conjunct melodic line that draws attention to the words, "'Tis visible silence, still as the hourglass." The first six words of this phrase are sung on a single pitch.

1:59   The piano interlude introduces a short section, marked "Quasi Recitative" ("Like a recitative"). The motion is temporarily suspended in order to draw your attention to a new mental picture: "Deep in the sun-searched growths the dragonfly hangs like a blue thread loosened from the sky."

3:12   The musical idea first given to you at the beginning of the song returns briefly, both in the piano and in the vocal line. This signals that the final quatrain of the poem is beginning. The voice picks up the opening melodic idea with "Oh, clasp we to our hearts . . ."

The song ends with a reminiscence of the opening rhythm; this time it is played with the left hand on the piano.

You probably noticed that the poem is asymmetrical in form. In keeping with the poetic structure, Vaughan Williams developed new musical ideas for each section of the lyrics. At the end, however, he gave the listener the chance to remember what the song sounded like at the beginning—a musical reference point that also suggests that the song was coming to an end. The composer's deliberate consideration of the meaning of the words is reflected in the rhythms, harmonies, accompanimental figures, and shape of the melody. This love song is lyrical, tender, and thoughtful. The style of the music captures the mood of the poetry in a most artful manner.

TIN PAN ALLEY: AMERICAN SONGSTERS COME OF AGE

The mainstream European/American musical culture was well acquainted with the art song tradition in which a poem is set to music for a solo voice and piano accompaniment. It was only logical that this practice would soon give rise to a related type of music that would encourage popular music trends. Popular song, based on art song traditions of the past, was thus born in America and literally exploded into the musical environment of the early twentieth century.

What factors came together to create the biggest popular music industry in the history of America thus far? The popularity of the piano as a household instrument and the availability of private instruction for amateur musicians provided an ideal setting for the sale of sheet music. You will remember that similar conditions gave rise to lieder, the German art song some 100 years earlier (see Chapter 7).

During the last decade of the nineteenth century, conditions in the United States were perfect for the flowering of popular love songs. Songwriters and publishers, capitalizing on several trends of popular music that were emerging almost simultaneously, developed a market for music that could be sung and played by amateur music makers. An early song hit was *After the Ball,* written by Charles K. Harris in 1892, which sold over 1 million copies.

An additional influence was the rise of several related vernacular genres: the blues and ragtime. This music also involved piano as well as other instruments—sometimes the guitar, and sometimes various wind instruments, string instruments, and percussion. Ragtime, with its syncopated rhythms, and the blues, with its bending of notes within a framework of standard chord progressions, became trendy expressions for people looking for new musical experiences. Although we are accustomed to identifying ragtime with either the piano or a small jazz band, early ragtime also was a very popular vocal genre. Composers, arrangers, and performers furnished an ever-expanding repertoire of music to the eager consumer.

In the 1920s, publishers in New York gravitated to a central district in lower Manhattan where they established a center for the popular song industry. **Tin Pan Alley,** as this area was known, soon became a musical metaphor not only for the district where the music was published but for the music itself. Tin Pan Alley songs acquired a stereotypical style, and often the term denoted love songs that were sung with piano accompaniment. Sometimes the sheet music was a reduction of music originally sung with the accompaniment of an orchestra on the stages of Broadway.

The rise of the Broadway musical in the early twentieth century also contributed to a series of song hits that were singled out for performance and separate publication. A type of song known as the **ballad** soon emerged. The ballad was a slow, often sentimental love song; it usually had an introduction, called a "verse," which was then followed by a "refrain." Eventually many ballads were written in the song form A-A-B-A (which we have already witnessed in previous musical selections), while still others were composed in a freer, less formulated structure of repetition and contrast. The most successful composers of this love music were Irving Berlin, Cole Porter, Hoagy Carmichael, Jerome Kern, and George Gershwin. Working in various genres ranging from full-production works for the musical theater to individual ballads with piano accompaniment, these composers produced literally thousands of love songs. The love song occupied the center stage of popular music. Singers became famous singing them (witness the careers of the late Frank Sinatra or Tony Bennett, for example), and jazz performers borrowed tunes for their performing medium.

This musical phenomenon of creating jazz from popular songs has lasted for decades. The foundation of the jazz ballad is the love song. Originally jazz ballads were virtually always drawn from vocal tunes; in recent years, the term ballad has been used by jazz performers to signify any tune that is slow and expressive in nature.

To illustrate the love song and its jazz adaptation, we will now examine the tune *A Sleeping Bee,* first sung by Tony Bennett in an early recording and then played by accomplished jazz pianist Bill Evans.

Sheet music: *Last Night on the Back Porch* by Lew Brown and Carl Schraubstader. Courtesy of the Library of Congress.

Listening Guide 62

"A Sleeping Bee," from *House of Flowers*	Love song from a Broadway musical
Harold Arlend, lyrics by Truman Capote	1959
	Recorded by Tony Bennett
	CD No. 4, Track 9 (3:25)

This song has an introductory verse that establishes the premise of the love song. It refers to an imaginative test that one can take to determine whether or not one's love for another is true. It suggests that a person should find a sleeping bee and hold it in the palm of the hand. If the bee does not waken but continues to sleep peacefully, one has indeed found true love. The "verse" presents the premise of the song:

> When you're in love and you are wonderin' if he really is the one,
> There's an ancient sign sure to tell you if your search is over and done.
> Just catch a bee and if he don't sting you you're in a spell that's just begun,
> It's a guarantee 'till the end of time your true love you have won.

The second part of the song (sometimes called the "refrain," or, "chorus" because it is this section that is often repeated if the singer wants to extend the performance) functions to personalize the love test and to bring it into the experiential realm of the poet/singer:

> When a bee lies sleeping in the palm of your hand
> You're bewitched and deep in love's long-looked-after land.
> Where you'll see a sun-up sky with a mornin' new
> And where the days go laughin' by as love comes acallin' on you.
> Sleep on bee, don't waken, I can't believe what's just passed.
> She's mine for the takin', I'm so happy at last.
> Maybe I dream, but she seems sweet golden as a crown.
> A sleepin' bee done told me that I'll walk with my feet off the ground
> When my one true love I have found.[3]

To Consider

1. This love song is a bit unconventional in its structure. Can you extract the formal structure of this song as it unfolds? What patterns of repetition are evident to you?
2. Discuss the relationship between the words and contour of the melody in the opening phrase. Do you think the shape of the tune and the rhythm of the music may have been derived from the natural flow of the lyrics?
3. Do the alterations of "appropriate" English address a specific segment of the culture?

The interplay between patterns of repetition in the opening of the refrain and the interesting varied conclusions of each refrain gives it a constant freshness that appeals to jazz players wishing to adapt it to an instrumental jazz style. When you hear the Bill Evans rendition of this tune, you will notice that he repeats the love song several times and uses it as a basis for jazz variations.

*L*istening Guide 63

A *Sleepin' Bee*
Jazz adaptation of a Broadway musical song

Recorded by Bill Evans, piano
CD No. 4, Track 10 (4:39)

*T*ony Bennett, in his performance, retains a slow tempo for the entire song. The jazz version created by Bill Evans, however, slips into a relaxed steady beat during the fifth line of the song. He thus uses the opening part of the refrain as an introduction to his arrangement. A more conventional treatment of the song would be to play the verse in a slow manner without a steady bass beat, thereby setting up the anticipation of a steady beat for the refrain.

The remarkable aspect of the popular songs coming from the Tin Pan Alley era is their amazing adaptability to various individual styles and genres of performance, due to the fundamental melodic structure and the interesting chord progressions underlying the tunes themselves. The great songwriters had a sophisticated command of the harmonic vocabulary that transcended the almost total dependency on the primary triads (I-IV-V-I). One of the major features of the jazz adaptations of these songs is the expansion of those harmonies to include what is commonly referred to as "substitution chords"—many times these expanded harmonies included chromatic variants of triads—added notes not drawn from the major scale of the tonic key.

To Consider

1. When you listen to the Bill Evans rendition of *Sleepin' Bee*, try to hear the melody of the song as the jazz trio takes you through various improvisations on the tune.
2. If you listen carefully to the bass line, you can detect that the pianist is using some alternate chords when you hear the chromatic bass lines (lines that move by half steps).
3. What is the function of the final statement of the tune?

0:00 The music begins without a steady beat in the character of an introduction; the melody of the refrain is stated from the opening bar.

0:38 Toward the end of the fifth line of the lyrics "Sleep on bee, don't waken, I can't believe what's just passed," Evans changes key and "goes into tempo" (a jazz term for beginning a steady beat that remains constant for the main part of the tune), reinforced by the string bass. Finally, before the first statement of the tune is over, the drums kick in to reinforce the beat.

1:11 The second time through the tune, you can barely recognize the melody. If you sing the melody as you hear the chords, you will realize that it all fits together. Once in a while you will find that some melodic notes in the piano match those of the original melody.

2:12 With the third statement of the *Sleeping Bee* tune, the bass plays a solo to the accompaniment of simple chords. Once more, if you sing the tune, you will realize that the harmonies are true to the original tune.

3:13 The bass continues a solo with the fourth statement and goes so far afield that the piano drops out and allows the bass to improvise so much so that the original melody is lost.

4:28 The tune returns in its recognizable form the middle of the fifth time around. ("Where you'll see a sun-up sky . . .") When this happens in a jazz piece, it is a signal that the performance is coming to an end.

ROMANCE AND THE BLUES TRADITION

Diversity and change are central themes that continually recur in our encounters with music. So far we have seen that styles of music continually emerge in order to address the changing aesthetic needs and tastes of a particular segment of culture. Furthermore, it seems that, as soon as they find their place in the mix of music in modern society, they begin a process of adjustment, and new variations of the styles become the norm.

Rhythm and blues, a musical expression that grew out of the African-American styles of the spiritual, gospel, and black folk music known as the blues, came to prominence concurrently with the rise of Tin Pan Alley music. It is one of the most versatile and constantly evolving genres of the popular music of our times, for it shows an amazing flexibility and persistence in the face of an ever-changing culture. This music, characterized by a strong backbeat (an accent on the second and fourth beats of a 4/4 measure), searing vocals often assisted by a honking saxophone, and always accompanied by electric guitars, was the primary vehicle for black expression for several decades in the first half of the twentieth century. Some rhythm and blues was the music of love, and some described the woes of the common African American who had to cope with everyday struggles in life. At times the music was a celebration of life, as in the James Brown hit *I Got You* ("I Feel Good"). The blues provides for us a social portrait of the composers and performers within this vibrant musical subculture.

Black musicians rose to prominence in the early 1940s, when a Harlem Hit Parade column was added to *Billboard* magazine—the country's leading periodical devoted to popular music. By 1945, **jukebox** ratings followed, which increased the market and popularity of this ethnic expression. (Jukeboxes were record players placed in restaurants, bars, and so on, activated by inserting coins into the machine.) "Rhythm and blues" was coined in 1949 by *Billboard* writers in an attempt to replace **"race music,"** the generic name for all music emanating from the black community. By the middle of the century, rhythm and blues, along with its sister musical form, the spiritual, was making great inroads into the broad musical culture of America.

Today, rhythm and blues is a well-established form—ever changing, to be sure, but a living expression in our diverse culture. In keeping with the current musical practices of blending several musical styles into fresh sounds, modern rhythm and blues singers often incorporate into their music elements of rock, jazz, and even rap.

Blues singers such as Chuck Berry, James Brown, Charles Brown, and B.B. King laid the foundation for modern rhythm and blues. For our musical selection featuring romance and the blues, we sample a song by Charles Brown, *Driftin' Blues*. This song was introduced by Brown in the late 1940s, when he was part of a band, Three Blazers, led by Johnny Moore. *Driftin' Blues* was the hit that launched Brown's career as a twenty-three-year old singer—a chemistry major from Prairie View College, Texas, who was trained in classical piano. (You will hear a recording made in 1993, almost fifty years after Brown's public entrance into the world of rhythm and blues.)

Through this song you will come to understand the basic harmonic and formal structure of blues music, and you will gain knowledge about musical nuances that represent the blues culture. The lyrics express the forlorn emotions of a lost love in terms of an analogy to a ship being lost at sea. Its imagery is uncluttered but poignant.

The genre of music known as the blues developed out of plantation songs dealing with the everyday troubles of the Negro slaves. Eventually the blues evolved into a musical pattern characterized by a chord progression that commonly occurred over a 12-measure time frame. The blues was both sung and played:

Measures: 1 - 2 - 3 - 4;   5 - 6 - 7 - 8;   9 - - - 10 - - - - - 11 - 12

Chords: I - - - -   IV - - I - -   V - - IV - V - - I

Or: I - (IV) - - I

"Driftin' Blues" follows this simple formula, known by all blues musicians as the "12-bar blues." It is one of hundreds of songs in which both the lyrics and chords are structured specifically to fit into a predictable structure. After you hear the first few measures of this song, you will probably begin anticipating the next chord and the next line of the lyrics, in such a way that you will want to become part of the music making. (You may want to write your own set of lyrics and have a musician play the blues progression while you sing your own version of the blues.)

istening Guide 64

Driftin' Blues   12-bar blues
Charles Mose Brown, Johnny   1946
Dudley Moore, and Edward E. Williams   Recorded by Charles Brown
                                                              CD No. 4, Track 11 (4:03)

Driftin' Blues

0:00   I'm driftin' and driftin,' like a ship out on the sea
            I - - - - - - - - - - - - - IV - - - - - - - - - - - - - - - I
            I'm driftin' and driftin,' like a ship out on the sea
            IV - I
            Well, I ain't got nobody, in this world to care for me.
            V - - - - - - - - - - - - IV - - - - V - - - - - - - - - - - - -I

0:48   If my baby would only take me back again!
            If my baby would only take me back again!
            No, I'm not good for nothing, Well, I haven't got no friend.

1:35   Instrumental interlude: guitar solo

2:22   I give you all my money, tell me what more can I do?
            I give you all my money, tell me what more can I do?
            You're just a good little girl, but you jist won't be true!

3:14   Bye, bye, Baby, Baby Bye, Bye,
            Bye, bye, Baby, Baby Bye, Bye,
            It's gonna be too late pretty mama, I'll be so far away.[4]

To Consider

1. Can you hear the 12-bar structure divided into 4-bar phrases? It soon becomes easy to feel this phrase structure without thinking about it.
2. Notice the instrumental fill at the end of the opening phrases for each verse.
3. What is the significance of the "double time" that the combo goes into after the singer sings "Baby, bye-bye, bye-bye"?
4. Describe the inflections Brown uses to give meaning to the words.

*T*HE BEATLES AND LOVE SONGS OF THE SIXTIES AND SEVENTIES

In February 1964, an English rock group came to the United States for the first time—a visit that began a new era in pop music and further expanded the boundaries of musical experience in the twentieth century. Their first American release *I Want to Hold Your Hand* (1964) topped the charts within two weeks of its release. Aided by their appearance on the *Ed Sullivan Show,* where they performed to an estimated audience of 73 million viewers, this group established a presence that even caught the attention of the classical world. Within five years of their first appearance in the United States, the Beatles succeeded in placing thirty songs on *Billboard*'s Top 10 popular music chart. Their varied stylistic approach to song writing had become familiar to millions of listeners. According to a Broadcast Music Industry (BMI) report, the Beatles song *Yesterday* (1964) inspired more than 2,500 cover versions during a twenty-five-year period following its release. Furthermore, it is the most performed song of the entire BMI repertoire, topping 5 million performances and still running close to a quarter of a million performances a year. (BMI functions as the principal clearinghouse and licensing organization for popular music in the United States. Headquartered in Nashville, it has been a central force in supporting the entire commercial music industry from its inception in 1940.)

What was different about the Beatles? They came on the American scene during a period of change, and they brought international perspectives to a culture often accused of being provincial. Their fresh approaches to song writing combined the rock influences of 1950s rock composers/singers such as Chuck Berry, Buddy Holly, and Little Richard with the sophisticated melodic styles of the music of Tin Pan Alley. Although the early songs were rather straightforward and simple, the Beatles soon exposed the country to both international concepts (such as their interest in the sitar—a stringed instrument of India—in *Norwegian Wood*) and innovative electronic idioms. Some of their songs can be classified as "rock," while others defy categorization. *Tomorrow Never Knows* was recorded with a four-track recorder and contains a repetitive phrase structure not dependent upon melody but upon an incessant rock backbeat with short, distorted lines of text, backed by an electronically produced accompaniment. Their 1967 album *Sgt. Pepper's Lonely Hearts Club Band* was a collection of songs related to a central theme—a vernacular version of the song cycle of the nineteenth-century German lieder. This collection represents a "coming of age" of vernacular music—a style that incorporates a wider perspective of experience than the music of simpler times. Through it all, the subject of love—a force that transcends all cultures and historical epochs—remained the primary vehicle for the Beatles' new musical expressions.

The all-time hit *Yesterday* serves well as an illustration of the freshness of Paul McCartney's writing. Although the Beatles performed the song at concerts that were dubbed "rock concerts" by producers and the public, this song does not qualify as a rock tune. It is much more strongly rooted in the tradition of the love ballad. Let us examine some of the musical gestures that make this love song particularly interesting to the ear.

Literally thousands of songs emanating from the Tin Pan Alley era commonly used phrase structures established by the European classical masters. Typically traditional song lyrics are written in rhyme schemes that fall comfortably into 8-measure phrases when set to music. If you count the beat patterns as they occur in well-known Broadway songs such as "*On the Street Where You Live* from *My Fair Lady,* or the title song from *The Sound of Music* (beginning with the lyrics "The hills are alive with the sound of music"), or the love ballads *Misty* and *I Left My Heart in San Francisco,* you will discover that each of these songs falls into easily defined 8-bar phrases. They all have a common formal structure—the now-familiar song form A-A-B-A.

Both the phrase length and formal structure of *Yesterday* stem from the common practices of the love ballad style—but they also contain elements of irregularity—

unconventional enough to alert the musically trained ear, but familiar enough to the casual listener to not upset the élan of the music. Herein lies the charm of this song.

The Beatles' success lies not only in the fresh approach of their musical practices which clearly stands out from their contemporaries, but more importantly, in the way in which they wrote songs that became classics in the world of trendy pop music, which seemed to be disposable music. Songs such as *Michelle, A Little Help from My Friends, Let It Be, Got to Get You into My Life, Eleanor Rigby,* and *The Fool on the Hill* have not been forgotten in the decades since their creation—they have become classics. The Beatles' influence on the pop music of the second half of the twentieth century was once more affirmed by the success of the 1995 retrospective album *Anthology,* which quickly became one of the best-selling albums in recording history. Volume two of *Anthology* (1996) enjoyed a similar fate.

The Changing Style of American Country Music

While some Americans were interested in being "hip" and exploring popular music styles representing the convergence of rock 'n' roll with international influences, others were directed toward down-home musical expressions. Country music, since its beginning, has always held a special attraction for people in our society who identify with the music of the common citizen, unaffected by the influences of art music or international styles. Just as the music of the blues was originally associated with the African-American subculture, country music was first considered a product of white America. Like the blues, which later expanded its horizon of influence and practice outside of its ethnic origins, country music in recent years has also broadened its appeal.

In the early post–World War II years, what is now known as country music was referred to as "hillbilly" or "folk" music. Interest in hillbilly music spread from its home in the South to other parts of the country as USO (United Service Organizations) performers representing this style sang to the geographically and culturally integrated audiences of U.S. servicemen. The recording industry and its inseparable companion, the radio, also played a significant role in the propagation of this spontaneous, accessible style of music. In 1948, the music industry created pop charts; in the following year, radio airplay charts for country music were established, which kept accounts of the songs being performed and also their frequency of performance. Eventually "hillbilly" music became known under the more user-friendly rubric "country and western music." In recent decades, it is firmly established as a national musical expression under the heading "country music," without the designation of "western."

In the earlier years, country-and-western lyrics typically described real-life love situations, full of everyday imagery. To accommodate this down-to-earth approach to music, the choice of chords, rhythms, and patterns of repetition was simple. These songs, often designed to be accompanied by a guitar, frequently used only three or four chords, making it extremely accessible to the amateur guitar player/singer. The country song *I'll Walk the Line,* made famous by Johnny Cash, for example, uses only three chords: the I, IV, and V chords. (In the key of C, this would consist of the C major, F Major, and G Major chords.) Similar simplicity was found in earlier songs such as *The Red River Valley.*

Straightforward lyrics and fundamental musical gestures became the hallmark of country music, as did a style of performing where singers adopted a nasal vocal style, retained any regional accents of language, and approached melodic skips by sliding into the pitch. Love lyrics expressed frank sentiments, broken promises, depression, or joy, without any pretense of sophistication or esoteric poetic metaphors. The aesthetic of traditional country music is that of unadorned simplicity and directness. And of course the lyrics frequently reflect the cultural tastes and attitudes of the people from which this music originates.

This is true for *Stand By Your Man,* written by Billy Sherrill and made famous by Tammy Wynette, whose recording rose to the top of the charts, and along with *D-I-V-O-R-C-E,* earned her an indelible place in country music. When *Stand By Your Man* was chosen to be used in Jack Nicholson's movie *Five Easy Pieces* (1970), feminist critics singled out the song as an example of male chauvinistic concepts and anti-feminist sentiments.

The entire premise of this song, according to them, underlined the time-worn attitude that a woman's role in life was to be accepting, long-suffering, and tolerant of her man, no matter what his behavior (much to the dismay of both Wynette and Sherrill). A retrospective look at this controversy calls attention to the conflicts brought about by social change in the 1970s. By attacking country music—the bastian for traditional down-home values (including the relationship of man to woman in our culture), the forward-looking feminists stirred up strong emotions on both sides of the argument. Shortly thereafter, the Lynn Anderson hit *Rose Garden* (written by Glenn Sutton) appeared, which portrayed woman as independent and self-sufficient with the opening lyrics, "I beg your pardon, I never promised you a rose garden."

When Wynette's recording of *Stand By Your Man* was used again in the sound track of the 1993 film *Sleepless in Seattle,* feminist versus anti-feminist conflicts were not raised.

And so the traditional genre that changed from "hillbilly" and "folk" to "country and western" and then to "country" became a vehicle to reflect social change in the modern world.

Stand By Your Man reflects more than old-fashioned social mores. Its musical style is typical of traditional country music:

1. The melodic/poetic phrases are shaped in short phrases, the last note of which is the longest of the phrase ("Sometimes it's hard to be a womannnnnn, Giving all your love to just one mannnnn").

2. Melodies are diatonic (drawn from the major scale, without chromatic alteration).

3. The harmonic structure predominantly centers on the I-IV-V chords.

4. The poem consists of verses of text with a refrain.

Listening Guide 65

Stand By Your Man
Billy Sherrill and Tammy Wynette

Country music song
1972
Sung by Tammy Wynette
CD No. 4, Track 12 (2:40)

Verse:
Sometimes it's hard to be a woman,
 Giving all your love to just one man,
You'll have bad times and he'll have good times
 Doin' things that you don't understand
But if you love him, you'll forgive him
 Even though he's hard to understand
And if you love him, aw, be proud of him
 Cause after all, he's just a man.

Refrain:
Stand by your man
 Give him two arms to cling to
And something warm to come to
 When nights are cold and lonely
Stand by your man
 And show the world you love him
Keep givin' all the love you can
 Stand by your man.
(Repeat last four lines)[5]

To Consider

1. What vocal/language inflections are used in Wynette's performance that are commonly associated with country music?
2. Do any of these performance techniques intensify the meaning of the lyrics?
3. Are there parallel musical gestures performed by the instrumental accompaniment that also link this piece to the country repertoire?

The term *crossover* came into use in the pop world during the late 1960s, referring to performers and their songs who were successful in two or more performing arenas. For example, Billy Sherrill established his career as a songwriter in the area of country music. While remaining active in country music, he achieved recognition in the pop world with the hit *The Most Beautiful Girl in the World.* His songs caught the attention of pop singer Charlie Rich, who recorded with Sun Records. Sherrill also wrote songs for David Houston, George Jones, Johnny Paycheck, Tanya Tucker, and Barbara Mandrell.

The concept of artists and composers expanding their audiences by becoming versatile with their musical styles was the genesis for a new approach to country music that became popular in the last decades of the twentieth century. A style known on the street as "new country" emerged—music that was designed to appeal to an eclectic audience. This style is not as easily stereotyped by its simple chords, melodic style, and performance practices as is traditional country music, but it still retains some of its aspects.

To be sure, new country music was a brilliant marketing gesture on behalf of publishers, performers, and the recording industry. But to attribute this change merely to economics is to deny that all parameters of musical style are constantly undergoing change in keeping with a continually evolving culture.

Part of the change centered on the lyrics. Instead of concentrating on the most basic experiences of day-to-day life, often told with a vocabulary that appealed predominantly to the lower middle class, writers of new country music looked to rock music to discover a language more in touch with the younger generation of listeners, who had been conditioned by an international rock culture.

Kris Kristofferson is such a writer. Kristofferson, a former Rhodes scholar and army helicopter pilot, gained recognition in Nashville in 1969 when he wrote *Me and Bobby McGee* and *For the Good Times.* Since then he has had more than 100 songs recorded by over 450 artists.[6] Two of his other best-known hits are *One Day at a Time* and *Help Me Make It through the Night.*

During the 1970s, a series of performing artists drew upon country inflections while maintaining positions in the pop and folk mainstream. Glen Campbell, John Denver, and even Harry Chapin allowed themselves to be directly or indirectly influenced by country music in some of their songs. By the 1980s, country music had become an acceptable genre of music for millions of listeners.

DULCE AMOR: THE LURE OF ROMANCE IN HISPANIC MUSIC

Hispanic Americans share a common ancestry linking them to countries whose principal language is Spanish. Most trace their roots to countries in Central and South America and, whether they come from places as varied as Peru or Puerto Rico, they often find identity through their Latin heritage. In reality, the Hispanic culture is one of the most diverse. Its ethnic identity has been retained to the present time (see the Musical Encounter that follows). Another element Hispanic cultures share is a strong musical environment in their homelands. Modern Hispanic music reflects these strong traditions; it also reflects the diversity of the people who originally colonized each Latin American country.

For example, some Hispanic music contains elements from Arabian music, dating back to the presence of Moors in southern Spain during the Middle Ages. Some is influenced by African sources, drawn from the importation of slaves from Africa during the period of colonization. And other musical expressions have features that suggest musical dialects from Central Europe. All of these outside influences, when mixed with local indigenous cultural expressions, result in musical styles that may be different from region to region, but that still show some common stylistic features that we call "Latin music."

Musical Encounter

The Musical Heritage of the Hispanic Culture

*I*t is estimated that by 2025, 50 million Americans living in the United States will be of Hispanic origin. The significant infusion of the Hispanic culture into the Northern Hemisphere began in the 1770s with the establishment of Spanish settlements in California. Today's cultural community reaches from coast to coast and is a mixture of subcultures with roots in countries as varied as Argentina, Chile, Columbia, the Dominican Republic, El Salvador, Ecuador, Mexico, Nicaragua, Panama, Peru, and Puerto Rico.

Mexican Americans account for about 60 percent of the U.S. Hispanic population; another 25 percent of Hispanic America traces its roots to other Central and South American countries; and the remaining mixture is from Puerto Rico and Cuba.

When Spain colonized the New World, it brought with it a rich musical culture steeped in a tradition that had been formed over the centuries, with several dominant influences. Andalusia, in southern Spain, gave rise to the **flamenco** tradition, a song and dance style that arose from a centuries' old gypsy culture. Flamenco traditions often include finger snapping, hand clapping, and foot stomping in complicated rhythmic patterns and changing accents. Many times you can hear three pulses in one part set against two in another. Another feature of this Andalusian music is the use of quick arpeggio-like ornaments that add colorful flair to the music and remind one of the ancient Arabic influences of this culture.

However, Spain is not the only musical ancestor in "Latin" music's rich heritage. The rich native cultures that the early explorers encountered were often not destroyed but were blended with several influences. Even today the flutes of the Andean Indian culture are found playing alongside the drums of African origin—a historical documentation of the Congolese background, from which slaves were imported in the seventeenth century. The Hispanic heritage is evident in the widespread use of the guitar throughout Latin America. The African heritage brought with it a variety of drums and marimbas.

Thus "Hispanic music," like "Hispanic culture," represents a composite of heritages. This acculturation process created a fertile atmosphere for the development and growth of various musical expressions and practices throughout the last three centuries.

Many forms of Hispanic music are part of the popular music culture. Two prominent singers are Gloria Estefan, whose music you will hear later, and Selena, the Mexican-American artist whose music continues to sell in spite of her untimely death in 1995. The fusion of Hispanic rhythms, instrumentation, and energy with virtually every current style of pop music in recent decades shows the vitality and adventuresome spirit found in the modern Hispanic culture. It is a culture interested both in preserving aspects of its heritage and surging forward to new experiences.

Perhaps the most exciting aspect of contemporary Latin American popular music is that it is always in transition and development. Modern groups from the Hispanic culture combine strong musical influences from the past (rhythmic patterns, melodic styles, dance forms, combinations of modern and indigenous instruments) with world movements in music such as rock, punk, reggae, and rap.

A popular style of Latin music stemming from a tradition of romance is known as *el vallenato*. **Vallenato** is a popular music expression coming from Colombia, specifically from the Valle de Upar. Its rhythmic structures are influenced by four traditional dances—the son, paseo, merengue, and puya—dances that each have their own unique tempos and are associated with certain instruments. The **son** is a slow dance usually played by an accordion (an instrument originating in Germany) and accompanied by bass instruments. The **paseo,** which can either be played in a slow or a moderately fast tempo, uses a guiro, a gourd-like percussion instrument with notches carved into it. The player scrapes a stick across the notches. Like the **merengue,** the paseo has complex rhythms. The accordion, bongos (originating from Africa), and guiro play the very fast dance, the **puya.**

Vallenato music is music of romance, for it carries with it romantic customs and traditions. The "romancero" vallenato is a man who highly values his woman and his native town and its customs. His songs are almost always about the woman he loves; at times he serenades her at midnight outside of her bedroom window.

It is against this broad cultural backdrop of courtship traditions that modern vallenato music is created. Current traditional vallenato groups usually are made up of a lead singer and two harmony singers, who are accompanied by an accordion, bongos (an instrument made of two small drums linked together and played with the hands), a conga (a larger drum), a guiro, a bass, a guitar, and timbales (a set of two drums played with sticks). Techno vallenato groups often add jazz drum sets, keyboards, and wind instruments. Most often the subject of their songs is love. Colombian native Carlos Vives is a well-known recording artist of vallenato music. This popular style has also been recorded by the Cuban-born Gloria Estefan, a popular Hispanic singer who now resides in Miami.

Listening Guide 66

Dulce Amor (Sweet Love)
Emelio Estefan Jr. and Kike Santander

Love song in the vallenato style
1995
Recorded by Gloria Estefan
CD No. 4, Track 13 (3:44)

The music for Estefan's 1995 album *Abriendo Puertas* (*Opening Doors*) was created and chosen specifically to celebrate the many styles of Latin American and Caribbean music. *Dulce Amor* (*Sweet Love*) is one of the songs from this recording and will be our musical selection from the Hispanic culture. The lyrics are full of references to the beauties of the countryside and speak of the love inspired by these images. Its music, far from being calm, is reflective and gentle, a mixture of the Colombian vallenato music infused with musical references to the Cuban **son** and the **cumbia.** The cumbia is a Caribbean rhythm of African origin that descended from a nineteenth-century "slave dance." Women dancing the cumbia traditionally dress in long, flowered skirts with brightly colored shirts, or white skirts with bright red fringes and ribbons.

Dulce Amor

Todas las noches cuando miro al cielo
brillan tus ojos como dos luceros
ojos tan puros como el agua clara
que calma las heridas
de mi pobre corrazón.

Te llevo anclado a mi pensamiento
paloma blanca que da el amor
amor que riega las ilusiones
como arroyito en el alma.

Aurora fresca de la mañana
tibia caricia, rayo del sol.
Coro:

Va saliendo la luna
reflejada en el rió (*repeat*)
Ay que buena fortuna
es tenerte amor mío. (*repeat*)

Es el perfume que me dan tus besos
dulc fragancia que en mi pecho anida
pasión que brota como blance espuma
cuando mueren al viento las olas del mar.

Te llevo escrito en mi firmamento
suave caricia que da el amor
amor que riega las ilusiones
como arroyito en el alma.
Aurora fresca de la mañana
tibia caricia, rayo del sol.
Coro:

Va saliendo la luna
reflejada en el rió (*repeat*)
Ay que buena fortuna
es tenerte amor mío. (*repeat*)

Eres canción que nace con el viento
inpiración cuando te doy un verso
eres la brisa que me alegra el alma
que lleva la fragancia de tu dulce amor.

Te llevo atado a mi pensamiento
paloma blanca que da el amor
amor que riega las ilusiones
como arroyito en el alma.

Aurora fresca de la mañana
tibia caricia, rayo del sol.
Coro:

Va saliendo la luna
reflejada en el rió (*repeat*)
Ay que buena fortuna
es tenerte amor mío. (*repeat*)[7]

Each evening when I look at the sky
your eyes shine like two stars,
Eyes so pure, like clear water
that soothes the wounds
of my poor heart.

I carry you anchored in my thoughts
White dove that brings love
Love that waters dreams
like a brook in my soul.

Fresh flush of the day,
warm caress, ray of the sun.
Chorus:

The moon is coming out,
reflected in the river (repeat)
What good fortune
it is to have you, my love. (repeat)

It is the perfume that your kisses give me
Sweet fragrance that is nestled in my breast.
Passion that bursts forth like the white foam
when the waves of the sea die in the wind.

I carry you written in my firmament
soft caress that brings love.
Love that waters dreams
Like a brook in my soul.
Fresh flush of the dawn,
warm caress, ray of the sun.
Chorus:

The moon is coming out,
Reflected in the river (repeat)
What good fortune
it is to have you, my love. (repeat)

You are the song born with the wind,
the inspiration when I give you verse.
You are the breeze that delights my soul,
carrying the fragrance of your sweet love.

I carry you bound to my thoughts
White dove that brings love,
Love that waters dreams
like a brook in my soul.

Fresh flush of the dawn,
warm caress, ray of the sun.
Chorus:

The moon is coming out,
Reflected in the river (repeat)
What good fortune
it is to have you, my love. (repeat)[8]

To Consider

1. What is your feeling regarding the relationship of the musical style to the lyrics? Do they relate well to each other?
2. Can you describe the rhythmic activity of the music? (What is the meter? Which instruments establish the beat, and which performers add syncopation to the music? Which beats of the measure receive accents (or stress)? Is this consistent throughout the song, or does it vary?)
3. What is the musical role of the accordion while the singer is singing?
4. Describe the general mood of this love song.

0:00	The song begins with a short instrumental introduction. The melody of the introduction is played by the accordion. A strong bass line and rhythm is established, and complex rhythmic patterns are defined by various percussion instruments.
0:11	The singer enters, stating the text with quick rhythms, and moves quickly through 11 lines of the text. The accordion makes a musical commentary at the end of each phrase of the lyrics.
0:38	The "chorus" is sung by the lead singer and backup singers. An alto voice sings a duet with the soloist.
0:58	The instrumental interlude is reminiscent of the vallenato style; the accordion plays the melody in this section.
1:18	The second verse of the lyrics begins by folding into the established rhythm without pause. The music is the same as in verse one, with the accordion commenting at the end of each phrase.
2:04	This instrumental interlude is different from the first one; the horns (trumpet, trombone, tenor saxophone, and baritone saxophone) lead in the style of cumbia. Soon the accordion takes over the melody. Now the bass line begins to add syncopated gestures.
2:25	The third stanza of the lyrics begins, once again playing basically the same music as before. If you listen carefully, however, you can detect some added syncopations in the rhythmic texture.
2:50	The chorus enters once again with the refrain, "Va saliendo la luna." It is repeated, signaling the end of the piece.
3:33	The band plays an ending. Notice that the principal instruments are the accordion, percussion, and bass. The full horn section, which you heard in the middle of the work, remains silent. This piece is more in the spirit of vallenato than cumbia.

As Latin music's popularity grew during the last four decades of the twentieth century, styles of popular music emerged, and a new vocabulary was formed for Hispanic musical expressions. These new forms were invariably formed by combining existing indigenous elements with current trends in international popular music. Some of these styles, such as vallenato, were direct descendants of dance rhythms and song styles, while others showed stronger outside influences, such as rock.

For example, in the late 1990s, a nouveau punk style emerged known as *rock en español*, which fused elements as diverse as heavy metal with folk traditions such as the bolero, samba, reggae, waltz, and ska. The result was an energetic musical celebration of international pop culture. The creation of this music was described by the co-leader and bassist from the Colombian group Aterciopelados:

> Our influences are English and American rock, no doubt, but also the music we've heard since we were little kids in Colombia: cumbia, salsa, musica carrilera. You don't have to force it. At the time of sitting down and composing, it's rare when that doesn't come up. In fact, you have to make an effort for it not to appear.[9]

The timeless subject of love, so frequently the aesthetic inspiration for folk music and dance, provided a link between the indigenous and international elements of this new music. But love was only part of the stimulus for pop music coming from a teenage world culture. Punk rock expressions, for example, were often rebellious in nature. Hispanic musicians wishing to adapt concepts of punk rock to their own cultural accents created their own style of music and called it **ska.**

Ska grew out of Jamaica in 1962, when Cecil Bustmente Campbell (also known as Prince Buster) started writing and performing dance band music that emphasized the after beat instead of the downbeat. A youth counter-culture movement called the Rude Boys adopted this music and changed it into a slow dance style with menacing gestures. In the 1970s, ska was mixed with reggae and punk. Groups such as Madness, the Beat, and the Bodysnatchers wore their hallmark black and white clothes and sang music that spoke loudly for the youth culture. Today, ska remains an outspoken rock movement that still draws upon punk, reggae, and the steady beat of rock for its basic musical expression.

When you begin to explore this exciting modern world of musical energy, another style you will encounter is **salsa.** This is a commercial name given to a variety of rhythms coming from dances such as the son montuno, mambo, and bomba y plena, the cha-cha, and the guaguanco—all are commonly referred to as "hot" or "sensuous." The actual birthplace of the term *salsa* is not Cuba or Puerto Rico, as one might guess by listening to the music, but New York. In the mid-1970s, some enterprising Puerto Rican musicians in New York recognized a market for Latin disco music and created a hot music and dance practice that has now become internationally recognized.

If we were to look for a common element that unites the multifaceted music of the various Latin American countries and generations, it would no doubt be romance. A common bond between much of the song and dance music from the Hispanic culture involves a male dancer who leads his partner through intricate steps and dance maneuvers. The dances, and the complex rhythms of the music supporting them, often can be traced back to various gestures and rituals of courtship. This link between music and romance is decidedly Latino.

$\mathcal{S}$UMMARY

Songs that are inspired by love and romance are found throughout all cultures and in all periods of music history. Whereas the subject of love is universal, musical expressions vary greatly.

In modern times, the music of romance exists both at the popular music level and in the arena of art music. Singers and composers of various styles and from different ethnic groups reflect a wide variety of musical expressions. Each style of music carries with it certain performance practices appropriate to that expression and gives it identity. These important features often stem from the cultural heritage of the particular style, providing life and meaning. When we understand these nuances of expression, we become meaningful participants in the music itself.

Since love is experienced by all people, regardless of historical time, location, or ethnic origin, it serves as an effective window through which we can gain a perspective on the way in which various cultures use music to express this universal sentiment. In the musical selections in this chapter, you have seen how some concepts can be generally held by all people but can be expressed in culturally specific musical languages.

$\mathcal{K}$EY TERMS

cumbia	puya	son
flamenco	race music	song cycle
jukebox	rhythm and blues	Tin Pan Alley
merengue	salsa	vallenato
paseo	ska	

CHAPTER 14

Music of War
and Peace

*I*N our musical encounters so far, we have seen the social and cultural influences of music and have come to understand that music exists in a variety of musical styles and venues, and that it can affect us in diverse ways and help intensify our thoughts about a wide spectrum of life's experiences. Now we will hear music and discover lyrics that focus on music's power both as a driving force in time of war and as an expression of humankind's desire for lasting peace. In the first part of this chapter, we discuss traditional musical ideas of war and see how war surfaces as a subject in music. We begin by temporarily diverting our attention away from the listening experience and examining a medieval literary masterpiece, the *Song of Roland,* in which the magic powers of music are referenced. Next, we encounter a curious musical practice in the late medieval era in which a popular war song was used as a melodic basis for a polyphonic Mass, the principal form of sacred music in the fifteenth century.

As we venture into later periods of music history, we sample a Mass composition by Franz Joseph Haydn, a cantata by English composer Ralph Vaughan Williams, and a serial piece by Arnold Schoenberg, all of which deal with some aspect of war and peace. Finally, we see how composers outside the venue of concert music use music to express anti-war ideas and to champion peace. Our study ends with a choral arrangement of an Australian folk song about war—a fitting blend of folk and concert music practices.

For centuries, music has been used to incite soldiers to war, to praise its heroes, to relieve the tedium of military life, and to provide a vehicle for expressing homesickness and loneliness invariably connected to a soldier's life. Ancient traditions from around the world have used chants, often connected to drumming and dancing, as an aid in war. The documented histories of Greek and Roman cultures also indicate that war songs were used to prepare men for battle. Some accounts even ascribe magical powers to music. In recent times, music has been composed that, instead of supporting the energies of war, focuses on hopes for peace.

The power of music as a social commentary is perhaps the strongest in music that is inspired by war. This chapter examines some of these works and shows how composers are able to appeal directly to the emotions through the medium of sound in order to arouse reactions in the listener. Music addressing specific causes, such as supporting a war effort or protesting a war, can rightly be called propaganda; although it may be a personal expression of the composer, such music also reflects the sentiments of a large segment of the population.

Contemplating the texts and listening to this music also brings history alive, for it gives us yet another way to perceive the thoughts and emotions of others during a given time.

With this in mind, we will examine several works that are effective commentaries on world events related to war and peace. We also observe the role that several musicians have played in supporting a specific position relating to military activity. Our sample is broad, for it ranges from the folk music of immediate appeal to an intense statement composed using the serial technique. Its historical scope exhibits the timelessness of music as a vehicle for political and emotional expression.

$\mathcal{T}$HE SONG OF ROLAND

Music of war and peace has a long history. The Old Testament account of Joshua conquering Jericho tells how Joshua was instructed by the Lord to choose seven priests who were to surround the city of Jericho, and on a given signal, they were to blow trumpets made of rams' horns, all at the same time. Upon hearing a long blast from the trumpets, the people gave a loud shout, and the walls of Jericho crumbled to the ground. This story is the basis of the spiritual *Joshua Fit the Battle of Jericho*, a song contained in Chapter 3.

Our next musical selection is a literary reference that also tells of the magical power of the trumpet. (We will temporarily digress from a listening experience to consider this interesting link between music and literature.) The *Chanson de Roland* (The *Song of Roland*) is an epic poem written circa 1130 by a Frenchman, Turoldus. Probably drawn from a series of existing popular ballads, it tells the story surrounding the death of Roland, the Emperor Charlemagne's nephew, in the Pyrenees Mountains in 778. Roland's magic trumpet, called the **oliphant**, plays a central part in the tale (verses 1753–95) and is identified with a series of emotions and powers.

According to the poem, Roland's return from the military campaign in Moorish Spain goes awry when he is betrayed by Ganelon and attacked while crossing a narrow mountain pass. Roland, although he is urged to sound his horn to summon help, proudly refuses. Finally, after the battle goes against him and many of his men are slaughtered, Roland blows his horn. Roland's sounding of the horn carries thirty leagues (a league, in modern equivalents, is estimated to be somewhere between 2.4 and 4.6 miles) and is heard by King Charlemagne (Charles), who concludes that Roland is in battle (verses 1753–60); the Duke of Niemes, upon hearing the trumpet's sound, interprets the music to mean that Roland has been betrayed and that he is in dire distress (verses 1785–95), for Roland has already been mortally wounded:

> 1753   Roland hath set the oliphant to his mouth,
> He grasps it well, and with great virtue sounds.
> High are those peaks, afar it rings and loud,
> Thirty great leagues they hear its echoes mount.
> So Charles heard, and all his comrades round;
> Then said that King: "Battle they do, our counts."
> And Guenelun answered, contrarious:
> "That were a lie, in any other mouth."

> 1760   The Count Rollanz, with sorrow and with pangs,
> And with great pain sounded his oliphant:
> Out of his mouth the clear blood leaped and ran,
> About his brain the very temples cracked.
> Loud is its voice, that horn he holds in hand;
> Charles hath heard, where in the pass he stands,
> And Niemes hears, and listen all the Franks.

> 1785   The Count Rollanz, through blood his mouth doth stain,
> And burst are both the temples of his brain,

His oliphant he sounds with grief and pain;
Charles hath heard, listen the Franks again.
"That horn," the King says, "hath a mighty strain!"
Answers Duke Niemes: "A baron blows with pain!
Battle is there, indeed I see it plain,
He is betrayed, by one that still doth feign.
Equip you, sir, cry out your old refrain,
That noble band, go succour them amain!
Enough you've heard how Rollanz doth complain."[1]

The *Song of Roland* figures prominently in the Battle of Hastings (in 1066, nearly 300 years after the events chronicled in the epic poem), for legend has it that a Norman jongleur by the name of Taillefer went before the Norman army, threw his sword in the air, and started to sing the *Song of Roland* before the enemy. Whether or not this was a gesture protesting the war or the jongleur was singing the song to rally the troops (England was conquered by William the Conqueror, a Norman, in this battle), the survival of this legend suggests that the song played an important psychological function in the events of the day.

The *Chanson de Roland* is an example of the *chanson de geste*, a French epic poem that was either recited or sung by minstrels (called **troubadours,** and later, **trouvères**) who functioned as entertainers, poets, and chroniclers of the events and legends of the times.

A SONG OF WAR AND SACRED MUSIC OF THE RENAISSANCE

During the mid-fifteenth century, an interesting folk song emerged in France that retained its popularity for over 150 years. The song *L'Homme armé* (*The Armed Man*) is immortalized in history because its melody was commonly used in polyphonic Mass compositions during the Renaissance. The folk songs of the late Medieval and early Renaissance eras (often referred to as "secular music") were often short tunes built on the strong rhythms of poetic meter. These simple melodies originated as single-line tunes, but gradually they became part of the polyphonic compositions that gained popularity, both in the sacred and secular music of this time.

The curious practice of using a preexisting tune as a source for the Mass originated with composers using Gregorian chant melodies for the foundation of their polyphony; gradually, in the mid-fifteenth century, a few popular secular songs were used as *cantus firmus* melodies (meaning "fixed song"). *L'homme armé* was the most popular of these songs. Over thirty *L'homme armé* Masses by composers ranging from Guillaume Dufay (1400–1474) to Giovanni Pierluigi da Palestrina (ca. 1525–1597) have been preserved.

The basic technique of using a cantus firmus involved using the notes of the tune in one voice part, such as the tenor, and writing counterpoint around that melody in the other voice parts. Sometimes the presence of the tune was obvious to the listener; at other times, the cantus firmus is not apparent.

The *L'homme armé* text addresses the intimidating power of a person dressed in armor. Its tune is a simple A-B-A structure, with the final section functioning as a closing statement of the first phrase.

Free translation:	The man, the man, the man at arms,	"Find if ye could, a coat of mail!"
	Fills the folk with dread alarms.	Oh, the man, the man at arms
	Everywhere we hear them wail,	Fills the folk with dread alarms![2]

L'Homme Armé melody.

It is highly doubtful that the use of this song related in any way either to support war or to protest it. However, its popularity as a folk song and its widespread use as a cantus firmus in Mass compositions attest to a strong consciousness of military power, medieval style. The use of a secular cantus firmus in the holy Mass was also an interesting phenomenon, for it gave evidence of a practice that was unusual in the tradition of the Catholic Church. In fact, a series of conferences were held in the middle of the sixteenth century, called the **Council of Trent**, where the practice of using secular songs in the Mass was discussed and eventually banned from future compositions intended for use in the Church.

Three of our musical selections in this chapter are centered around text drawn from the Mass of the Catholic Church. They all involve the text, "Lamb of God, who takest away the sins of the world . . . grant us thy peace," the "Agnus Dei" section of the Mass. The first is an early Renaissance setting of the *L'homme armé* folk song by Guillaume Dufay. The second is taken from Franz Joseph Haydn's *Mass in Time of War*. And last, we examine a work by the twentieth-century English composer Ralph Vaughan Williams. His *Dona Nobis Pacem* (*Grant Us Peace*) is clearly a statement against war; its title is taken from the Catholic Mass.

By the time Dufay was writing polyphonic settings of the Mass, the Catholic Church had established a standard order of worship, complete with certain texts that were used each time a Mass was celebrated. (Remember, a Mass is the central worship service in the Catholic Church in which communion is celebrated.) One of these standard sections of the service is the "Agnus Dei," a part of the service leading up to the holy moment of communion. The text is a plea to God to show mercy and to grant peace to humankind.

Agnus Dei, qui tollis peccata mundi,	Lamb of God, who takest away the sins of the world,
miserere nobis.	have mercy upon us.
Agnus Dei, qui tollis peccata mundi,	Lamb of God, who takest away the sins of the world,
miserere nobis.	have mercy upon us.
Agnus Dei, qui tollis peccata mundi,	Lamb of God, who takest away the sins of the world,
dona nobis pacem.	grant us thy peace.[3]

istening Guide 67

"Agnus Dei" ("Lamb of God"),
   from *Missa L'homme armé*
   (The *Armed Man Mass*)
Guillaume Dufay (1400–1474)

Polyphonic Mass movement
Recorded by the Oxford Singers
CD No. 4, Track 14 (1:27)

*T*he use of a war tune as a central melody for the "Agnus Dei" is a curious one, for it appears that the Latin text and the secular melody are at odds with each other. If one examines the use of secular songs as cantus firmus in much of the repertoire during this time, however, it becomes apparent that the Church did not view this practice as unusual until a much later date.

Dufay may have been the first to incorporate a secular song into the Mass. Whatever his motivations were, he no doubt captured the attention of the churchgoers of his time, for the tune is very obvious when the music is performed.

We will listen to a movement from Dufay's Mass setting to experience how this song of war emerges from the counterpoint of the music. As you listen to the "Agnus Dei," allow your ear to take in each voice part as it enters, and then notice the prominent *L'homme armé* tune emerge from the texture.

To Consider

1. The most important element to listen for is the use of the *Armed Man* tune. When do your ears first notice the tune?
2. Notice how the parts weave in and out of each other in a very independent way. Do you feel a kind of flow of motion and energy when some voices rise to their higher ranges? This is part of the charm of Renaissance vocal music.
3. Dufay's "Agnus Dei" setting is structured in three sections. The form is derived from patterns of repetition in the text. Is this structure obvious to you as you listen to the music?
4. Notice how the *Armed Man* tune is passed around between the lower parts of the ensemble. Sometimes you hear fragments of the tune, and sometimes you hear entire phrases.

*M*USIC OF PEACE AND THE CULTIVATED TRADITIONS

Although Dufay was probably not making a political statement about war by using a military song in his Mass composition, composers from later periods of history used the sacred venue as a vehicle for anti-war commentary. We will experience two of these works, one from the late eighteenth century and the other from the first half of the twentieth century.

The intensity with which anti-war statements occur in these works varies greatly. The commentary on war that Haydn makes in his *Mass in Time of War* (*Missa in tempora belli*) is subtle to the modern ear; his use of drums to signify the cannons of war probably had a stronger impact on the ears of his contemporaries than they do on our ears, which are accustomed to the loud noises of amplified sound. The *Dona Nobis Pacem* of Vaughan Williams, on the other hand, takes a more obvious position against war.

Schoenberg's *Survivor from Warsaw*, our last example from the concert repertoire, disturbs both our ears and minds with the horrors of war. Our encounter with this work will leave us realizing once more that music is capable of making a strong impact on our minds and emotions. Its powerful message is a fitting finale to the concert repertoire of *Musical Encounters*.

Considered together, they show not only the vast variety of musical styles commonly found in our classical music repertoire but also indicate degrees of directness concerning the source of their inspiration.

Franz Joseph Haydn: The Mass in Time of War

The European political arena was in the midst of conflict when Haydn wrote his *Mass in Time of War*. France, the center of a popular revolution in the 1790s, had witnessed massacres (a two-day rampage in Paris in 1792 produced over 1,200 casualties), and the guillotine became the symbol of justice. It claimed Louis XVI in January 1793. His wife Queen Marie Antionette—sister of Emperor Joseph II of Austria and daughter of Austrian Archduchess Maria Theresa and Holy Roman Emperor Francis I—suffered the same fate in October of the same year. Even Robespierre, a leading revolutionary who had demanded that the king be put to death, was himself guillotined in 1794.

In 1796, France was at war with Austria, and Napoleon, on the rise toward becoming emperor, was chalking up a string of victories. The citizens of Vienna were mobilized for war and forbidden to talk of peace until the French were defeated. Haydn—a man in his sixties, a conservative who believed in the monarchy and political stability, and by now the most prestigious musical presence in Vienna—wrote his first composition to reference war, the *Missa in tempora belli*.

Haydn's *Mass in Time of War*, at first glance, is a typical treatment of the five items from the Ordinary of the Catholic Mass—sections that are commonly used regardless of the Church calendar year. The practice of extracting the texts comprising the Kyrie, Gloria, Credo, Sanctus, and Agnus Dei was already well established by the time Haydn and his contemporaries wrote Masses, since it dates back to the fourteenth century. (Incidentally, composers are still writing music to these liturgical texts. The five items from the Ordinary of the Mass constitute the textual sources for the largest body of choral music in history.) In the Classical Era, these Mass settings were typically thirty to forty-five minutes long and used a chorus, soloists, and an orchestra.

To one who is acquainted with the classical aesthetic and musical practices, *Mass in Time of War* is not overtly programmatic, nor does Haydn alter the text of the Mass by adding lyrics that address war directly. And although the Kyrie opens with a steady thumping of the timpani—which perhaps could be interpreted as the sound of marching or of cannons—the direct references to war do not occur until the final movement, the "Agnus Dei." We will see how his prominent use of the timpani has been identified with cannon fire and the trumpet fanfares have been associated with the military. Although Haydn did not speak or write of this symbolism, the assumption that he referenced war with these devices rises from the fact that such specific practices of orchestration were unique to this music. We also know that he was fond of making subtle references to various events and objects in several of his other works. Furthermore, the title *Mass in Time of War* indicates Haydn's interest in making musical references part of his composition.

Haydn's cry for peace was not to be answered in his lifetime. He died on May 31, 1809, when Vienna was occupied by enemy troops. Shortly before he died, the city was under bombardment and a shot fell close to his house. He told his servants, "Children, don't be frightened; no harm can happen to you while Haydn is near." Five days before he died, he asked to be carried to the pianoforte, where he played three times his Emperor's hymn *Gott erhalte Franz den Kaiser*, which was to become Austria's national anthem. It was his last musical gesture.

istening Guide 68

"Agnus Dei," from *Mass in Time of War*
Franz Joseph Haydn

Movement from a polyphonic Mass
1796
Conducted by Leonard Bernstein
CD No. 4, Track 15 (6:28)

*A*s you listen to this work, review in your mind the basic elements of Classical style you
learned in Chapter 5 regarding melody, chord progression, and texture. Since the text de-
lineates the form of this movement, the following listening guide is referenced according to the
sections of the text.

To Consider

1. As you listen to this composition, be aware that Haydn's use of the timpani here is programmatic, and that this is his way of reminding the listener that this work is written to draw attention to issues of war and peace.
2. Notice how the orchestra establishes the general mood and harmonic structure so that when
   the chorus enters it folds logically into the work.
3. How does the form of the text dictate the structure of the music in this work? Describe its
   overall musical form.

Adagio

0:00   The first line of the "Agnus Dei" text is set homorhythmically, with the chorus and orchestra presenting a 9-measure statement. Notice that the first two "Agnus Dei" statements are quiet; the third statement that follows is suddenly forte.

1:10   After a 3-measure interlude in which the basses begin an agitated rhythm, the words "miserere nobis"
("have mercy upon us") are presented by the chorus. The timpani now enters, signifying the cannons
of war; it will continue to play prominently throughout this movement.

2:08   The second section begins in similar fashion to the opening of the movement, but now the orchestra
breaks into a steady eighth-note accompaniment.

2:37   In the sixth measure of this statement, the trumpets enter with the first fanfare rhythm, serving as a
link to the "miserere nobis."

3:10   The third statement of the "Agnus Dei," which sounds like a quiet plea for mercy, is only eight measures long. The timpani, however, maintains its ubiquitous presence.

Allegro con spirito

4:00   Now the fury of the war begins! This section, a repeat of the "dona nobis pacem" text, pounds away
with timpani and orchestra playing incessant rhythms, while the choir sings a loud, prolonged cry for
peace.

4:26   Soon the loud dynamics give way to a quiet vocal trio—which becomes a quartet four measures
later. This classic technique of contrast builds anticipation for a more flamboyant section to
come.

4:50   The final section, marked piu presto (even faster), is a section of fury, with trumpet calls, rapid scales,
and throbbing timpani. It is now not a gentle supplication but an emotional cry for peace. A grand
pause stops the motion abruptly, in preparation for the final section.

6:39   The movement (and the Mass) ends with four statements of the word "pacem," which provide an appropriate conclusion to this musical masterpiece.

Ralph Vaughan Williams: *Dona Nobis Pacem*

Some 100 years after Haydn had died, during the Napoleonic assault on Vienna, a composer emerged in England who, like Haydn, had strong connections to his country and to concerns for citizenship. Unlike Haydn, Vaughan Williams had firsthand experiences with war. In 1914, at age forty-two, he joined the medical corps in the British army and ended his service in France as an artillery officer. His *Dona Nobis Pacem*, the subject of our next musical selection, expresses emotions born out of the composer's experience.

Vaughan Williams said that a composer should not be isolated from his people, but that he should "cultivate a sense of musical citizenship." His music remains true to this creed, for the titles of his compositions often disclose his English roots—*English Folk Song Suite, Five Tudor Portraits, On Wenlock Edge, Fantasia on Sussex Folk Tunes,* and *In the Fen Country.* His first three symphonies have programmatic titles reminiscent of England—*The Sea,* the *London,* and the *Pastoral* symphonies.

Vaughan Williams's works, which are diverse in style and form, are frequently performed in today's concert halls. His songs with piano accompaniment, his works for chorus—both sacred and secular—and his symphonic works are the most popular. His style, which grew out of nineteenth-century harmonic practice, was not considered part of the "modernist" movement that was seeking new directions in music. Rather it communicated to a broad audience of musically educated listeners—a musical language that elevated Vaughan Williams to the forefront of English composers in the first half of the twentieth century.

His favorite texts for his vocal and choral works were those of English authors. His *Dona Nobis Pacem,* a forty-minute cantata for soprano and baritone soli, chorus, and orchestra, draws heavily upon English texts. Although its title is taken from the well-known supplication of the "Agnus Dei" of the Mass ("Grant Us Peace"), three of the six movements of this work are based on poems by Walt Whitman.

The cantata, whose title could be translated, "Give Peace in Our Time, O Lord," unfolds in six movements, according to the following organization:

I. A simple statement of the Mass text, "Dona nobis pacem," first sung by a soprano soloist and then echoed by the chorus.

II. Choral movement based on Whitman's "Beat, beat, drums! Blow, bugles, blow."

III. *Reconciliation,* text taken from the Whitman poem of the same name, for baritone solo and chorus.

IV. *Dirge for Two Veterans,* words by Whitman, for chorus.

V. For chorus (with baritone solo) consisting of several text sources, drawn from John Bright ("The Angel of Death has been abroad throughout the land") and Old Testament passages from Jeremiah, Daniel, and Haggai.

VI. Chorus: this grows directly out of the previous movement and is also based on texts from the Old Testament (selections from Micah, Leviticus, Psalms, and Isaiah). The work concludes with the "Glory to God in the highest" from the New Testament Book of Luke.

Whitman's text comes from a series of poems, *Drum Taps,* which he wrote in reaction to the American Civil War. No doubt Whitman had strong personal reasons to write these verses, for his brother was wounded in the war, and he worked in a hospital for soldiers in Washington during the Civil War years. Whitman's words provide fertile images and sounds for elaboration by a composer—an ideal text for musical composition:

Beat! beat! drums!—blow! bugles! blow!
Through the windows—through the doors—burst like a ruthless force,

Into the solemn church, and scatter the congregation,
Into the school where the scholar is studying;
Leave not the bridegroom quiet—no happiness must he have now with his bride,
Nor the peaceful farmer any peace, ploughing his field, or gathering in his grain,
So fierce you whirr and pound you drums—so shrill you bugles blow.

Beat! beat! drums!—blow! bugles! blow!
Over the traffic of cities—over the rumble of wheels in the streets;
Are beds prepared for the sleepers at night in the houses: No sleepers must sleep in
    those beds,
No bargainers; bargains by day—would they continue?
Would the talkers be talking: would the singer attempt to sing:
Then rattle quicker, heavier drums—you bugles wilder blow.

Beat! beat! drums!—blow! bugles! blow!
Make no parley—stop for no expostulation,
Mind not the timid—mind not the weeper or prayer,
Mind not the old man beseeching the young man,
Let not the child's voice be heard, nor the mother's entreaties,
Make even the trestles to shake the dead where they lie awaiting the hearses,
So strong you thump O terrible drums—so loud you bugles blow.[4]

Vaughan Williams turned to other text sources for the last two movements. The fifth
part of the cantata opens with a baritone solo singing words that originally were spoken by
John Bright before the House of Commons during a debate on the Crimean War in 1855.
Bright's comments refer to the Old Testament account of Passover:

> The angel of death has been abroad throughout the land; you may almost hear
> the beating of his wings. There is no one as of old . . . to sprinkle with blood
> the lintel and the two side-posts of our doors, that he may spare and pass on.[5]

The composer then cleverly turns to several biblical texts to further the mood set by the
opening solo:

> We looked for peace, but no good came; and for a time of health, and behold
> trouble! The snorting of his horses was heard from Dan; the whole land trembled
> at the sound of the neighing of his strong ones; for they are come, and have
> devoured the land . . . and those that dwell therein. . . . The harvest is past, the
> summer is ended, and we are not saved. . . . Is there no balm in Gilead? Is there
> no physician there? Why then is not the health of the daughter of my people
> recovered?

(Jeremiah VIII: 15–22)

> "O man greatly beloved, fear not, peace be unto thee, be strong, yea, be strong."

(Daniel X: 19)

> "The glory of this latter house shall be greater than of the former . . . and in this
> place will I give peace."

(Haggai II: 9)[6]

When approaching such powerful texts as these, the composer must decide how
much literal image painting to use and how to shape the music to fit the emotional flow
and climax of the text. These considerations also form a most appropriate approach to listening. Just how the music fits, complements, and breathes life into the text is important
here, because the words make such a strong statement.

Listening Guide 69

Dona Nobis Pacem (excerpts)
"The Angel of Death" and
    "O Man Greatly Beloved"
Ralph Vaughan Williams

1936
Recorded by the London Symphony
    Chorus and Orchestra.
Richard Hickox, conductor
CD No. 4, Track 16 (4:45)

To Consider

1. The opening of the "The Angel of Death," with its recitative style, is intended to immediately establish a sad, profound sentiment. What vocal techniques does the composer write to achieve this? What inflections does the soloist add to intensify the meaning of the words?

2. If you follow the words closely, you will see that the composer follows the emotions of the lyrics by exaggerating musical changes—from loud to soft, from solo passages to choral passages, and from strong, accented orchestral sound to quiet passages. When you listen to these abrupt changes, do you feel that this mixture of text sources, musical devices, and dramatic elements is successful?

3. Describe the relationship of the orchestra to the solo and choral parts. How much doubling, if any, do you hear? How does Vaughan Williams balance the textures of sound between the voices and orchestra?

Based on the experience that you have had listening to previous selections throughout this book, you will no doubt find yourself discovering points of reference even upon your first listening. The following program notes are intended to enhance your perception.

0:00	The baritone solo begins with a bare-bones accompaniment. With the entrance of the timpani, one can hear the Angel of Death's wings beating.
0:56	Suddenly the chorus cries out, "Dona nobis pacem" . . . the fundamental supplication that ties together the entire cantata. It is echoed by the soprano solo.
1:39	A contrasting lyrical text establishes a link to the feeling of anticipation described in the words, "We looked for peace." Soon, however, this gives rise to the frustration of war. Notice that the composer builds tension by the use of dynamics, chromaticism, and a general thickening of the texture during the most intense lines of the text.
3:27	The fifth section flows directly into the baritone solo, an affirmation of peace in a recitative-like statement of the words, "O man greatly beloved, fear not, peace be unto thee, be strong, yea, be strong. . . . The glory of this latter house shall be greater than the former, And in this place will I give peace."[7] The rest of the last movement (not included in the recording accompanying this text) focuses on the promises of peace.

Arnold Schoenberg Remembers the Holocaust

Ralph Vaughan Williams and Arnold Schoenberg shared the common experience of having lived in countries that were part of the war arena. Their perspectives on war were not shaped from history books but were firsthand experiences, and, although they wrote just a few works dealing with the subject of war and peace, their anti-war sentiments are clearly apparent in those compositions.

Schoenberg's musical theories leading toward the serial technique of composition have been discussed previously. Although many of his works seem to be too esoteric for much of the concertgoing public and are not frequently programmed, his work for narrator, men's chorus, and orchestra, *A Survivor from Warsaw, Op. 46*, contains a direct, easily understood message in spite of the complex serial techniques making up its musical structure. Its message addresses directly and emotionally the horrors of the Holocaust in the ghettos of Warsaw.

Written in 1947, this composition was an early contribution to the long list of books and artistic expressions in reaction to the Holocaust. These vivid images are chronicled in books such as *The Diary of Anne Frank, Inside the Third Reich, Memoirs of Albert Speer,* Herman Wouk's two novels, *The Winds of War* and *War and Remembrance*, and the film *Schindler's List,* which all serve as emotional reminders of inhumanity in recent history.

A Survivor from Warsaw is based on reports that Schoenberg had heard concerning the treatment of Jews in Warsaw while the city was under Nazi control during World War II. Schoenberg, himself a Jew, had wisely left Germany before the Holocaust. In May 1933, a mere four months after Hitler came to power, he quickly left Berlin for Paris. Earlier that year, he had left the Prussian Academy of Arts when it became apparent that Jews were no longer welcome, and he was officially dismissed in September. In October 1933, he came to the United States, where seven years later he was granted citizenship. Even prior to Hitler's rise to power, Schoenberg had been aware of the growing anti-Semitism in Germany. In a letter to artist Wassily Kandinsky, he wrote:

> I have at last learnt the lesson that has been forced upon me during this year, and I shall not ever forget it. It is that I am not a German, not a European, indeed perhaps scarcely even a human being (at least, the Europeans prefer the worst of their race to me), but I am a Jew.[8]

Schoenberg's life experiences during the early years of the Third Reich inspired him to renew his Jewish faith and at the same time they intensified his anxiety over the blatant persecutions brought about by the Hitler regime. It was not until the war was over and Schoenberg had become more fully informed about the Holocaust's extent that he translated these feelings into a masterpiece of musical expression in the form of a mini-drama.

The text of *A Survivor from Warsaw* is Schoenberg's own and is given a harmonically dissonant and rhythmically complex setting, but one that nevertheless allows the narrator's voice to be heard over the often ear-wrenching sounds. The rhythms in this work are inspired from the words and underline their intensity, beginning with the rather distorted bugle call of the trumpet, continuing through passages such as the painful rhythmic accellerandos supporting the words, "I heard it though I had been hit very hard, so hard that I could not help falling down," and ending with the men's choral statement of the Shmà Israèl, the ancient Jewish prayer.

istening Guide 70

A Survivor from Warsaw, Op. 46
Arnold Schoenberg

Work for narrator and symphony orchestra
1947
Recorded by the BBC Philharmonic and Chorus.
Pierre Boalez, conductor
CD No. 4, Track 17 (6:51)

To Consider

1. As you listen to this work, your ears will naturally be drawn to the narration. How does Schoenberg regulate the momentum of the work, and how does he control its dramatic intensity?

2. Can you detect points in the work where the orchestra plays music that is directly descriptive of the words?
3. Comment about the length of the piece in relationship to the consistency of tension that this composition creates. What would be your reaction if this piece were as long as a movement of a Beethoven symphony, for example?

Schoenberg's use of the orchestra is extremely precise. Every note is carefully measured and notated. Its discordant sounds and uneven rhythms are calculated to disturb. (Who says that all music should be "beautiful"?)

In *A Survivor from Warsaw*, Schoenberg altered the technique of *Sprechgesang* that he had used in earlier works, where the notation was very specific, to one that allowed the narrator more freedom. His notation for the narrator simply suggests the rise and fall of the vocal contour in relation to a simple line, representing the middle of the voice. The composer designates precise rhythms, however. The effectiveness of this technique lies in the clarity that is achieved; the voice, unencumbered even with approximate pitches, assumes the dramatic qualities of speech. The Shmà Israèl is sung in Hebrew. Its translation is as follows:

Hear, O Israel, the Lord is our God, the Lord is one.
You shall love the Lord your God with all your heart and all
    your soul and with all your might.
And these words which I command you today shall be in your heart.
You shall teach them diligently to your children,
And you shall speak of them when you are sitting at home and when
    you go on a journey.[9]

Reports from the premiere of this work at the University of New Mexico indicate that the audience was deeply moved by the performance. After the applause subsided, the conductor, Kurt Frederick, led the musicians in an encore performance.

Other prominent composers have written compositions inspired by either the patriotism of war or as a reaction against the effects of armed conflict. The following select list is a guide for those wishing to pursue further studies in music related to war: Benjamin Britten, *War Requiem* (1961); Aaron Copland, *Symphony No. 3* (1944–1946); Roy Harris, *When Johnny Comes Marching Home* (1935); Darius Milhaud, *Ode pour les morts des guerres* (1963); Krzysztof Penderecki, *Polish Requiem* (1959–1960) and *Threnody for the Victims of Hiroshima* (1960); Michael Tippett, *A Child of Our Time* (1942); and Randall Thompson, *Testament of Freedom* (1945).

*M*usical Encounter

John Philip Sousa and the Military Band in the United States

*W*hen John Philip Sousa (1854–1932) assumed the leadership of the U.S. Marine Band in 1880, he joined an organization that had already been in existence for eighty-two years. On July 11, 1798, President John Adams signed a bill that paved the way for an official band for the United States. This band, which Thomas Jefferson later called "The President's Own," was composed of thirty-two fife and drum players and a drum major and a fife major. It was the first professional band supported by the U.S. government. This new band saw active duty during the French Naval War, and some of its original members were killed aboard warships. Their first public concert was held in Philadelphia for the Independence Day celebration of 1800. Shortly thereafter, the U.S. Marine Band relocated to Washington, the new site of the nation's capital. It performed for Thomas Jefferson's inaugural in 1801, and it has performed for every president's inaugural ceremony since.

Over the centuries, the instrumentation of the military band has expanded to include a full complement of woodwinds, brass, and percussion instruments, but, more importantly, the function of military bands has also changed. Historically, bands were used for recruiting men into service, to inspire troops into battle, and even to support them during the conflict. Music was part of the noise of war; it aroused excitement, it caused the soldiers to move together and think together, and it gave the men focus. In modern times, military bands assume ceremonial roles and play music designed to enhance the image of a dedicated, well-trained body of men and women ready to answer the call of their country when the need arises. The U.S. Army, for example, advertises that military music supports concepts of loyalty, duty, respect, selflessness, and honor in the service of one's country. The many military bands affiliated with all branches of the armed forces perform concerts throughout the country and are present whenever patriotic ritual is called for.

As the new millennium begins, the music of war, represented in the United States by over eighty different service bands, has become the music of ceremony and cultural enrichment. It can be found wherever the military presence of the United States is felt, and it serves as a constant reinforcement for feelings of patriotism in a peacetime culture.

The composer whose name is most frequently linked to the military band is John Philip Sousa, the "March King." When he was thirteen, his father enlisted him as an apprentice in the U.S. Marine Band after he had tried to run away to join a circus band. John Philip was well acquainted with band music, for his father, John Antonio Sousa, had been a trombonist in the U.S. Marine Band. Furthermore, the young Sousa had studied voice, violin, piano, flute, cornet, baritone horn, trombone, and alto horn beginning shortly after his sixth birthday.

After his discharge from the U.S. Marines in 1875, John Philip joined several touring groups as a violinist; he also conducted Broadway performances of the Gilbert and Sullivan hit of the day, H.M.S. Pinafore. However, his fame and fortune were won as a band leader.

Sousa assumed the leadership of the U.S. Marine Band in 1880, and over a period of twelve years, he established the reputation of this ensemble as one of the nation's finest musical organizations. His first experiences with this group were unpleasant, for he found the band to be a demoralized collection of tired musicians waiting for their discharge. Shortly after his appointment, he ordered what he considered the best of music literature of the time—including music by Berlioz, Grieg, Wagner, and Tchaikovsky—and he conducted rigorous rehearsals. His demanding performance standards resulted in the early retirement of many of the older, unenthusiastic players (in fact, Sousa was able to convince the U.S. Marine headquarters to make special arrangements for the early discharge of these musicians), and he began to build his improved ensemble with only thirty-three men.

Soon, Sousa's U.S. Marine Band was giving regular concerts at the White House, at the Marine barracks, and on the Capitol's grounds. The band's marching discipline was strict, their marching tempos were brisk, and they became the ideal embodiment of military pomp and circumstance. Sousa's fame as a conductor was

Portrait of John Philip Sousa, band master and composer of popular marches at the turn of the century. c. 1900. Source: Archive Photos.

enhanced as his reputation for composition grew. His most successful genre was the march, and many of his 135 marches quickly set the standards for military marches. (Sousa also wrote fifteen operettas, eleven suites for instruments, seventy songs, twelve compositions for trumpet and drums, and many other works, including 322 arrangements and transcriptions.) Some of his most famous marches bear patriotic or military themes: *Stars and Stripes Forever, The Black Horse Troop, El Capitan, The Gallant Seventh,* and *Semper Fidelis.*

In 1892, Sousa left the U.S. Marine Band to form a professional touring band of his own. He first called it "The New Marine Band," but he later had to change the name when government officials suggested that its title too closely paralleled the U.S. Marine Band. When Patrick Gilmore, a famous showman and band director, died in 1892, Sousa hired some of the world's best-known instrumentalists, former members of the Gilmore Band, to join his group, including famous cornet virtuoso Herbert L. Clarke and saxophonist E. A. Lefebre.

During its long tenure, the Sousa band made many appearances across the United States, and it toured Europe on three separate occasions (in 1900, 1901, and 1905). In 1910, Sousa expanded his tour horizons to include a greater part of the world: Great Britain, the Canary Islands, South Africa, Australia, New Zealand, the Fiji Islands, Hawaii, and Canada.

Sousa remained an avid showman, conductor, composer, and patriot throughout his life. During World War I, he enlisted as a lieutenant in the U.S. Naval Reserve—at age sixty-two—and he served at a salary of one dollar a month. After the war, he was a strong advocate for music education; he received several honorary degrees and championed composer's rights. He died at age seventy-seven, shortly after having conducted his most famous composition *Stars and Stripes Forever.*

POPULAR SONGS IN TWENTIETH-CENTURY AMERICA: THE TWO SIDES OF WAR

Schoenberg's *A Survivor from Warsaw* and Vaughan William's *Dona Nobis Pacem* represent powerful commentaries about war and peace in the modern concert music repertoire. Art music composers were not the only creative artists to write on this subject, however; composers of popular songs also found a voice in communicating about and reflecting on the glories and atrocities of war in their works. In Chapter 13, we underscored the importance of Tin Pan Alley, the twentieth-century publishing industry, as a voice for the music of romance. Although Tin Pan Alley composers most commonly focused their attention on love, their works also show a sensitivity to world situations and to the social and political environment of their time.

With the advent of the two twentieth-century World Wars, it was only natural that tunesmiths would turn their efforts toward songs of war. Some were patriotic songs that inspired participation, showed support for the boys in uniform, and rallied the country to the cause, while others spoke of the loneliness of deferred love relationships, of a mother's worry about her son's going off to battle, and of death. During World War I, songs such as *America, Here's My Boy, After the War Is Over, All Aboard for Home Sweet Home,* and *He Sleeps Beneath the Soil of France* expressed through music the intense personal feelings connected to war; they also reflected a time when popular songs were highly sentimental.

The Second World War gave rise to several hit songs: *The Caissons Go Rolling Along* (published first in 1921 but revived in a 1945 edition), *Comin' in on a Wing and a Prayer, Bell Bottom Trousers, Rally 'Round the Flag, Boys, Rosie the Riveter* (a tribute to the working women of the war effort), *You're a Grand Old Flag,* and *God Bless America.* These popular songs inspired patriotism and became part of the American vernacular song tradition. In 1942, Irving Berlin (composer of "God Bless America") wrote the Broadway musical *This Is the Army.* His tunes soon became familiar to millions of Americans. And his tune *White Christmas*—now a standard song of the Christmas season—was very popular with American soldiers around the world who were spending the season away from home.

The cover of George M. Cohan's *Over There,* illustrated by Norman Rockwell, depicts four soldiers singing around a campfire. This song was so successful that other songwriters wrote tunes using the phrase "over there" in the titles (such as *Say a Prayer for the Boys Over There*) in the hope of sharing some of the success of Cohan's best-seller.

Verse 1:

Johnnie get your gun, get your gun,
　　get your gun,
Take it on the run, on the run,
　　on the run;
Hear them calling you and me;
　　Ev'ry son of liberty.
Hurry right away, no delay, go today,
Make your daddy glad, to have had
　　such a lad,
Tell your sweetheart not to pine,
To be proud her boy's in line
(Refrain) Over there, over there,
　　　　Send the word, send the
　　　　　word over there,
　　　　That the Yanks are coming,
　　　　　the Yanks are coming,
　　　　The drums rumtumming
　　　　　ev'ry where.

Verse 2:

Johnnie get your gun, get your gun,
　　get your gun,
Johnnie show the Hun, you're a
　　son-of-a-gun,
Hoist the flag and let her fly,
　　Like true heroes do or die.
Pack your little kit, show your grit, do your bit,
Soldiers to the ranks from the towns
　　and the tanks,
Make your mother proud of you,
And to liberty be true,
(Refrain) So prepare, say a pray'r,
　　　　Send the word, send the
　　　　　word to beware,
　　　　We'll be over, we're coming
　　　　　over,
　　　　And we won't be back 'till it's
　　　　　over over there.[10]

Prior to the Vietnam conflict in the mid-1960s, popular songs in America relating to wars avoided statements of political dissent. One exception was *I Didn't Raise My Boy To Be a Soldier* from 1915. The words to this song, in spite of their dated romantic sentiment, foreshadow expressions heard later in the century:

(Verse 1)　　Ten million soldiers to the war have gone,
　　　　　　Who may never return again.
　　　　　Ten million mothers' hearts must break
　　　　　　For the one who died in vain.
　　　　　Head bowed down in sorrow in her lonely years,
　　　　　　I heard a mother murmur thro' her tears:

(Refrain)   I didn't raise my boy to be a soldier,
   I brought him up to be my pride and joy,
Who dares to place a musket on his shoulder,
   To shoot some other mother's darling boy?
Let nations arbitrate their future troubles,
   It's time to lay the sword and gun a-way,
There'd be no war today, if mothers all would say,
   "I didn't raise my boy to be a soldier."

(Verse 2)   What victory can cheer a mother's heart,
   When she looks at her blighted home?
What victory can bring her back
   All she cared to call her own.
Let each mother answer in the year to be,
   Remember that my boy belongs to me![11]

During the 1960s, people in the United States were brought to an increased awareness of the power of music when protest songs played a major role in expressing and shaping public opinion about the presence of the U.S. armed forces in Vietnam. Led by singers/songwriters such as Bob Dylan (b. 1941), whose songs protesting nuclear weapons (*Hard Rain's a-Gonna Fall* and *Talking World War III Blues*) as well as songs about other war-related issues (*The Times They Are a-Changin'* and *Blowin' in the Wind*), these protest songs were beginning to gain an audience and became hits on popular music charts in America.

The urban folk movement of the 1960s was distinguished by a flourish of original songs, often composed by the performers themselves; many sang the songs of Dylan or of

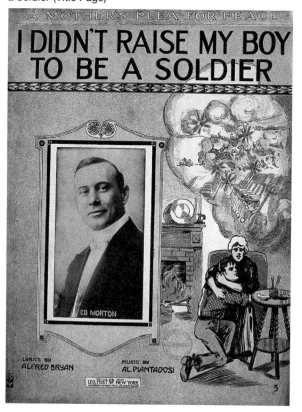

Alfred Bryan\Al Piantadosi,
I Didn't Raise My Boy To Be a Soldier (Title Page)

Pete Seeger. Groups such as the Kingston Trio, the Staple Singers, Simon and Garfunkel, and the Chad Mitchell Trio produced recordings based on their personal experiences and observations. Figuring prominently among these were songs of peace.

Joan Baez, a contemporary and a close companion of Dylan who had helped him become established as a performer, became the leading musical voice during the anti-war campaigns of the mid-1960s and early 1970s. Baez came to the peace movement as a well-established folk singer; her debut at the 1958 Newport Jazz Festival began a whirlwind rise to prominence that resulted in recording contracts and major concert engagements. By 1963, she performed before an audience of 20,000 at the Hollywood Bowl. In 1964, Baez, an international star, turned her efforts toward anti-war activities; millions heard her voice of protest as they listened to her music.

In December 1972, Joan Baez made a controversial trip to Hanoi, where she found herself in the center of bombing raids. During her visit, she exchanged songs with the Vietnamese and visited a POW camp. Upon her return to the United States, she recorded the album *Where Are You Now, My Son?* which contained vivid images and a strong commentary on the Vietnamese conflict. The last verse of the title song illustrates the intensity of her music:

10/16/67, Oakland, CA:
Singer Joan Baez arrested at
a drafting demonstration.
© Bettmann / CORBIS.
ID # BWE061000.

Oh, the people of the shelters what a gift you've given me
To smile at me and quietly let me share your agony
And I can only bow in utter humbleness and ask
Forgiveness and forgiveness for the things we've brought to pass.
The black pajama'd culture that we tried to kill with pellet holes
And the rows of tiny coffins we have paid for with our souls
Have built a spirit seldom seen in women and in men
And the White Flower of Bach Mai will surely blossom once again.
I've heard that the war is done
Then where are you now, my son?[12]

AN AUSTRALIAN SOLDIER'S SONG

One tune coming from a time when war songs regularly spoke more of patriotism than of protest is *And the Band Played Waltzing Matilda*, an Australian folk song that was recently arranged for men's chorus by Eric Bogle. Its text is based on the battle of Suvla Bay, Turkey, which took place on August 6, 1915, and it describes the horrors both of death and of being a maimed survivor of war. The reference to the then-popular tune *Waltzing Matilda* alludes to the underlying indifference of the general populace to the plight of the soldier. The "business as usual" attitude is interrupted by the poignant commentary of the soldier, injured for life, who must live with his memories as he wonders who else will remember the lessons of Australia's disastrous military effort in Turkey.

The folk song unfolds in the now-familiar pattern of A-A-B-A, this time with a refrain. The third line (B) of the text consistently carries the most intense line of each verse; the melodic line also represents the climax, for its phrase begins on a higher pitch, thereby drawing attention to itself. The arranger of this piece also uses an additive principle to deepen the meaning of the poem, by first having a solo state the first verse and refrain, and then adding the chorus for the following material. An excerpt from the popular tune *Waltzing Matilda* serves as an appropriate ending for the arrangement.

Listening Guide 71

And the Band Played Waltzing Matilda
Australian folk song

Eric Bogle, composer/arranger
Recorded by Chor Leoni.
Diane Loomer, conductor
CD No. 4, Track 18 (4:50)

When I was a young man I carried a pack, and I lived the free life of a rover.
From Murray's green banks to the dusty outback, I waltzed my Matilda all over.
Then in 1915 the Country said "Son, there's no time for rovin', there's work to be done,"
So they gave me a tin hat and gave me a gun, and they sent me away to the war.
    And the band played Waltzin' Matilda as the ship pulled away from the quay,
    And amidst all the cheers, the flag waving, and tears, we sailed off for Galipoli.

How well I remember that terrible day when the blood stained the sand and the water.
And how, in that hell they called "Suvla Bay" we were butchered like lambs at the slaughter.
Johnny Turk he was waitin', he primed himself well, he showered us with bullets and rained
    us with shell;
And in ten minutes flat he'd blown us to hell, nearly blew us right back to Australia.
    And the band played Waltzin' Matilda as we stopped to bury the slain.
    We buried ours and the Turks buried theirs, then we started all over again.

They collected the crippled, the sounded, and maimed, and they shipped us back home to
    Australia.
The armless, the legless, the blind and insane; all the brave wounded heroes of Suvla.
And when our ship pulled into Circular Quay, and I looked at the place where my legs used to be
I thanked God there was nobody waitin' for me, to grieve, and to mourn, and to pity.
    And the band played Waltzin' Matilda as they carried us down the gangway,
    But nobody cheered, they just stood there and stared and then turned their faces away.

And now every April I sit on my porch and I watch the parade pass before me,
And I see my old comrades how proudly they march, reliving old dreams and old glories.
But the old men march slowly, their bones stiff and sore, tired old men from a tired old war,
And the young people ask "What are they marchin' for?" And I ask myself the same question.
    And the band played Waltzin' Matilda, and the old men they answered the call.
    But year by year the old men disappear, soon no one will march there at all.[13]

To Consider

1. In this long, narrative ballad, how does the composer draw you into the story? What musical techniques are used to capture your ear?
2. In each verse, the line "And the band played *Waltzin' Matilda*" returns. When you hear this in the second verse, does this device of repetition establish your anticipation for future verses? What happens to your sense of musical structure when you hear it again in the third verse?
3. What is the general mood of the poem, and how does the composer support this mood with his musical setting?

SUMMARY

In this chapter you have seen how musical expressions related to war can range from a subtle statement of a culture's attitudes toward warfare (such as in Dufay's *L'homme armé* Mass setting) to a blatant statement representing the horror of war activities (such as Schoenberg's *A Survivor from Warsaw*). Although our musical settings represent a 500-year time span, they reinforce the fact that connecting ideas about war to music is not a recent phenomenon.

The musical references to war found in these works can provide us with some clues about the attitudes and compositional practices of composers in various periods of history, however. There can be no doubt that statements from the twentieth century are stronger than those during Franz Joseph Haydn's time. The musical statements that you encountered here from the past century, whether lyrical and sentimental or forceful and grotesque in design, speak strongly for the composers and cultures that the composers represent.

It is through the medium of music that poets and composers speak poignant messages of social consciousness. The communication symbols of words are always intensified when coupled with the sounds of music.

KEY TERMS

Council of Trent
oliphant
troubadours
trouvères

A P P E N D I X A

Glossary of Musical Terms

absolute music: music that does not depend on outside literary references or physical functions for its existence (also called **abstract music**).

abstract music: see **absolute music.**

accelerando: a gradual increase in the tempo or speed of the basic pulse.

accent: a slight dynamic stress on a note.

accidentals: the process of altering a pitch by adding a sharp (which raises the pitch one-half step) or a flat (which lowers the pitch by one-half step). A natural sign cancels earlier accidentals.

acid rock: a style of rock music, popular in the 1960s and 1970s, characterized by extremely loud dynamics and piercing timbres.

acoustical instrument: musical instruments that initially generate sound without the aid of electronic amplification.

adagio: a common designation for a very slow tempo.

aerophones: musical instruments that generate sound by air being blown through them.

aesthetics: a branch of philosophy dealing with the nature of beauty. In music, the term often relates to the interplay between the emotional and intellectual stimuli that the listener experiences upon hearing a composition.

afterbeat: the weak pulse in a meter (such as beats 2 and 4 in a 4/4 measure).

allegro: an indication designating a fast tempo.

allemande: a Renaissance dance in duple time.

alternative music: recordings that fall into this category of music are typified by songs with lyrics that can be understood upon first hearing; a general evenness of dynamic level; and which represent a relatively conservative mode of social expressions.

alto: in vocal writing, the alto is the voice range immediately below the soprano.

American musical: popular musical theatre in America, characterized by a mixture of spoken and sung dialogue.

andante: literally, "walking"; a tempo indication calling for a moderately slow pulse.

aria: a type of song, often characterized by emotional content, in which the singer often has an opportunity to display either advanced vocal technique and virtuosity or extreme lyricism.

arpeggio: the linear presentation of the notes of a chord.

art song: poems set to music for voice and accompaniment (commonly referred to by the German designation, **lieder**).

ayre: a stophic song in simple homophonic style.

backbeat: the practice of accenting the after beats, or weak beats, of a measure.

ballad: a general term for a narrative song.

ballade: (1) an extended poetic and musical form employed by trouvères in medieval times; (2) a solo character piece for piano often in ternary (A-B-A) form used by nineteenth-century composers of piano music.

bass: the lowest voice range; the lowest range of musical instruments.

bass clef: a designation of pitches on the staff in which the bass note "F" is found on the fourth line.

bassoon: a double reed instrument capable of playing in the tenor and bass voice ranges.

beat: the pulse of music.

biniou: a bagpipe found in Brittany.

blues: a form of jazz that developed out of plantation songs expressing the everyday problems of Negro slaves, which eventually evolved into a musical pattern commonly characterized by a chord progression occurring over a 12-bar phrase. Blues are either played or sung:

Measures: 1 - 2 - 3 - 4;   5-6-7-8;   9 - 10-----11 -12
Chords: I---------   IV - I   V - VI - V - I - -
         (Or: I - IV - I - - -)

brass quintet: a chamber group usually consisting of two trumpets, a horn, a trombone, and a tuba.

cadence: the melodic lines and/or chord progressions that either end a phrase, section, or composition.

cantata: a composition for a small choir, soloists, or an instrumental ensemble. Consisting of five to seven movements (called numbers), the cantata was a popular genre in the Lutheran Church in Germany during the Baroque Era. It was cultivated extensively by J. S. Bach and his contemporaries.

cantus firmus: literally, "fixed song," the cantus firmus is a pre-existing melody that was used as a melodic foundation for a sacred polyphonic composition during the Renaissance and Baroque eras. Popular sources for canti firmi were Gregorian chants in the Catholic tradition and chorales in the Lutheran tradition. During the fifteenth and sixteenth centuries, it was also popular to use secular tunes (such as "L'Homme Armé") in polyphonic Masses.

Celtic music: folk music coming from Ireland, the Scottish Highlands, Wales, and Brittany.

chance music: a compositional technique originating in the mid-twentieth century in which the composer uses random operations to determine pitches and other parameters of the composition (made famous by John Cage).

chanson: French for "song." A form of chamber vocal music popular in France during the Renaissance, typically written for four voice parts, with careful attention to the text.

chanting: the singing of a single-line melody, without harmony, counterpoint and, originally, without the accompaniment of instruments.

character piece: a generic description for a large variety of relatively short compositions mostly written for the piano, which may appear under various titles (such as Scherzi, Album Blätter, Impromptus, Études, etc.). Character pieces were popular in the nineteenth century and were cultivated by Schubert, Chopin, Schumann, Brahms, and their contemporaries.

chorales: Lutheran hymns. The term is also used as a synonym for choruses and for an organization of singers.

chorale preludes: organ works based on Lutheran hymns.

chord: The simultaneous sounding of three or more notes. In its more conservative context, chords refer to harmonic units that are primarily third related but that may have additional notes of varying consonance or dissonance.

chord progression: a pattern of chords played consecutively.

chordophone: instrument in which the sound is produced by strings resonating.

chorus: (1) a choral ensemble; (2) a section in a composite work, such as the cantata and oratorio in which the chorus sings; (3) a performance practice in jazz where all musicians join together to play or sing the main refrain; (4) a refrain.

chromatic scale: an arrangement of pitches consecutively in half steps.

chromaticism: intervallic relationships of half steps, or semitones. The original meaning of the term refers to color ("chroma").

classic rock: rock 'n' roll emanating from the 1960s and early 1970s.

clef sign: a symbol that indicates the location of a specific pitch on the staff. With the use of clef signs, it is possible to notate a wide range of pitches in a readable format. The treble clef (𝄞) encircles the pitch "G"; the bass clef (𝄢) locates the pitch "F" on the staff.

coloratura: in eighteenth- and nineteenth-century operatic tradition, coloratura signifies a voice type that is capable of singing rapid scales, trills, arpeggios, and other ornaments that are freely used in virtuoso arias.

comic opera: English comic opera, characterized by a mixture of spoken and sung dialogue.

composer's style: the manner in which a given composer utilizes the basic parameter of music, such as melody, harmony, rhythm, texture, form, dynamics, orchestration, and so on.

composite sound: a fundamental pitch and several overtones.

compound duple meter: 6/8 meter.

compound meter: a metrical arrangement in which the basic pulse and primary pulse have differing subdivisions.

compound triple meter: 9/8 meter.

concert band: an ensemble consisting of complete families of woodwinds, brass, and percussion instruments. The concert band is popular in public schools, colleges, and universities throughout the United States.

concert choir: a large group of singers commonly organized into sections of soprano, alto, tenor, and bass.

concertino: the designation for the solo group of instruments in a baroque concerto grosso.

concerto: an extended composition for a solo instrument and an orchestra. Classical concertos frequently are made up of three movements.

concerto grosso: a form of instrumental music in the Baroque Era that features a small group of solo instruments (concertino) pitted against the ensemble as a whole (ripieno).

conjunct (melody): a melody whose pitches are connected by small, intervallic units.

consonance: a term used to signify an agreeable effect caused by certain intervals. Music from the Western European/American traditions commonly considers music arranged in thirds (triads) to be consonant.

contemporary Christian music: a musical expression that uses lyrics and titles drawn from religious topics and expresses them in the modern music of rock and pop styles. Its appeal is to the young, its audience mostly in the United States.

contour: the shape of music, as in the shape of melody. A disjunct contour designates a pitch arrangement with wide intervals; a conjunct contour designates a succession of pitches that is organized with narrower intervals.

Council of Trent: a series of conferences held in the middle of the sixteenth century, where the practice of using secular songs in the Mass was discussed and eventually banned from future compositions intended for use in the church.

counterpoint: the simultaneous presentation of two or more independent musical lines.

courante: a dance that originated in the sixteenth century, characterized by a running or gliding step. The courante became part of the Baroque suite. It is usually in a moderate tempo and in a 3/2 or 6/4 meter.

crescendo: a gradual increase in volume.

cubism: an artistic movement in the early twentieth century that emphasized abstract structure at the expense of other pictorial elements. Often several perspectives of the subject were presented simultaneously, producing a unique fragmentation of that subject.

cumbia: a Caribbean rhythm of African origin that descended from a nineteenth-century slave dance. Women dancing the cumbia traditionally dress in long flowered shirts with brightly colored shirts, or white skirts with bright red fringes and ribbons.

cycles per second (cps): a measurement of the number of oscillations per second that a tone-producing body makes when emitting a specific pitch. Specific pitches of the chromatic scale are identified by acousticians as having a designated number of cycles per second, or frequency. Thus A = 440 cps (or its multiples, depending on the octave); C = 512 cps and so on.

cyclical melody: the use of one melody or motive in various movements of a multimovement work.

da capo: a notational marking directing the performer to repeat the beginning of the work (literally, "to the head").

dada: a twentieth-century movement in art and literature based on deliberate irrationality and the negation of conventional artistic values and standards.

decrescendo: a gradual decrease in volume.

diatonic organization: a melody that is fundamentally stepwise (extremely conjunct) in nature.

disjunct (melody): a melody that is characterized by large, intervallic leaps.

dissonance: a term used to signify a disagreeable effect caused by intervals such as those of the second or seventh.

Dixieland jazz: a jazz style of instrumental music that originated in New Orleans, characterized by music in duple meter and involving improvisation on melodic and harmonic material played by a small ensemble (frequently trumpet, clarinet, trombone, saxophone, tuba, banjo, and percussion).

dominant: the designation of a chord built on the fifth scale step of the tonic key (the V chord). Its most common resolution is to the tonic (or the I chord).

dotted rhythms: basic rhythms that are altered in length by a dot. The dot increases the duration of a note by one-half of its value.

doubling: a compositional practice in which a melody is presented by two different performing entities (such as voice and violin).

drone: a continually sounding pitch (usually in a low pitch range).

duple meter: an organization of pulses in even beats (2, 4, etc.).

duration: (1) the rhythmic value of a note; (2) the length of a composition.

dynamic markings: symbols that indicate the relative loudness or softness of music.

elements of music: the basic parameters of music, such as melody, harmony, meter, rhythm, texture, and form.

English anthem: a form of sacred choral music emanating from the Church of England in the Renaissance Era, characterized by four to six voice parts, an English text, and a mixture of homorhythmic and polyphonic textures.

English madrigal: a form of secular chamber vocal music from the Elizabethan era. A striking feature of this compositional style is the clarity of the individual voice parts. Whether the texture is woven with independent voice parts or is presented in homorhythmic chords, one can easily hear each part.

episodes: contrapuntal sections of texture in the fugue that do not contain the subject or main fugue theme.

exposition: a section in the sonata-allegro form in which the main themes, or subjects, are first presented. The term is also used to describe the part of the fugue where the subject is stated.

expressionism: a theory and practice in the arts that seeks to emphasize and elaborate on the subjective emotions that the art arouses in participants.

falsetto: an unnaturally high-pitched register, especially in the male voice, which allows the singer to extend the normal range of the voice.

figured bass: a musical shorthand to notate the outside parts of the music. The melody was notated on one musical staff, while the bass line was written on the lower staff along with symbols that indicated the chords. Harpsichord players reading this music partially improvised by adding chord notes of the chords, as suggested by the figured bass system.

fixed idea (idée fixe): a cyclical musical gesture (usually a melody) that recurs throughout a piece of programmatic music linked to either a character or an idea drawn from a literary reference.

flamenco: a song and dance style that grew out of a centuries-old gypsy culture. Flamenco traditions often include finger snapping, hand clapping, and foot stomping in complicated rhythmic patterns and changing accents.

flat: lowering a pitch by one-half step.

flute: a woodwind instrument in which the tone is produced either by blowing over an open hole (as in the modern flute) or into a beak (such as the recorder and other whistles).

folk music: traditional, vernacular music that originates from the common people. In many instances, it is not composed by formally trained composers (although that possibility exists), but it often grows anonymously from people who communicate their everyday emotions, rituals, and pleasures in song.

form: musical structure created by the organization of the various components of the composition.

four-part harmony: a common term in music that is organized for four voice parts—soprano, alto, tenor, and bass.

French chanson: a form of chamber vocal music popular in France during the Renaissance, typically written for four voice parts, with careful attention to the text.

fugue: a form or style of music characterized by imitative entrances of a melodic subject, (exposition), sections of free counterpoint (episodes), and often a section toward the end in which the imitative entrances of the subject are overlapped in short succession (stretto). The fugue first became popular in the Baroque Era and has remained one of the principal structures of contrapuntal music.

futurism: a movement in the arts, begun in the early nineteenth century in Italy, which sought to give formal expression to the energy and impetus created by the mechanization of culture at the time.

gaita: a Spanish bagpipe, traditionally played at weddings and feasts.

Gebrauchsmusik: a term coined by Paul Hindemith (1895–1963) to indicate music that was performable by a majority of musicians. Hindemith championed performable music to counter a trend toward very difficult music in early twentieth-century music. Literally, Gebrauchsmusik means "music for use."

genre: a French term that has gained universal popularity, indicating the type or form of composition (i.e., symphony, opera, motet, cantata, etc.).

gigue: a dance movement popular in the Renaissance and Baroque eras, characterized by a fast tempo and compound meters such as 6/8 or 9/8. The gigue is part of a musical suite.

glissando: "sliding" from one note to the next as opposed to beginning each note at its exact frequency.

gospel choir: a group of musicians dedicated to singing arrangements of gospel music.

gottan: a stringed instrument, popular in traditional Japanese music, which is plucked or strummed (also called **shamisen**).

grand staff: the system of lines and spaces upon which pitch is commonly notated. The grand staff is a combination of two staffs—one containing the treble clef and the other containing the bass clef.

half step: the interval between one note and its adjacent note within the chromatic scale.

hard rock: mainstream rock, coming out of the 1970s. Its driving backbeat is reinforced by high-tech electronic amplification, often reaching the levels of intentional distortion.

harmonic minor scale: a minor scale in which the third note is flatted and the seventh pitch is raised.

harmonic rhythm: regularity of chord progression.

harmonics: overtones or partials of a fundamental pitch.

harmony: the simultaneous sounding of pitches.

heterophony: the practice of presenting two variants of the same melody simultaneously.

hip-hop: a movement that broadly describes the New York City, mostly black, pop scene (especially rap) and includes break dancing, body popping, electronic sounds, and modern graffiti.

homophonic texture: a type of writing in which one predominant melody, or part, is supported either by an accompaniment of chords or by chord configurations.

homophony: music that employs a homophonic texture in which one predominant melody is supported by a figuration of chordal accompaniment.

homorhythmic texture: a type of rhythmic organization in which the various parts or voices play or sing identical rhythms simultaneously. A common example of homorhythmic texture is the American hymn, where soprano, alto, tenor, and bass have the same rhythms.

hymn: a song in praise of God.

Hz: (Hertz): a measurement of the the number of vibrations, or cycles per second (cps), of a pitch. Also called frequency, this common designation for this unit of measurement in cycles per second is named after Heinrich Hertz (1857–1894), the physicist whose theories led to the development of the wireless telegraph and the radio.

idée fixe: a cyclical musical gesture (usually a melody) that recurs throughout a piece of programmatic music that is linked either to a character or an idea drawn from a literary reference (often associated with the nineteenth-century French composer Hector Berlioz).

idiophones: music instruments in which sound is produced by striking or scraping on the instruments (commonly known as "percussion" instruments).

imitation: the repetition of a melodic gesture (subject or phrase) in close succession to another part of a contrapuntal texture.

impressionism: a movement in art in which objects were represented by the subtle use of colors and brush strokes that simulated actual reflected light. In music, the term designates a style in which subtleties are created by the **planing** of chords in parallel motion, the melding of rhythms and phrases into each other, and the blurring of formal schemes.

indeterminate music: produced by chance operations (see **chance music**).

intensity: the volume level in music.

interval: the distance between two notes. Major intervals are those derived from the major scale built on the lowest note—with the exception of the intervals of the fourth, fifth, and octave, which are by tradition called "perfect." Minor intervals are those derived from half steps or semitones—

chromatic pitches that are not part of the major scale based on the lowest note of the interval.

intonation: the manner of producing musical tones in relation to an established system of a musical scale. Musicians often speak of "playing in tune," meaning, "playing with the correct intonation."

Introit: a section of the Catholic Mass containing the entrance chant.

inversion: in serial, or twelve-tone music, an inversion is a permutation of the original tone row in which the intervals of the inverted row (or set) move in the exact opposite direction from that of the original tone row (either up or down).

jongleurs: minstrels who, during the Middle Ages, were employed in a feudal household.

jukebox: a coin-operated record player.

key: the central harmonic focal point (tonal center) in a section or a composition.

key signature: a symbol placed at the beginning of a musical line that indicates the pitches that are to be altered chromatically.

Klangfarbenmelodie: a twentieth-century compositional technique in which linear continuity is achieved through the constant changing of timbres. Literally, "tone-color-melody."

koto: a long zither used in the traditional classical music of Japan. The koto is a type of chordophone with numerous strings stretched over a basically flat, box-like body. It also has bridges that can be adjusted along the body of the instrument to tune it; the player plucks the string on one side of the bridge while pressing on the string on the other side of bridge, thereby causing slight changes in intonation.

layering: a compositional device whereby several musical gestures are presented simultaneously.

ledger lines: short lines added either above or below the staff to extend the normal range of the five lines and four spaces.

leitmotif: a musical gesture (melodic segment, harmonic progression, or rhythm) in music drama that identifies a specific character or emotion (associated with the operas and music dramas of Richard Wagner).

lento: a tempo indication meaning "slow."

lied (lieder): A German indication for art song.

liturgy: a form of public worship ritual. Music often plays a significant role in liturgical worship.

long zither: a type of chordophone with numerous strings stretched over a basically flat, box-like body. The Japanese koto belongs to the family of long zithers.

lute: a stringed instrument having a pear-shaped body, a long, fretted neck, and a vaulted back.

lyrical: a style of music that describes smoothly flowing, often song-like musical gestures.

madrigal groups: small choral ensembles whose main repertoire stems from singing music of the Renaissance and other chamber choir music.

major intervals: major intervals are those derived from the major scale of the bottom note—with the exception of the intervals of the fourth, fifth, and octave, which are by tradition called "perfect."

major scale: a linear organization of pitches according to the following intervals: T, T, S, T, T, T, S (T = tone or whole step; S = semitone or half step).

major second: a note separated from another note by one whole step, or tone.

mandala: a graphic symbol of the universe, used by Buddhists in religious ritual.

Mass: the form of worship in the Roman Catholic Church that culminates in the Eucharist (or communion) ritual.

measure: the notes and rests occurring between two vertical bars in musical notation.

meistersingers: a member of one of the German guilds in the fourteenth, fifteenth, and sixteenth centuries dedicated to music and poetry.

melisma: a melodic segment in vocal music where several notes are sung to one syllable of text.

melodic sequence: the repetition of a melodic segment at a different pitch level.

melody: the consecutive (linear) ordering of pitches.

membranophones: instruments whose sound is made from hitting a skin or other membrane stretched over a resonating drum or frame.

merengue: a dance, popular in Haiti and the Domincan Republic, characterized by a stiff-legged limping step and complex rhythmic structures.

meter: the organization of pulses into regular groups.

meter signature: the notational symbol that indicates the measuring of time and the relative rhythmic values of the notes in music.

Methodism: a religious denomination of Christianity founded in the eighteenth century by Charles and John Wesley.

minimalism: a theory and practice in the art of using the fewest elements to create the greatest effect.

minnesingers: German lyric poets and musicians in the twelfth, thirteenth, and fourteenth centuries.

minor intervals: minor intervals are those derived from the minor scale of the bottom note. This term is used to designate lowered intervals of the 2nd, 3rd, 6th, and 7th, and their octave doublings.

minor scale: a consecutive ordering of pitches according to the following formula of tones (whole steps) and semitones (half steps): TSTTSTT. (The natural minor scale is shown here; other variants—namely the harmonic and the melodic forms—are frequently used, but all forms of the minor scale are characterized by a semitone between the second and third notes of the scale.)

minor second: a note separated from another note by one-half step, or semi-tone.

minor triad: a chord of three tones consisting of a root, a tone a minor third above the root, and a tone a perfect fifth above the root.

minuet: a dance type in triple meter, found in the suite and as an internal movement in multimovement forms of the Classical era, particularly the music of Haydn, Mozart, and their contemporaries.

minuet and trio form: a three-part musical structure found in symphonies of the Classical Era in triple meter and moderate tempo.

mixed meter: metrical groupings which change frequently in a given composition.

moderato: a tempo indication meaning moderate.

modernism: a movement in the early twentieth century that sought to repeal the aesthetic codes of the Romantic Era by introducing new techniques of composition and new expressions.

modes: various organizations of scale patterns, first developed in ancient times by the Greeks and restructured throughout the development of liturgical music in the early Christian (Catholic) Church.

modulation: the shifting from one tonal center to another within a movement or a composition.

monody: single-line music, often accompanied by a keyboard instrument. The term was first coined in the early seventeenth century and formed the basis for early opera.

monophony: music consisting of a single, unaccompanied melodic line.

monophonic texture: a single, unaccompanied musical line.

motive: the smallest recognizable element of a melody. Motives have distinct rhythmic and intervallic properties.

motoric rhythm: music that included a regular beat, where some instruments play the fundamental beat of the music while others play faster notes, subdivisions of the basic pulse. This type of rhythmic organization is commonly found both in the music of the Baroque Era and in jazz.

multiculturalism: an awareness of the many-faceted blend of cultures that makes up various modern social and political structures.

music drama: Richard Wagner's (1813–1883) designation for large operas.

musical: see **American musical.**

musical style: the manner in which the basic parameters of music (such as melody, harmony, rhythm, texture, form, dynamics, orchestration, etc.) are manipulated to form a cohesive whole.

Muzak: a commercial term coined in the 1950s to describe recorded background music.

nationalism: the intentional expression of patriotism in music.

natural: a note that is not altered by an accidental, either by a sharp or a flat.

natural minor scale: a scale with the interval arrangement of T-S-T-T-S-T-T.

neoclassicism: a movement in the music of the early twentieth century in which composers based their works on forms and structures of pre-nineteenth-century music.

noise: a sound without a specific frequency.

Northumbrian small pipes: a bagpipe that is blown by a bellows.

notation: expressing music in written form.

note value: the rhythmic duration of a note.

oboe: a double reed woodwind instrument whose range approximates that of the soprano voice.

octave: the interval between one note and a second pitch created by doubling the frequency of the lower note.

oliphant: a large medieval trumpet made from an elephant's tusk, often ornately carved.

Ondes Martenot: a keyboard instrument with two loops of wire, called ribbons, which emit slurred, sweeping sounds.

opera buffa: comic opera in which both sung and spoken Italian dialogue occurs.

opera comique: comic opera in which both sung and spoken French dialogue occurs.

oratorio: an extended composition for chorus, soloists, and orchestra, first popular in the Baroque Era.

orchestration: (1) the technique of writing for instruments; (2) a list of instruments used in a specific composition.

ordres: the French term for keyboard suites, used by Couperin and his contemporaries.

organum: the earliest form of sacred polyphony in Western civilization, first appearing ca. 840 and continuing with innovative textural and rhythmic features until the thirteenth century. Organum was sacred music used as a substitute for sections of the Gregorian chant in the Catholic Church.

ornamentation: the embellishment of melodies using rapid trills, turns, and other figures.

oud (also known as ud): a plucked lute; one of the most significant stringed instruments in the Arab world.

overtone: a higher pitch produced by and sounded with a fundamental pitch (also called **partial,** or harmonic).

overtone series: the composite acoustic effect produced when a resonating body (such as a string or a vocal chord) creates a pitch, thus producing a fundamental pitch and partials, or overtones.

overtone singing: a technique cultivated by some cultures whereby a single person is able to sing simultaneously a fundamental, guttural melody and a higher melody, thereby producing both a fundamental pitch and its overtones.

overture: a type of single-movement composition that originally was the instrumental work preceding an opera. In the nineteenth century, the concert overture emerged independent from operatic music. In its more recent form, the concert overture frequently begins with an extended introduction in a slow tempo and is followed by a principal section in a faster tempo.

Pa: in Indian classical music, the fifth tone above the fundamental pitch (the **Sa**).

partial: a higher pitch produced by and sounded with a fundamental pitch (also called **overtone,** or harmonic).

paseo: a dance stemming from the Hispanic culture with complex rhythms, played in either a slow or a moderate tempo. The instrumentation accompanying it often uses a guiro (a gourd with notches in it which are scraped by a stick to produce sound).

performance style: appropriate interpretation of music based on a consideration of historical practices contemporary to the music being performed.

performer's style: specific mannerisms and interpretations that the individual performer brings to the performance of music.

performing rights organizations: businesses designed to represent composers and publishers and their right to be compensated when their music is performed in public.

permutation: a technique used in serial composition in the twentieth century, whereby a tone row or series is altered either by stating it in retrograde, inversion, or retrograde inversion. These forms also can be transposed to any level.

phase shifting: a technique of composition involving short musical gestures that are played in unison by several players and, gradually, one or more of the parts begins to change until there are several closely related rhythmic patterns that sound out of sync. This type of music was written by minimalist composers beginning in the 1970s.

phrase structure: logical units of thought in a melody.

piano concerto: a multimovement work for piano solo and orchestra.

piano quintet: a classical instrumental ensemble consisting of a piano and a string quartet.

piano trio: a classical instrumental ensemble consisting of a piano, a cello, and a violin. (In a few instances, woodwind instruments such as the oboe or clarinet are used in place of the violin.)

pitch: the frequency of a sound.

pizzicato: plucking the strings on a violin, viola, cello, or string bass.

planing: the presentation of chords in parallel motion. A technique of composition associated with impressionism in music and the music of Claude Debussy.

polarity of outer voices: a musical feature frequently found in Baroque music which emphasizes the top (soprano) and bottom (bass) parts.

polyphonic Mass: musical settings of selected items of the Catholic Mass for several voice parts (commonly soprano, alto, tenor, and bass).

polyphonic texture: a musical texture in which the various parts move with independent rhythms.

polyphony: music combining more than one individual voice part.

pops orchestra: a symphony whose repertoire is formed from the "light" classics. Groups such as the Boston Pops Orchestra have wide audience appeal and often present music in a less formal atmosphere than found in traditional symphony concerts.

post-modernism: an artistic movement in the arts originating in the mid-twentieth century in which artists and their works exhibit diverse directions and orientations. Plurality—the existence side by side of a range of differing approaches and reactions to modern life and thought—is its major feature.

prelude: (1) a Baroque form of keyboard music designed to be played either before a church service (such as an organ prelude) or a separate form that precedes a fugue; (2) a character piece for piano cultivated in the nineteenth century by Chopin and later used by Debussy.

presto: a tempo indication meaning very fast.

primitivism: a short-lived movement in art that expressed and represented untamed, or native, human conditions. This connection is represented in music through the subject matter that inspires the work and at times through the use of driving, repetitive rhythms that recall primal images.

program music: music that is inspired by and depicts events or stories or other extra-musical material.

program symphony: a symphonic work that describes a story or program, popular in the nineteenth century and cultivated by Hector Berlioz.

progression: the movement from one chord to another in logical succession.

pulse: the basic beat in music. The pulse is used as the basis for all movement in music.

punk rock: a style of rock music, first attached to youthful groups who came to the United States in the wake of the Beatles and the Rolling Stones. Originally identified by greased hair and clothes with padded shoulders, this movement in the 1970s came to represent socially offensive behavior where members blatantly set out to capture the attention of society through their behavior, appearance, noise, and language.

pure sound: a pitch without overtones, or partials. Practically, this is an impossibility, since partials, or overtones, are part of every pitch produced by instruments or voices.

puya: a very fast Hispanic dance that typically uses a combination of accordion, bongos (originating from Africa), and the guiro as accompanying instruments.

quadruple meter: 4/4 meter.

race music: a generic name for all music emanating from the black community in the first decades of twentieth-century America. It was eventually replaced by "rhythm and blues," which was coined in 1949 by the *Billboard* writers. By the middle of the century, rhythm and blues, along with its sister musical form, the spiritual, was making great inroads into the broad musical culture of America.

rāgas: the melodic system in Indian music comprised of several hundred entities, or gestures. A rāga actually includes a variety of concepts in a unique relationship: a selection of pitches, often in a distinctive melodic shape, a system of ornamentation, a basic scale of pitches varying from five to nine notes, and concepts of emotion that relate to the ordering of pitches in the melody.

ragtime: a type of jazz, popular in early twentieth-century North America, which featured "ragged time," or syncopated melodies accompanied by a steady beat pattern. Ragtime music was originally written solely for piano but later was played by ragtime bands. Scott Joplin (1868–1917) is the best-known ragtime composer.

range: a consideration of pitches in the melody from the lowest to the highest.

rap: a type of music originating from the recitation of rhymed street poetry with a strong backbeat.

recapitulation: a section in a composition where original thematic material is repeated. This term relates especially to the sonata-allegro form.

recitative: a type of solo vocal music originating in opera, declamatory and syllabic in nature. The term is used infrequently to describe instrumental music that resembles a vocal recitative (such as the opening of the final movement in Beethoven's *Symphony No. 9*).

recorder: a type of whistle flute, originating in the late Middle Ages, where the sound is produced by blowing over a beak.

referentialism: an aesthetic concept referring to the stimuli that the listener feels—such as emotions, the recollection of memories, feelings, and sensations—upon listening to a specific musical composition.

regular harmonic rhythm: music in which chords change in regular rhythmic patterns (such as on the first beat of each measure).

resonance: the ability or quality of a body to produce a sound by reverberation.

retrograde: a permutation, or altering, of the original tone row in serial music by stating it backwards.

retrograde inversion: a permutation, or altering, of the original tone row in serial music by both stating it backwards and by presenting each interval in the exact opposite direction from that of the original row.

rhythm: (1) the overall sense of movement in music; (2) the temporal value of a note.

rhythm and blues: a musical expression that grew out of the African-American style of the spiritual, gospel, and black

folk music known as the blues, which came to prominence concurrently with the rise of Tin Pan Alley music.

ripieno: the entire ensemble (also called "tutti") in a Baroque concerto grosso.

ritardando: gradually becoming slower.

rondeau: a medieval form of chanson, characterized by the form A-B-a-A-a-b-A-B (capital letters indicate the refrain where both the music and text are repeated).

rondo form: a structure that involves a principal melody that returns each time after contrasting melodies are stated (A-B-A-C-A, etc.). Although several variants of rondo exist, they all have in common a returning refrain.

round: a simple form of imitation where one performer begins a melody and subsequent performers enter at specifically designated time intervals with the same melody in an unaltered form.

Sa: in Indian classical music, the fundamental pitch.

sacred music: music written for worship.

salsa: a commercial name given to a variety of rhythms coming from dances such as the son montuno, mambo, and bomba y plena, the cha-cha, and the guaguanco—all of which are commonly referred to as hot or sensuous.

sarabande: a dance originating in the sixteenth century whose rhythmic patterns and meter formed the basis for a musical movement of the suite. The sarabande is typically in 3/2 meter and is played in a moderately slow tempo.

SATB: the common abbreviation for soprano, alto, tenor, and bass in choral music.

scales: a gradual ordering of pitches, either ascending or descending, which is organized according to specific intervallic patterns.

scat: a practice in jazz singing in which various speech syllables are used to present the sounds of instrumental jazz.

secular music: music not associated with religious worship.

semitone: one-twelfth of an octave, or the interval represented between one note on the piano and its adjacent note.

serialism: a technique of composition developed by Arnold Schoenberg (1874–1951) in which a work is based on a **tone row** or **set.** This fundamental group of pitches most frequently uses all twelve notes of the chromatic scale and is presented, both melodically and harmonically, throughout the work either in its original form, its retrograde, its inversion, or its retrograde inversion. By employing the serial technique, Schoenberg was able to free himself from conventional harmonic organization, and he succeeded in emancipating dissonance from consonance.

series: see **set,** below.

set: a series of pitches drawn from the twelve notes of the chromatic scale upon which serial compositions are founded. (Also called **tone row,** or **series.**)

shamisen: a stringed instrument originating in Japan, having three strings and played by plucking or strumming.

sharp: raising a note by a half step.

Shema Yisroel: also Shmà Israèl (Schema Israel), one of the cornerstone texts of Judaism, an ancient creed of the Jewish faith.

show choir: a group of singers that combines music with choreography to sing arrangements of popular jazz and romantic ballads or cabaret music.

singspiel: the German form of comic opera using both sung and spoken dialogue.

sitar: a lute of North India with a small, pear-shaped body and a long neck.

ska: Hispanic punk incorporating concepts of punk rock and Latin rhythms.

smearing: a performance practice found in spirituals, jazz, and blues, in which the singer or player "slides" into pitches.

solo concerto: a composition with several movements for solo instrument and orchestra.

solo sonata: a composition with several movements for a keyboard instrument, for a solo melodic instrument, or for an instrument with piano accompaniment.

son: a slow dance usually played by an accordion (an instrument originating in Germany) accompanied by bass instruments.

sonata: a composition containing several movements either for keyboard solo or for a melodic instrument and piano accompaniment.

sonata-allegro form: a musical structure emanating from the Classical Era, containing an exposition, where the themes are presented, a development section, where the material is manipulated through various keys, and a recapitulation, where the themes are presented again in their final statement. Many sonata-allegro structures are framed by an introduction and a coda—an ending.

song cycle: a collection of songs related by a common concept and character, designed to form a musical entity.

songs without words: nineteenth-century character pieces for the piano (cultivated mainly by Mendelssohn) that are lyrical in nature and thereby related to the song.

soprano: the highest female voice range.

spiritual: a religious song stemming from the African-American slave tradition. Although melodic sources of the spiritual exhibit both African and European roots, the texts of this large repertoire are highly personalized interpretations of the Christian faith and experience.

staff: a system of lines and spaces that forms the basis for musical notation.

string quartet: (1) a composition in several movements for two violins, viola, and cello; (2) a chamber ensemble consisting of two violins, viola, and cello.

string quintet: usually a string quartet with an added cello.

style: see **musical style.**

subdominant: a triad built on the fourth scale step of a given tonal structure (the IV chord).

suite: the gathering together of several different types of dance movements or music of differing tempos and meters to form a cohesive composite composition.

surrealism: the creation of incongruous or fantastic imagery in music, art, and literature and in theatre by the use of uncommon combinations of artistic elements.

sutra: the sacred discourse of Buddha, often used as a principal source of liturgical ritual.

symphonic poem: a genre of music for symphony orchestra, popular in the nineteenth century, that linked music to a literary source. Symphonic poems are single-movement works that are nonetheless sectionalized.

symphony: (1) a composition of several movements (traditionally four) for strings, woodwinds, brass, and percussion; (2) an instrumental ensemble consisting of the following families of instruments: strings (violins, violas, cellos, string basses); woodwinds (flutes, oboes, clarinets, bassoons); brass (horns, trumpets, trombones, tuba); and percussion (both pitched and nonpitched).

syncopation: the interruption of the natural relationship between meter and rhythm by accenting fractional parts of the pulse.

tāla: rhythmic formulas found in the music of India.

tempo: the speed of the pulse.

tenor: the highest male voice range.

ternary form: an A-B-A musical structure.

texture: the weave of musical lines in music (see **homophonic, monophonic, homorhythmic, polyphonic**).

theme: a recognizable melody that often serves as a primary structural device in a composition.

theme and variations: the presentation of a fundamental idea, theme, or melody, using that theme for a series of elaborations.

Theremin: a pioneer electronic device for creating sound in which both the pitch and the intensity were controlled by moving a hand between two projecting electrodes.

timbre: the characteristic tone quality or color of a sound.

time signature: a symbol at the beginning of a staff that indicates the number of beats per measure and designates which rhythmic unit receives the pulse.

Tin Pan Alley: a musical metaphor for both the district where popular music was published in New York City in the early twentieth century and also for the music itself. Tin Pan Alley songs acquired a stereotypical style, and often the term denoted love songs that were sung to piano accompaniment. Sometimes the sheet music was a reduction of music originally sung with the accompaniment of an orchestra on the stages of Broadway.

toccata: a form of keyboard music that originated in the Renaissance and flourished in the Baroque Era, characterized by free elaborate scales and virtuoso figures, often alternating with fugal or contrapuntal music.

tonal center: the principal pitch—and, consequently, the primary chord built upon that pitch—which serves as the harmonic foundation of a given composition or section.

tone: (1) the interval of a whole step—one-sixth of one octave; (2) the specific quality of timbre produced by a voice or an instrument (as in tone quality or tone color).

tone color: the specific timbre, or tone quality, of a sound.

tone row: a series of pitches drawn from the twelve notes of the chromatic scale upon which serial compositions are founded. (Also called **set,** or **series.**)

tonic: (1) the first tone of the scale; (2) the triad built upon the first tone of the scale.

transcription: an arrangement in which an original piece of music is transferred to a different performing medium (i.e., Tchaikovsky's *1812 Overture*, originally for symphony orchestra, also exists in several transcriptions for concert band).

transposition: changing, or shifting, from one key center to another.

treble clef: a designation of pitches on the staff in which the note "G" is found on the second line.

triad: a harmonic structure of three notes based upon the tonic, third, and fifth scale steps.

triadic melody: a melody that is structured around the consecutive presentation of notes in a triad.

trill: a musical ornament consisting of the rapid alternation of one note and its adjacent pitch (either a whole step or a half step).

trio: (1) music designed for three parts; (2) a musical ensemble of three performers.

trio sonata: a baroque musical genre consisting of several movements for two melody instruments and continuo (most commonly harpsichord and cello).

triple meter: the arrangement of pulses or beats into units of three.

troubadours: medieval minstrels from southern France.

troubairitz: women poet/musicians of the Medieval and Renaissance eras.

trouvères: medieval minstrels from northern France.

tutti: (1) in musical scores, this indicates that the entire ensemble is to perform where indicated; (2) the name for the entire ensemble in the **concerto grosso.**

umngqokolo: a technique of singing by the Xhosa culture in South Africa in which women produce a fundamental, gut-tural melody and simultaneously sing a higher-pitched melody. (Also called overtone singing.)

Uillean pipes: bellows-powered bagpipes that have a quieter sound than the Scottish bagpipes.

vallenato: a popular music expression coming from Colombia, specifically from the Valle de Upar. Its rhythmic structures are influenced by four traditional dances—the son, paseo, merengue, and puya—which each have their own unique tempos and are associated with certain instruments.

vīna: a stringed musical instrument of South India having a long neck and one or two gourds attached to it for resonance.

virelai: a medieval form of the chanson having the structure A-b-b-A-A (capital letters indicate repetition of both music and text).

virginal: the English version of the harpsichord, popular in the Renaissance and early Baroque eras.

vivace: a tempo indicator meaning fast and spirited.

vocables: any sounds in a musical composition or performance produced by the human voice but not associated with actual words or tones, such as clicks, grunts, shouts, hissing sounds, and nonsense syllables.

Vodun: a polytheistic religion practiced chiefly by West Indian cultures, which contains a mixture of African cult traditions and elements of the Catholic religion.

whole step: an interval containing two semi-tones, or chromatically related pitches.

wind ensemble: a band consisting of woodwind, brass, and (frequently) percussion instruments.

woodwind quintet: a chamber ensemble consisting of flute, oboe, clarinet, bassoon, and horn.

word painting: creating musical gestures that help underline, or illustrate, key words or concepts in a piece of vocal music.

work songs: vernacular songs that were sung by workers performing physical labor.

APPENDIX B

A Listener's Guide to Musical Criticism

Have you ever met someone who does not have an opinion about music? Because music is so ubiquitous in our society, it seems that everyone, no matter how qualified, has strong opinions about it. The ability to evaluate music with intelligence is an acquired one, a topic that deserves comment. It is essential that the music lover develop a sense of criticism, not only for the style and quality of the composition, but also for the competence and effectiveness of the individual performance.

How many times have you heard someone react negatively to a piece of music by saying, "Do you call *that* music?" or "Music is supposed to be beautiful! *That* junk you are playing is ugly! It's not even music!"

More appropriate questions concerning music are: "Is it effective music?"; "Does this music express any interesting ideas?"; "Does it speak to me?"; "Will this music wear well on the listener's ear?"; "Does this work exhibit continuity—does it work as a musical structure?"; and, "Is this worth hearing again?"

Musical criticism, like musical perception, can be exercised at different levels. When one is listening to a high school musician singing at a district music contest, for example, the expectation of expressive ranges (control of dynamics, subtleties of phrasing, tone control, etc.) is certainly lower than that same listener would have for a professional concert artist. One could contend that there exists a hierarchy of performance expectations that has emerged in the realm of music performance. Although the following order certainly does not represent a standardized hierarchy, it does attempt to isolate several aspects of performance that can function as a working list for the student of musical perception:

1. Does the performer play or sing in tune? Is the performer capable of executing each pitch accurately?

2. Is the performer's sense of rhythm accurate? Does the singer's or player's use of timing correspond to the demands of the composition? Can the performer maintain a steady tempo, or do tempos feel uneven?

3. Does the performer have the adequate technical skill to perform the composition? Can the instrumentalist play fast melodic passages so the notes fall with equal rhythm and emphasis? Does the performer play wrong notes, hesitate on entrances, hit specific notes exactly with the desired articulation, dynamic level, and pitch level? Do you hear noticeable "breaks" in the singer's voice, where one hears a change of tone color in different ranges, or is the tone quality consistent throughout the range of the voice? (This consideration also applies to wind and, to a lesser extent, string instrument performances.)

4. Does the general sound, or tone quality, of the performer match the needs of the music? Is the sound projected well? Is it rich and full? When the person is playing or singing in the extreme dynamic ranges, does the tone quality maintain its intensity?

5. Is the performer using nuances of musical expressions effectively? The shadings of tone color, tempo, dynamics, and even pitch are components of an excellent performance in music. Some of these subtleties are notated by the composer, but many are left up to the performer's abilities and interpretation.

6. Are the various parts of the ensemble balanced well with each other? Does the soloist project over the accompaniment when necessary? Are there times when the accompaniment should be louder? Do any sections (or individual performers) of a large ensemble dominate others, or is there evidence of an essential flexibility in the dynamic prominence of parts?

7. Does the performer interpret the composition using the appropriate stylistic conventions of the work, or does the performer take too many liberties with the composer's intentions? (This is a most sophisticated consideration and occupies much of the professional music critic's time. Musicologists and other scholars of performance practice have expended great energy to determine the correct interpretations of the music of the past in an attempt to reconstruct the exact intentions of the composer.)

Judging the quality of a musical composition is a much more subjective exercise than is the evaluation of a given performance. Here is where the experience and the individual taste of the listener come into play. Fundamentally, one judges music by comparing it to other examples in that genre—but, of course, that is not a complete solution to the question, "Is this good music?"

In successful compositions, a few elements or ideas usually exist that leap out at the listener or performer. Some compositions are noted for their beautiful, well-constructed melodies, others for the manipulation of harmonic language. Artful construction with regard to the relationship of voice parts is another factor. With all music, however, one consideration is constant: the composer must be able not only to state an idea but to sustain the interest of the intended audience throughout the composition.

If you could eavesdrop on experienced musicians discussing music, certain terms would be used to describe the ways in which the quality of a musical composition is interpreted. Many times you will hear comments about the "effectiveness" of the composition. This rather nebulous concept usually refers to whether or not the composer has shaped the entire composition into a cohesive whole. Another word from the imprecise vocabulary of criticism is "interest." Is the work interesting? This frequently refers to the germinal ideas themselves that serve as the foundation for the composition. For example: Are the melodies (or themes) distinct—do they grasp the attention of the listener? Is there anything unique about the phrasing, shape of melodies, or pitches involved? Does listening to the melodies make the listener anticipate further manipulations, or is the melody simply boring and commonplace? Does the composer organize the materials in his or her composition in a manner that both stimulates anticipation and surprises the realization? In short, would you as the listener want to hear this work again?

SOME HINTS FOR CONCERT ATTENDANCE: CONCERT ETIQUETTE

To lessen the uneasiness that some people feel who may have never ventured into the concert hall, we will consider a few of the commonly accepted courtesies of concert attendance.

Common sense dictates most concert etiquette. Since sound is the primary concern in music, anything that disrupts the ability to concentrate on the sound of the music becomes an irritant to other listeners. Coughing, whispering during a performance, entering or leaving while the music is playing, and making any sound whatsoever during a performance are certainly good ways to irk your fellow concertgoers.

For some reason—perhaps for artistic continuity—it has become the convention to applaud only after the end of the composition. In America, audiences almost never applaud an excellent performance between the movements of a multimovement work.

In short, concert etiquette is dictated by the consideration of the musicians performing and by the rest of the audience. Other than the rather artificial convention of applause, there should be no mysteries surrounding the attendance of a "classical" music performance.

Music History

An Overview of Composers, Forms, and Styles of Music

THE MEDIEVAL PERIOD (800–1450)

Composers (In the early music of this era, especially in the music of the Church, it was common for writers of music to remain anonymous.)

Hildegaard von Bingen (1098–1179)
Lenonin (ca. 1135–1201)
Perotin (fl. 1190–ca. 1225)
Francesco Landini (1325–1397)
Guillaume Machaut (ca. 1300–1377)
John Dunstable (ca. 1390–1453)

Forms of Music

Gregorian chant
Organum
Motet
Chanson (Rondeau, Ballade, Virelai)
Madrigal (early secular form developed in Italy)
Caccia
Polyphonic Mass
Liturgical drama
Monophonic songs sung by troubadours, trouvères, trobaritzs, minnesingers, meistersingers

General Styles and Practices of Music in the Middle Ages

Sacred music dominated by monophonic (Gregorian) chant
Development of polyphony occurs through organum (ca. 850–1200)
Motet features music of three parts, each often containing different texts (sometimes in different languages)

Late in the Medieval period, the polyphonic Mass (3- and 4-part settings of the texts from the Mass) emerges as common practice

Use of "rhythmic modes"—rhythmic formulas taken from poetic forms

Scale systems called "Ecclesiastical Modes" are the basis for chant compositions

THE RENAISSANCE (1450–1600)

Composers

Guillaume Dufay (1400–1474)
Johannes Ockeghem (ca. 1420–1496)
Josquin des Prez (ca. 1440–1521)
Heinrich Isaac (1450–1517)
Jacob Obrecht (1452–1505)
Adrian Willaert (1490–1562)
Jean Mouton (1470–1522)
Jacob Arcadelt (1505–1560)
Thomas Tallis (1505–1585)
Jacobus Clemens (1510–1556)
Antonio de Cabezon (1510–1566)
Cipriano de Rore (1516–1565)
Andrea Gabrieli (1520–1586)
Giovanni Pierluigi da Palestrina (1525–1594)
Roland de Lassus (1532–1594)
William Byrd (1543–1623)
Thomas Luis de Victoria (1549–1611)
Luca Marenzio (1553–1599)
Giovanni Gabrieli (1554–1612)
Thomas Monley (1557–1603)

Major Forms of Music in the Renaissance

Sacred Vocal Forms
Polyphonic Mass
Motet
Lutheran chorale (Germany)
Chorale motet (Germany)
Psalm settings (France,
    Netherlands, Switzerland)

Anthem (England)
Villancico (Spain)

Secular Vocal Forms
Madrigal (Italian)
Madrigal (England)
Lute song (England)
Ayre (England)
Ballett, Baletto (England, Italy)
Chanson (France)
Program chanson (France)
Musique mesuree (France)
Lied (Germany)

Instrumental and Keyboard Forms

Canzona
Fantasia
Dance forms (Pavanne, Galliard,
    Allemand, Cournate, Basse-danse)
Chaconne
Prelude

Ricercar
Tiento
Sonata
Variations
Passacaglia
Fantasia

General Stylistic Concepts of Music in the Renaissance Era

- Vocal music usually consists of four to six parts
- Two basic textures:
  (1) Equal-voiced polyphony
  (2) Homorhythmic texture
- Melodies are usually conjunct, based on vocal styles
- Harmonic structure:
  (1) Full triads
  (2) Strong cadences (V-I)
  (3) Emergence of a major/minor tonal basis (not yet recognized by theorists of the time)
- Use of *musica ficta* (the addition, during performance, of accidentals to notes according to an established set of rules, thereby avoiding certain melodic and harmonic irregularities)
- Points of imitation (each line of the text is set to a new imitative series of entrances)
- Use of word painting (*musica reservata*), a technique of composing in which melodic, harmonic, and rhythmic gestures were used to highlight the meaning of selected words or sections in the text of vocal music

Additional Practices of Music in the Renaissance

- Absence of measure bars, dynamic markings, tempo indications
- Music is notated in part books (not score format)
- Sacred vocal music is often doubled by instruments
- Mensural notation (the precursor to modern notation) is now very specfic with regard to pitch, meters, and rhythms

*T*HE BAROQUE ERA (1600–1750)

Composers

Guilio Caccini (ca. 1545–1618)
Claudio Monteverdi (1567–1643)
Girolamo Frescobaldi (1583–1643)
Heinrich Schutz (1585–1672)
Jean Baptiste Lully (1632–1687)
Giovanni Battista Vitali (1632–1692)
Diedrich Buxtehude (ca. 1637–1707)
Archangelo Corelli (1653–1713)
Giuseppi Torelli (1658–1709)
Henry Purcell (1659–1695)
Elisabeth-Claude Jacquet De La Guerre (1666–1729)
François Couperin (1668–1733)
Antonio Vivaldi (1678–1741)
Georg Philipp Telemann (1681–1767)
Jean Philippe Rameau (1683–1764)
Domenico Scarlatti (1685–1757)
Johann Sebastian Bach (1685–1750)
George Frideric Handel (1685–1759)
Francesco Geminiani (1687–1762)
Giovanni Battista Pergolesi (1710–1736)

Major Forms of Baroque Music

Vocal Forms:

Opera	Mass
Recitative	Motet
Aria	Magnificat
Oratorio	Psalm settings
Cantata	Passion

Instrumental Forms:

Concerto grosso	Accompanied sonata
Trio sonata	Unaccompanied sonata
Suite	Overture
Solo concerto	Chaconne, Passacaglia

Keyboard Forms:

Prelude	Fugue
Chorale prelude	Toccata
Suite	Invention
Partita	Theme and variations
Ordre	

General Stylistic Concepts and Practices of Music in the Baroque Era

- Chord progressions form basis of melodic/harmonic movement
- Regular harmonic rhythm (frequency of chord progression)
- Melodies are frequently "spun out" from a basic melodic/rhythmic idea, often resulting in long phrases that meld into each other (especially in instrumental music)
- Basic types of musical texture:
    (1) Contrapuntal texture founded on a concept of chord progression
    (2) Homorhythmic texture
    (3) Monody—solo melody accompanied by continuo (a combination of a keyboard instrument or lute and a bass instrument such as a cello, string bass, or bassoon)
- Styles of rhythmic organization:
    (1) Motoric rhythm (a continuous rhythm in which one can experience simultaneous presentation of the fundamental beat and its various levels of subdivisions
    (2) Improvisatory practices in which a regular pulse is momentarily suspended to allow for rapid scale passages, ornamentation, and so on
- Use of ornamentation (an elaborate system of trills and turns) to embellish the melody
- An aesthetic code, often referred to as the "Doctrine of Affections," is created by the composer, setting a general mood of the text with appropriate melodic, harmonic, and rhythmic figures; often an entire movement or section of a work reflects this approach; "word painting"—a practice inherited from the Renaissance—also occurs in music by Baroque composers.
- Ensemble and choral music is supported by the continuo—most often a harpsichord or an organ in combination with a melodic bass instrument—which provides a strong feeling of chord progressions and bass line.

THE CLASSICAL ERA (1750–1825)

Composers (including "pre-Classical" composers who represent a transition between the Baroque and Classical eras)

Carl Philip Emanuel Bach (1714–1788)
Johann Stamitz (1717–1757)
Johann Christoph Bach (1735–1782)
Luigi Boccherini (1743-1805)
Christoph Willibald Gluck (1714–1787)
Franz Joseph Haydn (1732–1809)
Wolfgang Amadeus Mozart (1756–1791)
Ludwig van Beethoven (1770–1827)

Major Forms of Music in the Classical Era

Instrumental:
Symphony
Concerto
Overture
Serenade
Divertimento
String quartet
Piano trio
Piano quintet
Woodwind quintet
Solo and accompanied sonata

Vocal:
Opera
Mass
Oratorio
Lieder
Aria

General Stylistic Concepts of Music in the Classical Era

- Aesthetic concepts influenced by the Enlightenment; concepts of "the art of pleasing by the succession and combination of agreeable sounds" govern the general approach to musical style
- Emphasis on cosmopolitan influences as opposed to regional styles
- Emphasis on structure, balance, formal considerations
- General economy of materials
- Influence of Nature and Reason to guide aesthetic approaches
- Primary triads (I-IV-V) become the predominant harmonic framework
- Slow, harmonic rhythm
- Musical form is often delineated by modulations to the dominant key and a subsequent return to the tonal area
- Melodies are often constructed in symmetrical phrases
- The 8-measure unit becomes the standard for musical phrases ("period structure")
- Homophonic texture prevails

THE ROMANTIC ERA (1825–1900)

Composers

Carl Maria von Weber (1726–1826)
Giacchino Rossini (1792–1868)
Franz Schubert (1797–1828)
Hector Berlioz (1803–1869)
Fanny Mendelssohn Hensel (1805–1847)
Felix Mendelssohn (1809–1847)
Frédéric Chopin (1810–1849)
Robert Schumann (1810–1856)
Franz Liszt (1811–1886)
Giuseppe Verdi (1813–1901)
Richard Wagner (1813–1883)
Clara Wieck Schumann (1819–1896)
César Franck (1822–1890)
Bedřich Smetana (1824–1884)
Anton Bruckner (1824–1896)
Johannes Brahms (1833–1897)
Modest Mussorgsky (1839–1881)
Peter Ilyitch Tchaikovsky (1840–1893)
Antonín Dvořák (1841–1904)
Nicolas Rimsky-Korsakov (1844–1908)
Hugo Wolf (1860–1903)
Gustav Mahler (1860–1911)
Richard Strauss (1864–1949)

Major Forms of Music in the Romantic Era

Continuation of all classical forms
Character pieces for piano:
    Prelude, Étude, Songs without Words, Mazurka, Polonaise, Waltz, Album Blätter,
    Scherzo, Ballade, Impromptu, Nocturne
Variations
Lieder
Music drama
Program symphony
Symphonic poem
Concert overture

General Stylistic Concepts of Music from the Romantic Era

- Emphasis on uninhibited emotion
- Aesthetics based upon youthful attitudes, longing, the exotic
- Lyrical melodies
- Freer phrase structures than before
- Expanded harmonic practices (chromaticism, distant modulations, color chords)
- Expanded concepts of formal organization
- Extensive virtuosity
- Expansion of orchestration and use of orchestral timbres as primary features of sound
- Popularity of program music and music linked to literary concepts

TWENTIETH-CENTURY MUSIC

Major Composers

Claude Debussy (1862–1918)
Erik Satie (1866–1925)
Amy (Mrs. H. H. A.) Beach (1867–1944)
Scott Joplin (1868–1917)
Ralph Vaughn Williams (1872–1958)
Arnold Schoenberg (1874–1951)
Charles Ives (1874–1954)
Maurice Ravel (1875–1937)
Ottorino Respighi (1879–1936)
Béla Bartók (1881–1945)
Igor Stravinsky (1882–1971)
Edgard Varèse (1883–1965)
Anton Webern (1883–1945)
Alban Berg (1885–1935)
Sergey Prokofiev (1891–1953)
Arthur Honegger (1892–1955)
Darius Milhaud (1892–1974)
Paul Hindemith (1895–1963)
William Grant Still (1895–1978)
George Gershwin (1898–1937)
Francis Poulenc (1899–1963)
Edward Kennedy ("Duke") Ellington (1899–1974)
Aaron Copland (1900–1990)
Harry Partch (1901–1974)
Dmitri Shostakovich (1906–1975)
Olivier Messiaen (1908–1992)
John Cage (1912–1992)
Benjamin Britten (1913–1976)
Ulysses Kay (1917–1995)
Leonard Bernstein (1918–1990)
Pierre Boulez (b. 1925)
Karlheinz Stockhausen (b. 1928)
George Crumb (b. 1929)
Pauline Oliveros (b. 1932)
Krzysztof Penderecki (b. 1933)
Steve Reich (b. 1936)
Philip Glass (b. 1937)
Joan Tower (b. 1938)
Ellen Taafe Zwillich (b. 1939)
Libby Larsen (b. 1940)

Major Trends and Movements in Twentieth-Century Concert Music

Continuation of past traditions and forms
Impressionism
Neo-classicism
Expressionism
Neo-romanticism

Serialism
Electronic music
Indeterminacy
Instrument exploration
Multimedia
Minimalism

Stylistic Features and Concepts

- Dissonance becomes emancipated, no longer relates necessarily to consonance
- Many types of music(s) exist for a broad spectrum of listeners in a diverse cultural and aesthetic environment
- The creation of "new" sounds occupies high priority
- Competition from past composers drives modern composers to develop new expressions
- Mass media allows expansion of audience
- Educational institutions constitute primary opportunities for musical composition and performance
- An understanding gap widens between the composer, the performer, and the audience

Endnotes

CHAPTER 1

1. American Symphony Orchestra League, *Annual Report* (New York: American Symphony Orchestra League, 1996).

2. Aaron Copland, *What to Listen for in Music* (New York: McGraw-Hill, 1957), 15–25.

3. Leonard Bernstein and Stephen Sondheim, *West Side Story* (New York: Boosey and Hawkes), by permission of Boosey and Hawkes, Inc.

4. Quoted in Vadim Prokhorov, "Will Piano Lessons Make My Child Smarter?" *Parade Magazine*, 14 June, 1998.

5. Robin Doveton, trans., from the brochure notes for *French Chansons*, NAXOS 8.550880, by permission of HNH International Ltd.

CHAPTER 2

1. Amanda McBroom, "The Rose," (Los Angeles: Warner/Chappell Music, 1977), by permission of Warner/Chappell Music.

CHAPTER 3

1. Foster's original lyrics have been lost. This version has evolved to present time by oral tradition.

2. Traditional text of unknown origin.

3. David Dargie, "UMNGQOKOLO: Xhosa Overtone Singing and the Song Nondel'ekhaya," *African Music*, Journal of the International Library of African Music, 7, no. 1, (1993): 39.

4. Translation by David C. Nichols.

CHAPTER 4

1. Traditional slave lament. Setting by Hall Johnson, *Albert McNeil Jubilee Singers, Live*, Albert McNeil MFOOX3.
2. Translation by David C. Nichols.
3. Berry, Chuck. "Oh, Baby Doll," Arc Music Corp., by permission of Arc Music Corp.
4. Bobbi Jean Lewis, "R & B Tells It Like It Is," *Soul*, June 9, 1966, p. 5. Quoted in Carl Belz, *The Story of Rock*, (New York: Oxford University Press, 1972), 184.
5. James Brown, "Try Me," Jadar Music Corp., by permission of Jadar Music Corp.
6. W. W. Norton, from *Source Readings in Music History*, by Oliver Strunk. (New York: W. W. Norton, 1950), 281-282, by permission of W. W. Norton.
7. Jane Bowers and Judith Tick, *Women Making Music: The Western Art Tradition 1150–1950*. (Urbana and Chicago-University of Illinois Press, 1986.)
8. As reported in the *New York Times*, 8 March 1999, E1.

CHAPTER 5

1. Quoted in H. W. Janson (Horst Woldemar) *History of Art*, 3rd ed. (New York: Harry N. Abrams, Inc., 1986), 513.

CHAPTER 6

1. H. C. Robbins Landon, *Haydn, The Years of The Creation 1796–1800, in Haydn: Chronicle and Works*, IV (Bloomington: Indiana University Press, 1977), 278, by permission of Indiana University Press.
2. Alexander Wheelock Thayer, *Thayer's Life of Beethoven*, rev. and ed. Elliot Forbes (Princeton, NJ: Princeton University Press, 1967), 304–305.
3. For a succinct introduction to classical music of India, see Bonnie C .Wade, *Some Principles of Indian Classical Music. Musics of Many Cultures, An Introduction*. ed. Elizabeth May (Berkeley, Los Angeles, London: University of California Press, 1980), 83–110.

CHAPTER 7

1. Janson, *History of Art*, 583.
2. Arthur Loesser, *Men, Women & Pianos*, (New York: Simon and Schuster, 1954), 385–392.

3. Ibid., 458–468.

4. *The New Grove Dictionary of Music and Musicians*, 6th ed., s. v. "Schubert, Franz."

5. Translation by David C. Nichols.

6. Cairns, David, trans. and ed., *Memoirs of Hector Berlioz*, (New York, Alfred A. Knopf, 1969) 31.

7. *The New Grove Dictionary of Music and Musicians*, 6th ed., s. v. "Berlioz, Hector."

8. Cairns, *Memoirs of Hector Berlioz*, 497.

9. Quoted in *The New Grove Dictionary of Music and Musicians*, 6th ed., s.v. "Berlioz, Hector."

10. Public Domain.

11. Cairns, *Memoirs of Hector Berlioz*, 37.

12. *Figaro*, London, (May 28, 1883). Quoted in Nicolas Slonimsky, *Lexicon of Musical Invective* (New York: Coleman-Ross Company, Inc., 1954). This cricitism, although from a time long after Berlioz's death, was typical of general attitudes that many nineteenth-century critics had toward Berlioz's writings.

13. Quoted in *The New Grove Dictionary of Music and Musicians*, 6th ed., s. v. "Chopin, Fryderyk Franciszek."

14. Ibid.

15. George R. Marek and Maria Gordon-Smith, *Chopin* (New York: Harper & Row, Publishers, 1978), 80.

16. Henryk Opieński, *Chopin's Letters*, trans., E. L. Voynich (New York: Vienna House, 1971), 154.

17. Ibid., 138.

18. Translation by David C. Nichols.

CHAPTER 8

1. Johann G. Herder. *Samtliche Werke*, ed. B. Suphan, IV, (Berlin, 1877–1913), 161 f.

2. Translation by David C. Nichols.

3. Ernest Newman, *Stories of the Great Operas and their Composers*, (St. Clair Shores, Michigan: Scholarly Press, 1977), 3.

4. Translation by David C. Nichols.

5. Edward Agate, trans., Nicolay Rimsky-Korsakov, *Der goldene Hahn: Oper in drei Akten* (Bonn: P. Jurgenson Musikverlag, (19--), by permission of Rob Forberg, Musikverlag, Germany.)

6. Mrs. H. H. A. Beach, "Must Music Forsake Emotion?" *The Musician* 37/2 (February, 1932) p. 6. Quoted in Brown, Janell Wise. *Amy Beach and Her Chamber Music* (Metuchen, N.J: Scarecrow Press, 1994), 333.

7. Carol Nuels-Bartes, *Women in Music: An Anthology of Source Readings from the Middle Ages to the Present* (New York: Harper and Row, 1982). Quoted in Janell Wise Brown, *Amy Beach and Her Chamber Music* (Metuchen, NJ.: Scarecrow Press, 1994), 12.

8. Ibid.

CHAPTER 9

1. U.S. Constitution, amend. 19.

2. *Modern Poetry*, eds. Maynard Mack, Leonard Dean, and William Frost (Englewood Cliffs: Prentice-Hall, 1962), 142–143, by permission of Prentice-Hall.

3. Igor Stravinsky, *An Autobiography* (New York: W. W. Norton, 1936), 31.

4. *Musical Times*, London, August 1, 1913.

5. Slonimsky, *Lexicon of Musical Invective*, 152–153.

6. Alfred Einstein, "War, Nationalism, Tolerance," *Modern Music*, 27, no. 1, (1939): 9.

7. This excerpt was filmed in a 1985 interview and appeared in the Arts and Entertainment television production, *Aaron Copland: A Self Portrait*, STAGE, aired December, 1991.

8. Ibid.

9. Taken from a presentation given by Libby Larsen to music students at Truman State University, April 19, 1994.

10. Ibid.

11. Ibid.

CHAPTER 10

1. John Cage, "On Robert Rauschenberg, Artist and His Work," in *Silence, Lectures and Writings* (Middletown, Connecticut: Wesleyan University Press, 1961), 101.

2. Pauline Oliveros, from her instructions for *Pacific Tell,* quoted in Von Gunden, Heidi, *The Music of Pauline Oliveros* (Metuchen, N.J.: Scarecrow Press, 1983), 114.

3. *New York Times*, September 13, 1970.

4. John Gutman, trans., *Madame Butterfly* (New York: G. Schirmer), by permission of G. Schirmer.

5. Crumb, George, *Ancient Voices of Children* (New York, C.F. Peters, 1973), by permission of C. F. Peters.

PART III: MUSIC AS A SOCIAL FORCE

1. Charles Burney, A *General History of Music, from the earliest ages to the present period (1789)* (New York: Harcourt Brace and Company, 1935), 21.

CHAPTER 11

1. Mars Bonfire, "Born to Be Wild," Songs of Universal, Inc., by permission of Songs of Universal, Inc.

2. Lawrence Grossberg, "Is There Rock After Punk?" quoted in Simon Frith and Andrew Goodwin, *On Record.* (New York: Pantheon Books, 1990), 116–117.

3. Alan Bloom, *The Closing of the American Mind.* (Chicago: University of Chicago Press, 1987), 73, by permission of the University of Chicago Press.

4. Charles P. Alexander, "A Parent's View of Pop, Sex, and Violence," *Time,* May 7, 1990.

5. Maya Bell, "Martinez says 2 live 2 lewd, no more sales 2 minor dudes," *Orlando Sentinel,* February 23, 1990.

6. Ed Vogel, "Rock song at center of lawsuit," *Las Vegas Review Journal,* June 8, 1988.

7. Ibid.

8. Committee on Commerce, Science, and Transportation, Congressional Hearing, September 19, 1985.

9. Committee on Commerce, Science, and Transportation, Congressional Hearing, September 26, 1985.

10. Michael Straight, *Twigs for an Eagle's Nest* (New York/Berkeley: Devon Press, 1979), 11.

11. Fannie Taylor and Anthony L. Barrese, *The Arts at a New Frontier* (New York and London: Plenum Press, 1984), 240.

12. CBS Sunday Morning, April 12, 1992.

13. "Caution, This Art May Offend," *New York Times,* August 11, 1989.

14. Ibid.

CHAPTER 12

1. Plato, *The Republic*. Quoted in Strunk, *Source Readings in Music History* (New York: W. W. Norton & Company, 1950), 8.

2. Brochure notes for *Sacred Ceremonies, Ritual Music of Tibetan Buddhism, Zen*, Fortuna Records, 17074-2.

3. Brochure notes for *Buddhist Liturgy of Tibet*, King Record Co. KICC 5137.

4. Willi Apel, *Gregorian Chant* (Bloomington, Indiana: Indiana University Press, 1958), 46.

5. Joyce Irwin, *Neither Voice nor Heart Alone*. (New York: Peter Lang, 1993), 103.

6. Martin Luther, *Sämmtliche Schriften*, herausgegeben von Dr. J. G. Walch, Neue revidierte Stereotypausgabe, trans. Carl Halter and Margaret Hermes (St. Louis: Concordia Publishing House, 1880) X: 1424, by permission of Concordia Publishing House.

7. Luther, *Sämmtliche Schriften*, XIV: 439, by permission of Concordia Publishing House.

8. Catherine Winkworth, trans., (1863), in *The Lutheran Hymnal* (St. Louis: Concordia Publishing House, 1941), 609.

9. Ibid.

10. Paul Henry Lang, *Music in Western Civilization*. (New York: W. W. Norton & Company, 1940), 209.

11. From John Wesley's *Select Hymns*, 1761. Reprinted in *The United Methodist Hymnal* (Nashville: The United Methodist Publishing House, 1989), vii., by permission of The United Methodist Publishing House.

12. Emory Stevens Bucke, ed., *The History of American Methodism* (Nashville: Abingdon Press, 1964), I: 29.

13. Ibid., II: 632.

14. John Wesley included chapter and verse citations of scriptures alongside the hymn verses in his published hymnals. In doing so, he not only documented his philosophy concerning the importance of bible-based hymns but also furnished both individual lay-persons references for private worship and ministers texts for their sermons. See Franz Hildebrandt and Oliver A. Beckerlegge, eds., *The Works of John Wesley, Volume 7: A Collection of Hymns for the Use of the People Called Methodists* (Nashville: Abigdon Press, 1983), 79-81, by permission of Abingdon Press.

15. Ibid., 563.

16. Abraham Zebi Idelsohn, *Jewish Music in Its Historical Development*. (New York.- Schocken Books, 1929, Third printing by Holt, Rinehart and Winston, Inc., 1975), 21.

17. Kay Kaufman Schelemey, "Mythologies and Realities in the Study of Jewish Music," in *Enchanting Powers, Music in the World's Religions*, ed. Lawrence E. Sullivan, (Cambridge: Harvard University Press), 303.

18. Idelsohn, *Jewish Music in Its Historical Development*, 358.

19. Pete Strayer and Robert Sterling, "Take Me Back," from the brochure for *The Whole Truth*, Word Records EK67049, by permission of Word, Inc.

20. Elsa Youngsteadt is a 1999 graduate of Truman State University, where she majored in biology and played viola in the TSU Symphony Orchestra. Her study on the Vodun culture of Haiti was originally prepared for Music History II. It is presented here in a reduced form.

21. Gerdes Fleurant, *Dancing Spirits: Rhythms and Rituals of Haitian Vodun, the Rada Rite* (Westport: Greenwood Press, 1996), 8.

22. Lisa Lekis, *Dancing Gods* (New York: Scarecrow Press, 1960), 111.

23. Maya Deren, *Divine Horsemen: The Living Gods of Haiti* (New York: Thames and Hudson, 1953), 235.

24. Harold Courlander, *Haiti Singing* (Chapel Hill: Univ. of North Carolina Press, 1939), 114.

CHAPTER 13

1. William Shakespeare, *Twelfth Night*, act 1, scene 1, line 1.

2. Rossetti, Dante Gabriel, *Collected Works* (London: Ellis and Elvey, 1897) I, 186.

3. Harold Arlen and Truman Capote, "A Sleepin' Bee" from the Broadway production *House of Flowers*, MPL Communications Inc., by permission of Hal Leonold.

4. Charles Mose Brown, Johnny Dudley Moore, Edward E. Williams, "Drifting Blues," EMI-Unart/ BMI, by permission of EMI-Unart.

5. Billy Sherrill and Tammy Wynette, "Stand By Your Man," EMI Al Gallico Music Corp., by permission of EMI Al Gallico Music Corp.

6. BMI Report, 1990.

7. From the brochure for *Gloria Estefan, Abriende Puertas*, Epic EK 67284, by permission of Sony Music Entertainment Inc.

8. Translation by Katalina Sanchez Bulen.

9. Fernando Gonzalez, *Miami Herald*, 1 January 1997.

CHAPTER 14

1. Charles Scott Moncrieff, *The Song of Roland* (New York: E. P. Dutton & Company, 1920), 58-59.

2. Translation by David C. Nichols.

3. The "Agnus Dei" is a traditional text from the Roman Catholic liturgy.

4. From *Dona Nobis Pacem*. Text arranged by R. Vaughan Williams. ©1936 by the Oxford University Press, London. Renewed in U.S.A. 1964. Used by permission. All rights reserved.

5. Ibid.

6. Ibid.

7. Ibid.

8. Erwin Stein, *Arnold Schoenberg Letters* (New York: St Martin's Press, 1965), 88–89.

9. The "Shema Israel" is the universally recognized creedal statement of the Jewish belief in one God. It is comprised of three paragraphs taken from Deuteronomy 6:4-9; Deuteronomy 11:13-21; and Numbers 15:37-41.

10. George M. Cohan, *Over There,* (New York: Leo. Feist, Inc., 1918).

11. Alfred Bryan and Al Piantadosi, "I Didn't Raise My Boy To Be A Soldier," (New York: Leo. Feist, Inc., 1915).

12. Joan Baez, *And A Voice to Sing With* (New York: Summit Books, 1987), 225. "Where are you now, my son'" copyright by Chandos Music, by permission of Chandos Music.

13. Eric Bogle, brochure notes for Chori Leoni, *Songs of War,* Skylark 9501, by permission of Skylark.

Selected Bibliography

Alexander, Charles P. "A Parent's View of Pop, Sex, and Violence," *Time*, May 7, 1990.

Apel, Willi. *Gregorian Chant*. Bloomington, Indiana: Indiana University Press, 1958.

Baez, Joan. *And A Voice to Sing With*. New York: Summit Books, 1987.

Bell, Maya. "Martinez says 2 live 2 lewd, no more sales 2 minor dudes," *Orlando Sentinel*, February 23, 1990.

Berlioz, Hector. *Memoirs of Hector Berlioz*. Translated and edited by David Cairns. New York: Alfred A. Knopf, 1969.

Bloom, Alan. *The Closing of the American Mind*. Chicago: University of Chicago Press, 1987.

Bucke, Emory Stevens, editor. *The History of American Methodism*. Nashville: Abingdon Press, 1964.

Burney, Charles. *A General History of Music, from the earliest ages to the present period (1789)*. New York: Harcourt Brace and Company, 1935.

Brown, Janell Wise. *Amy Beach and Her Chamber Music*. Metuchen, NJ.: Scarecrow Press, 1994.

Cage, John. *Silence, Lectures and Writings*. Middletown, Connecticut: Wesleyan University Press, 1961.

Copland, Aaron. *What to Listen for in Music*. New York: McGraw-Hill, 1957.

Courlander, Harold. *Haiti Singing*. Chapel Hill: Univ. of North Carolina Press, 1939.

Dargie, David. "UMNGQOKOLO: Xhosa Overtone Singing and the Song Nondel'ekhaya," *African Music*, Journal of the International Library of African Music, 7, no. 1, (1993): 39.

Deren, Maya. *Divine Horsemen: The Living Gods of Haiti*. New York: Thames and Hudson, 1953).

Einstein, Alfred. "War, Nationalism, Tolerance," *Modern Music*, 27, no. 1, (1939): 9.

Fleurant, Gerdes. *Dancing Spirits: Rhythms and Rituals of Hailian Vodun, the Rada Rite*. Westport: Greenwood Press, 1996.

Grossberg, Lawrence Grossberg. "Is There Rock After Punk?" quoted in Simon Frith and Andrew Goodwin, *On Record*. New York: Pantheon Books, 1990.

Herder, Johann G. *Samtliche Werke*. Edited by B. Suphan, IV, Berlin: 1877–1913.

Idelsohn, Abraham Zebi. *Jewish Music in its Historical Development*. New York. Schocken Books, 1929. Third printing by Holt, Rinehart and Winston, Inc., 1975.

Irwin, Joyce. *Neither Voice nor Heart Alone*. New York: Peter Lang, 1993.

Janson, H. (Horst) W. (Woldemar). *History of Art*, 3rd ed. New York: Harry N. Abrams, Inc., 1986.

Landon, H. C. Robbins. *Haydn: Chronicle and Works*, IV. Bloomington: Indiana University Press, 1977.

Lang, Paul Henry. *Music in Western Civilization*. New York: W. W. Norton & Company, 1940.

Lekis, Lisa. *Dancing Gods*. New York: Scarecrow Press, 1960.

Lewis, Bobbi Jean. "R & B Tells It Like It Is," *Soul*, June 9, 1966. Quoted in Carl Belz, *The Story of Rock*, New York: Oxford University Press, 1972.

Loesser, Arthur. *Men, Women & Pianos*. New York: Simon and Schuster, 1954.

Luther, Martin. *Sämmtliche Schriften*. Edited by Dr. J. G. Walch. Newly revised and translated by Carl Halter and Margaret Hermes. St. Louis: Concordia Publishing House, 1880 X: 1424.

Marek, George R., and Maria Gordon-Smith. *Chopin*. New York: Harper & Row, Publishers, 1978.

Modern Poetry, edited by Maynard Mack, Leonard Dean, and William Frost. Englewood Cliffs: Prentice-Hall, 1962.

Moncrieff, Charles Scott. *The Song of Roland*. New York: E. P. Dutton & Company, 1920.

Newman, Ernest. *Stories of the Great Operas and Their Composers*. St. Clair Shores, Michigan: Scholarly Press, 1977.

Nuels-Bartes, Carol. *Women in Music: An Anthology of Source Readings from the Middle Ages to the Present*. New York: Harper and Row, 1982.

Opieński, Henryk. *Chopin's Letters*. Translated by E. L. Voynich. New York: Vienna House, 1971.

Prokhorov, Vadim. "Will Piano Lessons Make My Child Smarter," *Parade Magazine*, 14 June, 1998.

Schelemey, Kay Kaufman. "Mythologies and Realities in the Study of Jewish Music," in *Enchanting Powers, Music in the World's Religions*, edited by Lawrence E. Sullivan, Cambridge: Harvard University Press.

Shakespeare, William. *Twelfth Night*. Edited by S. Musgrove. Berkeley and Los Angeles: University of California Press, 1969.

Slonimsky, Nicolas. *Lexicon of Musical Invective*. New York: Coleman-Ross Company, Inc., 1954.

Stein, Erwin. *Arnold Schoenberg Letters*. New York: St Martin's Press, 1965.

Straight, Michael. *Twigs for an Eagle's Nest*. New York/Berkeley: Devon Press, 1979.

Stravinsky, Igor. *An Autobiography*. New York: W. W. Norton, 1936.

Strunk, Oliver. *Source Readings in Music History*. New York: W. W. Norton, 1950.

Taylor, Fannie, and Anthony L. Barrese. *The Arts at a New Frontier*. New York and London: Plenum Press, 1984.

Thayer, Alexander Wheelock. *Thayer's Life of Beethoven*. Revised and edited by Elliot Forbes. Princeton, NJ: Princeton University Press, 1967.

Vogel, Ed. "Rock song at center of lawsuit," *Las Vegas Review Journal*, June 8, 1988.

Von Gunden, Heidi. *The Music of Pauline Oliveros*. Metuchen, NJ.: Scarecrow Press, 1983.

Wade, Bonnie C. *Some Principles of Indian Classical Music. Musics of Many Cultures, An Introduction*. Edited by Elizabeth May. Berkeley, Los Angeles, London: University of California Press, 1980.

Wesley, John. *The Works of John Wesley, Volume 7: A Collection of Hymns for the use of the People called Methodists*. Edited by Franz Hildebrandt and Oliver A. Beckerlegge. Nashville: Abingdon Press, 1983.

PHOTO CREDITS

INDEX

*Page numbers in italics refer to illustrations. CP followed by number refers to Color Plate.